CLOUDS AMONG THE STARS

2004

Victoria Clayton is the author of four previous, highly acclaimed novels. She is married and lives in Northamptonshire.

By the same author

Dance With Me
Out of Love
Past Mischief
Running Wild

VICTORIA CLAYTON

Clouds Among the Stars

HarperCollins*Publishers*

HarperCollins*Publishers*
77–85 Fulham Palace Road,
Hammersmith, London W6 8JB

www.harpercollins.co.uk

This paperback edition 2004
1 3 5 7 9 8 6 4 2

This novel is entirely a work of fiction. The names,
characters and incidents portrayed in it are the work
of the author's imagination. Any resemblance to actual
persons, living or dead, events or localities
is entirely coincidental.

A catalogue record for this book
is available from the British Library

ISBN 0 00 714255 2

Typeset in Sabon by Palimpsest Book Production Limited,
Polmont, Stirlingshire

Printed and bound in Great Britain by
Clays Ltd, St Ives plc

ONE

The day my father was arrested for murder began promisingly.
It was early November. Usually by mid-autumn the walls
of my attic room were spotted with damp and the ancient
paraffin heater had to be left on all night. On this particular
day the sky was like opaline glass faintly brushed with
rose and there was a seductive mildness in the air. I felt
unusually hopeful about my life and prospects. I was young
– twenty-two – almost certainly in love, and I had a vocation.
I was going to be a poet. I could not remember who said that
all was for the best in this best of all possible worlds but I
was prepared to put money on it.

Through the window beside my bed the remaining leaves
on the topmost branches of the tulip tree looked as though
they had been dipped in bronze. I began to compose a
line. 'Bronzed leaves unfurled like faerie banners –' Banners?
Perhaps 'pennants' was better. I got out of bed, put on my
writing robe, sat at my desk and sharpened my pencil while
I thought.

Pennant, banner, flag, burgee – no, wholly unsuitable,
making one think of pink gins and yacht clubs – what about
'oriflamme'? That was a beautiful word and perfect for a

pastoral epic. I abandoned the leaves altogether and thought about my work in progress, entitled 'Ode to Pulcheria'. Since I had given up writing poetry about myself I seemed to be getting on much better. I had written twelve stanzas and was gratified and disgusted in equal amounts. It had quite a zip to it, but it would keep turning into a poem by somebody else.

I turned again to Nature for inspiration and saw that Mark Antony was stalking a sparrow. I banged on the glass. He looked up in annoyance as the bird flew off. Considering Mark Antony's remarkable girth and the brightness of his ginger fur it would have to be a particularly stupid, short-sighted bird to allow itself to be caught, but I do hate Nature's predatory schemes. I waved to show all was forgiven and caught the sleeve of my writing robe on the edge of my desk.

I looked sorrowfully at the long tear. It was a beautiful robe and one of my most treasured possessions, dark-blue silk velvet embroidered with silver stars and gold lozenges. My father, Waldo Byng, had worn it playing Prospero in an acclaimed production of *The Tempest*. He had received wildly enthusiastic notices and been much lionised for a time. It would not be putting it too strongly, even allowing for family partisanship, to say that my father was still one of the most famous actors of his day. But the Prospero role had been in 1973, five years ago. Since then, things had not gone quite so well with him.

It is difficult to say what had gone – not wrong exactly, but slightly awry. Experimental theatre was all the rage so there were a lot of classical actors wanting the few good parts available. Probably being made a fuss of went to my father's head. He had turned down several leading roles on the grounds that they were insufficiently 'mesmeric'. He had thought himself so deeply into the part of Prospero that he could not stop being him. He was convinced he possessed magic powers and for a time our house was crammed with amulets, scarabs, lamps, rings, wands, pendulums and philtres. He offered to lay hands on every invalid he met. A Russian painter, who had TB, actually got better and my father exhibited Serge's miraculously pink cheeks and red lips at parties as though he were a hermaphrodite chicken or a two-headed lamb. We were all sorry when Serge died a few months later.

I looked out of the window again and saw Loveday, our gardener, weeding round what my father claimed was an antique bust of Shakespeare. It was indisputably a man with a bald head, whose features were indistinguishable from burst blisters. It stood at the centre of Loveday's maze. Originally it had taken up only a small part of what was a large garden for Blackheath, where we lived. Then Loveday had become obsessed. He had extended the maze, making it more and more elaborate until it filled almost the entire three-quarters of an acre behind the house. He had begun it in yew but in later years went over to privet because it grew so much faster. Of course it needed trimming more often as well. During the summer the drama of our daily lives was played out to the sound of clashing shears as Loveday clipped from dawn till nightfall.

Loveday had constructed the maze with the idea of baffling the Devil. He believed that all difficulties in this world were the works of Satan. Despite the ubiquity and industry of the Lord of Pandemonium Loveday was confident his maze would go some way to confound him. We children were frequently required to test the ingenuity of the newest layout and, to keep Loveday happy, even if we weren't lost, we pretended to be. My father said Loveday was a man in a million and, though a hopeless gardener, was a wonderful illustration of Rousseau's thesis of the boundless creativity of the untutored mind. Honestly though, when it came to wild credulity, I sometimes thought it would be difficult to choose between Loveday and Pa.

'Harriet!' It was Portia's voice. She rattled the door handle. 'What are you doing?' I put the 'Ode to Pulcheria' in my desk drawer, whipped off my writing robe, stuffed it under my bed and unlocked the door.

There are seven of us in my family. My mother, Clarissa, was also a Shakespearean actor, much fêted in the fifties and sixties but now retired. The eldest of us children, and the only male, is Oberon, twenty-six years old at that time, and known to everyone as Bron. Then comes Ophelia, twenty-four, followed by me, Harriet, and then Portia, aged twenty. Then a long gap before Cordelia, now aged twelve.

Portia's eyes looked past me, scanned the room and then returned, disappointed, to my face. 'You're such a dark horse. Whatever do you do up here all alone? I think you've got a shameful secret. You're not in the pudding club, are you?'

Though Portia was two years younger than me, people usually thought it was the other way round. She had a fierce self-assurance while I was – am – prone to self-doubt. Beneath an ancient beaver coat my mother had put out for the jumble, Portia was wearing a white dress, not very clean, that was cut low in front. A slick of scarlet lipstick hid her pretty mouth.

'Not as far as I know,' I said. 'Where are you going? You'll die of heat in that coat.'

'It's going to rain later on, Loveday says. Anyway, I can take it off if I have to. I'm going to have lunch with a delicious man.'

All men were, initially anyway, delicious to Portia. I looked at my watch. 'Isn't it rather early for lunch?'

'I'm going to Manton's first to borrow some jewellery.' Manton's was a theatrical costumier. 'This man is a bloated capitalist,' Portia continued. 'I don't want him to think I'm hard up.' She slipped her foot from her high-heeled patent leather shoe and bent to rub her heel. 'Ow! These shoes are hell! Why should Ophelia be blessed with small aristocratic feet and not me? It's so unfair.' She looked up from behind a fall of pale yellow hair, her expression half laughing and half cross.

'You've nothing to complain about, I should say. Even dressed like that you look gorgeous.'

My three sisters and Bron had all inherited my mother's looks, the same shining fair hair, huge deep blue eyes and marvellous mouth. Ophelia was generally thought to be the beauty of the family, having, in addition, my mother's perfect nose, but I thought there might be some who would prefer Portia's more animated features and friendlier disposition. Cordelia was already shaping up to rival the other two. I had dark hair and dark eyes like my father and the same bony frame. While my sisters were voluptuous, I was completely bosomless, to my great sorrow.

'Thanks for the compliment, I *don't* think.' Portia took a mauve scarf from her coat pocket and tied it round her head, Red Indian fashion. On anyone else it would have looked ridiculous but it gave Portia a seductive air I really envied. 'There's nothing the matter with the way I'm dressed. You're a fine one to talk, anyway. I never see you in anything but black these days. I suppose it's all because of that frightful Dodge. That reminds me what came up to tell you. He's on the phone.'

Dodge had been my boyfriend for the last year. Everyone disapproved of him, which was one of the things I liked about him. It is difficult to assert oneself in a large family of beautiful people overflowing with self-confidence.

'You might have said! He has to ring from a call box.'

'I'm surprised he condescends to use such a bourgeois means of communication,' she called after me as I ran down the stairs. 'I'd have thought a note written in blood and wrapped round a bullet would've been more in his line.'

I had brought Dodge home to have supper with us some

weeks after meeting him in a bus queue. It had not been a success. Usually people adore the zany glamour so liberally dispensed by my family. My father is a marvellous storyteller and my mother likes all young men to fall in love with her.

Claremont Lodge – this was the name of our house – was Regency and very large and handsome for the suburbs. It looked out over the park and was furnished in a manner both theatrical and *dégagé*, on the lines of Sleeping Beauty's castle after a decade or two of slumber. There was a great deal of peeling paint, crumpled velvet, cracked marble, tarnished silver and chipped porcelain. As much of it had been rescued from stage sets, things constantly fell to pieces and were repaired rather badly by Loveday. My mother was a keen decorator with a taste for dramatic tableaux. When Dodge came to dinner she had arranged a corner of the hall with a harp, entwined with ivy where the strings should have been, and a stool made from a Corinthian capital on which stood a clock without hands, a crown – possibly Henry IV's – and a stuffed partridge hanging from one claw. A guttering candle lit the scene, which my mother called *Caducity*. I looked it up later. It means transitoriness or frailty, a tendency to fall apart. It seemed appropriate, considering the state of the furniture.

Dodge had taken all this in with cold eyes, and when my mother had invited him to sit beside her on the sofa before dinner he had said he preferred to stand. Champagne was offered but he asked for beer so I had to raid Loveday's supplies. During dinner my father entertained us with stories of touring Borneo with *The Winter's Tale*. He described a feast of woodworms, considered a delicacy but tasting like the sawdust of which they were composed, and told of an embassy dinner where guests in white tie and long dresses were politely offered a pair of pillowcases to tie on to their feet as protection against the bites of mosquitoes. He drew a vivid picture of natives launching little rafts bearing rice, eggs and flowers into the sea, a custom intended to propitiate the gods of fishing.

My mother had said she was sure Dodge was frighteningly clever and she longed to hear all about his fascinating political views. He had scowled at his plate and answered her in monosyllables. After he had gone home my mother gave an elaborate yawn, flapping her hand at her mouth in a parody of boredom.

My father, with one of the darting, caustic looks he had perfected playing Iago years ago, said, 'What an extraordinary choice, Harriet. I think he may have given Mark Antony fleas.'

Dodge had black hair that stood up in spikes. His eyes were grey and generally filled with scorn. Just occasionally I saw this level stare of defiance waver and a look of doubt creep in, and then I felt sure that I loved him. At least I wanted to put my arms round him, which was probably the same thing.

Dodge was an anarchist. He wanted to rebuild the world and he was making a start with me. It was hardly possible to remark on the weather without provoking a diatribe on my hopelessly class-bound attitudes. He lectured me about my feeble capitulation to society's attempts to abort the creative expansion of my spirit. In protest I had shown him some of my poetry and he had verbally torn it to shreds. Milton, Spenser and Shakespeare were merely propagandists for corrupt regimes. He threw my gods to the ground and trampled on them. I was not to despair altogether, though. He could teach me to free myself from the bondage of erroneous constructs. By going to bed with him I would take the first steps towards enlightenment. I was only too ready to believe that I was hopelessly in error and I was grateful for his interest.

Dodge lived on a piece of waste ground by the river in Deptford, in a disused lighterman's hut. In one corner was a pile of ropes and tackle, and in another was Dodge's bed, the frame made from flotsam picked up on the shore. Instead of a mattress there were heaps of sacks. Beside his bed he had a homemade bookcase filled with anarchic texts. It was all rough, damp and pretty uncomfortable. Yet it had, for me, a strange attraction. When we sat together on the steps of the hut, frying sausages over a driftwood fire and throwing pieces of bread to the seagulls while Dodge outlined his plans for the world, I was happy. He was a seeker after truth and there are not too many of these.

When we made love Dodge changed altogether from his austere public persona. Without the regulation black jersey, donkey jacket and jeans his body was soft and white and his hands were gentle. He would growl like a dog as he got excited and yelp at key moments. I have always liked dogs. I loved it when he lay with his head in the crook of my arm afterwards, sleeping like a child, his expression unguarded and a smile on his lips. I knew it could not last, that Dodge was not the man with whom I wanted to spend the rest of my life but there was something about the rank smell of the river, the scream of the gulls, the hooting of the river craft and the scratchiness of the sacks that made me feel alive, a real person living in the real world.

I picked up the receiver.

'Hello, Ekaterina.' Dodge objected to Harriet on the grounds that it was too upper class. He was a great admirer of Prince Kropotkin, the famous anarchist, and almost anything Russian, apart from Communism, met with his approval. Of the social connotations of Ekaterina we were both in happy ignorance. 'I suppose you were asleep. Dissipation will kill you in the end, you know.' Dodge thought lying in past six o'clock was immoral. One ought to be in the streets, destroying the fabric of society. No doubt it is easier to rise early from damp hessian. 'We're having a meeting. At Nikolskoye. Twelve o'clock. Be there.'

There was a click followed by buzzing. Dodge was always terse on the telephone in case MI6 was tapping the line. Nikolskoye was the code word for 14A Owlstone Road, Clerkenwell, headquarters of SPIT, the Sect for Promoting Insurrection and Terrorism. I sighed. I had hoped to spend the morning peacefully mending my writing robe and reading Emily Dickinson for inspiration. I went down to the kitchen.

Next to my own attic fastness, I liked the kitchen best. It was a large room running the length of the basement, with windows at each end, and it was always warm because of the boiler, which stood in one corner. Loveday considered the boiler one of the Devil's more fiendish creations. It required constant feeding and riddling and spewed fine ash everywhere, but I associated the smell of coke and the screeching sound of the door swinging on its hinges with the long, sweet days of childhood. In the wall opposite the boiler was the dumb waiter, a useful piece of equipment like a small lift worked by ropes that brought food piping hot into the dining room on the floor above. We children used to give each other rides in it on wet days. It marked a boundary between childhood and adolescence when our legs grew too long to be squeezed into the shaft.

The decoration of the kitchen had been entirely neglected, as my mother hardly ever visited it. Its homely fifties wall-paper – yellow blobs like scrambled egg against a grey background – and red Formica counter-tops, blistered by hot pans, were tasteless and friendly. A large table was marked by pen-nibs, scissors and poster paints. Almost my happiest times had been spent at that table, making glittering Christmas cards that buckled with too much glue or lumpy potholders knitted in rainbow wool.

Maria-Alba was frying mushrooms and bacon. She shot me a glance from small black eyes. She was cook and house-keeper to our family but to me she was far more than that. Maria-Alba's plump breast had been my first pillow. I had insisted on entering the world feet first and my mother had been ill for a long time afterwards. Maria-Alba had fed me, bathed me and rocked me to sleep. Bron and Ophelia had been pretty babies but I was fat and plain so probably Ma was relieved that we got on so swimmingly. Maria-Alba's nature was prickly and suspicious, but having got hold of me in a raw state, she could not doubt that my motives and intentions were innocent. From the first moment that I was capable of entertaining a feeling of confidence in anything, my trust had been in Maria-Alba.

Though she ran the household Maria-Alba was not treated as a servant. My parents had an intellectual prejudice against caste. When she wished she ate with us. Usually she preferred to eat alone in the kitchen or in her basement room, which was cosy with brightly flowered curtains and chair covers and embellished with lace mats, plates depicting windmills in relief, china donkeys and fat children peering into wishing-wells or sitting under toadstools. When I was little I loved these ornaments passionately and it was a sad day when my taste evolved to the point when I could no longer look on them with uncritical affection. From the age of about fifteen I preferred the carved ivory crucifix and the reproductions of religious paintings, which as a child I had found gloomy.

Maria-Alba's Catholicism was quite unlike the kind prac-tised by the nuns of St Frideswide's Convent where we girls had been to school. The saints were her friends, good-natured and capricious, only tuning in to her incessant demands when the mood suited them. She wore her faith like a second skin and constantly upbraided God and his henchmen for their mistakes. The nuns who had taught us were placatory and subservient to God. Their saints were unsympathetic taskmasters and their religion was a system of pleasure-proscriptive rules.

Perhaps the differences had something to do with climate. Maria-Alba had spent her childhood in the broiling hills of Calabria, where the earth was the colour of cinnamon and violent storms rolled in daily from the sea. Maria-Alba's mother had been a prostitute and had died from syphilis. I thought this might account for Maria-Alba's abhorrence of sex and distrust of men, though she never said so.

Maria-Alba liked to cook and she was good at it. She enjoyed eating as all good cooks do and, by the time the events I am about to describe took place, she was generously proportioned even for her height, which was just under six feet. She had trouble with her legs, and her ankles had spilled out over her shoes like proving dough. Her black hair, now streaked with grey, was always a little greasy. Her best feature was her nose, which was large and curved like a parrot's beak and gave her face distinction.

No doubt the reason Maria-Alba put up with us was because we understood and sympathised with her illness. She suffered from agoraphobia and the older she grew the worse it became. Once I was with Maria-Alba in Marks and Spencer – I must have been about twelve – surrounded by cheerful woollens and bright mirrors and comfortable smells of newness and cleanness. To my surprise, I saw Maria-Alba clinging with closed eyes to a rack of tangerine botany twin-sets. She was panting and trembling. When, in the taxi going home, I asked her what had frightened her she said that people were looking at her and thinking her crazy. She feared she had been *iettata* – in other words, that someone had cast the evil eye on her. Her belief in this superstition was quite as strong as her devotion to the Virgin. Frequently she made the sign to protect herself against the *iettatore*, the first and little fingers outstretched and the middle ones curled. After that Maria-Alba rarely went out, groceries were delivered, and I bought most of her clothes, with varying degrees of success.

'Egg?' Maria-Alba pointed her spatula at me.

'No, thank you.'

'You lose weight. *Troppo frequentare* with the Russians.'

I had told Maria-Alba several times that Dodge had been born and brought up in Pinner. I had been touched to discover that his real name was Nigel Arthur Wattles. The staid character this suggested was reassuring whenever Dodge, in militant mood, talked of Bond Street running with blood. But Maria-Alba persisted in believing that all anarchists were Soviets, dangerous political animals bent on the corruption of virtuous females.

'Wearing black makes one look thinner.'

'*E troppo lugubre.*' Maria-Alba liked to wear orange, yellow or red, which made shopping for her extremely difficult in these days of punk for anyone under twenty-five, and pastels for anyone over.

'It's a badge of solidarity with the workers in the textile industry who have to slave all day making gorgeous clothes for the idle rich and who can only afford to clothe themselves in rags.'

'*Sciocchezze!*' Maria-Alba put down a plate of food in front of me and frowned. 'You been doing bad things with that Russian.'

'Honestly, Maria-Alba. I'm twenty-two. Years beyond the age of consent.'

'*Allora, bene!* You admit!' Maria-Alba's glance was triumphant. 'He give you a baby, *certo, e poi un scandalo*!'

'How could there be a scandal? Everyone expects actors' families to have babies out of wedlock. Pa would just be annoyed with me for being careless. Probably Ma would think it rather vulgar.'

Maria-Alba widened her eyes with indignation. '*E il bambino*? You bring him into the world, with no name and despise by the grandmother! Ah, *povero bebè*!'

'Harriet! You're going to have a baby!' Cordelia, my youngest sister, had come down into the kitchen. 'Oh, good! I've been longing to be an aunt for ages. I thought it would have to be you. I can't imagine Ophelia letting that stupid Crispin stick his thing into her. Ugh!' she shuddered elaborately. 'I'd better find the pram and try to get the rust off.' She had run upstairs before I could protest.

'*Senta*, the young mind of Cordelia is *macchiata*. I ask Father Alwyn to come to talk to her. It is not right she think of sex like she do.'

Father Alwyn was a reedy, stooping young man with a nervous manner and when, recently, our paths had crossed on the heath, he had jumped when I said 'Good morning' and scuttled back towards the presbytery as though pursued by a hellish host.

'I think possibly Cordelia knows more than he does about sex,' I said.

'Golly, Harriet!' Cordelia had come back down again, her speedwell-blue eyes dismayed. 'Isn't it going to be agony? I saw this film and the woman having the baby was screaming the place down. She was sopping with sweat and practically tying the bars on the bed-head into clove-hitches. I don't think I could bear it to be you.' She flung her arms around me and began to sob.

'What's going on?' Bron had come down after Cordelia. He sat at the table, snatched up the fork I had put down in order to comfort Cordelia and speared my rasher of bacon. 'Any more where that came from, Maria-Alba, my darling?' he said, between mouthfuls.

'Harriet's having a b-baby,' Cordelia's voice rose to a wail.

'A baby?' My eldest sister, Ophelia, who had drifted in after Bron, wrinkled her elegant nose in disgust. 'My dear Harriet, how *ghast*ly for you. I can't bear the way they smell. Cheap talcum powder, milk and sick. It's put me off breakfast.' She floated upstairs again.

'Really?' Bron began on my mushrooms. 'How idiotic. You'll never get your figure back. And your mind will go to jelly.'

'No, not really,' I said a little crossly. 'I wish you'd leave my plate alone. I've got to go out in a minute. Thank goodness I'm *not* having a baby if this is how my family receives the news.'

'I don't know whether to be pleased or sorry you aren't,' sniffed Cordelia, wiping her nose on my napkin. 'It would've been fun to teach it tricks.'

TWO

Owlstone Road was not one of the most attractive streets in Clerkenwell and 14A was the most dilapidated house in the row. As I gave the secret knock – three quick raps followed by two at longer intervals – at the flaking front door I held my breath, for the basement area served as the local *pissoir*.

The letter box opened and a wisp of smoke drifted into the street. I smelled marijuana. 'Password,' said a female voice.

'Oh, um, wait a minute – I've forgotten. Is it "The Paris Commune"?'

'That was last week.' I heard the sound of bolts being drawn. In the gloom of the hall the kohl-encircled eyes of Yelena, known as Yell, glittered with animosity. 'It's too much trouble for you to remember the sodding password, isn't it?'

'Sorry,' I said humbly. I knew when the revolution came Yell would denounce me as a patrician spy faster than you could say *The Conquest of Bread*. This was the title of Prince Kropotkin's monumental work, which had been Dodge's Christmas present to me. To my shame I was still on the second chapter.

Avoiding the sliding heaps of pamphlets on the floor and

15

a newspaper parcel of chips that lay open on the lowest step, adding a sharp vinegary smell to the general bouquet, I followed her up to the main office of SPIT. Dodge, who was sitting on his desk holding forth to a group of admiring neophytes, turned his head to give me a nod of acknowledgement before continuing his attack on Marx's theory of the division of labour. As I had already heard it before, several times, I felt free to wander into the kitchen to put on the kettle.

On the wall above the stove was a large photograph of Emma Goldman, the famous nineteenth-century anarchist, known in America as 'Red Emma'. Dodge had told me all about her. By day she had toiled in the sweatshops of New York, making corsets, and after work she had been a fiery orator on behalf of anarchist ideals. She had suffered imprisonment, humiliation and brutality from the police. She had been persecuted and slandered by the press and obliged to sleep in public parks and brothels. Her only crimes had been her uncompromising honesty and measureless sympathy with the labouring poor, but she had been driven to a state of complete physical and mental wreckage. Looking at her small angry eyes behind round-framed spectacles, her heavy jowls and turned-down mouth, I felt the weight of her reproach. I knew myself to be a fribble, incapable of self-sacrifice for a great cause. One night on a park bench would have delivered the deathblow to my zeal. I withdrew my eyes from Emma's gimlets and took from my bag a tin of Vim and a cloth I had brought from home. While I waited for the kettle to boil, I attacked the disgusting accumulations of grime in the sink.

'I suppose you think being a drudge in the kitchen and a whore in bed is the way to get a man.' Yell had followed me into the kitchen. She bent to take a cake from the oven. She was the only person at SPIT who ever bothered to cook and was really much more domesticated than I was. I looked hungrily at the delicious golden dome from which rose puffs of scented moisture.

'Sorry, what?' I scrubbed harder. I wanted to give myself time to think. Yell always made me nervous. She began to scratch with her thumbnail at a blob of congealed egg on the enamel of the cooker.

'Can't you see you're betraying the sisterhood when you concentrate on the menial tasks and neglect the great ones?'

'Surely there's nothing political about cleaning a sink?'

'Everything's political.' Yell scraped more energetically at the egg, so presumably drudgery was a question of scale. 'You want Dodge to abandon his principles so he can go on screwing you. You want him to marry you and become a wage-slave in the suburbs. I'd rather be celibate than betray my ideals.'

I stopped scouring to glance at Yell. She didn't look well. She was very thin and her skin was pasty, apart from some red spots under her eyes. I decided to try appeasement. 'I'm sure he'd never even consider doing such a thing. I know how important all this is to him. And the brotherhood. He often says what a support *you* are to him, particularly.'

Yell sucked hard on the homemade cigarette she was smoking and blew the smoke straight into my face. 'You little bitch!' she said before marching out of the kitchen.

'Can't you women manage to get on?' complained Dodge, as we walked to the appointed place of demonstration. 'I'm fed up with all the rowing that goes on in the Sect.'

'I think I'm beginning to hallucinate. I breathed in two whole lungfuls of whatever Yell was smoking. I feel most peculiar.' I was hungry, having had hardly any breakfast, thanks to Bron, and nothing for lunch but Yell's cake. I stumbled a little beneath the burden of two stout poles on which were fixed cardboard placards proclaiming our beliefs.

Several of the brethren had not turned up and we were having to double up with the banners.

People stared at us as we walked towards Parliament Square. Their expressions were unfriendly. I had not realised before how many variations there are on the human physiognomy. All had the regulation two eyes, nose, mouth, ears and chin but there were so many squints, wall eyes, crooked noses, misaligned jaws and deranged expressions that it was like being in a painting of hell by Bosch or Brueghel. 'I do try to get on with her but some people are impossible to please. She seems to hate me but I don't know what I've done.'

'It isn't you, you dumb cluck.' Dodge gave me that look of stern condescension I had become accustomed to. 'She's in love with me, of course.'

I looked at Yell's angular figure marching in front of me. Like me she wore scruffy black, but her hair was short and ragged, which suggested proper commitment to serious issues. 'Oh,' I said. 'Are you at all in love with her?'

Dodge brandished his placard at a passer-by who was shouting insults at us. 'I'm sleeping with you, aren't I?' Which was an unsatisfactory answer.

On reaching the square Dodge mounted the wooden box brought along for the purpose by Hank and Otto, our two burliest partisans, and began his speech.

When he was delivering a harangue, I found Dodge quite irresistible. He was magnificent, fierce and solemn by turns. He began by flinging up his arm to direct, with an imperative forefinger, our sights to higher and better courses. Then he rolled his head forward, shoulders drooping, hands outstretched, oppressed by the apathy of the world. He looked marvellous from a distance. Because he considered taking pleasure in food selfish and hedonistic, he ate very little, so his cheekbones were sharp and his eyes smouldered in deep sockets. Also, from a distance, you could not see the sprinkling of acne on his chin.

'Order is slavery,' he began. 'Thought in chains. Order is the continuous warfare of man against man, trade against trade, class against class, country against country. Order is nine-tenths of mankind working to provide luxurious idleness for a handful. Order is the slaughter of a generation on the battlefield. It is the peasant dying of starvation while the rich man dies of obesity. It is the woman selling herself to feed her children. Order is the degradation of the human race, maintained by the whip and the lash.'

As I listened to these now familiar words I felt the customary surge of indignation. As Dodge cited revolution after revolution that had been crushed by tank and gun, my dissatisfaction with the state of the world grew. Why should wealth and land be held by the few while the masses starved? Capitalism was undoubtedly a mistake. 'Hurrah!' I shouted with the others whenever Dodge made a particularly telling point. But when he described what anarchy could do to right the wrongs of mankind, I felt less certain. Would people really work more productively because they knew it would benefit their neighbours? I hoped so but I had to admit to a crumb of doubt.

A crowd gathered. Among them was a bad-tempered-looking policeman. At once I felt guilty, an absurd reaction bred of a childish fear of authority. I shook one of my banners vigorously and gave a cry of pain as a huge splinter from the stick drove itself deep into my thumb. It was then I heard the uplifted voice of a newspaper vendor, crying, 'Read all abaht it! Famous actor arrested for murder! Read all abaht it!'

I hardly took in the sense of it as I attempted to grasp with my teeth the end of the splinter, which had disappeared in welling blood.

'Here, before you, is the walking, breathing demonstration

of my thesis,' said Dodge, really warmed up now. He pointed to an old lady in a battered black straw hat, who stood just in front of me, crouching over her cane as she twisted her arthritic neck to stare up at him. 'Well, Mother, you could tell us a thing or two about capitalist repression, I should think! How many times have you had to put your children hungry to bed while you laboured sorrowfully over some wearisome task for which you were paid a pittance?'

'Shame!' yelled one of the brotherhood. The old woman stared round at us, cackling and displaying toothless gums, apparently enjoying the attention.

'How many times has your body been numb with cold because the coal mined by brave men, dying of silicosis, has gone to power the great factories that provide wealth only for their owners?'

'Scandal!' roared the revolutionists. The old lady waved her stick at us and screamed with laughter.

'How many times have you had to scrape and contrive to put a decent meal on the table for your husband when he came home, weary and sore oppressed?'

The crowd murmured sympathetically but, in a lightning change of mood, the old woman seemed suddenly to resent being the object of universal pity.

'My 'usband was a no-good drunken layabout. 'E never did a honest day's work in 'is life. When 'e ran off with the tart from the Co-op I was pleased to see the back of 'im!'

'So put that in your pipe and smoke it!' heckled one of the crowd.

'Yeah! What choo got ter say ter that?' jeered the old woman with consummate ingratitude. I noticed for the first time that she seemed a little drunk. 'You blinking lefties think you can tell us all what to do but we ain't 'aving none of it!'

Dodge opened his mouth to reply but at that moment one

of the placards I was cradling in the crook of my arm, so I could suck my throbbing thumb, toppled over and fell on the old lady. It knocked her hat over her eyes and sent her staggering round in circles until she sat down with a thump on the pavement while her basket went spinning.

''Ere!' shouted a spectator. 'There's no call for violence just 'cause she don't agree with you!'

Dodge jumped from the podium. He and the policeman helped the old lady up but as soon as they put her on her feet she began to swipe at Dodge's legs with her stick. She possessed a surprising amount of strength for such an ancient old thing. In the confusion I accidentally let go of the second placard. It knocked the policeman's helmet from his head. He swore loudly and blew his whistle.

What happened then was terrifying. It began as an exchange of insults between the anarchists and the audience, accompanied by the jabbing of fingers and some pushing and shoving. Then like a flame creeping through dry twigs it flared into violence. In seconds there was a whirling mêlée of fists and boots and flying objects. A fat old man, his eyes glaring and his lips stretched back from his teeth in hatred, kicked me hard on the knee. I staggered against the railings. An egg, presumably from the old lady's shopping basket, struck my eyebrow. Surprisingly, it hurt quite a lot. As I tried to wipe away the strings of white a youth with long matted hair aimed a blow at my cheek, snatched my bag from my shoulder and ran off with it. I was much too frightened to put up a fight. Someone was screaming. I wanted to scream too, but I was breathless with shock and fear. I stared in awe as Yell climbed the statue of Abraham Lincoln, shouting defiance and waving a banner before someone hit her smack on the forehead with an orange and knocked her from the pedestal into the crowd. A police car, with lights flashing and siren blaring drew up at the perimeter of the scrimmage. I saw a gap between the combatants and before I had time to think what I was doing I was through it and running hard.

I ran for what seemed like miles until the pain in my knee forced me to stop. I sank onto a step in a doorway, almost weeping with pain and despair. Although some of the brotherhood considered it their bounden duty to be militant whenever possible, and there had been much talk of previous bloody scrums, I had never witnessed them. This was only my second demonstration. The first had taken place on a hot July day in St James's Park when everyone had been too good-humoured to care much about anything but sunbathing and ice creams.

Violence at first hand was unfamiliar to me. I had lived all my life in peaceful Blackheath and Maria-Alba disapproved of smacking children. At St Frideswide's the nuns had patrolled the playground and even the sticking out of tongues was strictly forbidden. The crazy, indiscriminate aggression I had just witnessed was deeply disturbing. But none the less I was ashamed of myself. I had enrolled myself in the cause and at the first hint of danger I had run away. I had deserted not only my comrades but also the man I loved. At this moment he might be lying helpless while the battle raged about him, badly hurt or – terrible thought – even dead.

A car drew up at the kerb and a woman with bleached hair and a hard face stepped out. She looked at me with an expression of loathing. 'This is not a public bench. I shall fetch the porter if you don't move off.'

I hobbled as fast as my knee would allow me back to Parliament Square. It took some time as blood was seeping through the leg of my jeans and the rubbing of fabric on flesh was agony. 'Actor on murder charge,' shouted the man who had a kiosk near the Sanctuary. It went through my mind that my parents would be very interested in this piece of news, as they knew every thespian of any reputation. Then the square came in sight and I forgot about it.

The fighting was over. People stood about, talking, but of Dodge and Yell and the other members of SPIT there was no sign. I spotted a Black Maria disappearing into the traffic. The pavement was littered with squashed oranges and broken eggs and trampled placards. A packet of lard oozed and glistened on the pavement. The only person I recognized was the old woman with the black straw hat. She was trying to persuade a policeman, who was attempting to get her into the police car, to dance with her.

'Anyone see what happened this afternoon?' Another policemen addressed the crowd. 'We'd like to take statements from some of you.' The crowd thinned rapidly and I joined the exodus.

The warmth of the day had gone now and Nikolskoye looked particularly uninviting in the fading light. I almost turned back when I saw Hank and Otto walking up the steps but I knew I ought to face up to having behaved badly. I steeled myself to bear their resentment.

'Hey! Look who's here!' Hank called when he saw me. 'You were great, Harriet! Ha, ha! When I saw you hit that policeman! I'd never have believed it! I had you down as a stuck-up bourgeoise coquette.'

I grinned feebly as Otto gave me a clenched-fist salute. 'Come in, Sister, and ve shall drink you a toast. It vas a good day's work, *nicht war*? Leetle old ladies must take care ven Harriet is about. She vill knock them down!' He mimed a punch aimed at my shoulder.

I noticed that Otto was missing an earring and that his lobe was a nasty mess. Hank's nose was swollen to twice its usual size. We went upstairs, the two men congratulating each other on the blows they had managed to get in, in the name of freedom. What had seemed to me to be a disaster, bordering on farce, was apparently another glorious chapter in the history of heroic resistance to the forces of oppression.

23

My appearance at headquarters met with cries of approval. Dodge and Yell were absent, having been taken to the police station, but it was generally agreed that neither of them had been much hurt.

My health was drunk in warm beer and my fearless militancy made much of. We finished Yell's cake and then Hank went out for fish and chips, and we had a greasy feast of celebration. Though it was hard to see wherein lay the victory exactly, I went along gratefully with the general mood of self-congratulation. I had never in my life been fêted for anything and it was a heady experience.

It was half-past six when I got home. I looked wildly dishevelled, almost villainous, in the hall mirror – the personification of caducity. My hair was hanging in strings from the egg and the blood from a cut on my cheek had dried in a streak of blackish-red blobs. My knee was agony and my thumb was sore.

'*Ehilà*, Harriet! *C'è da impazzire!*' Maria-Alba's head appeared in the lighted doorway that led to the basement stairs. Her eyes and mouth were large with anguish. 'Clarissa is having the fits and Ophelia is lock in the bedroom. Bron is gone to The Green Dragon and Portia is nowhere found! *Non so più che fare!*'

'Harriet!' Cordelia flung herself at me. 'I'm going to kill myself! I've made a potion of laburnum seeds and deadly nightshade for us all to drink . . .' The rest was drowned by sobbing.

'What is it? What's the matter?' I was used to my family's dramatics. I expected Maria-Alba to tell me the boiler had gone out, and Cordelia that she had been given a C for Latin.

'*Waldo sarà impiccato per omicidio.* Your father is to be hang! For murder!' Maria-Alba sank to her knees and wrung her hands above her head.

Cordelia screamed and fainted.

THREE

We laid Cordelia on the ebony and gilt day bed, which had come from the set of *Antony and Cleopatra*. Its frame was made of writhing snakes with leopards' heads supporting the scrolled arms. The coats, lacrosse sticks, cricket bats and school satchels that had been carelessly chucked on to it over the years had chipped off most of the gesso, and Bron, when a small boy, had indelibly inked spectacles round the leopards' eyes, but it made a striking effect as you walked in through the front door. Next to it, a life-sized statue of Anubis, the Egyptian god with the head of a jackal, acted as a hat stand.

Maria-Alba snatched several feathers from an ostrich boa that was draped round Anubis's neck, set a lighted match to them and held them under Cordelia's nose. Cordelia came to immediately, complaining volubly about the disgusting smell. She gazed up at me with tragic eyes.

'Don't kiss me goodbye, my dearest sister, lest you take the poison from my lips. I love all my family but you're my favourite. Portia was a pig yesterday when I asked if I could borrow her mohair jersey.'

'Stop acting at once, this minute, and tell me truthfully. Did you swallow any nightshade and laburnum mixture?'

I spoke sharply because Cordelia frequently told lies. Also I wanted to bring myself back from the immense distance to which Maria-Alba's broken sentences had sent me. I saw myself bending over my sister in one of those out-of-the-body experiences people have when they nearly die. My sight was dim and I seemed to be intermittently deaf.

'I – I – don't remember.' Cordelia pressed her hand to her head and fluttered her lashes.

'*C'è bisogno di emetico*. Salt and water,' said Maria-Alba grimly. 'I go make it.'

'You'll be wasting your time because I won't drink it.' Cordelia sat up, looking cross. 'I hate this family. Isn't it bad enough that my own darling father is a prisoner and a captive and perhaps even going to be hung without you trying to make me sick?'

'Hanged,' I corrected automatically while muffled shock waves boomed in my head like the tolling of a submerged bell.

Cordelia glared at me. 'I expect if someone strapped you to a table and swung an axe over your naked quivering flesh like in *The Pit and the Pendulum*, you'd be correcting his grammar.'

'Probably. Anyway, they don't hang people any more in this country.'

'Don't they? Really not? Because I saw this film and the man was going to be hung – oh, all right, hanged – and the priest asked him to pretend to be afraid so that all the people who looked up to him as a hero would despise him and turn from their villainy and it was so awful when he started to cry and tried to get away – I wanted to be sick, it was so horrible. You see, you don't know whether he's pretending or he really *is* frightened –'

'It was only film.' My voice echoed as though my ears were stuffed with cotton wool. 'Hanging is against the law.'

26

'The law! Fie!' said a voice from above. We looked up. My mother stood at the head of the staircase, dressed all in black. 'The bloody book of law you shall yourselves read in the bitter letter.'

'*King Lear*,' said Cordelia.

'*Othello*,' I said at the same moment.

It was our parents' habit to quote extensively from Shakespeare's plays because, naturally, they knew reams of it by heart. As if this was not bad enough we were supposed to respond with the source of the quotation. In a spirit of rebellion against this pernicious cruelty we had agreed years ago to attribute any quotation to the particular play from which our Christian names had been taken (I had taken to using my second name to avoid embarrassment) and, naturally, sooner or later, we were bound to be spot on. Our parents never tumbled to this stratagem as they lived on a more exalted plane from our juvenile utterances and never really listened to us. Bron scored the fewest hits and Ophelia was most often right, which says something about *Hamlet*.

'The quality of mercy is not strained –' my mother began.

She delivered the speech very slowly with plenty of pomp and circumstance for the bit about the thronèd monarch and the sceptred sway. I hoped she would stop when she got to 'Therefore, Jew', as it was hardly relevant, but she carried on.

'Somebody's got to tell me what's happening,' I said as soon as she had finished. 'It *can't* be true that Pa's been arrested!'

My mother looked pained by my lack of sensibility. 'They say the owl was a baker's daughter.'

Ophelia's mad scene – Shakespeare's Ophelia, I mean – was a favourite of Ma's. She descended slowly, singing the mildly lewd songs that had put Sister Paulina, our English mistress, so painfully to the blush. I felt I would go mad myself if I had to listen to much more of it. As soon as Ma turned into the drawing room, still reciting, I ran up to my eldest sister's bedroom and knocked on her door.

'Ophelia!'

There was no answer. I turned the handle but the door was locked. I looked through the keyhole. Ophelia lay on her bed, hair trailing across the pillow, eyes closed. She looked very beautiful, framed by the primrose brocade curtains that hung from the gilded corona high on the wall. Her eiderdown was ivory silk and the carpet was a needlepoint extravaganza of flowers. A vase of pale yellow florists' roses, probably from Crispin, stood on the table beside the bed. Ophelia had gone to much trouble to make her room pretty and comfortable, and she spent a lot of time there. The moment anything vaguely demanding or tiresome occurred she would go to bed, whatever the time of day and regardless of the inconvenience to others.

I rattled the handle. 'Ophelia! Do talk to me! I *must* know what's happening. I can't get any sense out of Ma.'

I put my eye to the keyhole again. She stirred, but only to pull the sheets over her head.

I was standing irresolute, wondering if there was anything to be gained by going down to The Green Dragon to find Bron, when the doorbell rang. I went down to answer it. Two men stood on the doorstep, one of them in police uniform. I remembered the policeman's helmet and my heart gave a leap of fright. The one who was dressed in a fawn mackintosh pulled a badge from his pocket and showed it to me. I could make nothing of it. My eyes read but my mind refused to take it in.

'Miss Byng? I'm Chief Inspector Foy and this is Sergeant Tweeter. May we come in for a moment? I'd like to talk to you about your father.' A shudder of terror did something to my knees and the streetlamp by the front door seemed to jig about, in time to the rapid beating of my heart. I felt as though years were passing as I stood staring at the buckle of his belt, hearing only a faint beeping of a car horn streets away. 'It is Miss Byng, isn't it?'

I stood back to allow them to come in. Ma was declaiming still, in the drawing room. Though my family frequently drove me to despair I hated people to be critical of them. Probably these custodians of civic order would be puzzled by, perhaps even contemptuous of, my mother's response to a crisis. So I showed them into Pa's library.

We stood about awkwardly while I tried to recover my wits. I had a pain in my midriff as though I had been winded. I tried to smile but my lips stuck to my teeth. The mackintoshed man – I had already forgotten his name – pulled up one of the faux bamboo chairs that stood either side of the secretaire and tucked it behind my knees. I sank on to it. He took the other one for himself.

The uniformed sergeant perched on the end of the chaise longue where my father was accustomed to lie with closed eyes when he was trying to 'get into character'. The sergeant was a big man whose thighs strained at the seams of his trousers. He had a pitted nose, full red cheeks and tight black curls. He looked incongruous against the rich curtains made from the purple sails of Cleopatra's barge held back in elegant loops by gilded rams' heads. My stomach chose that moment to rumble with hunger. I smiled, then put my hand over my mouth because I was embarrassed to be smiling at such a time, and felt the bracing sting of the cut on my face.

The plainclothes man had very regular features and neat brown hair brushed straight back from his face. He had a cleft in his chin like Cary Grant. I saw his eyes travel round the room and pause at the skull, which was part of a tablescape composed by my mother called *Obsequy*. As well as the skull there was a graceful draping of white linen representing a shroud, an hour-glass and a lock of David Garrick's hair.

Glass lustres hanging from the table's edge suggested tears. It had been there for some time and there was plenty of dust.

'It's only a stage prop. The skull, I mean.' I was afraid he might be drawing sinister conclusions. 'Yorick. You know, *Hamlet*.' The inspector's eyes travelled to a dagger that lay on the table in front of him. 'That's from *Macbeth*. It's got a retractable blade. It couldn't hurt anyone.' My stomach made extravagant hollow noises, which we all pretended we could not hear.

I followed his glance to a bowl of apples on the table. Among them was a core, which had turned brown. My father must have eaten it before leaving for the theatre that morning. There was a poignancy in this that made my chest ache.

'Now, Miss Byng. Would you mind telling me your first name?'

'Yes. I mean, no. Harriet.' I heard the scratching of the sergeant's pencil.

'And the other members of the household – could I have their names, please?'

'Ophelia, Portia, Cordelia and Oberon. And my mother, Clarissa, and Maria-Alba.'

The inspector lifted a pair of tidy eyebrows. 'A relation?'

'Our housekeeper – more of a friend, really.'

The sergeant's pencil paused. 'Half a mo, sir. Is that O-f-e-e-l-y-a?'

The inspector spelled Ophelia for him.

'And would it be P-o-r-s-c-h-e, sir?'

I looked down at my lap to suppress a shocking desire to laugh. I was startled by the grubbiness of my hands and fingernails. Dried blood from the splinter mingled with the dirt. The inspector was examining the room when I looked up again. I tried to see, with his eyes, the automaton of Harlequin dancing with Columbine, the copy of the Reynolds portrait of Mrs Siddons, the porphyry urn containing the ashes of a Chinese emperor's favourite ape. There was a decoupage screen of Edwardian bathing beauties peeping through foliage, over which hung a petticoat and a pair of stays supposed to have belonged to Fanny Kemble. On the marquetry bombé chest lay Othello's scimitar and hanging above it, like a hunting trophy, an ass's head with a wreath of roses round its ears from *A Midsummer Night's Dream*.

'This is a very attractive room. Someone has a flair for interior decoration. Your mother?'

I was grateful for this praise. For the first time I had noticed that the library was not altogether clean, that one end of the curtain had slipped from its pole and that there was a damp stain on the ceiling. The veneer was missing in several places on the bombé chest, one of the ass's eyes had fallen out and the chaise longue had a depressed circle covered with fur at one end where Mark Antony had made a nest. Now things seemed to glide back into soft focus and look charmingly original again.

'Yes. She used to be an actress. But I think she likes decorating better.'

The sergeant's pencil continued to scratch, recording these pleasantries for posterity.

'I once saw your father play Coriolanus,' the inspector went on. His voice was deep and agreeably fruity. 'Must have been twenty years ago, when I was an undergraduate. He held the audience in his hand. You saw it from his point of view, how he was cut to the heart by the ingratitude of the proletariat. You felt they were ill-mannered, boorish, unreasonable. And yet, as Plutarch says, Coriolanus was a man of mistaken passion and self-will. An ill-educated prince, unfit to govern. Your father presented the crux with every line. It was a wonderful performance.'

'Thank you. Thank you very much,' I said with what I

immediately felt to be excessive warmth. I wondered if an interest in literature was usual in a policeman.

The inspector smiled as though we were making polite conversation over teacups and sandwiches. He was really rather good-looking, with twinkling, sympathetic eyes. I liked the way the tips of his ears bent outwards a little.

'Mind if I smoke my pipe?' I shook my head. He took out the pipe and a leather pouch and began to stuff shreds into the bowl. Then he struck a match and applied it to the tobacco between puffs. A sweetish smell floated towards me. The process was strangely enthralling. I stared at the little curls of smoke. 'You know, don't you, Miss Byng, that your father has been placed under arrest?'

My temperature seemed to shoot up until my ears were practically in flames while my face grew cold with sudden perspiration. Until that moment I had not believed it.

'Why – when . . . ?' I could not finish the sentence.

'The police were called to the Phoebus Theatre this morning. Sir Basil Wintergreen was found lying on the stage with a fractured skull.'

'Sir B-Basil Wintergreen? Is he . . . ?'

'I'm afraid so.'

I wanted to groan. I may even have done so. My father was currently a member of the newly formed Hubert Hat Shakespeare Company. They were to open with *King Lear* in two weeks. Sir Basil Wintergreen was Lear and Pa was the Duke of Gloucester. Pa had told us many times that the casting was a triumph of mediocrity. Apparently Sir Basil, since his knighthood the previous year, could not get the self-satisfaction out of his voice, however sad, mad or angry he was supposed to be. His Lear sounded like a bank manager delivering an after-dinner speech to a Masonic Lodge. He had grown so fat he could barely do more than fling out an arm or waggle his head. Soon, according to Pa, Sir Basil would have to be brought on and off stage in a cart. With his eyes dwindling to sly gleams in his swollen cheeks, he could express no nobler feeling than the comic posturing of Falstaff or Sir Toby Belch.

The lifelong rivalry between Pa and Sir Basil had been both a spur and a scourge. For many years Pa had been satirical at Basil's expense, deriding his eagerness to court impresarios, directors, critics and anyone who could help him rise. My father had insisted, in a proud-spirited sort of way, that audiences were the proper arbiters of genius. It had been an unpleasant shock when the laurel crown had been placed on Basil's receding brow. It was not the knighthood Pa resented but the immediate clamour for Basil's presence on every stage that stung him. My father's insults became less jocular and more venomous. It would be true to say that he was in a fair way to hating Basil.

'This has been a terrible shock for you.' The inspector's manner was that of a story-book uncle, genial, reassuring, safe. Probably the pipe and Burberry helped. 'I'm afraid there are one or two questions I must ask. Your mother – is she at home?'

'I – she's in the drawing room. I'm not sure whether . . . She suffers from, um, neurasthenia.'

I did not know what this was exactly, only that my mother complained of it. The sergeant's pencil paused and I heard him give a cluck of distress.

'You needn't write that down, Tweeter.' Inspector Foy nodded and hummed thoughtfully to himself. 'Are you the eldest, Miss Byng?'

'No. My brother – we call him Bron – is twenty-six and Ophelia's twenty-four. I'm twenty-two.'

'Can I have a word with them?'

'Bron's gone to the – out. Ophelia's in bed.'

'Is she ill?'

'No. She always goes to bed when she's upset.'

He squinted down the end of his pipe and hummed some more. 'Pom – pom – pom,' up and down the scale. 'And Portia? How old is she?'

'She's twenty. But she isn't here. I don't know where she is.'

'I see.' The inspector drew thoughtfully on his pipe and blew a cloud, his expression noncommittal. 'I was hoping that someone would come back to the station with me. Your father'll need some overnight things, and no doubt a visit from a member of the family will cheer him up. His solicitor's been with him all day, of course. Your father'll be moved in the morning. Probably the Shrubs.'

'The Shrubs?' I echoed stupidly.

'Winston Shrubs. The wing for prisoners on remand.' When he said 'prisoners' I wanted to be sick. I must have looked green for the inspector said, 'You're rather young for all this. I think I should have a word with your mother.'

'I – I'll ask her.'

My mother was alone, pacing the length of the drawing room, the back of one hand pressed to her forehead, the other clutching her left side. 'Ma.' I tried to speak calmly but my voice was breathy and unnaturally high. 'There's a policeman in the library who wants us to go to the station to see Pa.'

She paused in her pacing and crossed her hands over her chest as though cradling something small and vulnerable. 'Waldo! Poor wounded name! My bosom as a bed shall lodge thee till thy wound be healed!'

'*Othello*. Are you coming then?'

'*Two Gentlemen*. Why, he is whiter than new snow upon a raven's back!'

'Yes, I *know*. But we ought to go and see him.'

She widened her eyes. 'This is the very coinage of my brain. It harrows me with fear and wonder.'

I saw the policemen hovering at the door of the drawing room. 'This is Inspector ... um,' I still could not remember his name.

'Good evening, Mrs Byng. I'm Chief Inspector Foy.'

My mother looked wildly at me. 'Alas, how is't with you that you do bend your eye on vacancy?'

The inspector spoke in a slow, calming sort of way as though announcing the next item of a concert on the radio. '*Hamlet*, isn't it? Gertrude's speech, if I'm not mistaken. This is my sergeant. We'd like you to come with us to the station, if you wouldn't mind.'

My mother groaned and clasped her throat. 'This fell sergeant, death, is swift in his arrest.'

The sergeant coughed respectfully. 'Beg pardon, ma'am, but the name's Tweeter.'

My mother made a small sound of impatience. Brushing past us, she paused on the threshold and pointed a finger at each of us in turn. 'Hence, horrible shadow! Unreal mockery, hence!' She swept into the hall and I heard her walking upstairs with slow majesty.

'It had better be me,' I said.

I went into the hall to find my coat.

'I come with you.' In the dim light of the stairs Maria-Alba's complexion, always sallow because of all the nerve-stabilising pills she took, looked yellow enough to be jaundiced.

'Oh, but Maria-Alba – you can't. You know it'll make you – upset. Besides, they need you here.'

'Cordelia is with the television.' Maria-Alba was buttoning her cape, a voluminous garment in scratchy tartan, which she wore winter and summer. 'The others is all right. And Bron, when he return home, *è ubriaco fradico, certo*.'

I hoped the policemen would not know the Italian for stinking drunk. I had not the presence of mind for argument. I went up to my father's dressing room to pack a

35

bag. Shirts, pyjamas, pants, socks, washing things, razor, shaving soap. Eau-de-Cologne, two silver hairbrushes and the hairnet he wore in bed. He was extremely particular about his appearance. I folded up his dressing gown carefully. It was made of saffron-coloured marocain and had once belonged to Noel Coward. As an afterthought I took two cigars from his humidor, his cigar cutter, his sleeping pills and the book of sonnets from his bedside table.

The car was an unmarked black saloon. Sergeant Tweeter drove, Inspector Foy sat next to him and Maria-Alba and I sat in the back. The inspector kept up a stream of small talk – the unseasonably mild weather, the effect of roadworks on traffic flow, the Lely exhibition, the new play by Harold Pinter, the latest novel by Günter Grass. No doubt my replies were lame but the effort required to make them was steadying. Sergeant Tweeter confined his remarks to the odd grunt of dissatisfaction with other people's driving, and Maria-Alba sat in silence, looking stern. As chance would have it we drove round Parliament Square.

'Bit of a row here today,' said the inspector.

'Really?'

'Just some silly kids with nothing better to do than make a nuisance of themselves. But apparently they attacked an old woman. This sort of thing sends the press into overdrive. They'll insist it's proof of declining morality. There'll be sentimental talk of the past when hardened East End villains paused in the act of shooting each other full of holes to help dear old ladies cross the road.'

'Oh. Yes. Of course,' I murmured.

'But think what life was in the so-called good old days. A couple of world wars for a start. A hundred years ago children starved to death in the streets. Two hundred years ago dear old ladies were burned as witches. Plenty of things have changed for the better. In my job it's all too easy to be cynical. But there's a great deal of good in the world if you look for it.'

I understood that he was trying to keep my spirits up. In the half-darkness, coloured lights from shops and advertisements streamed across Maria-Alba's face. It was shining with sweat. Searching for a handkerchief in my pocket, I found the remains of Yell's cake, which Hank had given me. It was composed chiefly of golden syrup and had made a horrible mess of my coat. The stickiness seemed to get worse the more I licked my fingers.

The police station was modern and anonymous. As we walked in I was assailed once more by the disorientation that had threatened all afternoon. Sound and vision were subtly distorted. People's faces were crooked with bulging foreheads and noses out of proportion with their chins. Overhead neon strips made buzzing sounds, pulsating, now dim, now glaring, as though they were extraterrestrial beings attempting to communicate across light years.

We walked down corridors that swayed and jiggled like the elephants' cakewalk at the funfair. I kept my eyes fastened on the nape of Inspector Foy's neck. When he stopped and spoke to me his voice boomed and broke over my ears in waves.

'He's in here. We've made him as comfortable as we could.' He was frowning at me. 'Are you all right?'

'*Sta bene.*' Maria-Alba's voice was gruff. '*Senta, sputa.*' Her handkerchief appeared in my line of vision like a great white wing. 'On the cheeks is what you eat in the car. *Lo sa il cielo, chissà!*' I spat obediently and did not protest as Maria-Alba dabbed vigorously, hurting my cut cheek.

'Here we are.' Inspector Foy spoke with a hearty cheerfulness as though ushering his nieces into a box at the theatre for their annual pantomime treat.

37

FOUR

My father was sitting at a table with a glass in his hand and a nearly empty bottle of red wine at his elbow. The room had originally been painted a harsh yellow. Now, up to shoulder height, it was dimmed by dirt and defaced by graffiti. The ugly plastic chairs, metal filing cabinets and printed notices were depressing. In this setting my father, with his beautiful, sensitive face and his dark hair, grown long for the part of Gloucester, looked like an exotic creature trapped in a down-at-heel circus. This was despite wearing a jacket and trousers that plainly did not belong to him. Not only were they too small but they were of a Terylene respectability that Pa would never have chosen. A policeman was standing to attention by the door, presumably in case my father decided to make a run for it. He was grinning all over his face for my father was in full flow.

'So there she was, without a stitch on and holding this thing as though it was a bomb about to go off, when the lights went on and the duchess said – Ah, Harriet!' He broke off as we were ushered in. 'And Maria-Alba. My dears, this is truly heroic.' He stood up and came from behind the table to kiss our hands and then our cheeks with the graceful ceremony of a Bourbon prince welcoming guests to his Neapolitan palazzo. 'I was just telling the constable the story of Margot Bassington and the Prince of Wales' cigar case.'

I was astonished to see him apparently in the best of spirits. A shiver ran down my back and into my knees, which was probably relief. I had been afraid this terrible shipwreck might have changed my father into someone unrecognisable. I wanted to put my arms round him but I saw at once that this would be inconsistent with the style in which he had chosen to play the episode.

'We've brought you some things.'

'Thank you, my darling. Ridiculous as it may seem, my clothes have been impounded. Of course they are covered in blood and naturally the blood is Basil's. I do not wear clothes dabbled with gore, as a rule.' He looked more closely at my begrimed appearance. 'Your sympathy with the oppressed does you credit, Harriet, but is it absolutely necessary to take on their slipshod condition? Where is your mother?'

'She's . . . distressed. Lying down.'

'Good, good. I should not like to see her against this – pedestrian background. And Ophelia? Have you met my eldest daughter, Inspector? One ought not to praise one's own children, but she is remarkably beautiful. Very like her mother.'

'Ophelia's gone to bed.' I could not keep a note of apology from my voice though I knew it would annoy him.

'Of course, of course. The sensible thing.' He frowned. 'Is your brother with you?'

'He had to go out.'

'My son, Oberon,' he addressed the inspector again, 'is a fine actor. But sordid commercial considerations must prevail over beauty and truth.' Beauty and Truth were our household gods and my father had a special face he put on when speaking of them, lifting his eyebrows and lengthening his upper lip.

39

'As a suckling actor Oberon is obliged to turn his hand to toil of a more prosaic kind. He has a flourishing career in – ah – property.'

Bron, who had not had an acting job for more than a year, had been working for an estate agent but had been sacked only last week. An American to whom Bron had sold several miles of the River Thames for a gigantic sum had complained to the ombudsman when he discovered the sale was fraudulent. There was the threat of a court case.

'Portia's staying with friends,' I said. 'She probably doesn't know what's happened – otherwise she'd certainly be here.'

I knew I had put too much eager assurance into my voice. My father betrayed his displeasure by drumming his fingers on the tabletop. Then he shook back his hair and showed his excellent teeth in a smile in which good humour was mildly flavoured with regret. 'I understand perfectly, Harriet. You need not prevaricate. You see, Inspector, my children have inherited a sensibility so acute we may even call it excessive. They do not wish to see their father in this painful predicament. They dislike unpleasantness, the dark passages in a man's life, the sordid whys and wherefores of our mortality. They prefer to frisk and frolic in the sun, to banquet on felicity. It is a family weakness but is it not better to be thin-skinned than to be unfeeling? I confess I think so.'

Maria-Alba put his overnight bag on the chair with something of a thump. 'Fortunate for you there is someone of the family without feelings. Or you have no toothbrush.' She sat on a chair beside the constable, folded her cape around her though the room was stuffy, and closed her eyes.

'Is there anything I can do for you, Pa?' I asked, still standing by the table, wanting but not daring to take his hand.

'No, Harriet. These gentlemen,' he waved in the direction of the constable, 'have done their best to supply the few requirements a man can have in such unprosperous circumstances. My supper has been brought to me and simple though it was – and, let us be truthful, rather too early to be perfectly agreeable – it was wholesome and fresh.'

'Well, sir,' Inspector Foy brought a chair up to the table for me, 'would you have any objection to running through a few details in the presence of your daughter? Informally, now, without Mr Sickert-Greene.' Henry Sickert-Greene was our family's solicitor. 'No tape recorder. Nothing that'll be used in court. While I understand Mr Sickert-Greene's anxiety that you might incriminate yourself, his refusal to let you say anything doesn't get us any further, does it? Sergeant Tweeter will write down anything you care to tell me and it needn't go beyond the walls of this room. I want to get a clearer picture of what exactly happened this morning.'

I was pretty sure old Sickly Grin, as Bron had christened Mr Sickert-Greene years ago, would have disapproved strongly of this suggestion. I wondered if Inspector Foy was to be trusted. Looking at his nice straight nose and firm chin and intelligent grey eyes I felt almost certain that he was.

'Do you mind a pipe, sir?' Inspector Foy reached inside his coat.

'Yes, I do. My voice is the chief tool of my trade, Inspector, and it is extremely susceptible to tobacco fumes.'

No one could accuse my father of trying to curry favour, at all events.

The inspector took his hand out again. 'Would you tell your daughter what happened? Take as long as you like.'

'Could you bear to talk about it?' I asked timidly. Mentioning Sir Basil's death seemed as insensitive as asking a stranger straight out how they had lost all their arms and legs.

'Poor old Basil, do you mean? Oh-oh-oh!' My father ran through two registers with the exclamation. 'Murder most

41

foul, strange and unnatural!' He shook his head but there was a gleam in his eye I hoped Inspector Foy could not see. 'Ha! What a lesson was there! Reduced from a strutting cock to a blood-boltered corpse in one tick – tock – of Time.' He jerked his finger to imitate the minute hand of a clock. 'Farewe-e-e-ll! A lo-o-ng farewell to all his greatness! Today he puts forth the tender leaves of hope, tomorrow, blossoms, the third day comes the *killing frost*.'

You had to hand it to him. The lightning change of expression from gentle introspection to malevolence as he spat out 'killing frost' was masterly. I did not dare to look at the inspector.

'Oh dear! Was there much blood?'

'Yes, Harriet. I was in blood stepped in so far that, should I wade no more, returning were as tedious as go o'er.'

'*Othello*,' I said automatically, then blushed, fearing the inspector would think I was trying to show off.

'Tst! *Macbeth*.'

I could hear Sergeant Tweeter's pencil, scribbling frantically.

'What happened just before you found Sir Basil?' asked the inspector.

'There was the usual delay before the rehearsal. I generally use the time to warm up. I decided to run through the gouging scene – the one in which they put out my eyes – on my own. I was still undecided about the cry of pain for the second eye, whether to rise to a shrill scream or to stay in the lower register, a bellow of agony like a creature of sacrificial offering –'

'Were you struck by anything unusual?' the inspector put in. 'Something about the stage that wasn't quite as it should be?'

'A theatre in rehearsal is always a mess.' My father seemed irritated by the interruption. 'Had the stage *not* been a clutter of heterogeneous objects then I might have thought it unusual. I expect there were props, flats, carpenters' tools, scripts, paint pots, swords, lanterns, tea trays – the usual clutter of crude implements with whose assistance we actors conjure the illusion of man's genius and depravity.'

'Did you touch anything on your way?'

'Nothing. Nothing at all. The auditorium was in semi-darkness, the stage lit by a single spotlight. I walked towards centre stage and, blinded by the light that was in my eyes – some fool had trained a single spot there – I stumbled across something that lay in my path and fell. I put out my hand. The thing was warm, unpleasantly sticky. It was poor Basil – his head quite crushed. I sprang to my feet with a cry of "Give me some light. Away!"'

'Just a tick, sir,' said Sergeant Tweeter. 'When you said "away", was you meaning one word or two? Away with the body or you was going away or you was hoping to find a way, sir?'

My father sighed impatiently. 'It is a quotation from *Hamlet*. Doubtless had I been capable of thought at that moment I would have intended all three interpretations you put upon it. It was a horror, an abomination!' He gave a shudder I was convinced was genuine. He was extremely squeamish.

'What happened then?'

'Several people came running onto the stage in response to my shouting.'

'Can you remember who they were?'

'Haven't the least idea. The women were screaming at the tops of their voices and the men were nearly as bad. Wait a minute, I remember there was that little understudy among them – Sandra, I think her name is – who was flatteringly relieved to discover that it was Basil and not I who lay incarnadined and mute.'

43

There was a grunt of protest from Sergeant Tweeter but the inspector swept on.

'Was there bad blood between Sandra and Sir Basil?'

'It had nothing to do with poor Basil. She has a crush on me. Of course, I don't take it seriously. She's a sweet little thing, hardly out of school. You know how impressionable girls are at that age.' If the inspector knew he wasn't telling. He hummed up and down an octave. 'But,' continued Pa, 'the theatre is an adder's nest of jealousy and insecurity. And Basil, poor man, did not have the art of endearing himself to others. I dare say I could name several who actually hated him. But of course,' he put on his noble Brutus face, 'I shan't.'

'Very laudable, sir.' The inspector's voice was admiring. 'But it might be in your own interest, as this is a case of murder, to put such scruples aside. This afternoon I interviewed several members of the cast. They none of them hesitated to mention a quarrel yesterday between you and Sir Basil.'

For a brief second Pa looked rather hurt by this treachery but then rapidly assumed a mask of world-weariness.

'I have no secrets from you, Inspector. It was a childish row over a suggestion of Basil's. He thought I should have my eyes gouged out offstage, to save messing about with blood bags.'

'You didn't think that was a good idea?'

'Certainly not. In some second-rate productions the horrid deed is done in the wings. But that's throwing away a great dramatic climax, for the lack of a little ingenuity. It was obvious that Basil was desperate to hog all the audience's compassion for Lear. In many ways Gloucester is a much more sympathetic character.'

'You quarrelled?'

'I called him a fat, greasy lickspittle – or something like that. He called me a Casanova, an ageing lady-killer – among other things, I forget what.' He lifted his chin, which was still firm and well-defined. 'Spiteful nonsense, of course.'

'So you were angry. Did you feel at that point you wanted to kill him?'

My father laughed as though indulging the inspector's sense of drama. 'I'm not a violent man nor is it my habit to assault people who call me hard names.'

'But why *have* you been arrested?' I asked.

My father gave a superior sort of smile. 'You have to see it from a policeman's point of view, to understand why such a hopeless bungle has been made of the business. Imagine yourself a young constable – about seventeen years old to judge from the down on his cheek – whose most exciting job of the day has been to take a lost puppy to the dog pound. You are informed that a famous actor has been found dead in suspicious circumstances. You come bounding in, almost swallowing your whistle with excitement. At last, a chance to use those handcuffs! Something to tell mother when you go home for tea! You see a possibly even more famous actor – it is not for me to say – prostrate at the scene of the crime – for Sandra's eager embraces had prevented me from rising – and dripping with the corpse's vital fluids. Naturally – because you are young and foolish and have no comprehension of human nature – you assume it was he who dispatched the man with all his crimes broad-blown, as flush as May, his heels kicking at heaven.'

'Hang on a bit.' Sergeant Tweeter was breathing hard now in his efforts to keep up. 'Who was it kicked the dog?'

'Never mind, Tweeter.' Inspector Foy looked at his notebook. 'We mustn't forget that when PC Copper questioned you, your answers were, to say the least, ambiguous. When asked what you knew about Sir Basil's death, you said, "Blood will have blood. Never shake thy Goldilocks at me."' The inspector frowned. 'I think that must be gory locks. "Will

45

all my great-nephew's" – great Neptune's, I think – "ocean wash this blood clean from my hand?"'

'They were re*mark*ably bloody.' My father looked down at his spread fingers, now mercifully clean.

'But you can't arrest him for saying that,' I protested. 'He was in shock. He just said the first thing that came into his head. It didn't mean anything.'

'If you remember *Macbeth* as you ought, Harriet,' said my father reprovingly, 'you will know it is a moment of exquisite nuance in a scene crammed with meaning and expressed in the finest poetry: No-o-o! This my hand will rather the multitudinous seas –'

'I understand, Miss Byng. But PC Copper is not a student of English literature. It sounded to him like a confession. When your father refused to say he didn't do it, the constable placed him under arrest.'

I leant across the table and put my hand on my father's arm. 'Pa, tell them you didn't kill Basil.'

'Thy wish was father, Harry, to that thought. Of this alone I am guilty.' My father spoke in a slow dreamy voice. 'I may not have been the instrument but I confess I was, God help me, frequently angry enough to wish him – no, not dead, but – out of my way.'

For my father other people's prime duty was to be an audience. Being looked at and wondered at and talked about was as necessary to him as breathing. He was enjoying giving a bravura performance of a man wrongfully accused. One of his first roles as a child actor had been the eponymous character in *The Winslow Boy*.

'There you are!' I looked at the inspector. 'He's just said he didn't do it.'

'Sergeant, read out what you've just written.'

'I'm getting it down as fast as I can.' The sergeant's tone was injured. He read out in a slow monotone. '"Father Harry

46

– I am guil-ty. I may not have been a hinstrument but I confess –" Blast! Excuse me, ladies. My pencil's just broke. It's all them long words.'

The inspector sighed. 'You see how it's going to sound in court, Miss Byng. What we need is a clear statement. A straightforward denial. And there's also the business of the fingerprints.'

'Fingerprints?' I began to feel frightened.

'The autopsy report's just come in. Sir Basil was struck once, a heavy blow, centre skull, from above. According to PC Copper's notes there was a metal rod lying beside the body. It was sent immediately to Forensic. Two feet six inches long, weighing several pounds, with a point at one end. And covered with blood. Forensic say Mr Byng's prints were on the handle.'

'Naturally they were. That was the gouger,' explained my father. 'I took it with me to get me in the mood. Think of it, Inspector. Your arms are tied, you are helpless before your enemies. Their grinning, exultant faces are the last things you will see in this world. But not quite! The very last thing of all is the cruel tip of obdurate iron as it makes it way through the soft jelly of your eye into your very brain! A-a-a-rgh!' My father flung himself back in his chair and gave a blood-curdling scream that made me drive my nails into my palms. Maria-Alba opened her eyes and crossed herself fervently. A policeman put his head round the door and asked if we were all right.

The inspector waved him away and stuck to his point. 'Did you use this – gouger to kill Sir Basil, Mr Byng?'

'Of course I didn't! I must have dropped it when I fell over the body. Naturally there was blood on it. Everything within ten feet of Basil was covered with it. Ugh!' He gave another shudder and drew together his dark-winged brows.

'Got that, Tweeter?'

Sergeant Tweeter, licking the point of his pencil, muttered that he had some of it.

'What did you mean when you called Sir Basil –' he consulted his notes again, '"a dreary old queen, bloated with bombast"?'

'Did I really say that? I don't remember.'

'According to Miss Marina Marlow. Was Sir Basil a homosexual, to your knowledge?'

My father put on his I-know-a-hawk-from-a-handsaw face, a combination of abstraction and cunning. 'Don't start a hare, Inspector. I neither know nor care if Basil was queer. He's dead. Let his secrets die with him. *De mortuis nil nisi bonum* – good advice and I shall stick to it.'

Was it possible? I wondered, watching my father as he swept a lock of dark wavy hair from his forehead. His expression was one of pained virtue. Could he actually be a murderer? My father – who would cross the road to avoid seeing rabbits with bloody muzzles hanging in the butcher's shop window? Who would not allow Loveday to kill the moles that ruined the grass? Who, when fishing had enjoyed a brief vogue with Bron years ago, objected violently to the cruelty of skewering live worms with hooks.

'Thank you, sir. I think we'll leave it there for today. Miss Byng, I'll arrange for a car to take you and Miss Petrelli home.'

For a moment I couldn't think who Miss Petrelli was. Then I remembered it was Maria-Alba. I was fairly sure I had not got round to introducing them. My anxiety was increased by this display of police omniscience.

'Have you a message for Ma?' I asked my father.

'Tell her to be brave. All will be resolved. Tomorrow and tomorrow, and tomorrow creeps in this petty pace . . .'

I stood politely and waited for the end of the speech, my knee aching and my cut stinging. Shakespeare had suitable observations for every occasion. He really was inexhaustible. The last sight I had of my father was of his face turned to the window displaying his famous profile while the young constable applauded.

Maria-Alba held my arm tightly as we walked back along the corridor.

'This is very hard on you.' The sympathy in Inspector Foy's voice was almost my undoing. 'He's bearing up very well, considering. Try not to worry.' But he believed my father to be guilty of murder and was therefore the enemy. I felt confused.

We heard voices raised in anger. I averted my eyes from a quarrelsome group of people by the reception desk. I had had enough of human life in the raw for one day. Then someone shouted, 'Order is Slavery!' I saw, handcuffed to a policeman apiece, Dodge and Yell. Dodge had a swollen eye that was nearly closed and Yell's nose was dripping with blood. Despite this there was evidence that the fight had not been knocked out of them. A broken chair lay on its side and several posters had been torn from the walls.

'Pigs! Capitalist zombies!' screamed Yell.

'Harriet!' Dodge must have forgotten about the opprobrious middle-classness of my name. 'Have those fascists been beating you up? Hey! You!' He addressed Inspector Foy. 'You leave my girlfriend alone! I know what our rights are!' The inspector looked hard at me. I felt myself grow hot.

'Where're you taking those two?' he asked one of the handcuffed policemen.

'Down the nick. They've made a nasty mess of the nice cell we put 'em in. They're asking for a bit of rough treatment. I think we can arrange that.'

'Don't let the bastards intimidate you, Harriet.' Dodge's voice was almost tender. 'Refuse to say anything. They'll have to let us out on bail. See you in court.' He waved his free fist. 'Fight for freedom!'

'Are you all right?' I looked from Dodge to Yell. She raised two fingers, discreetly so Dodge could not see. 'They won't be hurt, will they?' I asked the inspector as they were led away, chanting slogans. 'It isn't a crime to try and make things better for other people, is it?'

'If you'll take my advice you won't go to Owlstone Road tomorrow.'

'Oh. No.' I was too taken aback by the compass of the inspector's knowledge to dream of rebelling against his authority. 'I won't.'

'Good girl. Sergeant Tweeter will take you home. Good night, Miss Petrelli.'

Maria-Alba's reply was inaudible.

'Drat it!' said Sergeant Tweeter, pushing ahead of us through the vestibule. 'Them para-patsies are on to us. Inspector Foy had the idea of sending 'em to Hammersmith. He set up a decoy car but o' course it was only going to fool 'em for a bit.'

I crossed the threshold and was dazzled by the bursting of flashbulbs. 'Just look this way, miss. How's your father, Miss Byng? Has Waldo Byng been charged yet? Over here! Which daughter are you?' There was extraordinary menace in these demands and questions. Now I understood why primitive peoples believed that cameras stole their souls. The explosions of light in my face greedily sucked up all my reserves of strength. Maria-Alba was sick without warning on the top step and, taking advantage of the gap that opened up as the reporters backed away from the pool of vomit, I put my arm round her and followed Sergeant Tweeter, who was breasting his way through the photographers. He pushed Maria-Alba into the car. Hands pulled at my arms, even held on to the collar of my coat. I felt the helpless paralysis of nightmare.

The next moment I·was inside the car and Sergeant Tweeter had slammed the door painfully against my hip.

Maria-Alba was sick again, this time into the foot well, and Sergeant Tweeter swore loudly but it may have been in reaction to the faces pressed against the windows, the popping of bulbs and the banging of fists on glass as we moved slowly forward. Maria-Alba held her handkerchief to her face and drew sobbing breaths, hyperventilating. With a proficiency born of experience I emptied the contents of my bag on to my knees and pressed it over her face to restrict her intake of oxygen and increase the level of carbon dioxide in her blood. We left the crowd behind and sped away through the dwindling evening traffic. I rubbed Maria-Alba's shaking hands and tried to give her words of comfort. It seemed a long way to Blackheath.

A succession of thoughts, half formed, slippery, disappearing the moment I defined them, raced through my brain. My father was alone in that dreary place, acting like mad to an almost empty auditorium. I felt that I had abandoned him. From childhood, from that first moment when I was able to isolate one distinct feeling from the flood of sensations that constitute infant consciousness, I had known intuitively that my parents needed protection from a hard, ungenerous world. That intense love that children have for their parents was never, afterwards, untouched by fear.

As I grew in experience the sense of danger increased to include their own excesses. They enjoyed living dangerously, being either *aux anges* or in the depths of despair, and they rarely troubled to conceal their state from us. They saw emotional extravagance as living life to the full and perhaps they were right. But I was a changeling. Circumspection, one might fairly call it cowardice, was part of my character. I seemed to have everyone else's share of prudence and I was often afraid on their behalf. I was fairly sure the performance I had just seen was the product of euphoria generated by shock. My father's confidence must have received a fearful knock. What if his courage should desert him in the long hours of the night?

We crossed Tower Bridge without my noticing it. Was Inspector Foy convinced of Pa's guilt? Would he sift the evidence carefully or did he hope for a quick conviction? How many innocent men were serving sentences in prison for crimes they had not committed? Was my father innocent? The idea that he might not be was so frightening that I had to clench my jaw to stop myself from screaming. After an unhappy fifteen minutes we were in Blackheath and Sergeant Tweeter was saying, 'Is there a back way in, miss? Them buggers – pardon the language, miss – the ladies and gentlemen of the press are here an' all.'

At least a dozen people stood in the shadows around our gate. I could just make out Bron in their midst. He was turning his head from side to side, posing and smiling. I directed the sergeant into the mews. No sooner had I hauled a gasping Maria-Alba from the car than I heard running feet and what sounded like baying for blood.

'You get in, miss. I'll hold them off. Now then, you lot!' Sergeant Tweeter shouted as he got out of the car. We scuttled through the gate, sprinted through the convolutions of Loveday's maze and dashed into the house. I locked and bolted the back door.

'*Madre di Dio*!' wheezed Maria-Alba. '*Sono le pene dell' inferno*!'

She did not exaggerate.

FIVE

'I can't go *on* saying I'm sorry.' Bron stood before the drawing-room fire, smoking a Passing Cloud through a long cigarette holder. It was later that same evening. He sounded aggrieved. 'How was I to know you were in Garbo mode? They seemed like rather good types to me. They'd been hanging around our gate for hours. It was common courtesy to ask them in.'

'All right.' I must try to keep calm, be reasonable. Above my right eye throbbed a severe pain as though someone was boring a hole with a brace and bit. 'Let's forget it. Only it was rather like finding a herd of snapping crocodiles in one's bed. It must have been obvious I didn't want to talk to anybody. I'm not at all-surprised Maria-Alba had a screaming fit. I wanted to have one myself.'

'How like a girl to say "let's forget it" and then go on about it. I sent them away when you asked, didn't I?'

It was true that Bron had got rid of the reporters with the promise of an extended interview the next day. Later, he had gone out to rescue the hapless journalist who had been wandering about for ages, lost in Loveday's maze. I knew Loveday would be delighted.

'All I ask is that you don't let them back in.'

'I'm going to give my press conference at The Green Dragon. The landlord's thrilled to have the free publicity. My agent'll be pleased too.'

'Have you understood what's happening? Pa's about to be sent to prison for the rest of his life and all you can think about is promoting your career.'

'Not really?' Bron looked quite anxious. 'That would be awful.'

'That's an understatement!'

'I must say I'm surprised. I consider myself a good judge of character.' I wondered on what grounds he made this entirely unsubstantiated boast. But as, despite everything, I loved my brother I did not contradict him. 'I mean, actually smashing a man's skull. I know Pa's always hated Basil but it's taking rivalry a bit far.'

'Of course he didn't do it!'

'Oh. No. That is, if he didn't, why's he been arrested?'

'I've explained all that.' I had, at length, as soon as the press had gone. The trouble was, Bron was full of Manhattans, and black coffee can only do so much. 'Of *course* he didn't do it. And we've got to go on telling everyone that, however bad things look. What'll the police think if even his own family doesn't believe he's innocent?'

'Righto.' Bron nodded solemnly, his fair hair flopping elegantly over one eye. 'I'm with you there, Harriet. Pa didn't do it. I'm prepared to stand up in court and testify to that.' He was silent for a moment and I knew he was seeing himself as a character in a courtroom drama.

'What on earth is that?' I stared with distaste at a swan fashioned from white carnations, sitting on the piano. Its beak was made of orange chrysanthemums and turned up, like a duck's. Until that moment I had been too agitated to register that the drawing room resembled a cemetery. There were vases of lilies and roses on every table.

'Oh, people keep sending Ma flowers. She's very annoyed. They're all the wrong colours.'

The telephone rang. I went into the hall to answer it.

'Hello. This is the *Daily Champion*. I take it you are a member of the family? Can I have your first reactions to the arrest of Waldo Byng?'

I put the receiver back on its rest as a violent surge of misery made me almost too weak to stand. The telephone rang again immediately. I felt cornered by it as if it were a wild, snarling animal. I held my breath and lifted the receiver cautiously.

'Hello, hello? This is the *Examiner* –'

After that, though our number was ex-directory, everyone in the world seemed to know it and be bent on seeking our opinions, so I unplugged all the telephones. The front doorbell rang incessantly. I was deputed to answer it, which I did by calling through the letter box. Usually it was a reporter and he was asked politely to go away. I was afraid if I allowed myself to be rude I would lose all self-control.

Occasionally it was a neighbour, wondering if they might do anything to help. A perceptible curiosity unpleasantly mixed with relish was channelled like a bad smell through the slot between us. We had never been popular locally. I think people were torn between pride in having a famous actor living in their neighbourhood and umbrage that my parents had nothing to do with them. No slight was intended. It simply never occurred to my parents that the residents of The Avenue might be in any way interesting. According to Bron, who fraternised down at The Green Dragon, they were enthralled if my mother appeared in a different hat, but she never noticed if they were sporting a new pram complete with twins. I expect it seemed that ours was a gay and privileged life. Faces familiar from the stage and screen came constantly to our house. Parties went on until the early hours of the morning and there was much laughter to be heard over the garden wall.

Now our neighbours had some kind of reparation for the years of neglect. I thanked everyone and said I would be certain to call upon them if there was anything they could do. After a while I got thoroughly sick of this so I fetched a stepladder, put a wedge of paper between the bell and the clapper and tried to ignore the urgent knockings and flappings of the letter box. In the drawing room Bron was reading Ophelia's copy of *Harpers and Queen* and playing *The Rite of Spring* at full volume, which made my head, already pounding, want to burst. I turned it down a little.

'What? Sorry?' Bron looked up at me enquiringly. 'Couldn't stand that bloody row going on.'

'I wish I knew where Portia was. If she's seen the newspapers or television she must be frantic with worry.' I dithered. 'Perhaps I ought to plug one of the telephones back in.'

My mother thought television sets too hideous to be seen so ours was shut away in the small room where the fuel for the boiler was stored. Cordelia, who spent much of her time sitting in the coal-hole, greatly to the detriment of her clothes, had come running upstairs the minute the reporters had been got rid of, to say that Sir Basil's death was on the nine o'clock news. Bron and I had gone down to watch. I did not want to, in the least, but a confused sense of loyalty seemed to require that I should know what was being said about Pa behind his back.

As we crowded in, slithering about on pieces of nutty slack, there was an interview with someone who had seen Pa being driven away from the Phoebus Theatre in handcuffs. The newsreader said, in what sounded to me like a sneer, that the police were refusing to confirm that Waldo Byng had been arrested on a charge of murder. A résumé of Basil's career, with accompanying stills, had lasted nearly ten minutes. There followed fulsome tributes to Basil from people with tremulous voices and tear-filled eyes and an interview with the producer of *King Lear*, saying what an absolute disaster his sudden departure would be for theatre in this country.

Anyone who didn't know would have thought from all this that Basil was dearly loved, but actually he was a cold, proud man with a sharp tongue and generally unpopular. He never went to theatrical parties and rumours abounded that his only hobby outside the theatre was an unhealthy interest in little boys. But he had died a violent death and I had a sick, sad feeling, watching him in a clip from an ancient film, playing Henry V. After that they had shown a recent press release photograph of Pa and Basil together as Gloucester and Lear.

'It's not a very good one of Pa,' Cordelia said critically. 'His teeth look enormous. He's baring them as though he's going to bite Basil's neck.'

'I expect that's why they chose it,' said Bron. 'The bags under Basil's eyes are shocking! I wonder why he didn't get them fixed? Still, it's too late now.'

I looked at my watch. I continued to worry about Portia, in the brief intervals when I wasn't worrying about Pa. 'Ten o'clock. I suppose she's gone out to dinner with this new man. But usually she lets me know if she's staying out all night.'

'Oh. Yes.' Bron fished about in the pockets of his jacket. 'I found this letter on your bedside table earlier.' The envelope was addressed to me, in Portia's writing. 'I thought you'd probably be keen to read it straightaway so I brought it downstairs. Then I went to The Green Dragon and forgot about it. Sorry.'

'What were you doing in my room?'

Bron looked guilty. 'I needed a few quid for the pub. I haven't bought a round for ages.'

I decided to let this pass. Considering the state of things we couldn't afford to fall out over trivial matters. I tore open the envelope.

> Darling Hat, Have come back for some clothes. Dimitri's asked me to spend a few days at his country house at Oxshott. I think it's in Devon. It sounds terribly grand. Fifteen bedrooms and simply acres of land. I've borrowed your old yellow silk. I hope you don't mind.

I had bought that particular dress just before meeting Dodge and had worn it only once so it hardly qualified as 'old'. But it was certainly too frivolous for a dedicated revolutionary, so it would have been niggardly to mind.

> Dimitri is incredibly sexy. He practically made love to me in the lift though there was an attendant. He has lots of men working for him – three bodyguards, no less! – and they all seem devoted, which must be a good sign. He only has to raise a finger and they leap to attention. We went to Gerardi's for lunch and had oysters and champagne in a private room! It made me think of Edward VII and chorus girls. Dimitri says he's been having an affair with a member of the royal family. He wouldn't tell me who but apparently she chain-smoked all the time they were between the sheets. Also he had to call her ma'am even in bed. He said this put him off. As an anarchist you will understand this. Tell Ma and Pa that I'm spending a few days with a friend from school. Make up someone suitably respectable, bye for now, Portia.

'Is Oxshott in Devon?' I asked Bron, my anxiety increased rather than allayed by this letter.

'Haven't the foggiest. Did you say ten o'clock? Long past my din-dins. Do you think Maria-Alba's recovered enough to cook some grub?'

'Oh, damn! How awful, I'd forgotten about her.'

I ran downstairs to see if she was all right. She was lying on her bed beneath an eiderdown, reading a cookery book.

'*Così, così*,' she replied in answer to my enquiry. She shut the book and slowly swung her huge legs over the side of the bed. Her lids were swollen and dark, like two black eyes. 'You need to eat, *tesora mia*. No, no,' she went on as I protested that she should rest. '*Mi farà bene*.'

I peeled potatoes and made a salad while Maria-Alba put on partridges to roast. Cordelia came out from the coal-hole and sat at the table doing her French knitting. This is done by winding wool round a cotton reel with four little nails in the top. You hook the wool over the nails and from the hole at the other end of the reel emerges a knitted tail. So far all my efforts to think of something she could make from this had been fruitless. The tail was now four feet long and distinctly grubby from falling into Mark Antony's bowl and being trodden on, but Cordelia kept doggedly on. She was unusually silent. Maria-Alba made a sauce for the partridges and heaved long, sad sighs. I knew I must pull myself together. I tried to find things to talk about that had nothing to do with murder or prisons but ideas slipped like bars of wet soap from my deliberative grasp before I could put them into words.

'I'm starving.' Bron came into the kitchen just as we were loading hot dishes into the dumb waiter. He peered into the lift shaft. 'It's a very good sauce.' He withdrew his head, licking his fingers.

'Oh, Bron, you pig!' protested Cordelia.

Bron patted her cheek with his just-licked finger.

'A lady there was in Antigua

Who said to her spouse, "What a pig you are!"
He answered "My queen!
Is it my manner you mean,
Or do you refer to my figua?"'

Cordelia giggled. Sometimes I got the impression that other people found Bron's ebullience a little trying, but often, as on this occasion, I was glad of it.

'*Lascia solo*.' Maria-Alba looked up from unmoulding the blackberry bavarois she had made that morning, when the serene skies over Blackheath were untroubled by so much as a single cloud. 'It is well for you to make joke. When the things go wrong you abandon the boat. When Harriet want you to visit *il povero* Waldo you are rotten drunk! She have to look only to me for help!' Bron's full soft mouth drooped and he looked perfectly angelic. '*Senta, io sono debole*. She need a strong man. You do not think of other than yourself.' With hands that trembled, Maria-Alba arranged a few whole blackberries round the pale-violet, speckled pudding. 'You are *egoista* – selfish like a peeg –'

'That will do, Maria-Alba!' My mother had broken her general rule of pretending the kitchen did not exist and that food in our house was provided by unseen spirit Shapes, as on Prospero's island. She descended the last few steps into the basement, her progress impeded by her long black evening dress and a tiara of jet and feathers like the crest of a giant bird, which collided with the plastic shade of the overhead light. Her High Renaissance features manifested pain. 'I hardly think abusing poor Bron will help in this predicament. You know how loud, discordant voices upset me. Use your chest tones. Fingers here –' she tapped her own impressively small waist – 'and breathe from the stomach.' She bent her plumed head to examine the bavarois as though she was going to peck it. 'Darling,' she patted Bron's cheek, 'don't look so woebegone. Let's have a cosy supper together on trays in the drawing room and leave these nasty, cross people to get on by themselves. Afterwards you shall turn the pages for me while I play.'

Bron considered the proposed plan. Staying at home rated low in his estimation of an amusing evening. Various expressions flitted across his face before it assumed something like compliance. 'That would be fun. I may have to pop out later on, though.' As they went upstairs I heard him say, 'Mama dearest, could you possibly let me have a bob or two? I find I've run rather short —'

Maria-Alba slammed two trays on to the dumb waiter. I took up a tray to Ophelia.

'You can come in,' she said in answer to my knock. She lay on her back across the bed, her head hanging over the side as though she had been strangled, her long hair running over the carpet like liquid gold. 'Oh, food,' she went on in tones of disgust. 'I shan't be able to eat a *thing*. Has Crispin telephoned?'

'I don't think so.'

'You realise what a disaster Pa's going to prison is for me?' She blinked rapidly several times. People's faces, and their eyes particularly, look strange and rather unpleasant, upside down. I felt a return of the disturbing, hallucinatory sensations that had affected me on and off throughout the day. 'Crispin's mother is a complete bitch. She's crazily jealous and she'll use this to turn Crispin against me.'

'But if he loves you . . . ?' The Honourable Crispin Mallilieu had never struck me as the passionate type. He was small and rather weedy, with pale crinkly hair and rabbit teeth. To be fair I did not think Ophelia was much in love with him. She had told me that his elder brother's liver was marinating in alcohol, his skin was perforated with needle marks and that he resorted to public lavatories for passages of love, so

Crispin stood an odds-on chance of inheriting the title and the estate.

'That cow –' I understood her to be referring to Lady Mallilieu – 'wants him to marry Henrietta Slotts. Her father wallows in filthy lucre like a hog in muck.'

'Does Crispin like her?'

'He says she reminds him of a dog he was very fond of as a boy. Certainly she has a long snout-like nose and a great deal of facial hair.'

'Poor girl. In that case she doesn't stands a chance against you.'

'I wouldn't be so sure. Crispin's mental development received a severe check at prep school. If la Slotts looked like a one-eared teddy bear with a darn on its stomach I wouldn't have a prayer.'

'I expect he hasn't rung because he hasn't heard yet. Why don't you have something to eat and then telephone him?'

'My dear, sweet sister, you know nothing about men. I've never rung one up in my life. It's quite fatal to show the least interest. I never accept two invitations in a row and I make a point of being frosty and difficult at least once a week. On Saturday Crispin threatened to throw himself off the battlements of Mallilieu Towers because I said his pathetic attempts to kiss me made me think of a monitor lizard. It's true. He's got a very reptilian tongue, long and thin and flickering.'

I thought of Dodge's face after we'd made love. Happy, peaceful and momentarily reconciled to an unjust world. 'I don't think I'd be very good at that kind of thing.'

'No, I dare say not. That's why I have hundreds of eligible men after me and you've got one spotty crackpot beatnik.'

This wounded, though I tried not to show it. 'It's because you're beautiful, Ophelia. If other girls behaved like you they wouldn't get asked out again.'

'Oh Harriet!' Ophelia's voice sharpened with annoyance. 'Don't fish. It's *so* boring. You're as good-looking as any of us. Different maybe, but there are plenty of men who'd prefer your style of beauty. I do *hate* it when you get humble and saintly.'

'Sorry. Well, anyway, eat before it gets cold.' I put the tray on her bedside table. 'I'm worried about Portia. Do read this.'

I handed her the letter. Ophelia ran her eyes quickly over it and then threw it down. 'Oxshott's in Surrey. Rather parvenu.'

'I don't like the sound of Dimitri.'

'Obviously he's a gangster who breaks people's legs if they displease him. Portia's an idiot.'

I ought to have known there was no point in asking Ophelia for comfort. It seems to me that family life consists of endless repetition of the same misunderstandings and stalemates like a sort of round game. Because I was insecure I was always seeking reassurance and because Ophelia was easily bored she always wanted to shock.

'Will you come with me tomorrow to see Pa?'

'Whatever for? I should think he'd hate to be gawped at behind bars like a chimpanzee in the zoo.'

I decided not to press the point. Ophelia usually said no to everything at first but she could sometimes be persuaded to change her mind. I left her to pick at the partridge and went downstairs slowly, wondering if she could be right about me being sanctimonious. I could be as mean as anyone when angry. Was I lacking the necessary art of dalliance, as she seemed to suggest? It was true that Dodge had been my first real boyfriend but he was not my first lover.

At the age of sixteen Portia had decided that she wanted to get rid of her virginity. She had put the names of all the men she knew between the ages of twenty and sixty into a hat and asked me to pick one. The name on the scrap of paper I had pulled out was Roger Arquiss. This made us giggle, not just because Roger was gay but because the idea of anything remotely passionate in connection with him seemed ridiculous. Sadly, the best-looking of my father's friends were all homosexual, but Roger was not in the former category. He was in his mid-fifties, had a large Roman nose, a fleshy upper lip above crooked teeth and resembled a friendly old horse. When young he had had great success on the stage playing decent self-sacrificing Englishman who never got the girl, but later on he was reduced to playing idiot clergymen in popular farces.

'Why on earth did you put the buggers in?' I asked. 'Let's take them out and do it again.'

'Without them there'd be precious few names. Besides, I was hoping to get Hugo Dance. I'm sure he stroked my bottom last Christmas when he was helping me into my coat. He pretended it was accidental but I saw something like a glint in his eye. I think he just needs the right woman. Still, it's too late now. Roger it will have to be.'

'But, Portia, you're not serious! He's so horrible, the poor old thing. I mean, sweet but!'

'It's no good picking names out of hats if you aren't going to stick to it.'

Portia was nothing if not stubborn. We took the tube to Albany, Piccadilly, where Roger had a set of rooms decorated in a cosy English style with mahogany furniture, green leather chairs, elegant bibelots and masses of books. Roger was very well connected, and judging from the portraits on the walls all his family would have looked at home nodding over a stable door. As luck would have it Hugo Dance was there. They were enjoying tea and crumpets and gallantly pressed us to join them, though it was obvious they were surprised to see us. It was not a little embarrassing. I wondered if poor old

Roger had been trying to get Hugo into his bed. Hugo was certainly a dish. He had black hair, long curly eyelashes and a dark red mouth. I saw Portia giving him longing looks as she smothered her crumpet with quince jelly.

Roger, whom we had known for years, brought out all his tame, child-friendly jokes for our benefit. Portia, instead of laughing politely, slid down her chair so that her skirt rode up over her knees, breathing deeply to make her bosom conspicuous – already it was much bigger than mine – and smouldered. Roger looked more and more surprised. Hugo stared at her a lot, I noticed. Time wore on. It was quite dark outside and soon we'd have to be thinking about going home. Roger got out a bottle of whisky. I stuck with tea because I hate whisky but the other three had plenty. Roger's jokes began to get more daring and then Hugo told some really filthy stories. I laughed, though they did not seem particularly amusing.

'Roger.' Portia stood up, cutting Hugo short. 'I've never seen your bedroom. I bet it's pretty.'

Roger liked to be complimented on his taste. He followed her meekly from the room.

'What's going on?' asked Hugo, chummily.

I couldn't think of a convincing lie so I told him the truth. Hugo thought it was very funny. We giggled together and I thought how attractive he was and what a shame he didn't like girls. He walked up and down before the fire, grinning.

'I wonder if Roger will be able to – what a hoot! Your sister's a little devil, isn't she? I could see she wasn't wearing any pants. Christ! How old is she?' I stopped wanting to laugh. For some reason the fact that Portia wasn't wearing knickers, which I hadn't known before, made it seem real. Despite the brightness of the fire, the elegance of the furnishings and the smartness of the address, everything seemed suddenly tawdry and sad. I heartily wished we weren't there.

Hugo came over and put his hand on my breast. His cologne smelled of lemons and pencil boxes. 'Are you wearing pants, Harriet?' I was horrified and became rigid and tongue-tied with embarrassment. I could not look at him. 'Mm-m-m. You're as flat as a boy. I like that. I think it would be only friendly to follow suit, don't you?'

He shoved me down on to Roger's chesterfield and began to kiss me. His tongue was in my mouth and it seemed enormous. I couldn't think what I ought to do. I wanted him to stop but I was afraid of making him angry. Perhaps it was better to go on. Portia and I could laugh about it afterwards. What was virginity but a nuisance, a badge of immaturity? This was my chance to get rid of it. If only it weren't all so horrible. When he put his hand between my legs I don't think I could have stopped myself from screaming if my mouth had not been full of his tongue. I closed my eyes, terrified I was going to be sick. Amid waves of heat and sweat and pain and drowning in aftershave, Hugo rid me of my virginity before it had begun to be troublesome. Afterwards, as he lay panting on top of me, a hateful stranger, my throat ached from trying not to cry.

'You lucky swine!' shouted Portia as we ran down the escalator at the underground station. 'God! Roger was the last word in utter wetness. When he couldn't manage to have an orgasm he cried, the silly old Dobbin, and I had to tell him it was all right. I think he managed to penetrate all right, though. There was blood. That counts, doesn't it?'

My own thighs were sticky and I had a sharp pain in the pit of my stomach. Hugo and I had been sitting silent in our chairs when Portia had come back, alone, into the drawing room, tugging a comb through her hair. Hugo was smoking a cigarette. We did not look at each other. He saw us to the door and patted my arm, before turning quickly away and shutting us out. Though the thing had not been of my doing I felt deeply ashamed.

'You are lucky!' said Portia again as we rattled through dark tunnels on the way home. 'Fancy! The divine Hugo! There can't be many girls who've had the pleasure.' Then she peered at me. 'You've got lipstick all over your cheeks.'

Even now, years later, when I remember Hugo I want to groan aloud. For a long time afterwards, when anyone kissed me, I wanted to retch. Portia had described in intimate detail what it had been like making love with Roger. She was a good mimic and conjured up a vivid picture of his fumbling awkwardness and her attempts to be nice about his incompetence. The incident did not appear to trouble her in the least. In some ways I envied her profoundly.

Maria-Alba, Cordelia and I ate the partridge in silence. I could think of nothing to say.

When we were halfway through the bavarois Cordelia suddenly said, 'Are you going to see Pa tomorrow? Because I want to come too.'

I looked at Maria-Alba. She shrugged her plump shoulders. '*Perché no?*' she said, wiping blackberry-stained lips with her napkin. 'The mistake has been too little of the reality.'

I wondered which particular mistake she meant. At that moment the opening chords of Chopin's Funeral March, played with the sustaining pedal held firmly down and the occasional wrong note, came floating through from the drawing room. I rested my aching head on my hand. Oh, Pa, I thought, I do love you.

SIX

The sound of the telephone woke me. I opened my eyes, aware that something was terribly wrong. Then with the violence of a fist in the face, I remembered everything. For the first time for years I said the waking prayer the nuns had taught us, as fervently as when I was a child. From the age of sixteen I had declared myself an atheist but now I could not afford intellectual pride. I stared gloomily through the window. All the brightness of the previous day had dissolved in swollen grey clouds, piled ominously high.

I listened to the insistent monotone, hating it, hoping it would stop or that someone else would answer it. For the first part of the night I had been unable to sleep for more than a few minutes before a subconscious prompting had made my eyes snap open to confront some awful danger. I had had to visit the lavatory several times, whether because of the indigestibility of Yell's cake or the affect of terror on my bowels I did not know. My mind was in rags.

When the telephone went on ringing, I rolled out from beneath the weight of Mark Antony and ran down two flights to the first-floor landing, my bare feet recoiling from the coldness and hardness of the stairs.

'Hello?'

'Chief Inspector Foy speaking.'

The cleft in his chin flashed into my mind. 'It's Harriet.'

'Ah. I was hoping to speak to your mother.'

'What's the time?'

'A quarter past eight.'

'Could you ring back later? She doesn't like to be disturbed before half-past ten.'

There was a pause followed by some pom-pomming up and down the scale. 'Perhaps you'll tell her that Mr Byng is due to appear in court this morning at nine fifteen.'

'Oh. Oh dear!' I immediately felt sick. I could not deal with reality following so swiftly on sleep.

'Don't worry. It's only a formality. He'll be put on remand. No need for you to be there.'

'Isn't there any chance they'll find him not guilty?'

'This is only the preliminary hearing. The case won't come to court until we've had a chance to sift the evidence. Probably not for months.'

'He didn't do it. He's not the sort of man who could kill someone.' A crushing misery made my throat tight. Tears began to roll down my face.

'Harriet, listen to me. Can I call you Harriet?' I let out a kind of bleat because I was suppressing a howl. He took it as assent. 'You've got to be brave, Harriet, both for him and for you. British justice is slow and often the way it goes about things seems pretty asinine but it's the fairest legal system in the world. I know that perhaps isn't saying much but, believe me, the idea of sending an innocent man to prison is as abhorrent to me as it will be to the judge and the twelve men and women of the jury. Be patient, and trust me.'

It did not seem to me that I had any alternative but I was grateful for the kindness in his voice. 'All right. Thank you.' I tried to sniff quietly.

'Good girl. He won't be without friends. Mr Sickert-Greene will be with him.' The cleft in Inspector Foy's chin was swiftly replaced by a mental snapshot of Sickly Grin's neck, which bulged in a fleshy roll over his starched collar. I could not imagine him being a comfort to anyone. 'If I were you I'd spend the day quietly at home. The press will be merciless for the next few days. You might get Mr Sickert-Greene to give them some sort of statement on behalf of the family.'

'All right. Thank you,' I added, though probably it was silly to thank the man who was accusing my father of murder.

'Chin up.'

The line went dead. I put back the receiver and the telephone rang again immediately.

'Hello, it's Crispin. Who's that?'

'Harriet.'

'Oh, good.' There was a shade of relief in Crispin's cultured tones. 'I hoped it might be you.'

'Shall I go and get Ophelia?'

'Ah – no. Hang on a sec – don't disturb her. Just tell her I called, will you?'

'Any particular message?'

'Er – just say I've gone down to the Towers for a few days. Awful bore – m'uncle's birthday. Mother insists I show the phisog for a spot of celebrating. He's nearly ninety and expected to pip out before long.'

'Oh.' I did not know whether to sound pleased or sorry.

'Tell Ophelia I'll ring her when I get back. By-ee.'

'The low-down, snivelling, craven wretch,' said Ophelia when I gave her the substance of the conversation. 'He's going to rat!' She punched her pillow violently. 'Well, I hate that hideous Mallilieu Towers, anyway. All pinnacles and gargoyles and nasty blue bricks. Henrietta Slotts is welcome. I don't care.'

She put the pillow over her face and refused to say another

word. After I had closed the door behind me I heard what might have been a stifled sob. I went downstairs to make myself some tea.

Maria-Alba was washing up the supper things.

'*Che c'e?* You look beaky.'

'Peaky, I think you mean. I'm all right.' I could feel my chin trembling 'It's delayed shock or something. It seems worse this morning but I expect I'll be better when I've woken up properly.'

I managed a smile, which changed to a scream as a man with several cameras round his neck jumped from the front garden down into the area outside the kitchen window. He pressed his face against the glass, which clouded with his breath.

'*Basta così*!' exclaimed Maria-Alba, picking up a soup ladle that lay to hand. She threw open the kitchen door and ran out. '*Va fottere la cucina della Mamma*!' she screamed. It was one of her favourite insults. I heard the man yell as Maria-Alba hit him hard on his bald head. He tried to take a photograph of her but she pelted him with blows. He ran off. Maria-Alba came in again, her normally sallow face dark red.

'*La feccia*!' She was panting with anger.

'You gave him a good thrashing. I bet *he* won't come back.'

'If he do I take a knife to him. I keel him!'

I wondered if the world had gone mad. I did not want to spend the rest of my life travelling between maximum-security prisons, visiting those I loved.

Cordelia came down, looking pale but determined. She was wearing jeans, though it was a school day.

'You don't think I'm going to that stinking convent so those beastly girls can be foul to me? Drusilla Papworth'll be thrilled to bits. She's jealous as hell of me and now my father's a criminal she'll be able to leave me out of everything.'

'He isn't! You mustn't believe that. I can understand that some of them might be unkind but surely your friends –'

'You've obviously forgotten what school's like.' Cordelia thrust out her lower lip and shook her silky curls. 'I won't have any friends after this. Ever again. I shall be ostrichised by everyone. When all my family are finally dead there won't be anyone left speaking to me. But by then I'll probably be used to it.' A faraway look came into Cordelia's eye. 'I shall live in a cave in a forest and tame wild animals. People will come and make offerings of food and wine and call me Cordelia the Holy Woman. It might be fun to make a hole in the rock and tell people's fortunes, like an oracle. You have to say things in an amphibious way so you can't be caught out. Pa told me all about it.'

'Ambiguous. But it would be very difficult to think up clever answers if you hadn't been to school and acquired some sort of education.'

'What a poisonous remark!' Cordelia glared at me. 'Just the sort of sneaky, trapping thing the nuns say.'

There was some truth in this but I was not in the mood to be generous and admit it.

'I hate school,' Cordelia continued with passion, 'and particularly those nasty nuns. Their only happiness in life is to punish helpless children. I bet when they're supposed to be saying prayers they're dreaming up new forms of torture. Camilla Everard had to kneel on a broom handle for an hour because she forgot her gym pants. Her parents were furious and she wasn't allowed back after that. She goes to school in Switzerland now and her skiing instructor buys her chocolate cake in return for favours – you know.' Cordelia assumed her grown-up, knowing face.

'Some people come cheap.' I suppressed a smile, not believing a word of it.

'Well, poor Camilla has braces *and* glasses,' Cordelia conceded. 'It's a dump and I'm never going back. I shall kill myself if you try and make me.' I sighed, unable to contend with so much violence. Cordelia scented victory. 'I'm going to make Pa a cake.' She fetched the flour jar as she spoke. 'That'll cheer him up. I'll put it in a tin so the rats can't get at it.' She found Maria-Alba's folder of recipes and began to weigh ingredients.

I was touched by this instance of thoughtfulness in one so young. It seemed a good example to imitate. I began to cast about in my mind for something I could do to console the weary prisoner. I wondered if he would be allowed music. I could take along my portable gramophone and some of his favourite records. Prison furniture was probably uncomfortable. Perhaps they wouldn't mind a very small bergère armchair. The piece of Brussels tapestry that hung on the stairs would conceal ugly paint or wallpaper. I began to form a picture of quite a cosy cell with pictures and books and a few pieces of his favourite Vincennes porcelain.

It occurred to me that someone ought to inform Cordelia's headmistress that she would not be coming to school. My mother's voice, issuing from the receiver as I lifted it, said sharply, 'I am *try*ing to have a private conversation. Whoever that is, put it down at once.' I was disappointed. I had assumed the telephone's silence was because the reporters had given up using it as a medium to contact us. It shows how naïve I still was.

When I wandered down again an hour later, having refreshed myself with a bath and a few lines of Gerard Manley Hopkins, I was surprised to find Max Frensham in the drawing room. Max was a member of the cast of *King Lear* and a friend of my parents'.

'Harriet!' He came towards me and took my hand in both of his. 'I had to come and see you were all right. How is Waldo bearing up?'

'How did you get in?'

'Through the back door. I expect you've forgotten, but last year at your mother's birthday party, you let me in on the secret of the maze.'

I remembered that Max and I had spent half an hour last summer exploring its intricacies and I had told him Loveday's masterplan. Caroline Frensham, Max's wife, had been waspish when we re-emerged and had devoted the rest of the afternoon to flirting with my father. She was good-looking, if one overlooked the blankness in her eyes. In fact the Frenshams were considered a handsome couple and were much in demand socially. Max was auburn-haired with a pale, ascetic face, in which hazel eyes burned, and one of those thin, finely modelled noses with a slight dent at the tip. He had considerable charm. Being Edgar to Basil's Lear was the high point of his career so far but he was only thirty-four and great things were foretold.

'It *is* good of you to come.'

'This is so terrible for you. Of course he didn't do it. Waldo would be the last person on earth to hurt anyone. He is quite simply, and without any qualification, my hero. He can act anyone else off the stage. Certainly poor old Basil. But you mustn't worry. The police have made a stupid mistake. We'll all testify to the fact that Waldo is incapable of murder.' This was like a lungful of oxygen to one who had been breathing thin, foetid air. I was ready to tell anyone who would listen that my father was innocent, but to hear someone else say it was balm to the soreness of my heart. 'Poor Harriet, you must be having a wretched time of it.'

'Max! Dear boy!' My mother glided towards us across the drawing room carpet, her lilac *peignoir* fluttering like a sail head to wind, one arm held out before her like a bowsprit. 'You find us supping full with horrors! Harriet,' she added, in her ordinary voice, 'ask Maria-Alba to bring us some coffee.' She shook out a fan. 'Time has been my senses would have cooled to hear a night-shriek.' She fluttered her hand. 'And, darling, some of those delicious little almond biscuits.'

'What do you think?' Bron was up unusually early. It was not yet eleven o'clock. He was looking *soigné* in his best suit with a blue silk shirt and a scarlet tie. He twirled on the spot. 'Elegant or what?'

'Elegant,' I said, though Maria-Alba and Cordelia said 'what' in unison. After all it would do no good if we allowed ourselves to *marcher à la ruine*. This was one of my mother's most damning phrases and applied to anyone who had allowed a centimetre of fat to accrete to their hips or the tiniest wrinkle to quilt their cheek. 'Are you going out?'

'My press conference.'

'What are you going to tell them?'

'I shall point out how few decent parts there are for good-looking young classical actors. Rudolf Rumpole is playing Romeo at the Tivoli and he's nearly forty. What chance is there for the rest of us? I'd like to know.'

'I meant, what are you going to tell them about Pa?'

'Oh, I don't know. Something will occur to me.' He waved his hand in a lordly way. 'Is there something to eat? I don't want to look pale.'

Maria-Alba, Cordelia and I had breakfast together in the dining room, with the curtains drawn against the photographers, who were back, jostling for place like thirsty buffaloes round a water hole. I lifted a corner of the curtain and counted sixteen of them milling about among the clipped box and bay trees in the front garden. Probably this was trespass but ordinary citizens' rights no longer seemed to belong to us. One reporter sat on a gate pier, his legs either side of the stone ball and another shinned up the lamppost to get a bedroom shot. One of them spotted me and immediately they were shouting and pointing cameras. Cordelia turned to look at me in surprise as I dropped to the floor, my heart beating fast. Her huge blue eyes, in a face as yet unmarked by weal or woe, looked angelic. Supposing this terrible experience had a permanent affect on her happiness?

'This is silly.' I got up and tried to laugh. 'Like being besieged in a Royalist stronghold during the Civil War. With hordes of Roundheads camping beyond the barbican.'

'We wouldn't hold out for long with only Bron to do the fighting.' Cordelia cracked the top of her egg with a spoon.

'Women fought too, even in those days. At least they helped with dropping boiling oil and quicklime on the enemy's heads. Though sometimes the sieges went on for months or even years with nothing much happening. The worst thing must have been running out of food and having to eat dogs and cats and candles and soap and things.'

'I'd rather starve to death than eat Mark Antony.' Cordelia punctured the yolk of her boiled egg with a toast soldier. We were drinking hot chocolate with whipped cream. Maria-Alba's instinctive response to any crisis was to try to fatten us up. 'Think of his dear little whiskery face poking out of a pie.'

'How stupid it all seems now, looking back,' I said, in a vain attempt to turn our thoughts from our own difficulties. 'All those young men killed in battle and then poor King Charles having his head chopped off. He put on an extra shirt so he wouldn't shiver. He didn't want people to think he was afraid – it was so unfair.' I paused, remembering Pa, and felt a twist of pain in my stomach. It was odd how one managed to forget for nearly a minute at a time and then memory would come lurching back, to terrorize.

'How's he going to go to the lav?' asked Cordelia anxiously. I realized she meant Mark Anthony not Charles II. 'You know how he hates doing it if anyone's looking.' A fastidious propriety in such matters was one of Mark Antony's good points.

'He'll have to nip into the maze when no one's looking. What's that?'

'It is the front door. Some man is got in.' Maria-Alba stood up and seized the poker from the fireplace. I ran to get ahead of her. Leaning against the front door, his coat disarranged, the carnation in his buttonhole crushed and his toupee crooked, was Ronald Mason.

'Harriet, my dear girl! I hope I didn't alarm you,' His voice, once a mellow baritone, had the graveliness of a long-term smoker. 'I remembered where you keep the spare key.' He held it out to me. 'You'd better have it indoors for now.'

Ronald Mason had been a heart-throb of the silver screen during the thirties and forties when he was hardly ever out of slashed doublets and diamond-buckled knee-breeches. His characters' speeches were punctuated by antique expressions such as ''pon rep' and 'i'faith' and 'have at thee, varlet'. When he saw Maria-Alba holding the poker his protuberant eyes and small girlish mouth grew round with dismay. '*Sono io, Maria-Alba*,' he cried with pure Oxford vowels. '*Il tuo anziano amico* – Ronnie.'

'*Anziano, vero*,' said Maria-Alba with uncharacteristic brutality, but she put down the poker.

'Ronnie! How good of you to come!' I kissed his wrinkled cheek, which smelled of lavender water. 'But you look a little . . . Have they hurt you?'

'No, no.' Ronald panted as he straightened his toupee. 'Bron coming out distracted them. Had to come. Clarissa asked me. Couldn't let her down.' His eyes were watering with the cold, and perhaps with emotion, for he clutched my arm and added, 'This is a ghastly business. Poor Waldo. I've never been more upset.'

I felt ashamed of all the times Portia and I had made fun of Ronnie behind his back, imitating his mincing walk and his mannered laugh and stagey speech. He had been my mother's lover years ago and had remained worshipping at the shrine despite being replaced by a stream of younger actors. It struck me for the first time that these suitors were conspicuous by their absence. Where was Jeremy Northampton, her current *cicisbeo*? Recently he had been in the habit of dropping in almost daily. And where were those other friends who had so often gathered round the dining table, making assignations in the drawing room and love in the garden?

The doorbell rang. I peered through the letter box into the eyes of an unknown youth.

'Perdi'a's Pe'als. I go'a lo'a flahs fer yew.'

'What?' Then I remembered that Perdita's Petals was our local flower shop. 'Oh. Yes, wait a minute. Maria-Alba, stand by with the poker. I'm going to open the door.'

I tried to ignore the yelling that broke out the minute I put out my head. Lenses were thrust into my face as the press shouted questions about my father's guilt, his reaction to prison life, and was it true that my father had been staying with Princess Margaret on Mustique?

Luckily the delivery boy was fiercely voluable. ''Ere! Don' you go pushing me, ma'ey. '*Ere*!' He was inflamed from indignation to outrage when his hair was rumpled by a fur-covered microphone. 'Naff orf or I'll push tha' fucking thing down yer throa'!'

While he was arguing with them I was able to gather up the bouquets and pass them back into the house to the others. Then I slammed the door, bolted it and put on the chain.

'Hyenas! Vipers! Wolves!' Ronald passed a handkerchief across his brow. 'I am sorry for modern youth. They are uncultured yobs, wallowing in ignorance. Their understanding is superficial and their tastes are banal.'

'Come and have some coffee.' I guessed his pride had been hurt by one of the reporters asking if Ronald was my grandfather.

'Thank you, Harriet, but I have a cab waiting.' He bowed his head. 'I except you and your dear sisters, of course, from the general censure.'

'What we do with these flowers?' asked Maria-Alba. 'I use every vase yesterday.'

Cordelia read one of the notes accompanying what the woman in Perdita's Petals would probably have called 'floral tributes'. '"Darling Clarissa. You must be going through hell!!! It's too maddening our having to go away just now. Our thoughts are with you. Binny and Oscar, with our love."'

Binny and Oscar had been friends of my parents for years. When Oscar had temporarily left Binny for a double-jointed Olympic sprinter, as black as ink and with hair like a thunder cloud, Binny had found consolation in eating Maria-Alba's food, gossiping with my mother and, I was almost certain, sleeping with my father. Certainly when Oscar had turned up at our house several weeks later with dark circles under his eyes and a slipped disc, there had been some difficulty in getting Binny to go home with him. She had declared that my father was twenty times the man Oscar was and then this was certainly true. Now it seemed all this was forgotten.

'I don't like the house looking like a wake,' I said. 'Oh no, someone's actually sent a wreath!' I looked at the label. It said, 'Darling Clarissa from Jeremy. I shall never forget.' 'How horrible! They all believe he did it! We'll give them to Loveday for the compost heap.'

'Think of the cost of those orchids!' moaned Ronald.

We often joked among ourselves about Ronald's little economies. He never entertained but was always the first to arrive at a party and the last to leave. More than once he had been seen pocketing the remaining canapés and sometimes a bottle of wine or whisky. And always after Ronnie's visits the soap disappeared from the downstairs lav. Once even the towel. My parents were amused rather than irritated by these lapses. Ronnie still occasionally appeared in films, in cameo roles, and probably earned enough to live on, but these days his fees were as crumbs to the cake he had once commanded. Advancing age made him fearful of poverty and as my father charitably said, who could blame him?

'What difference does it make?' I said, with reference to the flowers. 'They'll be dead in a week anyway.' I tried to sound careless. I was disappointed that, with the exception of Ronnie and Max Frensham, my parents' friends had found it easier to dial the number of the nearest florist rather than come themselves to offer sympathy. But perhaps they were giving us time to adjust.

'If you're quite sure you don't want them . . .' Ronald replaced his spoiled carnation with an orchid and rearranged his hair and clothing in the hall mirror. He looked critically at his reflection. I could see that his velvet-collared coat, which must have been expensive long ago, was worn at the lapels and he was no longer able to fasten it across his stomach. He looked rather longingly at the clothes brush before putting it back into the drawer of the console table.

'There you are, Ronald.' My mother was coming downstairs, wearing her leopard coat and a pair of tinted spectacles. She was carrying a suitcase. 'I was beginning to wonder what had happened to you. A traffic accident or – something.' She made it sound a matter of supreme indifference.

'I set out the minute you rang off,' Ronald said, with a slight air of injury. Then he straightened his tie, braced his shoulders and lifted his chin. 'How *rav*ishing you're looking, my darling! The bloom on your cheek would put a rose to shame.' He flung up his hand in a graceful gesture, just as he must have done years ago when he first said the line in front of the camera.

'That wig wouldn't fool a blind man,' replied my mother,

very nastily, I thought. 'And the dye you're using on the rest of it looks purple in this light.'

I had been struck myself by the odd effect of the aubergine tufts of hair above Ronnie's ears.

'Well! You certainly don't believe in robing naked truth with the silk of courtesy.' Ronald looked pardonably annoyed.

'You're getting a paunch,' was my mother's rejoinder. 'You'd better go and see Bo-Bo Lascelles. She's opened a new clinic in Bruton Street. Her special diet is a week of raw beetroot juice three times a day combined with three tablespoons of kush-kush stalks from the Andes. Apparently it *pul*verises the fat cells.'

'Knowing Bo-Bo I bet it costs an arm and a leg,' muttered Ronald peevishly. 'Raw beetroot! Never mind the damned grass!'

'If you're going to be moody and difficult I shall be sorry I asked you to go with me.'

'Where *are* you going?' I asked.

'I'm going to see Bo-Bo's plastic surgeon. She says Mr Moffat-Rime is a genius and very reasonable, and luckily he's managed to squeeze me in. I'm having a little tuck here.'

She pressed her hands to her jawbone. Cosmetic surgery was my mother's recourse *in extremis*.

'But what about Pa?'

'I shall be over the bruising by the time he comes out. It's all fitting in quite well.' Her mouth smiled with satisfaction. She seemed to have forgotten about his name being wounded and her bosom being a bed to lodge it in until it was healed.

'Aren't you going to see him? I think he was sorry you didn't go yesterday.'

She turned her dark lenses towards me. 'Harriet, I have noticed before that you have a tendency to *wallow*. Mawkishness is extremely vulgar.' She tossed her head, petulantly. 'I expect

Marina Marlow will be delighted to have the publicity. You know how *I* dislike it.'

I was surprised into silence. Marina Marlow was playing the part of Regan in *King Lear*. She did not look much older than me. Was it possible that she and my father . . . ? I turned the thought away.

'I'll be back next week. Goodbye, Cordelia, my sweet one.' My mother blew a limp-fingered kiss in her direction. 'Give my love to darling Bron. I shall take this opportunity to have a com*plete* rest.' She gave a little hum of pleasure. 'Goodbye, Harriet. Do keep an eye on Ophelia. When I spoke to her just now, I thought she seemed *un peu distrait*. Goodbye, Maria-Alba. I know you'll look after my chicks for me.' She pecked the space above Maria-Alba's ear. 'My fortress. My harbour in a time of storm.' Maria-Alba gave a grim smile of satisfaction, which I doubted had anything to do with my mother's patently insincere praise. 'Ronald, there is nothing for it but to face those vultures. God knows, they have picked me to the very bone often enough! But, arm in arm, we may yet triumph.'

'Ah, yes.' Ronald put a good deal of solemnity into his voice 'Fame is indeed a twin-headed monster. As it creates, so it devours.'

They almost banged heads trying to see themselves in the looking-glass. Then they sucked in their cheeks and stomachs, Ronald flung open the door and they exited together. There was an awkward little moment of anticlimax as the garden was found to be quite empty. Presumably all the reporters were at Bron's press conference. Nevertheless, as they titupped elegantly down the path – Ronald's heels were nearly as high as my mother's – they turned their heads from right to left as if greeting the crowd. Ronald's bow as he handed my mother into the waiting taxi would have struck an echo in the bosoms of those fans who had seen him as Sir Walter Raleigh conducting his sovereign across that celebrated puddle.

'*Bravo! Ben fatto!*' Maria-Alba's dun-coloured cheeks had points of pink in them, which was unusual. '*Dio mi è giudice* . . . but all of heaven and hell is not know till when we die.'

With this inscrutable utterance she went down into the kitchen.

I brought Mark Antony downstairs and put him out into the front garden. Then I went back upstairs to make what I was almost sure would be a useless attempt to console Ophelia. I knocked on the door and called her name but she ignored me. I put my eye to the keyhole. If I had believed for one moment that she loved Crispin I would have been most upset, for she lay pale and still on her bed, the picture of dejection. Now and then she sniffed despondently and once she said, 'Bugger, bugger, *bugger*!' with great emphasis. I imagined she was thinking of Henrietta Slotts as the future Countess of Sope.

While I was on my knees at the keyhole strange noises broke out downstairs and then Mark Antony, his ginger fur stiff with feeling, shot past me on his way to the attic. I looked over the banisters. Bron was standing at the foot of the stairs, his arms extended, holding the loop of a lead with both hands. At the other end was a dog, brown and white and very furry, with feet like dinner plates. Deaf to Bron's commands and in defiance of a throttling choke chain, it was trying to climb the stairs.

'Good dog! Who's a beautiful girl, then?' I said ingratiatingly as I descended. It is hard to prevent oneself from extravagant gushing in the one-sided conversations imposed by animals and babies. The dog jumped up to lick my jerseyed chest with an enormously long tongue, and whined with every appearance of love.

'That's good. He likes you. His name's Derek.'

'Derek? Poor thing. I don't think it suits him at all. The only Derek I know sells office furniture and is a terrible lech.'

'You can call him what you like. But he answers to Derek. When he answers at all, that is.'

'Why should I want to call him anything?' I began to be suspicious.

'Because he's a present for you. To make up for getting drunk yesterday and not going with you to the police station to see Pa. Maria-Alba was quite right. It was very bad of me and Derek's to say sorry.'

'Oh, but . . . Really, Bron, you shouldn't have – I'd forgotten all about it. I don't think I can . . . You know how Pa hates dogs.'

'Haven't you always said you wanted one? Well, now Pa's in the clink this is your chance.'

'But, Bron, imagine what he'll think when he comes home – as though we were taking advantage of him being away. Of course I *have* always wanted a dog, but not now, when things are impossibly difficult as it is –'

'Well, I must say . . .' Bron's handsome face was despondent. 'It's extremely hurtful, you know to have one's presents rejected. I was so pleased when I had the idea. I thought. I know what will make Harriet happy again. A dear little dog she can love, to make up for Pa being banged up.' He lifted a hand to shade his eyes and his voice was broken. 'I don't think I was ever more unhappy –'

'Oh, Bron, I'm sorry! It was kind of you and I'm very grateful but –'

'Not another word!' Bron heaved a sigh and dashed away an invisible tear. 'I'll take him away. Though the man I bought him from has already left the country. He was on his way to the airport. That's how I managed to get him for such a good price. He's a very rare breed, you know. I'm afraid it's the

84

dogs' home for Derek. He won't like it. Apparently he hates being alone. They'll put him in a concrete pen and he'll howl until his poor little chest hurts and then at the end of the week, when no one's claimed him, they'll take him to the vet. He'll be so happy, thinking he's going to a good home, and instead they'll fill his veins with poison –'

'All right, all right!' When we were children Bron used to enjoy telling me sad stories to make me cry, about overburdened donkeys and starving robins frozen to branches, and it always worked. 'I'll keep him – for the moment, anyway. Just until Pa gets home.' I fondled Derek's soft brown triangular ears that lay flat against his head and he wrinkled his brow comically. He was the colour of muscovado sugar, with a white muzzle and a black nose. I made up my mind to put an advertisement in the local post office straightaway before I got too fond of him. 'And – thank you.' I spoke a little gruffly because I was not feeling particularly grateful but Bron didn't seem to notice.

'Righto. Here you are.' He handed me the loop of the lead. 'He likes bacon and eggs to eat.'

'What? Oh, don't be silly, Bron. You know nothing about dogs.'

'It's what the man said. I wasn't aware that you were an authority.'

'I'm not, but surely he eats raw meat and tins of Scoffalot and that sort of thing.'

'I didn't say you had to cook the bacon, did I?'

'Well.' I tried not to sound ungracious. 'What sort of dog is he, then? I hope he isn't going to get any bigger.'

'Oh, no, he's fully-grown. The man said so. He's a – a Cornish terrier.'

'Really?' I looked at Derek with interest. 'I've never heard of such a thing.'

'You've still got a lot to learn, Miss Harriet Byng.' Bron

spoke sarcastically as though still smarting at my ingratitude. 'Expert though you are, in so many fields.'

'I'm not going to call him Derek, though.'

'Whatever you like. I'm going out. Tell Maria-Alba I shan't be in for supper.'

'But, Bron, you'll come with me to see Pa today, won't you? Ma's gone to have her jaw tightened and Ophelia's in a state about Crispin's desertion and Portia still isn't back and I don't like to ask Maria-Alba – she was so upset yesterday.'

'Look, we can't *all* go trooping along as though it was some kind of party. A little tact is called for.' Bron pressed his chin into his neck and looked at me reprovingly. 'I'm going to see Wanda.' Wanda was Bron's agent. 'There should be some good piccies in the evening papers. They took hundreds from every angle and wrote down everything I said, like bees sipping nectar. I don't suppose they often get the chance to interview someone highly articulate. Wanda particularly wants me to go to this party tonight to meet an important film director. It would be madness to hurl away all my chances just to visit Pa. Ten to one Marina Marlow will be there, and Pa won't want grown children at his knee when he's trying to lure the bird into the cage. Honestly, Harriet, you *must* try to put yourself in other people's places. It's no good just thinking about what would suit *you*.'

My mother must have been right about Marina. It was selfish of me, perhaps, to be depressed by the idea. Derek suddenly took it into his head that down in the kitchen was the one thing for which he had been searching all his life and that nothing must hold him back from immediate consummation. His paws windmilled on the polished floor and my arms were pulled painfully in their sockets. I went downstairs with him, leaving Bron with the moral high ground.

SEVEN

'I shall call him Byron,' I said. 'After the poet.'

'He doesn't look a bit like a nasty old poet.' Cordelia was feeding Derek with glacé cherries, which he was gobbling greedily. 'I wish Bron had given him to *me*. He's such a sweet little snookums. I'd call him Honeypot.'

'You wouldn't!' I was revolted. Derek blinked and panted and laid his chin gratefully on Cordelia's knee, showing a regrettable lack of taste.

'Why not? Better than calling him after a boring, wrinkly old man.'

'Byron was only thirty-six when he died. He was stunningly attractive and women fell in love with him by the lorry-load, even though he had a club foot. Besides he was a first-class poet,' I added, attempting to redress the trivial aspects of my argument.

'A club foot? Now that *is* romantic,' Cordelia became dreamy. 'Like Richard the Third, do you mean?' This was Cordelia's favourite film and every time it came to the arty little cinema down the road she made me sit through practically every performance. Laurence Olivier's improbable wig sent shivers of delight through her and she made noses like shoehorns out of Plasticine for all her dolls. Now she got up from her chair, brought one shoulder up to her ear and walked about the kitchen, limping. Derek – Byron, I should say – was driven into a frenzy by this performance, racing several times round the table, jumping up at Maria-Alba and knocking the whisk from her hand.

'*Uffa! Senti!*' she said, fetching a cloth to wipe zabaglione from the table, chairs and floor. '*Le cose vanno di male in peggio*!'

By which I understood her to mean that things were going from bad to worse. Derek was sick at her feet, the glacé cherries being conspicuous on their return. Maria-Alba flung me the cloth wordlessly.

After a lunch that was rich even by Maria-Alba's standards – *chiocciole* with walnuts and mascarpone, braised guinea fowl, tomatoes stuffed with rice and the zabaglione – for Byron's sake as well as our tightened waistbands, we dragged ourselves out for a walk. The only thing I knew about dogs was that they needed plentiful exercise. Also Derek was such a tiring dog indoors that by the time he had gnawed the legs of the furniture, fought the rugs, eaten the lock of Garrick's hair and knocked over almost every vase of flowers in the house, we were quite prepared to brave the newspaper men. That is, Cordelia and I were. Ophelia had appeared briefly for lunch, dry-eyed but subdued. She had confined her remarks to unfavourable comment on Derek/Byron, who, it must be admitted, behaved quite badly. He insisted on lying under the table, snatching our napkins from our knees and trying to take off our shoes. When we put him outside the room he cried continuously with a high-pitched whine until we allowed him back in.

'This was a very bad idea of Bron's,' Ophelia said, some-what savagely as I tied the dining-room curtains into loose knots to discourage Byron from thrusting up his head inside them and pulling down the interlinings with his teeth.

'I expect he'll settle down soon,' I said. 'You must admit he's terribly sweet.' There was about Byron a floppy, panting appeal that I was beginning to find quite irresistible. His nature was affectionate to a fault.

'I admit nothing of the kind,' said Ophelia, as she wrested her shoes from Byron's jaws and placed them with the entrée dishes on the sideboard.

Our walk was not particularly enjoyable. For one thing I was suffering from indigestion, having grossly overeaten to keep Maria-Alba happy. Also I had been obliged to jump up between each mouthful to rescue our goods and chattels from Derek. For another, the weather was damp and chilly, with water droplets condensing on one's hair, face and hands. The reporters stuck to us like blowflies to a corpse as we wandered through the park, Byron pulling on the choke chain until his eyes were starting from his head.

'You ought to let him have a good run, miss,' said one of the reporters, wearying of my reply of 'No comment' to all his questions. 'It's cruel to keep them always on a leash.'

I was cut by this accusation and, against my better judgement, I unhooked his lead. Byron at once changed down, revved up and sped away into the mist. It was a good hour later when Cordelia and I and the two reporters who remained loyal to the search, sank down hoarse and exhausted on the bench beside the war memorial drinking trough. The fog was much thicker now and we could see barely ten yards in front of us. My hair clung wetly to my forehead and my shoes were ruined.

'This is a rum do,' said the nicest reporter, whose name was Stan. 'Likely the little blighter's halfway home by now. Where did you say you got him from?'

'I didn't. I've no idea where he lived before. Perhaps he'll be run over before he gets there.' Low spirits dipped past the point of what was tolerable at the dreadful idea of Derek – we had given up calling him Byron – smoothed extensively over the surface of Shooter's Hill Road.

'I'd better go back now,' said Cordelia, looking dutiful. 'I promised Maria-Alba I'd help her make the *strozzapreti* for supper.' Though *strozzapreti* literally means priest-stranglers, it is nothing more homicidal than a kind of pasta. I suspected there was a favourite television programme about to come on. 'Don't get all mopy, Hat. He's probably waiting for us on the doorstep. Whatever anyone else says, *I* think he's very intelligent.'

During the last half-hour Derek's reputation had been much sullied by the other reporter, whose name was Jay.

'See if you can persuade Maria-Alba to cook something simple,' I begged. 'Sausages would be nice. I don't know when we'll be back from visiting Pa.'

'I'd better come with you,' Jay said to Cordelia, relief evident in his tone. 'You'll get lost in this fog.'

'It's just like that film with Doris Day, called *Midnight Lace*,' said Cordelia. 'It begins with her walking across a London park and it's foggy and this voice says from behind a fountain – only you can't see anyone – "Mrs Preston –" that was Doris Day's name in the film, – "Mrs Preston! I'm going to kill you." It's a really spooky voice – sing-song Welsh – and Doris Day is terrified. Her husband's incredibly swave and sexy, played by Rex Harrison . . .' They were hidden from view by the drifting vapour long before I ceased to hear Cordelia's voice describing the plot in fine detail.

'Cheer up, young lady,' said Stan to me. 'Probably the little girl's right and the dog's gone home. I've got a dog meself – a Westie, cute as a button – and I shouldn't like not knowing where she was. They're part of the family, aren't they? My

Melanie – that's my daughter, only six but she's got me twisted round her little finger – she'd break her heart if Snowy got lost.'

He told me all about Melanie, how pretty and bright she was, and then about Annette, his wife, who had multiple sclerosis and had been forced to give up her job as a clerk in a solicitor's office and was very depressed in consequence, and about their house in Purley Oaks that they were struggling to pay the mortgage on, and Annette's mother who lived with them. Her name was Ivy, and Stan called her Ivy the Terrible because she was so disagreeable. I was sympathetic about all these difficulties and Stan said it was as good as a tonic to talk to someone who really understood.

In return I told him a little about my family. Despite the awfulness of my father's arrest and wrongful imprisonment, I realised that our life sounded much more fun than Stan's and I felt embarrassed by our comparative good fortune. Because he had been so honest with me I felt obliged to do a little unburdening myself. So I told him about Bron's dormant acting career and Ophelia's engagement, which looked unlikely now and Portia's having gone off with a sinister-sounding man, and Stan was very kind and made all sorts of consoling and boosting remarks.

'Tell you what,' Stan shook his head and little starry drops of water fell on my knees, 'it's getting dark and I could do with a drop of sustenance. What say we finish me sandwiches leftover from lunch and then have one last holler for the hound?'

I was not at all hungry but I didn't want to hurt his feelings as he'd been so decent, so I agreed it was a good plan. Stan undid the unappetisingly soggy parcel and a split second later Derek materialised at his knee. His coat was silvered all over with fog but he was quite unharmed. I was so pleased to see him I forgot to be angry about the wasted time spent searching. I snapped on the lead and begged Stan to give Derek my share of the fish-paste sandwiches as he had fixed the package with his large brown eyes and was drooling unbecomingly.

By the time we had walked back across the park, exulting in a shared sense of relief, Stan and I were the best of friends. Though he thought it wouldn't come out because the light was bad, he took a photograph of Derek for his daughter because Melanie loved dogs and would be interested to hear how her father had spent the afternoon. He hoped it would cheer Annette up a little to hear that the dog had come at once in response to the sandwiches.

'Laughter's the best medicine, when all's said and done,' he said, with a wink.

As I was waving a fond farewell a black car drew up and Inspector Foy and Sergeant Tweeter got out. At once I felt guilty because I had been smiling at Stan and forgetting, for a moment, my father's predicament. Actually, I think now that it is impossible to keep sorrow continually before one's eyes, and almost the worst thing about unhappiness is constantly remembering it, so that you realise your grief a thousand times over with the devastation of a fresh shock each time.

Derek took a shine to the inspector at once and made lengthy smears over the immaculate mackintosh with his muddy paws. I apologised profusely but the inspector said it didn't matter a bit. This confirmed my opinion that despite his calling as a fascist instrument of proletarian oppression he was a nice man.

'Is your mother coming with us?' he asked, attempting to wipe his coat with his handkerchief and making a worse mess.

'I'm afraid not. She's – having an operation.'

'I'm sorry to hear that.' He looked so concerned that I almost told him the truth. 'What about your brother and sisters?'

'Cordelia's coming. Portia's still away, Bron's got a – business appointment and Ophelia, my eldest sister, isn't well.'

Just as I said that the front door opened and Ophelia came down the front steps. Even by the light of the streetlamp, which was refracted into a halo by the excessive moisture in the air, she looked stunning. She was wearing a white wool coat, a diaphanous silver scarf and a black Juliet cap. The fairy-tale romance of her appearance was exaggerated by her golden hair, which was knotted loosely behind her head and tumbled down her shoulders in elegant waves, like the youngest of three princesses, who is always the most virtuous and kind-hearted. Ophelia shrank back from Derek's overtures.

'For God's sake, don't let that bloody animal near me.' She ignored the inspector. 'I'm going out to dinner with Peregrine Wolmscott. I can't stand another minute in that depressing house of horrors. Woe, woe, woe! All those ghastly flower arrangements – nobody cheerful to talk to. As for Maria-Alba, she's sinking so fast into depression, I think she's going to have to go in for another sizzle.' She meant the electroconvulsive therapy that Maria-Alba so hated and feared.

'It's awfully early for dinner.' I looked at my watch. It was not yet six. 'Do come with me and see Pa.'

'I thought I'd go to a news cinema and cheer myself up watching the Libyans blasting one another to bits.'

'I'd be grateful if you'd give me a few minutes of your time.' Inspector Foy looked gravely at Ophelia and I longed to explain to him that she only talked like that because she was unhappy.

'You are . . . ?' Ophelia turned her eyes towards him for the first time with her most crushing look of boredom and indifference, which she had spent years perfecting.

The inspector reacted only by the merest contraction of his

eyebrows. 'If you'll just step inside, Miss Byng. It shouldn't take long.'

'As I just said, I'm going out.' She turned to walk away but the inspector made a sign to Sergeant Tweeter, who placed his large bulk in her path.

'Don't let's play games, Miss Byng.' The inspector looked very calm. 'My time is valuable. I want to speak to all the members of Mr Byng's family. I can interview you at the police station if you prefer.' He nodded towards the car and Sergeant Tweeter took a step forward and opened the door.

'Are you going to arrest me?' Ophelia gave a contemptuous laugh.

'You'll look less ridiculous if you come with me into the house of your own free will.'

'You wouldn't dare!'

'The choice is yours.'

Something in the inspector's face persuaded Ophelia, for once, to capitulate. She flounced up the steps to the front door and stalked in ahead of us. I went down to the kitchen. Maria-Alba had just finished making the *strozzapreti*.

'Is there anything for Derek to eat?' I asked. 'I'm going to creep out to the police car. Probably he won't whine if he's got food. Where's Cordelia?'

'She watch the television. *Sì*, I give him the *faraona* from lunch and the bones of the *coscetto d'abbachio* we have for dinner.'

This was one of her specialities, a boned leg of lamb stuffed with onions, liver, sage and pearl barley, delicious but bloatingly rich. Evidently Cordelia had forgotten to give her my message. She opened the fridge door and Derek gave little shivering growls of anticipation. 'Sausages!' I heard Maria-Alba mutter. '*Cos'altro! Dio ci scampi e liberi!*'

I had collected Cordelia from the television in the coal-hole and my hand was on the front door when Derek gave voice

94

to several ear-splitting bars of painfully high notes, like an amateur Queen of the Night. I could hear Ophelia's voice in the drawing room, though not what she was saying. I heard her laugh scornfully. Cordelia and I sat in the car with Sergeant Tweeter and I tried not to worry. Five minutes later Inspector Foy ran down the steps and got into the front passenger seat. 'All right, Sergeant.' He sounded almost savage. 'Let's not dawdle. We haven't got all night.'

Cordelia and I exchanged glances. It seemed that Ophelia had, after all, won the encounter. I could detect anger in the tilt of the inspector's head. Even the bristles on his neck seemed to express a contained fury. No one said anything until we drew up outside a massive, red-brick Victorian gateway that was closed to the world by giant wooden doors. The inspector showed something to the uniformed man at the wicket, who looked carefully at each of our faces before he pressed a button that opened the huge gates and waved us through.

We stood in the brilliantly lit courtyard and, selfishly, I wished myself far, far away. Our household gods, Beauty and Truth, were conspicuous by their absence. Lights shone between bars from curtainless windows in high walls. They illumined nothing but dirt and barrenness. A black van, with its engine running, filled the air with sickening fumes. Not a trace of starlight could penetrate the polluted haze that composed the square of dripping sky above. Not a skeleton leaf nor a straggling weed softened the concrete paving blocks below. Several men in shirtsleeves were brushing a tide of water towards gratings in the centre. I found out later that there were several details of prisoners appointed to this task throughout the day. The slop buckets in the cells, built for one man and occupied by three, were emptied in the mornings only. Not unreasonably the prisoners were unwilling to be confined at close quarters with a pail overflowing with excrement so they threw the contents out of the window.

Truth, also, was reluctant to put in an appearance in this breeding ground of despondency. It seemed obvious to me that if one were weak, stupid or wicked before, one would undoubtedly be weaker, more stupid and more wicked after spending any length of time here.

Inside, the shiny green paint of the corridors reflected the neon lighting with a glare that made me blink. There was a reek of disinfectant laced with urine and sweat that overlaid the smell of boiled greens. Every ten yards or so we stopped and the prison officer who was leading the way unlocked a gate in a grille that barred our path, then fastened it again behind us. I kept my eyes on the floor, which someone had washed with a dirty mop, leaving streaks of grime. I dreaded to see an eye glaring through one of the square peepholes that were in every door. I felt sick with horror at the prisoners' plight and at the same time I was afraid of them. Surely those who are imprisoned can only feel violent hatred for those who are free? I was close to tears but anxious not to alarm Cordelia, who was walking ahead of me, lugging her cake in a plastic carrier. I had a ridiculous longing to hold the inspector's hand but, thanks to Ophelia, he too was an enemy. Just as I thought this, he turned to look at me, said, 'Are you all right?' and winked.

That brief instance of kindness was exactly what I needed. Panic subsided and I felt, if not calm, at least able to control myself. I was thankful that the door to the interview room was not locked. The idea of my brilliant, princely father caged, was intensely hurtful; I did not want to see it.

He was standing by the window. It took a moment to realise that it was he. He was still wearing the borrowed clothes, and his hair was fastened into a ponytail. But more unfamiliar than this was his demeanour. His shoulders drooped forward and his hands hung loosely by his sides. There was none of the *élan* that characterised his bearing. His face was grey and puffy.

'Pa, darling.' Cordelia went towards him, her arms held wide. 'You look just like Sydney Carton.' Several times during the journey I had regretted allowing Cordelia to come, afraid that it was too harrowing an experience for a child. Now I saw that the theatricality of her nature was just what was needed. Except for the ponytail Pa did not look in the least like Sydney Carton, but it was a happy thought and his face brightened. Cordelia took his hand, assumed a frightened expression and a French accent. 'Citizen Évremonde, will you let me 'old your 'and? I am but a poor, leetle creature and it will give me ze courage.' Then she looked at him and did a dramatic double take. 'Sacrebleu! Zoot, alors! Do you die for 'im?'

'And his wife and child. Hush! Yes.'

'Oh, you will let me 'old your 'and, oh brave, brave stranger?'

'Hush! Yes, my poor child. To the last.'

'Am I to keess you now? Is ze moment come?'

'Yes. God bless you! Very soon we shall meet again in a better place than this. Go ahead of me. I shall follow swiftly.'

Sydney Carton took the little seamstress, alias Cordelia, in his arms and kissed her. Then she kneeled and extended her neck, her arms thrust out behind her with a professionalism acquired from the many films about Anne Boleyn, Lady Jane Grey and Mary, Queen of Scots she had sobbed through at the Hippodrome, Blackheath.

My father kneeled in his turn and lifted his eyes to a vision of the future. 'I see the lives for which I lay down my life, peaceful, prosperous and happy in that England which I shall see no more. I see her with a child upon her bosom that shall bear my name. I see that I hold a sanctuary in their hearts and in the hearts of their descendants, generations hence. I see that child who bears my name, a man. My name is made illustrious there by the light of him. I see the blots I threw on it faded away.' He closed his eyes and his face became radiant. 'It is a far, far better thing that I do, than I have ever done. It is a far, far better rest that I go to, than I have ever known.' He allowed his head to drop slowly forward.

I felt my throat tighten. I can't ever read about Sydney Carton going to the guillotine without crying, and my father managed to get into his voice all the triumph and despair of that moment. He was, without doubt, truly a great actor. After he and Cordelia had embraced passionately I kissed his cheek more diffidently. I wished I was less inhibited. It wasn't because I was more truthful, far from it. I was the only one of my family who was no good at acting and if I felt self-conscious there was nothing I could do to hide it.

We brought my father up to date on the condition of the family. I would have avoided any mention of Ronald Mason but Cordelia, to her credit, was not sophistical and blurted it out. Luckily my father was inclined to be condescending rather than jealous.

'Poor Ronnie. It *is* loyal of the old war horse to muster to the sound of trumpets. You may not remember, Inspector, the only Bonnie Prince Charlie with a strong Irish brogue. Every housewife from Sunderland to Wimbledon longed to be Flora Macdonald nestling in Prince Charlie's manly arms, crooning love songs into his lace jabot, crossing the sea to Skye against a purple sunset. The truth was less romantic. Apparently it was filmed in the studio pool with a wave machine but even so, poor Ronnie was sick as a dog.'

There is nothing so effective in the short-term as sneering at someone else to make one feel better about oneself. Pa seemed to recover his spirits a little.

Inspector Foy smiled. 'I remember he was a great favourite with my mother. 'Now, sir, one or two more questions, if you don't mind. I understand from Mr Sickert-Greene that you want to appeal against committal and change your plea to not guilty.'

'Of course I didn't do it! No one but a simpleton could imagine that I, Waldo Byng, am capable of murder! Sickert-Greene made a hopeless mull of it in court this morning. What on earth made him plead guilty but insane? Do I look crazy?' Pa inflated his chest and narrowed his nostrils, as though indignation and insanity were mutually incompatible. 'He actually believes I did it! I can't think why I go on employing that silly old fool.'

The reason was because old Sickly Grin was a fearful intellectual snob. No ancient rabbi daring to pronounce the forbidden name of Yahweh could have looked more awe-stricken than Sickly Grin when he uttered the sacred moniker of Shakespeare. His voice dropped along with his several chins and even his knees appeared to bend in their Savile Row trousers. He was prepared to look after my father's interests for practically nothing so he could boast of his intimacy with Waldo Byng, the great Shakespearean actor.

'Mm.' The inspector got out his pipe and stroked the bowl tenderly. He had nice square, strong-looking hands. 'If I may say so, sir, I think it was a mistake to tell the chief magistrate that he was as guilty as you were of the murder.'

My father laughed bitterly. 'The fellow's a philistine. When I gave him the speech from *Measure for Measure* where Isabella pleads for Claudio's life, he went as red as fire and started to gobble.' My father began to recite. '"Man, proud man, Dressed in a little brief authority, Most ignorant of what he's most assured, His glassy essence, like an angry ape, Plays such fantastic tricks before high heaven, As makes the angels weep."'

'It was the angry ape that annoyed him, I think.' The inspector's expression was reproachful and I believed, then, that he wanted my father not to be guilty. Pa looked sulky and folded his arms across his chest. 'Well.' The inspector seemed to have packed his pipe with tobacco to his apparent satisfaction. 'It's too late to worry about that. Let's look again at the question of motive. Who might have wanted Sir Basil dead? The most common motive for homicide is sexual jealousy.' He sucked wistfully at his unlit pipe but my father was unmoved. 'Somebody discovers his or her other half's been unfaithful and there's a violent reaction. The killing's unpremeditated. Those cases are relatively straightforward. Sir Basil's housekeeper says he rarely went out and had no close friendships with either sex, as far as she knows. We can't exclude sexual jealousy entirely but at the moment it seems unlikely. Having looked at Sir Basil's will, I'm sure it wasn't money.' Inspector Foy stopped, looked at his pipe with something like disgust and thrust it into his pocket. 'Let's consider more complex motives – killings intended to protect some discreditable secret, for example. Blackmailers get bumped off because their victim can't or won't go on paying out. Since the legalisation of homosexuality, this sort of crime is on the decline. Was Sir Basil the kind of man who might hold other men to account for their sins or indulge in a little gentle blackmail?'

'I should say there was no man less likely to do such a thing.' Pa looked amused at the idea. 'He wasn't interested in other people. He was much too self-absorbed. But you could say that of most actors.' It was evident that Pa considered himself an exception.

Inspector Foy selected a pencil from the pen tray on the table, took a penknife from his pocket and began to make a fine point. Balked of his pipe, he needed another focus for his attention. I wondered whether this was a ploy to soothe the nerves of his suspects and distract them into making damning confessions. I dismissed at once the idea that he might be jittery himself. The inspector was almost monumentally calm as he smiled at Cordelia, then at me. The situation seemed quite unreal. We might have been discussing the plot of a film.

'So we're left with a mixed bag of motives – let's call it personal animosity. This includes everything from disputes between neighbours rowing over the height of a hedge to professional jealousy.'

Pa looked scornful. 'I can assure you that Basil's small talents were insufficient to make me lose a moment's sleep.'

'All right. But I have to examine even the remotest possibilities. I've interviewed every member of the cast. They all described your relationship with Sir Basil Wintergreen as being – well, the mildest expression was "competitive". Apparently there was no love lost.'

'My dear Inspector, it is clear you know nothing of the theatre. All actors are toxically jealous and grudging of others' success. Sometimes friendships survive despite it. Often there is unqualified dislike and contempt. But never, as far as I know, does it lead to murder. Sooner or later, along comes a critic who will do one's dirty work far more effectively. Now look here. I've had enough of this. I've gone along with things pretty well, I think, but I'd like to go home now. This is a ghastly place, quite unfit for even a hardened criminal. Get me out of here, will you?'

'It's not as simple as that, sir. The law moves slowly. It has to, to avoid making mistakes.'

'But I didn't do it!' There was something like panic in Pa's voice. Cordelia leaned against him and tucked her hand through his arm. He patted it absently.

'There was something else, wasn't there, that came out at this morning's hearing? Something which Harriet won't know about.' The inspector frowned at a notice instructing anyone who cared to read it that all articles of furniture, stationery and crockery were the property of HM Prison

101

Services and removal of ANY item would be counted as theft. 'Evidence that, when combined with your fingerprints on the only possible weapon, would have made any bench in the land decide to commit you for trial, regardless of the plea entered. Let's run over it again, just in case there's something we haven't thought of. Do you remember passing anyone as you went on stage to rehearse the putting out of your eyes?'

Pa looked impatient. 'Must we? I went through it all in court. I'm sick of talking about it.' The inspector folded his arms and gave my father the look he had given Ophelia – a firming of the lips and a drawing together of the eyebrows. It was surprisingly effective. 'Oh, all right,' said Pa very grumpily. 'You know perfectly well that Sandra was there, with Gemma, the wardrobe mistress. And there was a blonde girl, probably another understudy. New, anyway. Not bad-looking. A bit flat-chested. Can't remember her name. They were chatting together. Sandra was leaning against the cyclorama –'

'That's the curved wall at the back of the stage?'

'Yes.'

'But they couldn't actually see the stage itself from there?'

'Not unless they had X-ray eyes. The backcloth was down. What I didn't tell the magistrates was that Sandra leaned forward as I went by, so I accidentally brushed against her breasts. They all twittered like starlings.' Pa smiled as though the memory was an agreeable one. The inspector continued to run the blade of his knife up and down the lead of his pencil as though nothing was so important to him as getting the point needle-sharp.

'You went on from stage left?'

'Yes.'

'Why? Stage right was more accessible. You wouldn't have needed to go round the back.'

'I *told* them in court . . . Oh, all right.' Pa sighed and

continued with exaggerated emphasis as though speaking to someone of limited understanding. 'There was an A-frame trolley stacked with flats carelessly parked at stage right, blocking the wings.'

'No one could have got on to the stage that side?'

'Not without an element of risk. Those trolleys are notoriously unstable. Full of flats, the weight is enough to kill a man.'

'Sandra says that just before the murder she went on to the stage to retrieve her knitting. Sir Basil was on the stage, running through some lines. She remembers this clearly because he glared at her as though she had no right to be there and she was annoyed. She's quite certain he was alone. A minute or two later you came along. She says she remembers that because you smiled at her and pinched her – cheek.'

'I may have done.' Pa put on his supercilious face. 'If you mean I squeezed her behind, I probably did. These things mean nothing in the theatre.'

'No one else passed them, either entering or leaving the stage. The next thing anyone remembers is hearing you shout. They ran on stage to find you kneeling by the body.' The inspector looked at me. 'You see the inference the court was bound to draw from that?'

The blade of the knife slipped and the point of the pencil snapped. I felt the hair on my scalp rise. I would have taken Pa's other hand but he was smoothing his hair with his palm as though comforting himself.

Yes,' I said slowly. 'It means that Pa *must* have been alone on the stage with Basil.'

My father forgot to be superior. 'But he was already dead, I swear it!'

Inspector Foy looked regretful. 'But you see how awkward it is.' He sighed. 'I understand how you must be feeling. But we shall do everything in our power to bring the killer to justice, you can be sure of that.' There was a sinister ambiguity about this promise. 'I'll leave you with your family now. We'll have another talk later. Goodbye, young lady.' Inspector Foy smiled kindly at Cordelia and laid a reassuring hand on her shoulder.

'Uh-oh,' said Cordelia, pointing at the notice. 'It won't do for a police inspector to be put in gaol for stealing.'

Inspector Foy restored to the pen tray the pencil he had absent-mindedly put in his pocket.

'Goodbye, Harriet. We'll keep in touch.' For a moment it looked as though he was going to pat my arm too, but evidently he changed his mind and instead felt in his pocket for his pipe. I searched his face for clues to what he was thinking. He looked as though he had nothing more on his mind than what Mrs Foy was going to give him for supper. I wondered if there was a Mrs Foy and, if there was, what she was like.

'I brought you this cake. I made it myself,' said Cordelia when the inspector had gone, offering up the bag with pride.

My father took it on his knee. 'Good heavens, what've you put in it? Cakes are supposed to be light, my girl. And what's this metal thing sticking out —'

'Shh!' Cordelia, apparently in agony, rolled her eyes at the constable on duty.

'Ha, I see!' My father smiled and for a moment looked almost his old self. I blessed Cordelia for coming with me. 'But what shall I do when I've filed through the bars? My cell's on the first floor. I'd be human jam if I jumped. You'd better make another cake with a rope inside. Though what Loveday will say when he sees his precious tools smothered in icing and currants, I wouldn't like to say.'

'You aren't taking it seriously.' Cordelia was cross. 'But I saw this film called *Heaven is where the Heart is*, where this man was in gaol though he hadn't done the murder —

he'd been stitched up by his best friend – and his childhood sweetheart was dying and they wouldn't let him go and see her and he made a file in the prison workshop –'

'I've brought your post,' I said as Cordelia paused to draw breath.

My father looked through the envelopes. 'Half these are bills.' His momentary good humour evaporated. 'And there'll be your mother's chin to pay for. They've cancelled the play. Had to, of course, without me and Basil.' He swore a decorative Elizabethan oath. 'Here's a letter from the bank. My God, they're quick on the draw when it comes to calling in the dibs! This fellow,' he glanced to the bottom of the letter, 'Potter, he calls himself, says he wants to know what I'm going to do about reducing my overdraft.' He threw the letter down. 'Well, he can take what steps he likes. They can't do anything to me while I'm in here.'

He set his face mutinously. I picked up the letter and put it in my bag. While my father and Cordelia played the farewell scene from Romeo and Juliet, I went to find Sergeant Tweeter.

We arrived home to find our neighbours mingling with the reporters who had reappeared with the cessation of rain, like flowers blooming in the desert.

'Someone ought to ring the RSPCA.' Mrs Newbiggin from next door, whom I had never liked, had a penetrating voice but even she was almost drowned out by the howling that was coming from inside the house. Seeing me, she pointed a finger. 'That's one of the girls. This used to be a respectable neighbourhood. What's going on? I'd like to know. Is some poor animal being tortured in there?'

'Sorry. It's only our dog.' I squeezed past the cameras and rang the bell. The howling changed to barking over three octaves, from a high-pitched whine to a deep Baskerville bay. I pushed open the letter box to call out to Maria-Alba and a large pink tongue laved my hand affectionately.

'*Grazie al cielo.*' Maria-Alba brandished her ladle threateningly as she let us in. Under the other arm she held two cushions. 'Now I understand the cruelty to animals.'

'What are the cushions for?' asked Cordelia.

Maria-Alba held them over her ears in demonstration. 'He has not stop since you go out.'

'But look how pleased he is to see us.' I patted Derek, who was jumping up in an attempt to get his front paws on to my shoulders. 'It's really very touching. He's going to be an excellent watchdog.'

'Perhaps he's going to perform deeds of heroism.' Cordelia was willing to join me in a little dog-worshipping. 'He might rescue me from a raging torrent or you from an axe-murderer. He'd be famous then, like Greyfriars Bobby. They might put up a statue of him in the street. Wouldn't that be lovely?'

'I'm not entirely sold on the idea, since you ask. There don't seem to be quite so many reporters as usual. I wonder if they're getting fed up? There can't be a worse job in the world than working for a newspaper. Out at all hours in all weathers, making an absolute nuisance of oneself and being loathed and reviled, just to get a story that's identical to everyone else's. Making up sordid lies about other people's sadness to get something exclusive. I should hate it.'

'I'm going to have to get used to the paparazzi, though,' said Cordelia. 'When I'm a famous film star I shall never know a moment's peace.'

'It may not be that easy.' I did not want to be discouraging but I knew acting was a cruelly disappointing occupation for most people.

'It will be for me.' Cordelia said with confidence. Looking at the calm smile on her ravishing little face, I thought she might be right. Cordelia had my father's ability to draw your eye and hold your attention. She had Ophelia's beauty with the added charm of warmth, and Portia's spontaneity, with – so far anyway – less reckless self-destructiveness in her nature. 'I shall have a white Pekinese like Marina Marlow,' she went on, 'that I can carry around under my arm. I shall call it Yum-Yum after the girl in *The Mikado*. You needn't look so snooty. At least *I* haven't got a dog called Derek.'

'A palpable hit,' I acknowledged.

'I've just had a brainwave!' Cordelia looked pleased. 'You remember the film of *A Tale of Two Cities*? They've got the same gorgeous doggy brown eyes. Derek and Sydney Carton, I mean'

'Isn't it rather a mouthful? Imagine calling, "Come here, Sydney Carton!" across the park. Beside sounding a little pretentious –'

'No, you ass! You can call him Dirk – after Dirk Bogarde. It'll sound just the same to a dog but it's got *bags* more style than Derek.'

This was undeniable, but I was still not enthusiastic. Dirk sounded assertively masculine; it lacked poetry. Cordelia pointed out that it was a sort of Highland dagger, which was romantic enough for anyone, even a loopy poetess. It made her think of wild, wet mountains, bottomless lochs, ruined castles, skirling bagpipes. When I begged her, perhaps unkindly, to stop sounding like The Highlands and Islands Tourist Board, she lost her temper and hard words were exchanged. I think we were both tired and under a strain. Anyway, Cordelia got her way as she always did and, by a process of attrition, Dirk he became.

EIGHT

'So! The worm has turned.' Ophelia flung down a letter among the toast crumbs on the breakfast table.

'What worm?' Cordelia was interested as, indeed, was I.

'Which worm, you dunce.' Ophelia's lips were curved with a smile of satisfaction. 'That soft squirming thing called Crispin Mallilieu. He's written to ask me to marry him.'

'Can I wear white with a pink sash and a wreath of pink rosebuds?' said Cordelia instantly. 'That's what Janice Thatcher wore when her sister got married and Janice has hair as straight as stair rods and tiny, tiny eyes like ink blots.'

'I'm so pleased!' I said mendaciously, for the idea of Crispin as a brother-in-law was not one to gladden the heart. 'How wrong we were to accuse him of cowardice.'

'Actually, what about yellow sashes? And yellow rosebuds? We'll all have to look the same and Harriet looks foul in pink.'

'Do I?' I remembered that we were discussing an event of great moment. 'I suppose you'll have to wait a bit, though – till Pa can give you away.'

'Of course I'm not going to marry him.' The light in Ophelia's eye became scorching. 'He says his mother's begged him not to throw himself away but he can't give me up, whatever the world may say. Pah! I don't imagine the world ever gives Crispin a second's thought. He's much too dull and stupid. He suggests a quiet ceremony in a register office followed by a short honeymoon in a little *pension* he knows in the Pyrenees. The very idea of spending a weekend in a second-rate hotel with Crispin makes me want to kill myself. He thinks his mother will come round when it's a *fait accompli*. He's worse than a worm. I believe worms have guts.'

'Oh, yes,' said Cordelia. 'I saw this nature programme on the telly and it said that worms are just muscle and intestine, jesting and execrating, rather disgusting actually.'

'But, poor Crispin – he must be very much in love with you,' I said.

'So? Plenty of people are in love with me. I can't marry them all. Apparently his mother says I'm heartless and decadent. Ha! *Merci du compliment*.' I could see that Ophelia, despite her expressions of derision, actually minded. I stopped feeling quite so sorry for Crispin. It was very stupid of him to repeat his mother's remarks. 'He says he's sure she'll come round eventually to our marriage if we show her we're repentant. If he thinks I'm going to bed forgiveness from that ghastly old countess, he must be even more stupid than I thought!' I had rarely seen Ophelia so moved. 'If *I* were covered with warts, I'd think twice about abusing other people. I'd hide under a stone and hope that people would be kind to me.'

'Is she really covered with warts?' Cordelia looked fascinated.

'She has two. On her chin. Huge and hairy.'

'Poor thing. She can't help that, I suppose,' I said.

Ophelia turned on me, her eyes blazing. 'Why are you always sorry for everyone but me? I suppose *you'd* like me to marry Crispin and be bored to death and patronised by that hateful old woman. I'm sick of you being holier-than-thou!'

'I'm not!' I very felt near to losing my temper. 'It's just that you despise people who aren't beautiful – as though they wouldn't be if they could. No one *wants* to be ugly –'

'Christ!' Ophelia got up from the table and slammed out of the room.

'Don't mind it,' said Maria-Alba, who was washing up at the sink. 'She is looking for a goat.'

'A goat?'

'Sì. *Espiatorio*. A thing to blame.'

'Oh, I see, a scapegoat. Am I irritatingly goody-goody?'

'Not *all* the time,' Cordelia said kindly. 'Sometimes you're a bit wet but you're still my favourite sister, by far.'

'Thank you very much.' I felt gloomy. We were getting terribly on each other's nerves. Quite apart from the fact that I hate rows, surely when everything was so miserable we ought to try to stick together? Anyway, during a quarrel our family always fell into the same divisions, which had more to with temperament than the merits of the argument so the rows were pretty pointless. Perhaps this is the case with all families. My mother and Bron were generally in league, and my father, Ophelia and Cordelia were usually on the same side. Portia was my ally on these occasions of family feud but God only knew where she was now. I wondered, not for the first time, if I ought to consult Inspector Foy but I was afraid Portia would be angry with me for making a fuss.

Wherever one turned one's thoughts there seemed to be doubt and difficulty. I took a covert look at Maria-Alba as she bent to give Mark Antony and Dirk their breakfast biscuits. At least they were settling down together. Mark Antony had established ascendancy the day before by springing claws like flick knives and hissing like a maddened cobra. Dirk had rolled on to his back and ratified the peace treaty before the ink was dry, like a dog of sense.

110

Maria-Alba began to dry the cups. She had black rings under her eyes and her hands were shaky. She had made delicious little custard and raisin buns for breakfast so she must have risen early. Insomnia was one of the first signs with Maria-Alba that things were going seriously wrong. I hated the idea that she might have to go back into the psychiatric unit. For all our sakes we could not afford to allow what was left of our domestic structure to break down. I resolved not to lose my temper or provoke any more quarrelling, even if it meant knuckling down under insult. I was given the chance to put theory into practice immediately.

'You bitch, Harriet! You bloody little traitor!' Bron was standing beside me, clad in his dressing gown, his hair ruffled from sleep. He thrust a newspaper into my face. 'I'm sacking you as a sister! From now on you're no relation of mine! I don't think I'll ever be able to bring myself to speak to you again! And nor will the others when they see this!'

I was bewildered. But one glance at Bron's face convinced me this was not play-acting. My heart began to race. 'What is it? What have I done?'

Bron slammed the paper down in front of me and pointed to a headline. 'Read it!'

'My Unhappy Family. Waldo Byng's Daughter Confesses All. An exclusive story by Stanley Norman.' Under the caption was a large photograph of me grinning into the camera, my chin resting on the top of Dirk's head.

'Oh, but I didn't. I only said "no comment" whatever they asked me –'

'So where did they get this?' Bron real aloud in a voice modulated by fury.

'Oberon Byng, aspiring thespian and young man-about-town seems likely to follow in his jail-bird father's footsteps in more ways than one. After being expelled

111

from school for impregnating the matron he has had a chequered career. A few undistinguished stage roles have been interspersed with nefarious dabblings, receiving stolen goods and drug trafficking. He is now being investigated by Scotland Yard with regard to a serious charge of fraudulent land deals.'

'Oh! Oh dear! I only said – Stan was telling me about his family and it seemed polite – I *didn't* say you'd been dealing in drugs, only that you were suspended for a term for taking that hookah to school that Pa brought back from an opium den in Shanghai, and smoking it in the junior common room. And I just mentioned the car you bought that turned out to be stolen, though it wasn't your fault, and you lost all the money for it. He's just turned everything around and made it all sound terrible! He seemed so nice and friendly and I was sorry for him. Oh God, I'm so sorry!'

'You absolute imbecile! Don't you know that's what journalists always do? It's the oldest trick in the book.'

'I wasn't thinking. I'd forgotten about him being a reporter and he was so depressed. His wife's an invalid and they haven't got any money. I was trying to cheer him up.'

'What a sap you are! Well, I hoped you're pleased to have your photograph splashed all over the *Daily Banner*. There isn't even the smallest one of *me*.'

I hung my head in shame.

'I say, Ophelia's going to be hopping mad when she reads this.' Cordelia gave a whoop of glee. 'Jolly well serves her right. Listen!

'I have it on the authority of her sister that Miss Ophelia Byng, formerly an actress, was jilted at the altar by the Hon. Crispin Mallilieu. He is the second son of the Earl and Countess of Sope. When the Earl brought the

marriage service to a halt by voicing his objection to
the alliance of his son with the daughter of a suspected
murderer, the bride-to-be fainted and had to be carried
from the church by four of the officers who were to have
formed the guard of honour. According to her sister,
Ophelia has locked herself in her bedroom, still dressed
in her bridal finery, surrounded by magnificent wedding
presents from England's most aristocratic families, which
she refuses to return.'

'He's making it all up!' My indignation was unbounded. 'It's
a crib from *Great Expectations*! Of course I didn't say any
such thing!'

'I'm sure Ophelia will be comforted to know that,' said
Bron drily.

'If I could get hold of that hateful liar I'd – I don't know
what I'd do to him. It's all wild invention – apart from the
bit about you getting Matron pregnant. I wish I hadn't told
him that.'

'Golly! Look at all this about Portia.' Cordelia's voice
was awed.

'Even worse is the present predicament of Portia Byng
who, her sister reports, has left the country in mysterious
circumstances, escorted by a man who is wanted by
the police for crimes ranging from illegal immigration
to homicide. According to a reliable informant, Mr X,
thought to be of Albanian extraction, is known to his
associates as The Gravefiller. Chief Inspector Charles Foy
has been in touch with Interpol, acting on a tip-off that
she has been taken to Albania. The informant has also
revealed that Mr X has a harem of girls in his mountain
hideaway, kept under guard to satisfy his unbridled
sexual depravity.'

113

Cordelia gave a scream. 'Is it true? My poor darling sister! What do you think unbridled sexual depravity means, exactly?'

'Oh, Lord! You don't think . . . No, Portia can't have gone abroad; she would have telephoned. He's made it all up. It's just nonsense like the rest.' I read the article again, wanting to reassure myself. Supposing there was even the smallest amount of truth in the story?

'There isn't anything about me.' Cordelia sounded disappointed.

'No doubt there'll be something in the evening edition.' Bron was bitter and I couldn't blame him.

'I don't suppose I'll ever be able to make you see how sorry I am,' I said sorrowfully.

'I shouldn't think so, no.' Bron took a plate, filled it with buns and went slowly upstairs with the mien of a man betrayed.

I felt deeply remorseful. I had been an idiot and I deserved all the vituperation that would no doubt be coming my way. Dirk put his paws on my knees and tried to lick my face. I was grateful for his solicitude.

'Don't worry, Hat,' Cordelia patted my arm, smearing my sleeve with custard. '*I* shall go on speaking to you even if everyone else in the world refuses to. There was a sad film I saw once called *The Angry Silence* about this man who was sent to Coventry by his workmates . . .'

I stopped listening to Cordelia's recital of the plot as my eye fell on another, smaller item on the same page.

Drugs Seized at Headquarters of Rebel Political Organisation.

Acting on information received, police yesterday raided a house in Owlstone Road, Clerkenwell. They took away several packages, believed to be cannabis, and the remains of a cake. The officer in charge said he could

114

not confirm the presence of illegal substances until these items had been subjected to laboratory tests. Several arrests were made and an injunction has been served prohibiting the group known as SPIT to hold further meetings on the premises.

'. . . I mean, nothing could be *that* important, could it?' asked Cordelia. 'I'd have given in at once – What's the matter?'

'This is the worst day of my life.' I groaned and put my head in my hands.

'You can't possibly know that. You might have something really awful going to happen to you later on. All your children burned to death or your nose cut off in a revolving door.'

I was too depressed to argue. The telephone rang and went on ringing. There had been an offended silence since I had dared to plug it back in, the night before. And the gang of pressmen outside the front door was considerably depleted. It seemed they were busy digesting Stanley Norman's scoop. Now the telephone bell seemed to have a new tone, insolent and at the same time imperative.

It was Mr Potter, the bank manager. When I said my mother would not be able to answer his letter for at least two weeks he sounded cross. He kept saying that it was all 'very irregular', to which I could make no answer, having no idea what, in a bank's eyes, constituted regularity. I have never been good with money. In this I am a true Byng. I always hope some will come from somewhere and, so far, it always has. I waited patiently, mostly in silence, while he remonstrated with me. Sometimes I said 'I see' when he seemed to require a response. I suppose this was irritating for he got more and more tetchy. When he began to talk of solicitors and bailiffs I felt alarmed but continued to say 'I see' because I really couldn't think of anything more appropriate. It would hardly do any good to

beg him for mercy, or a donation to the fund for indi-
gent Byngs.

'I'm sorry, Miss Byng, but I don't think you *do* see. Unless
funds are immediately forthcoming, I'm afraid the bank will
have to freeze the account.'

I was suddenly annoyed beyond bearing by the hypocritical
tones of regret he put into his voice. I was certain that the
fall of the House of Byng was brightening his dreary life
immeasurably. Why should he have all the fun, lecturing
and threatening and making himself out to be a model of
deportment when he probably fiddled his business expenses,
bullied his children and neglected his poor old mother, if he
had one? 'Why don't you give yourself a well-deserved rest
from these onerous duties?' I said in my sweetest voice. 'Go
and – make love to your mother's cook.'

I could not quite bring myself to use an obscenity so it lost
something in translation but I put the receiver down with a
sense of triumph. It was a cheap victory but nothing better
was likely to come my way.

The arrival of the post brought more unhappiness. I saw
at once, among the bills and circulars, a letter addressed to
me, in Dodge's handwriting.

I never would have believed it of you. My confidence in
my own judgement is severely undermined. You grassed
on your friends to save your own skin. You are a traitor
and that is the kindest thing I can say. You are expelled
from the society – and my heart – for ever, with effect
from this moment. D.

There was a postscript: 'Yell says she saw you let that pig put
his arm round you. I hope there was nothing worse.'

The ink grew faint at the end as though the pen was
spluttering with indignation. I had felt too many things too

116

violently in the last forty-eight hours for this latest blow to my happiness to have much immediate effect. Dodge's pale, angular face, fierce with polemic, loomed up in the forefront of my brain from time to time and there was an intensification of the gnawing sensation in my stomach that had been there since I heard of Pa's arrest, but I was incapable of anything like serious reflection.

Dirk followed me up to my room and stretched himself out on the bed next to Mark Antony, his head pillowed on my pyjamas, while I sat at my desk and wrote several stanzas of verse. I knew the poetry was bad but I didn't care. Anything was better than thinking about life.

Maria-Alba brought lunch up to my room. I rushed to take the tray from her so she could recover her breath, for the last flight of stairs was steep.

'I call and call but you not answer so I think Harriet like to be alone. Perhaps it is better. Ophelia is in *cattivissimo umore, eccome*!' She flapped her fingers and blew out her cheeks, to denote tempestuous rage.

'I can't say I blame her.'

'*Certo.*' Maria-Alba settled her huge frame on my bed. Mark Antony removed himself to the windowsill but despite the circulation in his paws being cut off, Dirk merely smacked his lips and continued to snore. 'It is not a thing a woman enjoys to be know – to be abandon by a man. And a woman like Ophelia – *mio Dio*!'

'I'd better resign myself to being extremely unpopular for several years.' I felt my chin wobble.

'*Su, su, Harriet!*' Maria-Alba stroked my arm with her large yellow fingers. 'It will come better. We are all in troubles but they will go away.'

'It isn't only Bron and Ophelia. The bank's going to stop our money. And I'm very worried about Portia. Supposing that beastly, bloody Stan didn't make it up? I mean, what does a

117

man have to do to be nicknamed The Gravefiller? And Dodge thinks I informed on him to the police. He doesn't want . . . to see me . . . any more.'

I burst into tears and sobbed on Maria-Alba's comforting bosom, as so many times in the past. '*Che stupido!*' she hugged my head. 'You are too good for him. He is lucky you speak him in the street, besides you allow him to kiss you. He is a bad boy, *e disordinato*.' Maria-Alba had not forgotten that Dodge's shoes had left a deposit of Deptford river mud on the drawing-room carpet and that he had stubbed out his cigarette among the sugared almonds in the silver *bonbonnière*.

'He isn't bad,' I sobbed. 'He really cares about people and wants to help them. I do love him.' And just at that moment I did. There is nothing like being handed notice to quit to fan the flames of passion, even if you were only lukewarm before. Never had Dodge's virtues been so desirable and his faults so negligible.

'*Cocca mia*, you are tired. Eat your good lunch that Maria-Alba brings despite the poor legs, and you feel better.'

I was obliged to try though I was not in the least hungry and after a while, whether it was the rich risotto, unctuous with beef marrow, or the figs baked in marsala-flavoured custard or the utter kindness of Maria-Alba, petting and coaxing me as though I were a child, I certainly started to feel braver and stronger.

'We're going to have to make some economies.' I wiped my greasy chin with the napkin. 'No new clothes or taxis for anyone until Pa's out of prison.'

'*Va bene. La cucina italiana* is the peasant cooking, simple and cheap and good. We have pasta and polenta and gnocchi. I go see to the larder. And,' she paused as though struck by inspiration, 'we say go to Mrs Dyer. I tell her in the morning.' Maria-Alba and Mrs Dyer, our daily, had never got on. Mrs Dyer was openly xenophobic when my parents

118

were not in earshot, muttering about wogs, eyties, japs and darkies, usually with the prefix 'dirty'. Maria-Alba clapped her hands together in a manner well satisfied and smiled for the first time for days.

'What do you think?' Bron stood with his hips thrust forward and his chin sunk on his chest so that his eyes looked brooding and sultry as they met ours. Well, everyone's but mine. I was still less popular than Napoleon on the retreat from Moscow. Bron was wearing a long black coat with an elegant fur lining.

'Amazing!' Ophelia was moved to unusual enthusiasm. 'It looks like mink.'

'It is mink.'

'No! How much?'

'Just fifty pounds on account. Bloke I met in the pub is selling them cheap. Warehouse closing down. I'm paying in monthly instalments.'

I wondered where Bron had got even so much as fifty pounds. The telephone call with Mr Potter was much on my mind but I was reluctant to give them the opportunity to snub me, so I said nothing.

'Do they have them in women's sizes?' Ophelia's eyes were sharp. 'Can you get me one?'

'Got fifty smackers?'

'No, but I could borrow from Peregrine.'

'Consider it done.'

The curtailment of family spending seemed to have got off to a very poor start.

The doorbell began to ring persistently, which made Dirk howl and, for some reason, attack Bron's coat.

'Get your dog off me!' he yelled. 'He's got his teeth into the lining.'

'I go tell them *va' farsi fottere*!' Maria-Alba picked up the ladle.

'You get on with supper,' I said. 'I'll go.'

I was overtaken by Dirk, who hurled himself at the front door with a scream of rage. 'No comment,' I shouted when I could get near the letter box. 'Please go away.'

'For God's sake, let me in!' cried Portia's voice.

I undid the chain and the lock and drew back the bolts. Portia fell into my arms. Dirk displayed wonderful intelligence by allowing Portia to enter before baring his teeth at the reporters who were trying to follow her in, and growling ferociously, until I managed to shut them out.

'Who are those bloody people? Has the world gone mad?' Portia sank down on the Cleopatra day bed, her head drooping as though exhausted. Then, as Dirk gave her a hearty, reassuring lick, 'What's this dog doing here?'

She looked up. Even in the scattered light from the chandelier I could see that Portia was a mess. She was wearing a black leather blouson, much too big for her, and enormous, baggy jeans. Her face was extremely dirty.

'Where have you been? I've been so worried!' I was so relieved, I probably sounded cross.

'Don't scold me. I've had the most awful time. I'm as weak as ditchwater.'

I sat down and put my arms around her. 'I'm so thankful to see you. I'd made up my mind to ring the police.'

'Ow! That hurts.' She winced and pulled away. I saw that what I had assumed to be dirt on her cheeks and lips was bruising.

'Portia! Who did this to you?'

'That bastard Dimitri, of course. We went to his house. You never saw anything like it – an absolute scream – a circular bed, nylon furry cushions and a television that popped up and down when you pressed a button, a cocktail bar – and I thought it was going to be fun.' Portia was talking fast, as though she was nervous. 'But when I laughed at the erotic

120

murals on the ceiling – they were really awful – Dimitri got huffy. We had a bit of a row. Then I said I didn't want to go to bed with a bad-tempered dwarf – I may not have mentioned that he's stocky, with short legs. And other similarities to Toulouse-Lautrec, as I discovered later. The most enormous prick you ever saw.' Portia laughed but her expression was anguished. I realised she was trying to recapture her usual breezy, cynical manner but also that it was a huge effort.

'Portia! You didn't really say that! I mean, you didn't call him a dwarf?' I had always admired her blasé attitude to sex and her flippant attitude towards the male ego. 'What did he say?'

'He smacked me across the mouth and broke my tooth. Look!' Portia lifted her swollen top lip to show me her front tooth, broken in half. 'I tried not to cry but I do so hate the dentist!'

Portia closed her eyes and hugged herself, shaking her head as though to rid herself of the memory. Her fingernails were grubby as usual, which made her small white hands look childlike. I took one of them in mine. 'Poor darling, what an ordeal! The brute! Hitting a girl! He ought to be locked up.'

She smiled and shrugged. 'That isn't the worst of it. But don't let's go into detail. Only I'm conditioned now, like Pavlov's dogs. I shan't be able to see a pair of sunglasses ever again without wanting to throw up. Dimitri wore them all the time, even in bed. I've no idea what colour his eyes are.'

'In bed! You slept with him? Why didn't you come home straightaway?'

'He had a gun, that's why.'

'A gun!' Cold waves of fear ran up and down my legs. 'Oh, Portia!'

'For God's sake, Hat, keep your voice down! I don't want the entire neighbourhood to know. He put the gun against my head –' Portia gave me a look that was shamefaced – 'I

121

know I always say I'm not frightened of anything but I was really scared then. So I let him do what he wanted.'

'Only a fool wouldn't have been scared! I'd have screamed!'

'I expect you would have. You always were a terrible coward.' Portia tried to regain her old spirit, but added, 'I may have let out a small scream myself. The bodyguards – they took it in turns to sit outside the door – had guns too.'

'Portia! You might have been killed!' I tried to put my arm round her again but she gave a gasp of pain. 'Darling, what a risk to take! I can't bear to think about it!'

'All right, all right! I know I was a fool to go off with him. You needn't pretend to be so worldly-wise.' Portia sounded offended. 'Who was it who had to ask what fellatio meant?'

'That was ages ago – anyway, never mind. So he raped you!' I had forgotten all my prejudices against violence. I felt murderous. I could easily have killed Dimitri with my bare hands if he had presented his throat. I tried to stifle my anger for Portia's sake. 'Stan was right. He is a gangster. We must tell Inspector Foy at once.'

'Inspector who?'

'Foy. He's – Oh, never mind for the moment. But what happened then? And how did you manage to get away?'

'I had to go along with whatever he wanted or he hit me. It was – No, I'm not going to think about it. Only if I ever see another furry cushion I can't answer for the consequences. Luckily he was out a lot so I was left for hours with nothing to do but read this dreadful book about a girl who goes to Hollywood and gets hooked on drink and drugs. She dies in the end, and a good thing too. Anyway, this morning Dimitri said he was going to be away all day. He said he'd bring me a fur coat and jewellery, but I must be nice to him when he got back because he was tired of threatening. I knew I had to escape, then or never. So I seduced Chico, one of the bodyguards. I'd seen the way he looked at me when he

122

brought in sandwiches and things. I expect he'd indulged in quite a few fantasies sitting outside the door, listening to Dimitri yodelling like an alpine goatherd every time he had an orgasm. I told Chico I was so sore he'd have to take all his clothes off so as not to rub against the bruises. Ugh, God . . .' Portia clutched her head and shuddered. 'The smell of sweat and garlic and the blubber, possibly worse than Dimitri's blackheads and dandruff – except he came at once, thank God. Then, afterwards, he sort of drifted off for a bit, you know how men do. Well, when he was lying there, all passion spent, I grabbed his jeans and jacket and ran. Of course he came after me but he couldn't move nearly as fast. I ran, stark naked, across fields full of cows and woods full of brambles and stinging nettles until I got to a road. I put on Chico's clothes, and the first lorry I put up my thumb to stopped. He was coming into London and dropped me in Camberwell. I bussed the rest of the way. I told the lorry driver I was a lesbian, just in case, and he was quite interested. Actually it isn't at all a bad idea. Thanks to Dimitri, I'll probably be frigid for the rest of my life.'

'Hello, Portia.' Bron came into the hall. 'Where have you been? What do you think of my coat?'

'She's been kidnapped by a homicidal sex maniac!' I was so upset by Portia's recital that I had forgotten about being an outcast.

Bron gave me a glacial look. 'I call that a joke in poor taste.'

'No, really, she has been! We must ring the police and a doctor.'

'Oh, no you don't!' Portia snatched back her hand, which I had been holding. 'If you think I'm going to go on talking about it to a lot of prurient busybodies, you must be crazy. All I want to do is lie in a hot bath for a very long time and then go to my own chaste, sweet bed and forget it ever happened. I've never been so tired in my life.'

'But, Portia! You must see a doctor! Supposing you've got a horrible disease? Or you're pregnant?'

'What a comfort you are, Harriet.' Portia, in her turn, began to look coldly at me.

'You must, at any rate, report it to the police. If he isn't stopped, Dimitri will find some other unsuspecting girl.'

'That's her lookout. If I'd known you were going to be so community-spirited I wouldn't have told you. I thought as my sister you'd be concerned for me. It seems I was mistaken.'

'Don't be angry.' I tried to take her arm but she shook me off, her mouth turned down mulishly. 'All right, whatever you say. I still think we ought but – well, never mind. Dear, dear Portia, I'm so glad have you back. Come on, I'll run the bath for you and bring you up some supper.'

'Promise no officious telephoning?'

'Promise.'

Portia was mollified sufficiently to let me accompany her upstairs. When I saw her without clothes on, I was tempted to break my word, there and then. She was covered in blackening bruises and red weals. Despite her attempts to be insouciant, I was sure she must be suffering the aftereffects of extreme fear so I decided to say nothing about Pa for the moment. Fortunately, she seemed to have forgotten about the cameras outside the front door. While she bathed, I sat on the laundry basket and we talked and made silly jokes as we always did. But there was an atmosphere of strain.

Dirk was a useful distraction, trying to get into the bath with Portia, then attempting to eat the sponge. Portia was not particularly fond of animals but she admitted that he had a wayward charm all his own. She ate very little of the supper I brought her, saying she was too tired to be hungry. I left her tucked up in bed, her hair stretched across the pillow, her damaged face very calm. I thought she seemed remarkably composed in the circumstances.

But during the night I was woken by Dirk, whining and scraping with his paw at my pillow. Before I could tell him to be quiet I heard a blood-chilling scream from Portia's room, which was directly below mine. I raced downstairs, my heart puttering with fright. She was sitting up in bed, shrieking, her eyes and mouth wide open.

'What's the matter with her?' Cordelia, her face white from sleep, came in with Mark Antony in her arms.

'Will whoever's making that infernal racket kindly shut up?' called Bron's voice from across the landing.

'She's having a bad dream.' I went over to Portia and spoke soothingly. 'It's all right. You're at home. You're quite safe. I'm here, darling.'

Portia closed her eyes and then opened them again. 'Hat? Oh, thank God! I was dreaming – horrible – horrible!' A tear slid from one eye. She closed her eyes again and took hold of my hand. 'Stay.'

I could have wept myself at this admission of need from my most dauntless, spirited sister. I sent Cordelia back to bed. Pulling up a chair, I sat beside Portia and made her lie down. After a while Dirk settled on my feet and I was grateful for the warmth from his body for slowly the house became very cold. Portia slept again but badly, turning her head from side to side and grinding her teeth, her eyes always a little open as though she could not trust the world enough to relax her vigilance even in sleep. More than once she sat up and cried out. When she heard my voice, she lay down again, muttering things I could not decipher.

The imp of anxiety that had taken up tenancy in my stomach chewed away. When I wasn't worrying about Portia being permanently affected, physically and mentally, by her appalling experience, I worried about Pa. Luckily the nuns at

St Frideswide's had made us learn large tracts of poetry by heart. By the time I had got through a good chunk of *Goblin Market*, I felt exhausted and numb. I fetched blankets from the linen cupboard and made myself comfortable. Gradually the night wore away and I dozed, off and on. Towards dawn, when she seemed to be sleeping more peacefully, I crept upstairs to my own bed. I thought Portia might not like to find me beside her when she woke, a reminder of the terrors of darkness.

NINE

'That's a new photographer, isn't it?' said Cordelia, three days later, lifting swollen eyelids to look into the street. She was sitting cross-legged on the window seat in the drawing room, with a box of paper handkerchiefs at her elbow, reading her favourite bit in *Little Women* where Beth March almost dies of scarlet fever. She had *Good Wives* beside her with a marker at the page where Beth finally joins the choir invisible.

Idly I strolled over to have a look. We were all extremely bored with our lives. It was difficult to be purposeful with a cohort of reporters dogging our steps and quite impossible to think expansively, confronted as we were at every turn by insuperable problems. Cordelia and I had been to the cinema the evening before to see Robert Mitchum in *The Big Sleep* but it had been hard to lose ourselves in the story while the press chortled at the seduction scenes, rustled bags of Butterkist and blew so much cigarette smoke over us that our hair and clothes reeked like the snug at The Green Dragon.

Bron was the only one of us who did not mind having his photograph taken whenever he bought a bar of soap or went to collect his dry-cleaning. But, to his annoyance, photographs of him never appeared in the newspapers. Not a word of the interview he had given had been printed. We no longer merited headlines. Instead, articles about our clothes and our hairstyles and whether we were looking pale and haunted (Bron) or aristocratic and forlorn (Ophelia) or sparky and irrepressible (Cordelia) appeared in the society gossip columns, a whispering that continued to fan the flames of notoriety. According to the *Clarion*, Ophelia was suing Crispin for breach of promise and Bron was out on bail, paid by a female member of the royal family whose playmate he had been until scandal touched him.

Because she had not set foot outside the house since her return from Surrey three days ago, the wildest conjectures were made about Portia. The *Clarion* revealed that she had signed a lucrative contract to star *en travestie* as Mozart in a new play called *Amadeus*. The *People's Exclusive* had it from a reliable source that she had been the mistress, successively, of Prince Rainier, Lord Snowdon and Ziggy Stardust. The *Herald* insisted that she was due to fly out to join Lord Lucan, who had taken refuge in a Nazi colony in Tierra del Fuego.

Probably it was my lack of resemblance to my brother and sisters that fuelled the rumours circulated by The *Daily Examiner* that I was the lovechild of my father and Maria Callas. I have to admit that I was pleased to be described as svelte and enigmatic.

Portia joined us at the window. Her bruises were beginning to turn yellow and the swellings to go down, but the broken tooth was startlingly incongruous with her beautiful face. She had not been able to bring herself to confront the outside world in order to visit the dentist. Her sleep had been so troubled by nightmares that she had moved to a camp bed in my room. She refused to say a word more about her experiences and had made me promise not to tell the others. She insisted she was nearly over it but I was worried about her. She glanced indifferently in the direction of Cordelia's pointing finger and then ducked down beneath the sill.

'It's one of Dimitri's bodyguards!' She clutched my ankle. 'Not Chico, the other one! I think his name was Dex.'

'Are you sure?' The man, who was leaning against the lamppost, rolling a cigarette, looked quite ordinary. 'I can't see, Cordelia, if you're going to put your head there.'

'Would I say so if I weren't sure? You think I'm having hallucinations? Or going mad, perhaps?' Portia was extremely snappy these days, which was unlike her. 'He's got a birthmark on his cheek. I can hardly make a mistake about that, I suppose.'

'*Some* people think it's rude to push,' said Cordelia bitingly.

'Well, I can't see one.' I was studying the man's profile as he fiddled about with a box of matches. 'He's so undistinguished, I bet thousands of people look just like –' I broke off as the man turned his head to stare up at the house and I saw a dark red mark running from temple to chin. 'Oh. Oh dear. It's Dex, all right. But what can he want?'

'I expect he wants Maria-Alba's recipe for minestrone. Honestly, Harriet, you seem to be particularly stupid at the moment. Of course he's looking for me.'

'Poor man! I think it's very sad,' said Cordelia. 'Imagine having people stare at you all the time. There's a girl at school –' Cordelia stopped speaking and begun to hum.

I was well aware that Cordelia had been deliberately avoiding all mention of school because she was afraid someone would insist on her going back.

I stared down at Portia. 'Why?' Portia had turned round so she could sit on the floor, out of sight. She shrugged her shoulders and spread her hands wide in a gesture of bafflement. 'I know you don't want to talk about it,' I went on, 'but I've been wondering – how did you meet Dimitri?'

'Bron introduced us. He suggested we went down to The

Green Dragon for a drink. He pointed Dimitri out the minute we got in there and said he was incredibly rich.' Portia went faintly pink. 'I thought at the time it was something of a set-up. Bron shuffled off the minute Dimitri started talking to me.'

I was silent for a moment. An unpleasant idea had at once presented itself. This might be the explanation for Bron's new-found riches. No doubt selling one's sister was a time-honoured method of raising the wind in many parts of the world but I was incensed with my own brother for doing it. 'The low-down louse!' I said aloud.

'That's putting it mildly, I think.' Portia thought I was referring to Dimitri and I didn't bother to enlighten her. 'What's Dex doing now?'

'He's talking to one of the reporters.' Cordelia kneeled on the window seat to get a better view. 'He's looking very bad-tempered. I expect it's his birthmark that makes him grumpy. If he was a girl he could wear his hair across his face like Veronica Lake in *I Married a Witch*. You remember, the one which starts off with a thunderstorm and the lightning strikes the tree Veronica Lake's buried under. She and her father, who's also a witch – or would that be a wizard? – were burnt by the Puritans two hundred years ago and the two witches come out as puffs of smoke –'

'Oh, mercy!' cried Portia. 'Just tell me what's happening, will you?'

'He's shaking his head. He's looking at the house – he's looking at me!' Cordelia pulled her hair half across her face and began to pout. 'Golly, he's really staring at me. I wonder if I remind him of Veronica Lake? I love the bit when they're going to be married and the woman keeps singing, "I love you truly" and he says, "Oh, shut up!"' Cordelia began to giggle helplessly.

'If you don't want to be tied to a railway track and have your Veronica Lake locks cut off by the wheels of a passing express, you'd better shut up yourself.' Portia put up her hand and got hold of Cordelia's skirt. 'Move over and let Harriet see.'

'Don't pull! He's getting out a little book and writing something in it. Now he's tearing out a page. He's walking up the path – he's coming up the steps!' We heard the flap of the letter box clang and Dirk, who had been sleeping off his breakfast on the sofa, went from nought to sixty in one point eight seconds and was at the door attempting to remove the paint from the panels with his front paws. 'I'll get it. You beast, Portia, you've torn my skirt. I hope it's a love letter. Or a poem. I shan't mind about the birthmark. I wish he was a bit more swave, though.'

She ran off, ignoring Portia's unkind laughter. She returned, frowning over the note. Written in crooked capitals, bunched together like a cipher was the legend, 'GIVEUSTHECLOBER-ANDWELLEVEYOUALONE OTHERWIZYOULBESORY-YOUWAZBORN.'

Cordelia looked disappointed. 'It's not a very good letter. I expect he was an orphan and was made to work in a blacking factory instead of going to sch – O-ho, a-ha . . . What's a clober?'

We puzzled briefly over this until the general absence of double consonants suggested 'clobber'. Bron came in at that moment, wearing only a towelling robe. His hair was wet and sleeked back from his noble brow. He looked every inch a splendid specimen of modern manhood.

'Hello, Portia. Your face is turning quite a fetching shade of gold, like Tutankhamun's mask. But whatever you do, don't grin. That tooth really spoils the effect.'

Now I thought about it, I realised that Portia had not smiled once since her return. Bron wandered to the window, pointedly ignoring me, but I was too angry with him to be hurt.

'Cordelia,' he went on, 'be a good girl and ask Maria-Alba to make me a chicken sandwich. I've got a date with a girl whose father owns a merchant bank. Just the thought of all that tin is making me hungry. Hello, what's that bloke doing out there?' He stabbed a finger at the pane. 'Geezer who sold me the coat. Fellow with the birthmark. I paid the first instalment in cash so there can't be anything wrong about it. He's lowering the superior tone set by the gentlemen of the press. I'll tell him to go away.'

'No, don't do that,' we girls cried in unison as Bron made to throw up the sash.

'It must be Bron's coat he's after,' cried Cordelia. 'I'll run and fetch it, shall I?'

'What are you talking about?' Bron took hold of Cordelia's arm. 'Keep your mitts off my gear.'

'But Dex wants it. He's going to make us sorry we were born if we don't give it to him,' Cordelia explained. 'You're pulling my jersey.'

'One step further and I'll pull your head off. You don't mean to say that you're actually considering handing that ape my beautiful new coat?'

'Read this.' Portia gave him the note.

Bron turned it sideways and upside down before finally interpreting the crude capitals. 'Go and get it,' he instructed Cordelia. 'Chop, chop!'

'I'll come with you,' said Portia, crawling across the floor towards the door. 'I'm getting tired of this *ventre à terre* existence.'

Bron watched Portia's progress with an air of puzzlement. 'What's the matter with her?' he asked me, forgetting that I was in Coventry. Dirk was so enchanted to find a human face at his own level that he followed Portia into the hall, pawing at her bottom and barking loudly into her ear.

'Thanks to you, pretty well everything.' I regretted breaking

132

my promise to Portia but I was so furious with Bron that I found it impossible to keep silent any longer. 'How much money did that brute Dimitri give you for an introduction to Portia? You ought to be ashamed, Bron! Selling your own sister to a gangster! She might have been killed! As it is, she may never get over what he did to her. How *could* you?'

'I don't know what you're talking about!' Bron put on his injured expression, to which I was only too well accustomed.

'Where did you get that money I've seen you flashing about recently? Dimitri gave it to you, didn't he? Portia told me you set the whole thing up. He raped her several times at gunpoint and kept her prisoner in his house. She had to let some other thug make love to her in order to get away. That man you got the coat from is one of Dimitri's gang. You absolute bastard, Bron!' I was shouting now. All the anxiety I had been feeling on Portia's behalf poured out as uncontrolled anger and Bron, for once, looked abashed.

'Is it true? You're not having me on?' Seeing my face he went on, 'All right! No need to scream at me! Naturally, I had no idea he was going to do that. I just thought there'd be something in it for Portia. You must admit she's never been exactly fussy about who she takes into her bed. Dimitri said he'd seen Portia several times in The Green Dragon and was crazy to meet her. It seemed harmless enough. Of course I'm sorry if he hurt her. But I didn't take a penny from him, I swear.'

'Where did you get that money then? I don't believe you. I know what a liar you are!'

'I don't see why I should keep you informed of my pecuniary dealings.'

'I'm going to the police. I ought to have done it days ago.' I was halfway to the door when he called me back.

'All right, Goody Two-shoes. But you won't like it. I got

the money from Derek's last owner. He was mad keen to find him a good home. He said if I'd take the dog he'd give me a hundred pounds. Apparently his wife was kicking up hell because Derek barked all night and stopped the baby sleeping and she told him not to come home until he'd got rid of him. The poor bloke was desperate. He said he couldn't reconcile it with his conscience to abandon Derek in the streets because he'd grown fond of him. But the missus was threatening divorce. Well, it seemed to me we'd all benefit. He'd be restored to domestic bliss, you'd have the dog you've always wanted and I'd have a hundred pounds. What are you doing? Don't mess up my hair! I've just combed it the way I want it to dry. Look, Harriet, remember men don't like girls who throw themselves at their heads.'

'I'm just so thankful!' I was halfway between laughing and crying. 'I couldn't bear the thought of you being a – procurer.'

'Pimp is the *mot juste*, I fancy.' Bron waggled a finger at me. 'Let that be a lesson to you, Harriet, not to jump to conclusions. You've got a nasty censorious nature. Were you really going to tell Plod all my evil doings?'

I shook my head. 'Not really. I wanted you to tell me the truth. Dear Bron, let's make it up. I'm sick of quarrelling. I'll forgive you if you'll forgive me?'

'What are you forgiving me for, exactly –' Bron broke off as something dark and voluminous dropped past the window. He pushed up the sash and put out his head. 'There goes my wonderful coat. Straight into a dustbin.'

We heard Cordelia's voice from the upstairs window, yelling, 'It's yours. Take it and go away! If you wouldn't mind!' she added as an afterthought.

'What a shame. I'm so sorry. But if you bought it from Dex, it was probably stolen.'

'So? *I* didn't steal it. Damn it, look at those reporters!'

The press were jostling each other to get down the area steps. There was an ugly scene as they fought for possession of the coat. Instead of joining the scrum Dex was back at the lamppost, rolling another cigarette.

'I don't get it. Why isn't Dex interested?'

'Presumably, though you girls were so eager to fling my raiment to the wolves, it is not the clobber referred to in the note.'

'But what . . . ?' Light dawned. 'It must be Chico's clothes he's after.'

'Where are they?'

'I gave them to Maria-Alba to give to Loveday to burn in his incinerator.'

'You muff!' Portia was standing in the doorway, her expression alarmed. 'You absolute fathead!'

'I'm sorry. I just hated having the nasty smelly things around reminding – me.'

'Let it be a lesson to you to stop bloody tidying up! Now we're going to be made sorry we were born and I can tell you, in my case, it won't take much.' Portia put her head in her hands.

'That does it! I'm ringing Inspector Foy.' I went into the hall and picked up the receiver. It seemed like weeks until I was finally put through.

'Hello, Harriet. How are you getting along?' I felt comforted at once by the jolly uncle manner. I launched immediately into the tale. 'What was there about the garments in question to justify a threat like that?' he asked when I had told him everything I knew. All the avuncular cheer had gone out of his voice.

'I don't know. Nothing as far as I could see. The jacket was leather but it was worn and the collar was filthy. And the jeans were just ordinary.'

The inspector made his characteristic pom-pomming noise.

Then he said, 'Stay indoors and don't let anyone in. I'll be an hour at the most.'

He was as good as his word. I happened to be standing at the window as his car drew up. Though it was his usual plain black, unmarked saloon, Dex took one look at it and melted into the ether.

'Now, Miss Byng.' The inspector looked at Portia. 'You'd have done yourself and us a favour if you'd come along straight away and told us all about it. We'd have had some evidence then.'

'If you mean presenting myself knickerless on a table to be groped by a sadistic doctor in full view of a bevy of sniggering female police officers so that you can earn another pip, thank you, but no.' Portia gave him a glare of defiance. 'Nothing would persuade me.'

'Well, I can understand that.' Inspector Foy sat down, got out his pipe and lifted an eyebrow at me. I nodded. 'I've always thought the victim of a rape gets a thoroughly raw deal. Not just the physical examination, though that's bad enough, but all the questioning afterwards. Her past life raked up, counter-accusations from the defence, public humiliation – no, things are stacked against the victim from the start. And, naturally, when you've been through an ordeal like that, the last thing you want to do is talk about it with a lot of strangers who are bent on trying to prove you wrong. I agree, you've suffered enough already.' Portia's stern gaze softened fractionally. 'If you'll co-operate with me I'll see your privacy's protected. But I'd like you to help me put the culprit away.' Portia looked noncommittal. 'Do you recognise any of these men?'

He handed her a portfolio of photographs. She began to go through them. 'No, no, no,' sigh 'no, no – wait a minute. My God! I think it's him! I can't be sure. I never saw him without sunglasses.' Inspector Foy took out a pen and scribbled black circles over the eyes, then handed the photograph back. 'It's him. That's Dimitri.' Her eyes filled with tears and her mouth trembled but she continued to fix the inspector with a mutinous look that made me feel tremendously protective of her.

'Well done, Portia – if I may call you that?' There was a breezy kindness in his voice as he waved the stem of his pipe at her. Portia shrugged and quickly wiped the corner of one eye. 'This fellow's been on our books a long time. He's done time for fraud, embezzlement and robbery. A couple of his chums are still inside for GBH. It's likely he's involved with drugs. The vice boys are very interested in him. Anyone else you recognise?'

'Chico.' She threw the photograph of a man with cheeks like cushions on to the floor. 'And that's the man who was lurking outside, ready to make us regret our birthdays.' She held up a photograph of Dex.

'The birthmark doesn't look so bad, does it?' Cordelia held her head on one side, considering.

'I could get him straight away for loitering with intent. But I don't want to warn off the big boys. Could you find the house again?'

'I don't think it was in Devon. It didn't seem far enough away.'

The inspector pom-pommed a little.

'It was near Oxshott,' I said. 'That's Surrey, according to Ophelia. Oh, here she is.'

Ophelia came strolling into the drawing room, wearing her new fur-lined coat and a great deal of shimmering eye-shadow that made her eyes appear startlingly large. She looked extra-ordinarily lovely, even for her. Inspector Foy stood up politely. When she saw him she sighed. 'I'll be home late so don't bolt the back door.' She turned to go out again.

'Just a minute, Miss Byng.' The inspector spoke sharply.

'There's a man lurking who's been making serious threats against your family. You'd better not go out.'

'Why don't you arrest him?' Ophelia allowed her eyes to glide over the inspector's face before training them on the fireplace in a bored way. 'Isn't that your job?'

'I don't plan to do that yet.'

'Well, that's your business.' Ophelia lifted a brow. 'Kindly mind it. I'm going out.'

The inspector moved between her and the door. I admired the way he managed to look bigger suddenly, like an animal when challenged, though he had no fur to fluff up or hackles to raise. 'Don't be a fool.' It was quietly said, but with an undertone of contempt. 'I don't want to have to fish your body out of the river in a few hours' time. It doesn't take long for a water-logged corpse to swell to four times its usual size. They're a great deal of trouble to get to the morgue.'

Ophelia stared at him as insolently as she could, which was plenty and then some, as Americans say. The inspector held her gaze with one equally forceful.

'Life is rapidly becoming a dead bore.' She took off her coat and let it drop to the floor. She walked slowly from the room and I heard her going upstairs.

If the inspector felt victorious he had the grace not to show it. 'If Chico's clothes weren't worth anything then there was something in the pockets, or perhaps the lining, that was. Can I have a word with your gardener?'

'I'll go and get him,' said Portia.

'I don't think Loveday's the easiest person to question,' I said apologetically, aware as never before that our family must be quite infuriating to the methodical mind. 'He's rather – odd.'

'We see all sorts in this job.' The inspector was helping his pipe to draw by placing his matchbox on the bowl. I was becoming familiar with the habits and mannerisms of pipe-smokers. I was convinced now it was all a distraction so he could control the tempo of any conversation. 'From genius to madman and everything in between.' He got out his notebook and a Biro.

'Have you seen the film *Dr Jekyll and Mr Hyde*?' asked Cordelia eagerly. 'It's about a man who's both. This scientist invents a potion that makes him grow hideous and sinful and go out killing people. He's good, you see, but his other self is as wicked as can be. It's absolutely terrifying – particularly the bit when you see this horrible hairy hand come creeping round the door and she's brushing her hair in front of the mirror and she sees it and tries to scream only she can't get any sound out –' Cordelia paused for breath – 'but I expect being a policeman, nothing scares you.'

'Don't you believe it!' Inspector Foy laughed. 'The man who tells you nothing frightens him is whistling in the dark. Besides, fear is not necessarily bad. It may guard you from harm. And I suspect that fear of being caught, punished and disgraced keeps many more of us from committing crimes than does the voice of conscience –'

The arrival of Loveday interrupted this philosophical discourse. He was a small man with a large pointed nose and small eyes, rather ratty-looking, in fact. He had been giving the maze one last trim before the onset of winter so his hair and his clothes were sprinkled with leaves. His eyes gleamed cunningly against his speckled green skin in a way that made me think of those sinister wild men in medieval literature, forces of Nature and all that sort of thing.

'Thank you for coming to see me, Mr Loveday. I'm Chief Inspector Foy of –'

'I know who ye are. I seen it all writ in the clouds, se'en nights ago.' Though Loveday had been born and bred in East Hackney, he had a strange Loamshire accent that suggested a childhood on a heather-tufted moor or a sheep-bitten crag.

139

'Oh.' The inspector smiled, so far undeterred. 'Well, Mr Loveday, I believe Miss Byng gave you some clothes to burn.'

'Ah ha. Cloth made fro' devil's dust, spun into threads on Queen Mab's wheel.'

'Well – perhaps.' The inspector blew noisily down the stem of his pipe. 'Did you do so?'

'No, milord.'

The inspector forgot to puff and suck, and leaned forward on his chair. 'Where are they?'

''Twas the flames that burned them. I am but a mortal man. I cannot combust.'

'So they *are* destroyed?' The inspector could not hide his disappointment.

'Tha's a deep question, milord. Who knows where things go that are consumed by fire? Mayhap they become smoke-imps that ride the backs o' will-o'-the-wisps to mislead travellers in the dark. There's only one can answer that.'

The inspector frowned, and I sensed that Loveday's particular brand of whimsy was beginning to pall. 'Who?'

''Tis the man in the moon with a dog at his feet and sticks on his back.'

'Right. Well, thank you, Mr Loveday, that'll be all for the moment.'

Loveday went back to his maze, leaving a trail of leaves across the carpet. The inspector put away his notebook, humming tunefully and spent some time examining the tobacco in the bowl of his pipe. When he spoke again it was to ask me how I thought my father was bearing up in prison. The inspector was very kind and assured me that being on remand was nothing like as bad as serving a sentence. I hoped this meant he thought it unlikely that my father would have to do so. I was afraid to ask him outright.

He waited with us until a police car delivered a uniformed

bobby to stand in our front garden. PC Bird had round, grey, guileless eyes. A manifest sense of duty stiffened the large chin that braced the strap of his helmet. I noticed this at once for the events of the last few days had bread an increased sense of caution and mistrust in things generally, and in men in particular. I watched from the window as Loveday remonstrated angrily with him about treading on the emerging hellebores. This was sheer bloody-mindedness on Loveday's part, for the journalists had long since crushed every living thing to stalks and mud resembling a small-scale Passchendaele.

It was about then that things – already, I had thought, about as bad as they could possibly get – got suddenly worse. We were told by Inspector Foy that we should limit our excursions into the outside world. If we really had to go out, it should be during the hours of daylight and only to public places where there were plenty of people about. We had to inform the policeman on guard of our destination and appoint an hour for our return. Having to log in and out was curiously discouraging to enjoyment, and anyway, it was difficult to have a good time when we were jumpy and suspicious of every stranger. We all began to behave as though we were characters in *Wuthering Heights*, digging up old scores, seeing slights where there were none, and generally doing a good deal of brooding, sulking and scowling.

Absolutely the worst thing of all – apart from Pa being in prison, that is – was the disappearance of Mark Antony. He had become quite a favourite with the, by now, very bored reporters. So when, one rainy night, he did not return from his evening session at stool I went out to ask the last stragglers if they had seen him. They told me that the fellow with the birthmark had put in a brief reappearance an hour earlier with a 'dish of scraps for the kitty'. It had struck them as odd at the time for he had not seemed the sort of person to be fond of animals and, anyway, it was apparent from the size of Mark Antony's girth that he was already well catered for.

I spoke urgently to the policeman on duty, not our nice PC Bird but the grumpiest of the three who took it in turns to prevent us being made sorry we had been born. He had noticed the man but assumed he was a crank. When I rang Inspector Foy he was sympathetic but regretted that resources would not permit him to send out a police car to search for Mark Antony.

I had recently failed my driving test for the fourth time for being insufficiently in control of the vehicle but this did not prevent me from taking out Bron's car illegally, with only Cordelia as passenger, and combing the streets of Blackheath. After an hour of hopeless searching we were both crying so much that I failed to see a bollard and we had to drive away hastily, leaving confirmatory evidence of the justice of the last examiner's pithily worded strictures.

After this, life looked as black as could be and I think it was this that prevented me from seeing what was happening to Maria-Alba. At first I thought her extreme volatility was due to distress at the disappearance of Mark Antony, of whom she was very fond. But when she started seeing the Virgin Mary on the basement stairs and having long hectoring conversations with her about the rights and wrongs of the Catholic Church, I became seriously worried. The others were no help at all in this latest crisis.

To while away the hours of their incarceration Bron and Ophelia played Honeymoon Bridge in the drawing room for enormous if imaginary stakes. Portia spent all her time in her room, reading things like *Swallows and Amazons* and *The Magic Pudding*, chosen, she explained because she could be certain there would be no sex scenes, as she could not bear the idea of even the chastest kiss. Cordelia and I occupied the dining room where we were constructing a cat-sized four-poster bed for Mark Antony to sleep in when he came home. This was to distract Cordelia from her first plan, to keep a candle burning in every window of the house. I was certain this plan would result in him having no home to return to. Secretly I was convinced that he would not come back and whenever I thought of what might have happened to him I felt miserably sick, and scowled and brooded and sulked as much as anyone.

I was just stitching some gold braid to the delicious blue velvet we had found for Mark Antony's curtains when I heard screams of rage coming from the basement. I ran down to discover Maria-Alba beating the stair carpet with the soup ladle, so violently that the handle broke and the bowl flew off, hitting me painfully on the shin.

'*Diavolo! Diavolo!*' she howled, almost incoherent with angry weeping. When Cordelia appeared at the top of the stairs, her golden locks illuminated by the hall chandelier, Maria-Alba fell on her knees and implored *il Spirito Santo* to be merciful.

Reluctantly I rang her doctor. He was out, and by the time he called back, a few hours later, Maria-Alba was her old self again, exhausted but perfectly rational. But the next afternoon, at about the same time, Maria-Alba was on her knees before the washing machine, weeping and begging it to forgive her for strangling Father Alwyn. I tried to reason with her but she was convinced I had come to arrest her. When PC Bird, who was on duty that afternoon and with whom we had become friendly, came to the back door to thank her for the tea and to return his mug, she shrieked with terror. To my surprise he turned pale and put his hands over his ears. Considering what ghastly things police officers are required to witness it struck me that PC Bird was going to have to toughen up. I went to call Maria-Alba's doctor.

143

I had to hang on for ages while the doctor's receptionist rang round his various haunts. I returned to find PC Bird, glassy-eyed and gibbering, wandering about the kitchen declaring that he could see tiny faces of beautiful girls on the cupboard doors. I assured him they were just door knobs but when he began to clutch his head and moan that he was being blinded by brilliant stars exploding like fireworks, that were something ruddy marvellous but at the same time bloody awful, then I began to put two and two together.

By the time Inspector Foy and Sergeant Tweeter arrived, one of the reporters had joined us in the kitchen, exclaiming that everything in the world had turned a bright, beautiful yellow and that he was floating in the scent of lemons. This encouraged PC Bird to assure us earnestly that he *was* a lemon.

'All right. So it's some kind of hallucinogenic substance.' Inspector Foy began to pick up bottles at random and sniff the contents. 'Obviously taken unintentionally.' He looked at his watch. 'Four thirty. Who had cups of tea?'

'Everyone except Cordelia and two of the reporters who bring flasks. I had a mug of tea and I feel fine. Oh, I know – of course! It's the sugar! Maria-Alba always has three spoons. Only two of the reporters take sugar. And poor Dicky, I mean PC Bird – sorry, but everyone calls him that – has four.'

The inspector dipped his finger in the blue-and-white sugar jar and licked it. 'Tastes all right to me but I'll take it for analysis. I wonder, though . . .' He got out his pipe while he was thinking but when he lit a match poor Dicky knuckled his eyes and whimpered that a big fiery dragon was coming to eat him up, so the inspector was forced to abandon it. 'Look after that man,' he instructed Sergeant Tweeter.

Dicky began to sob brokenly into Sergeant Tweeter's tunic, which embarrassed its owner horribly. Meanwhile Maria-Alba was cradling the pieces of the broken ladle in her arms and singing it a lullaby, while the reporter, under the impression that the kitchen table was a large chocolate cake, was trying to eat it with a spoon.

The inspector sounded just a little rattled. 'I can't think with all this noise going on. Get that man into the car and wait for me. Calm him down. Sing him a nursery rhyme or something.' Sergeant Tweeter's ruby-coloured face darkened further and he dragged the poor sufferer away. 'It's something like LSD. That's it. Sugar lumps!' We opened every jar and box in the place until we found a large cache of lump sugar in an old biscuit tin.

'We never usually have sugar in lumps,' I said, puzzled. 'Maria-Alba, shush a minute!' I showed her the tin. 'Where did you get them?'

Her expression grew solemn and wondering. '*Diamanti! Scintillanti! Siamo ricchi!*'

'No, not diamonds – unfortunately. Sugar. *Zucchero.*'

'*Sì, sì.* Jack! Jack!'

'Jack who? We don't know anyone called Jack.'

'No, no, no!' She shook her head emphatically. '*Jack!*'

Suddenly I got it. 'I see! Not Jack but *giacca*! It means jacket. They must have been in Chico's coat! We've been trying desperately to save money. She probably thought it would be wasteful to throw them away.'

'If they're all impregnated with LSD there must be a thousand pounds worth here,' said the inspector. 'Dex and his chums would be keen to recover them. Who else takes sugar in their tea?'

'Not Ophelia – nor Portia – oh dear, Bron!'

The inspector picked up the biscuit tin. 'You go and see to your brother. I'll check on the other reporter. Come along with me,' he addressed the one who was trying to eat the table. 'We'll see you safely home.'

The reporter looked at the inspector with astonishment.

'Why, if it isn't Rita Hayworth! Well, I never!' he giggled. 'I've always fancied you rotten.'

I ran up to see how Bron was. He was lying on the sofa in the drawing room, screeching with laughter.

'I've never known him be so stupid.' Ophelia was sitting at the table, building a house of cards. 'I can't get any sense out of him at all. I suppose he must be drunk but I do think he might have shared it round. He's always *so* selfish. There!' The construction collapsed with the last card. 'I wish I knew what was funny. I'm bored to sobs.'

'He's on a trip. The sugar lumps in the tea had LSD in them.'

'Really?' Ophelia was interested for a moment. 'How long will it last? Where did you get them from?'

'Several hours, I should think. Maria-Alba found them in the pockets of Chico's clothes.'

'Who's Chico?'

'Oh dear, I'd forgotten. I promised Portia I wouldn't tell anyone.'

'All right, don't bother, then. I'm not really interested in her sordid pick-ups.' Ophelia looked gloomy. 'I'd better have a sugar lump, then. I could do with a laugh.'

'The inspector's taken them away. Anyway, it wouldn't do you any good. Honestly, I think it's dangerous. People jump out of windows thinking they can fly, and often they have a really horrible time.'

'I may as well go to bed then, until he's sobered up.'

'You aren't supposed to leave people alone when they're on trips.'

'I shall have a migraine if I have to listen to that noise.'

Dirk and I sat with Bron while he chortled and cackled and chuckled for hours without a break. I was glad for his sake that my brother seemed to have no inner demons, but whether this was good or bad for the rest of the world, I couldn't make up my mind. Portia and Cordelia played draughts in Maria-Alba's room while she slept deeply, having been given a sedative by her doctor. By evening we were all in a state of extreme lassitude. Bron finally stopped laughing and demanded supplies of wine, lemonade and throat lozenges, as he was painfully hoarse.

There was a general, plaintive call for food. I tried to poach some eggs but it was more difficult than I had imagined. A plate was piled high with failures – too hard, broken yolks, stringy whites like rubber bands – and I was heated with feelings of inadequacy and annoyance, when a row broke out at the front door. The bell rang repeatedly, the knocker banged violently and Dirk let the front door know what he thought of it in a succession of ear-splitting barks. All the journalists had gone home hours ago, no doubt to write lurid exposés of everyday life in a famous actor's narcotics den. I went up to see.

On the doorstep were two figures of sinister appearance, disguised in swathes of clothing so as to conceal their features.

'Cut along now!' said the policeman who had replaced poor Dicky. 'Let's have no argy-bargy, madam, if you please. The family doesn't want to be disturbed.'

'Now, look here, my good man,' said a male voice that was familiar. 'This lady lives here and if you know what's good for you you'll let us in without delay.'

'A likely story,' said the PC, who seemed to have learned his lines from *Dixon of Dock Green*. 'You reporters have plenty of cheek, I'll give you that.'

'But this is my daughter!' said my mother's voice from behind a veil. A gloved finger emerged from among the wraps to point at me. 'Harriet, tell this blundering fool who I am!'

TEN

'Confusion now hath made his masterpiece!' said my mother, with feeling. 'Ronnie, I need a drink. No, Harriet, *Macbeth*! You can't think,' she continued to address me, 'what a *fright*ful time we've been having. Ow-how! Gently!' I drew back in alarm, having attempted to kiss the veil masking her cheek. 'What is this dog doing in the house? Can no one stop it barking?'

'Sorry. Be quiet, Dirk! At once!' Dirk barked on. 'Shall I take your coats? There's a bottle of wine open in the drawing room. I'll get more glasses.'

'I think double Scotches would be more the thing.' Ronnie helped my mother out of her coat and then took off his own. They retained their scarves, hats – a smart blood-red turban in my mother's case, pulled well down over her ears – and sunglasses. 'It's chilly, isn't it?' He shivered, though the house felt warm to me, and drew his scarf tighter round his face. 'I think I'll hang on to this for the moment.'

'Me, too.' My mother went into the drawing room.

I ran down to the kitchen and poured two generous whiskies. 'Ma's home,' I said to Portia and Cordelia.

'Your eggs have boiled dry,' said Portia. 'Was that meant to happen?'

There followed a short scene of which I was immediately ashamed. After I had apologised we went up together to the drawing room.

My mother seemed touchingly pleased to see her children but repelled affectionate overtures with cries of pain. She and Ronnie crouched by the fire in their mufflers and head-dresses, like Russian peasants round a samovar. Dirk was evidently worried by their suspicious appearance, for he flashed his eyes from one to the other and kept up a continuous growling.

'I hope Maria-Alba has something good for supper,' said my mother as she gulped down the whisky. 'That bloody clinic has kept us on famine rations. Only the thought of getting home and having something decent to eat stopped me from throwing myself into the river.'

'Maria-Alba isn't well,' I said. 'I'm trying to poach some eggs. But it's trickier than I thought. I've got two out of the eight that are probably edible. You should have telephoned.'

'Naturally we'd have done so if we'd had two pennies to rub together. When we arrived at the clinic – Ronnie decided, as the prices were so favourable, to have a little work done too – they made us strip down to the last hairpin and put on their overalls. They took away our clothes and locked them up. Then the minute we came round from our operations they presented us with exorbitant bills. Eighty pounds for champagne that was scarcely drinkable! Of course we refused to pay. Had Ronnie not been very resourceful and stolen the key from Matron's desk we'd be there still. All our pockets had been emptied and there was no sign of my bag or Ronnie's notecase. We had to walk all the way from Bethnal Green. I had no idea that London could be so unpleasant. The inhabitants were positively abusive and some of the children threw things at us. Poor Ronnie received a nasty blow on the shoulder from a brick. Not a policeman in sight, naturally. They are all too busy obstructing the doorways of the upper classes.'

'Why *are* the myrmidons of the law encircling the house?' Ronnie sat cradling his glass in one hand while the other tenderly massaged his upper arm.

'It's all Portia's fault,' said Ophelia. 'Her penchant for rough trade has had its inevitable consequence. This house is now notorious for every vice and vileness in the *Thieves' Almanac.*'

'That's unfair.' I looked at Portia but her chair was empty. When, later, I went up to her room she explained that two pairs of sunglasses were too much for her and she would forgo supper. I descended to the kitchen with the forlorn hope of making something of those wretched poached eggs. Ronnie was already there, his features still hidden by scarves and sunglasses, but with his shirtsleeves rolled up and wearing Maria-Alba's apron. He was chopping an onion with speed and expertise.

'We cannot all afford a cook,' he said with a degree of hauteur when I expressed surprise. 'I am going to make a cottage pie. It will be simple but good. Your mother needs nourishment.'

'How kind you are, Ronnie.'

'Not really.' Ronnie's lenses flashed as he bent to crush a clove of garlic. 'I've always adored her. I simply can't help wanting to do things for her. It's as natural as tides being drawn to the moon or the hen returning to her coop at dusk. Irresistible forces compel each of us to our destiny . . .' I sat down, my hand on Dirk's head to dissuade him from growling as Ronnie continued his speech to the end. 'And how is your poor papa?' he asked when he had finished, his good humour apparently restored. 'You know, your mother's feelings have been so painfully lacerated by his misfortune that she cannot bring herself even to mention it. Some people might misunderstand this but we, who know her delicate, sensitive nature, will not condemn it as weakness. Great artists are as different from us ordinary mortals as a Ming vase from a flowerpot.'

I wondered if he really believed this. My mother had not acted for ten years. Not since a reviewer wrote that her portrayal of Lady Macbeth put him in mind of an exasperated society hostess burdened with unmannerly guests who had lost the new tennis balls, left the bathrooms in a mess, and finished the gin. My mother was inclined to recite the review verbatim accompanied by peals of mordant laughter, when she had had a little too much to drink.

'But surely you are no mean actor yourself?' I said politely.

'I was, in my day, a skilled journeyman of the stage. I could charm and I could menace. Girls, the length and breadth of England, dreamed of being taken in my arms and bent to my will. My performance as Lord Sylvester Steel, the *Man in the Scarlet Hood*, was, I believe, definitive. But I could not have played Hamlet to save my life.'

'Ma has always said you've the best profile of any man she's ever met.'

'Really?' Ronnie sounded pleased. What she had actually said was that Ronnie had done very well with nothing to recommend him but a handsome profile, but it was nearly the same thing. He offered Dirk the remains of the leg of lamb he was cutting up. 'That's a nice puppy you've got there.'

'He is sweet, isn't he?' Dirk did not at that moment look specially sweet, tearing the flesh from the bone with huge white teeth. 'But he's fully grown, thank goodness.'

'Mm.' Ronnie considered him. 'I wouldn't be too sure.'

I fetched potatoes and carrots from the larder and together Ronnie and I chopped and scraped and scrubbed in a warm, steamy atmosphere of domestic harmony. From time to time I looked at Dirk as he lay slumbering, one ear folded across the glistening picked-clean femur. Now Ronnie had drawn my attention to it, Dirk did seem larger than when he had arrived.

'I'm afraid the clinic wasn't all it was cracked up to be,' I said. My father and I sat facing each other, in the middle of a long row of prisoners and their visitors. Two prison officers patrolled the room, looking bored. Between Pa and me was a battered table, over which crawled an out-of-season fly. Neither it nor my father looked well. 'The bruising's very bad. They're still refusing to take off the scarves and sunglasses. You remember *The Invisible Man*? It's almost the same except for the turban and Ronnie's purple hair. Apparently because it was so cheap and the surgeon was awfully persuasive, they got carried away and had far more done than they'd originally planned.' I was chattering on in this inconsequential way, hoping to cheer Pa up. His skin looked colourless, almost flabby. I wondered if he was eating properly. I paused, then plunged on. 'Ronnie's staying with us for the time being. He's being very useful because he knows how to cook. Maria-Alba has had to go and stay with the nuns again.'

Poor Maria-Alba had had upsetting flashbacks from her involuntary experience with LSD and her doctor had decided that she should have a rest. She had a love-hate relationship, mostly hate, with the sisters at the Convent of St Ursula, in Bushey Heath, whose guest she had been several times in the past. She was convinced they wanted to get possession of her soul so they could barter with God to improve their own lot in the life to come. The more Maria-Alba raged the more saintly the sisters became, which inflamed her to greater heights of scurrilous invective. On the other hand

152

Maria-Alba's sanity was invariably restored by the peaceful rhythm of conventual life.

Maria-Alba had been in no state to survive a long journey on public transport so I had bribed Bron – with the offer of doing all his laundry for the next six months – to drive us to the convent. I was pretty sure I would be doing it anyway, so it was cheap at the price. Despite what Maria-Alba said, the sisters who welcomed us seemed much saner and sweeter-tempered than my old schoolmistresses, no doubt because they didn't have horrible little girls to look after. It was a closed order so we would not be allowed to visit her, but as she was a guest, she would be allowed to send and receive letters.

'Poor Maria-Alba,' said my father in a lacklustre way.

I wondered what I might say to cheer him up. I had met Marina Marlow at the prison gates. She had been posing for photographers and giving an impromptu interview. I heard her say that it was a matter of indifference to her whether my father was guilty or not. Friendship meant commitment through thick and thin. I got the impression she would prefer him to be guilty as this would show her in a more praiseworthy light. Her hair was a bright shade of platinum, like tinfoil. A low neckline and a thigh-length split in her skirt seemed tactless when visiting men obliged to be celibate. But she was magnetic. I felt a shudder of apprehension and pretended not to see her matey little wave.

The truth was, no matter how many affairs my parents entered into, I always bitterly resented their paramours. I was wounded on behalf of whichever parent was left out in the cold and I was fearful each time that the temporary sexual attachment might turn out to be something more important. No matter how hard I tried to be an obedient daughter and teach myself the lesson that monogamy was unnatural, illogical and deplorably lower middle class, my feelings of insecurity were painful. One of the things I had loved about Dodge was that he held fiercely puritanical views about everything, which included constancy in love.

'I saw Marina outside.' I tried to sound matter-of-fact. 'It was good of her to visit.'

'She brought me a bottle of L'Equipée Pour Hommes. Very expensive. It doesn't seem to have occurred to Marina that making oneself smell attractive is the last thing one wants to do in a place like this.'

'You mean –' I lowered my voice – 'the other men?'

'You bet. I go in fear of my virtue. That's why I got the barber to cut my hair.' I had managed to suppress a gasp when I first caught sight of his shaven head. It made his eyes and jaw look much bigger. 'You see that bloke with the scars and the broken nose two tables down?' I looked surreptitiously at a man who seemed to have spent his whole life running his face into sharp and dangerous objects. 'That's Slasher O'Flaherty. He's offered me a whole month's snout – that's tobacco – if I'll drop into his cell one evening to discuss acting techniques.'

Unluckily the man happened to glance in my direction before I could look away. He winked and smiled, exposing a solitary brown tooth.

'Oh, Pa! Do be careful! Can't the prison officers protect you?'

'Some of the screws are worse than the prisoners.' He laughed in a depressed way. 'So Ronnie's seized the opportunity to lay siege to your mother. Not that it will do him any good. He's about as virile as a pink-eyed rabbit in a conjurer's hat.'

I thought he was entitled to be catty in the circumstances. 'Ronnie's really very domesticated. He's hardly ever out of apron and rubber gloves. And I think he's enjoying it.'

'He always was an old woman.' My father looked gloomy

154

and rubbed his hand over the bristles on his head. 'I suppose you're all having a wonderful time without me.'

'We certainly are not! Portia still won't go out anywhere, though the police found Dimitri's house and arrested him and discovered masses of drugs and things and they're all in prison – luckily not this one – and the police guard's been called off.' I knew Portia had written to my father, giving an edited account of her escapade, but I had not seen the letter so I kept the details vague. 'All except Dex.'

I felt a sinking of spirits, recalling this disappointment. When Inspector Foy had telephoned to tell me about the successful police raid on the house in Oxshott I had hoped that he might have found Mark Antony as well, but there had not been so much as a bowl of Kittichunks or a clump of ginger fur. Or Dex. The inspector assured me there was a nationwide watch for Dex and he would not be able to leave the country. I had not told my father about Mark Antony being missing. The news could only depress.

'Ophelia's as grumpy as she can possibly be.' I wanted to reassure him that we were not disporting ourselves, indifferent to his plight. 'Peregrine Wolmscott hasn't asked her to marry him and she's worried in case her looks are going. She reckons to enslave any man within two weeks.'

'That's my girl. Your mother enslaved me in less than one. How is Cordelia?'

'At rather a loose end.' I felt guilty and I expect I looked it. 'She hasn't been to school since you were arrested. I had a bit of a row with Sister Imelda.'

Sister Imelda, headmistress of St Frideswide's, had telephoned to ask why Cordelia was not at school. When I said I thought Cordelia needed a little time at home to recover from the shock of my father's arrest, Sister Imelda's voice had grown cold. It was her considered opinion that children brought up as we had been needed discipline, not coddling.

Cordelia already had a distressing disregard for truth and a vulgar tendency to dramatise herself, and if she were to escape a life given over to flagrant immorality it was important that home influences be kept to a minimum.

'Honestly, just because she's a nun she thinks she can get away with any amount of rudeness,' I said, feeling aggrieved all over again.

Though none but the bare facts of the case had been made public, it was obvious that nearly everyone believed that my father must be guilty of the murder of Sir Basil Wintergreen or he would not be in prison. The old adage that there is no smoke without fire was persuasive. What had been admired in Pa before as the eccentricity of artistic genius had been transformed at a stroke to the vicious traits of psychopathy.

Sister Imelda did not doubt that we were the children of a cold-blooded assassin and therefore she despised us. I had been so hurt by her disparagement of my family that I was prompted to strike a blow in return. I asked her if she was aware that her relationship with Sister Justinia had been the subject of malicious gossip throughout the school. If so, she would know how painful it was to be condemned without a hearing.

Sister Imelda had given a satisfying scream of affliction at the other end of the telephone and the line had gone dead. For several hours I had felt quite buoyed up by the success of my revenge. I had said nothing that was not true. According to Cordelia, Sister Imelda's passion for the novice teacher had been common knowledge for weeks and the more censorious parents were beginning to mutter. But when my indignation had cooled I repented. Sister Imelda was an unhappy woman and her spiteful behaviour was proof of this.

I wrote to Sister Imelda, saying she was probably right about Cordelia needing more discipline. I would see that she returned to school within a few days. I apologised unreservedly for losing my temper and asked her to put it down to the strain of my father's arrest and imprisonment, which, naturally, had made us all very unhappy. I received a letter by return of post, which said that the Byng family would be *personae non gratae* at any future school occasion and would I send a cheque immediately for a term's fees, in lieu of notice? It concluded with a request for an additional forty-five pence to replace the light bulb that Cordelia had broken a few weeks before.

'She's an extremely silly woman,' said my father absently. 'I've always said so.' This was true. My parents had been consistent in their ridiculing of the school and its preceptors. Their attitude might go some way to explain why – except for English at which we excelled – we were all so undistinguished academically and athletically. 'You'd better ring up a few schools,' was my father's reply, when I asked him what I should do about Cordelia.

'What about the bank?'

'Tell them to do their worst. The worst is not, so long as we can say, "This is the worst."'

'*Othello*,' I said, to please him, though it seemed a singularly discouraging remark. 'But, really, Pa, we must do *some*thing. We don't want them to take away the furniture.'

'*King Lear*. We'll have to borrow a couple of thousand from someone, just to tide us over. Let me see. Edgar's a decent, generous chap.'

'He's just married again,' I reminded him. 'He'll be paying Celia vast amounts of alimony. We can't possibly ask him.'

'Roddy and Tallulah.'

'They've gone to Tibet for six months, don't you remember? They're getting spiritually aligned.'

'All right. Cosmo and Alfred, then.'

'They've moved to Bath to write a verse play about Beau

Nash. They won't make any money for months. If ever. They'll need all their capital.'

'Very well. Mortimer Dunn.' A tetchy note had come into my father's voice and I didn't blame him. It was unpleasant work, raking through one's acquaintances to see to whom one could go cap in hand.

'His obituary was in yesterday's paper.'

'Oh bugger!' Pa put his shorn head in his hands, whether with regret at Mortimer's demise or his disqualification as a possible milch cow, I did not know. I racked my brains, unsuccessfully, for something comforting to say. When he looked up, my father's expression was fierce. 'You must ask Rupert Wolvespurges.'

I stared at him in astonishment, wondering if imprisonment had turned his brain.

Rupert Wolvespurges was the illegitimate son of my father's best friend at Cambridge – the product of an undergraduate discretion with a pretty young Armenian waitress. The waitress had gone back to Armenia after Rupert's birth, leaving the baby and no forwarding address. After Rupert's father had been shot in mistake for a grouse less than a year later, the responsibility for Rupert fell to his paternal grandmother. Her nature, said Pa, was severe and exacting, a good match for the bleak, uncomfortable castle on a windy mountain in Scotland in which she lived. Lady Wolvespurges was delighted to accept my father's proposal that Rupert, as soon as he reached preparatory school age, should spend his holidays with us. A household composed of two struggling but glamorous young actors and their hopeful offspring must have been a lot more fun than that of a high-nosed widow who thoroughly disapproved of her dead son's liaison.

Rupert was ten years older than me. When I search for memories of him I remember a tall, thin boy with dark eyes

158

and black hair, whose features denoted his Indo-European rather than his English ancestry. He was different from us in every way. Compared with our extrovert rowdiness, Rupert seemed introspective, uncommunicative and something of an outsider, which I think was his choice.

He was kind to us children. My mother maintained that he was a difficult boy, always shutting himself up with books, brooding and writing bad poetry, but to me he was a godlike being. When he condescended to play with us, I can say without exaggeration that those were the happiest times of my childhood. Of course he was much older even than Bron, so it was not surprising that we all admired him without reservation.

There was a corner of the park made gloomy by a circle of trees. It was a long way from any path and here we set up our kingdom, named Ravenswood by Rupert. At that time he was devoted to the novels of Sir Walter Scott. It was made entirely from what we thought of as valuable finds and what others would have called junk – old boards, broken deck chairs, tea chests, sheets of corrugated iron, even the prow of an old boat we had dug from the mud by the river. Rupert nailed and glued these riches together to create an eccentric structure that seemed to my infant eyes a palace.

The entrance was by way of a home-made ladder up to the lowest branches. When you had climbed up, collecting a new set of splinters each time, you found yourself in a baronial hall. Rupert had brought back several pairs of antlers from his grandmother's estate. He hung these on the walls that we painstakingly constructed from mud and sticks mixed with animal hair. Rupert said that was how houses had been made for centuries until they thought of bricks. Sometimes the walls dried out too much and broke down. Rupert said this was because there was not enough hair binding the mud. We carefully trimmed the fur from Mark Antony's predecessor and took surreptitious snips from the coats of dogs we befriended in the street. My parents were mystified and annoyed when we insisted on returning from a holiday in Devon with three large bags of sheeps' wool collected from barbed wire fences.

Rupert was furious with Bron for cutting off a horse's tail. He gave us all a lecture on cruelty, and reduced Portia and me to tears with a harrowing picture of a poor animal tormented by flies and unable to chase them away. He received my donation of two plaits that I had cut from my own head with proper expressions of gratitude and they were immured in mud with suitable ceremony. Predictably, my mother was angry about my sadly altered appearance and blamed Rupert. Bron made me unhappy by refusing to be seen with me in public until my hair had grown to a more becoming length but Rupert said I had the Dunkirk spirit. It was some years before I knew what that was but I was comforted. Naturally my parents knew nothing of Ravenswood. We had all cut our fingers and sworn in blood not to divulge the whereabouts of our hideaway. I remember Rupert losing his temper with Bron over a bottle of red ink.

Many blissful hours were spent excavating for shards of broken china to decorate the walls of the refectory, which was built higher up and could be reached only by a perilous scramble along a rickety walkway between two trees. On one occasion Portia fell and broke her arm. There was an almighty row, with Rupert once again getting the blame. He said Portia was a great gun for not telling and gave her his brass inkwell that was shaped like a frog as a reward for bravery. After that I tried to pluck up the courage to hurl myself to the ground but I always funked it.

Almost the best bit of Ravenswood was the dungeon. One of the trees was hollow and you could slide right down inside it. We covered the floor with an old rug and lit our secret chamber with candle ends, and Rupert read us bits from *The Bride of Lammermoor*, his eyes glittering in the lambent light. I barely understood one sentence in ten. But my imagination was fired by that far-off place, hemmed about with dark forests and peopled with quarrelsome characters of compelling beauty.

Rupert was very fond of my father. His relationship with my mother was always complicated. My mother really only liked people who were in love with her and Rupert, even at that age, was not fond of women. I don't know how I knew that.

When Rupert left school and went up to Oxford it was the end of things. I suppose he spent his holidays abroad. I remember him coming to the house for dinner several times, occasions from which we children were excluded. Once when he was standing in the hall saying goodbye, I crept to the head of the stairs in my dressing gown and whispered his name. He looked up and caught sight of my face pressed against the banisters. He had waved, a gesture no one else saw. I treasured that secret communication for a long time.

Bron and Ophelia grew too old for the pleasures of Ravenswood and so it came to belong to Portia and me. It wasn't the same without Rupert. We visited it infrequently and let it fall into disrepair. Years later, when Cordelia was five or six, I took her to see it. I had to search for a long time before I found it. All but two of the trees had been cut down and only the discovery of several pieces of china and a broken antler convinced me this really was the place where I had spent so many glorious hours of my childhood.

I was thirteen when Rupert came under sentence of excommunication from the Byng family. The severance was, on the surface, conducted with civilised calm but as with a banked-up fire, there were fiery gleams that threatened to combust. For weeks my mother went silently about with a face carved from stone. We avoided her, depressed by the charged atmosphere of imminent storm. The decorators were called in and the strawberry-coloured walls of the dining room were painted pewter, with black skirting boards and silvered shutters and doors. The effect was chic but chilling. For a few days my mother insisted on food to match the new scheme but it was too expensive and troublesome to keep up. Everyone except Cordelia, who was still more or less a baby, liked caviar, olives and sardines but we children refused to eat prunes and even Ma couldn't manage the black pudding. Whenever we gathered for lunch or supper the silence was broken only by my father's vain attempts to pretend that nothing was wrong. He talked of literature, architecture, painting, music and even the weather – of everything in fact except the theatre – while we children sat mute and cowardly, afraid of freezing reproofs from the personification of Bale who sat at the end of the table, smiling at grief.

Rupert Wolvespurges, always precocious, had, at the age of twenty-three, been appointed drama critic for the *London Intelligencer*. It was he who had made the comparison between my mother's Lady Macbeth and the fraught society hostess. My mother had never forgiven him.

ELEVEN

A canal, bordered on each side by a leafless framework of pleached trees, flowed between two rows of terraced houses. Gas lamps, placed sparingly along the cobbled pavements, cast ribbons of light on the water and moving shadows across the soft red-brick façades. The houses had severely plain sash windows and graceful fanlights. This small Georgian utopia on the cusp of Richmond, where Beauty frolicked, was called Horn-on-the-Green, presumably because one end of the terrace adjoined a park. This I had discovered from my *A–Z*, for now it was too dark to see it. At the town end was a pair of wrought-iron gates, padlocked and admitting pedestrians only, through a wicket gate.

For reassurance I felt in my pocket for the sheet of paper my father had given me. I had read it several times and was familiar with its message. In a large hand, in black ink, beneath an engraved address on thick cream paper, were the following words: 'Dear Waldo, I have read with distress of your misfortune. If I can be of any service to you, I am yours to command, Rupert Wolvespurges.' Though well-expressed, the letter lacked warmth. Remembering it now, I felt thoroughly discouraged from asking a virtual stranger if he would lend me two thousand pounds.

I had been amazed to discover that my father had kept in touch with Rupert Wolvespurges all this time, without saying a word to anyone. My mother would have been absolutely furious if she had known. From the moment of his exclusion, visitors had quickly learned not to mention Rupert's name in our household if they wished to avoid the permafrost of her displeasure. It had seemed strange to me, then, how rapidly he had passed out of our lives. Only Portia and I had felt, apparently, that the sentence of permanent exile had been too harsh. Bron and Ophelia, precociously attractive to the opposite sex, were already profoundly absorbed by their own lives. Anyway, neither of them had been more than vaguely attached to Rupert. Maria-Alba's dislike of men was too deeply ingrained to permit her to take any man's side against a woman. Cordelia was just a baby. In a house so filled with sociable comings and goings Portia had soon lost interest in someone she never saw. As the years passed, I thought of Rupert only occasionally, in disconnected images, as someone almost imaginary like a character in a book, for ever lost.

The sound of voices strained to shrillness came from number 10, which was Rupert's house. The escaping warmth from the open front door sent wisps of steam into the night. I walked into the hall, threw my scarf on to the pile of coats and asked myself if I would rather be at the dentist. I usually answer this question with an unequivocal 'no' and feel heartened as a result. But for once I was in two minds. A cheque signed by my mother and marked 'Return to Drawer' had been brought round that morning by the local butcher. He had made a plaintive appeal through the letter box. My errand could not be put off.

'How'th the chick?'

A girl with a large bust and blue sequins on her upper eyelids kissed my cheek and put a glass of something sparkling into my hand. I recognised her voice. A few hours earlier I had telephoned in a state of trepidation and asked to speak to Rupert. A girl with a lisp and an inability to pronounce her Rs had answered. She said Rupert – only she called him Woopert – and Archie were expecting one or two people for drinks. I had made polite noises about not liking to turn up uninvited. She had said not to be a thilly ath and come. Apparently Rupert was flying to New York the next day so if I wanted to see him urgently I must take my chance.

It was after nine now and the racket suggested large numbers of *la jeunesse dorée* warming up for a night of revel. I recognised a decadent Weimar Republic chic, brought into vogue by the film *Cabaret*. Two men wearing basques, stockings, high heels and bowler hats leaned against a piano on which a black man in a pink suit was playing something jazzy.

I was conscious that the hem of my skirt was hanging down at the back, that there was a run in my tights and that Portia's suede jacket had a blob of makeup on the sleeve, which I had tried, unsuccessfully, to scrub off. My yellow silk dress would have done wonders for my self-confidence but Portia had left it at Dimitri's house and the police had impounded it.

'I'm Harriet Byng.' I tried not to stare at her breasts. 'I telephoned earlier.'

'Hello, darling. I'm Wothalind.' Rosalind's freckled bosom swelled within the bodice of her dress as she leaned over to pour herself another glass of champagne. There is nothing sexual about my interest in other women's breasts. But it is difficult not be curious when you have next to none of your own. 'Who did you thay you were?'

'Harriet.'

'Hello, Harriet darling.' She took a swig and looked at me over the rim of her glass with large swimming eyes. 'Isn't

165

thith fun? Woopert and Archie alwayth have thuch lovely partieth.'

'Actually I was hoping to be able to talk to Rupert. But perhaps this isn't the right moment –'

'I do love Woopert. *Tho* much! But he never taketh me theriouthly.' Her eyes swum a bit more.

'I'd probably better go – another time –'

'Don't be bashful, darling. Woopert'th over there, being nithe to evwybody.' She pointed to the corner of the room. 'Exthept me.' She hiccuped sadly and turned away.

A fair young man of epicene beauty who wore a dinner jacket and tiger-skin shorts, winked at me and blew me a kiss. An equally gynandrous figure with long red hair and a stubbly chin offered me the cigarette he or she was smoking. I did not like to refuse, though the butt was uninvitingly soggy. I was careful not to inhale.

Peering between the heads of the crowd gathered around him, I had a chance to observe Rupert. He was dressed in a striped blazer with a bow tie and his black hair was slicked back from his forehead with glistening pomade. His face was covered with white makeup. His eyebrows were upside-down Vs, pencilled starkly in black, and his lips were cherry red. He was recounting a story that was drowned by explosions of laughter from his audience. His was an interesting face, expressive, mocking, almost wicked. I wondered which of us had changed most during the intervening years. It ought to have been me, since I had grown from a child to a young woman. Trying to get a better view of Rupert, the man next to me trod hard on my foot without noticing. As soon as I could I limped away to the other end of the room where it was less crowded.

A pair of French windows revealed a garden of wavering beauty. I cupped my hands round my face and pressed my nose to the glass to see it better. Lanterns in jewel colours were strung from dark masses of trees. A helmeted statue, perhaps Hermes, stood on one leg in the centre of a long rectangular pond. As my eyes grew accustomed to the darkness I saw stone fish – dolphins, probably – on each corner, spewing water.

'Well? What do you think?'

Beside me stood a man with silvery-grey hair. He was wearing a plain suit and a conventional tie, loosely knotted round his unbuttoned collar. He seemed out of tune with the razzmatazz of the party and did not look as though he was enjoying himself.

'Of the garden? It's lovely. Town gardens are usually so dull. But this makes you want to go out and explore. It's what I'd have imagined Rupert's garden to be like, though he's not at all what I expected.' I looked again at Rupert, who remained the focus of attention. The whistles and catcalls suggested that the story had become salacious. The movements of his face and hands were exaggerated and fluent, like a mime artist's. He seemed to possess an undeniable, almost dangerous glamour, though he was not at all handsome. I must have confused him in retrospection with the heroes from the stories he read to us. 'I didn't think he'd be quite . . . I imagined someone more . . .' I stopped, unable to come up with a word that didn't sound disapproving. 'I haven't seen Rupert for a long time. He used to be so reserved.'

The man looked me up and down in a rather bored way, then turned his eyes to watch Rupert's performance. The lighting was dim but I thought his smile was cynical. 'You aren't drinking.' He filled my empty glass from the bottle in his hand. 'Do you mind if we sit down?' he said. 'I've just got back from a meeting. I'm exhausted. And rather drunk.'

We sat together on one of a pair of sofas beside the fireplace. It had a curved back and high arms and was covered with something silky and slippery.

'It must be a good story.' I adopted an animated tone that

sounded painfully false. I was feeling uncomfortable, hip to hip with this unsympathetic stranger.

He yawned behind his hand. He looked very far from drunk but perhaps he had already reached the gloomy stage. 'Shall we ask him to repeat it?'

'No, don't! I don't want him to think I'm a nuisance.' I hesitated. His expression was discouraging but it would be more embarrassing to sit in silence so I went on. 'I meant to ask Rupert for a huge favour but now I don't know if I've the courage. It probably isn't a very good idea. Perhaps I ought to go home.'

My companion made a half-hearted attempt to smother another yawn. 'That would be throwing the game away altogether, wouldn't it? Nothing venture, nothing have.' He folded one long leg over the other and looked at me in what I felt was a measuring way. I was thankful it was too dark to see the smear of makeup on my sleeve. 'You're an actress, are you?' I detected something like contempt in his voice. 'Let me guess – you're in a play that's flopping badly and you want a puff.'

'No!' I felt indignant before I remembered that the favour I intended to ask was considerably greater. 'No. But, oh dear, I think I *will* go. He hasn't seen me for years. There was a terrible row.' I paused. He raised his eyebrows but didn't say anything. At least he had stopped yawning. 'I used to know Rupert very well.'

'Yes?' I could tell that he did not believe me.

'Oh, yes. *Real*-ly well,' I said, perhaps rather gushingly. 'He was practically family.' I saw I had his attention now. 'He was ten years older than me but he played with us sometimes. We had a castle in the trees, called Ravenswood.'

'Ravenswood? Good God!' He frowned at his kneecap as though it had offended him. His cool reception of my confidences was crushing. I made up my mind to leave. Then he gave a crack of laughter. 'Walter Scott. I used to admire him so much but I haven't looked at him for years. Does anyone read him nowadays?' He closed his eyes, leaned his head against the back of the sofa and recited in exaggeratedly theatrical tones,

'When the last Laird of Ravenswood of Ravenswood
    shall ride,
And woo a dead maiden to be his bride,
He shall stable his steed in the Kelpie's flow,
And his name – his name –'

He opened his eyes. 'I'm too drunk to remember any more.'

I felt protective of Rupert's youthful passion. 'Charlotte Brontë admired Scott enormously.'

'What has that to say to anything?'

'Well, she was a good writer and something of a judge, I should've thought. Anyway, *our* Ravenswood I remember as being glorious. It was the sort of place you long to get back to, sometimes, when you're grown up. But you never can. I expect you think that's ridiculous.'

He seemed to me the sort of man who would find a good many things ridiculous. I wondered if he had stopped listening. He studied the marble chimneypiece, his dark eyebrows drawn together as though doubtful of its architectural merit. But he no longer looked bored. Then he said, softly, 'Harry?'

Only one person had ever called me that. I must have looked like a caricature of astonishment.

'Oh, how mean! You might have said! What a rotten, low-down trick –'

Rupert – for of course it was he – waved his finger at me. 'Careful. Weren't you going to ask me to do something for you?'

'Oh. Yes. But it *was* unkind of you to let me go on making a fool of myself.'

'It was unkind of you to mistake Archie for me, I consider.'

'It was the hair. You look so much older than I'd – Sorry, I didn't mean –'

'You're not doing very well, are you?'

'Honestly, I didn't mean to be rude. I like grey hair on men.'

'I'm not sensitive about it. It's a family characteristic – going grey early. So my grandmother tells me.'

I examined his face. The picture of Rupert I had retained for so many years dissolved and reshaped itself. It was not only the alteration in hair colour. This man was broader, stronger and more confident than my indefinite imaginings. He had straight black brows, an authoritative nose and a square chin. The only part of him I recognised, now that I knew, were his eyes – dark, slanted and set wide apart, evidence of his Armenian ancestry. I looked for other traces of the boy but found nothing. I felt, absurdly, a sense of loss.

'Is she still alive?'

'Very much so. Like Lady Ashton in *The Bride of Lammermoor* she's as proud as Lucifer and every bit as unrepentant and will probably outlive all those she's made miserable.' He folded his arms and turned his whole body to face me. 'All right. What brings grown-up Harriet – how fortunate you've lost that tendency to podginess – to petition for my favour?'

'I was never fat!'

'You were a fright – a dumpy little thing, no front teeth and head shaved like a convict's.'

Evidently he had forgotten about the Dunkirk spirit.

'It's clear you *are* drunk,' I prevaricated. 'Or you've a hopelessly bad memory.'

'Oh ho! You require my good offices, remember.' He

dropped his tone of mockery. 'It's about Waldo. Tell me everything that's happened so far.'

All I could add to what he had read in the newspapers were the incriminating facts about the gouger and the fingerprints, and the damning evidence of the wardrobe mistress and the two understudies, which established the impossibility of there being a third person on the stage at the moment of Sir Basil's death.

'What I don't understand,' said Rupert, almost savagely, 'is why the hell Waldo didn't say straight away that he didn't do it.'

'Well, you know, he rather enjoyed it at first – being the centre of attention, high drama, tragic irony, all that sort of thing.'

Rupert stood up. 'I need to be able to think clearly. I'm going to run my head under the tap. Stay where you are,' he added peremptorily, walking off.

I did as I was told. The party seemed to be gathering zip. The pianist was playing Kurt Weill hits, a girl began to croon and the other guests to dance. Rosalind elbowed through the crowd with a plate of food, which she thrust it into my hand. By candlelight the black ovals looked suspiciously like kidneys, which I hate.

'Having a lovely time, darling? What did you thay your name wath?'

'Harriet. Yes, thanks.'

'Where'th Woopert? I thaw you talking to him.'

'He's gone to put his head under the tap.'

'Lithen to me, Harriet.' Rosalind wagged a finger and nodded her head with solemn emphasis. 'Don't fall in love with him, becoth you'll only be mitherwable. I'm mitherwable. Ath mitherwable ath thin.' To my dismay she started to cry. A couple of sequins and trickles of black mascara transferred themselves to her cheeks.

'Oh, dear! Poor Rosalind!' I felt in Portia's pockets for a handkerchief. All I could find was a screwed-up piece of newspaper. It smelled rather of vinegar but I offered it anyway. Rosalind wiped her eyes, not improving her appearance. 'Why don't you sit down until you feel better?' I suggested.

I meant on the sofa next to me but Rosalind plopped down on to the floor, her legs sticking out straight in front of her, like a doll's.

'Get me a dwink, darling, would you?'

I filled my own glass from the bottle Rupert had left on a nearby table and held it out to her but a hand – Rupert's – came down to intercept it.

'Rosalind's had enough. I'll get her some orange juice.'

'You beatht!' said Rosalind when he returned. 'What'th thauth for the gooth ith thauth for the gander!'

Rupert laughed. 'What's that supposed to mean, you ridiculous girl?'

'It meanth I've oftcn seen you ath pithed as a newt. But if anybody twied to get bothy with you you'd be cwoth ath two thticths.'

'True. But the day I'm found sitting on the floor with makeup on my chin and newsprint on my nose, I hope someone will be good enough to take me in hand. You'd better eat something. I'll find someone to look after you.'

He disappeared into the crowd.

'Have a kidney.' I offered her the plate.

Rosalind screeched with laughter. 'Thilly! They're devilth on hortheback!'

The name was alluring – I thought of horned, caped fiends galloping furiously to hell – very Walter Scott. I ate one. It was delicious – an almond wrapped in an anchovy fillet inside a prune, rolled up in a rasher of bacon.

'Have another,' I suggested.

'No, thankth.' Rosalind sagged against the leg of the

opposite sofa. 'I'm feeling thleepy. I think I'll have a little thnoothe . . .'

A beatific smile spread across her stained face. I managed to catch her glass of orange juice before it fell from her relaxing fingers. I sat with the plate on my knee and tried to prevent people treading on Rosalind as they danced by. To while away the time I ate several more devils on horseback. Prunes are generous with their essences, but having travelled to the party by tube I was reluctant to lick my fingers. Maria-Alba regarded London's underground system as a pit of brimstone seething with pathogens, and early indoctrination is hard to throw off.

'Hanky?'

I looked up. It was Max Frensham.

'I do seem to have got rather sticky.' I took the handker-chief. 'Thanks. Have one?'

He sat down beside me. 'I saw you when you came in but I was stuck in the dining room with Marina Marlow. That woman's a black hole where flattery's concerned.'

'I didn't know she was here.' I felt again that constriction of the heart at the thought of her. 'Do you have to be nice to her?'

Max shrugged. 'She's a narcissist – capricious enough to insist on having me as her leading man in her next play if she thinks I worship her body.' I wanted to ask if he did, but thought better of it and ate another prune. 'I suppose that sort of duplicity shocks you? It ought to. I feel rather disgusted with myself.' He grimaced and ran both hands through his hair as though shaking off something objectionable. Some people can do this without making themselves look a complete mess. I am not of their number.

'How's – Caroline?' I remembered his wife's name just in time.

'Not well. Actually I'm really worried about her.'

173

I popped in another devil and tried to look sympathetic, not easy when your cheeks are bulging with food.

'What do you think's wrong?' I asked thickly.

'Too many pills, probably. She takes a handful to send her to sleep at night and another to keep her awake during the day. She has pills for slimming, for depression, for imaginary illnesses. It's awful to see such unhappiness.' I was surprised. Caroline Frensham had always seemed to me about as soft and sensitive as a chisel. I saw sorrow in Max's eyes and I no longer doubted. The greasiness of the bacon had transferred itself from my fingers to the handkerchief and back again, preventing any demonstrations of sympathy like patting his hand. 'Believe me, Harriet, an inheritance is nothing but a curse.'

'I didn't know she was rich.'

'Her father owns a chain of department stores in New Zealand. Imagine what it's like to be able to have whatever you want.' It sounded all right to me. 'It's by testing yourself and winning through that you become self-confident. Caroline's never had to work. She's bought her way out of every difficulty. As a result she's crippled by self-doubt. Of course she covers it up brilliantly. She should have been an actress. God, when I think how much in love with her I was –' He broke off and shook his head. 'How's your dear papa?'

'Not too good.'

Max took my hand and bravely did not recoil from its stickiness. 'You know he didn't do it, don't you? I'd stake my own life on it. There never was a man less capable of killing anybody.'

I was so grateful for this testimonial that I did not mind when he squeezed my fingers and crushed them painfully against my ring.

'It must be agony for you.' I realised he meant my father being in prison. 'Why don't we have dinner together next week? Somewhere small and quiet where we can talk.' I must have looked doubtful for he said quickly, 'Don't get the wrong idea. You're a beautiful young woman but I'm a happily married man. Well, married, anyway. And I'm not such a conceited idiot as to think you'd ever look at me.' This surprised me for Max Frensham was, by anyone's standards, attractive, and I had thought he knew it. 'I'd like to help you through this dreadful business with Waldo. I can't offer much, I know – just a sympathetic ear. You needn't be grateful,' he added when I started to mumble my appreciation. 'It would be a treat for me to talk to someone who isn't in the theatre. Someone who's straightforward and rational. But you're probably much too busy.'

He laughed but his face was sad. I looked down at the empty plate balanced on my knees, wishing I had not eaten so many prunes. I felt extremely thirsty and a little sick. The room was suddenly too warm.

'Quite a few of my guests have got to the hand-holding stage.' Rupert was beside us. 'But I want to talk to Harriet if you wouldn't mind disengaging.'

The man in the tiger-skin shorts hauled Rosalind up from the floor, swung her over his shoulder in a fireman's lift and carried her off. Max stood up.

'Hello, Rupert. I thought you were in Italy.'

'I got back this morning.'

'Whereabouts were you?'

'Florence.'

'When I was there they'd just cleaned all the Veroneses in the Uffizi. Stupendous colours. Did you see them?'

'No.' Rupert made no effort to continue the conversation. I felt embarrassed but Max seemed unruffled.

'Perhaps I'd better be going.' He smiled at me. 'Don't forget what I said.' He turned back to Rupert. 'Thanks for an excellent party. Original. As always.'

175

'You must thank Archie. He does everything.'

'Goodbye, Max.' I would have offered my hand but I was sure he would not want to touch it again. 'I hope Caroline will feel better soon.'

'I'll telephone you tomorrow.' He kissed my cheek. I realised Rupert would conclude from this that Max and I were on more intimate terms than was in fact the case. I acquitted Max of blame, for men are always rather dim about these things. Anyway, it didn't matter.

'Come on. We'll go too.' Rupert led me through the throng in Max's wake.

Everyone was dancing now. A girl wearing a spangled leotard, like a trapeze artist's, clapped her hands and shouted, 'Be careful where you tread, people. Rover's given me the slip.'

'What does Rover look like?' someone asked.

'He's about two feet long. And bright green. No, you ass, whoever heard of a green dog? Rover's an Indian water snake.' There was a burst of screaming and most of the girls and several men got on to chairs. 'Don't do that, you dopes,' cried Rover's owner. 'He's mad about getting under cushions. You're probably squashing him to death.' More screams as everyone hastily got down.

'Really, Loelia,' said Rupert when the yelling had died down a little, 'you ought to give that poor creature to a zoo.'

Loelia clasped her hands round his neck. 'Can I be your pet, Rupert? *Please* let me into your bed. You don't know what the love of a good woman can do.'

'Take some aspirin.' He removed her arms unceremoniously. 'You'll have a shocking head tomorrow.'

'Won't your friends be offended if you leave now?' I said as we reached the front door.

'Don't be ridiculous.'

We walked along to the main road and Rupert hailed a taxi. He gave my address to the cabby. I thought I was being dismissed but Rupert got in after me. 'All right, let's have it,' he said as the taxi drew out into the stream of traffic. 'No beating about the bush. What do you want me to do?'

He listened without saying anything as I described as succinctly as I could what had happened since my father's arrest. 'You see,' I concluded, 'we can't pay the butcher or the greengrocer or the milkman and there are six of us – seven counting Ronnie – to feed. I absolutely *hate* asking you but Pa couldn't think of anyone else who might – who might –' I could not bring myself to suggest, as my father had done, that Rupert might feel himself to be under some kind of obligation to my family. It sounded so crudely calculating – 'be in a position to lend us something to tide us over.'

Rupert did not look at me. I couldn't tell if he was angry or commiserative. 'How much did Waldo suggest you ask for?'

'Two thousand pounds.' It sounded an impossibly large sum once I had said it aloud. I grew hot with shame. How hateful is the necessity to have money! How guilty you feel when you have more than other people, how wretched when you have less. Banks, overdrafts, loans, chequebooks, pounds and pence – I felt I should burst into tears if anyone mentioned any of these things ever again. I had a horrible pain in my stomach – probably the result of eating a whole plateful of prunes.

Rupert was silent for what seemed a long time. Just as I was going to ask him to forget I had ever mentioned it, he said, 'I'm not going to give it to you.'

'You're absolutely right!' I said eagerly. 'It was a terrible idea! I knew I shouldn't have asked. It was the most awful cheek –'

'Shut up a minute and listen. If I give you two thousand pounds it'll be gone in a couple of months and you'll be in the same mess as before. It's obvious that nothing's changed.

None of you has the least idea about money. You simply can't be trusted with it.'

I bent my head humbly. His judgement was harsh but I could not deny the truth of it.

'What I'll do is this. You can send me the butcher's bill, and the baker's and the candlestick-maker's, and I'll pay them. On certain conditions. You, Bron, Ophelia and Portia must find jobs. I'll give you two weeks to get some kind of employment. Of course it won't be well-paid but that's not important. What matters is, you've all got to stick to it. Any slacking, getting the sack – by any one of you – and the wellspring will dry up.' I said nothing. I was trying to imagine Ophelia getting up to go to work. 'I'll expect some simple accounting from each of you. Bus fares, clothes, books – whatever seems essential to you must be shown to be necessary to me. You must all of you contribute three-quarters of what you earn to the kitty, which I shall have charge of. That'll go towards food, rates, electricity, telephone, and so on. I'll make up the shortfall. The remaining quarter you can spend on cigars, crocodile luggage, diamond telephone diallers, what you will.' I failed altogether to picture Ophelia getting on a bus, or Bron either. 'Clarissa and Maria-Alba can be your pensioners. Ronnie, I assume, can pay for his board and lodging. Cordelia, naturally, will go to school. I've no intention of paying couturiers' bills or exorbitant demands from interior decorators or plastic surgeons. You must all practise economy. If any of you knows what the word means.'

'I'm afraid we're going to be a terrible nuisance to you,' I said meekly.

'I'm certain of it. Don't let it worry you, though. You'll suffer more than I will, I imagine. It seems to me quite extraordinary that you are all, at your respective ages, still living at home, financially dependent on your father.'

'Well.' I paused, unable for the moment to explain just

why this was so. 'I suppose it *is* rather lazy and selfish of us.'

'Not only is it lazy and selfish, it's thoroughly detrimental to your own lives and happiness.' He sighed and pressed his hands to his temples. 'I'm tired of moralising. It's been a long day. Let me know about the jobs. I'll be back in London by Thursday. Two weeks, mind.'

'But what shall we do?' I felt helpless in the face of these demands, which, though I knew them to be entirely reasonable, I saw no way of meeting.

Rupert looked at me with an expression of barely suppressed irritation. 'All right. Let's begin with you. What do you most enjoy doing?'

'I've written a lot of poetry. But it isn't nearly ready for the public gaze.'

'You may as well attempt to colonise the moon with white mice as publish a volume of poetry. But if you like writing – let's think.' He thought while my mind wandered ineffectually, revolving vague, indefinable anxieties. 'I'll give Sidney Podmore a ring before I leave tomorrow. He's a subeditor on the *Brixton Mercury*. He'll take you as a cub reporter as a favour to me.'

'A journalist?' I thought of Stanley Norman and all the others who had staked out the house and gone through our dustbins, hoping to discover, among fishbones, vegetable peelings and butter wrappers, the web and woof of the Byng family life. 'I couldn't possibly!'

TWELVE

Mr Podmore, subeditor of the *Brixton Mercury*, had a large nose that was reddish. The rest of his face was putty-coloured, as though he spent too much time cloistered from the light of day. His eyes were hidden behind small blue-lensed spectacles. A crop of grizzled hair was parted in the middle, ending below his ears in an exuberant burst of curls. His clothes, particularly the crumpled silk cravat and stained, embroidered waistcoat, proclaimed the Bohemian.

His office, which I had leisure to examine as he kept me waiting several minutes while he finished what he was reading, bore testament to pantheistic views. A crude painting of Kali, the goddess with a necklace of skulls and more than the usual complement of arms, hung on one wall, hanging out her tongue at a large green plaster Buddha, smiling fatly above rolls of flesh, which stood on the desk. Distributed about the room were sacred symbols and fetishes galore – masks, beads, bells, crucifixes, pyramids, something wizened that might have been a shrunken head, corn dollies, wooden snakes, a brass pyx and a small totem pole. The room smelled strongly of incense, cigarettes and perspiration. It was not at all what I had expected.

'Name?' said Mr Podmore, without looking up.

'Harriet Byng.'

'Byng? Oh, yes.' He raised his voice as though he was shouting banner headlines from a windy street corner. 'Famous Actor Arrested for Murder!'

I winced. 'He didn't do it.'

'Daughter Protests Innocence!' He dropped his voice to a volume more suitable for a conversation between two people in a small office. 'Relationship to Rupert Wolvespurges?'

'Um – a family friend, really. He used to live with us but we hadn't seen him for years until –'

'Experience?'

'None, I'm afraid.'

'Previous job?' A violent blowing of nose in a far-from-clean handkerchief.

'Well, I've written some poetry –'

'Shorthand?'

I watched with horrid fascination as Mr Podmore burrowed in a nostril with a skinny forefinger. 'I'm afraid not –'

'Spelling?'

'S-H-O-R-T – oh, I see. Well, a bit erratic, to be truthful, but with a dictionary –'

'You can do my business expenses.' Mr Podmore found whatever he was looking for and brought it out for inspection. He got up, stuffing his handkerchief into his trousers pocket and went out, leaving the door open. After a few seconds he put his head back round the door and threw up his chin at an angle of forty-five degrees, which I interpreted as a signal to follow him.

His office led into a larger one in which two women of indeterminate age were attacking typewriters as though they were engaged in a race and the loser was to be executed the next morning. They did not raise their eyes from the page to look at us but continued to pound the keys and every few seconds to clout the thing like a black rolling pin at the top of the machine as though they were determined to teach it a lesson. I wondered how they could keep up such furious activity without fainting, for the gas fire was full on and the room was a shimmering stew.

'Desk.' Mr Podmore pointed to a table, which was bare but for a typewriter. I smiled keenly and sat down. He threw a folder in front of me. 'Sort them into headings, itemise and total. You can add, I suppose?'

I recognised sarcasm in his tone but I did not blame him. Of course he resented having to give a job, however lowly, to someone as ill-qualified as me. I reflected briefly on Rupert's power and importance in the world of journalism with increased respect. Mr Podmore went back into his office and slammed the door. The two women stopped typing as abruptly as though they had been plugged into the mains and the trip switch had been thrown.

'I'll have an extra sugar in mine,' said the one with dyed blonde hair and a kingfisher-blue cardigan.

'Fancy a marshmallow tea-cake?' asked the thin one in ginger slacks, getting up and going to the corner where there was a tray with a kettle and some cups. They avoided looking in my direction.

'Hello,' I said. 'I'm Harriet.'

Ginger slacks looked at me over the top of her spectacles. 'How do you do? I am Muriel Minchin.' Her accent was suddenly breathtakingly refined. 'And this,' she indicated the kingfisher cardigan, 'is Eileen Feather. Would you care for some refreshment?'

'That would be lovely.' I smiled, almost showing my wisdom teeth, but it was no good.

'I'm afraid we only have PG Tips or Nes-caif. Probably it is not to what you are used. You may prefer to bring your own.'

'Oh, no, either of those would be marvellous.'

'Would you care for a digestive biscuit or a rich tea?'

I would have liked a marshmallow teacake but I did not dare to say so. 'Nothing to eat, thank you.'

'You'll pardon us if we nibble, I'm sure. We are obliged to get up so very early, you see, to travel by public transport.'

Now I understood. Bron had insisted on dropping me off at the *Brixton Mercury* in a silver and blue Bentley Continental. 'Oh, that car doesn't belong to me,' I said eagerly. 'My brother's got a job as a salesman and he was delivering it to a customer in St John's Wood. He wanted the excuse to drive it around a bit.'

Miss Feather gave me a cool smile. 'I do not know to what you are referring.'

Naturally they were not pleased by the insinuation that they had been craning out of the window when I arrived. They sipped their coffee with pursed lips and little fingers extended.

'Mr Podmore has told us that you are a debutante in need of pin money.' From this I gathered that Rupert must have suggested to Mr Podmore that I work incognito at the *Brixton Mercury* to save me from painful notoriety among my co-workers. 'Evening gowns are so expensive, are they not?' Muriel took a tissue from her bag and daintily patted her lips to remove a crumb of chocolate.

'I'm not a deb. I've only ever been to two balls in my life and I really hated them. I was longing to go home by ten o'clock. Honestly, we're as poor as church mice.'

Muriel and Eileen exchanged little smiles of disbelief.

'My mother was used to have her gowns made by a very select shop in Bounds Green,' Muriel went on, having taken charge of the conversation. 'My grandfather had a flourishing business in domestic wares. My grandmother had everything she wanted. Fitted carpets in every room. A cook-general living in.'

'Gosh!' I said.

'What happened to all the money?' asked Eileen.

'My father, God rest his soul, was unlucky in his invest-ments. My mother said he was the plaything of fortune.' She looked solemn. I imagined that Eileen felt, as I did, that it would be impertinent to ask for details.

'Another cup of coffee, Eileen dear?' Muriel shook herself from the sad reverie into which she had momentarily fallen.

'I think I will partake. Though it is only instant, it does perk one up no end. Did I tell you about Auntie and I going to the whist drive last evening? It is only the British Legion Hall but there is always a very nice sort of person attending.'

They chatted between themselves and soon relaxed into ordinary voices. With fingers dampened by anxiety and the tremendous heat in the room, I opened the file and stared at a sheaf of bills and bits of paper covered with illegible writing. I had not the faintest idea what to do with them.

'Excuse me,' I said, when Eileen paused during a breathless résumé of her aunt's doings, 'I know it's stupid of me but I don't understand what Mr Podmore wants me to do.'

'Eileen, I am sure, will be delighted to assist you,' said Muriel. 'She has seen to Mr Podmore's business expenses for the last ten years and I can say with absolute confidence that her accounts were without error.'

'Thank you, Muriel,' said Eileen in stately tones. 'I have done my poor best.'

She walked over to my desk and picked up one of the bills. 'Hotel Astoria, Brighton, double room, bed and break-fast. That'll be when he took that nasty little piece from the printers, Marietta something or other, common as they come. Mind you, I should have thought even *she* might have objected. Mr Podmore has –' she lowered her voice – 'perspiration problems which make him not very nice to know. Put it down as single room and dinner. That'll make the cost about right. And don't forget the rail fare.' I stared at her blankly. She sighed. 'Dear me, what a lot you have to learn. Left hand of the page, capital letters, underlined in red, "TRAVEL".' I looked at the typewriter, my eyes wandering over the keys. I saw the letter T and struck it nervously. In my agitation I hit two other keys by mistake. Eileen freed the tangle of metal strips with fastidious fingers. 'I don't know where *you* was trained – no doubt somewhere in the West End – but *I* was always taught it was advisable to put some paper in first.'

Muriel tittered.

'I don't know what you're complaining about,' said Bron, swinging his legs up on to the sofa in the drawing room. 'At least you've still got a job to go to. I've had an unspeakably dull afternoon and now I've got to hunt around for another dreary little hole to hide my talents in for the nonce.'

After dropping me at the *Brixton Mercury* Bron had been unable to resist picking up a pretty girl he had spotted at a bus stop and they had got on so well that he had taken her for a spin. They had stopped for a snifter at cosy little place he knew in Putney and the snifter had become a long lunch. It was not his fault that some bloody idiot had stopped without warning at a zebra crossing and destroyed the Bentley's radiator and the front offside wing. He had taken the car back to the showroom and explained that this had happened just after he had parked outside the customer's house to effect the handover. The manager had been suspicious but Bron had got away with it. He had been told to stay in the showroom for the rest of the day and look after browsing punters. Bron had got on very well for a while and actually made a sale by promising extremely favourable credit. Then a tolerably good-looking woman had arrived and Bron had made a pass at her. How was he to know that she was the manager's wife?

'Oh dear.' I swung my arms and flexed my shoulders to relieve the cramp that had set in after a miserable day spent crouched over the typewriter. I had finally managed a page of expenses, laid out as instructed by Eileen and without spelling mistakes. I suspected that she had deliberately omitted to tell me I was supposed to be making carbon copies of the beastly thing, so it would all have to be done again in the morning. Dirk, who had only been pacified in my absence by being allowed to sleep *in* my bed with a large, greasy bone, was disturbed by my muscle-stretching exercises and started to bark so I stopped. 'What will Rupert say?'

'Naturally we shan't tell him,' said Bron.

'But won't that be breaking our agreement?'

'Rupert doesn't want to be bothered with the minutiae of our dealings. He's a busy man with more important things to think of. Anyway, I shall have another job in no time. You're always straining at gnats, Harriet. It's very tiresome in a sister. I blame those nuns. Now, be a good girl and fetch a bottle of plonk. I'm in need of fortification.'

'Do you think we ought? Rupert did say we had to economise –' A flying cushion struck me on the nose. I went down to the kitchen with watering eyes, conceding that the reform of Bron was a hopeless task.

Ophelia was spread-eagled in a chair, still wearing her coat, scarf and gloves when I returned to the drawing room. As with Bron and me, it had been her first day as a member of the working classes. 'God! Give me a glass at once before I faint.'

I took one over to her. 'Bad day?' I enquired sympathetically.

'No-o-o,' she said slowly. 'Actually, rather fun. But shattering. Fay is a vortex of energy. By lunchtime my feet were killing me and I could hardly keep my eyes open. I explained that I'd had to get up at eight to be at her house by nine and she told me she gets up at six every day! I mean, really, have you ever heard of such a thing?'

Fay Swann ran a successful interior decorating business and had agreed like a shot to take on Ophelia. She had been a friend of my mother's for years but the relationship was somewhat half-hearted on my mother's side. She knew that Fay was a toadeater who enjoyed being able to talk about her intimacy with a famous actor. My mother said that Fay had excellent taste but there was a smell of the shop about her. My mother said this about everyone whose occupation was unconnected with the theatre. I still have no idea what she meant by it. I thought Fay quite terrifyingly grand.

I was relieved that Ophelia's mood was cheerful. When I had tentatively set forth the conditions Rupert had laid down in return for subsidising the Byng family Ophelia had laughed contemptuously and said that nothing would persuade her to be party to such a ridiculous scheme. My mother had been indignant on Ophelia's behalf and demanded to know whether Rupert was so determined to humiliate them that he expected Ophelia to stand in rags in Oxford Street, selling matches from a tray. During the period of his absence in New York my family indulged in much extravagant satire at Rupert's expense.

He had called on us the very next day after his return from New York. I thought it was kind of him to come all the way to Blackheath. Though it was noon the curtains were closed against the wintry sun and the drawing room was lit by candles. My mother received him with great stateliness, sitting on a throne from *Richard II* – or was it *King John*? – and wearing a black mantilla that covered her face. Though their stitches had been taken out by the local GP, she and Ronnie were still under wraps. They claimed to be still too bruised to reveal themselves in their full glory.

'Well, Rupert. It must be five years since we met.'

187

I was willing to bet she knew to the day when that merciless review had been published. She extended a couple of fingers. Rupert shook her hand briefly, then dropped it.

'Hello, Clarissa. It's nearer ten.'

'Really?' My mother gave her stage laugh, which was pretty convincing until you heard her real one. 'It seems only yesterday that you were a dirty little boy with *farouche* manners and a sad little stammer.'

'I don't suppose much has changed.'

Cordelia came up to him and peered rather closely, perhaps looking for dirt. 'How do you do? I'm Cordelia. I'm going to be a film star.'

He looked down at her gravely. 'Have you the hide of a pachyderm and the brain of an amoeba? If so, you'll do.'

'I assume you don't mean that liberally,' said Cordelia with dignity.

'Cordelia, ask Ronnie to bring us some sherry,' said my mother quickly, perhaps unwilling that any member of the family should seem comical in the eyes of this repulsive Nemesis who had thrust himself among us. 'And tell the others to come.' She addressed herself to Rupert. 'I can't tell you how much we have all looked forward to seeing you again.'

She delivered this with a tremendous weight of irony but Rupert appeared not to have heard. He had turned his back on us and was examining a portrait by Corot. 'I'd forgotten you had this. Charming. But it's a copy, of course.'

'It happens to be genuine –' began my mother heatedly, forgetting to be icily remote.

'Ah, ha, ha!' Bron strode in and shook Rupert's hand vigorously. 'How are you, old chap? Marvellous to see you! Never better, thankee, never better!'

He put his hand to his eye to adjust an imaginary monocle. For some reason Bron had decided to conduct the interview in the guise of a P. G. Wodehouse toff.

'Good,' said Rupert in rather a deflating way.

'I say, old boy, jolly decent of you to rally to the call – appreciate it no end. Quite right, we've all got to pull together now the pater's down on his uppers. I'm as ready as the next man to put my shoulder to the wheel but the question is, as what? I suppose you couldn't get me a snug little billet on the *Guardian* as restaurant critic, could you? I'd be prepared to eat anywhere if it'll help the old man get on his legs again. Even Greek.'

'No,' said Rupert.

'Here we are.' Ronnie bustled in with a tray of tiny glasses, meanly filled with sherry. He had retained his dark spectacles and wore a red and white spotted bandanna over the lower part of his face, like a bank robber. 'Hello, Rupert. It's been a long time. Excuse the get-up. Clarissa and I had a little motoring accident and we aren't quite better yet. Oh, bugger that bloody dog!' He clutched at the skidding glasses on the tray and managed to save them. 'Sorry, Harriet, but he will get under one's feet and I didn't see him in the dark. Come on, my dear.' He offered the tray to my mother. 'Drink up,' he said kindly. 'This'll make you feel more the thing.'

She held up the glass before her veiled eyes. 'There's hardly enough to wet one's lips. I don't see why you feel the need to stint us when it's Waldo's sherry.'

'We mustn't give Rupert the wrong impression, Clarissa. It's very good of him to come to the rescue. We must do our bit and make little economies where we can.' He turned his spectacles in Rupert's direction. 'We're running a tight ship here. We've got to if we don't want to founder. There'll be a stiff breeze to the Cape and a storm or two before we're round it! It's a cruel sea, an unforgiving sea, a sea that'll never be tamed! It'll take all we men can give in seamanship and sweat and sheer damned guts and then, by God, it'll ask for more! Our hands'll be raw – our eyes stinging with the salt –'

189

'Do shut up, Ronnie!' My mother carefully manoeuvred the glass beneath her veil. 'You gave us Hornblower yesterday. Whoever wrote that script had as much idea of life at sea as a carpet-beetle.'

What there was visible of Ronnie looked hurt. I got the impression that he was rather in awe of Rupert. Of course, drama critics are Olympians where actors are concerned, with the power to set a fair wind behind them or sink them without trace. I stole a glance at Rupert. He was standing next to me and for a moment I thought I saw something in his eyes that might have been amusement. Ophelia and Portia had come in then and his expression became grave. Portia said hello but did not offer to shake hands. She went to sit on the window seat, parted the curtains fractionally and stared moodily through the gap into the street.

Ophelia made no attempt to greet him but threw herself down on the sofa. She tossed her head and glared at Rupert. 'I suppose you think it's very amusing to come here and make absurd demands. It's an odd way to show gratitude for all you had from us, I must say. You'd better know at once that I've no intention of dancing to your tune like the organ grinder's monkey.'

'Certainly not. You would look quite ridiculous,' returned Rupert smoothly. It seemed he was master of the dusty answer.

I longed to say something to show that we were grateful for his generous offer of assistance but I was afraid they would all be angry and accuse me of sucking up, so I kept quiet. Rupert looked at his watch.

'Has anyone got a job yet?'

'I'm going to work as PA to a romantic novelist called Jessica Delavine,' said Portia, turning away from the window to look at him for the first time. 'Luckily she doesn't want any typing done, just answering the telephone and organising

190

meetings and things. She's an ardent feminist and only writes novels to fund the cause. She's going to pay me one pound fifty an hour.'

Rupert nodded. 'Good. Harriet, we know, is fixed up.' I tried not to look despondent. 'Bron?'

'There's an advertisement for a car salesman in today's paper but it doesn't exactly excite. If you can't help me with the *Guardian*, I wouldn't mind going into banking, though it is the death of the soul –'

'Right, garage job for you. Ophelia?'

'Pah!' said Ophelia.

'I repeat my terms. Should any one of the four of you fail to get employment, or lose it, I shall wash my hands of all of you. So I suggest you start trying to make Ophelia see sense. I don't envy you the task. Harriet can telephone me next week to let me know how things stand. Goodbye.'

He had put down his glass and walked out. I had run after him to the front door. 'Don't be angry, please, Rupert. I'll make Ophelia understand that she's got to get a job. I know you're doing this for our own good and we *are* grateful, though we don't behave as though we are. It's really so kind of you to help us.'

'I'm not angry.'

'Really not?'

'I know what actors are like. I spend a lot of time with them. The worse they are at acting the more arrogant they become.'

'You *are* angry.'

He sighed. 'Not yet, Harry, but if you keep me here, fruitlessly debating my state of mind and making me miss my train, who knows?'

I felt crushed. Only his use of my old nickname gave me any hope that there was a watery milk of human kindness in Rupert's breast.

'Oh, boy!' cried Cordelia when I returned to the drawing room. '*Che uomo affascinante!* I wonder if he'll want to make love to me when I'm a famous film star. Of course he'll be quite old by then, but frantically experienced.'

I did not attempt to defend Rupert against the chorus of denunciation that followed. I was thinking, for the hundredth time since she had gone to stay with the nuns, how much I missed the stout bosom and sympathetic presence of Maria-Alba.

THIRTEEN

Mr Podmore threw open the door of his office and faster than you could lick a stamp Muriel and Eileen were thundering at the keys. 'Slim in yet?' he barked.

Muriel and Eileen continued to attack their keyboards as though they were playing Rachmaninov. Without raising her eyes Muriel said, 'He rang in to say he's got a bad cold. Bad hangover more like.'

'It's a bloody nuisance, whatever the cause. Body found in sewer's being buried this morning. The coroner gave accidental death. Cops wanted first-degree murder. Something smells. Gangland Killing! Corruption In High Places! Someone'll have to report it. It's only a question of getting the names of the mourners and what sort of police presence there is.'

'It's no good looking at me.' Muriel stopped typing to stare indignantly at Mr Podmore. 'My doctor says my sciatica ought to be reported in the *Lancet*. If you think I'm going to stand around in that cold wind –'

'It isn't any use my going,' said Eileen. 'Funerals always make me cry, even if it's a stranger what's being interred and once I start I can't always stop.' She fumbled in her bag and brought out a handkerchief. 'I'm that soft-hearted.

When my next-door neighbour's budgie died I had to have the district nurse in. I sort of swelled up.' She gulped and blew her nose.

Mr Podmore's eyes rolled up to the ceiling as though seeking inspiration from above, and then they travelled round the room to rest on me. 'You. Byng. Four Lamps Cemetery, eleven o'clock. You can take the bus fare out of petty cash.'

'Oh, but I wouldn't know what to –'

'Two hundred words'll do. Put in a bit of atmosphere. Weeping relatives, slanting rain, that kind of thing.'

'But really I –'

Mr Podmore had retreated into his office.

'Well, I *am* glad it isn't me going.' Muriel got up to put the kettle on. 'Rain's forecast. I don't know about slanting. Some people are always ready to push themselves forward. Like a Cadbury's orange sandwich, Eileen?'

'Yes, please.' Eileen smothered a sob in her handkerchief. 'It's ever such a liability having a tender heart like what I have but I shouldn't care to be *hard*.'

They looked at me disapprovingly. 'What was it he said your name was?' said Muriel, thoughtfully as she dropped tea bags into flowered china cups. 'Byng, wasn't it? Now where have I heard that name before? Quite recently, wasn't it?'

The bus dropped me outside the cemetery gates, which was lucky as rain was beginning to fall in chilly drops and darken the concrete drive. The cemetery was large and by the time I found the funeral party, I was uncomfortably wet. I spotted a police car parked behind a large yew. The mourners, dressed to the eyes in deepest black, with preposterously dressy hats, were sheltering under an enormous cedar while the vicar stood with open prayer book some ten feet away at the head of the grave. His surplice billowed to expose a pair of ancient paint-splashed flannels beneath.

The vicar spoke quietly, depressing his chin and muttering into his chest. The others had stopped bothering to listen and were chatting among themselves. I sidled up behind a large woman in a short skirt that revealed an underground map of blue veins on the backs of her knees. 'We thought the Seychelles this year,' she was saying to her neighbour. 'On account of our Dawn wanting to go to Lanzarote with her boyfriend so Fred said, what the hell, let's go somewhere decent for a change, just the two of us.'

'Very nice,' said the other woman, an unrealistic redhead in extravagantly patterned black tights that made her legs look gangrenous. 'Gerald wanted to go to Barbados. But I said to him, Gerald, I said, have you forgotten my stomach? Show it an unwashed lettuce leaf and it rebels. Everyone we spoke to last year who'd been to foreign parts had gippy tummy. I said to Gerald, it isn't worth making yourself ill, just to show off.'

'So where're you going then?' said the fat woman sharply.
'Blackpool.'

The vicar signalled to the chief mourners to come forward to throw a trowelful of earth over the coffin. A woman started to hand round a basket of artificial flowers but a strong gust of rain sent her scuttling back under the tree. I got out my notebook.

'Excuse me,' I said to the fat woman. 'I'm from the *Brixton Mercury*. Would you mind giving me your name and relationship to the deceased?'

'Ooh, that's nice. Think of Vildo having the papers to his burial! He was anxious enough to keep out of them when he was alive, that's for sure!' She let out a squawk of laughter and then made a face of apology when she caught the vicar's eye. 'It's true, though. He was a pain in the underpass, when all's said and done, and there isn't anyone here that gives a toss. Not what you could call a credit to the family either, was it, drowning in a sewer? He was my uncle.'

'Vildo? That's an unusual name.'

'It's Serbian. His dad came over here from Sarajevo after the last war.'

'Would you mind giving me his surname?'

'Surely. It's –' She made an explosive sound and then spelled it for me. It had seven letters and not one was a vowel.

As I struggled with fingers numbed by cold, to write to dictation half a dozen impossible names, it occurred to me that they looked like typing mistakes and no one would be any the wiser if I made them all up. The vicar hurried off, holding his prayer book open over his head in a last-ditch attempt to keep off the rain. I looked desperately about for atmosphere. The flowers, beheaded and tortured into hideous shapes, were already limp with rain. The artificial turf lining the hole was spattered with mud. The glossy black headstones, with lettering picked out in gold, set off by green chippings in granite corrals, looked bravely gay.

I noticed a man standing alone in the shadow of the cedar. The mourners ignored him, gathering into groups to make dashes for their cars, which were parked along the drive. When every one, including the police car, had driven off, the man walked over to peer into the grave. He looked dreadfully ill, his cheeks a ghastly greyish-white, his lips blue. A few black hairs straggled across his bald head. It was a battered sort of face, perhaps foreign, probably Serbian. He ignored the freezing rain blowing into his face. 'A friend from the past, a mysterious stranger,' I wrote, hoping this might qualify as atmosphere. As I sucked my pencil and thought how best to describe him, the man put his hands to his head and uttered a keening sound. I was glad that Vildo had someone to mourn for him. The man certainly seemed upset. He got out his handkerchief and put it to his eyes while his shoulders heaved. 'Never again. Never again,' he said. 'As God is my witness, this is the last time.'

This had some poetry about it as from the grave's edge, so I wrote it down, intending to embellish later. When I looked up the man had gone. I stared about in bewilderment. He was absolutely nowhere to be seen. I even looked up into the branches of the cedar in case he had swung himself up, Tarzan-style, but the tree was empty, even of sparrows. For miles around there was nothing but rows of memorial slabs, wilting blossoms and tattered grass. There was no one in the cemetery but me.

A damp mist coiled about the graves. The branches above my head dripped mournfully. A sudden blast of wind sent the black clouds scurrying and a wreath bowling down the drive. I clutched my coat tightly round me for comfort. From within the grave there came a sepulchral groan. Once I had started to run I couldn't stop for fear of a skeletal hand on my shoulder. I reached the gates, wet to my knees from landing in puddles, and in a sad state of breathlessness. I flagged the bus that was approaching, and hopped on, hurling myself into a seat with such speed that the other passengers looked at me in surprise.

Once my heart had slowed to a reasonable rate and my nerves had been soothed by the ordinariness of the old lady sitting next to me, grasping a string bag filled with Brussels sprouts, I started to wonder what I might make of the extraordinary phenomenon I had just witnessed. I had heard plenty of stories about people appearing in photographs of their own funerals. That I had just seen Vildo's ghost I was almost ready to take my oath on. Ignoring the motion of the bus and the jerks of its stopping and starting, I began to write.

I continued the narration in the hothouse of the office and, by the time my shoes and coat had dried, I had finished what

197

I hoped was a masterpiece of reporting. In case Mr Podmore was disposed to be sceptical I had added a few extra details. I made the apparition transparent and had him gliding through a couple of headstones and a tree before vanishing. Also I dressed him in a white shroud rather than a grey mac. As soon as I had checked in the office dictionary whether 'wraithlike' was one word or two, I delivered my article in person to Mr Podmore.

He took it from me without a word and began to read. I watched his face eagerly and was pleased to see his expression changed from its customary sneer to one of surprise.

'Good God!' he said quite a few times. When he got to the end he let the paper fall on to the desk while he leaned back in his chair and cleaned out one ear with a paperclip, in a distracted sort of way. 'Incredible, quite incredible. After all these years – when I've not seen so much as a wisp of ectoplasm – that you, a young, ignorant –' he checked himself – 'I mean, unversed in parapsychology – well . . .' He went on looking at me but he seemed to be talking to himself. 'It might validate the theory that paranormal manifestations prefer to reveal themselves to adolescents and simpletons. Or else that the unformed mind is a sort of wet clay, perfect for taking impressions, to which the more developed intellect is unreceptive.'

There was a confirmatory tinkle from his wind chime.

'Now, look here,' I began, not a little annoyed to be called ignorant, a simpleton and mentally unformed, in three consecutive sentences. 'I'd like you to know that far from being stupid I have in fact read a great deal and I could recite loads of Shakespeare if I wanted –'

'All right.' He held up his hand. 'I'm sure you're a clever little girl. Deb Claims Brains. And, now I think of it, this is better than I expected, but you've got a lot to learn about writing articles.' He snatched up a pen and bent over it. 'First rule, establish the facts. Who, what, where and when. Then get on to the why and how. We'll get rid of the obscure adjectives and adverbs –' he swiped through all the lovely words I had spent so long thinking up – 'and we'll cut out the bit about "the almost palpable miasma of etheric malignity rising from the tombs of the departed". We don't want our readers to think that staff of the *Brixton Mercury* has collectively had hysterics – Mental Health Scare At Newspaper Office! Doctors Baffled! Atmosphere, Byng, does *not* mean a novel of manners by Henry James.'

He began to scribble all over my precious work, and my spirits, which had soared during its composition, folded their wings and plummeted earthwards. 'If I'd known you wanted me to write like Raymond Chandler . . .' I began, but I could see he wasn't listening.

'Just a minute.' Mr Podmore held up a finger as I turned to go. 'I've had an idea. I want you to write a series for the paper.'

I could not believe my ears. 'What, me?'

'Yes, you. Unless there's someone else in this office that only you can see.' He put extra sarcasm into his voice but I was too amazed to object. 'One thousand five hundred words every week until further notice for the Friday edition. Eight pounds an article. Entitled –' he tilted his chair on to its back legs and gazed thoughtfully at the fly-filled globe that encased the light bulb – '"The Ghostly Habitat". No we don't want them thinking of anything as mundane as a department store. We want to titillate their imaginations. "The Revenant Revisited"? Too clever by half. "Spectral Sleuthing"? Too much of a tongue-twister. We want this to become part of the nation's patois.' You had to allow that there was nothing small about Mr Podmore's ideas. 'I have it! "Spook Hall". That's got a friendly colloquial feel that won't frighten even those readers who think the Red

Brigade is an Italian fire-fighting service and Kenyatta is a kind of African boating party.'

'But what am I to write about?'

'Haunted houses, of course. Give your imagination free rein. Get their spines shivering. Make their follicles contract. I want you to visit every house the length and breadth of England that's had so much as a unattributable footfall. You can indent for expenses. But keep it cheap, mind. No four-star hotels.'

I was bewildered by the suddenness of my promotion and extent of the project. 'But I can't – I couldn't possibly –'

'I'll say one thing for you, Byng. You drive a hard bargain and that's no bad thing if you want to get on. All right, I'll raise you to ten pounds an article. But the copy's to be on my desk every Thursday lunchtime *without fail*. You get flu, or your auntie falls off a cliff, that's tough. We'll make a journalist of you.' For the first time he smiled, disclosing two long incisors like fangs.

'When shall I begin?'

'You can start next week.'

'But where shall I –'

Mr Podmore gave me an unfriendly look over the top of his blue spectacles. 'Are you a resourceful, stop-at-nothing newshawk or an incompetent feeble-brained nymphet?'

'Oh, the former, certainly,' I lied.

'Good. Now hop it.'

I hopped. In a dream I sat at my desk and fiddled with the lever that wound up the page on my typewriter, wondering how I was going to fulfil my brief. I could not imagine myself wandering up to people's front doors demanding to become intimate with their domestic poltergeists. And how was I to discover suitably spectre-ridden dwellings? Could there be a guidebook of such things? But quite quickly I fell to glorying in the increased contribution I could make to the family kitty and to thinking how pleased with me Rupert would be.

Some time passed before I became aware that silence had fallen. The atmosphere was usually peaceful for, unless Mr Podmore's door was open, Muriel and Eileen typed like idly pecking birds already stuffed with crumbs, and their tea intervals were lengthy and numerous. But there was always a steady mutter of conversation, a rasping of emery boards, a rattling of the toffee tin, or a rustling of magazines. Now the silence was complete. I looked up.

Muriel and Eileen shifted their gazes from my face as soon as I did so and Muriel made a curious motion with her head and neck like an ostrich swallowing a cricket ball. 'Some people have a nerve, you've got to hand it to them. My sainted mother would turn in her grave if she knew the sort of riffraff I'm obliged to associate with.' I stared at her in astonishment. 'Oh, yes!' Muriel spoke more fiercely as though angered by my incomprehension. 'I've read all about it in the *Daily Banner*. Not only murdering in the family but prostitution, thievery and goodness knows what else! But that doesn't seem to matter to some people! No! They come flaunting themselves among people who've never even had a library book overdue, bold as brass, as though butter wouldn't melt in their mouths. Disgusting I call it.'

'Yes.' Eileen had flushed a dark red. 'You'd think those what are intimately acquainted with convicts would be ashamed to go about.'

I couldn't think what to say. Cheap though the taunts were, yet I was wounded. I didn't care what they thought about me but the idea that these silly, small-minded women despised my family cut me to the heart. They must have seen this for they looked at each other and smiled spitefully.

'Did I tell you, Muriel dear,' said Eileen in a low voice, 'about the time my auntie was stopped in the street and this man with a microphone asked her if she could tell Stork from butter? It was ever so exciting.'

An hour later I was close to tears. It had nothing to do with Muriel and Eileen, for I had entirely forgotten their unkindness in the struggle to get the expenses to make anything like sense. I was supposed to lose the cost of Mr Podmore's holiday in Morocco in things like pints of beer with ex-mistresses of alcoholic footballers, lunches with renegade MPs, B&Bs in Manchester, Biros and staples. But the hotel bill had been so large that Mr Podmore would have had to have lunched at Wilton's seven days a week for at least a year to get anywhere near the total.

'Byng.' Mr Podmore stood in the doorway. 'Haven't you finished those accounts yet?'

'Sorry. I don't seem to be very good at, um, adjusting –'

'Give them to Eileen. I want you in my office. Now.'

He slammed the door.

'Well!' said Eileen, ceasing to storm at the keys as I handed her the untidy sheaf of papers, much scribbled on. 'And they say crime doesn't pay.'

'Sit down,' said Mr Podmore. I did as I was told. Mr Podmore strolled about the room, smoking a cigarette, an armpit smell much in evidence. 'It will surprise you to know that I have for some years been writing a book about psychical exploration.' I was not particularly surprised. Knowing absolutely nothing about Mr Podmore I had formed no ideas about what he did for fun. 'I'm aware,' he went on, 'that an interest in such things might seem at odds with a substantial intellect. However, it's the case.' I continued to look solemnly at him as befitted an employee, regardless of the ass her boss might be. 'I'm interested in your claim to have psychic powers.' I smiled modestly. 'I don't say I believe in the existence of such any such thing,' Mr Podmore continued. 'My mind's entirely open. I've never seen anything of a supernatural nature myself that could begin to convince me. But as I say, probably an active, sceptical intelligence is a barrier. I want you to attend a séance tomorrow afternoon. Four o'clock.'

'Will I get paid? I'll have to do overtime.'

Mr Podmore looked pained. 'There are other gods besides money, you know. I'll show my gratitude in other ways.' Mr Podmore's gratitude was something I was quite prepared to live without. 'All right, five pounds.'

'Done. Where will the séance be?'

'At the house of Madame Eusapia, the well-known medium.' Our social circles evidently did not overlap. 'Be punctual. Madame Eusapia is highly sensitive to any disruption of her mental preparations –'

There was a knock at the door and a head appeared around it. 'Hello, Sidney,' it said, blinking its bleary eyes as though the light in the office was too bright. 'Sorry I'm a bit late. I've been ill – flu, I think it was.' He coughed pathetically to illustrate the point and a blast of beery air filled the office. Luckily Mr Podmore had already stubbed out his cigarette.

'You can't have flu and recover in twenty-four hours,' snarled Mr Podmore. 'You've been drinking again.'

The rest of the body followed the head. I looked at the visitor, aghast.

'You always were inclined to think the worst of a fellow,' he whined. 'It's not enough that I've dragged myself from my bed to bring you that piece on that gangster funeral you were so insistent on having. And with a fever on me so I could hardly see straight. I had a nasty accident. I should think my knee-cap's dislocated from falling into the gr – a ruddy great hole.'

'You needn't have bothered.' Mr Podmore remained unsympathetic. 'This young woman's done your work for you.' He looked at me. 'This is Slim Brewer, our chief reporter. When he's sober – which isn't often.'

A scowl appeared on Slim's pallid countenance. His flabby mouth drooped and a skinny hand pushed back a thread of black hair scraped across his shining white skull. I made a resolve on the spot that absolutely nothing, not money, expediency, common honesty nor bamboo shoots under the fingernails, would make me confess to having mistaken the chief reporter of the *Brixton Mercury* for Vildo's incorporeal shade.

FOURTEEN

'Come in, young ladies.' The woman who opened the door had a good deal of caked rouge in her wrinkles and lipstick on her teeth. A curious odour drifted out from the hall of number 74 Philadelphia Avenue. I detected disinfectant mixed with damp, overlaid by the rank smell of flowers that have been too long in their vases.

'Thanks very much.' Portia moved ahead of me. 'I'm Portia Byng and this is my sister Harriet.'

'Pleased to meet you.' She smiled, in a tried sort of way. 'We weren't expecting two girls. Mr Podmore said only one.'

Though Portia's ability to smile had been curtailed by the broken tooth, she could still be charming when she chose. 'When Harriet told me about you I *begged* her to let me come too. I've always longed to attend a séance. It's so thrilling to meet someone who's actually talked to dead people. You must be *aw*fully clever.'

What Portia had actually said was, 'A séance? What a hoot! If you don't let me come with you I'll never, ever forgive you.'

As it was the first time for ages that she had sounded remotely enthusiastic about anything, I had decided to risk Madame Eusapia's displeasure and bring her with me.

'Oh, *I'm* not Madame Eusapia. I'm Miss Judd. I help Madame Eusapia on her séance days. The spirits are very troublesome often, quite nasty and spiteful. She's fit for nothing after.' The woman looked despondent. 'Madame Eusapia says I haven't any psychometric gifts so I'm an ideal assistant.'

The narrow hall was further constricted by a mound of carrier bags spilling over with clothes, with a note pinned to one of them, which said 'Vicar, 4.30', and an old-fashioned lady's bicycle. An ancient fur coat reeking of mothballs hung from a row of hooks and on the telephone table stood a cut-glass vase of dying bronze chrysanthemums. We followed Miss Judd into the sitting room. The curtains were drawn to exclude every scrap of daylight. An oil lamp burned smokily at the centre of a circular table draped with a black cloth. Four people sat round it.

'Hello,' said Portia. 'This is my sister Harriet and –'

There was a chorus of 'Sh-h-h!' A man with a bald head and a little black beard pointed to an empty chair. Miss Judd drew up another next to it. We sat obediently and surreptitiously examined our fellow seekers after truth.

The two women were grey-headed, one with a tight perm, the other with an uncompromising pudding-basin haircut. They wore sensible woollen garments and I could imagine them being very efficient librarians or perhaps devoted secretaries. After a cursory glance at us they had returned their eyes to the lamp, at which they gazed with fierce eyes as though hoping to stare it out of countenance. The second man was small with a fringe brushed forward over his eyes like a thatched roof. He was staring slack-jawed at Portia. The moment she returned his look, he dropped his eyes to the lamp. I stole a glance at the bearded man on my right. He sat with folded arms, chewing his lower lip with a disgruntled expression, eyes closed. He smelled very strongly of whisky.

As my eyes adjusted to the darkness I noticed a Victorian

chiffonier with curtained doors and an upright piano with fabric-backed fretwork, both very useful for hiding tape recorders. I had bought a book about spiritualism called *Behind the Veil* from a second-hand bookshop and had discovered, greatly to my disappointment, that mediums are almost invariably fraudulent. But there had been many interesting little snippets of information. I had enjoyed the story about Arthur Conan Doyle, a staunch believer, who was furious because his spirit control insisted on calling him Sir Sherlock Holmes. I suppose he thought that ignorance should not persist beyond the grave.

As I learned more about it, it became clear that there must be a lot of money involved. One medium went so far as to have her vagina made larger so that she could hide large quantities of butter muslin in it, supposed to be ectoplasm. The novelist, Thomas Mann, said that spiritualism was a Sunday afternoon diversion for the servants' hall. But this had not stopped him experimenting frequently with it – in a patrician manner for the purpose of determining scientific truths, naturally. Perhaps, like me, he yearned to see or hear something that would sweep aside dull reason and boring old common sense. Probably we would all like proof that death will not snuff us out entirely.

As we sat shrouded in mystic gloom, listening to the ticking of the clock and each other's breathing, I told myself firmly that despite a tendency to be easily persuaded – to the point, said my family, of hopeless gullibility – on this occasion I would not allow myself be duped.

The chair nearest the door remained empty. A coal fire was sending out a great heat and the atmosphere of the parlour was frowsy. The bearded man's feet were beginning to make their presence known.

'It's very hot in here, isn't it?' said Portia, in her normal voice. The beard turned glinting eyeballs in her direction.

'This isn't a tea-party,' he whispered. 'Try to get yourself into a receptive state. Make your mind a void.'

After another minute's silence Portia said, 'I've tried. It's impossible. I keep wondering what that peculiar smell is.'

'For heaven's sake!' said the man with the thatch. 'You've broken my thread of concentration completely. Now I shall have to begin all over again.'

'Would you kindly cease talking!' whispered the pudding-basin haircut. 'It makes me feel positively unwell to be disturbed when I am floating on the aerial tide.'

'I do beg your pardon,' the thatch replied with bitter insincerity. 'It may interest you to know that you're not the only one. Though some people are all self.'

Portia giggled and they both turned to glare at her.

'It's just this kind of thing that upsets the spirits,' began the perm indignantly. 'It's ever so hard for them to come back into the world and we ought to give them proper respect –'

'Stop yammering, woman,' hissed the beard. 'Here she is!'

Miss Judd threw open the door with an air of ceremony and Madame Eusapia came in. I was disappointed. I had expected someone exotic and mysterious, perhaps inspiring. Her face was round and pudgy with a snub nose, and her figure was dumpy. She wore a gaudy robe, with jingling bracelets on her arms and a crooked turban of knotted scarves on her head. Could this unpromising material really be the conduit for communication with departed souls across the Great Divide? She made me think of Widow Twankey in a provincial pantomime.

'I hope it's all right me coming too, Madame Eusapia,' said Portia.

'Hush, dearie.' The medium held up her hand and her bracelets clattered down to her elbow. 'Just you sit quiet and try not to get in the way of the business.' Then she looked at me. 'This is the girlie with the gift.'

'Well, not really,' I said, feeling uncomfortable. 'I'm afraid – perhaps I imagined –'

Madame Eusapia waved away my modesty with a plump hand. 'I know these things. You've got it. I can see a light hovering about your shoulders. Blue and sparkly, like a necklace. It'll be a blessing and a burden to you, dearie, but I hope you'll always try to do good with it.' I lowered my eyes, my face burning from the heat of the fire and feelings of shame at my own duplicity. 'That'll be three pounds each, before we start.'

Miss Judd travelled fast round the table, pocketing notes discreetly, and stopped at my elbow.

I took out my purse. I had ten pence besides the five pounds that Mr Podmore had given me, out of which I had intended to buy some of Pa's favourite garlic-stuffed olives and two cigars, as well as some ink for myself. And there was the tube fare to get home. Portia had seventy-five pence.

'Five pounds, then, for you two girls,' said Madame Eusapia, 'A special discount, seeing as one of you's got astral influences.' I put the note into Miss Judd's outstretched palm, not without a sense of grievance. 'All right, Judd.' Madame Eusapia sat down, massaged her temples with the tips of her fingers and then spread her hands on the table, palm up. 'I'm ready to begin.'

Beard placed his large paw over my right one and Portia held my left. Miss Judd drew a curtain across the door and turned down the wick in the lamp to a crimson glow. There was an unpleasant smell of oil vying for ascendancy with socks and whisky. For what seemed like ages we sat in silence. I could hear Beard's breath whistling in his nostrils.

My stomach began to rumble. Always troublesome, it had got much worse since my father's arrest, and these days only a slight increase in nervous tension was needed to get it going.

I tightened my abdominal muscles but that seemed to make it worse.

'Ah-h-h!' sighed Madame Eusapia in unison with a particularly loud rumble on my part. Portia snorted. 'There is an intelligence present. Please make yourself known to us. One rap for yes, two for no.' Portia made another explosive sound, which she disguised as a cough. She must have frightened off whoever was attempting to penetrate the malodorous murk of Philadelphia Avenue, for Madame Eusapia again fell silent. My arm and thigh were growing uncomfortably warm from the heat from the fire, and Beard's hand was sticky. I tried to distance myself from the idea that he was giving mine sly little squeezes. A tinkling sound, like harness bells, from somewhere in the blackness overhead, made the hairs on the back of my neck stand up. Something light and soft drifted across my face, like blowing cobwebs.

'I can hear you,' cooed Madame Eusapia. 'Come and join us and don't be shy. I've got a name coming through. Jack?' Silence, all round. 'Not Jack? Peter?' Another spell of silence. 'Harry, is it?'

'Harry?' gasped Pudding-basin haircut. 'My husband?'

'Hello, Harry. I can hear you. Come in, dear.'

There was a sudden sharp rap that made my heart patter with alarm. It appeared to come from beneath the table.

'Are you Harold Leadbetter?' asked Madame Eusapia.

Another rap.

'He was Henry when I was married to him.'

'Yes, Henry, to be sure. I can't always hear perfectly. Sometimes there's a lot of interference. Other spirits trying to get through.'

'Can you see him?' asked Mrs Leadbetter. 'How's he looking?'

'He's floating just behind the young lady with the psychic gift.' I shrank my head down into my shoulders, not

210

daring to turn round. 'He doesn't want anyone else to see him but me,' continued Madame Eusapia. 'He's fading in and out a lot. But he's looking very well. A nice fresh colour.'

'Is he in uniform?' asked Mrs Leadbetter.

'Let me see. RAF, I think. Or is it army? One of our brave boys, anyway. I can hear music. It's a march. Listen, can anyone hear that?'

It was faint and slightly scratchy but I distinctly heard the sound of a brass band from somewhere above my head. Madame Eusapia began to trill, '"Some talk of Alexander and some of Hercules . . ."'

'He wasn't in the forces,' interrupted Mrs Leadbetter. 'He was a commissionaire at the Green Park Hotel.'

Portia stifled laughter, not very successfully. I was too embarrassed by this hopeless ineptitude to find it funny.

'Well!' said Madame Eusapia. 'All that braid and the cap, I quite thought . . . Never mind. Have you a message, Harry, for your dear wife?'

Something brushed my knee. I stretched out my foot, half expecting to encounter Miss Judd crawling under the table. It came into contact with something that at once returned the pressure with unpleasant insistence. Beard's nostrils were whistling like a high wind. I shifted in my chair towards Portia.

'*I'd* like to say something to *him*.' Mrs Leadbetter raised her voice, the better to penetrate the astral barrier. 'Henry? It's me, Audrey. I'd like to know what that Cora Smith – the one that works at the travel agent – is to you. Turning up at your funeral with a heart-shaped wreath of red roses and crying her eyes out so we couldn't hear the vicar's address – I was never so humiliated in my life!'

'Oh dear, he's going,' cried Madame Eusapia. 'They don't like to be attacked. They're very sensitive.'

'He's sensitive, is he?' said Mrs Leadbetter grimly. 'Being dead's changed him, then.'

I would have felt sorry for Madame Eusapia, had it not been for the five pounds. We sat in silence once more. Beard twitched the hand that was enfolding mine and there was a sucking noise as our flesh parted briefly.

Just as I was thinking what a nuisance it was that men were incapable of leaving sex out of any proceeding, the clock stopped ticking and the lamp went out. My stomach stopped rumbling and I could no longer hear Beard's nostrils. The sudden silence, like putting one's head under water, seemed to expand in a sort of wave and I felt a tremendous pressure on my eardrums. I looked around, surprised. The coals were burning with an intense blue light. 'Oh-h-h!' groaned Madame Eusapia in a quite different voice. 'You sulphurous and thought-executing fires, Vaunt couriers to oak-cleaving thunderbolts.'

Beard gripped my hand tightly.

'*Merchant of Venice*,' whispered Portia in an excited voice but I was too alarmed to speak.

'Oh, blood, blood, blood!' said Madame Eusapia in a growly baritone.

'Who are you?' asked Beard. 'Are you a spirit control?'

'I am a very foolish, fond old man,' replied Madame Eusapia in the same deep tones. 'Revenge my foul and most unnatural murder!'

Miss Judd must have opened the window at that moment for an icy wind blasted my hot cheeks, sucked open the door and blew it shut again with a slam. I felt the draught tug at my hair. The woman with the perm gave a little scream.

'Who are you?' repeated Beard, who seemed to have taken charge.

'I am – Sir Basil Wintergreen,' continued the fruity voice

from the throat of Madame Eusapia. Portia seized my arm. I felt a trickle of terror.

'What do you want to tell us?' asked Beard peremptorily.

'But that I am forbid to tell you the secrets of my prison house,' began Sir Basil, 'I could a tale unfold whose lightest word would harrow up thy soul, freeze thy young blood, make thy two eyes start from their spheres, thy knotted and combinèd locks to part –'

'Yes, yes,' interrupted Beard, 'but can you tell us what actually happened?'

'Dost thou not read the newspapers?' Sir Basil sounded grumpy. 'A vile blow cut me off even in the blossoms of my sin, unhouseled, disappointed, unaneled, no reckoning made, but sent to my account with all my imperfections on my head.'

'But who did it?' persisted Beard.

'Ah, he – he with his sharp and sulphurous bolt split'st the unwedgeable and gnarled oak –'

'Facts first, *if* you please,' Beard was probably something like an actuary or a solicitor. 'Who did it?'

'Since I was a man,' said Madame Eusapia in a voice of gravel, 'such sheets of fire, such bursts of horrid thunder, such groans of roaring wind and rain –'

'If we'd wanted the weather forecast we could have turned on the wireless,' said Beard rudely. Probably he was one of those people who become aggressive when alarmed.

'O Fool, I shall go ma-a-ad!' raged Sir Basil.

The curtains streamed out. A violent wind whooshed over us and made the flames leap in the grate until the entire room was incandescent with glittering blue fire. Madame Eusapia screamed. There was a crash and the table shuddered.

The wind dropped as suddenly as it had risen. Beard struck a match with a hand that shook, lit the lamp and turned it high. Madame Eusapia lay with her face pressed to the

213

tablecloth. Miss Judd said, 'Oh, crumbs!' and ran over to her. With the help of Thatch she pulled Madame Eusapia back into her chair. Her head, with eyes closed, lolled to one side. We all looked at each other in silence for a moment or two. My heart was racing and my limbs were tingling with fright.

Beard was the first to speak. 'Well! What do we make of that?' He sounded uncertain, almost cowed. His scalp was glistening with sweat.

'I think we have been granted a glimpse behind the curtain that separates us from the hereafter,' said Thatch, who was shaking, either with rage or fright. 'And if you hadn't been so hectoring we might have been privileged to learn something that would have put a very different complexion on our understanding of life and death.'

'What did you want to go bullying it for?' cried the woman with the perm, putting her handkerchief to her eyes.

'If it weren't for you being so impudent to it,' said Mrs Leadbetter, her face working with emotion, 'we might have learned something to our advantage. We've never had such a good connection. But there's always some man *has* to be a smart aleck and spoil everything.'

'I take exception to that remark!' said Thatch, sticking out his chin.

'Oh, you can go boil your head –' began Mrs Leadbetter but Miss Judd interrupted her with a wail.

'Whatever am I going to do about poor Madame? I can't get her to wake up.'

Madame Eusapia's turban had fallen off, exposing a head of grey curls. A bubble of saliva glistened at the corner of her mouth.

'We'll put her on the sofa,' said Beard, with a return of his usual bossiness and, though he was the object of collective dislike, we did as he said.

While he and Thatch struggled with the heavy limbs of

the unconscious Madame Eusapia, and the women fluttered about, fanning her and patting her hands, Portia and I looked under the table, behind the curtains, on the shelves of the chiffonier, inside the lid of the piano. I found nothing but dust, dead spiders and a bar of chocolate, its white bloom proclaiming its age. Inside a large Chinese vase was a tin of face powder and half a bottle of vodka.

'I was scared,' admitted Portia later as we sat in the kitchen at home, drinking tea and eating toast and pork dripping, sprinkled with salt. This was Ronnie's idea, to save on butter. Actually it was delicious. 'Of course it must have been faked. Mr Podmore told her who you were and she'd read about it in the papers. But how did she know all that Shakespeare?'

'She mugged it up, of course,' said Ronnie, who was making dumplings from suet paste, 'and then recorded it. It's what they all do.'

'The voice seemed to come straight out of her mouth,' I said. 'I looked very carefully all round her chair and felt underneath it. There were no wires or anything. And when she went off into a swoon Miss Judd undid her clothing – Madame Eusapia's, I mean – and I saw down to her vest. There was no microphone. Could Miss Judd be a ventriloquist?'

'I wish I'd been there.' Cordelia got up to put on more toast. 'Do you remember *Blithe Spirit*? It had Margaret Rutherford in.'

'No,' said Portia. 'I suppose Miss Judd must have chucked something on the fire to make it blue. But when the clock stopped there was a weird sensation – a sort of – well the opposite of an explosion. A sort of sucking in of air.'

'An implosion.' Ronnie put potatoes and mutton chops into a large pot. 'That's what a television set does if you throw a brick at it. And the very best thing one can do,

215

in my opinion. Such horrid, vulgar people appearing on it, these days.'

'I felt it too!' I said. 'As though my head was being cracked like a nut.'

'You must remember *Blithe Spirit*,' persisted Cordelia. 'There's this man who's married again and when they hold a séance his first wife who's dead comes back to haunt them and she makes fun of the second wife all the time, who isn't nearly as nice and she gets very angry because she can't see Elvira – that's the first wife – and –'

'What would be the point of it all?' I wondered aloud. 'Madame Eusapia meant it for us – me, I suppose, because she didn't know you were coming. But why? If she thinks I'm going to give her a lot of money her hopes will be sadly blighted.'

'I remember it.' Ronnie paused in the act of chopping an onion. 'In the end the second wife dies in a car crash – the ghost tampers with the brakes. And then he dies and ends up trapped between the two of them. Poor Noel had a very low opinion of marriage.'

'Perhaps she wants you to tell all your rich and influential friends?' suggested Portia.

'Even if Mr Podmore was in on it, it couldn't have been a recording,' I pondered. 'I mean, it was a real conversation, wasn't it? There weren't any awkward pauses.'

'I'm surprised at you girls being so gullible,' said Ronnie as he bent to put the stew into the oven. 'You sound as though you really believe all that poppycock.'

'Honestly, if you'd been there, you'd have been convinced,' said Portia. 'It was extremely alarming. I'm almost ashamed to admit it but I went cold all over.'

'I wouldn't have been frightened at all,' said Cordelia. 'I'd have asked it questions about what it was like to be dead. And whether there's such a thing as hell. Because if there is

I don't give much for Sister Imelda's chances, the mean cow. You two were idiots not to say anything. I wouldn't *ever* be scared of a ghost.'

As it happened, later events proved this to be a vain boast but I was too fond of my little sister ever to remind her of it.

FIFTEEN

'Honestly, it *did* sound like Sir Basil's voice. Voices are as distinctive as faces, really, aren't they? I mean someone's only got to say hello on the telephone and you know who they are.'

'It's a ridiculously easy voice to mimic.' My father put on his Basil Wintergreen face, which involved screwing up his eyes and protruding his tongue slightly between his lips. '"I prithee, daughter, do not make me mad ... thou art a boil, A plague sore, or embossèd carbuncle In my corrupted blood –"'

Pa projected his voice, tremulous and lisping, to the acoustic tiles and the other prisoners and their visitors turned to stare. A warder moved hastily in our direction, and lingered watchfully, fingering the whistle on his belt. The nice old lady sitting next to me, clucked sympathetically and said, 'Don't you take it personal, love, they've a lot to try 'em here when all's said and done.' She was visiting her son, who had hairy backs to his hands and "knock twice' tattooed on the narrow expanse of his forehead.

'That sounded just like Basil,' I said. Actually it wasn't nearly as good as Madame Eusapia's impersonation but

I did not want to upset Pa, who seemed gloomier than ever.

'How's your mother?'

'Oh, pretty well. Still not going out of doors because of the bandages. But she sends you her fondest love. She's very anxious about you and always asks me how you're looking, whether you're eating enough, getting exercise, all that sort of thing.'

My father frowned at me. 'If I believed a word of this tar-radiddle, I should be seriously worried that your mother was showing signs of a personality disorder. That idiot Ronnie's always telling me how concerned she is and I let it go because I know all actors have trouble with the truth. But I expect more of you, Harriet. I wouldn't be surprised if her hairdresser isn't more often in Clarissa's thoughts than I am.'

I felt myself blush, remembering that Ma, only that morning, had grumbled about her enforced separation from Stefano, the colourist at Turning Heads. 'Ronnie's awfully kind, really.'

'Yes, he is,' said my father unexpectedly. 'He visits more often than anyone.'

'Oh, Pa, I'm so sorry! It's just that Mr Podmore often doesn't let me go home until after five, so I can't get here before the end of visiting hours. And you know what Rupert said – I've *got* to keep my job.'

'I know, darling. Don't take any notice of my bad temper. It's just this place getting on my nerves. You can't imagine what it's like to be shut in with unrelieved ugliness. The window in my cell is so high up you have to stand on a chair to see out. There's nothing to look at, anyway. More barred windows, brick walls as grey as the square of sky. I've stopped bothering. You're very sweet and loyal and come more often than any of the others.'

'It's difficult for Portia,' I rushed to defend her. 'She has to work even longer hours than I do. Jessica Delavine likes her to go with her to feminist rallies and usually they're in the evening.'

'How does she like the sisterhood? I suppose they're all as plain as suet puddings.'

'Oh, Pa! It's just that sort of remark that makes them cross. You men have got to learn to value us for our characters and brains, instead of the way we look.' My father smiled cynically. I had to admit it was about as likely as pigs learning to prefer *Beowulf* to a roll in the mud. 'Anyway, they aren't all plain by any means. Jessica took Portia to this women's club, somewhere smart in Pall Mall. There were lots of women in suits and ties with short haircuts who tried to make assignations with her. Portia said she must have been very dim not to realise Jessica's a lesbian. Apparently she's ferociously ancient and has a little white beard so Portia didn't think of her in connection with any kind of sex.'

'So I'm not the only one who judges by appearance.' My father's eyes brightened a little. 'That sounds interesting.'

'Portia said the atmosphere was amazing. The women were all intelligent and stimulating and fun to talk to. I can't see why sexual orientation should have an effect on personality. Perhaps only women with strong characters will admit openly to homosexuality.'

'It's true that gay actors are as plentiful as blackberries but not many actresses own to it. So Portia approved these monocled sapphists.'

'She was introduced to this girl called Suke – she's a writer, I'm not sure what kind – Portia said she was the most fascinating person she'd ever met. They had lunch the next day, at Suke's flat. Apparently Suke makes all her own furniture. She's very good at carpentry and all her curtains and things are hand-dyed and hand-woven. She's got a workshop and a big loom in the garage. Suke disapproves of things made

220

in a factory. She thinks machines are evil because they deny people the joy of creation. Portia says Suke could easily sell the rugs and cushions and things but she isn't interested in money – only Art and Truth. They ate brown rice and miso, with berries and nuts that she'd gathered in the park for pudding, served in shells she'd found on a beach in Bali. I assume she walked and swam there rather than flying in an evil, joyless plane. Portia says Suke's so high-minded she makes her feel ashamed. Suke has explained some fundamental errors in her thinking – Portia's, I mean. Suke's thinking is, of course, beyond criticism. This afternoon they're going to the dentist together. Suke's going to hold her hand and read poems by Sylvia Townsend Warner to her while she has her tooth fixed.'

'My poor Harriet. It seems it's not only me who's suffering.'

'What do you mean?'

'Dear girl, of course you're bound to be jealous. You and Portia have always been so close.'

'I don't know what you – Well . . . Oh dear, I suppose you're right. I *am* rather jealous. Naturally I've never minded about her men. But I've always taken it for granted that no other woman could be as important to her as me.'

'It may be just the friendship that Portia needs. She looked wretched, last time she came. Not just the broken tooth but something about the eyes. Disenchanted with the world.'

'It's very selfish of me to mind.'

'Portia's always needed excitement. Imagining she's in love with this girl will be the distraction she needs. And probably she'll get something in return, for a change – kindness, attention, affection. I've always wondered why more women aren't lesbians.'

'Oh, Pa, you are a wonder!' I looked at him with love. 'There can't be many fathers who are so tolerant and wise.'

221

'Thank you, Harriet.'

Pa looked pleased by the compliment and I had the glorious feeling that we perfectly understood each other. I knew I had never been his favourite daughter. Strangely, for an actor, my father was not good at dissimulation when it came to his children. Cordelia and Ophelia were his darlings, with the former perhaps a nose in front. Unsurprisingly, as he was her only son, Bron was my mother's favourite. That left Portia and me to champion each other. We had accepted this state of things and had not resented the favourites. But I treasured those times when I felt Pa and I were in harmony.

'How's Marina?' This was the moment to be generous.

'Haven't seen her this week. Now I'm no longer headline material there isn't much point, from her point of view.' It was true that for several days now there had been no more than two or three reporters hanging about outside Winston Shrubs.

'Have you quarrelled?'

'No. There never was an affair, you know. We played around a little but it wasn't in earnest. Marina's too much of a narcissist to want hot breath melting her mascara.' I tried not to show my relief. 'Actually I'm rather sick of all that sort of thing,' he continued. His voice took on a confidential tone. 'I've had the devil of a time recently with a very tiresome woman who won't let go. I never meant the thing to be serious, never even liked her above half, to tell the truth, but she was quite pretty and very enthusiastic in the bedroom. Now she keeps threatening to kill herself if I don't leave Clarissa. I think she's more than a little crazy. I've forbidden her to visit me any more, so she sends the most ridiculous presents instead. The caviar's welcome, I admit, but there are three of us living, sleeping and defecating in a cell twelve feet by ten. The quadraphonic loudspeakers and the badminton set had to be sent straight back.'

'How did you manage to stop her coming?'

My father looked a little shame-faced. 'I told her we must be discreet. A scandal just now might prejudice public opinion against me and affect the outcome of my case.'

'But, Pa, if you don't intend to have anything more to do with her wasn't it unkind to mislead her?'

'I know. But can I help it if she's besotted? She was a perfect pest, making scenes, insulting the warders and insisting on abusive interviews with the governor. She's mad, I tell you. Supposing she does kill herself? Imagine what the press would say. It wouldn't exactly help things.'

I forgave my father this egotistical view. I knew from experience how hard it is to think of others when you are miserable. I kissed him goodbye and promised to go immediately to the police station, to ask Inspector Foy how his investigations were progressing and to urge upon him my father's pressing need to breathe the purer air of freedom.

The inspector greeted me as an old friend when I knocked on his door. His desk was piled with papers and half his filing cabinets were open. Both telephones began to ring the moment I went in but he assured me he was not in the least busy.

He dealt with the calls swiftly and then clapped the pockets of his jacket, searching for his pipe and pouch. 'How do you think he's bearing up?'

'Considering everything, not too badly. But . . . you know.'

'Yes, I know. Even old lags can go stir-crazy.'

'I don't suppose there are any new developments?'

He shook his head. 'I'm going through the statements of the cast again in case I've missed something. If we could only find a motive.'

'You don't think my father did it, do you?'

The inspector took a long pull on his pipe to get it going. The tobacco in the bowl glowed red. 'The circumstantial evidence is very strong against him. But we all flatter ourselves that we're good judges of character. I've met a good many murderers and I find it hard to believe your father's a killer. But if your father didn't hit him over the head with the gouger, who did? There was no other possible weapon and there are three witnesses to swear that there was no one else on the stage.'

'According to Sir Basil it was a thunderstorm that killed him.'

'What?'

I told the inspector about the séance. I made a joke of it and expected him to be amused or politely dismissive. But he listened very carefully to everything I could remember that Sir Basil had said, and then made me repeat it so he could write it all down.

'Surely you don't think there's anything in it?' I asked, when he fished out a battered copy of Shakespeare's tragedies and attempted to pinpoint the actual quotations.

'One thing I've learned in fifteen years of doing this job is that nothing's too insignificant to be disregarded. We once brought in a conviction on a particular brand of cigarette paper. If nothing else, that woman's probably a fraud and she ought to be stopped. I don't suppose for a moment that it was Sir Basil's perturbèd spirit. But this case is so lacking in leads of any kind I'd be prepared to analyse the lick on a stamp if only we had one.'

He asked a lot of questions about Mr Podmore and laughed when I told him about my first assignment for the *Brixton Mercury*. I felt cheered up as I always did after talking to him. I wondered, not for the first time, whether there was a Mrs Foy. If so, she was very fortunate to be married to someone who always seemed able to inspire confidence.

'I don't suppose there's any news of Dex? I know a cat isn't important when you're dealing with murders and rapes and armed robberies but we do miss him dreadfully.'

'We'll get him sooner or later, don't you worry. It just takes time in a place the size of London.' I did not say that it might be too late for Mark Antony but the inspector must have read my thoughts. 'Don't forget, a dead cat is no use as a bargaining tool. I'm very surprised he's made no attempt to contact you. You won't be silly and try to deal with it yourselves, will you? Promise you'll let me know straight away if Dex gets in touch?'

I promised.

Walking up The Avenue from the bus stop I saw a large and elegant car parked outside our house. The sole reporter who was hanging on despite the chill wind and the lateness of the hour, was peering in through one of the windows, admiring its interior.

'Hello, Harriet,' said Frank of the *Scrutineer*. We were on familiar terms with all the journalists by now. 'How's Dad?'

'A bit fed up.'

'I bet! It doesn't seem right for a gent like your father to be banged up with the scum of society.'

'Have you had some tea?'

'Mr Mason brought me out a mug. It isn't every day you get your cha served up by Bonnie Prince Charlie. He's a good sort, I must say.'

'Absolutely the best.'

'He and your mum look a proper picture together in their veils and scarves and hats and whatnot. Why the cloak-and-dagger act?'

By this time I was standing on the top step looking for my keys. Indoors Dirk was turning himself into a canine battering ram. 'Protection from cold winds. They're as bad as too much sun for making wrinkles.'

225

'My father, who's a bit of a film buff, says Mr Mason and your mum saw a lot of one another in the fifties. Rumour was they ran off to the South of France together.'

'He's always been a close friend of the family.'

'Come on, Harriet. Strictly off the record, he's still holding a torch, isn't he? You can tell, the way he talks to her. I like a bit of romance myself. There isn't enough of it in this hard, cynical world. Cross my heart and hope to die, I wouldn't publish anything.'

'Their relationship is as brother and sister.'

I closed the front door behind me with a gracious smile. I had learned my lesson.

'Hello, Hat,' Cordelia was in the hall, carefully negotiating the Anubis hat stand with a tray of drinks. 'Rupert's here. And his friend.' She opened her eyes and mouth wide and mimed astonishment. It was Archie's first visit to our house. I would have liked to linger in the hall to compose a favourable account of our first week as members of the nation's workforce but Dirk's effusions made this impossible. I went into the drawing room with the same sensations of guilt and anxiety I had experienced when, as a schoolgirl, I had been summoned to Sister Imelda's office.

Rupert, still wearing his overcoat, was standing by a window looking out, his shoulders hunched against the cold, while Archie walked up and down, flapping his arms. He was much shorter than Rupert. His arms and legs were spindly by contrast with his barrel-shaped trunk. He wore a three-piece suit in a bold black-and-white Prince of Wales check, with a watch chain stretched across his stomach. The upper parts of his shoes were covered by pale-yellow spats.

'My *God*!' Archie rolled his black eyes, which were made more striking by the white makeup that covered his face, from a pronounced widow's peak to sharply pointed chin. '*Now* I know how a *pen*guin feels when its flippers are *fro*zen in the ice and it has a *py*ramid of *snow* on the top of its head.' He spoke very rapidly, with exaggerated emphasis on key words and syllables.

'I'm awfully sorry.' I went to the fireplace and took the matches from behind the ormolu clock crowned by a pair of lovebirds, which had not kept time for years. 'Ronnie says we must save money on central heating.'

'When I told you to make economies I didn't mean you to live like beggars.' Rupert took the matches from my hand and kneeled to light the fire.

'We keep our coats on in here nowadays. But most of the time we live in the kitchen.'

'Want to borrow my scarf?' Cordelia unwound it from her neck.

Archie held up the scarf between finger and thumb for inspection. It was knitted in garish stripes and had large holes in it. '*Too* sweet of you but I prefer to shudder. Did you rob a sleeping tramp, you *naughty* girl?' He put his head on one side and smiled provocatively.

Cordelia giggled. 'I made it myself in craft lessons at sch – last year,' she amended.

'Take my advice, dear girl, and give up the manual arts forth*with*. Your talents lie *else*where.'

'Are you back at school yet, Cordelia?' asked Rupert, without turning round. He was busy piling logs on the kindling but it was clear nothing escaped him.

Cordelia began to trip towards the door. 'I promised Ronnie I'd help him make the faggots for supper.'

Archie pursed his crimsoned lips. '*Fag*gots! Oh, how horrid! All those little *tubes* and gristly bits. Teeth and claws and pancreatic *juice*s. Surely you aren't going to eat such *beast*liness?'

But Cordelia had gone.

'I haven't found a school, yet, that will take her at short

notice,' I said guiltily. 'Sister Imelda refused to have her back. I'm afraid it was my fault. We had a row.'

Rupert stood up and brushed splinters of bark from his overcoat. Dirk evidently thought he wanted to play and sprang at him, placing two large paws on his chest, which made Rupert fall backwards and crack his elbow painfully against the marble chimneypiece. 'Ah-ow! Damn! Get *down*, will you? He nursed his arm, glaring first at Dirk and then at me, as I tried to express my concern. 'All right, there's no need to fuss. I accept it was a playful gesture. Though why anyone should want to keep such an animal in London . . . Well, how's the job?'

'Going quite well. I've got a rise, actually. But it was a fluke and I expect I'm going to come unstuck. I nearly made a complete ass of myself but luckily it turned out in my favour.'

'Tell all,' instructed Archie, drawing a chair close to the fire. 'And make it funny. *You*, sir,' he looked sternly at Dirk, who was eyeing Archie's shoes hungrily, 'one *drop* of saliva on those and I shall personally drive you to the dog pound.'

I did my best to be amusing and Archie was a good audience. He gave a gasp of surprise when I described Slim's sudden disappearance and a shout of laughter when I revealed his true identity. Rupert remained silent. He kept his eyes fixed on me with a gravity that I found discouraging and if it had not been for Archie's expressed desire to be entertained I would have cut the whole thing short.

'So what's your first article going to be about?' asked Rupert when I had finished my recital.

'I haven't any idea. Are London houses haunted? It seems rather a country thing somehow.'

'Of *course* they are,' said Archie. 'Near the Vauxhall Bridge a bollard marks the spot where prisoners were kept until they could be loaded on ships and transported to Australia. One young woman *threw* herself into the water rather than be banished from her native shores. *Not* surprisingly, as her hands and feet were shackled, she drowned. Several people have claimed to have met her *drip*ping figure. Apparently she *glows* with a green light.'

'I'm not surprised,' said Rupert. 'The Thames in those days was little better than an open sewer.'

'But that isn't a building,' I objected. 'I don't think it'll count.'

'There's the Church of St Agnes and St Margaret in Cheapside, named after two young *virg*ins who were beheaded in the fourteenth century. According to legend, on All Hallows Eve they play ninepins, with *thigh*-bones for skittles and their *own* skulls for balls.'

'That might do. But I'm not sure if I can write about a church under the heading "Spook Hall".'

'You *are* hard to please,' complained Archie. 'All right. What about the Red Cow Inn at Cripplegate? Named after the landlord's wife, who had hair of that colour and was a *shrew*. She discovered her husband *rav*ishing the barmaid in the marital bed. She *stabbed* the girl with a poisoned bodkin, then accused *him* of the crime. He was hanged at Tyburn.'

'That seems very unfair. Did the police just take her word for it?'

'This was the eighteenth century, you *i*gnorant girl. They didn't *have* policemen. Only rather inefficient Bow Street Runners. The inn became famous for being haunted. The landlady got rich by charging visitors half a crown to see the bedroom where at certain hours of the day, the ghostly couple could be heard fornicating, *ham*mer and *tongs*.'

'What happened to the landlady?'

'She got smallpox soon after and died in that *very* room, her last hours a *tor*ment because of the tiresome creaking and shaking of the bed and ghostly sniggers of *car*nal gratification. But it goes to show that sometimes crime *does* pay.'

'It was hard on the barmaid.'

'Don't waste your pity, Harriet.' Rupert was examining a Meissen shepherdess, which stood on the table beside him. 'The whole thing is a fabrication. There are no such things as ghosts.' He looked dismayed when the shepherdess's head came off in his hand.

'Please don't worry,' I said. 'It was only stuck on with Gripfix.' I took from Dirk the cushion he was chewing. 'I would have been inclined to agree with you. About ghosts, I mean. Until two days ago.'

'O*ho*!' cried Archie. 'Tell all, my frippet, and don't delay. Make my jaw *lock* with *ter*ror.'

'It isn't as frightening as all that. Unless you were there.'

Archie listened to my account of the séance with rapt and solemn concentration.

'Marvellous how clever people can be when it comes to chicanery,' said Rupert dampeningly. 'It never seems to occur to them to apply the same skills to a proper line of work for which they'd probably earn more money and be safe from the risk of prosecution.' He frowned at the chimneypiece. 'That clock wasn't working ten years ago.'

'Take *no* notice of Rupert,' said Archie. 'He's a *wet blank*et but he can't help it. There has been no benign *fe*male influence in his life. Being an orphan with a wicked grandmother has curdled his *soul*.'

I remembered then those times, long ago, when my mother had been unkind to Rupert. I think she was jealous because my father and Rupert were so fond of each other. On one occasion – I must have been four or five years old – I had clung to Rupert, in a storm of childish tears, while she lashed him with sarcasm. I had felt an overwhelming desire to protect him. Rupert had not been at all grateful for my sympathy. He had told me sharply not to be a little silly and that he didn't mind a row. But the next day he had given me his old prep school belt that I had always coveted. It was navy and red striped elastic with a buckle shaped like an S, and I had it still, rolled up in the drawer of my desk. When I looked at him now, grown up, wise, impregnable, it was difficult to believe that he had once stood silent, head down, dark hair falling untidily over shuttered eyes, playing with a piece of cord from a broken window sash, while my mother scolded.

'What about the others?' asked Rupert. 'How's Bron's career with Burlington Motors?' I noticed that abrupt redirection of the conversation seemed to be a habit of his.

I was spared the necessity of varnishing the truth by the return of Cordelia, bearing a small parcel. 'Look, Hat, this must have come by the afternoon post. It's addressed to 'MISBING'. Who does he mean, do you think?'

I took the parcel from her. From the number of crossings-out and readdressings on the dirty brown paper, it had been delivered all over London. Every word of the original address had been misspelt in an illiterate hand. With a presentiment of anguish, I ripped off the string. Out fell a piece of paper and a ginger tail. Cordelia closed her eyes, clenched her fists, and began to scream. I put my hand over my mouth to quell the rising nausea.

'Oh, oh!' I cried through falling tears. 'Mark Antony! Oh, no! The – bastard! How *could* he! His beautiful tail!'

Archie skipped over to the window, putting as much distance between himself and the dreadful object as possible. 'You mean – is that part of an *an*imal? I feel faint.'

Dirk, perceiving that the hank of fur was responsible for this aberrant human behaviour, seized it and shook it violently.

'Let go, you stupid creature!' Rupert wrested it from him and examined it. 'Be quiet, all of you! You're behaving like idiots. This is clearly part of something long dead,

231

probably a fox tippet. It smells of mothballs. See for yourselves.'

He held it towards me. Trembling with horror, I forced myself to look at it. My legs grew weak with relief.

'It's all right, Cordelia.' I tried to grab her hands but she broke away, yelling hysterically. 'It *isn't* Mark Antony's tail. Honestly, it's darker and much coarser. Look!'

I showed her the battered and now damp piece of fur but she kept her eyes shut and only bawled more loudly.

'She's hysterical,' said Rupert, and struck her, none too gently, on the cheek. Cordelia stopped crying and stood blinking with shock. I put my arms round her and pulled her down next to me on the sofa.

'Are you *cer*tain it isn't a recently severed limb?' Archie eyed the tail with distrust.

Rupert was examining the note. 'This is indecipherable.'

'Let me try.' I said. 'I'm familiar with the style.'

BRING2000KWIDTOTHEHATEBELZWOPPING-
NARSKFORDEXIFYUTELTHEFUZILRINGITSNEK

'He must mean the Eight Bells pub in Wapping,' I said, after some thought. 'Oh dear!' My mind raced round possible outcomes. 'I haven't got two thousand pounds. I haven't even got twenty. But supposing he means it about wringing Mark Antony's neck?' I had a sick feeling as I said the words and Cordelia squealed.

Rupert gave her a flinty look. 'Don't start that again.'

'I promised Inspector Foy if I heard from Dex I'd let him know at once. Oh, what shall I do?'

Rupert took the letter from my hand. 'We can call at the police station on our way home. I'll tell the inspector for you. Let me have this week's bills and we'll be off.'

'I haven't finished my *drink*,' protested Archie. 'Damn it, it's a very good Pouilly Fuissé.'

Rupert held up the bottle. 'An excellent year. I don't think Waldo will be pleased to find you've been offering his best wines to all and sundry. I'll get my wine merchant to send you something suitable for drinking every day.'

I was too anxious about Mark Antony to be properly grateful. 'It must mean he's still alive, mustn't it?'

'Of course,' said Rupert. 'Even the most witless criminal would not expect to be given the money before handing over the animal.'

Cordelia gazed beseechingly up into his face, her eyes sparkling, her long lashes clumped together by tears. 'If anything happens to Mark Antony I shall never, *ever* be able to be happy again. You will make the inspector see it's important, won't you?'

'I'll do my best. But you'll have to go back to school, you know.'

Cordelia left the room, frowning mightily.

I went with them to the front door. 'It's so kind of you to go to so much trouble for us.'

'The labour we delight in physics pain.' Archie made a dignified bow. 'And I am *not* all and sundry.'

I spent the rest of the time before supper in Pa's library, trying to distract my thoughts from Mark Antony's neck in the hands of the hateful Dex. I was running my eye down the first page of one of M.R.James's ghost stories when I noticed that Dirk was nibbling the head of the mummified Egyptian cat that stood on the cigar cabinet. I was attempting to re-attach the four-thousand-year-old ears when the doorbell rang. I threw the ears into a drawer, left Dirk shut in the library and went to answer it. Rupert and Archie were on the doorstep, their breaths steaming in the cold. Rupert held something wrapped in a grey army blanket, which he put into my arms.

'The brute's scratched me several times already.'

The bundle fought hard to unwrap itself. A paw shot out from the folds and attempted to hook out my eye. Then, with a snarl of rage, Mark Antony sprang from his prison house on to Cleopatra's day bed. I gazed at him with incredulous joy.

He was a changed creature. His embonpoint had disappeared, his shanks were shrunken. His fur was matted, his white bib was grey, his precious tail was tattered. As he surveyed the hall with a look of strong disapproval, he staggered a little. Cordelia, reaching the head of the basement stairs at that moment, let out a blood-chilling scream. The tea and toast she had been carrying went everywhere, Dirk barked madly on the other side of the library door and Mark Antony ran under the day bed. In a trice Cordelia was on her stomach in the dust, with only her legs sticking out, weeping words of blandishment.

I closed the front door. Rupert, Archie and I stood together in the hall, our faces dappled by the light from the chandelier that swung in the draught. In my heartfelt relief and gratitude I wanted to hug them both, but feared even the chastest embrace from a woman might be repugnant.

'How did you manage it?' I asked.

'Rupert was im*mense*ly brave,' said Archie.

'You mean – Dex was violent?'

'He *reeked* of pickled onions.'

'You went to the Eight Bells in Wapping?'

'A thoroughly *fourth*-rate pub,' Archie said while Rupert applied a handkerchief to his scratches.

'But how did you persuade him to hand over Mark Antony?' A terrible thought occurred. 'You didn't have to give him two thousand pounds?'

'Certainly not,' said Rupert. 'I offered him fifty. I pointed

234

out that it was not my cat and I was indifferent to its fate. If he preferred to wring its neck and forgo the money, that was fine by me. He blustered for a while but when he saw I meant it, he changed his tune. He said we could have the vicious animal and welcome.'

'He took us to his lodgings in a neighbouring street,' continued Archie. 'A *hell*hole, smelling of *gas* and *lav*atories. Charles Dickens would have written an exposé immediately. The cat was shut up in a cupboard.'

'How can people be so cruel?' I was unable to prevent a few tears, of anger and relief. 'Shall I get some sticking plaster and Dettol?'

'Don't bother,' said Rupert coolly. 'My great consolation is that, judging from the state of Dex's hands, Mark Antony was an unco-operative room-mate.'

'Here he is!' Cordelia scooped him out from under the day-bed. 'Oh, poor, sweet darling! He's just skin and bone. I'm going to take him downstairs at once and find him something lovely to eat.'

Ophelia came downstairs, a pair of shoes in her hand, just as Dirk increased the volume of his protest to *sforzatissimo tonante*.

'Harriet! That wretched animal! Look what he's done! Forty pounds from Chiaralino, the new shop in Bond Street. I only bought them yesterday and – Oh!' She paused when she saw Rupert and Archie in the hall. Then she threw up her chin. 'You needn't look so stern. I can hardly go about with bare feet, can I? And if the clients see me wearing horrid, cheap things they'll think I don't know any better.'

'I'm not looking stern,' said Rupert. 'This is my usual expression.'

'All right, I'll say I'm sorry,' said Ophelia very grumpily. 'I knew I shouldn't have bought them but everything's so beastly at home and they were so divine and I wanted to cheer myself up. And now they're spoiled. He's chewed one heel practically off!'

Rupert looked at his watch. 'Nine o'clock. We must go.'

'We've an appointment with Vera Vice,' said Archie excitedly. 'Dex's fingerprints will be all over the ransom letter.'

'Vera Vice?'

'Your life has been *too* sheltered Harriet. It's slang for the vice squad.'

I followed them to the front door. 'But we haven't thanked you properly.' I caught Ophelia's arm as she was about to go back upstairs. 'Rupert and Archie have rescued Mark Antony. Wasn't it marvellous? They went all the way to Wapping to a dreadful pub and gave a hateful man fifty pounds! It was the kindest thing anyone has ever done for me.' Greatly daring, I approached Rupert, stood on tiptoe and kissed his cheek. 'I shall remember it all my life.'

Rupert looked down at me, his eyes cold and sceptical. Archie, on the other hand, put his arm about my waist, gave me a brotherly squeeze and offered his cheek with every appearance of complaisance.

'Fifty pounds!' Ophelia's tone was regretful. She glanced down at the ruined shoe in her hand. Then she smiled and looked suddenly beautiful and kind. 'That was decent of you, Rupert. I can't pretend to be particularly fond of animals but I shouldn't have liked anything unpleasant to happen to him.'

Rupert gave a half-smile. 'How are you surviving employment?'

'It's perfectly foul getting up in the morning. It's completely dark, you know, at half-past seven.' I thought I detected something like a flash of amusement in Rupert's slanting dark eyes. I might have been mistaken. 'But actually,' Ophelia went on in considering tones, 'it's really very interesting. The job, I mean. People are extraordinarily unsure when it comes to

236

matters of taste and very happy to be told what they ought to have. I enjoy that.'

'One's *clothes* may be a moment's aberration,' said Archie, 'but one's *draw*ing room is one's character revealed in *all* its nakedness.'

'Supposing you don't happen to be interested in the way things look?' I asked.

'Then the *mis*erable deficiency will be exposed beyond the *shad*ow of a doubt.'

The telephone rang. Ophelia, who was nearest, picked up the receiver. 'Hello? Who did you say? Oh, how are you? This is Ophelia. Do you want to speak to my mother? Oh.' She sounded surprised. 'She's here. Hold on.' She held the receiver towards me. 'For you, Harriet. It's Max Frensham.'

SIXTEEN

'This is fun,' said Max. 'I'm feeling better already.' He looked to me in the pink of health. When I had tried to refuse his invitation to dinner, his voice on the telephone had taken on subtle inflections of melancholy. He had made considerate attempts to disguise his disappointment but the more charming he was, the more guilty I felt. Unlike the rest of the cast of *King Lear*, who had been richly inventive with their excuses, Max had been several times to see my father in prison and had been generous with books, wine and cigars. I had accepted his invitation at last, out of a sense of obligation. It was not that I did not like Max. On the contrary, I was aware that he was a very attractive man. But I had not wanted to desert Mark Antony on the first evening of his return.

'It's wonderful to be able to relax.' Max smiled at me. 'It's been a frantic day. Now what will you have?'

I was not feeling particularly relaxed. When Max had suggested a quiet little supper I had imagined a friendly bistro, not the *Cinq Tours*, where there seemed to be two waiters for every guest and my shabby appearance was reflected *ad nauseam* in the mirrored walls and even in the domed carving trolley. I was thankful that yards of starched napery hid my denim skirt and scuffed boots.

Max was looking spruce and expensive. His shirt, his tie, his suit all looked as though they had just emerged from cellophane. It was not quite in the English style. I remembered that his wife was from New Zealand, which would explain it. His long curling hair was a shade of chestnut any woman would have killed for. The dent at the end of his nose was fascinating.

'*Eh bien, Monsieur.*' An important-looking man with fierce eyes appeared beside our table, with a notebook and pencil in his hand. 'May I soo-gest for Madame ze oyster cocktails to begin?'

We never had oysters at home. Maria-Alba's childhood had frequently been blighted by eating things fished out of the Bay of Naples, and in consequence she thought all molluscs were *malsano*. It was time I threw off the indoctrination of my early years. Besides, I had a craven desire to conciliate this panjandrum whose very moustaches seemed to disdain my lack of sophistication. 'Well. Yes, please –'

'And would Madame care for the *filets de levraut chasseur* to follow?'

'What is that, exactly?'

'It eez the tiny baby hare cook wiz brandy and wine –'

'Oh no, thank you.' I have always been very fond of hares.

'Non?' The *maître d'hôtel*'s look grew cold. 'Then perhaps Madame would enjoy ze *pieds et langue d'agneau*? Eez lamb's feets and tongue –'

I shook my head.

'*Eh bien*, we have *cochon de lait Saint-Fortunat*. Eez little peeg taken from its muzzer after few days and roast wiz chestnuts.' Visions of tiny creatures with milky lips, woken from innocent slumber to be butchered for the dinner table,

239

made my mind recoil. I shook my head again. 'I have eet! Madame will enjoy ze *crêtes de coq à l'aurore*. It eez the crests of the young cocks – how you say, combs – cooked with ze kidneys and ze truffles. Very light and deelicious – a favourite dish of the great Escoffier –'

'Oh, no, I really couldn't!'

He frowned awfully at the point of his pencil. Then he turned to Max. 'Perraps sir can soo-gest somzing for ze young lady?'

'We'll both have *sole meunière* and a green salad.'

He wrote down our order with the corners of his mouth turned down in disgust. Then he snapped his fingers to summon the sommelier.

'What do you think?' said Max, when we were alone. 'One of those fish with a huge lower lip that feeds on the bottom of the ocean?'

'Oh, no! The sole will be fine, thank you.'

'I meant the head waiter.' Max imitated his frown so perfectly that I laughed and felt happier. 'We ought to have gone somewhere else. They're getting too big for their boots.'

'It looks terribly expensive.' These days I was unable to buy so much as a postage stamp without worrying. Max lifted his eyebrows and I blushed, realising I had been gauche, perhaps even rude.

'Don't you like expensive restaurants?' he asked, having sent the wine waiter, possibly an even more august personage than the *maître d'hôtel*, for champagne.

'Well. I hardly ever go to them. Never, to be absolutely truthful. Pa says we children cramp his style. He says he can't flirt properly under our disapproving eyes.'

'Don't your boyfriends take you to decent places?'

I smiled when I thought of Dodge at the *Cinq Tours*. 'I've only had one real boyfriend and he was an anarchist.'

Max looked marvellous when he laughed. His teeth were

240

perfect. 'No, I see. It wouldn't be quite the thing, would it? You amaze me, Harriet. Only one boyfriend? But you're so beautiful.'

No man had ever complimented me on my appearance. Pa had several times said it was a pity I had not inherited my mother's looks. Dodge thought it was a derogation of purpose to give thought to trivial externals, such as whether someone was beautiful or not. Though I noticed he always looked at pretty girls if there were any. He had said once that he loved me because my mind was unsullied. Also that I was remarkably free from artifice, for a female. I much preferred to be told that I was beautiful.

'I've never minded not going out. I like being at home.'

'There must be another reason.'

The memory of Hugo Dance loomed and at once I pushed the image away. 'How lovely these flowers are. Lilies of the valley are my favourite.' I lowered my face to the arrangement in the silver vase. 'Oh, the scent! And in November!' I was about to say how much they must have cost but I pulled myself up in time.

'I'm sorry.' Max looked suddenly serious. 'It's none of my business.'

'What?'

'Nothing. Let's forget all about it. I want you to be happy. Tell me about your new job.'

I expect it was the champagne, and the fact that it was the fourth time of telling, but I seemed to myself to be actually quite witty as I recounted my experiences at the *Brixton Mercury*. At least Max did not looked bored. I was about to start on the séance, the recital of which I was confident I had got down to a fine art, when the oyster cocktails arrived. I had hoped they would be mostly cocktail and not much oyster but it was very much the other way round. I prodded one with my fork and it seemed to shrink up.

'Are they raw?' I asked Max.

'Not only raw but breathing.' Then he saw my face. 'Sorry. I didn't mean to put you off. Never mind. Don't eat them.'

'Oh, I must. I'm sure they cost – I mean, I hate to waste things.'

'I'll have yours if that'll make you feel better. Really, it isn't important in the least.'

I put down my fork. 'It's very hypocritical of me to mind. I really must face up to brutal truths like the food chain.'

'"But four young oysters hurried up, All eager for the treat. Their coats were brushed, their faces washed, Their shoes were clean and neat – And this was odd, because, you know, They hadn't any feet."'

Max's expression was teasing. It was lovely being with someone good-humoured. Dodge was always serious and in earnest about things. I could not remember him laughing at anything, except once when we went to see a Marx brothers film. He had been beside himself with mirth and then it was I who was straining to smile, with that unpleasant sense of alienation you get when you can't see the joke.

'That's "The Walrus and the Carpenter"; isn't it? I've always loved *Through the Looking-Glass*. Rupert gave it to me for my birthday years ago.'

'Rupert Wolvespurges? I'd no idea you were intimates.'

'Oh yes, when I was a child. But there was a falling-out. We've only just met again. Now I don't feel I know him at all.'

'I don't imagine many people know him very well.'

'Don't you like him?'

'I don't *dis*like him. As I said, one can't get near him. Of course, he doesn't like actors because they court him. I can understand that. Now he's directing as well as reviewing people are willing to wash his socks *and* blow on them until they're dry. I prefer Archie. He's much more easy-going. And the truth is, I'm really much too lazy to make the kind of effort that would convince Rupert I wasn't trying to butter him up.'

Max smiled at me and I found myself thinking lucky, lucky Caroline. I noticed that the woman on the next table was shooting covert glances at Max while her companion talked.

'I didn't know Rupert was actually directing plays.'

On those brief occasions that I saw Rupert we always talked about my life and, by implication, its shortcomings. So subordinate was my position as almswoman and apologist for the Byng family that I would not have dared to ask him questions about himself. It would have seemed as impertinent as asking the Queen whether she was weary of exercising the royal prerogative and becoming bored by the Duke of Edinburgh.

'He did a very good *Hedda Gabler* in New York recently. And last year he produced a controversial but respected *Fidelio* for Opera of the West.'

'Gosh!' I was impressed and ridiculously gratified, though not by any stretch of the imagination could Rupert's consequence reflect any glory on me.

'Hello, hello, hello?' said a voice at my elbow. 'Is this London's best-kept secret? Don't worry, I shan't tell a soul.'

Bron, looking elegant in a dinner jacket, had on his arm a woman with fluffy hair and a revealing bronze lamé dress. I felt very conscious of the ginger cat hairs on my black polo-necked jersey.

'Hello, Elsa, hello, Bron.' Max stood up and introduced me to Elsa. He had marvellous manners. Dodge thought standing up for women, holding doors for them and guiding them across busy roads was an insult to their intelligence and competence. Until this evening I had agreed with him.

'I can see we're *de trop*,' said Bron, absently running his hand to and fro over Elsa's bottom, as though he was not in

243

the middle of a large and crowded dining room. 'We'll push on to our table. The champers must be getting warm. By the way, Max, I'm urgently seeking employment. You might put in a word for me with your uncle. Max's uncle's a very important man in the Foreign Office,' he explained to Elsa. 'Though I shouldn't care to be sent somewhere outlandish. Paris or Rome would be fine. Madrid, just about OK.'

'I hope Bron isn't really having champagne.' I watched them waving to acquaintances as they wove between tables.

'Are you hard up, Harriet?' Max put down his fork and laid his warm hand on mine. I noticed his nails were elegantly shaped and clean. The strain of having an employer to satisfy had driven me back to old, bad habits and mine were looking ragged and nibbled. 'I wish you'd trust me. I could lend you something to tide you over.'

'It's terribly kind of you. We're managing, just about. But Bron's already lost his job and he's got to get another quickly or –' I had been about to mention Rupert but suddenly I thought he might not care to have tidings of his philanthropy broadcast. 'Pa's never been very good with money and Ma's even more hopeless.'

'Well, promise you'll let me know. There's nothing I wouldn't do for Waldo. I had my first part in one of his plays. *Twelfth Night*. He was Orsino and I was Valentine. I had something like a dozen lines. When it came to the opening night I was so frightened I could hardly walk. My knees were literally knocking together and my face was twitching, like this.' Max blinked and grimaced, making me laugh. The woman on the next table looked absolutely fascinated. 'Your father held out his hand to show me that he was trembling too. "This," he said, "is the capacity to feel, made visible. Without it we cannot make magic. We'll weave the spell together." Do you know, whenever I've had stage fright I've always thought of Waldo and it's helped no end.'

244

I was accustomed to people idolising my father. I could not remember a time when he had not been the centre of attention, almost an object of worship. But these days, hearing praise of him was like a drug of which I could never have enough. Max seemed very willing to feed my addiction. This, combined with the relief of knowing Mark Antony to be safe, made me happier than I had been for weeks. At any time, in fact, since my father's arrest. The sole arrived, glistening with speckles of brown butter, and was delicious. Max described his early career with much wit and, for an actor, a most unusual modesty.

'How's Caroline?' I asked while we were eating the most heavenly cold, crunchy *meringue glacées*. I had been putting off mentioning her, for no good reason that I could think of.

'She flew to Auckland this afternoon to stay with her sister. I think the change'll do her good.' There was a pause. 'Things have been a bit – tough, recently. I expect it's my fault. Of course, acting's never going to pay as well as a department store. What a nuisance money is!'

'Oh, isn't it!' I agreed fervently.

Max had picked me up that evening in a racy sports car. I don't know anything about cars but something about the leather seats and the feeling of being punched in the spine when he accelerated, suggested this was a luxury model. Max had expensive tastes and Caroline must be tired of paying for them. I envisaged sordid rows about bills across the breakfast table. My exhilaration dwindled a little.

'The trouble is, we like quite different things. I'm not boring you?'

I shook my head.

'Caroline can't understand that I'd rather do without something than have my wife pay for it. She's incredibly generous, gives me clothes, cars, paintings, books, anything I could possibly want. But I'm a simple man, really. Before I married her I used to live in jeans and ancient jerseys and drive a clapped-out Morris Minor. Perhaps it's disloyal of me to say so but I really don't like so much emphasis on consumption. I don't mind if our furniture's scruffy, I'd just as soon eat boiled eggs as caviar and I don't want to fly about the world to lie on the private beaches of smart hotels. I'd rather sit under a tree in a field reading poetry.'

'Oh, so would I!'

'What sort of poetry do you like?'

This was the beginning of a most satisfactory conversation. Max turned out to like all the same poets. He quoted his favourite bit of Keats, from *Endymion*, and the woman on the next table gave up any pretence of not listening. Max's voice was beautiful and full of expression. He said the lines as though he really felt them. I could have listened for hours. After that we talked about anything and everything as though we had known each other for years and I was astonished to find, when I looked at my watch, that it was half-past ten.

'I must go. I promised Cordelia I wouldn't be late.' She had disapproved of my desertion of Mark Antony so soon after his return and I had pacified her by swearing to cut the evening short. I had not realised then how much I was going to enjoy it.

'That's the youngest one? Is she always so tyrannical?'

'It's because of our cat.'

I explained about Mark Antony's abduction and restoration. Max was sympathetic and agreed it was particularly important not to break one's word to children. He summoned a waiter for the bill. When he stood with his hand on the back of my chair so he could pull it out for me, the woman on the next table practically bit the bowl off her spoon with longing. He took my elbow as we walked to the door and I was conscious of female attention from every side. I expect they thought I was his kid sister and he was being kind to me.

'To tell the truth,' Max said as we purred through the traffic on our way back to Blackheath, 'things have been very bad lately between Caroline and me. I suppose this sounds like a variation on "my wife doesn't understand me".'

'Not at all,' I said politely, watching the first spots of rain begin to trickle down the windscreen. They sparkled colourfully, changing from red to yellow and to green with the traffic lights.

'There isn't anyone I can talk to about it.' Max changed up as he sped across the junction. 'All my friends are more or less Caroline's friends too. You know what gossips actors are. And they're mostly so insecure that they're delighted to have something to bitch about. I'd trust Waldo, of course, but at the moment it would be unfair to burden him with my own problems. The fact is,' he slowed to let an old woman and a dog over a zebra crossing, 'Caroline tried to kill herself a few days ago.'

'Oh! Oh, I'm so sorry!' I looked at him with concern. His expression was blurred by rolling shadows but I saw that his eyes were bright.

'She'd taken barbiturates and she'd been drinking. She knocks back a bottle of whisky a day now, has done for several months. Luckily I got home unexpectedly early. I found Caroline unconscious in the bathroom. I called an ambulance and they pumped out her stomach and – well, I needn't go into details. She was pretty groggy for twenty-four hours but she's all right now.'

'Poor Caroline!' I said. 'Could it have been an accident?'

'She'd written me a note. Saying she was sorry and that she loved me but she felt she was a drag on my life.' He was silent for a moment while negotiating a right-hand turn. A beam of light fell on his hands as they turned the wheel

247

and I experienced something that was so unfamiliar and, in the circumstances, so entirely inappropriate that I felt a sense of shock. It was desire. When I had made love with Dodge I had wanted to please him. I enjoyed the feeling that he wanted me, that for a while I was his equal. I had felt no physical sensations but a vague periodic flutter of excitement. But just then, when I had looked at Max's hands, I thought I had something of a clue to what all the fuss was about.

'I didn't want her to go to Auckland on her own but she said she was homesick.' I jerked my mind back to what he was saying. He drew up outside our house and we sat for a while, the engine running, the windscreen wipers making streaky fan shapes in the flowing water. 'Of course I feel as guilty as hell. When she asks me if I love her I always say yes. And I try to make it sound convincing. But I suppose there's a part of her that doesn't want to be convinced. Someone who's depressed seeks a rational explanation for their state of mind, don't they?'

Did he mean, then, that he did not love Caroline? I watched the fan shapes dissolving between each wipe and tried to think of something comforting to say. 'It's torture watching someone you love suffer and not be able to help them, isn't it?'

'You're thinking of Waldo, aren't you?' Of course I had been. 'What's happening now? Are the police any nearer the truth?'

I told him what the inspector had said the last time we had spoken.

'It's an unhappy time for both of us,' said Max, taking out his handkerchief to wipe condensation from the inside of the windscreen. 'But tonight's been a wonderful respite. I hope I haven't spoiled the evening by burdening you with confidences.'

'Oh no! I've enjoyed myself so much. It was very kind of you to take me somewhere so elegant and glamorous.'

'And you'd have much preferred somewhere less pretentious and more interesting. It was a mistake but I hope to put it right. I've honestly never known a woman who didn't feel that her value ought to be measured in pound notes. The truth is I haven't known that many women. I'm rather shy though I try to put on a good front.'

He smiled. I saw the lamplight tremble in his eyes. It is extraordinary how one can get the wrong idea about people. Before that evening I had believed Max to be something of a lady-killer.

'Honestly, I loved it.'

'You're an adorable liar.' He leaned towards me and put his hand on my arm. 'If I promise not to bore you with my problems will you let me take you somewhere we'll both like much better?'

'That would be lovely. I mean – of course, you haven't been.' There was a silence filled with anticipation of an indecipherable kind. His face was very close to mine, his eyes half-closed. I looked away and felt for the door-handle. 'I'd better go in now.' He made a movement to open his door. 'Oh, don't get out, please! You'll get so wet. It's coming down in torrents. I can just run in.'

'Let me escort you under an umbrella.'

'No, really, I like rain.'

'All right.' He put out his hand to open my door from the inside and his arm brushed against my breasts. 'Run in then, my beautiful amphibian.'

I was glad it was dark and raining and he could not possibly see the expression of idiotic gratification on my face.

'What are you looking so starry-eyed about?' Ophelia's reflection appeared behind mine in the hall mirror.

'Nothing.' I was embarrassed to be caught staring at myself.

'Where've you been?'

'I've been out to dinner with Max Frensham.'

'Really?' I could see that Ophelia thought I might be joking. 'Whatever for?'

'Not *for* anything particularly. Just to talk.'

'Where did you go?'

'The *Cinq Tours*.' I was conscious of a certain satisfaction. I rarely had the chance to impress Ophelia.

'Harriet! Not dressed like that! A cross between a refusenik and a Sunday school teacher. Poor Max!'

'Sometimes I envy people who don't have sisters.'

'I know just what you mean.' Ophelia and I looked angrily at each and then curiosity got the better of her annoyance. 'So what did you talk about?'

'Nothing important. My job, how he started in acting, poetry, that sort of thing.'

'How riveting!' Ophelia allowed her eyelids to droop and gave a pretend yawn.

'And we talked a bit about Caroline.'

'She's a sot.'

'She's very unhappy.'

'I expect I'd be unhappy if my husband took girls half his age to the *Cinq Tours* the minute my back was turned. Particularly if I looked like Caroline.'

'She's generally considered good-looking. And I'm not half his age. He's thirty-four and I'm twenty-two.'

'You're not, are you? I must have missed your birthday again. You don't look twenty-two, anyway. Caroline Frensham has a nose a champion pig would be proud of. It's obvious that Max married her for her money. But what can he want with you?'

This was just what I had been wondering when I looked at myself in the mirror. 'I don't believe it was anything to do with money. You always think the worst of everyone.'

'Oh, don't lecture me, for God's sake! Your precious

inspector has only just left. I believe he's trying to break the record for the longest sermon ever preached.'

'Inspector Foy was here, this evening?'

'Rupert told him about his adventures in Wapping with the cat-napper. The inspector waxed wroth that he hadn't been let in on it from the beginning. I think he wanted to give you a nice cosy ticking-off. He looked annoyed when I said you'd gone out. I explained that I was entirely ignorant of any of the circumstances but he was determined to have an audience for his display of temper. Ma and Ronnie were in the coal-hole, watching one of Ronnie's old films. They made me promise to say they were out.'

'You didn't make him cross?'

'I?' Ophelia opened wide her wonderful blue eyes. 'I listened to the first few sentences to make sure that there was nothing worth attending to. Then I interrupted very briefly to ask if he'd mind if I stretched out on the sofa and closed my eyes while he talked, as I'd had a long and very tiring day. What there was in *that* to make him so ratty, I've no idea.' Ophelia smiled slowly as though the memory of his anger was pleasant.

'Hat? Are you awake?'

It was Portia's voice. I dragged my eyelids apart and saw the familiar dark shapes of my bedroom. I lifted myself on to my elbow. 'What time is it?

'Six, near enough.'

'In the morning?'

'Yes, you clot. If it were six at night you'd hardly be in bed, would you?'

I shut my eyes for a few blissful seconds and then opened them again. 'What's the matter?'

'Nothing. But I've only just got back and I couldn't possibly sleep. And you know you're always worried about your alarm clock not going off at six thirty so I thought I'd pop up and make sure.'

Back? Back from where? Then I remembered that Portia had been to a party with Suke. I thought for a while longer. 'It's Saturday.'

'Oh, damn, so it is. I'd forgotten. Sorry.' Then, when I said nothing because I was thinking longingly of being allowed to go back to sleep, Portia said in her special repentant voice, which we both knew was entirely put-on but somehow it always worked, 'Can I talk to you anyway?'

'OK. Keep your voice down, though. And don't put the light on. Mark Antony's asleep in the crook of my arm. He sicked up his supper but he did actually give two little purrs before going to sleep. Careful!'

Dirk gave a yelp as Portia trod on him.

'God! Sorry. I can't see a thing. And it's perishing in here. How do you stand it?'

'See if you can get the heater going.'

'What do I do?'

I explained the idiosyncrasies of the stove and soon we had a cheerful glow that outweighed the disadvantage of a penetrating oily smell.

'What's this? I'll sling it round my shoulders.'

It was my writing robe. Before getting into bed I had tried to write a poem about the evening and what I felt about Max. In vain. It sounded like an entry in the In Memoriam column of the *Brixton Mercury*. 'Dear Mum we miss you very much We miss your voice and kindly touch We miss your face and other things, Now you've got a pair of wings.' Honestly, that was one of the better ones.

'I've had an extraordinary evening.' I heard the excitement in Portia's voice. 'The party was terrific. It was held in this marvellous house in a sort of park. I've no idea where because Suke drove and we were stopped by a policeman because one of her headlights had gone. He was very sarcastic at first, the way they always are, and asked us if we normally drove about in our underwear in midwinter. Did I tell you it was fancy dress? We went as Orpheus and Euridice. Suke made me a dress out of an old sheet, with one bare shoulder and a silver girdle and a chaplet of roses. She was wearing the tiniest tunic and a curly black wig, with thick black lines round her eyes to make them doe-like, as on Greek vases. Her nose has a very straight bridge so it couldn't be more perfect . . .'

I must have dozed off for a few minutes. Portia was still talking when I came to. '. . . and grapevines trained right across this vast trellis ceiling with real grapes – I ate a few to see – and they'd made a sort of lagoon in the conservatory and there was a man dressed up as Neptune serving drinks . . .'

I was swimming in water that was wonderfully warm and people were cheering. I was swimming for the glory of St Frideswide's and suddenly I was able to do a miraculous crawl, lifting my head above the water at every fourth stroke which I had never been able to do before without nearly drowning. Sister Imelda was running up and down the edge of the school swimming baths, trying to scoop me out of the water with a giant hook . . .

'. . . so when we'd had enough to dancing we explored the house and on the landing, by a window that looked down to a lake with the moon floating on it, Suke put her hands on my shoulders and kissed me.'

I was suddenly much more awake. 'What was it like, being kissed by a woman?'

Portia sighed. 'Luckily I'd had a lot to drink or I'd probably have panicked. Her mouth was very light and soft and at first it just felt friendly and nice. As though we were chums. And of course not scratchy. But then she put her hand on one of my breasts and I had several seconds of absolute panic when I felt like a fly must feel on the end of a chameleon's tongue – trapped and going down for the last time. Then Suke whispered, "Oh, Portia, I've fallen in love with you." Hearing her voice, a woman's voice, made me feel safe again. I mean, you trust a woman in a way you'd never trust a man. In an extraordinary way it was as though I was kissing another self, a part of me, so I felt sort of safe. She went on talking to me, reassuring me, and everything she did was so delicate, so gentle – not pushy and urgent, like a man. It was quite different. A man only pretends he cares about you. And you have to pretend to believe him because otherwise it feels so – bleak. Suke made me feel loved for the very first time. And then, because there wasn't any forcing or grabbing, I felt it too – love, I mean. And gratitude, really, for making the past seem much less important. We danced for hours in each other's arms up and down the landing, and I stopped even thinking about . . .' Portia shuddered. 'It was such a relief. I only thought about her and I felt if someone so beautiful and good loved me then perhaps I wasn't so –'

Portia stopped talking suddenly and I guessed she was close to tears. She clasped her forearms and put back her head as though to recapture the ecstasy of the moment, and the sequins and lozenges on my writing robe winked in the light from the stove. She let out another sigh as though from a full heart. 'Well. Now I know. I'm a lesbian.'

Clearly so momentous a declaration required proper recognition. I searched for something intelligent and positive to say. It was difficult, so early in the day. 'Darling Portia.' I stretched out my free hand and patted her knee. 'I hope you and Suke will be very, very happy.' I was aware, even as I said it, that this response was paltry.

SEVENTEEN

'Look at this!' Cordelia kicked the front door shut behind her and negotiated Dirk's prancing with care. She held a bowl filled with flowers. 'It came just now by a special van. Isn't it pretty?'

'Did I hear the bell?' Ophelia emerged from the drawing room. 'Lilies of the valley! Peregrine's taste is improving. I had to give the carnations he sent to the woman who collects for the blind. Good Lord! This bowl is *famille verte*!' She looked triumphant. 'He's going to propose.'

Cordelia read the card. 'It says, "For Harriet, with my apologies and love." Look, they're real little plants in earth like a garden. Hat!' Her eyes gleamed with inspiration. 'You could put in a bit of mirror for a lake and make some flamingos out of Plasticene. I've got a bit of bright pink left you can have for the legs.'

'Well! What an extraordinary thing!' Ophelia was evidently disappointed, and I did not blame her. Between the stalks of trembling, scented bells the earth was covered by velvety emerald moss, charmingly complemented by the paler green of the flowered porcelain. 'Apologies for what?' asked Ophelia. 'It must have been one hell of a *faux pas*. That bowl's worth at least a hundred pounds. Who sent it? It doesn't look like something Grudge would choose.'

Ophelia had called Dodge 'Grudge' from the moment of meeting him at that unfortunate supper party when he had so conspicuously sulked and glowered. I had long since given up protesting. She took the card from Cordelia. 'Max Frensham!' She looked at me meditatively for a moment, then took the bowl from Cordelia. 'You're bound to drop it. I think it will look best on the red lacquer desk.' I followed her meekly into the drawing room. 'Yes. It covers that chipped place beautifully. Now, you little ass,' she fixed me with a look of disapproval, 'you'd better listen to me. Don't even con*side*r having an affair with a married man.'

I was surprised. Usually Ophelia had only contempt for conventional moral codes. I stood in attentive silence while Ophelia opened her budget on matters adulterous. 'They hardly ever leave their wives. The dog always returns to his vomit and it's the same thing with a man. He feels safe with the poor drudge who's willing to wash his underpants and have his ghastly mother for Christmas. But if he does leave her for you, then he feels quite justified in whining non-stop about his crippling guilt complex, while trying to throw all the blame on you. And when she rings in tears at two in the morning you're supposed not to mind having your sleep ruined. She'll send you vituperative letters and tell poisonous stories about you to anyone who'll listen. That's when she's not following you about and making scenes in Harvey Nichols. Worse, there may exist some disgusting sprogs, the spit of their mother. Either you have to spend weekends on your own or put up with the little beasts eyeing you as though you were an acid-bath murderer, while he spends ridiculous amounts of money on them to shut them up.' Ophelia spoke with unusual energy. Evidently this was a subject about which she had strong feelings.

I spoke firmly and I meant it. 'I'm not going to have an affair with Max.'

Naturally neither Ophelia nor Cordelia could be expected to keep to themselves the interesting news that I had a new suitor. Reactions were various and characteristic. Though Max had forever lowered his value in my mother's eyes for not paying court to *her*, she was prepared to acknowledge that he would be able to give me a little of the town bronze I so observably lacked.

'He's certainly good-looking, though a little effete for my taste,' she articulated carefully through her veil. 'I prefer something more rugged.' Ronnie expanded his chest and clenched his jaw. 'But,' continued my mother, 'Max should be able to teach you something of the ways of the world. Blushing, breathless innocence is perfectly *convenable* in young girls from country parsonages, whose only accomplishments are grooming dogs, serving over-arm at tennis and making a fourth at bridge, but you, Harriet, despite your social advantages, have elevated naivety to an art form.'

She made an exit, which was her own kind of art form, before I could think of anything to say in self-defence.

'Don't take it to heart.' Ronnie patted my arm kindly as he followed my mother. 'She's nervous. We've agreed to take the wrappings off after lunch. Promise you'll enthuse. As for Max Frensham – one should never look a gift horse in the mouth.'

'Why didn't you tell me about Max?' Portia asked me, after she had been entertained by Cordelia with a highly embellished account of my romantic adventures.

'There's nothing *to* tell. We had dinner together and that's all. Surely a man and a woman can be friends without everyone thinking of sex? He has a perfectly good wife. I don't expect he'll ask me again.'

'Come and see what he sent her,' Cordelia persisted.

We stood together in the drawing room and admired the bowl and the flowers.

'Oh, Hat!' Portia was impressed. 'You flipping little liar! And you expect us to believe that he doesn't want to get into your pants. I should think he'll be exciting, as men go. If you can stand all that scratchy stubble and sweatiness and seeing his rather revolting equipment.'

Portia had the exhortatory zeal of the newly converted.

'I've only ever seen Bron's cock,' said Cordelia thoughtfully. 'It's really small and floppy, like on statues. Not at all like the photograph Tania Vickers showed us in a magazine she pinched from her dad's desk –'

A smart slap on the side of her head cut her off mid-speech. 'You little stinker!' We had been standing with our backs to the door and had not heard Bron come in. 'If you ever repeat that I shall tear out your tongue, mince it up, fry it in butter and eat it smeared on toast.'

'Ow!' Cordelia rubbed her ear and glared at him, indignantly. 'That hurt!'

'Let it be a warning to you, you treacherous little blighter, not to discuss your brother's genitalia in public.'

'I only said it was small – ow, ow, *ow*!'

After Portia and I had intervened on Cordelia's behalf and she had gone away to sulk, Bron pinged his finger against the bowl.

'That'll fetch a bob or two. If he's really keen on you, perhaps he'll let me borrow his Aston Martin sometimes. You might ask him again about that job in the FO. Soften him up a bit first. Timing is everything, I've found.' He put on his worldly-wise look, which he had perfected playing Lord Henry Wotton in *The Picture of Dorian Gray*, when he had belonged to a touring company two years ago.

'I'm sorry to be disobliging but I have no influence over

Max.' I spoke a little coldly. 'I'm not going to have an affair with him.'

'That's sisters all over,' said Bron bitterly. 'Self, self, self. I'm not suggesting you devote all your working hours to it. You only have to get him into bed once. Tease him into a lather of desire and just before you let the fox go to earth, pop the question. I don't think it's much to ask.'

'You make it sound so enticing,' said Portia sarcastically.

'I heard that about lathers of desire and foxes,' called Cordelia, through the crack in the door.

Dirk was so excited by this disembodied voice that he knocked over the shepherdess. I was able to put an end to the speculation about my putative lovemaking by rescuing her head from beneath the chest against which Hamlet had once leaned, bemoaning the beastliness of life and wondering whether to put an end to it, or not.

I went upstairs to my attic room. Mark Antony was asleep on one of my jerseys before the paraffin heater. He refused to have anything to do with the four-poster Cordelia and I had made for him. Our hurt feelings had been assuaged by Dirk's electing to sleep with his head within it. It was all he could squeeze in for he had grown considerably larger in the last two weeks. His jowls were droopier, his ears longer, his chest more massive. I had looked up Cornish terriers in my *Observer's Book of Dogs* but they had not included the breed, presumably because it was so rare. I knew I must apply myself to instilling some discipline. After a day of the literary equivalent of picking oakum – that is, sorting out the ads section of the *Brixton Mercury* – it was disheartening to be met with a long and varied list of complaints about Dirk's behaviour.

Working conditions had taken a definite turn for the worse after Eileen and Muriel had circulated the news that I was the daughter of the celebrated actor-murderer. I had swapped inferiority for notoriety. The editor, Mr Walpole, who hitherto had been just a shadowy profile on the frosted glass of his office door, sent for me to ask if I would write an exclusive feature for the *Mercury* about what it was like to be the offspring of a crazed exterminator. These were not his actual words but, by implication, it was what he thought. I asked if I could think about it and rang Rupert immediately for guidance. Would he consider I was failing to keep my part of our financial bargain if I refused to write the article, thereby risking the sack? Or should I take this opportunity to declare my father's innocence to the world?

Rupert told me not to be a little idiot. I was not to say anything to anyone, let alone write it. The case was *sub judice* and for all he knew, I would be running foul of the law. Far from persuading people of my father's innocence I would create damaging speculation and make things worse. He said he would speak to Walpole, and rang off without saying goodbye. I was left with the feeling that I had behaved with wanton ineptitude. Anyway, Mr Walpole reverted to his former shadowy eminence and I did not hear from him again. Most of the rest of the staff confined their interest to staring a good deal and averting their gaze the minute our eyes met. A few were excited to a show of friendliness but when it became clear after a few days that I had nothing to tell them, their curiosity turned to resentment. Fortunately I was prevented from worrying about this by the daily struggle to remain employed.

When Mr Podmore had asked me to write a weekly article on haunted houses, I had imagined this would be the sum of my contribution to the paper and was consequently disappointed to be told I could have only one day a week away from the office for researching and writing up. On the remaining four days I was to make myself useful and learn the trade, which meant doing the jobs Muriel and Eileen most disliked.

Advising people how best to word an advertisement for 'baby bath, v.g.c. pushchair with hood, navy, exercise bike, as new', palled after two days and the lists of dreary appurtenances and all that they said about adult life began to depress me. There was sporadic interest in entries like 'ventriloquist's dummy, suit novice', and 'silk top hat and tailcoat, much worn, hence bargain price'. Occasionally I was sent out on my own to cover the closing-down of a long-established corset factory or an evening of jujitsu organised to raise money for the scouts' outing, but anything at all interesting that happened in Brixton was bagged by Muriel and Eileen.

I put on my writing robe and threw a blanket round my shoulders, for the warmth from the paraffin heater did not quite reach my desk. I had discovered a block of marzipan, one of my favourite things to eat, in the cake tin in the larder. It was past its best but, thanks to Ronnie's tight grasp on the family purse strings, rations were short these days. I nibbled abstractedly. I was supposed to be fine-tuning an account of the senior citizens' tea-party I had attended, but my muse was uncooperative.

It had been an occasion to make one dread one's decline. The middle-aged women running the event spoke to their charges in hard-edged voices and exchanged glances of exasperation and contempt. The poor old things were bullied into joining in the songs played by 'Uncle Billy' on his electric organ. Half of them wanted to go to sleep, the other half to the lavatory. A few tried to rebel but were swiftly reprimanded. Uncle Billy, whose heart did not seem to be in it, had galloped through to the end of 'My Bonnie Lies over the Ocean' while quavering voices were still mumbling the first words. Greasy ham rolls and bitter-tasting fruit cake were handed round, and anyone who spilled their tea was roundly ticked off. Bleary eyes with down-turned lower lids stared in bewilderment as

261

impatient hands wiped their chins and whisked away their cups. Instructions to sit up and stop looking miserable were audible above the distorting amplification of 'Danny Boy'.

I ate some more marzipan. A piercing draught from an imperfectly fitting sash window made my eyes water. When the shortcomings of my working conditions were brought thus to my attention, I always thought of Dr Johnson, one of my heroes. He had laboured at his marvellous dictionary in an unheated garret, by the feeble light of the few candles he could afford, while balanced precariously on a chair with only three legs. Whether this was due to dire impoverishment or just perversity it was difficult to be sure but at least I could congratulate myself on a light bulb and a solid chair. I found an old pair of tights to stuff into the gap, searched my desk drawer for my writing mittens, which were my old school gloves with the fingers cut off, and came across Dodge's letters.

I was unable to resist looking at them again, though their contents were well known. They were mostly terse notes of instruction, devoid of expressions of love. Occasionally they said that he had been thinking about me. Once, when I had been in bed for a week with tonsillitis, he had written to say that he was missing me and enclosed a pressed dog rose. My happiness on receiving this testimony of devotion had been immense. I still had the dog rose enclosed between the pages of *Hard Times*. Had Dodge not disapproved altogether of reading fiction, I felt certain this was a novel he would have liked.

When I had received my marching orders a few weeks before, I had been unable even to glance at the letters without a fierce pain and a welling eye. But in a surprisingly short time – so short, actually, that I accused myself of lamentable shallowness – I stopped being altogether sorry that the affair was over. Now, as I reread Dodge's letters, I felt what could only be described as unqualified relief. I still thought of him with affection but the unremitting effort to be other than I was had been irksome. While I agreed wholeheartedly with his principles, I was too selfish to devote my life to the class struggle. Nor did I like to be constantly on the receiving end of disapproval and rebuke. The realisation that I need never again attempt to disarm the suspicions of the inhabitants of Owlstone Road made my spirits lift.

I wondered if this surge of optimism had anything to do with Max. I would have liked to have had the lilies of the valley in my room, adding what scent manufacturers would call 'floral notes' to the smell of hot, damp animal fur and paraffin, but I knew my family would put the wrong construction on their removal from the drawing room.

I recalled Max's face as clearly as I could, given the brief nature of our friendship, and felt an agreeable flutter of excitement. Then I tried hard to conjure up a picture of Caroline. I could only remember that she was slender and extremely well-dressed. And that during our only conversation, at Ma's birthday party in the summer, her eyes had roamed constantly, as if seeking someone more interesting to talk to. I felt an instinctive prejudice against her but the idea of adding to her unhappiness, perhaps even to the point of sending her back to the barbiturate bottle, horrified me. No, no, no! Without meaning to, I found I had spoken aloud. Dirk withdrew his muzzle enquiringly from the curtains of Mark Antony's bed and Mark Antony stretched out a protesting paw. Anyway, wasn't I forgetting something? Max had not asked me to assist him in breaking the seventh commandment. Probably the idea had never occured to him.

'Hat.' Portia tapped on the door. 'Max on the blower.'

'Tell him I'm out.'

'What's the verdict? I wish I'd been there.' Despite the shaven head and the paleness of his complexion my father seemed to have regained something of his old sparkle. His shoulders were braced and his eyes were bright. I wondered why. 'So thrilling, the moment of denouement. Like that great dramatic climax in *The Winter's Tale* when the curtain is drawn back to reveal the statue of Hermione. '"O! she's warm."' he boomed suddenly, making the woman next to us on the visitors' side of the table spill her tea. '"If this be magic, let it be an art Lawful as eating."'

'I nearly screamed when I saw Ronnie's nose.' Cordelia was sitting on my left.

'Thank goodness you didn't,' I said. 'The atmosphere was quite tense enough. Ma's mouth is quite a lot smaller than it used to be. Ronnie says it's very aristocratic.'

Actually it looked as though she were perpetually sucking a straw. The best that could be said of it was that it made the most of her cheekbones.

'It reminds me of my gym-bag, you know, all gathered up,' said Cordelia. 'The string's got into a knot and now I shall have to cut it to get my school plimsolls – Ah, ha! I thought it was small feet that showed you were highborn. You couldn't say Ronnie's new nose was aristocratic, could you? It's exactly like Judy Garland's.'

'No, really?' My father started to laugh, then straightened his face. 'Poor fellow.'

'It's much shorter than it was and quite startlingly retroussé,' I said.

'One is tempted to say "I told you so" but that would be ill-natured. I mustn't let myself become embittered by misfortune. I've argued with your mother so often about putting herself into the hands of quacks. For myself I am resolved to put up with the ravages of time.' He turned his head a little to the left to exhibit his famous profile. Dutifully we reassured him that his good looks were unimpaired by

264

the march of years, which was largely true. I thought this might be the right moment to disclose something that had been troubling me.

'Ronnie's going to take Ma away for Christmas. To a little hotel he knows in Cornwall, so they can get used to their new faces among strangers.'

My father continued to look unconcerned, though as he was a good actor this told me nothing. 'What does Rupert say? He's footing the bill, presumably.'

'No. Ronnie's going to pay. He says he's got a tiny nest egg he's been saving in case he becomes quite helpless when he gets old. He's like that old woman in *Our Mutual Friend* who had such a dread of the workhouse that she preferred to die under a hedge. In Ronnie's case it's the NHS he dreads. But he says he's prepared to run the risk of filth, degradation and neglect if it'll make Ma happy. After all, he said, he might simply drop down dead in the street and not need nursing.'

'Ma said with his mauve complexion and increasing paunch he was certain to have a heart attack or a stroke before he got to be really old,' put in Cordelia. 'Ronnie looked a bit put out.'

My father drew his handsome features into a frown and then his eyelids creased and the corners of his mouth turned up and he burst into laughter. Cordelia and I joined in. It was marvellous to be laughing with Pa again. Everyone looked at us to see what the joke was. Slasher bared his tooth in a gesture of solidarity.

'Your mother's a wonderful woman.' My father wiped his eyes. 'There's really no one like her.'

'There's never anyone like anyone I know,' said Cordelia. 'I wish there was someone in the world exactly like me. Someone who doesn't want to boss me about or gang up against me and who isn't jealous of my beauty.'

My father looked at her kindly. 'That's what we're all

looking for in a way, Cordelia. But I'm afraid we're destined for disappointment. What about the girls at school? Aren't any of them soul mates?'

'Uh-oh, I'd better run to the lav.' Cordelia got up quickly. 'I think it was the rissoles at lunch.'

'She's hoping I've forgotten all about it,' I explained when Cordelia had gone. 'Of course I haven't but so far I haven't found anywhere willing to take her before the summer term.'

'Can't Rupert help?'

'I don't suppose he knows anything about schools. Anyway, I don't like to keep asking him for favours. He's doing so much for us already. He rang up just before we left. He's found Bron another job. As chauffeur to someone called Letizia. Apparently she doesn't have a surname. She's a fashion designer. Bron said he thought it was rather infra dig to be employed by a woman. But when Rupert told him she had a Ferrari he said he'd give it a go.'

'Good. How's the newshawk of Battersea, then?'

'Brixton. Just about keeping pace.' I tried to make the account of my doings entertaining but I could see his thoughts were elsewhere. I debated whether to tell him about going out to dinner with Max but decided against it. I was not perfectly confident of carrying off the 'just good friends' line. My father could be astute when he was sufficiently interested. 'Have you been given a date for the court case yet?' I asked.

'Should be some time in February, according to Fleur.'

'Fleur?'

'Fleur Kirkpatrick. My new barrister. Sickly Grin engaged this turgid old fool, so senile he couldn't remember my name for two minutes together. So I threw a tantrum and Foy put me in touch with Fleur. What a woman!' My father shook his head, smiling as though at some delightful memory.

'What's she like?'

'The loveliest eyes you've ever seen. Forget-me-not blue but needle-sharp with intelligence. Hair dark and gleaming like a blackbird's wing. Slender waist but a proper bosom and hips. Skin like ivory velvet. Mind like a precision tool. Incidentally, a great fan of my work.' I recognised the signs of the violent infatuation to which my father always succumbed on first meeting a new flirt. He was incapable of doing things by halves. If Fleur was the woman of the moment she would obsess his thoughts night and day. While I understood that this absorption would make his life more tolerable, selfishly I felt a sickening disappointment. 'It's impossible to convey that kind of beauty in words. The charm of the curve of a cheekbone, the fullness of a lower lip.'

'I'm starting to get the picture.'

'How goes it with the budding wordsmith?' Archie lifted his eyebrows, which wrinkled the white makeup on his forehead and made his widow's peak more pronounced.

It was Friday, and he and Rupert had come to Blackheath to conduct their weekly inquest on the Byng family's industry, accounting, and general probity. I had lit the fire in the drawing room, arranged a bunch of wilting chrysanthemums I had bought cheaply from the woman outside the tube station, and opened a bottle of the Sauvignon Blanc Rupert had kindly sent us.

'After I'd rewritten it about a hundred times I felt I was beginning to get somewhere,' I said. Though Archie's manner was always teasing, I was grateful for the interest he took in my career. 'Mr Podmore said it was promising but when I read it in today's paper I hardly recognised it.'

'*All* newspaper editors are *des*pots. It goes hard with them to let someone else top up the inkwells. Let me see it.'

I handed over the page that bore my immortal prose and watched Archie's face expectantly as his eyes ran along the lines. The haunted house I described was a rectory in

Cricklewood. I had been allowed half an hour to look over it. The owner, a Mrs Newt, pigeon-chested and with bulging, suspicious eyes, prowled close behind me every step of the way lest I should slip a china kitten or an onyx table lighter into my bag. The house, reportedly seventeenth century, had been extensively remodelled and redecorated. Outside it was Victorian. Inside it was Tudor cottage-cum-Regency villa. Magnolia walls and maroon-and-cream striped curtains were enhanced by mock beams and furniture painted black to look like oak and upholstered in dusty-rose Dralon. Mrs Newt said that the ghost of a former rector had been particularly troublesome when they had first moved in, rattling door handles, tapping on windows and sobbing in the dining room. Looking at the horrible reproduction dining suite with fake warming-pans on the walls and a Spanish dancer on the chimneypiece, I could see why.

'Oho! Aha!' cried Archie. '"At twilight the ghost of the Reverend Blenkinsop can be seen on his knees burrowing at his wife's womb." The filthy reprobate! In public, too.'

'That's a misprint.' I pointed out. 'It should be "sorrowing at his wife's tomb".'

'"His long beard and side whiskers, stove-pipe hat and frock have frequently alarmed pedestrians" – I'm not surprised! So the man was a transvestite as well as in*sati*ably libidinous!'

'The printers missed out a word. It should be "frock *coat*".'

'This is absolutely gripping! ". . . alarmed pedestrians taking a short cut through graveyard as the white-bellied owls flit overhead like feathered phantasms on their way to play bingo at what was formerly the Roxy Cinema." A sudden lowering of tone here. Was it the owls or the pedestrians who were on their way to the bingo hall?'

'You aren't taking it seriously!'

'I am, I am! I *prom*ise.' Archie put his hand on his heart.

'Honestly, I think it's *very* good. I can't remember when I've enjoyed a newspaper article more.'

'Mr Podmore put in the bit about the bingo,' I said resentfully. 'I wrote something rather telling about bats swooping like darts of conscience about the guilty man's head. His wife was an heiress who died suddenly in mysterious circumstances. Only years later his younger brother, who'd gone to Australia because he was in love with the heiress himself, and who happened by chance to see an old newspaper –'

'Stop! Archie held up his hand. 'Don't spoil the exquisite moment of revelation! "As the parish priest postured in the pulpit denouncing profligacy, insobriety and naked busts,"'

'Lusts,' I corrected. '"he little knew that Nemesis was speeding towards him on the bow wave of HMS *Albatross*." That's good! *Very* good!' Archie read on, with expressions of surprise and pleasure. 'So the rector was a skilled amateur chemist with an extensive knowledge of toxicology. *And*, before taking holy orders, he was a knife-thrower in a circus. I suppose he didn't have an earlier career as a merchant seaman, with access to blowpipes and curare?' Before I could accuse Archie of ridiculing my efforts, he said, 'No, honestly, Harriet, I'm im*pressed*! It's got a distinctive voice and that's what's important. Not a dull sentence in it. Plenty of people can write grammatical prose but that's not enough. It must *seize* the reader and run away with him like Tom the Piper's son and the stolen pig.'

I was delighted to have some praise at last. For some reason those of my family who had seen my debut in print had found it extraordinarily funny. Bron, especially, had gone about repeating phrases like 'his spectral tears moistened the moss' and 'as the setting sun steeps the Rectory in star-less dark' and screeching with laughter.

Mr Podmore stuck in the sentence about the new roundabout and the supermarket,' I explained. 'He said it had to be relevant to the modern reader.' I had already come to entertain a profound hatred for the modern reader, who seemed unable to understand anything not explained in terms of urban development.

'Here you are, Rupert.' Archie handed the newspaper across. 'Let's have the pro*fess*ional's verdict.'

I waited on tenterhooks while Rupert read the piece. I knew he would be a less indulgent critic than Archie. His face was expressionless as he read it. 'I've read worse,' he said, at last. 'I suggest you curb your fondness for alliteration.' He placed the newspaper on the table beside him and frowned at the hole that Dirk had chewed in the carpet. 'That dog is out of control.' When, finally, he raised his face to mine, I had a fleeting impression that there lurked in those smoke-brown eyes something that might have been a scintilla of a smile.

I had longed for praise from Rupert. 'Who'd like some marzipan?' I said brightly to cover my dashed hopes. I had found a second slab in the larder and had nearly amputated a finger hacking it into small cubes for our guests. Rupert examined the plate of small greyish-yellow lumps, then shook his head.

'Marzipan with wine?' Archie took a piece. 'How Middle *East*ern! We should be lying on cushions, wearing tarbooshes.' He popped it into his mouth and chewed energetically. It certainly was a little stale. I offered him some more. 'No, thank you, Harriet. *Too* delicious but I *must*n't spoil myself. It might lead to an awkward *crav*ing for those embalmed objects that lurk in dusty cases in the British Museum.'

'What are you laughing at?' asked Portia, walking in just then. Rupert and Archie stood up. She looked disdainful. 'You needn't get up for my benefit. That's one of the phoney-polite things men do, like opening doors and lighting cigarettes, to validate the concept of women as inadequate and dependent. 'Stop giggling, Cordelia, and share the joke.'

Cordelia, who seemed to find Archie exquisitely funny, was scarlet with streaming eyes. But when she repeated, between explosions of laughter, what Archie had said, Portia did not look amused. She seemed to have acquired a new seriousness with her espousal of feminism. I suppose her mind was on higher things.

'It's not too bad,' she said in answer to Rupert's enquiry about her job. 'Jessica Delavine is a remarkable woman. She's dedicated her entire life to fighting men's determination to subjugate and disempower intelligent, articulate women.'

'I'm sure we should *all* be *very* grateful,' said Archie solemnly.

'What about the unintelligent, inarticulate ones?' said Rupert. 'Surely they're even more in need of someone to take up the cudgels on their behalf?'

Portia gave him a cool glance. 'Suke and I are spending Christmas with Jessica in Edinburgh. She's going to give a lecture entitled "Where Eve went Wrong".'

'That *does* sound fun,' said Archie.

'Will one lecture be enough?' asked Rupert. I was practically certain then that there was a smile lurking. 'Who is Suke?'

Portia hesitated. Though she could hardly have had a more understanding audience than Rupert and Archie I suspected that a public declaration of her new sexuality required courage. But she was not someone who shirked difficulties. 'She's my lover.'

There was a brief pause.

'And what a *very* lucky girl she is,' said Archie, with commendable grace.

'Crikey!' Cordelia giggled. 'You don't mean – not really – you're joking.'

'There's nothing funny about homosexuality,' said Portia freezingly.

271

'But you've always laughed about Pa's queer friends. When I asked what they did together you said it was revolting – Ow!' Cordelia glared at me. 'That hurt!'

'Sorry. My foot slipped.'

'How can your foot slip when you're sitting down?'

Ophelia came in then, luckily. She waved a careless hand at Rupert and Archie who, despite Portia's snubbing, had stood up again. 'You'll be pleased to hear I've just taken on my first clients. They've made a vast fortune making plastic bottles for shampoos and things and they've just had an enormous house built in Sussex. Fay will help me with quantities and suppliers but I'm to be allowed to do as I like. Fay's mad about Empire but somehow I don't see it. I'm thinking of Louis Quinze. Bert and Marilee Drosselmeyer – they're the clients – have asked me to spend Christmas with them so I can get the feel of the place. 'Imagine! Proper central heating!' She hugged herself at the thought. 'It'll be wonderful to have something decent to eat. They probably have champagne every day.' She looked more beautiful than I had ever seen her. Her eyes were sparkling and her mouth no longer drooped at the corners. She was wearing a new dress, black-and-white silk and very smart. I wondered how much it had cost. 'My God, where did those hideous things come from?' She grabbed the chrysanthemums and rammed them headfirst into the wastepaper basket, from where the stems dripped water on to the carpet. 'I'd love a drink.' She threw herself into a chair and lit a cigarette.

Archie, who was nearest the tray, poured some and took it to her. 'Like a glass of wine, Portia?'

'Thanks. But if I want a drink I can get it myself.' She looked at Ophelia. 'I thought you were spending Christmas with Peregrine.'

'I was. But I'm delighted to have somewhere else to go. Peregrine's family think of nothing but hunting. Their chairs are like rocks because they have large, fleshy bottoms to sit on, they never shut a door because their circulations are in tiptop form and they don't feel draughts, at dinner they talk about snaffles and worms, and they go to bed at ten o'clock so they can get up at dawn. Lady Wolmscott's face is like pickled red cabbage and she smells of horse pee. And, when they aren't galloping about ripping up foxes, they're slaughtering chickens and ducks and drowning kittens in the yard.'

'No more.' Archie shook his head. 'I see it *all*. Better to spend Christmas in a commune in Wales, worshipping Vishnu and eating soya beans. Or at a railway hotel in Northampton with all one's aunts. Or *even*,' Archie's eyes brightened, 'rounding the Horn on a man-o'-war under the lash of a *brut*al admiral.'

'You could have spent Christmas at home with us,' I said to Ophelia, trying not to sound reproachful. 'There'll only be Bron and Cordelia and me now.'

'Terrific!' said Cordelia sarcastically, while sticking her toe into the hole in the carpet. 'Harriet will be mooning about stupid, dead poets and Bron'll be drunk.'

'Don't do that,' I said. 'You're making it bigger. 'It'll be horribly expensive to repair. And I don't moon.'

'You do. All the time. You've mooned all week about Max Frensham.'

'I have *not*!'

We looked at each other angrily. The vehemence in my voice woke Dirk from his doze beneath the piano and he began to bark.

'Girls, *girls*!' said Archie. '*Think* of the embarrassment of your guests as you tear into one another. I shall be obliged to create a diversion.'

'Harriet is twenty-two,' said Portia. 'By calling her a girl you're reinforcing the stereotype of women being like children – weak and incapable.'

273

'*Thank* you, dear Portia,' said Archie. 'You've saved me the trouble.'

I noticed that Rupert was looking at me thoughtfully. When he caught my eye he looked away.

'Hello, hello, hello!' Bron came in then and I could see at once that he had been drinking. 'A nice thing, everyone sitting about getting pissed while I'm out in the sordid world, going several rounds with Mammon.'

'How's Letizia?' asked Rupert while Bron poured himself a drink and threw several logs on to the fire.

'One touch on the throttle and she's off. Hroom! She's almost impossible to park without ramming bumpers. And she drinks petrol intravenously.'

'Letizia?'

'Oh, she's not a bad old thing either. Frighteningly clever and has her minions darting about like those little fish that clean sharks' teeth. She's got a violent temper and an autocratic manner but I don't mind that. You know where you are.' Bron gazed at himself in the mirror over the fireplace and combed his hair with his fingers while elaborating on his theme. 'What I can't stand is a women who falls into the sullens at the drop of a hat but when you ask what's eating her, she refuses to tell you. So you hazard a guess that she's discovered she's got cancer – or her mother's been run over by a train – but she just gets more moody and silent, until your fevered imagination has run out of possibilities. Then it turns out she's had half an inch cut off her fringe and is furious because you haven't noticed. Now Letizia is a woman who tells you exactly what she means. It's extremely restful. She's asked me to spend Christmas with her in Milan. Five-star hotel, a suite of rooms with a private roof terrace, dinner at the best restaurants, tickets for La Scala, all expenses paid. Unless a better offer comes up, I think I'll go. What's this noxious substance?' He bent to examine the plate. I snatched it from him.

'It's marzipan. Don't prod it if you aren't going to eat it. I happen to like it.'

'You eat this stuff voluntarily? What depraved tastes you have. I thought it was a pregnant woman's thing to fancy a nibble at outlandish grub like coal and dog biscuits.' His eyes narrowed suspiciously. 'You haven't let Frensham put a pudding in the oven, I hope?' He looked at Rupert and waggled his eyebrows. 'You have no idea what a responsibility sisters are.'

'Honestly, Bron!' I was very cross with him, though of course it never did any good. 'I think you do it on purpose.'

'What?' he looked injured.

'Oh, never mind!'

Bron looked at the assembled company and spread his hands wide as if to say that I had proved his point.

'Hat and I are going to be all by ourselves at Christmas.' Cordelia's tone was heavy with reproof. 'It'll be the worst Christmas anyone my age has ever had, in the whole history of the world. Even the Cratchits had people to pull crackers with.'

'We'll have Dirk,' I said. 'And Mark Antony. Remember, when Rupert brought him back you said you'd never be unhappy about anything ever again.'

'But I didn't mean being left all alone at Christmas! Can't we come with you to Edinburgh or Sussex?' She knew it would be useless to appeal to her brother's tenderness of heart.

'I shall be busy,' said Portia. 'Besides it won't be a suitable thing for children. You wouldn't enjoy it. And we couldn't afford the extra train fares.'

'No,' said Ophelia.

Rupert put down his glass and stood up. 'Has the electricity bill come? And what about that insurance premium?'

'I'll go and get them,' I said.

Cordelia began to sob. Though I knew she was adept

275

at weeping by design, I was sympathetic. My parents had always invited friends for Christmas and at least twenty of us sat down for lunch. Maria-Alba made the most wonderful things to eat and Pa organised games, like charades, in which everyone but me was able to show off their acting ability. We had enormous fun playing childish things like sardines and murder-in-the-dark, which are good with lots of people. We would never be able to play the latter again.

I felt profoundly miserable as I went through the papers on Pa's desk. Even thinking the M-word made my stomach hurt. This part of my anatomy had taken on an independent existence since my father's arrest. An imp of grief and carking care had taken up residence within and when I moved the tin painted to look like the Globe Theatre in which Pa kept his stamps, the unpleasant creature nipped and gnawed to let me know it was there. Christmas for the unhappy is worse than having one's liver torn out by eagles, like poor old Prometheus. How was I to get my little sister cheerfully through the long days of celebration without giving way to gloom myself? When I returned to the drawing room Cordelia was gleeful.

'Rupert says we can spend Christmas with him and Archie in – where did you say?'

'Derbyshire.'

'In Derbyshire. It's miles out in the country but there'll be lots of people and parties.'

'Do you mean it?' I asked. 'But won't we be terribly in the way? Whose house is it?'

'Taking your questions in order: yes, I mean it – no, you won't be in the way. It belongs to a distant cousin of mine,' said Rupert. 'There's a daughter of Cordelia's age. And a son of twenty or so. You'll fit in very well. Maggie will be delighted.'

'Maggie?'

'Lady Pye. My cousin's wife.'

I tried to imagine myself in the setting of a country house party and failed altogether. 'It seems so inconsiderate to land ourselves on complete strangers at Christmas. Cordelia and I can manage on our own perfectly well –'

'No, we can't.' Cordelia spoke decidedly. '*I* shall go anyway. Is this girl who's my age at all beautiful?'

Rupert looked down at Cordelia, his expression serious. 'I believe Annabel is considered to be pretty.' Cordelia's face fell. 'But not at all in your style. Don't worry, she won't cast you into the shade.' Cordelia smiled complacently.

'An added inducement,' Archie clasped his hands behind his back and looked at me impressively, 'is that Pye Place is said to be one of the most haunted houses in England.'

'No kidding? Really?' Cordelia and I spoke together.

'Of course that's all nonsense,' said Rupert. 'A lot of silly fairy tales. But you might get an article out of them.'

'I've always wanted to see a ghost,' said Cordelia, which was exactly what I was thinking myself.

'You're doomed to disappointment, then.' He spoke blightingly.

'It really is so good of you,' I said as I took Rupert and Archie to the front door. 'Promise you'll say if they don't like the idea.'

'Of course they'll *love* it,' said Archie. 'They're im*men*sely hospitable. And Maggie will do anything to please Rupert. We shall have a very jolly time.' He pinched my cheek. 'And we shall allow you to have a *teeny* little moon every day, just for five minutes or so, to keep your hand in.'

I blushed. 'It's all nonsense about Max.'

The telephone rang. 'I'll get it, shouted Portia. 'I'm expecting Suke to ring. Hello, it's Portia.' She listened for a moment then held it out to me. 'Surprise, surprise, Hat. It's Max.'

EIGHTEEN

'I'm not feeling sick any more,' said Cordelia, whose cheeks were now white instead of luminously green. 'You can close the windows. After the first hour I get my car legs.'

Archie pressed a button and the windows slid slowly shut. Despite the intense cold that prevented me from feeling my hands and feet and had undoubtedly made my nose scarlet, my mood was buoyant. The countryside is always even more beautiful than I remember it. We were driving through Northamptonshire now and the large brown fields of Bedfordshire had given way to smaller green fields with sheep. The flatness had softened into little hills broken by woods.

Rupert's car – I presumed it was his though Archie drove it – was so spacious and comfortable I could happily have lived in it for a week. Archie drove fast with an air of reckless excitement as though our suitcases were filled with bootleg liquor and the police were in pursuit. He crouched over the wheel, accelerated with a roar and braked with screeching tyres. When he came up behind another car he clung to its bumper, weaving about in the middle of the road to try to pass it. He would shake his fist and toot the horn. Several motorists, their nerves jangled to breaking point, drew into lay-bys to let him go by.

'Slow down, for God's sake,' protested Rupert. 'You'll kill us all.'

'Just putting her through her paces. We haven't had her on the open road for a while. Goes like a *dream*, doesn't she?' He sounded the horn at a herd of cows that were staring over a fence and sent them stampeding in terror.

'That was quite unnecessary,' said Rupert crossly. 'Toad had nothing on you.'

'Poop! Poop!' cried Archie. 'You, my dear Rupert, can be Ratty. It will suit you *very* well in your present mood.' He began to sing Madame Butterfly's famous aria about waiting for the Pinkerton, in a trilling falsetto.

I watched flocks of birds sweeping in circles in a sky that was daffodil-coloured, just as in Tennyson's *Maud* poems, and wished the journey could go on for ever. I shifted my feet on the case in the foot-well and smiled inwardly, imagining its delectable contents.

'You're mooning again,' said Cordelia.

It had pleased my family to continue the teasing about Max. In the absence of the others Cordelia had appointed herself guardian of the joke. I was too elated to mind.

'I was just thinking of my clothes.'

I looked down at the tobacco wool coat I was wearing and turned my head so I could feel with my chin the softness of the fur collar. Behind my seat on the back windowsill was a fur hat to match.

Archie had said, 'We *can't* take Harriet away with us looking like a character from a play about the Irish potato famine.'

'Certainly not,' Rupert had replied. 'She must do us credit.'

Archie and I had gone to Bond Street where the shops

were hot and scented. He had become autocratic and single-minded. He snatched things from rails and sent me into the changing room to try them on. I emerged, feeling self-conscious, and walked up and down while he appraised. Usually he shook his head but occasionally he nodded. I soon realised he was an excellent judge. My new wardrobe, though far more glamorous than anything I would have chosen for myself, had none of the outré flamboyance of his own apparel. The clothes seemed to me immensely elegant and stylish and they transformed my appearance.

Archie's enthusiasm for the task added to the pleasure of the experience. Indifferent to the curious glances of shoppers, he screwed up his eyes, sucked in his cheeks and supported his chin on the point of his finger to consider the effect, then waved it in a circle to get me to revolve slowly on the spot. 'Marvellous!' he would enthuse. 'Perfect! Now look at the swing of the skirt. Don't you a*dore* the cut of the shoulder?' Or, 'Perfectly *hor*rible. It makes you look like a tart who's married well. Expensive vulgarity. Take it off at *once*.'

This prompted me to examine some of the price tickets. At first I thought must have mistaken the number of noughts. I ran out of the cubicle. 'I can't possibly accept these clothes. It'll take me absolutely years to pay Rupert back.'

'Don't *arg*ue, Harriet. This is for our sakes as much as yours. We don't want to blush for our protégée. Rupert *hates* the sight of badly dressed women.' I was perfectly sure that Rupert was indifferent to my or anyone else's appearance. 'Now try on that primrose crêpe de Chine. I thought it was rather *you*.'

I knew that no pleasure of theirs could possibly match my own exultation as the assistant took away an armful of beautiful skirts, shirts, coats and dresses to enfold them in layers of tissue paper and shiny cardboard boxes.

* * *

'But you hate shopping!' said Portia, as I laid out the clothes on my bed for her to see.

'It's because I don't know what I really look like. In the mirror I see eyes and nose and mouth and the odd spot or untidy eyebrow or hair that needs washing but I can't get an overall view. It's like examining a picture through a small hole in a piece of paper that shifts about. When I see a rack of clothes I panic or feel depressed because they all look equally impossible. I've no idea how I want to look, even if I knew how to achieve it. Having Archie decide was like being a child again. Blissful!'

'I didn't specially enjoy being a child.' Portia stroked the sleeve of my new raspberry-coloured cashmere jersey. 'I don't like having to please other people. Except Suke. She has such high standards. When she approves of me it's like being given a million pounds. These glacé kid boots are heaven. They feel just like glass. Won't Ophelia be jealous when she sees these things!'

'I'm not going to show her. I don't want her to crush my new-found confidence. Not about the clothes – no one could think they were anything but wonderful – but about me in them. Her ideas of what's right are impossibly high. Even more than Ma's.'

'Poor Hat!' Portia looked superior. 'You've never been able to stand up for yourself, have you? You've let them squash you practically out of existence. I decided I wasn't going to let Ma and Ophelia boss me about as soon as I was physically capable of stamping my foot.'

I could not deny it, remembering the row there had been when, at the age of four, Portia had put her deeply hated velvet-collared tweed coat and matching velvet hat, which had cost twenty pounds from Harrods, into Loveday's incinerator.

'I suppose I've always had a contemptible longing for praise,' I admitted.

'But surely it has to be praise from someone who matters. Of course I love Ma and Pa no end but they aren't interested enough in me to make it worth while to try and win their approval. I've always thought we were lucky that they were so relaxed as parents, so eccentric and unmindful of us. I really felt sorry for the girls at school whose parents nagged them about working for exams, sucking up to teachers and being home by half-past ten. Of course I still think that's all crap. But now – since I met Suke – I'm beginning to see things differently. I wish I'd been made to see that some things *do* matter.' She held up an ivory silk shirt, piped in grey to match a cutaway jacket and pencil skirt in softest vicuna wool. 'You're going to look fabulous, Hat. I almost wish I was going to be there to see it.'

'What do you think?' While we were talking I had been busy at the mirror, applying the new wine-red lipstick Archie had chosen to go with my beautiful brown coat.

'Who'd have believed it! Harriet wearing makeup! After all you've said about cosmetics being a decadent tool of seduction for the idle rich!' I felt a little colour come into my cheeks at this reminder of the prig I had so recently been, but luckily this didn't show beneath the new Charles of the Ritz blusher. Archie had spent ages selecting exactly the right shade and we had had a lovely time choosing glittery eye shadow for each other. 'You look really beautiful,' Portia continued. 'It shows off the creaminess of your skin and somehow your eyes look darker and shinier.'

'I'm wearing mascara as well.'

'Brothers, the revolution is here! Max is going to do a triple toe-loop when he sees you.'

On the night before we left for Derbyshire a large parcel had arrived by Special Delivery, addressed to me. It contained a beautiful dark-red leather suitcase and a vanity case to match.

Archie had enclosed a note: 'Dear Harriet,' it said. 'Had a frightful dream last night that you had IMITATION leather luggage. Love R. and A.'

I smiled as I read it. Most of the decent suitcases the family possessed were already in Cornwall with my mother, and Ophelia had bagged the remaining one that was fit to be seen. A practical and prescient godmother had given Cordelia a respectable plain brown case for her last birthday, to her great disgust at the time. I had been about to pack my beautiful clothes in plastic carrier bags.

As Cordelia insisted on unwrapping the new luggage in the hall, Ophelia saw it. She spent some time examining it, stroking the leather outsides and the suede insides and fingering the glass bottles held in place by bands of elasticised satin before saying, 'I hope you're not going to be mean about lending these when the occasion arises?' It was praise indeed. I assured her eagerly that she could borrow them whenever she pleased. She smiled. Then her eyes fell on my jersey, which had a hole where the polo neck was departing from the rest. She sighed. 'It does seem a fearful waste.'

It was on the vanity case that I rested my frozen feet – stockinged, naturally, for fear of scratching it.

'I think my hands *may* be returning to life,' said Archie. 'I know what it feels like to be a laboratory assistant handling plutonium with electronic arms. Only Dirk's hot breath on the back of my head has forestalled frostbite and subsequent gangrene of the ears.'

'In that case it's mean of you to keep complaining you can't see in your rear-view mirror because of his head,' Cordelia reminded him.

'Like Mr Darcy, I have a resentful temper. I cannot justify my failings. You must take me as I *am*. Which at the moment is glacial.'

'You wouldn't want me to be sick?'

'I take it you are using Socratic irony?'

'What's that?'

'A famous old man called Socrates used to ask questions to which he pretended ignorance of the answer. It's a device for revealing to others their own faulty reasoning and innate stupidity.'

There was silence for some time as Cordelia worked this out. Dirk, made drowsy by the rapidly rising temperature inside the car, decided to roll over into his favourite sleeping position, on his back with his feet in the air. Rupert and Archie had been very good about his inclusion into the party. I had telephoned Rupert the day after the invitation to Derbyshire had been given, in something of a panic.

'It was so kind of you to ask me,' I said, 'but I honestly don't think I can bring myself to put Dirk into kennels. He can't bear being alone for a single solitary minute and I won't be able to enjoy myself, thinking of him being miserable. Would you mind just taking Cordelia?'

There had been a short pause and then Rupert had said, 'Bring him.'

'What about Lady Pye? Won't she think it ill-mannered of us to turn up with a large dog?'

'The house has two of its own. As long as Dirk doesn't fight with them it won't matter. I'll telephone to let them know to expect him.'

I had given Dirk a talking-to about the absolute necessity of not barking at other dogs, as he was inclined to do when he met them in the street. So that he would not disgrace Rupert and Archie, I invested in a smart blue collar and lead to replace the string and choke chain.

Rupert had been firm about Mark Antony, though. 'He will be much happier in his own house.'

I had to admit this was true. Luckily Loveday, who preferred animals to people, was very willing to feed him and as they voluntarily spent part of the day in each other's company, I thought it would be all right.

I had explained to Seamus and Joe, two of the journalists who frequently dropped in to have a cup of tea and a chat, that we would all be away for Christmas. Mindful of the ground I had to make up with various members of my family because of previous indiscretions, I told them all about Bron being whizzed over to Milan to help a leading couturier put together an important new summer collection and they seemed mildly interested. They jotted down everything I said about Ophelia being an internationally renowned interior decorator about to perform a multi-million-pound transformation on a client's house. I concluded my press briefing with the publication date of Jessica Delavine's new novel. I hoped this might make amends.

There remained only a last visit to my father to tell him where we were going and to assure him that he would remain uppermost in our thoughts. Pa accepted our desertion in a cheerful spirit. Apparently Fleur Kirkpatrick had arranged for a special Christmas lunch to be prepared by the head chef of Le Pain Perdu. She had ordered oysters, turbot, grouse, *îles flottantes* and Dom Pérignon. The prison governor, much in awe of my father's celebrity and keen to curry favour, had placed his job on the line by giving permission, off the record, for this feast to be consumed *à deux* in his office. *A deux* with Fleur, that is – the governor would be celebrating in the bosom of his family. I had to acknowledge that though my feelings for Fleur Kirkpatrick were painfully ambivalent, she had done wonderful things for my father's morale.

I had sent Maria-Alba my Derbyshire address in my Wednesday letter. I felt it was important to be both faithful

285

and consistent so I wrote twice a week without fail, though sometimes I could manage only a brief note. Her letters came erratically, sometimes two on the same day and then nothing for a week. The spelling was idiosyncratic, there was no punctuation and most sentences were incomplete. We had never corresponded before so I had no idea how much was due to difficulties with written English and how much to mental turbulence. She complained vehemently about the nastiness of the food and accused Sister Mary-Joseph, who was head cook at the convent, of putting poison in the tea. Apparently the convent was run as a brothel for the exclusive use of the Devil. Maria-Alba escaped diabolical violation by sitting up all night with the kitchen ladle at the ready. Her refusal to be parted from the ladle, which I had had repaired by the tinker who called regularly to sharpen knives, had caused considerable inconvenience in our household as cabbage soup was frequently on Ronnie's menu, but he would not let me incur the expense of buying another.

My letters, by comparison were tame. I had reported on Mark Antony's weight gain, Ronnie and Ma's departure to Cornwall, Dirk's very nearly responding to 'S-s-sit!', our continued employment and the good behaviour of the washing machine. I said that Pa was in reasonably good spirits but did not say why. Rereading the letter, we sounded a thoroughly united, enterprising and successful family. I wondered if there was anything in Coué's method of psychotherapy by auto-suggestion, which works by constant repeating the mantra that everyday everything is getting better and better. If I went on insisting what terrific achievers and all-round good eggs the Byngs were, might it become true?

'This looks like lunch.' Archie interrupted my thoughts.

He turned left by a sign which said 'Tallyho Towers, Hotel

and Restaurant'. We followed the drive through woods until the trees gave way to a gravelled turning circle before a large Victorian Gothic house.

'I suppose it's no good being fussy.' Rupert undid his seat belt and got out. 'They will have tablecloths, at least.'

'You go ahead,' I said. 'I shan't be long.' I put Dirk on his lead and led him a little way into the wood in search of a discreet peeing place. He was extremely interested in all the wood had to offer and took some persuasion to return to the car. A man with a brightly checked suit and long sideburns, who was loading suitcases into the boot of the car next to ours, smiled at me and said,

'Very swish motor. Weber carburettors? Turbocharger?'

I smiled back politely. 'I'm afraid I don't know anything about cars.'

'Nice dog, too.'

Here I felt on more secure ground

'Yes, isn't he. He's a Cornish terrier.'

The man laughed, showing very white teeth. 'A Cornish pixie, more likely. Don't try and pull my leg, young lady. My aunt had a St Bernard. Lovely temperament. But nearly ate her out of house and home. Hope you've got some family jewels to sell.'

I stiffened a little. 'It's a very rare breed.'

The man laughed again. 'Listen to this, Tracy,' he said to the woman who had just walked up to us. 'This young lady is asking me to believe that *that* pooch,' he pointed to Drik, who was sitting on the gravel, scratching his ear, 'is a rare Cornish spaniel.'

'Terrier,' I corrected.

The woman, who was a pretty platinum blonde with startlingly red lips, said, 'Well, sweetie, perhaps he is. I don't know anything about dogs.' She looked again at Dirk. 'But I must say he looks awfully like your auntie's old dog – the sort that wears a barrel round its neck and rescues people from the snow.'

'Exactly.' The man was triumphant. 'A St Bernard. This one's just a pup, of course.'

The woman saw my face. 'Anyway, poppet, you shouldn't go around accosting people you don't know.' She smiled at me. 'He can't resist a chin-wag. Take no notice.' She bent to pat Dirk, who simpered and panted. 'You're a ducky-dear, whatever you are.' She fluttered her fingers at me. 'Tra-la!'

They got into their car and drove away. I was feeling cold and flustered by the time I walked into the restaurant.

Our party was clearly the focus of all eyes. Waiters ran about, bringing drinks and menus, and the other guests stared and whispered. For a moment I saw us as others might. Rupert would always attract attention by reason of his height, his silver-grey hair and his handsome, slightly saturnine face. Cordelia was wearing a navy coat and pleated skirt that had once belonged to Ophelia. It was plain and well cut and showed off the bright gold of her hair. The cream jersey beneath made the most of her exquisite pink-and white complexion. I suppose it was superficial of me to care for appearances but I was proud of my little sister. Archie wore a thick tweed jacket and plus-twos of lovat green, his socks were tasselled, his brogues had an almost blinding shine. On the chair beside him was a Tyrolean hat, the band trimmed with colourful feathers.

A waiter approached me to take my coat.

'Reginald!' hissed a respectable matron to her dull-looking husband. 'That man is wearing lipstick!' They were sitting at the table nearest the door and were so intent on gazing at Archie that they had not noticed me.

Her husband snorted with laughter. 'I don't often venture to contradict you, my dear, but that *man* is, in fact, a woman. And a distressingly plain one at that.'

'What? Oh, nonsense! Of course it's a man.'

'You need spectacles, my love.'

'There's nothing wrong with my eyesight!'

'I wish you would remember, my dear, that asserting something, however violently, does not make it true. I'm afraid vanity makes fools of us all. It's high time you visited the optician.'

'Well, I like that! Who was it mistook my aunt for the lady gardener? I seem to remember you told her to stop buggering about on the lawn and bloody well get down to it. She has always disapproved of language –'

At this point the couple noticed that I was listening avidly, while taking an unconscionably long time to take off my coat. As I was already discovering, Archie had an unsettling effect on people. They crumbled their rolls in mute anger and I was obliged to join the others at the table. Another waiter bounded over to shake my napkin over my knee.

'I advise the roast beef,' said Rupert. 'There's little anyone can do to ruin a good piece of beef – except overcook it. And the crab salad to begin with, on the same principle.'

'I never normally get the chance to eat in a restaurant,' said Cordelia. 'Can't I have something more exciting?'

Rupert looked at her. 'Experience is good, they say, if not bought too dear. What would you like?'

'I'll begin with *coquilles St-Jacques* because it sounds pretty. And then I'll have *homard thermidor*, please. I know that's lobster. We had it in French.'

I frowned at Cordelia and slightly shook my head for it was by far the most expensive thing on the menu but she affected not to see. She was delighted with everything, the waiter who bowed to her and called her 'madam', the panoply of glasses and knives and forks, the ice-bucket on a stand, the silver pot full of toothpicks, the books of matches with the hotel's name on it. She was aware that people were staring at us and she played up to it, tossing her head and pouting and laughing rather loudly.

I heard a man on the table next to us mutter, 'Fetching little thing, isn't she?'

'Do you think *he* could be a relation?' whispered his female companion who had been mesmerised by Archie for some time. 'I mean it's such a *strange* little group.'

'I think you'll find, my darling Fiona, that pansies don't breed. Ergo, no relations. That's something to be said for it, anyway.'

'Don't be silly, Jerry. They have mothers and fathers at least.'

'Perhaps they're actors over from Hollywood. He's wearing makeup.'

'Yet their accents are good. Definitely upper-middle. The one who seems to be in charge reminds me of Rudolph Valentino. Not quite English. I think the fairy is rather sweet.'

'You used to think Mao Tse-tung was sweet. Anyway, actors are supposed to be able to do accents, aren't they? I suppose they might have escaped from somewhere. The circus. Or the funny farm.'

'Sssh! They'll hear you.'

I rather enjoyed our notoriety, with the attendant insights into other people's ways of thinking. It was much more interesting than the fawning tributes that strangers paid to Pa.

The crab salad was plain but good. Rupert and Archie grumbled about the dressing. Cordelia managed to eat nearly all the *coquilles St-Jacques* though I could see it was an effort. Scallops, mashed potatoes, breadcrumbs, cheese and cream are a rich combination and not the thing to choose when recovering from feeling sick in the car.

A welcome distraction was provided by the drama of the carving trolley with its shining dome, vat of steaming gravy and theatrical clashings of knife against steel. The beef, when it was cut, was only faintly pink, which was fine by me as I am not fond of blood, but Rupert and Archie looked at each other gloomily. Cordelia's face fell at the arrival of the lobster. It looked remarkably liked the *coquilles* except that the shell was a different shape and there was four times as much cream, breadcrumbs and cheese.

'Well.' Rupert put down his knife and fork, having worked through most of the beef, which was sadly tough. 'At least our nervous systems were not subjected to sudden shock by finding the meat properly hung and the vegetables lightly cooked.'

'We shall revive with pudding.' said Archie gaily. 'English hotels can usually manage to pull themselves together when it comes to confectionery. You groan, Cordelia? What about some trifle – layers of jam, custard and whipped cream with sherry and toasted almonds?'

'Ooh . . .' Cordelia moaned and pressed her napkin to her mouth.

A waiter propelled a trolley towards us, loaded with dishes decorated with glacé cherries, angelica and chocolate shavings.

Rupert waved him away. 'Just bring the cheese board. No, Archie. You'll never be able to get into those lederhosen you bought in Gstaad. Besides,' he looked at Cordelia, 'it's mean.'

When we were walking out of the dining room, a little later, the couple by the door observed Archie attentively. The woman broke what seemed to be a strained silence to mutter, 'A man. I told you so. But Mother was right. You always were a pig-headed old fool!'

'Your mother was a narrow-minded, sanctimonious, sexually frustrated old bitch,' returned her husband, 'and if you don't look out . . .' The rest of what he had to say was lost as the swing door closed behind us.

* * *

'Looks like snow ahead,' said Rupert. He consulted the map. 'Another thirty miles to go. It's getting dark.'

'I'll put my foot down, shall I?' Archie revved the engine. 'Dear *me*! What a lot of cowards you are! There's no need to scream. I read somewhere that fear is *good* for the human constitution. It keeps our instincts sharp and our appetites whetted.'

'For God's sake, Archie,' said Rupert as we skimmed by a lorry on the outside of a blind bend, 'if you care nothing for our shattered nerves, at least have some care for the paint-work.'

'I'm sorry.' Cordelia's voice had a note of desperation. 'I'm going to have to get out again.'

'Nonsense!' said Archie. 'There can be nothing left to spew.' Poor Cordelia had already been sick twice since leaving the hotel. 'Of course lobster is horribly rich,' he continued cheerfully, 'and together with a greasy combination of cheese and cream –'

In the darkness of the back of the car Cordelia's eyes grew agonised.

'Stop!' I cried.

Archie drew over to the left. Cordelia threw open the door and stumbled into the thicket of trees. Dirk, who had seemed to be deeply asleep, gathered himself and made a leap for freedom.

'Damn!' I said. 'I'd better go and get him.'

'Much though I relish the idea of prospecting a dark, damp wilderness, peopled by vomiting children, he is more likely to respond to your call.' Rupert sneezed several times. 'I think my sinuses may have been permanently damaged.'

We had had to have the windows open since leaving the hotel.

'I'm *cer*tainly not going.' Archie leaned across him to peer suspiciously into the wood. 'There could be adders in there, or rabid foxes or psychopaths armed with knives.'

I pulled on my boots and my fur hat and got out into the road. 'I thought you said fear was good for you.'

'Ah yes, but *not* after four o'clock. Evenings should be spent composing oneself peacefully for sleep. Scream if you're attacked and we shall valiantly set forth.' Archie slid the windows up.

The wood was larger than it had first appeared. I shouted Cordelia's name, then Dirk's and at once winged things sprang out of every bush, making me jump. Beneath the trees was impenetrable undergrowth so I was sure she would not have left the path. I walked briskly, calling every few seconds. There was no sign of either of them so I decided to turn back and explore the other way. I could have sworn that I retraced my route exactly but when I found myself in a small clearing beside an unfamiliar pile of logs I knew I was lost.

The sky was growing darker, and as I looked up something wet fell on my face. Snow. I told myself I had no reason to be afraid. I could not be very far from the road and Rupert and Archie would come to look for me before long. Probably Cordelia and Dirk were already back in the car. At this point I remembered that she had run off without her coat.

The flakes were falling fast now. With what was perhaps a reprehensible care for the material things of this world, I constantly brushed them from my shoulders and shook them from my beautiful hat. My hands grew cold. I thrust them deep into my pockets and found the mint imperials I had bought when we stopped for petrol. I pulled out the packet and immediately there was a pattering behind me and something damp thrust itself into my palm. It was Dirk's nose.

I was much too pleased to see him to be convincingly angry. I snapped the lead on to his collar and said Cordelia's name

293

several times in an urgent, entreating way. Dirk sat down and refused to move no matter how much I tugged him.

'Oh, really! What a dog you are!'

I gave him a mint. He devoured it with one swallow and nearly dislocated my arms at he set off at speed. I ran behind him and soon saw, in the distance between the trees, the welcome sight of headlights. Twice, before we reached them Dirk sat down and refused to move until I had given him another mint. Then he darted off again until the enticing flavour had worn off sufficiently to require another. As I approached the car the interior light disclosed two dark shapes that were the heads of Rupert and Archie. No Cordelia.

'We were beginning to think you had met a de*lic*ious prince on a magnificently caparisoned steed and had ridden away with him,' said Archie as I came panting up.

'Where's Cordelia?' Rupert sounded annoyed.

'I don't know! I've been calling and calling. And then I got lost. It's the most confusing place and it all looks the same in the dark.'

Rupert muttered something imprecatory beneath his breath on the subject of women and children. 'All right. Get in. We'll go and look for her.'

'But it's *snow*ing!' protested Archie. 'My shoes will be *ru*ined!'

I remembered how I had felt about my coat and hat and did not reproach him in my heart.

'There's a torch in the boot. We'd better hurry. The wretched child may be wandering further away every second.'

'I'm coming with you.' I stripped off my coat and hat, threw them on the back seat and enveloped myself in the car rug. 'Dirk brought me back to the car. He may be able to find Cordelia. Here, Dirk, good boy!' I offered him Cordelia's coat to sniff. 'Seek, seek!' Dirk was off like a pea from a

294

catapult. He bounded ahead while I hung on with difficulty behind.

'Give him to me,' said Rupert.

Dirk, feeling a less gentle hand on the rein, stopped dead but a mint fired him off again. Behind us Archie was calling, 'Oh, *do* wait, you mean things. I've got a stone in my shoe and it's *ag*ony!'

As we had the torch I suggested that we stop but Rupert said, 'We'll go back for him when we've found Cordelia. Oh, get on, you tiresome creature! Give him another mint, Harry, quick!'

The snow was whipping up into our faces now and it was completely dark. I continued to call Cordelia but my voice was weakened by breathlessness. Just as I was beginning to feel really frightened for Cordelia's safety, Dirk started to whimper with excitement and seconds later the torch-beam fell on a section of trunk and the sleeve of a jersey. Cordelia had climbed into the hollow of a tree to shelter from the snowstorm. She was voluble with fright and cold but her teeth were chattering too much for us to understand what she was saying. I pushed her arms into her coat.

'Put this round your shoulders.' Rupert was taking off his own coat as he spoke. 'You can stop crying now. Where's your spirit of adventure? Come on, walking will warm you up.'

Between us we coaxed her along, groping our way between the trees, faces screwed up against the snowflakes that melted on our cheeks and dripped down our necks.

'You *beasts*!' Archie was wrathful when we found him. 'Leaving me alone in the dark! I've probably got pneumonia . . .' He followed behind us, grumbling all the way.

The lights of the car were not less welcome than Ithaca must have been to the travel-weary Ulysses. Archie put the heater full on and soon the inside of the car was as steamy as a Turkish bath. Cordelia was inclined to be indignant with the world in general and the wood in particular.

'I never want to see a tree again. I'm surprised both my eyes aren't stuck on twigs. Look at my hands!'

They were muddy and scratched and there was a long red mark on her cheek.

'I think we should all pay homage to Dirk.' I was delighted to be able to feel proud of him. 'Without him you'd probably still be lost.'

'I have to admit,' said Rupert, turning in his seat to view Dirk with favour, 'much must be forgiven the hound from hell.'

'Give the dog a mint,' said Archie. 'I think my shoes *may* recover with some polish and buffing.'

'Ah, but Dirk was the reason I got lost in the first place,' said Cordelia. 'He was chasing a rabbit and I ran after him to save it only I couldn't keep up and then somehow I got lost.'

Dirk began to pant, no doubt wondering why our smiles had turned so swiftly to frowns.

'If there is one scratch on the upholstery . . .' The rest of what Rupert had to say was lost in a fit of sneezing.

We continued our journey. The snow drove itself horizontally into the windscreen in a distracting, hypnotising way, and Archie was forced to slow to something just above a crawl. The road became slippery and we slewed round bends as though on skis. Whenever we came to villages with streetlights I tried to see what the houses were like but my view was blurred by rivulets of snow sliding down the glass and forming themselves into miniature mountain ranges on the windowsill.

My thoughts did their customary round of the people who were always on my mind. I hoped my father was reasonably cheerful and that Maria-Alba was calm, that Portia was happy with Suke, that Ophelia was steeped in luxury and that Bron was enjoying the sophistication of *l'alta moda*. My mother had telephoned before we left to say that the hotel in Cornwall was surprisingly comfortable and attractive. They had rooms overlooking the bay and the food was good. I wondered whether there was snow in London and if Mark Antony was asleep in his favourite place on my bed or perhaps on his cushion in Loveday's potting shed.

My train of thought drifted from those who were dearest to me and turned to Max. When he had telephoned to ask me to have dinner with him again I had refused, explaining that I had work that must be finished before I went away. He had said, quite reasonably, that one evening could not make that much difference. I had remained firm and at last he had rung off, unable to hide his disappointment.

I was flattered. I lacked the courage to tell him I did not want to have dinner with him because he was married. For one thing, it would have sounded prim and ingenuous. And for another, it would have been an admission that I had been thinking of something more than friendship. What a pity, I reflected, that honesty in human relations is so rarely possible. We are compelled to approach, circle and retreat as though performing the steps of a complicated dance, neither trusting the appearance of truth nor daring to speak it.

'We should be turning right somewhere along here,' said Rupert. 'I just saw some lights.'

I peered into the night. For a second or two I saw something twinkling and yellow, impossibly high up.

'Is it a mountain?' I asked, feeling thrilled.

'It's called the High Peak,' said Rupert. 'It goes up to two thousand feet. We've been climbing for some time.'

I turned to Cordelia. 'How exciting, darling, isn't it?' But she was asleep.

NINETEEN

After the village of Pyenock, the road dwindled to a lane with what appeared to be high banks or hedges on each side. It twisted alarmingly and at one point rose at such a steep angle that the wheels began to spin and I was afraid we were going to slide backwards. Archie growled, gripped the steering wheel and with a scream from the engine we shot forward.

Stone pillars and then trunks of trees flashed past as Archie negotiated what must be the drive to the house with a final burst of speed that made Dirk lose his footing and by mistake strike me painfully on the temple with his bared teeth.

'Here we are!' Archie slammed on the brakes and Dirk plunged into the foot-well on Cordelia's side. Archie snapped on the interior light and grinned round at us triumphantly. 'Safe and sound.'

Rupert gave him an expressive look.

The snow streamed into our faces as we staggered stiff-legged from the car and stumbled up some steps. I had the impression of many windows, extravagantly lit. I thought I could hear, above the wailing of wind, the sound of rushing water. Rupert tugged at the bell pull and without waiting for an answer, opened the front door. Accompanied by a whirl of snowflakes that left wet marks on the stone flags, we walked in. A small vestibule gave on to a substantial inner hall. On a stepladder by the foot of the stairs a woman was reaching up to fasten a star to the pinnacle of a glorious, glittering Christmas tree.

'Rupert, my dear! And Archie!' She descended the ladder with surprising agility for she was no longer young. I guessed about fifty. 'What a night to be out in! You must be chilled to the marrow!'

She came to welcome us, putting out her arms to embrace Rupert. My first impression was of a large-boned woman, broad-shouldered and unfeminine, but her eyes, owlishly magnified behind thick-lensed spectacles, were mild and affectionate. She must have been nearly six feet tall. Her apron covered a generous expanse of hip, but she was muscular rather than fat.

'Pretty nearly.' Rupert kissed her cheek. 'How are you, Maggie?'

'Very well, dear, and all the better for seeing you.' She patted his face tenderly with a large hand. 'And Archie! Oh, you've caught me in my apron.' She undid the strings of it as she spoke, rolled it up and stuffed it into the pocket of her shapeless brown cardigan.

'Hello, Maggie.' Archie kissed her hand. 'You're as beautiful as a buttercup.'

This was a reference to Lady Pye's yellow dress.

'Get away with you, you flatterer!' But she looked pleased.

'This is Harriet Byng,' said Rupert. 'And attached to her a troublesome animal by the name of Dirk.'

Lady Pye took my hand and pressed it between both of hers. Her face could never have been called beautiful, for her nose was large and her teeth were prominent. Her mousy hair was fastened back in a bun from which curls like wisps of cloud escaped over her forehead. But her face was set in lines of gentleness and good humour, and I liked her at once.

'How d'ye do, Miss Byng. It's ever so kind of you to come and visit us. And in this weather!' Her voice was soft, with a strong northern accent.

'It's very kind of you to have us, Lady Pye. And so good of you to let us bring our dog.'

'I'd like it best if you'll call me Maggie, my dear.' She bent to pat Dirk's head. 'It's a grand breed, the St Bernard. There's something noble about them going out after folks in the snow. But Sir Oswald only likes pointers.'

Dirk panted and dribbled a bit, looking anything but noble.

'This is my sister, Cordelia.'

'What a pretty child! You're very welcome, dear. But you've hurt yourself!' Cordelia's face had dried blood on it and by the light of the huge brass lantern that hung from the rafters, her skin looked waxen. 'And you're wet through! You must come upstairs this minute and get out of them clothes. Oh, but I must introduce you . . . Janet, where are you, love?'

Janet stepped out from the behind the Chrsitmas tree, her hands full of coloured baubles and tinsel. They looked incongruous with her plain black dress, grey hair cropped to the top of her ears and her expression, which was unsmiling, almost sullen. Her only ornament was a silver cross on her unadorned bosom, which instantly made me think of the nuns. I felt guilty at once, though I knew it was irrational. It was easy to see that she had once been handsome but something – character or misfortune or both – had worn her face into harsh lines. Maggie took the decorations from her and laid them in a box on a nearby table. 'This is Mrs Whale, my dear friend and companion and someone I wouldn't know how to do without.'

Mrs Whale extended her hand so I offered mine but instead

of taking it she stooped to pick up my suitcase. She kept her eyes lowered, not looking at me.

'That's right, my dear, bring the doggy.' Maggie went ahead of us up the stairs. 'He'll feel strange downstairs on his own till he's got to know us.'

Dirk took the steps two at a time and showed none of the shy uncertainty his hostess attributed to him. I hoped his claws would not scratch the wood which, despite worn hollows at the centre of each tread, was polished to a deep shine.

At the head of the staircase was an extensive landing – like pictures I had seen of long galleries in large country houses – with windows in deep bays down one side. The sky was black and starless and the lights on the panelled wall opposite the windows were placed at distant intervals, dividing the landing into pools of brightness and shadow. Maggie's feet, shod in large corduroy slippers, made a slapping sound on the bare floorboards. I remembered that this was said to be the most haunted house in England. Something made me look round. Mrs Whale was some way behind us, leaning heavily to one side to balance the weight of my suitcase. I felt guilty again.

'Is this house very old?' I asked.

'Ever so old, my dear.' Maggie stopped at the first window, pulling on a pair of white gloves as she spoke and drew the curtains across the embrasure. 'The first Oswald Pye – he was plain mister – built the house in 1598. A clever man he must have been for he started life as a cowherd. When he died he owned all the mines hereabouts.'

She carefully stroked the folds of crimson brocade into place, then ran her gloved hand over the lower edge of a picture frame and examined the fingertips for dust.

'What sort of mines?' I asked.

'Lead, dear,' was the disappointing answer. I had been thinking of gold, perhaps even rubies and sapphires. 'Here he is. The founder of the family fortunes.'

We paused before a portrait of a weasely looking man with small eyes, a yellow, leprous skin and a dingy white ruff.

'Isn't he the saucy churl that slips his ice-cold, invisible members into one's bed without invitation?' said Archie.

Maggie drew in her breath, her eyes growing large behind the thick lenses. 'I wouldn't joke about it, my dear. Really I wouldn't! "Mr Oswald, hear my prayer, please don't give me a nightmare. Cease your groans and ghostly murmurs And keep your hands off my pyjamas,"' she muttered, half under her breath.

'What's that all about?' asked Rupert.

'It's something the children used to say before going to sleep. Jonno made it up when he was a lad. I say it myself whenever I start feeling a bit – nervy.'

'But it's terrible,' objected Archie. 'It doesn't even scan.'

'Well, no, but to my mind it's more comforting than a fine bit of verse'd be. Shakespeare and that – they'd be too grand to come to your aid if you needed them.'

I was interested in this point of view, having been brought up to consider Shakespeare as a reliable source of truth and wisdom, an infallible reference book for the human heart, a faithful friend and alter ego. I wondered who Jonno was.

I stopped before the next portrait. The subject was less, perhaps, of a scurvy knave. He wore a dashing plumed hat and his eyes were not so close together. 'Who's this?'

'Sir Galahad Pye, the first Oswald's son.'

'He seems to have benefited from his father's social eleva-tion,' said Archie. 'A brow less villainously low. All the same, I don't much care for him.'

'Ssh!' Maggie glanced up and down the landing as though she expected someone, or something, to spring out from behind a tapestry. 'Old Gally everyone calls him, so as not to muddle him with the Galahads that came after – he was a very fine gentleman. He fought bravely in the wars and didn't deserve to come to such an end.'

'Which wars?' I asked.

'The ones against King Charles. That nasty Oliver Cromwell ought to have known better.'

'What was his end – Galahad's, I mean?'

'His head was cut off by Commonwealth soldiers during the siege of Pontefract Castle and his body thrown into the river. What a way to behave!' Maggie sounded as indignant as though it had happened yesterday.

'What's this?' Cordelia pointed to a glass case on a chest beneath the portrait. It was fastened with a chain wound twice round it, the ends padlocked together. I could just make out something tube-shaped, perhaps eighteen inches long, that was ginger with rust.

'That's Old Gally's arm. He lost it fighting for Prince Rupert at the battle of Marston Moor. Hacked off at the elbow. That was four years before he died at Pontefract, you understand. Old Gally had this false arm made to his own design. Quite revolutionary it was, for in those days artificial limbs weren't up to much. It was said he could pick up even little things, like a playing card or a coin. He spent his last years trying to invent a way of putting them down again. That's why the family motto is "Hold Tight".'

I looked more closely and saw there were jointed metal fingers attached to one end. 'Why is it kept here in this box?' I wanted to know. 'It's a bit gruesome, isn't it?'

'The visitors like it.' Maggie took the apron from her cardigan pocket and used it to dust the top of the chest. 'We get a lot in the summer. They pay fifty pence to go round the house and you'd be surprised how it mounts up. Then there's the teas. I give them a good long talk about the history of the family and the estate so they'll work up a thirst and an appetite. The chocolate cake's always the most popular.

303

Last year we had a local history group act scenes from the Civil War on the front lawn. We made near a hundred and fifty pounds that afternoon. Of course we can't compete with Chatsworth and the other big houses. We're a bit out of the way and the parking's not easy. But the visitors like to hear tell of the hauntings and Old Gally.' She gave an extra hard rub to the glass. 'There's no accounting for taste.'

'Why is it chained up?'

'The story is that after Old Gally was killed at Pontefract his groom went to look for his master's remains, to give them a decent Christian burial. But all he found was the artificial arm, caught in a bramble bush on the river bank. A branch of thorns beneath a clenched fist is the crest of the Pye family. The servant brought the arm back to Pye Place and it were put in the chapel so's folks could come and pay their last respects, for Old Gally was a big man in these parts. They cleaned it up, of course. But the next morning it were rusty. Every time they dried it and cleaned it up, it was always rusty and wet the next time. So they reckoned it was the work of Old Gally's spirit from beyond his watery grave. That's what we tell them anyway.'

'How fascinating,' I enthused, beginning to construct the rudiments of an article in my mind. 'But that doesn't explain why it's chained up in a case.'

Maggie glanced at me and then at Cordelia. 'No reason. Just silliness, my dear. Now, where's Rupert and Archie?'

'I'm here.' Rupert had been examining a tapestry of the three Gorgons. Their snaky heads, fat scaly bodies and tusk-like teeth made them look like walruses with unsuccessful perms. 'Archie's gone to change. I presume we're in our old rooms?'

'You'll have heard all the stories before,' said Maggie, 'and you know how daft folk can be.'

'The willingness of otherwise sensible people to be gulled

into believing a lot of unsubstantiated nonsense never fails to surprise me.' Rupert looked at me sternly. 'But as Harriet's career may depend on it we had better be grateful that they are.'

'I'm writing a series for a local newspaper about haunted houses,' I explained to Maggie. 'Would you mind if I did a piece about Pye Place?'

'Not at all, my dear. I'll be glad to give you all the help I can. It might bring more visitors, you never know.'

'And have you ever actually seen a ghost?'

'Look at the time!' Maggie peered at her watch. 'Dinner's at eight sharp. We'd best get a move on. Here we are, my dear.' She opened a door. 'I thought you and your sister might like to share a room, this being a terrible place for noises in the night. It's nowt but the house being so old and so high up. There's a bitter wind most days. I hope you're both good sleepers.'

I assured her that we were. Our bed was a four-poster in which four could have slept quite comfortably. It had hangings of green silk embroidered with flowers and birds. A handsome stone fireplace threw out heat and light from logs that burned with the sweet scent of apple. The walls and floor were made from planks twisted and silver with age. If you discounted the light bulbs and switches there was nothing to show that any time had gone by since the house was built.

'This is such a beautiful room!' I moved closer to the fire to examine a painting of a house among hills that hung above the chimneypiece. 'Is this Pye Place?'

'It were painted in the seventeenth century. You can see how little it's altered. The chapel's a ruin now,' Maggie pointed to a building with a tower, 'and the garden's nothing like as fancy but the yews are still here, though growed out of shape.'

'It's the most wonderful house.'

'It's a fine old place.' Maggie stroked the gold and blue

305

threads of a fanciful needlework bird. 'I used to come here sometimes as a little lass and make believe I were a fine lady. I had to keep out of the way of the gentry and be careful not to scuff the floor or put fingermarks on the brass locks.' She put a log and some fir cones on to the fire and poked the embers. With her apron she whisked away some flakes of ash that had drifted on to the floor. 'This is the closet for your clothes.' She opened a jib-door hidden in the panelling.

'I'm glad I'm sleeping with you,' whispered Cordelia as we followed Maggie to be shown the bathroom. 'It's very cold, isn't it, when you're not being cooked by the fire.' She shivered and I noticed her eyes lacked their usual brightness.

The bathroom was large and you could have stored lumps of ice in it without them melting. The bath itself was the size of a sarcophagus and a small flight of steps had been thoughtfully provided to step into it. The lavatory was mounted on a platform and set within a wooden throne. A weighing-machine, like a giant balance scale with a set of weights in a pan on one side and a wicker chair on the other, was the kind of thing that normally would have delighted Cordelia. She looked around with lacklustre eyes and shivered again.

'Drinks in the drawing room from a quarter past seven,' said Maggie. 'Is there anything I can get you young ladies before I go?'

'Actually, Lady Pye, do you think I could have a bath and go to bed?' asked Cordelia. 'I couldn't eat a thing. I may have food poisoning,' she added importantly.

'Laws!' Maggie looked horrified. 'Had I better send for the doctor?'

'It isn't as bad as all that,' I said. 'But perhaps it would be better for Cordelia to have an early night.'

While the bath was running I unpacked our things. I marvelled at the sight of my beautiful new clothes, hanging from the rail. My own made-up face staring back at me from the mirror at the back of the closet startled me. Could that sophisticated creature really be Harriet Byng? My grey shapeless underwear dispelled any vain ideas of myself as a woman of the world. I selected an elegant black dress with a tight bodice, long sleeves and a low square neckline. Years ago my godmother had left me her garnet choker, which I had never worn. It filled up the bareness admirably.

Maggie came back with two hot-water bottles, the old-fashioned stone kind with a cork, which she put between the sheets. Cordelia returned from the bathroom and climbed into bed. But despite four blankets as well as an eiderdown she still shuddered with cold. I looked at her anxiously as I prepared to go downstairs. 'How's the tum?'

'Feels as though it's on a choppy sea . . . O-oh. Let's keep off the subject. I hope we're going to like it here. All the time I was in the bath someone was rattling the door-handle. When he got to hammering on the door and shouting, I unlocked it. This awful old fossil with a big white moustache said it was bad manners to hog the one and only bathroom. I said I thought it was *very* bad manners to spoil my bath by thumping on the door. He said in his day children were seen and not heard and I said I hoped he'd been better-looking when he was a child or his parents would have had a bad time of it. He went bright red and slammed the door. I'd have given him a taste of his own medicine but I was feeling too ill.'

'Darling, that was rather disrespectful. Well, never mind,' I said cravenly, seeing Cordelia look mutinous. 'It's just that the sort of people we know are unusually free and easy. People who live in the country are much more old-fashioned and –'

'How come you're such an authority? You can hardly tell a cow from a horse.'

This was true. My knowledge of rural etiquette was garnered from novels and was no doubt wildly out of date.

'I'll come to bed as early as I can,' I said pacifically.

'Your hair looks nice.'

I had tied it into a knot at the back with the long ends falling loose. I had nearly lost my temper with it as hair is not one of the things I have ever been good at. 'It said how to do it in *Vogue*.'

'It wasn't very long ago you and Ophelia had a row and you said *Vogue* was a piece of capital propagation for the fashion industry.'

'Capitalist propaganda. It means saying things to influence other people, not necessarily truthfully, in this case to make them spend money. Propagation is breeding plants and things –'

Cordelia gave a howl. 'Shut up lecturing. You ought to have been a beastly school teacher.'

'Sorry. You're tired. I should have thought.'

She stared at me resentfully from above the rim of the bedclothes. 'It's extremely aggravating at any time, tired or not. I suppose this new you that cares about clothes and idle luxury is because of Max.'

'Certainly not! If you must know, I don't want Rupert to feel that he's wasted his money on a slattern. It was so generous of him. I want him to feel it was worth it.'

'Sez you! Well, I think it's a pity it'll all be thrown away on two faggots and a lot of ancient old druids.'

'Cordelia! You shouldn't call Rupert and Archie something so unkind!'

'Why not? It's what Pa says. I didn't mean it unkindly. It's what they are. I really like them so what difference does it make? You're the one that minds about them being queer, obviously.'

'All right. Don't let's argue. Want me to bring you up something to eat? Some bread and butter or cocoa –'

Cordelia gave a scream and put her hands over her ears.

TWENTY

I identified the drawing room from the murmur of conversation that flowed from its open door. I wished Cordelia was with me. My mother was so good at entrances. She always came into a room in a rush, with her chin uplifted and her hands outstretched as though acknowledging ecstatic applause. '*Dar*lings!' she would say with a breathy decrescendo, 'How *thrilling* to see you all.' This created a stir of excitement and everyone would stop talking and look pleased and interested. This was much more successful than sidling up forlornly to the backs of people already engaged in conversation, hoping to be noticed.

I hesitated on the threshold, imitating my mother's mannerisms and mouthing the words to give myself courage.

'What on earth are you doing?' Rupert was standing behind me, holding an ice bucket. He had changed into a dinner jacket and looked tremendously 'swave' as Cordelia would have said.

'Nothing. Breathing exercises. I'm still stiff from being in the car.'

Rupert gave me one of his looks, combining disbelief with exasperation. Probably he was wondering whether I was a consummate liar or a congenital idiot. 'Go on in, then.'

The drawing room was very grand, with a marvellous old plaster ceiling from which hung bosses three feet long, like stalactites. Full-length paintings of men and women wearing doublets, ruffs, huge dresses and inimical expressions decorated the walls. Some people were standing by an enormous fireplace with glasses in their hands, talking. The smell of wood-smoke was mixed with the scent of hyacinths, of which there was a great bowl of white ones on a table.

Archie waved from the centre of the gathering. I felt so self-conscious that the blood rushed to my cheeks as I crossed what felt like a large expanse of Persian carpet to join them. He took my arm in a proprietorial manner and at once I felt better. Archie's evening clothes were distinguished by a violet-coloured cummerbund and pretty amethyst dress studs. A black patch shaped like a star near the corner of his mouth accentuated the lily-whiteness of his face. I was pleased to see he was wearing the sparkly lavender eye shadow we had chosen together. 'Now let me introduce you. Miss Harriet Byng, Colonel and Mrs Mordaker.'

I shook hands with a couple who definitely fell into the druid category. Mrs Mordaker was the sort of woman who considers personal adornment the mark of the harlot. She wore a woollen shirt-waister in an unbecoming shade of beige and stout shoes suitable for striding across moors in. Her only concession to feminine frippery was a kirby grip holding back her iron-grey hair. She practically threw away my hand in her eagerness to give Dirk a pat on the head.

'Ha! Now there's a splendid fellow! Can't abide little yapping dogs. Give me a St Bernard any day. Paw, sir!'

Dirk looked up, perplexed, before giving a piercing yip in Mrs Mordaker's ear that made her start backwards, knocking the colonel's arm and treading on his foot.

'For God's sake, woman!' her husband snarled as the whisky slopped about in his glass. He had a bony red face and a low thrusting brow from beneath which angry eyes gleamed like wild animals peering out from a rocky crevice. 'You've probably bust m' toe. Leave the brute alone.'

'And this is Georgia Bisset.'

My hand was taken by a woman with cold eyes, chestnut-brown like aniseed balls. She wore a smart glittery suit and shoes with high thin heels you could have performed surgery with. Her hair, streaked with platinum highlights, was lacquered into a stiff helmet. She could have been launched in the prow of a lifeboat without damage to her coiffure. She was not bad-looking except for being deficient in the chin department. She stared at my hair and my clothes and turned bored eyes away.

'Harriet is a *mad*ly successful journalist,' said Archie with a sly glance at me.

Georgia's eyes switched back to my face and her face softened into a pussycat smile. It was something that usually happened when people found out who my parents were, transforming me in a split second from a person of absolutely no importance into someone worth being nice to. 'Really? How clever.'

'Well, not actually –'

I had been going to say that I worked for a local rag but Archie said quickly, 'Harriet is a war correspondent and is obliged to be discreet so you mustn't pester her about her assignments because she won't tell you.'

I could see Georgia's mind was busy. Should she crush my pretensions or make a friend of me? She gave me a brilliant smile. 'How fascinating! I love your dress. French, isn't it? You must meet Emilio, my fiancé. Darling, this is . . .'

'Harriet Byng,' I supplied.

Emilio took my hand and held on to it. He was, I guessed,

ten years younger than Georgia. He had curly black hair smoothed down with brilliantine, and an olive, pock-marked skin. His eyes were dark, the whites an unusual shade of primrose. '*Hola*!' he said with a foreign accent, possibly Spanish. 'We should be frighten of you, yes? You must be very kind to poor Emilio and not use big words he not unnerstand.' He grinned like a friendly crocodile and looked meltingly into my eyes.

I shot Archie a look of reproach.

'Don't worry,' he said, evidently warming to his self-appointed task of making me either the most popular or the most hated person present. 'Harriet is e*norm*ously empathetic. In her work she meets so many unhappy souls in the most desperate plights – fathers shot, husbands tortured, children missing, mothers raped – it hardly bears thinking about. She can turn the most hardened guerrilla to putty.'

'M-hm!' Emilio lifted my hand to his lips and nuzzled it before bestowing a damp kiss. 'What a del-eecious idea.'

'Now, Emilio,' Archie tapped him on the arm and removed my hand, 'remember where you are. Harriet, this is Elfrida Gilderoy.'

'Do call me Freddie,' said a young woman with wonderful red curls and a bright, charming face. 'We've already met, in London, but it was years ago and you won't remember. Fay Swann's my stepmother. I used to help Fay with decorating.'

'Oh yes,' I said. 'Yes, of course.' I remembered a girl with red hair coming to our house with Fay. Portia and I used to run away and hide. We were always mistrustful of Fay's gushing manner and hated the asphyxiating scent she wore. Freddie was older than Ophelia so we had classed her as grown-up. My father had once said that Freddie was a cracking good painter and a thorn in Fay's side. 'Ophelia's working for Fay now, did you know?' I said. 'She's having a lovely time.'

'I didn't,' Freddie said. 'I don't see much of Fay these days.

How extraordinary to find you here. I recognised you the minute you came in.'

'Did you?' I was surprised and pleased.

'Oh yes. You've got a very distinctive look, those dark eyes exactly like – quite different from your mother and sisters.' I knew she had been about to mention my father and then thought better of it. I was glad she had decided not to. I still found it difficult to talk about his arrest and imprisonment in a social kind of way. My eyes always got watery and that mean little imp in my stomach had a nip and a chew, that I was afraid showed on my face. 'There were always so many people in your house,' Freddie went on, 'and you seemed to have such fun. I used to feel rather envious. Our house was always silent. You were the serious one, running round after your naughty little sister and rescuing her from coal buckets and window ledges.'

'Cordelia's here. She's having an early night but I hope she'll come down tomorrow.'

'She was another fair one with huge blue eyes. A very pretty baby.'

'She still is. Pretty, I mean. No longer a baby, of course.'

'But yours is the face I should like to paint.'

No doubt Freddie was being polite. 'Is that what you do?'

'I'm painting Sir Oswald. We arrived four days ago and I've been hard at work ever since.'

'I'd love to see it.'

'So you shall. But now you must meet Vere, my husband.'

As far as I knew, Fay had not mentioned to my mother that Freddie was married. Then I remembered that a year ago there had been something of – not a scandal exactly, but a subject for excited gossip, when Freddie had run away from her eligible, well-heeled fiancé on the eve of her marriage. Ma had been not a little annoyed as she had bought a beautiful hat for what was to have been an extremely smart wedding.

Freddie drew me over to where a man was standing apart from everyone else, studying a shelf of books. 'Darling, say hello to Harriet.'

Vere started as though his thoughts had been miles away. I was already suffering from an overburdened memory after so many introductions, but his name was unusual enough to fix itself in my mind, in association with a tall man with prominent cheekbones, a brown skin, as though he spent a lot of time outdoors, and short grey hair. He had dreamy eyes of an indeterminate colour. 'Hello,' he said. 'Do you like Fielding?'

'Oh, yes. That is, I've only read *Tom Jones* but I loved it.'

'You should try *Joseph Andrews*. Not such a good story but with characteristic Fielding touches. Let me see.'

He pulled a book from the shelves and began to leaf through it. Freddie took it from him and turned him round to face me. 'Darling, you're not supposed to be thinking about literary criticism just now. You must talk.'

He frowned abstractedly in my direction and pulled at his bow tie, which was crooked, making it much worse. 'Sorry. Was I being rude? I don't know how Freddie puts up with me.' He rested his eyes on her face for a moment. That glance changed my idea of him. I could not remember seeing such an expression of tenderness on a man's face before. Even Ronnie, the most steadfast worshipper I knew, lacked such ardent devotion when he gazed at Ma. I wondered if anyone would ever look at me like that. I feared, sorrowfully, that it was quite impossible.

After that I was introduced to an extraordinarily ancient old lady dressed in purple, her spine so bent I could only see the top of her head. I met a peer, Cordelia's bathroom adversary, and a bishop – with a moustache and a bald head respectively. After that I lost any hope of remembering anyone's name or a single thing I was told about them.

'Jonno!' Archie hailed a young man who slammed the door on entering, making the flames leap up in the sudden draught. 'How are you, you *ex*ecrable boy?'

Jonno was one of the young people with whom I was supposed to fit in. It was difficult to see what we might have in common, apart from the fact that we both had ponytails. Jonno's was fair, wispy and greasy. His beard was more luxuriant – than his hair, I mean; luckily I am beardless. It covered almost all of his face except for his nose and forehead. He reminded me of that hairy creature in *Star Wars* called Chewbacca – Cordelia made me see it three times – half-man, half-ape, whose repertory had been limited to agonised looks and incomprehensible groans. Jonno wore a dog-collar with brutal-looking studs round his neck. This was bad enough but worse was the chain of safety pins, one end attached to the belt of his tight leather trousers, the other end fastened through the septum of his nose. It made me feel sick to think of the consequences if he caught it on anything. It was a style statement intended to convey a message – something like 'You'd better look out.' What it said to me was 'I am afraid.' I did not make the mistake, however, of thinking this meant he was harmless. Fear makes people do terrible things. One only has to think of wars.

'Oh, my!' Archie looked Jonno up and down, then made him turn round. 'What a *roguish* little outfit! What's this emblazoned on your back? Now this you *must* see, everyone. A skull-and-crossbones! Really, Jonno, did you do it? I *love* the flames in the eye-sockets. And what is this message? "Kiss my Arse." Oh!' Archie gave an elaborate shudder. 'What an exciting creature you are!'

Jonno scowled, then laughed. 'Wotcha, Archie, you old bum-bandit. How's it going? Hi, Rupe.'

'Hi,' said Rupert with, I thought, an inflection of irony. 'Harriet, this is Jonno Pye.'

315

I held out my hand. Instead of taking it Jonno formed his own into a gun and pretended to shoot me. 'Bang! Hi, Harriet. Is there any whisky?'

'Over here,' said Rupert. 'Come on, I want to talk to you.'

'Don't worry,' said Archie to me. 'It's just a tiresome little phase. The spring tide of testosterone. Jonno will grow out of it. He's already greatly improved.'

'You amaze me.'

'He got in with some naughty boys at school and some even naughtier ones at university. He's all at sea. What Jonno needs is the love of a good woman.' He looked at me speculatively.

'No.' I am not often firm. By nature I am compliant to the point of utter spinelessness but on this occasion I was adamant. 'Surely you don't believe that men need women to make them into reasonable people.'

Archie pulled a rueful face. 'Oh, but I do. Women – when they have left the dizzy, splashing cygnet stage and become swans, that is – are so much more astute than men. They have a sense of perspective and can take the long view. I'm afraid charming little boy cygnets always turn into ducks. We are the *slaves* of impulse, unable to resist temptation. We throw away all that is precious for one juicy-looking worm. Afterwards, when it's too late, we're sorry. When I *think* what I could be if I could only love a woman. The *heaven* of knowing there was a firm hand on the tiller of my little craft. But,' he shrugged, 'it was not to be.'

'You have Rupert.' I glanced over to where he and Jonno were talking.

'My dear Harriet, no one has Rupert, or ever will. By comparison with Rupert, the sphinx is a rattle. Who knows what spirit inhabits his mind, tiptoeing about his hemispheres with subtle stealth, *shrou*ded in secrecy?' Archie looked more closely at my face. 'I do admire your lipstick. Is it, by any chance, Rhubarb Dash?'

I opened my evening bag, a small velvet purse with a diamanté clasp, borrowed from my mother. I peered at the words on the base of the lipstick case. 'Currant Bliss.' I saw that he was looking at it hungrily. 'Do have it, if you don't mind the germs.'

Archie pocketed the lipstick. 'It would be a pleasure to be blasted into eternity by one of your pathogens, you *gen*erous girl.'

Rupert came up to fill my glass. 'I'm glad you two are enjoying yourselves. What are you giggling about?'

'Harriet has made me the happiest of men,' said Archie obliquely. 'I see you've got Jonno to behave.' We watched Jonno shaking hands with the other guests. The men walked quickly away the moment the ceremony was over but Georgia Bisset put her arm through his to draw him apart.

'I *must* circulate, darlings.' Archie pinched his lips together and smoothed his eyebrows with a forefinger. 'Emilio has been sending me come-hither looks for some time. He's rather excitingly ole*ag*inous.'

'Where's Sir Oswald?' I asked Rupert.

'In the library. He likes to fortify himself before dinner.'

'Isn't that rather odd? Don't the lords and bishops mind?'

'Oswald never puts protocol before his own immediate comfort. Everyone knows that. The lords and bishops are only too pleased to be lavishly entertained with no obligation to return it. Oswald never goes anywhere to dine. He's very fussy about what he eats and drinks.'

'Oh.' I considered this. 'He's rather selfish then?'

'He's always had his own way. Spoiled perhaps, but amiable. And very generous.' I was relieved to hear this. Presumably, then, he would not mind having two strangers foisted on him for the Christmas period, at short notice. 'I've only seen him angry once,' continued Rupert, 'and I've known him all my life.'

'What made him angry?'

'The death of his first wife. He married Maggie within the year and recovered his temper.'

'Then Jonno isn't Maggie's son?'

'Both children are from his first marriage. Here's Annabel, Jonno's sister.'

A girl of about Cordelia's age had come into the room, carrying a plate and a bowl. Dirk, who had given every appearance of being delighted by Mrs Mordaker's petting and conversation, dropped her like a hot brick and presented himself at the child's knees. When Annabel saw Rupert, her eyes widened with an expression of joy and she flew towards him.

I knew Cordelia would require every detail of her rival's appearance so I took careful note. Annabel's brown hair was fastened into two tight plaits. Her bottle-green dress was hideous. She wore knee-length socks, another fashion atrocity in Cordelia's eyes, and her brown shoes, strapped across the instep, were clumsy and childish. Annabel would have been entirely eclipsed by Cordelia but for her eyes, which were the colour of storm-clouds, surrounded by dark lashes, and were really beautiful. She fastened them on Rupert with a look of adoration, blent with accusation.

'I've been waiting *all* day to see you. Maggie promised she'd tell me when you arrived but she broke her word.'

'Maggie's been much too busy to think about it. I hope you've been giving her a hand?'

'I walked the dogs. Anyway, I don't see why I should help her. It's her job.'

'You're an ungrateful little hussy.'

'Maggie's boring and stupid.' Annabel shook her head impatiently until her plaits flew out. 'Come for a walk with me tomorrow? I can recite two whole pages of *The Ancient Mariner* by heart. I spent hours during prep learning it. You said it was your favourite poem.'

'But I don't like tramping about in snow.'

Annabel's face fell. 'Please, Rupert.'

'Don't be a pest. Take those things round and make yourself useful. And offer them first to Harriet.'

I took a sliver of toast spread with what looked like scrambled egg and fish roe. 'I'll come for a walk with you,' I said, feeling that Rupert had been unkind. 'I'm very fond of *The Ancient Mariner*.'

Annabel looked me up and down, apparently with contempt. 'You wouldn't be able to keep up. Besides,' she wrinkled her nose, 'girls are a pain.'

Rupert took hold of Annabel's ear. '*You* can talk. Apologise to Harriet for being cheeky.'

'Ow! That hurts!'

'Go on!'

'All right. I'm sorry. There!' Annabel's eyes filled with tears, whether of pain or humiliation I could not tell.

'Good. Now go and do the rounds. And be polite.'

Annabel rubbed her ear and gave him a look of wounded love before going away, sniffing and wiping her nose on the back of her hand.

'Weren't you rather hard on her? I wasn't offended.'

'That's because you come from a large and outspoken family. Not everyone's accustomed to candour. It's time those children learned how to make themselves liked.'

This conventional attitude surprised me. Rupert glanced across at Jonno and I took advantage of the pause in the conversation to examine him. Rupert, that is, not Jonno. I had already seen quite enough of him. Evening dress is a sort of uniform and Rupert's plain piqué-fronted dress-shirt and small pearl studs were beyond criticism. But something in his face, most particularly in his eyes, told you he did not care what the world thought. From what I knew of him and the people he chose to associate with, I guessed he preferred eccentricity, that conformity bored him. And he was frequently less than polite himself. 'Of course, it's too late for me.' He returned his eyes suddenly to me. 'That's what you were thinking, wasn't it?'

'Certainly not!' I was indignant because he was right. 'Some people always imagine they are uppermost in other people's thoughts.'

Rupert laughed. 'How cutting, Harry.'

Before I could think of something really crushing to say our host came in and began a stately tour of his guests. He walked slowly of necessity for he was immensely fat. He turned his head from side to side as he advanced, nodding graciously and bearing a remarkable likeness to cartoons by Rowlandson of the Prince Regent in middle age. His hair touched his collar, and waved in a shade between gold and grey. As he waddled towards me I saw that the buttons of his dinner jacket were strained to bursting point across his enormous stomach. His eyes were glistening pits in shiny flesh and his little red mouth was crushed between pendulous cheeks.

'Introduce me, Rupert,' he wheezed, very out of breath.

Rupert did so. Sir Oswald pressed my hand between his great paws. 'Delighted you could come, my dear Miss Bung.'

'Byng. It's very kind of you to have us. My sister and I are so –'

'Charming!' He peered closely at my face and I smelled the alcohol on his breath. 'Really lovely and quite original. Something of the Russian look, I fancy. You read Tolstoy?'

'I'm very fond of *Anna Karenina* –'

'Yes, yes. But little Natasha Rostov – gazing at the moon from her bedroom window, a young girl on the threshold of experience – it was she you reminded of.' He ran a finger down my cheek as if feeling the texture of a piece of cloth. 'Hm! Soft and young. You're staying for Christmas?'

'Yes. It really is very good of you to –'

'Excellent! I look forward to many little chats with you.'

His chin disappeared into swelling folds as he bowed his head and made his way over to the other guests.

'I didn't make a very good job of that,' I said, when Sir Oswald was out of earshot. 'I hadn't realised how troublesome gratitude can be. I feel I ought to be making little speeches of thanks and finding innumerable ways to show how grateful I am but everything sounds gushing and insincere.'

'Oswald won't care about it either way. He'll take your appreciation for granted.'

'I wasn't thinking only of him. I'm so deeply in debt to you – for my beautiful clothes and bringing us here and getting me a job and paying the bills. There's so much, I don't know how to thank you.'

'Then don't try. Your parents were very good to me years ago. But for them my childhood would have been hell.' Rupert spoke quite coldly. I made a resolve that in the unlikely event of anyone feeling indebted to me, I would be extremely gracious. Rupert made a sound of vexation. 'I think we ought to rescue the olives – Oh, too late!'

'Dirk, how could you!' I spoke sharply and he came bounding over, wagging his tail. 'All the stones too. It'll serve you right if you have a stomach ache.'

Rupert beckoned to Annabel. 'Take this animal – his name's Dirk – to the kitchen and feed him, will you?'

Annabel's face was eager. 'If I do, will you let me unpack your things?'

'I've already unpacked.'

'Can I bring you breakfast in bed?'

'I hate toast-crumbs between the sheets.'

'Can I clean your shoes, then? Maggie showed me how to clean Father's. I'm really good at it.'

'Well, all right. But one smear of polish on the laces and you'll be in hot water.'

'I promise I'll be careful.' She beamed and took hold of Dirk's collar. He dropped to the ground as though felled by a blow. 'Supper!' I hissed. As yet, this was the only word Dirk definitely understood. He sprang up and strode purposefully to the door, Annabel running behind.

'Poor little thing!' I said as I watched them go.

'I don't see that either of them deserves your compassion.'

'Annabel worships you. And you're so hard on her.'

'Just an adolescent crush. But it's a nuisance. I'm trying to discourage it.'

I laughed. 'You evidently know very little about female psychology if you think that being mean to her is going to make her fall out of love with you.'

'Why you women want to be treated badly, I shall never understand.' Rupert frowned at me as though I were chiefly responsible for this feminine failing. 'I can only imagine such masochism has its murky origins in cave behaviour. Which reminds me, I want to talk to you about Max Frensham –'

'Dinner's ready, everyone.' Maggie looked heated and her hair was escaping its bun. She wiped her hands absent-mindedly on her hips and left smears of flour on her yellow dress.

The dining room was lit only by candles. Down the length of the table were some wonderful arrangements of black-berried ivy and red hippeastrum. They made me think of Maria-Alba, whose favourite flowers they were. My mother decried them as coarse but I liked the huge, artificial-looking trumpets of sickly pink or scarlet that flared all winter on Maria-Alba's windowsill. In the middle of the table was a magnificent silver galleon, about three feet long. It had square silver sails and a snaking silver pennant on top of each of the three masts. The rigging was silver too, a ravelled web of ropes. It occurred to me, even though I was possibly the least domesticated female in England, if one discounted my mother and sisters, that it must take hours to clean. Everything on the table, the knives and forks, the glasses, the salt and pepper pots, and the candlesticks, sparkled against the unblemished whiteness of the damask tablecloth. I wondered how many servants were required to maintain a large house to this standard. Except for Mrs Whale, who stood with downcast eyes, waiting for us to be seated, there was no sign of domestic staff.

My name was written on a card held between the paws of a miniature silver fox. I was delighted to find myself on the side nearest the fire, but less pleased to discover that I was sitting between Emilio and the bishop. I have nothing against bishops in general but something about this one was unalluring. His moist, pasty face bore an expression of pompous satisfaction, as though he thought that to be a bishop was everything, and also that he considered himself to be just the man for the job.

I counted the guests. Including Sir Oswald, Maggie and Jonno, there were twenty people for dinner. No, nineteen, for one chair remained empty. Maggie hurried to check the place card for the missing guest, then consulted her watch. 'Oh dear, one minute past – perhaps the weather . . . We won't wait,' she murmured to no one in particular. 'Bishop, will you say grace?'

We bowed our heads and the bishop began a homily about God's goodness and the prodigal plenitude of our teeming earth. Every time he paused a scraping of chairs on floorboards broke out as people tried to sit down but the bishop was only drawing breath. From the subject of Nature's bounty he passed on to our unfitness to receive it and his tone became accusatory. As I was standing next to the bishop I could open my eyes without him seeing me. Everyone was looking bored and cross. Except for Mrs Whale. Her eyes were screwed up tight and her hands were locked together as though she were standing on the lip of hell, praying like mad not to be dropped in. Freddie's husband, Vere, seemed to have forgotten that we were supposed to be praying, for he leaned forward to adjust something on the deck of the silver galleon. Mrs Mordaker coughed reprovingly.

'In the mouth it is sweet as honey but the moment it is eaten it is bitter in the belly,' the bishop assured us in well-bred tones. Vere caught my eye and made a face of mock-terror. I started to giggle.

The next few minutes were agony. Archie, who was opposite me, saw the difficulty I was in and began to titter. We were about to break down all together when Sir Oswald, raising his voice from the end of the table, said firmly, 'Amen. Thank you, Bishop, most enjoyable.' He sat down and everyone gratefully followed suit. The bishop was obliged to tail off lamely, his expression aggrieved.

'*Hola!* What a bore that man eez!' said Emilio a little too loudly. 'I like to put him to the inqueezetion.' He displayed his teeth. 'Long time I theenk I wish to talk to the beautiful Mees Harriet.'

There was much more in this vein. I wondered if Georgia was doing the right thing, marrying this jaundiced Don Juan. My attention wandered during the flow of compliments. I heard Mrs Mordaker say to Archie, 'When you have travelled as much as I have, you become thoroughly familiar with folly and improvidence. Nothing ever surprises *me*.' She ate a mouthful of soup with an air of complacency. 'The British Empire was the making of India and Africa but were they grateful? Not a bit of it! Though occasionally you do see a spark of decency despite everything. When we were stationed in Nzomiland, the officers' wives did sterling work setting up schools for the !Yu tribe and when we left the women held a special feast day and presented us with hats made from painted animal skins. They're a tiny people, extraordinarily primitive and ignorant and they speak in a series of clicks. Like this.' She made a series of clucking noises like a hen having difficulty with an egg. 'They're quite artistic in their simple way. Unfortunately the hats had to be thrown overboard on our way home as they weren't properly cured.'

'The !Yu of Nzomiland?' Archie clicked with gusto. 'Didn't I read somewhere that they are now extinct?'

'Well, there *was* an unfortunate incident.' Mrs Mordaker's face clouded. 'For which no one was to blame. Hereward – my husband – made the !Yu hand over their bows and spears. They were always warring with the other local tribes, you see, and it was difficult to establish law and order. Unluckily the !Qig chose that very night to attack. Someone always has to carry the can, of course. But I say the British Army *can*not be held responsible for the behaviour of the indigenous population.'

'*Fas*cinating, isn't it, the universal human impulse to create art?' Archie spoke with fatuous pomposity. 'Did you know, the males of certain tribes in New Guinea wear elaborately carved and brightly painted penis gourds to cover their genitals? Generally they are strapped in the upright position, sometimes as long as three feet, with tassels at the tip. For those of us who take an intelligent interest in anthropology,' he bowed courteously to Mrs Mordaker, 'there can be few more inspiring sights than a group of these men so garbed, *in naturalibus cum membris virilis erectis.*'

Something that looked like uncertainty disturbed Mrs Mordarker's composure and she gave her attention to a thorough buttering of her melba toast.

The ancient old lady in purple, on Archie's other side,

who had been browsing in her soup like a herbivore on the savannah, twisted up her head to direct her gaze at the bishop. 'Some men love the sound of their own voices.' Her features were lost in dropping flesh but her eyes were bright and her voices, though quavering, was distinct. 'Some men resemble nothing so much as a lump of mutton fat. But they are not as useful.'

Though I felt sorry for him as the target of general hostility I thought her description of the bishop's pale and sweating complexion had hit it off rather well. I was trying to think of something mollifying to say when the dining door opened to admit a man in evening dress, presumably the twentieth guest.

'Sorry to be late, Lady Pye,' said a voice I knew. 'The train broke down in the snowstorm. We were brought the last lap by bus.' He walked the length of the table to shake hands with Sir Oswald. I saw him clearly as he passed by. It was Max Frensham.

'Oho!' Archie leaned towards me across the table. 'Now the *fun* begins!'

TWENTY-ONE

Archie was mistaken when he predicted the beginning of fun. The bishop sulked disgracefully for a grown man. Emilio's English was not good but it was far better than my Spanish, so our conversation was limited, verging on the banal. At first I smiled a lot, to show good will. He must have taken this for evidence of banked fires, for he patted my hand, stroked my arm and paid me ridiculous compliments. Once he pretended to rescue his napkin from the floor so he could give my knee a squeeze. After that I shifted my chair by degrees nearer to the bishop and adopted an expression that was coolly neutral. There was not much fun in this.

The light in this encircling gloom was provided by Archie, who was having a lovely time baiting Mrs Mordaker. She was anxious to impress him with her knowledge of far-flung places. He trumped her every boast. She lectured him about the natives of Suetemala. He countered with an exhaustively detailed description of the ritual deflowering of virgins by the Rum-baba tribe. I was pretty sure he was making it all up, specially the bit about the corn cob and the eggs of the la-la bird. Poor Mrs Mordaker seemed to lose her appetite though the food was really good.

Throughout dinner I avoided catching Max's eye. I wanted time to adjust to the shock of his arrival. Luckily he was seated at the other end of the table. He had said nothing on the telephone about his Christmas plans. I tried to remember if I had told him the name of my host. I thought not.

When dinner was over, the women followed Maggie into the drawing room and I went upstairs to check on Cordelia. She was awake and complained of feeling sick and cold. Her forehead was burning. Fortunately I met Mrs Whale in the hall and she brought aspirin and barley water. She refilled the hot-water bottles and made up the fire, moving competently about her tasks, unsmiling and unresponsive to my attempts to be friendly. I asked her to make my excuses to Lady Pye and to tell her that I would remain upstairs for the rest of the evening.

Neither Cordelia nor I got much sleep that night. Dirk tracked down a tantalising smell to a box of biscuits beside the bed. He fixed it with his eye and barked until, foolishly, I gave him one. After that no peace was to be had until the contents of the box had been eaten. Then he lay down by the fire for a good scratch. This was followed by a thorough wash with much lip-smacking, licking and nibbling. Toilette completed to his satisfaction, he padded restlessly about the room and scraped at the door. I had tried to persuade him to go out into the garden while Mrs Whale was fetching the hot-water bottles but he had refused to leave the doorstep.

'You idiotic dog!' I whispered crossly, putting on my dressing gown.

My watch said ten minutes to midnight. It was quite likely that some members of the household would still be up. I was reluctant to meet anyone, but particularly Max, in my nightclothes. In a house this size there must be a second set of stairs. I attached Dirk's lead and we went in search of it. He behaved quite stupidly, wanting to scratch on every door we passed, until we came to what must be the servants' staircase. The stone treads had been worn into curves by centuries of traipsing up and down with coals, trays, hot-water jugs, chamber-pots and slop pails.

I was halfway down it when the lights went out. The blackness was complete, which for a Londoner was disconcerting. I tried to feel the steps ahead of me with my toe and managed to clock my eyebrow painfully on the newel at the turn of the stairs.

Then the whispering began. At first I thought it might be a water-tank filling or the wind blowing through a crack but I soon heard voices mingled with the susurration. The echo made it impossible to hear what they were saying. Dirk growled.

'Hello?' I called. 'Who's there?'

The whispering stopped. A horrid silence prevailed in which I imagined someone – or something – creeping stealthily down the stairs towards me. It was broken by a peal of maniacal laughter of which Mrs Rochester would have been proud. Dirk gave a howl that frightened me even more, and pulled frantically on his lead, his claws scrabbling on the stone. I launched myself forward, away from whatever it was, and missed several steps to land awkwardly at the foot of the stairs. Ahead I saw a faint greyish light. I ran towards it and found a half-glazed door. The handle turned under my hand. I yelled again as the door opened and a gust of freezing air hit my face. A dark shape gripped me by the elbows and shook me, none too gently.

'Is that you, Harriet? Stop screaming. You'll wake the whole house.'

'Rupert! Oh! Thank God!'

'It's all right. You're safe. There's nothing to be afraid of.'

I clung to him, shuddering with cold and fear, and he put his arms round me. The warmth of his body, the faint scent of cologne and the smell of smoke from his cigar were immensely reassuring. After a while I lifted my head, which I had been pressing against his chest.

'I'm OK now.'

He let me go at once and removed his cigar from his mouth. 'What are you doing down here?'

'Dirk wanted to go out. I was just coming downstairs when the lights went out. I heard whispering and laughter –'

I broke off as the passage was flooded with light. We stared at each other. I must have looked ridiculous, blinking in the glare, my hair practically standing on end with fright.

'There's no mains electricity at Pye Place. The generator is apt to cough from time to time. As for the rest – you're tired after a long journey and you've been imagining things.'

'I haven't! Someone, two people, I think, were whispering and when I called to them they didn't answer.'

'It was probably an adulterous couple making an assignation. Clandestine sex is as much a part of a country house party as bridge, boredom and too much to drink.' Rupert was maddeningly calm. 'Just a minute.' He opened the door, letting in a spiteful eddy of cold that shot up my dressing gown, and chucked away his cigar. 'Where's the dog?'

'I must have let go of his lead when I screamed.'

'It was a coloratura performance, then?'

I gave him a cool look though it is hard to be dignified when one has so recently clung to a person, sobbing with terror on his shirt-front. 'Anyway, what were *you* doing here?'

'I thought a stroll in the fresh air might clear my head. I shouldn't have had that last brandy-and-soda. Or the cigar. The idea's so much more pleasant than the real thing. Luckily I heard you screeching. We'd better go and find him.' I noticed for the first time that my ankle was hurting like hell. I decided to maintain a decent reticence but before

330

we had gone far Rupert said, 'Why the Long John Silver imitation?'

'It's nothing.'

Rupert smiled. 'Strange girl. Life must have a dreary sameness about it if you have to limp for fun.'

I couldn't help laughing. 'Brute.'

'Fathead!'

The ten years' separation was forgotten. We were friends as in the old days. I remembered Rupert's particular brand of teasing as distinctly as the taste of the fluorescent yellow sherbet lemons we used to suck while he read to us of Lucy and the Master of Ravenswood.

My pleasure in this sentimental reunion was spoiled when we reached the main landing. It had been transformed from an empty, echoing and slightly sinister place in which one could imagine dark shapes slipping between sliding panels, or even through them, into a busy thoroughfare.

'Look here!' expostulated the colonel when he saw me. 'I was just dozing off nicely when that blasted dog of yours tried to shoulder my door down!' A long strand of hair dislodged from his bald pate hung over one ear, his pyjama jacket was buttoned up the wrong way and his face was flushed with temper. 'If you own an animal you damned well ought to keep it under control.'

'Kindly remember that my husband is a clergyman!' The bishop's wife stood in the doorway of her room, her sensible camel dressing gown fastened to the neck, a hairnet pulled down to her eyebrows, her cheeks shiny with blobs of cold cream. 'I was always taught that swearing is the sign of an impoverished vocabulary.'

The colonel glared at her. 'I should appreciate it, madam, if you would keep your trite and worthless opinions to yourself.' He disappeared into his room and slammed the door.

'Shut up, Doris, and come to bed,' called the bishop from

within. 'How can I sleep with that bloody dog howling outside my room and you picking quarrels all night?' The bishop's wife retreated, with a face of wrath.

'Will whoever has been scratching at my door desist?' The old lady who had taken such a strong dislike to the bishop put out her head. 'At my age I expect to be excused the libidinal attentions of the opposite sex.' She withdrew her head without waiting for an answer.

'Is something wrong?' Maggie looked anxious. She wore an apron over her dress and her hands were wet and red. 'I heard voices.'

'I'm afraid it's my dog. He's been making a terrible nuisance of himself and now he's run off and I can't find him.'

'He's down in the kitchen.' Maggie sounded apologetic though it was hardly her fault. 'He seemed hungry so I've given him the remains of dinner.'

Ten minutes later we were all back in our rooms and the house was quiet, except for the sound of teeth clashing against bone as Dirk chewed his prize on the rug before the fire.

I slept intermittently. The sound of the wind, a sort of low hoo-hooing that sometimes rose to a scream, seemed to weave itself into my dreams, while Cordelia turned and kicked, radiating heat like a brazier. Sometimes she muttered in her sleep, frequently she threw out an arm, striking me in the face or stomach. During one of the few periods when I was deeply asleep, she was violently sick over the bedclothes. As it was only barley water it was not too horrible and at least my half of the bed was still dry.

'What time is it?' Cordelia pressed up against me, shivering.

'Half-past five. I'll put out the light and you try to go back to sleep.'

'OK.' We lay in the darkness for some time until Cordelia said, 'I'm freezing.'

I pulled the damp eiderdown over us. After about ten minutes she said, 'I'm too hot.'

'It's because you've got a temperature. Like a drink?'

'Yes.'

'Here you are. Don't drink it too fast.'

'OK.'

A further passage of time in which I tried to slide into unconsciousness.

'Hat?'

'Yes?'

'Sorry I woke you being sick.'

'S'all right. I was having . . . bad dream anyway.'

'What about?'

'I was being chased . . . by a big black bull . . . with red nostrils.'

'Ooh!' Cordelia clutched me sympathetically. We were silent for some time after that. I felt my mind slipping into irrationality. 'Hat?'

'What?'

'I'm awfully glad I'm here with you. After Pa and Mark Antony you really are my favourite person.'

'Good.'

'Who're your favourite people?'

'Tell you . . . morning.'

'It *is* the morning.'

'Not . . . yet.' I turned on my side away from Cordelia and felt myself fall slowly and blissfully towards oblivion. Beneath my feet were masses of primroses. I decided to lie down among them but, close to, they turned out to be miniature fried eggs on stalks, and their crinkled leaves were rashers of bacon. I was just about to eat some of them when something poked me hard in the back. Cordelia had her knee against my kidneys. I managed to manoeuvre her back to her side without waking her. I thought regretfully of the bacon and

333

eggs and the empty biscuit box. It would be hours before breakfast.

Then my heart began to beat very fast. It was too dark to see anything but I heard something creeping round the foot of the bed. There was no mistaking the stealthy nature of what were undoubtedly footsteps. The wind raised its voice to a wail. Dirk woke with a yelp and growled.

'Shh!' came a whisper. 'Don't wake the young ladies, there's a good lad.' I heard Dirk's tail thumping. I began to breathe again.

The sound of a match being struck was followed by crackling. I lifted my head and saw a flame leap in the fireplace. Someone was on their knees before it, adding fuel to burning paper. Slowly, expertly, the fire was built until that half of the room was filled with warm, red light.

'Maggie?'

'Bless me, you made me jump!' Maggie came over to the bed. 'How's the lass?'

'Feverish. And I'm afraid she's been sick. I'm so sorry.'

'Don't you worry. There's nothing in that way that can't be set right. But I'm sorry she's poorly. We'd best send for Dr Parsons straight way.'

'Thank you for lighting the fire. It's the most wonderful luxury.'

'It's a pleasure, my dear.'

I lay staring at the moving patterns made by the flame-shadows on the pleated silk ceiling of our bed and wondered why it was necessary for the mistress of the house to tiptoe about at dawn, lighting bedroom fires. There had been no other signs of economy. Dinner had been of the very best and the wine much praised. Accustomed to furnishings that were a little ramshackle I had been impressed by the orderliness of Pye Place. Though everything was marvellously old, it was in good order, shining and clean. Downstairs there were hot-house flowers, the latest magazines and silver *bonbonnières* of expensive-looking chocolates. Upstairs the sheets were linen, as smooth as glass and smelling of lavender, there were piles of soft towels and the sort of soap of which Ophelia approved. The spirit of the place, far from being penny-pinching, was sumptuous.

Twenty minutes later Maggie came in again with a tray of tea and, oh joy! two Chocolate Olivers. Seeing that Cordelia was asleep she put her finger to her lips and slipped away before I could thank her properly.

'Good morning, Harriet.' Archie was contemplating with pleasure a substantial plate of porridge and cream. 'You look a little pale.'

Rupert lowered his newspaper enough to look at me over the top of it, then, wordlessly, resumed reading. Colonel Mordaker, the bishop and his wife and the old lady, formerly in purple, now in maroon, were the only others present.

'I have always found a diet of water, poached fish and citrus fruit the answer for a muddy complexion,' said the bishop's wife to the table in general. 'That, and outdoor exercise. The young these days are too much inclined to *lounge*. When I was a child my best friend was my skipping rope, and I can assure you I never suffered from so much as a sniffle.'

A derisive noise, something like 'Tchah!' came from the colonel's lips as he banged his cup on to his saucer.

The bishop's wife looked at him in haughty surprise for a moment before continuing, 'If the young lady will condescend to take my advice and get out into the fresh air with a rope, I can guarantee she will find her appearance greatly improved.'

'There happens to be something like a foot of snow and ice outside,' said Rupert from behind his paper. 'I don't know that her appearance would be much improved by a broken leg.'

'I'm all right,' I said. 'I'll feel better when I've eaten something.' I went to the sideboard where spirit lamps kept several silver dishes hot, and helped myself to scrambled eggs, tomatoes, mushrooms and toast.

'Hello, Harriet.' Max was at my elbow. He looked poetic in a waistcoat, collarless shirt and jeans. The other men, except for Archie, were in tweeds. Archie was wearing a suit of large windowpane checks in yellow and brown, very like Rupert Bear's trousers. 'You *are* pale,' Max said in a low tone that only I could hear, 'but it's extremely attractive. That alabaster complexion with those dark eyes is stunning.'

No one had compared my skin to alabaster before. I was unaccustomed to so much concentration on my appearance. 'Tomato?' I held the spoon poised above the dish.

'Whispering's not allowed' called Archie. 'I must in*sist* on a thorough briefing.'

''Morning, Archie. Rupert.' Max went to the table, pulled out a chair and waited for me to sit on it. Rupert stared over his paper. I carried my plate across, trying not to limp, though my ankle was still sore. I felt Rupert and Archie's eyes focused upon me as critically as though they were casting directors and I was auditioning for an important role. 'Haven't seen either of you for a while.' Max pushed in my chair and sat down next to me. 'How are you both?'

'Well,' said Rupert.

'My bosom's lord sits lightly in his throne,' replied Archie.

'*Othello*,' I said without thinking.

Colonel Mordaker paused in the process of shovelling down kedgeree to say 'Tchah!' again, rather louder this time.

'Really, Harriet!' Archie frowned. 'You have *shocked* the colonel by your ignorance. It was, of course, a quotation from

336

Romeo and Juliet. I'm sure Colonel Mordaker will give you act and scene, if you ask him nicely.'

'I'll do nothing of the kind, sir!' A grain of rice trembled on Colonel Mordaker's upper lip. 'I know nothing of such twaddle! Fighting for Queen and country has kept me fully occupied without resorting to such stuff!'

'There, Colonel, you are wrong.' The bishop's wife spoke decidedly. 'I grant you there is a great deal of inferior prose and verse written these days, but the bard himself *must* be beyond criticism. Personally I have a great dislike for T. S. Eliot. As for D. H. Lawrence, I consider him fit only for degraded minds –'

'Madam,' the colonel's face grew red as he turned his angry little eyes towards her, 'when I want instruction during breakfast on the trashy jingles of dirty-minded nancy-boys I'll be certain to apply to you. Until then perhaps you'll be good enough to remain silent on the subject.'

'Well!' The bishop's wife sent an indignant glance in her husband's direction but he only crunched his toast more loudly and pretended to be engrossed in *Country Life*. 'Well!' She decided to enter the lists on her own behalf. 'Of course we all know the proverb that ignorance is the mother of impudence. And whatever else he might have been D. H. Lawrence was *not* a homosexual.'

'Madam, an old soldier knows better than to waste time bandying words with – ladies.' The colonel got up and helped himself liberally to scrambled eggs and bacon.

'When it comes to proverbs,' said the old lady in maroon, uncurling her neck to stare at the bishop's wife, 'he is an ass that brays against another ass.'

In the silence that fell as the colonel and the bishop's wife meditated replies Maggie came in with pots of coffee and tea.

'No, thank you, Lady Pye,' said the bishop's wife. 'Too

337

much caffeine is very bad for the temper.' The colonel snorted and held up his cup and saucer to be refilled. 'It is well-known,' she continued, 'that red-faced, choleric types often have an addiction to such stimulants. Dear Lady Pye, I must let you have *my* recipe for kedgeree. It was given me by my great friend, the Bishop of Bengal, so there can be no doubt of its authenticity. Rice should be the bulk of the dish, the fish being merely a flavouring. As for parsley in kedgeree, I never *heard* of such a thing.'

'I've sent for Dr Parsons, my dear,' said Maggie to me. 'He'll come as soon as the snow-plough's been up.'

'How is the poor child?' asked Max.

'Not very well but I'm sure it's not serious.'

'And Waldo?' He had lowered his voice so that only I could hear. 'I thought last time I saw him he seemed more cheerful. I hope the police are getting on with the job of finding the real murderer.'

'Thank you, he does seem better. You've been so kind visiting him so often. Inspector Foy said not to expect any progress for a week or two as it's Christmas.'

'I count Waldo as one of my dearest friends.' He looked at me and smiled. 'You were very much missed after dinner. A bevy of harridans and not a single pretty woman.'

'There was Freddie.'

'Ah, yes, true. Lovely, but firmly spoken for. A woman thoroughly in love with her husband becomes almost invisible to other men, I'm afraid.'

'And Georgia whatever-her-name is. She didn't strike me as being very much in love with Emilio.'

Max looked surprised. 'Do you call her pretty?'

'How are the roads, dear Lady Pye?' asked the bishop. 'We must catch the noon train. Painful though it is to drag ourselves away, a man of the cloth cannot call his soul his own.'

'No, indeed,' said the colonel. 'Particularly not when he is married to a busybody know-it-all.'

'Hereward, you've forgotten your heart pills.' Mrs Mordaker entered the dining room, waving a small bottle. She came over to inspect his plate. 'What did the doctor say about eating too many eggs?' The colonel bared his teeth and made swatting movements as though troubled by a fly.

'It's very difficult,' said Mrs Mordaker to Maggie. 'I try to make him do the right thing but he doesn't like to be fussed. The doctor says if he doesn't take his pills he could be struck down at any moment.'

The bishop's wife smiled an awful smile. 'How sorry we should all be in *that* eventuality.'

She left the room in triumph.

'Now, Hereward,' said Mrs Mordaker. 'What's happened to upset you? Remember what the doctor said about getting worked up –'

'For heaven's sake, will you *shut up*!' the colonel almost shouted. 'It's more than a man can bear, being lectured all the time by dim-witted females.'

The old lady unbent enough to say, 'A spurred ass must trot.'

The colonel almost split his waistcoat and his face darkened to mahogany. 'Madam!' He was sounding more and more like Dr Johnson. 'This is more than flesh and blood can stand!'

'Now, Ernestine,' said Maggie hurriedly.

'Now, Hereward,' said Mrs Mordaker at the same time.

'Another cup of tea, my dear?' asked Maggie, filling the old lady's cup before she could answer. 'And what about a nice drop scone? I made them myself this morning. You must keep up your strength for the great work.'

'That woman has twice called me an ass within ten minutes,' muttered the colonel to his wife as she sat down beside him. 'It's beyond sufferance!'

'Colonel, have a little more toast and my homemade blackberry jelly,' said Maggie soothingly. She bent close to his ear and added in an undertone, 'Miss Tipple is ninety-four, you know, and doesn't hear quite as well as she used to. I'm sure she had no intention of calling you names.'

'I heard that.' Miss Tipple said at once. 'And I have always found honesty to be the best policy.'

'Do tell me,' I said, liking this indomitable old lady, 'what is your great work about?'

'It is the *History of the Union of Female Franchise*,' said Miss Tipple, beating her twisted, freckled hand on the table for emphasis as she spoke. 'Which is the story of women's struggle to escape the tyranny of selfish and unscrupulous men.' Though her voice was shrill and variable in its register and her eyes just a gleam among folds of crêpe-like skin, I had no doubt of a still sparking mind.

'How interesting!'

'Oh, yes, Ernestine is ever so clever,' said Maggie. 'It's a wonderful book. But you must take care, my dear, not to overtire yourself so you can get it finished. I hope you slept well?'

'I did *not*! I was much troubled by some importunate wretch scratching at my door. Luckily I always take the precaution of locking it so he was forced to go away unsatisfied but I was unable to return to sleep until two o'clock.' She fixed her eyes on the colonel.

'You need not look at me, madam –' began the colonel wrathfully.

'No, no,' said Maggie. 'No one suspects you for a moment, of course, Colonel. What a pity the weather is so rough. There've been reports of blue-footed falcons on Doorknocker Tor this summer. I thought of you at once, knowing what a great expert you are on birds.'

'Really? Who says so?' The colonel was distracted at once.

'If it's that idiot gardener of yours I shall insist on seeing for myself before I believe it.'

The bishop, who had all this time been cowering behind his magazine, now ventured an opinion on the likelihood of blue-footed falcons coming so far south and soon he and the colonel were locked in disagreement. I found the disputatious style of the other guests extremely entertaining.

'Quite a raree show, isn't it?' said Max quietly, echoing my thoughts. 'It does one good to get away from London. And not just for the scenery, though this must be one of the most beautiful parts of the world.'

'I haven't seen anything of it yet. We arrived after dark and when I looked out of the window this morning everything was white, even the sky.'

'I was here two years ago. There are some pretty marvellous views, if you've got a head for heights. What about a walk when the snow stops?'

'Have you known the Pyes long?'

'I was Hotspur in *Henry IV* at the Bunton Festival two summers ago. Sir Oswald was extraordinarily generous, throwing parties for the whole cast and putting up the leading actors for two weeks. We had a wonderful time. Though I must say,' he added, 'it was rather hard on Maggie. She seems to do the work of ten. But when Cordelia happened to mention, over the telephone, that you were coming here for Christmas, the open invitation the Pyes had given me seemed suddenly extremely attractive.' In his look was a glow of appreciation that I could only interpret as being a tribute to my charms. I examined the tablecloth, embarrassed and delighted. 'What are your plans for the day?'

'I can't make any until the doctor has seen Cordelia.' I had dropped my voice to match his.

'Harriet,' called Archie, 'if you are forming a cabal I beg

341

you to let me in on it. I've always thought I might have a talent for intrigue.'

There was justice in this reproof, but before I could make amends Jonno appeared. He was wearing a coat of shaggy fur, and jeans with the knees ripped out. 'Hi, gang.' He sauntered over to inspect the dishes on the sideboard. 'Jesus, nothing but fucking rice. Who's pinched all the haddock? Maggie, there's no bacon left.'

'I'll go and get you some,' she said at once.

'Sit down, Maggie,' said Rupert. 'You've been rushing about for the last hour. Jonno knows where the kitchen is.'

Jonno looked sulky. 'What's the point of having women about the place if they can't make themselves useful.'

'And of what use are you?' Rupert spoke calmly but he looked cold.

'Well said!' put in Miss Tipple.

Jonno smirked. 'Come off it, Rupe. You weren't always such a tight-arse. I can remember you drunk as a lord on more than one occasion.'

'Being drunk is boorish, I grant you,' said Rupert, 'but behaving like an insolent puppy when sober is worse.'

'Well, of all the . . .' Jonno flushed deeply. 'Christ! I don't have to put up with this!' He looked at Rupert, indecision written clearly on his face.

'Well?' Rupert expression was icy. 'Do you refute the charge?'

'I'm not accountable to you for my behaviour.'

'It's not you I'm concerned about. But if you can't see that Maggie deserves your gratitude and consideration, then it's up to her friends to point it out to you.' He grimaced as though at some unpleasant thought, folded his newspaper and then smiled at Jonno. 'Now don't sulk. Come and sit down and tell us about university life in Manchester.'

Jonno hesitated.

'In my day,' said the colonel, 'we did as we were told by our elders and betters with no shillyshallying. Nor did we come late to breakfast looking like something the cat brought in.'

'Thank you!' said Jonno bitterly. 'D'you think I give a bugger about the opinions of blimps like you? All wars are evil and it's people like you who've perpetrated them. You're an anachronism, obsolescent, a deadbeat – and the pity of it is you can't even see it!'

He stalked out of the dining room.

'A whipping would be too good for that boy,' snapped the colonel as soon as he had mastered his temper sufficiently to speak.

Maggie looked ready to cry. 'Perhaps I'd better go after him.'

'Over my dead body,' said Rupert.

'Excuse me, Lady Pye but the doctor's here.' Mrs Whale was standing at the door. 'I've showed him up to the young lady. And Sir Oswald wants his breakfast. Now.'

TWENTY-TWO

'I'm so *bored*!' cried Cordelia. Considering how much effort had been put into entertaining her for the three days she had been bedridden, this was ungrateful. 'When's Max coming?'

'Darling, you can't expect a grown-up man to spend all his time in a sick room.' Particularly with a patient who was tetchy and imperious, I might have added, but did not. Cordelia's morale was at an unusually low ebb. She had been forced into the ignominious role of invalid when she had hoped to burst upon Pye Place as a star of extraordinary magnitude.

Cordelia had been quite unwell the day after our arrival. Dr Parsons, a physician of the old school, had given orders that she must stay in bed with hot-water bottles to sweat out the fever, aspirin for her headache and a light diet of beef broth and water biscuits to settle her stomach. He had been alarmed by her fluttering lashes, poignant farewell speeches and demands to be carried to the window for a last look at the moor, and had prescribed a tonic to settle her nerves. I was not too worried. The wind had not ceased to howl for a solitary second since our arrival and our imaginations had become hopelessly entangled with Emily Brontë's.

When Rupert had come to see Cordelia she had spoken in a strangled voice of her imminent departure for an early grave. Rupert had told her not to talk rubbish and get some sleep. For the rest of his visit Cordelia had kept her eyes closed and her hands folded on her chest, refusing to answer when he spoke to her. Archie sent a message to the effect that loath though he was to be deprived of her beauty and wit, he was extremely susceptible to viruses.

'It isn't any good pretending queers are just like other men except for sex,' said Cordelia grumpily, offended by this dereliction of duty. 'I think they're incredibly selfish.'

Like all my family, with the exception of Portia, Cordelia was a bad patient. Maggie was tireless in her efforts to tempt Cordelia's appetite. When she declared that the beef broth was disgusting, the water biscuits tasted like blotting paper and Dr Parsons was a warty toad, a succession of good things – tiny tomato sandwiches, chicken patties, glazed apple tarts, orange-scented custards and lemon possets – were brought up at intervals throughout the three days. Chocolate milk shakes and miniature buns with pink icing found most favour.

I had tried to persuade Maggie to let me provide for the invalid. She had been shocked by the idea of my going into the kitchen and making myself useful. Apparently Sir Oswald had strict notions of hospitality and prided himself on his excellence as host. He was used to hearing visitors say that Pye Place rivalled Chatsworth in comfort, beauty and gracious living in the old style. Though less ostentatious it had an unparalleled charm in its remoteness from the world's stain. He would have been seriously angered to discover that anyone staying beneath his roof had been allowed to dirty their hands with cabbages or gravy.

Maggie had admitted she did all the cooking for the household. Mrs Whale was only a plain cook but she was invaluable when it came to housework. She was a dab hand at laundry-work and could sew 'like an angel.' I said I hoped there was not too much needlework in heaven as I was terribly bad at it and the idea of unpicking stitches for eternity was depressing. Maggie said very seriously that she was sure the Good Lord would never be so cruel as that. I realised that the sort of irreverence that was the bread of life to my family had no place in Maggie's scheme of things and made a resolve to keep such silly jokes to myself in future.

Anyway, it was Mrs Whale who darned the linen with tiny stitches and kept the fragile textiles in good repair. Dingle, the gardener, lent a hand with 'the rough', such as cleaning silver and stoking the boiler. Cooking for twenty, Maggie said, held no terrors for her; she was strong and she was used to it. She had been brought up to work hard and she would not have known how to occupy her time otherwise. But none the less by the end of the day I saw her pinching her nose to hide yawns and often during dinner her eyes closed and her head nodded. She always got up before six to light the bedroom fires, and she and Mrs Whale washed up the dinner things after the guests had gone to bed.

Cordelia was pampered not only by Maggie. Max spent every afternoon with us and spared no effort to entertain the fretful invalid, for which kindness, even had he not been charming, amusing and good to look at, he would have earned my undying gratitude. Serious flirtation was out of the question for we were never alone. But, though he gave the greater part of his attention to Cordelia during these afternoons, playing consequences, cribbage and dominoes with us or reading to her, while I struggled with Cordelia's latest creative project, he never let me forget that I was the chief reason he was there. It would have been difficult to say by what means exactly he conveyed his intense interest – a look, a smile, a tone of voice – but I was certainly acutely conscious of it. As far as I could tell, I was not in love with him, but when he was near me it was peculiarly difficult to think of anything else.

Cordelia had spent the last two weeks before we left for Derbyshire making a tapestry along the lines of the Bayeux, which was to be a record of our family life. She planned to use a combination of appliqué and embroidery to illustrate people, places and events as they happened. I had bought a length of hessian for the background and we had raided every cupboard and drawer at home for scraps of fabric. It was to be a present for Pa, to brighten the dreary walls of his cell. Among the many memos he fired off daily to the Home Secretary, was a complaint about the remarkably vile shade of green he was made to live with, for twenty-three hours out of twenty-four. It was sickly, the colour of stagnant water, of creeping fungal growths, of putrescent matter. It jangled his nerves, depressed his spirits and offended his artistic sensibility. So far there had been no response.

Cordelia's idea was excellent but it was harder to do than either of us had envisaged. She had insisted on beginning with a portrait of Dirk. We had been brought to the edge of a flaming row, trying to get his legs right. Bron had said he looked like a lactating giraffe with a nasty attack of mastitis. Cordelia had said if he made one more unhelpful remarks she would leave Bron off the tapestry altogether. When, in later years, it was displayed to the marvelling world in a purpose-built museum, people would wonder at the absence of her only brother, but by then regret would be vain.

While Cordelia grumbled about being bored I tried to stitch Maggie's hair in place with a squiggle of French knots to imitate her curly fringe. Her face was a virulent shrimp-pink, cut out of the woollen vest I had bought from the Co-op, which was the nearest thing I could find to flesh colour. Just as I discovered I had sewn the whole thing to my skirt there came a knock at the bedroom door and, with the prevision one acquires when a single individual is the prism through which all things are viewed, I knew it was Max.

'How's the sufferer?' He stood at the end of the bed, smiling at Cordelia who stopped looking petulant and beamed up at him with bright eyes.

'Looking forward to coming downstairs, I can tell you. I'm sick of being in bed. If only Harriet weren't such an idiot I could come down right now. I can't see what difference a few hours makes.'

'Dr Parsons said she could get up for dinner this evening,' I explained. 'Maggie sets such store by Dr Parsons' opinions and has been so good to Cordelia, I think it would be unkind to ignore his advice.'

'Harriet always wants to please people. It's nauseating. Except for me, of course.'

Max looked at me and I thought I read in his eyes a question. Might he fall into the category of people to be pleased? If so . . . I stared, fascinated, at the dent in the end of his nose as though he were a snake charmer and I a cobra in a basket.

'Ah, but think.' Max turned again to Cordelia. 'If you want to stun the company, and particularly Annabel, by the impact of your beauty you'll do it far more effectively in evening dress than in a skirt and jersey.'

The girls had yet to meet. Maggie had suggested that Annabel might play snakes and ladders with Cordelia to help while away the hours. Cordelia had told me that if Annabel so much as set foot in the sickroom she, Cordelia, would throw herself out of the window. So it was as well Annabel had thought she might have a cold coming.

Now Cordelia chewed her lip and looked thoughtful. 'I think my blue thing is a bit babyish. Darling Hat, will you lend me your beautiful black dress that Rupert bought you?'

'But it's miles too grown-up for you. It's almost too grown-up for me.'

'I think I'll get up now.' Cordelia threw back the bedclothes. 'And I shan't eat that cake Maggie's making specially for my tea. I shall ask her to take it away because I'm too upset. I bet Elinor Dashwood would have lent Marianne her entire wardrobe if she'd wanted it because she was so sad that her favourite sister was nearly dying.'

'Oh, goodness, all right!'

Cordelia drew the bedclothes over her again. 'Now that's settled, what game have you thought of for today, Max?'

'It's called five senses. We each have to write down the five things that we would like best to see, to hear, to touch, to smell and to taste. I've brought pencils and paper. We'll start with sight. It's quite good fun, I promise you.'

It was surprisingly hard to decide on the things we really, *really* wanted to see. Cordelia's list was: Richard III, Mark Antony when a new-born kitten, a flying saucer landing in the garden, Shakespeare (so she could tell him exactly what she thought of him for writing all those long boring plays) and a vanity case exactly like mine with her initials on it. Mine was cautious and deliberately unrevealing: John Keats, eighteenth-century London, a polar bear cub, an angel, Michelangelo at work on the Sistine Chapel. Max's were typically masculine, except perhaps the last: Fangio winning the world championship, a Nuremberg rally, the earth from the moon, the Battle of Trafalgar, a look of love (from whom unspecified).

When it came to hearing it was even harder. Cordelia had gasps of admiration (at what she didn't say), the rustle of a hundred Christmas presents on the end of the bed in the middle of the night, a lion purring, Richard III's limp and the announcement of her name at an Oscar ceremony.

'How come you've both got Mozart playing his own piano

concertos?' she complained. 'What's with this Mozart? I think God's voice is good, Hat. I wish I'd thought of that. But a sigh of love is cheating, Max. At this rate you'll be saying the touch of her lips, the taste of her skin and the smell of her armpits for the other senses. I mean these are all things you could easily have. You said they mustn't be ordinary things like money or a sunny day.'

'Love isn't quite as commonplace as you seem to think.' Max glanced at me. 'Unfortunately.'

I sucked my pencil and examined my piece of paper, then suggested we got on with the five things we wanted to touch. An hour went by during which we were pleasantly amused.

'I'd better take Dirk for a walk before it gets dark.' I looked out of the window at the sky, which was beginning to lose its brilliance.

'I'll come with you,' said Max.

'You can't both go,' said Cordelia. 'Anyway, Max, you promised you'd finish reading *Far From the Madding Crowd*. I *must* know whether she goes back to that stupid Gabriel Oak. I hope Sergeant Troy turns out not to be dead, after all.'

'Yes, stay and read,' I said. 'It'll be horribly cold. I shall be twenty minutes at the most.' I knew that Cordelia had already finished the novel that morning but I had no intention of giving away her stratagem. Having accepted that Rupert was incapable of turning over a new leaf as far as women were concerned, she had made up her mind to be in love with Max. I thought he could be trusted to deal kindly with her infatuation.

Out of doors the wind left off its plangent wailing and became savage. The light, reflected by the snow, which had ceased falling, was still bright enough to hurt one's eyes. Though I had put on a quilted coat of Maggie's and wrapped a woollen scarf round my ears my extremities became numb almost immediately. After three days Dirk and I had established a route that took us down the drive to the cattle-grid and then left, following the line of a tumbled-down stone wall, to the most staggering view at the edge of a vertiginous drop. Whatever the weather I always paused by the cattle-grid and turned back to admire the house.

Pye Place was built of grey stone and was E-shaped, with a projecting wing at each end. The central porch was surmounted by two oriel windows, one above the other, making a shorter middle stroke. It had five handsome gables surmounted by ball finials and the roofline was broken by chimney stacks. On the central gable was carved the date of its construction. Later, when memories of the cow-herding had faded, someone had added the family's coat of arms between the first- and second-floor windows. The façade, three storeys high and roughly four times as long, was the embodiment of Beauty and Truth. It seemed to me as lovely a dwelling as man could have made for himself and yet it had withstood whatever Nature could throw at it over several centuries, with no sign of injury.

In front of the house lay a broad sweep, gradually declining towards the valley. This was now uniformly white but presumably some combination of grass and gravel lay beneath. Springing out of this plateau were odd excrescences, their lower halves showing dark green, their summits piled with snow. Some were like crouching giants, others like fabulous beasts. One was lean and slanted like a rocket-ship aimed at the stars. These were the yews Maggie had mentioned that had grown out of shape. Incontrovertible proof of the first Oswald Pye's genius in choosing this spot on which to build his house was its proximity to a projection of rock, some twenty or thirty feet high, which lay to the right of the house. A waterfall plummeted from its apex to disappear with a smoky fury into a dark and mysterious hole behind the yews. The spur was not near enough to cast the house into shade, but was sufficiently close to make the crashing of the water audible from the front door.

The study of noble architecture was Dirk's least favourite part of the walk. He liked to get into the field where he could dig holes. On the grounds of mutual incompatibility we agreed to separate. He continued with his excavations and I went on alone to admire the view. This we did twice a day. As Dingle took Dirk out for a good run every morning with Sir Oswald's corpulent pointers, Bouncer and Blitzen, my conscience was almost clear.

Approaching the cattle-grid on this particular afternoon I saw a crouching figure ahead, examining something on the ground. It was Vere, Freddie's husband. Though we only met at dinner, for he always had breakfast early and was out of the house all day, I felt I was beginning to know him. He was a man of moods, sometimes talkative, sometimes taciturn, but he was always very friendly once he was aware of you. I wondered what he found to occupy his thoughts so much of the time.

'Hello, Dirk.' Dirk, who rated Vere highly among his acquaintance, rolled over so Vere could rub his stomach with the toe of his boot. Dirk's stomach, I mean. 'Now, steady on or you'll scuff up the prints. Hello, Harriet,' as I came panting up, lead at the ready.

'Sorry, is he being a nuisance?'

'No, he's all right. I was just wondering if these were the tracks of an otter.'

I stared at the marks that looked to my untrained eye like cat's paw-prints. 'Don't otters live in water? Surely not in the waterfall?'

'Listen.' Vere held up his finger for silence. I heard only the shushing and phewing of the wind.

'What am I listening for?'

'Come and see.'

Vere set off and I had almost to run to keep up. The surface of the snow was iridescent with sparkling points that changed colour as I approached. Round the boles of trees lay pools of deep violet shadow into which dropped clumps of snow blown from naked branches. The crystals crunched satisfyingly beneath my boots like sugar. Dirk ran ahead, clods of ice flying from his heels. Our path became a crevice, constricted by overhanging trees, their trunks distorted by the interminable gales.

'Look at that!' Vere said as I clambered, puffing, over rocks glazed with ice to see within yards of me a torrent of water slipping between boulders down a ravine and tumbling into a silver and black river below. 'This is where the waterfall by the house comes out. I'd like to follow its path underground, wouldn't you?'

'Mm!' I enthused untruthfully.

'There'll be caves and stalactites. Derbyshire limestone is the perfect medium. There might be narrow places where you'd have to go under water. I suppose a canoe in summer when the riverbed's at its driest,' he mused, 'but you'd have to be careful not to get swept over this drop when you emerged.'

Somehow I could not get excited by the prospect. 'Do shut up, Dirk.' Dirk had been prompted by the energy in Vere's voice to bark loudly. The sound bounced off the cliffs and echoed about the valley.

'Listen,' said Vere again. 'A fox answering.' I heard a harsh scream that seemed to come from miles away. Vere took my arm and pointed up at the sky. 'Look! A mountain bustard!' I saw something black against the pearly sky before the brightness and coldness blurred my vision. 'I think I'll go after it. Perhaps there are some others. Want to come?'

He looked so eager that I felt I should disguise the sad truth that it would not be the most wonderful treat for me. 'I'd love to but I'm afraid Dirk would alarm them.'

'Oh, yes, you're right. I'd forgotten him. Can find your way back to the house all right?'

I could see he was desperate to be off. 'Absolutely. Go on, don't worry about me.'

I was not as certain of my route back as I had pretended, and the uniform whiteness made each boulder and tree look much like its neighbour. Dirk romped about, pleased to have our walk extended and stopped occasionally for a furious dig. After a while I realised we were lost. A fairly anxious few minutes later, I was relieved to see a woman trudging ahead of me, head down against the wind.

'Hello!' I shouted. 'Do wait a moment!'

Through watering eyes I saw her stop and turn. It was Jonno. We had had little to do with each other so far. He was pretty drunk when he came down to dinner and extremely drunk by the end of it. After that first morning he never came to breakfast, or lunch.

He waited for me to come up to him. 'Hi! You look cold.'

'I'm frozen, actually. And lost.'

'We aren't far from the house. I was going back anyway. Want a drag?' he waved a hand-rolled cigarette at me. 'It's good stuff.'

'Oh, all right. Thanks.' It seemed unsociable to refuse. Many of my parents' friends smoked cannabis and I had shared a few joints with Bron. I did not disapprove of it, but smoking anything seemed inappropriate in such unpolluted surroundings.

'Bloody awful here, isn't it?' Jonno shambled along, his eyes on the ground.

'I think it's extraordinarily beautiful.'

'Oh?' He lifted his head and looked around. 'Oh yeah, it's

OK scenery. But I was born here. I can't fuss about what I've always known.'

'That might make it more precious. Memories of childhood, that sort of thing.'

He gave a laugh that sounded bitter. 'Maybe, if those memories were anything but hell.' He laughed again, the cry of the tortured soul.

I was used to melodrama so I did not smile. 'However awful something's been, surely it's better to have it happen in a place that's beautiful rather than somewhere squalid and ugly? Imagine being unhappy in an inner-city slum with cockroaches and wailing police sirens. Or slaving underground in a Siberian salt mine.'

Jonno managed a proper laugh this time. 'You're a chick for extremes. Yeah, well, anyway, don't take any notice of me. I just get depressed sometimes. Particularly when I come home.'

'What's it like at university?'

'OK. The lectures are boring and I hate writing essays but there are some good clubs and bars. Only,' he hesitated and then went on in a rush, 'I bust up with my girlfriend last term. She went off with a mate of mine. I really miss her,' he added in a softer tone and my heart, previously granite where Jonno was concerned, was touched. 'And him.' He sucked hard at the reefer. 'It's a bitch, actually.'

'Certainly sounds like one.'

'I don't know why anyone lets themselves get fond of people. They always fuck off in the end, leaving you on your tod, bloody miserable.'

'Aren't you exaggerating? You aren't alone. You've got a father and a sister for a start. And I can't imagine Maggie deserting anyone.'

'Oh, great!' he spoke with heavy sarcasm. 'My father doesn't care about me. He's too busy caring about *him*.

And Annabel's just a silly kid. As for Maggie – you aren't seriously suggesting she could be a friend? She's barely literate.'

'I'd have thought that mattered a lot less than loyalty and decency.'

'Cant!'

'No, it isn't. I really like Maggie, as well as being grateful for everything she's done for Cordelia and me. I admire her. She works hard and she has tremendous self-discipline. She's utterly unselfish. And I know when I talk to her she'll always be truthful. She feels things deeply. That's important, isn't it? People might be able to recite all of Newton's Laws but if they're shallow everything's more or less the same to them. They just do or think or feel whatever seems most immediately attractive. Those are the people who rat on you when you need them.'

'Uh-huh.' Jonno kept his eyes trained on the ground.

'Yesterday Maggie said she was worried about you. She thinks you're unhappy.'

'Ten out of ten for observation.'

'She said, "I'd give my eyeteeth to know what I could do for the poor lamb."' Jonno gave me a look of angry impatience. I knew I was taking a risk but I pressed on, in hope of doing good. 'She said it was hard watching you what she called "turning in on yourself" but that you wouldn't allow her near you.'

'Well, I like that! I let her pin a pair of cords on me the other day that she's taking in down the seams. How much nearer does she want to be?'

'Not like that, silly. You don't talk to her, take her into your confidence.'

'It's never occurred to me. What point would there be? Our worlds are quite different. She's just a village drab Dad married to pay the bills and drudge for him.' He glanced at me then and looked a little ashamed. 'OK, I know that sounds snobbish.'

'Not only revoltingly snobbish but stupid as well.'

'Hey, you don't mind making enemies, do you?'

'I hate it, actually, but I'm fond of Maggie and I won't hear her spoken of disrespectfully.'

We walked up the drive towards the house in silence, Dirk running round us in circles. Suddenly Jonno gave a mirthless laugh. 'She called me a "poor lamb", did she? And I'm supposed to be grateful!'

'She also called you a "lost weakly lad who drinks more than is good for him to cushion his misery."' Having gone so far there seemed little point in holding back anything.

'Well, bloody hell! It's nice to know I'm treated so deferentially behind my back. Weakly! What the fuck did she mean by that? I may not be Mr Universe but I've my fair share of musculature.'

'You know perfectly well she meant morally.'

'Fucking cheek!'

As he maintained an offended silence, I went on, 'I don't suppose any of us would like it if we knew what other people said about us. A village drab, indeed! Only Maggie thinks so little of herself she'd probably just accept it. It's those of us who put on airs and graces whose pride is apt to be hurt.'

'Thanks very much. So now I'm affected.'

'I didn't say that, exactly. I know *I* am.'

'You? You're little Miss Perfectly Pretty and Pretty Perfect. I suppose all good-looking chicks are vilely conceited, though. It's unfair to blame you.'

I was moved by this tribute to my looks to feel I might have been a bit hard on him.

'The thing is, how many people do *you* care about?' I asked. 'I mean, you can't expect it to be all one way.'

'I care about plenty of people.' His tone was injured. I

waited while he stood still and thought. 'Well, I suppose I wouldn't like anything to happen to Annabel, even if she is a pain in the arse. And I was keen enough on Kate before she dumped me.' He thought some more. 'Ah!' he said triumphantly. 'I was in love with the prep school matron when I was a kid. Her name was Miss Prosser and she had untidy brown hair and reminded me of Tufty, my guinea pig.'

I smiled, relieved that on occasion he could forget the Dostoevskian pain and strike a note of self-mockery.

'I suppose it isn't exactly an impressive list,' said Jonno. 'But then I'm not into bleeding hearts. So, what about you? Who rates in your book?'

'Well, my parents and my three sisters and my brother, for a start. Naturally I really, *really* love them.'

'Naturally,' said Jonno drily.

'No, truthfully. They frequently drive me to utter despair but if it was my life or theirs, I'd give mine without a second thought. Or only a brief moment of reflection.'

'As I said, you're a girl of extremes.'

'Then there's Maria-Alba. She lives with us and I love her dearly. There are three girls I was at school with who I don't see much of because they're not living in London any more but none the less I'm deeply fond of. And there are plenty of people I know, like Ronnie, my mother's friend, who I'm always pleased to see. And Rupert and Archie –'

'All right, all right. You're a marshmallow, in love with the human race.'

'You asked me. Actually, when I meet people for the first time I'm much more inclined to hate them than love them. Just in case they hate me, you know.'

'Yeah. I know.' He inhaled deeply and handed the soggy joint to me but I shook my head. 'That sounds a prim, wholesome sort of list to me.' He mimicked a girlish, upper-class voice. 'Mummy, Daddy and all the nice people I know.

My former headmistress, dear Miss Bodily-Function, and Reverend Lickspittle, the vicar. Not forgetting Brown Owl, who taught me that singing round the campfire can bring on a nice clean orgasm with no danger of getting up the spout.'

'Oh, for God's sake! Look, you can go on ahead. I know my way now.'

'Don't get huffy, Miss Perfectly Pretty. OK, I'm sorry.' When I did not reply, he stopped and pulled my arm so that I was facing him. 'I really am sorry, Harriet. I'm a prat sometimes. I don't know why I have to be so stupid and I hate myself even when I'm being it. You're right to be angry when you were only trying to help. Give me another chance.'

There was something like real wretchedness in his face, despite the ridiculous beard and the unpleasant nose-chain, which made me relent.

'All right, you're forgiven. This time.' I smiled. 'Come on, let's walk faster. I'm cold.'

'But, really,' we were moving briskly now, 'isn't there some man languishing in London, desperate for a lusty glance from those dark doe eyes, who matters more than old school chums?'

I didn't answer then because I saw someone coming out of the house and down the steps on to the drive. Though the light was draining fast from the sky, flinging a cloak of ultramarine across the countryside, I knew it was Max.

'Don't be shy,' said Jonno. 'You can trust me to keep the secrets of your innocent girlish heart. Unless I'm drunk, of course, which, I regret to say, I very often am.' Then he saw Max. 'There's that actor bloke. A pearl of masculine beauty and doesn't he know it!'

'How can you say that? You've hardly spoken to him.'

'I know. I've been too smashed. But there were some chicks from the village up here yesterday wanting his autograph and practically wetting themselves at the sight of him. He put on the charm like he was Robert Redford. But I have to admit – reluctantly – surrounded by a pack of simpering giggling birds, I'd have done the same. Put it down to jealousy on my part.'

'There you are.' Max was within calling distance now. 'You said twenty minutes. It's been three-quarters of an hour. I was worried. But I see I needn't have been.' He smiled at Jonno. It was too dark to decide quite what sort of smile it was. 'Been clearing the head, Jonno?' Before he could answer, Max said, 'You ought to come in, Harriet. It must be below freezing.'

'I got lost.' I tried to walk between them, which was difficult because Max had taken my arm and was walking at a faster pace than Jonno. I was conscious of the pressure of Max's hand.

'So that's it, Miss P-P,' said Jonno, in a low voice. 'I ought to have guessed. I'd better tell the groupies hanging about the stable yard that they're wasting their time.'

He veered off abruptly and was swallowed up by shadows.

'Do you like that boy?' Max asked.

'I don't know. Yes, perhaps. I feel sorry for him, anyway.'

'He's an ass.'

'Mm. But I like some asses.'

Max seemed to be considering this. Then he said, 'Is that possible? Isn't respect part of liking?'

'Probably it ought to be. But the truth is, I usually like people if they seem to like me. Not very praiseworthy, I know.'

'So Jonno's been making advances, has he?'

'Not at all. He's pretty rude most of the time. But I get the impression he's very lonely.'

'He's a self-indulgent yahoo,' said Max dismissively.

We were nearly up at the house by this time. Lights from the ground-floor windows daubed the snow with yellow squares.

Maggie was in the dining room, unfolding the shutters, her hands encased in the white gloves she wore to protect polished surfaces and antique textiles from fingermarks. Such meticulousness was touching, as though Maggie poured into the house all the tenderness that was rebuffed by those she lived with.

'Can we extrapolate from that that it's enough for someone to be in love with you to have you return the feeling?' Max said as we stood in the porch among mackintoshes, gumboots and walking sticks. He turned me round to face him. The waterfall sounded very loud. I was thankful the porch was dark. It was dreadfully cold and I tried not to shiver. 'Harriet. Answer me.'

When I did not, he bent his head and kissed me on the mouth. I returned the kiss, out of politeness at first but then because a mixture of emotions, both pleasant and unpleasant, made me forget about being polite.

Dodge had kissed me in quite a different way, like a hungry dog that has lighted on a delicious snack and is impatient to wolf it down. Max kissed me with deliberation, a mindfulness that told me he was in charge and knew exactly what he was about. He would lead me where I was certain to like to go. I had only to relinquish my will and everything would follow. Something like happiness filled my mind and body briefly, and the sighing of the wind and the thundering of the water suggested that passion cannot be governed by resolve. Then I reminded myself that Max had a wife who had tried to kill herself. That was when my misgivings eclipsed the gladness.

I pulled away and leaned back against the door jamb. 'Max, please, this isn't a good idea.'

'You shouldn't be so damned seductive if you don't want to be kissed.'

Max put his hands on my shoulders, pinning me to the wall within the circle of his embrace and looked at me intently, without speaking. When I hung my head, in an agony of self-consciousness, he took hold of my chin, none too gently, and forced me to look up. This was weakening stuff. I was desperate not to sniff though I knew my nose was about to run catastrophically. I tried to keep the picture of an unhappy woman before my eyes, in place of Max's face.

'Harriet!' he said at last, a new note of urgency in his voice. 'I must be possessed. All day whatever I'm doing or saying I'm really only thinking of you. Even during the night that's all I think of. Especially during the night. When you're in the room I can't take my eyes off you without an effort of will. I've never felt like this about anyone before.'

The image of Caroline faded just a little. I was about to confess to being in a similar state when the front door opened abruptly and our tryst was illumined by the light in the vestibule. Max dropped his arms to his sides and stepped back.

'What an importunate pair you are!' Rupert was unsmiling. 'Miss Tipple is convinced you are either the police coming to warn us of the escape of a dangerous and insatiable rapist or – worse – the rapist himself. Maggie has gone to fetch her some brandy.'

'What do you mean?' I felt bewildered.

'You're leaning against the doorbell.'

TWENTY-THREE

Christmas Eve
Dearest Maria-Alba,

Thank you so much for your letter, which arrived safely this morning despite the postman having to walk all the way up from the village. We had another fall of snow in the night and his van was stuck. Cordelia is quite better and I can assure you she is getting the best food possible, so please don't worry. Maggie's cooking is nearly as good as yours only more English. I told you, didn't I, in my last letter what we had to eat out first evening at Pye Hall and I can only say that the standard hasn't gone down at all. We'll all be incredibly fat at this rate. Maggie looks so disappointed if you don't eat up. She's a really motherly sort of person and it's a shame she hasn't any children of her own. Jonno and Annabel take her completely for granted.

Anyway, for dinner last night we had crème Constance, which is a curried soup, followed by roast duck with a wonderful sauce. I particularly asked Maggie what was in it so I could describe it to you properly. It is made with shallots, that's a kind of onion, I think, and

red wine, orange juice, redcurrant jelly and something
called a demi-glace. With it we had roast potatoes,
carrots, leeks and an orange salad. For pudding there
were plums baked with rosemary and a white coffee
ice, perfectly delicious, and cheese afterwards. Then
everything is taken off the table, including the cloth,
which is made in strips so it can be done with minimum
disturbance and it's laid for dessert, fresh and glacéed
fruit and nuts. Maggie and Mrs Whale are tremendously
efficient but I'm always aware of how hard they work
while the rest of us sit about. But when Freddie offered
to help clear away the plates Sir Oswald nearly burst
a blood vessel. So we none of us dared move. For
lunch the day before yesterday we had eggs in a cream
sauce . . .

There was much more about food because I knew that apart
from the wellbeing of our family it was the only thing that
really interested Maria-Alba.

At this moment Cordelia is getting ready to come down
for drinks before dinner. She insisted on my waiting
downstairs as she wants to knock us all dead with envy
and admiration, even me. We are a smaller audience for
her now as the bishop and his wife have left, which is
disappointing as she was a very interesting and peculiar
woman. Lord Bevel and his wife have gone too. And
the two middle-aged women whose names I never did
discover. A really awful couple called Colonel and Mrs
Mordaker are staying until Boxing Day. At least they
are dreadful but you can't help feeling sorry for her. He
bullies her all the time and now Archie is giving him
a taste of his own medicine. Archie is unrepentantly
wicked but quite wonderful. So for Christmas there'll

be – apart from us four and the Pyes – Freddie and Vere, Georgia Bisset, Emilio, and Miss Tipple, a rather marvellous old lady, much given to speaking her mind. Oh, and someone I forgot to mention in my last letter, Max Frensham. Do you remember him? He used to come to Ma and Pa's parties.

We usually have a very amusing time when we all meet up for lunch or dinner – we in this context being Rupert, Archie, Freddie, Vere, Max and me. Sir Oswald doesn't care about anything but eating as far as I can tell, and Maggie is too busy to enjoy herself, except I think she likes housework. I hope so. Jonno is always drunk, poor Miss Tipple is deaf, Emilio's English isn't good enough to follow what's being said and Georgia is entirely without a sense of humour. She's engaged to Emilio but he's always busy trying to seduce anything on legs, with perhaps the exception of Dirk. He – Emilio, I mean – has a laborious kind of charm that he lays on thickly like train oil but without much success as far as I can tell. I can't help wondering why Georgia and Emilio ever got engaged because she, I've just realised, has *her* eye on Max Frensham. He is, of course, very attractive and quite well-known so perhaps it's not surprising.

I had firm evidence on which to base the last assertion – about Georgia having her eye on Max, that is. In order to get my letter-writing done without distractions I had retreated to what I was already coming to think of as *my* workroom. Anyway, no one else seemed to use it. A narrow flight of stairs led from the drawing room to what was called the Little Parlour. It was hardly more than ten feet square, with painted green panelling and an arched window that looked on to the waterfall. It had in it a desk, an armchair, a table lamp and a bookcase. There was a charming little fireplace with Delft tiles of scenes from Noah's Flood but, most important of all, it had an electric fire for instant, directable heat. Maggie said visitors always asked if it was a priest's hole and sometimes, without actually telling a lie, she let them think it was but really it was too large and easily discoverable for that. Probably it had been a steward's room or where the lady of the house did her accounts.

The Pyes had, in those days, been Catholics, which, according to Rupert, was the saving of the Pye Place as Catholics were not allowed to hold important positions, and so get rich and put up newer, more fashionable houses. In one wall of the Little Parlour was a wooden shutter, about twelve inches square, which you could open to get a view of the drawing room below. But unless someone knew of it, they wouldn't be aware of you observing them. Rupert told me they were called squints. Probably generations of Lady Pyes had kept a vigilant eye on the household from here.

Just as I had finished describing Maggie's cooking in my letter to Maria-Alba I heard someone come into the drawing room and chink the glasses on the drinks tray, which was brought in at seven fifteen on the dot and from which guests were supposed to help themselves. I only had to lean over the desk and look through the squint to get a bird's-eye view of what was happening below. Georgia, done up to the nines in diamonds – something very glittery anyway, perhaps paste – and a strapless red dress, was pouring herself a gin and tonic. From my eyrie I could see a good deal of lacy underwear. She must have been fearfully cold. Though Maggie and Mrs Whale rushed round all day like Chinese jugglers, hurling logs and coal into every fireplace, the temperature was not suitable for more than bare wrists and perhaps a couple of inches of neck.

I watched her as she paced up and down, glugging her drink and turning ornaments upside down to examine the factory marks. There was something purposeful about her that engaged my attention. Then Max came in. He helped himself to whisky and came to stand beside her, right under my peephole so I could hear everything.

'Marvellous old house, isn't it?' said Max.

'It's full of beastly draughts,' said Georgia. 'Anyway, I hate old places, they depress me. I'd rather be in the Caribbean any day. I've hardly any tan left from the summer,' she added in regretful tones, practically knocking out his eye with her elbow as she showed him her arm.

'I don't much like very tanned skin. Except on farmers and fishermen. People ought to have something better to do than lie about on beaches. It makes me think they must be rather stupid.'

Gosh, that was telling her, I thought gleefully.

'Oh, I agree with you. Deep tans are awfully common,' said Georgia without a blush. 'Minds are so much more interesting than appearances. Good looks are all very well but what I find more attractive than anything is a first-class brain. I like a man to be clever and – and mysterious.'

'Mysterious?' He laughed. 'I shouldn't think there are many of those.'

'Of course I can read all women like a book.' (A likely story, I thought, pun not intended.) 'But occasionally I meet a man I can't fathom.'

She gave him a pussycat smile and that is when I was certain she had designs on him.

Max shrugged. 'I think men are pretty easy to understand. Once they identify a goal they generally pursue it single-mindedly, not necessarily to their own advantage. I usually find women much more unpredictable and interesting.'

'Aren't you horribly bored being cooped up here with a lot of ancient old fogies and children?'

Max smiled at her. 'As long as there's one person present

to whom I'm strongly attracted and whose company I really enjoy, I can be happy almost anywhere.'

'Oh?' Her tone became arch. 'And may I ask whose company you're particularly enjoying at the moment?'

'Aha!' said Max in a teasing voice. 'That would be telling!'

This seemed to have a galvanising effect on Georgia. She prowled up and down, head thrown back, nostrils flared, sucking hard on a cigarette and looking dramatic. I realised that the person she'd been reminding me of all along was Bette Davis. Probably the protuberant eyes.

Her pacing was disturbed by Freddie and Vere, who came in with Miss Tipple between them. Georgia looked furious at having her tête-à-tête with Max interrupted. When Emilio and the Mordakers followed almost immediately and then Annabel – in her bottle-green dress again, I was sad to see – Georgia turned her back to them all.

She moved very close to Max and looked up at him, her lips parted and the tip of her tongue showing, like a snake about to strike.

'Tell me.' Her voice had become strangely husky. 'I must know who this interesting and unpredictable person is. Give me a clue. Is she a million miles away from where we're standing?'

'She's very near.'

She put her hand on his arm. 'Am I cold or warm?'

'You're very warm – burning, in fact.'

Georgia rolled her eyes and practically swallowed her cigarette. The lesson about eavesdropping was brought severely home to me. Naturally, the minute I realised Max was interested in someone else, he became a million times more desirable. The memory of that kiss on the doorstep filled me with miserable, uncomfortable rage. What a fool I had been! It seemed that any girl was fair game if she was stupid enough to believe his compliments. Besides, Georgia really wasn't someone one could remotely think of as unpredictable. Actually I couldn't think of anyone *less* interesting. For the first time in my life I experienced sexual jealousy. It was a sickening feeling, a punishing combination of a strong desire for the other person and a profound disgust of oneself. Just as I was debating whether I ought to close the shutter and make myself get on with some work, or go downstairs and show Max by my cold and dignified behaviour that I was no longer his plaything, Sir Oswald came in and waddled over to Max and Georgia. He wanted to tell her the history of a particular piece of furniture and of course she had to go with him. You could practically hear the ripping sound as she tore herself from Max's side. As she walked away Max turned round. He looked up, straight into my eyes. Smiling, he shook his head in reproof and blew me a kiss.

I shrank back out of sight, my heart thumping with excitement, gratification and shame at having been caught eavesdropping. Worse, I experienced an ignoble sensation of triumph. He had known I was there, listening. He had let Georgia think he was talking about her but he had intended every word for me. Hadn't he? As soon as I identified my state to be one of dizzy euphoria on finding myself preferred to Georgia, I asked myself whether I had completely lost my head. Was this frenzy of feeling nothing more than base competition for the attention of the only attractive heterosexual man available? Did I feel any of those softer, less egoistic emotions that might have something to do with love? Then I had remembered Caroline. I buried my face in my hands and sighed. I was losing sight of everything that mattered. I almost hated Max then for making me weak and assailable, a silly romantic girl without clarity of mind and strength of purpose.

Anyway, I'll finish by giving you a thumbnail sketch of

the house, as I wrote my first letter before I had any idea what it looked like from the outside. It's an amazingly building, stone walls and a stone tiled roof, quite large windows with small diamond-shaped panes, all set at different angles to let maximum light in, which Maggie says is called bombé glass. It's very touching how much she loves the house.

Here I described the waterfall and the scenery round about and the consequences, good and bad, of deep snow which, of course, we never had in London.

I've tried to write a poem about it but it wasn't any good. The textures and colours of snow are just too elusive. Do you remember you used to say it was the angels moulting? I've just heard the second gong, which means that dinner is in ten minutes so I'd better go down and be nice to people. I'm so glad the nuns are letting you take over some of the cooking. I bet they're glad too. I'm delighted you're feeling better. You know how much you mean to me, dear, dear Maria-Alba, I'll write again in a few days, fondest love, Harriet.

In the drawing room Sir Oswald was lecturing Freddie, Vere and Georgia about the seventeenth-century cabinet on stand, pointing out its exquisite 'seaweed' marquetry and blend of oyster veneers. Freddie was nodding attentively, Georgia looked frankly bored. Vere was staring at a painting behind Sir Oswald's head. He wandered over to take a closer look at it, unaware of Sir Oswald's vexation at having part of his audience stray. Miss Tipple sat alone, as was often the case. Her deafness, combined with her habit of speaking her mind, made her something of a social test. I brought up a stool beside her chair so I could shout in her ear, if necessary.

This was, I'm afraid, not as altruistic as it sounds. Though I could not prevent myself knowing exactly where he was standing and who he was talking to, even whether he was smiling or serious, I wanted to avoid Max. The super-cognisance that operated between us was productive of both pleasure and pain. All my life I had chided myself for being vacillating and irresolute. That inner voice that advises against the dictates of our vanity and weakness and would guide us safely if only we would let it, which perhaps is nothing more mysterious than common sense, took a dim view of my hurling myself into a romantic abyss.

Miss Tipple's deafness varied quite a bit according to her mood. This time, despite the growing buzz of conversation, she heard every word I said and told me what it was like to be on hunger strike in prison as a suffragette before the First World War and how sleep strike – walking up and down without pause day and night – was far worse than being hungry. Sir Oswald interrupted a very interesting conversation.

'Ah, Miss Tipple, you are warm enough there, by the fire? That is my favourite chair.' Actually it was everybody's favourite chair as it was closest to the only source of heat. 'It is very comfortable, is it not? In the reign of Queen Anne, when it was made, they were beginning to acknowledge the importance of such things. It has a particularly deep seat. That is what makes the difference. Old Gally's, on the other hand,' he indicated the ancient black oak chair that stood on the other side of the fireplace, 'makes few concessions to the requirement of the human frame for cushioning.'

This particular chair had caused a good deal of annoyance. Its proximity to warmth had made several guests overlook its shortcomings in the comfort department, but whenever anyone attempted to remove the clay pipe, tobacco jar and snuff box that lay carelessly disposed on its seat, Sir Oswald or

Maggie protested as vehemently as if someone had suggested the Holy Grail be used as a spittoon. The chair had belonged to the first Galahad Pye, he of tin-arm fame, and it had to be left exactly as it was with his favourite accoutrements at the ready or – the consequences were the more sinister for being left unspoken. This dog-in-the-manger-ish attitude on Old Gally's part was regrettable but it was impossible to disregard the genuine distress of our hosts so the plum spot went untenanted, except possibly by spectral shanks.

'No, no, you must not get up.' Sir Oswald waved a hand dimpled with fat to motion Miss Tipple back into her chair. 'Certainly not. I shall sit over there on the sofa and Miss Bung will perhaps be good enough to favour me with her views on the county of Derbyshire for which, I must confess, I have an unreasonable partiality.'

He really was Prinny to the life. Dutifully I followed him over to the sofa, belabouring my brain for tributes to his native soil. But I need not have worried. Sitting down for Sir Oswald was a lengthy business. It produced much gasping and puffing, crunching of human joints and ominous creakings from wooden ones as the sofa took the strain. When I had squeezed myself in beside him, pressed hard against the arm on one side and Sir Oswald's swollen thigh on the other, he began to talk.

'You can have no idea, Miss Bung, what pleasure it gives me to see young people about the place. This dear old house, simple and modest as it is,' I made disclaiming noises in my throat to which he nodded approval, 'needs the vitality of the new generation if it is not to sink absolutely into the past. Ah, Annabel, there you are. Come and give your father a kiss.' Annabel, her face expressionless, came over and planted a peck on Sir Oswald's enormous cheek. 'Sweet child! That will do now.' He waved her away. 'Now, my dear,' he placed the hand on my knee, 'you will not object to telling an ancient creature like me how old you are?'

'Not at all,' I said politely. 'I'm twenty-two.'

'Really? As much as that? I should not have thought it.' He looked disappointed. 'Are you married?' I shook my head. 'Catherine, my first wife, was just seventeen when I married her. Think of that! Hardly more than a child.' He gave my knee a hard squeeze. 'Her skin was of a delicious creaminess flushed with pink, like – like strawberry fool, with violet-blue veins on the insides of her wrists and the backs of her knees – yes, hmm. The rude blast of life was too rough for my poor sweet girl and the tender blossom withered on the bough. I have only a painting now to remind me of that gentle, innocent gaze, those cheeks with a faint, fair down of youth, that little dimpled chin, lips like the plump breasts of tiny birds – ah, me!' He sighed. I struggled to think of something sympathetic to say. 'We made a handsome couple though perhaps I should not say so,' Sir Oswald went on before anything occurred to me. 'But you will allow an old man to boast of past glories, my dear Miss Bong.' A smile broke across his cheeks like a knife cutting dough and he gave my kneecap a gentle massage. 'You know Mrs Gilderoy is painting my portrait now?'

'Yes, Freddie did tell me.'

'She has managed to capture something of the old dog, I fancy.' His small beaky mouth was round with silent laughter. 'The years have taken their toll and I'm a touch broader round the girth, of course. You must ask her to let you see it.'

'Yes, I'd like –'

'Something about the eyes isn't quite right, a little too small, I think.' I glanced at the tiny porcine twinkles enveloped in seamed blubber and wondered at man's ability to delude himself. 'Twenty-two, you say? I'd have guessed about eighteen. You're very slender. And firm.' He slid his hand, which was hidden by the folds of my dress, along my thigh. I could not help seeing that his face was reddening, I hoped with the effects of alcohol.

'My sister's coming downstairs for dinner. Perhaps I ought to go and hurry her.'

'No, don't do that. Not when we're so nice and cosy here, having our little chat.' His breathing quickened as his hand explored further.

I was seized by mental paralysis. There must be a thousand excuses for getting up and going away but I couldn't think of one. Rupert's voice over my shoulder said, 'Oswald, I must have a word with you. Harriet, would you mind giving up your place to me?'

I shot up from the sofa. Sir Oswald looked at him reproachfully. 'I am quite cross with you, Rupert, for interrupting our little talk just when we were getting on so well.' He seized my hand in his flabby paw and held on to it tight. 'We shall continue it after dinner, my dear Miss Bang.'

It was then that Cordelia came in. The black dress fitted very well as she had nearly as much bosom as I, and it didn't matter at all that on her it was ankle length. The dress, that is. Her hair hung about her shoulder in soft, shining curls. She had raided my supply of cosmetics and was wearing a great deal of makeup. It would have looked whorish, but Cordelia looked seductive and at least seventeen. Sir Oswald let go of my hand. 'Who is that girl?' His cheeks quivered. 'Where has she sprung from?'

'By heaven, that's a fine-looking gel!' I heard Colonel Mordaker say. 'Sort of creature one dreamed about in the trenches.'

Mrs Mordaker looked hurt.

'That's Cordelia Byng,' Rupert took away Sir Oswald's glass before he could spill it over himself. 'Harriet's sister. She's been ill and confined to bed since our arrival.'

Sir Oswald's feet scrabbled ineffectually at the floor before he panted, 'Bring her over here. I must bid her welcome.'

'Here's Maggie to announce dinner.' Rupert gripped his arm. 'Let me help you up, Oswald. You can say hello later.'

As we walked towards the dining room I heard Annabel say to Cordelia, 'Maggie said I'm to say I'm sorry you were ill.'

'You needn't be. It isn't every girl who has a film star to herself for hours and hours in her bedroom.'

'A film star?'

'Max's going to be in a film version of *Macbeth* this autumn. Of course I shall miss him *dread*fully while he's away.'

'Is he your boyfriend, then?'

Cordelia hesitated for a fraction of a second. 'Let's just say,' she tossed back her curls, 'it's a meeting of kindling spirits.'

'Are you really only twelve?' Annabel looked at her in awe. 'Emily Cutler-Biggs was voted the best-looking girl in the school last term but I think you're much prettier.'

'Really? murmured Cordelia, with a fair imitation of modest astonishment. 'Where did you come?'

'Nowhere. I never get picked for anything.'

Cordelia opened her blue eyes wide. 'That's the saddest thing I ever heard!'

I was delighted to find Vere on my left but rather less pleased to have Sir Oswald on my right. But he rarely spoke during the first two courses, preferring to give his attention to his plate. One's duty was to keep him supplied with sauces, salt and pepper and bread and butter. Max was at the other end of the table next to Georgia and Maggie. Cordelia was sitting between Emilio and Archie. Emilio was rolling his eyes at Cordelia and showing her all his teeth. He reminded me of Dirk in one of his less sensible moods.

'Did you see any more of those birds?' I asked Vere as we

began the soup, which I saw from the little menus Maggie put at intervals along the table, was called *Potage Alexandre*. It was smooth and creamy with grains of rice and green shreds, possibly leeks floating in it. I must not forget to tell Maria-Alba about the delicious little *croûtons* coated with sieved hard-boiled egg that accompanied it.

'The mountain bustards, you mean? Yes. Three. But I saw something even more exciting.' Vere put down his spoon and turned to look at me so I knew it was important. 'A blue-footed falcon!'

'No!'

'I'm positive. There's no mistaking it's black moustachial stripe and a densely cross-striped belly.'

'Good heavens!'

'And in flight the wedge-shaped, tapering tail makes it unmistakable. I think it was a young one, for the dorsal feathers were quite pale still.'

'Gosh! Really?'

I had overdone the incredulous excitement. Vere began to laugh. 'You haven't a clue what I'm talking about, have you?'

'I'm afraid I'm completely ignorant about birds. I'm so sorry.'

'No, it's I who ought to apologise for assuming that everyone cares about what interests me.'

'But I really am interested. Honestly, I'd love to know something about them. I wish you'd begin to educate me.'

'Well, if you really mean that –'

Colonel Mordaker interrupted Georgia, who was telling him about her last holiday in Jamaica, to lean across the table. 'A blue-footed falcon, you say? I don't believe it. It must have been a sparrowhawk.'

'No,' said Vere firmly. 'It wasn't.'

'I tell you, blue-footed falcons don't appear this far south in winter.' The colonel thrust his brick-red jaw at Vere.

'But my dear Colonel,' said Archie. 'One should never forget Nature's apostasy. If ice-caps can melt and rivers dry and volcanoes become extinct, if mountains can rise up from ocean beds and continents can move, we must allow that blue-footed falcons may, from time to time, change their habitat. Flux! Flux! All is flux! Just the thought of it makes one feel madly insecure, I know,' he added kindly. 'But we mustn't get into a tizzy about it. You, particularly,' he waggled a finger, 'must remember that troublesome old ticker.'

Colonel Mordaker, whose line of country had been action and not words, made his customary swatting motion as he struggled for speech. Archie goaded him mercilessly and the colonel was beginning to be afraid that he, a tough old bruiser of a war-horse might be got the better of by a namby-pamby pervert who wore makeup. Makeup, for God's sake!

'Now what was that bird I was reading about the other day?' continued Archie smoothly, as the colonel opened his mouth to resume his attack on Vere. 'A masked something-or-other – dear me, one's memory – that has suddenly appeared in great colonies in quite the wrong place. The ornithologists are in a rare old dither about it.'

'If, sir, you'll allow me, to speak,' said the colonel with slow emphasis, 'we might be able to have a sensible discussion.'

'Oh, of course, Colonel, dear. You press on while I have a teeny think.'

The colonel ground his dental plates together and questioned Vere in barking tones about what he persisted in calling the 'supposed' blue-footed falcon.

'What a fuss about a stupid bird,' said Georgia quite angrily. 'Can't we talk about something interesting?'

'Madam,' the colonel turned to her, 'when you have something interesting to say I shall be delighted to hear it.'

'Booby!' said Archie.

The colonel drew himself up and bared his teeth. 'I'll have

no more of it!' he shouted. Everyone stopped talking. A beetroot tide suffused the colonel's features. 'I won't put up with being insulted to m' face by a painted catamite who ought to be ashamed to call himself a man!'

We looked at each other aghast. Maggie half rose from her chair.

'Yes, that's it,' said Archie, beaming. 'The masked booby! A tropical marine bird of the same family as pelicans and cormorants. Colonel dear, as you're such an expert, I'm sure you can enlighten us as to its usual migration patterns.'

'Washa matter, everybody?' asked Jonno, sliding into the empty chair next to Annabel. 'Shorry I'm late.' He let out an ill-concealed belch. 'Cat got your tonguesh?' He fell into helpless giggling.

I caught Freddie's eye. She was making motions with her hand to imitate the eating of soup and pointing at Vere. I saw that his plate was still untouched while the rest of us had finished. I risked my first glance at Max since we had sat down. He was looking at me with an expression of amusement. As our eyes met, he threw back his head and laughed.

TWENTY-FOUR

After dinner, when we women gathered for coffee in the drawing room, leaving the men to their port, Freddie grabbed my arm. 'Come and talk to me. I have a dread of that Bisset woman.'

'Apparently she can read us all like a book.'

'From the conversations I've had with her, I doubt very much if she ever reads anything, human or paper and glue.'

Georgia was standing on the hearth to get warm, her *décolleté* covered by a shawl now there were no men to admire it. Her bold eyes wandered in a bored way about the room. 'She looks like a spider that's just eaten its mate,' I said cattily. 'The triumph of ascendancy faintly tinged with regret. She can't be bothered to struggle with Miss Tipple and she despises Mrs Mordaker. She certainly doesn't want to talk to little girls. Oh, no,' I turned my head to avoid catching Georgia's eye, 'she's looking at us. I think she's decided to while away the barren half-hour until the men come in by riffling through the pages of our dull, commonplace minds. Do let's go and look at your portrait of Sir Oswald.'

We went into the hall and up the stairs. Freddie paused

at the top and pointed to two paintings, full-lengths in the manner of Sargent but in more modern clothes.

'These are interesting examples of the art of portraiture.'

'I always look at them as I go by. He's so handsome and she's enchanting.'

'That, believe it or not, is Sir Oswald.'

I stared at the golden-haired Phoebus Apollo, his eyes large and bright, features that it would not be an exaggeration to describe as chiselled, a mouth firm and well-shaped above a decided chin. He stood slender and proud, a pointer at his feet, Pye Place and the waterfall on the skyline.

Freddie read the date on the frame. 'It's 1958. Only twenty years ago. If one needed an incentive to forgo a second helping of treacle tart, this is it.'

The other painting was of a sweet-faced girl in a white dress. Her dark hair was pulled smoothly back from her brow and fastened with a cluster of white flowers on the crown of her head. Her enormous eyes were childlike, her mouth a soft pout. She looked younger than Cordelia.

'This is by a different hand,' said Freddie, looking closely at the brushwork. 'It's shamelessly meretricious – denying truth, I mean, for the sake of appeal. Of course you *can* paint a basket of kittens well and capture the essence of the animal but the temptation is to prettify it so that judgement is suspended. All the viewer wants to do is pick them up and stroke them. It tells you nothing about the creatures themselves. Certainly most men would like to pick up this girl and give her a damned good stroking. See how her skin is painted in tones of quite unrealistic sugary pink, which make her face more doll-like than human. Eyes *that* big would be freakish in life. And look how tiny her hands are, on fat little arms without wrists, again like a doll's.'

'What sort of portrait are you doing of Sir Oswald?'

Freddie made a face. 'I've had to take at least six stone off him, I have to admit. It's always the way. Sitters don't want the truth. But I suppose one can hardly blame them.'

'Don't you like painting portraits?'

'It's a love-hate relationship. I like looking at people's faces in detail. There's a reward in uncovering hidden traits, which you invariably do after a while. But it's surprisingly unsatisfactory to paint a lie. Sir Oswald's still tubby but you could just about call him a fine figure of a man. The trouble is, it's hard to make any money painting other things. I'm putting together an exhibition of landscapes but that takes time. And though I no longer need to work to earn money, I like the feeling of making a contribution to the matrimonial jam jar. Also I never want Vere to become bored with me. I'm afraid he might if I don't challenge myself.'

I was surprised. Vere had not seemed, the little I knew of him, to be particularly demanding. 'Is he difficult to please?'

'Not in the least. He's the kindest man in the world and he'd never intend to let it be seen that he was bored but he's quite incapable of dissimulation. I'd know at once. His transparency is one of the things I absolutely love about him.'

I was amazed that Freddie could think that anyone would grow tired of her. I supposed it was just possible that a man might weary of eyes of an arresting shade of peridot green, a face like Botticelli's Venus, an elegant figure and flaming Pre-Raphaelite hair, had they been matched with a vapid, disagreeable personality. But Freddie was interested in so many things. She was not much older than Ophelia but I could not help seeing that they were as different as egg tempera and poster paint. Absurdly, this comparison wounded me as soon as I had made it. Though I was frequently cross with Ophelia, yet I could not bear any attack on her, even in my own thoughts.

Freddie opened the door of the housemaid's room that had been set aside as her studio. It was lined with cupboards and had a huge sink beneath the window. A dozen stone hot-water bottles were lined up on a shelf above a row of white china slop pails. A small table with a sewing machine on it, an armchair and an easel, with its back to the door, were the only items of furniture.

'Cosy, isn't it? There are two cylinders in this cupboard that keep me deliciously warm. I really enjoy working here. Painting's a chilly business, standing on the spot for hours until your blood has pooled in your ankles.'

'Maggie's a brilliant housekeeper, isn't she?'

'With her powers of organisation she could be a managing director of British Steel or Marks and Spencer. Not that she'd probably enjoy it as much as looking after this house. But it makes my blood boil to see her treated like a turnspit dog. Now, what do you think?'

I approached the easel with trepidation. Coming from a family almost morbidly sensitive to criticism about its artistic performances, I knew how a careless word could bring on a migraine or destroy a night's sleep. But when I saw the portrait the complimentary phrases I had been rehearsing deserted me. The canvas was as bright with blocks of colour as a Fauvist painting. I happened to know about this because my mother had been through a Fauvist phase of decoration and for at least a year our drawing room had been as colourful as a Matisse, with juxtapositions of vivid contrasts, pink sofas, red walls, emerald curtains and a blue fireplace with a carpet dyed in abstract shapes of purple and lemon yellow. It had had a very lifting effect on one's mood and we had all been sorry to see it go in favour of le Crépuscule, sophisticated and recherché though this had been.

Though his cheeks were chequered with mauve and blue, it was unmistakably Sir Oswald. It had caught exactly his brand of genial patronage. Something besides good humour lurked in the charcoal and crimson eyes, perhaps desire, certainly greed, and – was it discontent or could it be a deeper anguish? – in the sensual mouth. Despite Freddie's tactful omission of the grossest accumulations of flesh you saw clearly that he was a ruin of a man. I looked at it for a long time and my assumptions about Sir Oswald changed. He ceased to be a caricature and became a complex being.

'Poor man!' I said, at last. 'It's so awfully sad.'

'Ah! You've seen it. Vere says it's very like Sir Oswald but, perhaps because he's another man, he didn't see that. After he – Sir Oswald, I mean – had been sitting for a few hours I found I wanted to paint his face in a rictus of grief. Yet I don't believe he's truly aware of his own wretchedness. He probably considers himself a fortunate man. Just as well.'

'It really is good, Freddie! How talented you are! I feel in awe.'

'Glad you like it.' Freddie was looking at it, her eyes narrowed, head on one side. 'Oh, damn! Yes, I see now. Something about the chin – not quite . . .' She picked up a paintbrush and then put it down. 'The temptation to fiddle is almost irresistible but really I want to talk to you, Harriet.' Freddie leaned back against the sill. The sky through the unshuttered window was black against her fiery hair. She smiled. 'I enjoyed sitting next to Max at dinner.' I was annoyed with myself for blushing 'I won't say another word if you'd rather I didn't.'

'Why – what do you mean?' Freddie shook her head and smiled more broadly. I saw it was pointless to prevaricate. 'How did you know?'

'Perhaps it was because he hardly took his eyes off you for five courses. It rather undid any conceited ideas I might have got from his flirtatious manner.'

'Flirtatious?'

'Only of the most generalised kind. Men and women are

383

supposed to flirt with each other at dinner and Max plays the game. Very well.'

I could not help a *frisson* of pleasure at this praise, trifling though the accomplishment was. 'There isn't anything to know, really. I mean we haven't actually . . . Freddie, can I ask you something?'

'Go ahead.' Freddie's eyes veered over to her painting for a moment but quickly she returned them to my face.

'Do you think the fact that Max is married ought to make a difference to – anything? I mean,' I rushed on, 'Apart from Ophelia, who thinks married men a complete waste of time, the rest of my family consider people being married or not absolutely unimportant. They think being faithful is corny and middle-class and rather ridiculous and that everybody has affairs as a matter of course. But you see,' I rushed on without giving Freddie time to answer, 'Max says that Caroline – his wife – tried to kill herself. Not because of me. Honestly, we haven't done anything that could upset her even if she knew.' I paused, suddenly remembering the kiss on the doorstep. 'Well, *hard*ly anything. I know my family would think her wanting to kill herself was between Caroline and Max and nothing to do with me. But oughtn't it to have some bearing? At least on our behaviour, if not our feelings. Am I being hopelessly naïve?'

'I'd never thought of adultery as a class thing.' Freddie cupped her elbow with one hand and rested her chin on the other while she considered. 'Certainly the upper classes are adulterous almost to a man. And royalty are worse than anyone. I suppose monogamy *has* got a two-grey-little-people-in-a-dull-little-house sort of image. Boarding-house holidays, two children and a Labrador. Slippers by the fire and calling each other "dear" and a Rotary Club dinner-dance as the high point of the year. From a snobbish point of view, it does sound dreary.'

'Actually I think it sounds rather nice. With the right person. Particularly the two children and the Labrador. I could do without the dinner-dance.'

'You're a romantic, Harriet, and so am I. But to tell you the truth – bourgeois or not – I know if Vere had an affair I'd feel as though my back was broken. My happiness would be absolutely destroyed. It would be no comfort to tell myself that Vere making love to another woman was merely a well-bred convention. If he ended the affair and asked me to take him back, I expect I'd try to forgive it because, frankly, I can't bear to think of life without him.'

'It'll never happen.'

'One can't be sure of anything. I admit Vere's the last man I'd expect to be unfaithful. But if he were, then I'd have to face up to having been mistaken about him and find a way of living with a broken back. But I doubt if I'd try to kill myself. I think that's the result of a serious personality disorder. Max's wife is clearly sick, poor thing, and she needs help. If I were you I'd be reluctant to add to her troubles but I wouldn't hold myself entirely responsible for her behaviour. Better to ask yourself about Max.'

'About Max?' I echoed stupidly.

'One of the reasons I love Vere – if there are *reasons* for loving anybody – is because he's honest. He won't cheat me if he can help it, nor would he cheat himself. And I can't help feeling that an adulterous affair is, above all, an attempt to cheat oneself.'

'What do you mean, exactly?'

Freddie held up a thumb before the canvas and narrowed her eyes. 'Definitely it's the left-hand side of the chin that's wrong – more white, perhaps? Um, the justifications never quite add up, do they? Is being in love an involuntary state that can't be denied? I don't believe that. I think love's a matter of will. We can't escape the instinct that makes us act in our own

385

interest. But often we can't identify where our best interests lie. The woman who stays with the man who regularly beats her feels that life would be worse without him. But I doubt if it's love. More like habit. Or fear.' Freddie pounced on a tube of paint and squeezed a white worm on to her palette. 'We want to be "in love",' she continued, 'because it makes us supremely happy, and if someone's sufficiently attractive we abandon ourselves willingly to as much passion as can be generated. The difficulty is finding someone who meets our expectations.'

'So you think adultery's just about sex?'

'Lust's in the mind, isn't it? I don't believe it's uncontrollable. Even rapists are supposed to be driven by hatred and aggression rather than desire, aren't they? I think adultery is about vanity – the excitement and the gratification of being desired. At the worst, boredom or even wanting something someone else is enjoying. It's my guess that self-love makes Don Juan what he is.'

'My family would say that life without romantic adventure was dull.'

'But, Harriet, what does it matter what they think? You've got to make up your own mind, quite independently of them or me or anyone else.' I knew she was right. I resolved to try to be more self-reliant. Freddie turned slowly away from the canvas with an obvious effort as though it were a magnet. She might have been composed of those little iron filings that were so dear to Miss Pothole, our physics mistress. 'There's no law I know of,' she continued, 'that obliges anyone to commit themselves to one person. Why not stay single and have as many romantic adventures as there are hours in the day, if that's what matters to you?' She glanced quickly at the painting and frowned. 'I mean you can't have everything.'

'No. But I suppose it's only human to try.'

I was thinking about my father and Fleur Kirkpatrick.

Freddie was probably right about the vanity bit. Pa was so terribly in need of reassurance. I tried to imagine him giving up Fleur for my mother's sake and spending the rest of his life devoting himself to acting, books, friends, family. I gave up the attempt almost immediately. He would be bored and miserable.

'Also adulterous affairs absorb a lot of energy and time,' continued Freddie. 'Running two lives, almost. Constructing the lies. And the high-octane passion is fuelled by the excitement of its being illicit. The affair itself becomes the focus of interest. Does he know? Has she guessed? Will anyone see us? You can kid yourself you're really living life to the full.'

'An expense of spirit in a waste of shame,' I thought. I did not say it aloud because, though I acknowledged his unerring ability to put his finger on the exact spot, one of the few rules of life I had laid down for myself early on was never, ever to quote Shakespeare to anyone.

'Don't let yourself be persuaded into something you don't want, Harriet.' Freddie put her hand on my shoulder and looked at me intently. 'Max has a great deal of charm and he's quite a bit older than you. Don't be tempted to take his word for it that this relationship ought to be. I know how seductive it is to give up one's autonomy, to let someone else take responsibility. But you're still accountable even if you allow someone else to take the reins.'

'How extraordinary that you should say that.' I was impressed by Freddie's powers of divination. 'That *is* part of the attraction, if I'm truthful.'

'I was once guilty myself of mistaking despotism for destiny.'

Though I longed to question Freddie further I knew it would be positively cruel to keep her a moment longer from her work.

'I'd better go back to the drawing room and check that

Cordelia's OK. Thanks, Freddie, it's been a great help to talk.'

'I'll just be two minutes.' Freddie squeezed a shining coil of vermilion into the blob of white on her palette. Just as I was closing the door she turned her head from the canvas long enough to say, 'And don't forget, however much he wants to make love to you, you're under no obligation to satisfy his desire.'

I went downstairs, thinking of everything we had talked about. Was Max's interest in me nothing more than self-love, a rake's determination to add another conquest to his score? My own vanity shied away from the idea.

The men had joined the women in the drawing room. Archie was showing the children card tricks. Cordelia seemed not to notice that Sir Oswald was squeezing her hand. Emilio was leering at Mrs Mordaker. I noticed Jonno's feet sticking out from behind the sofa.

Max – ah, yes, Max, whom, of course, I had been aware of at once – was leaning against the piano with Georgia, looking through some sheet music. In point of fact, he was examining the music while Georgia, her shawl discarded, had her eyes fixed on his face. Max turned round as I came in and sent me a smile that instantly overturned the resolve I had just made to have nothing more to do with him. Georgia looked sharply at me, then put her hand through his arm and drew him round to face her.

'Freddie's in her studio, doing something to Sir Oswald's chin,' I said to Vere, who was standing in one of the window bays, holding a glass of brandy and looking rather lost.

'Ah. I *had* been wondering where she was. Well, at least I know she's happy.'

'It's a marvellous painting.'

'I'm very proud of her. Perhaps that sounds presumptuous. Of course her talent doesn't reflect any glory on me.'

'I don't agree. She's a monument to your good taste.'

Vere laughed. 'I'll take that as a great compliment.'

'She and I have had a very interesting talk. But there's so much else I long to ask her. Where you're both living now, for example? Not in London, surely, or I'd have known.'

'At my family home in Dorset. It's miles from anywhere. But she seems to love it.'

'What's the house like?'

Vere described it to me and I concentrated hard on not letting my eyes wander over to Max and Georgia. 'It sounds wonderful,' I said when he had finished. I wondered why they had left it to spend Christmas in Derbyshire. I didn't ask because there was an air of reserve about Vere that made me nervous of seeming to pry. But he was in a communicative mood.

'I was abroad for twelve years but I thought about the house and the valley every day. I began to doubt whether they could be as good as I imagined. When I finally came home everything was even better . . . more beautiful . . . than I'd remembered. I hate being away from it, to tell you the truth, but my brother asked a lot of people to stay and – well, Freddie and I knew we wouldn't particularly enjoy them, so we decided to take up Sir Oswald's extremely generous invitation and kill two birds with one stone. This'll be the last Christmas that we won't mind too much being away.'

'Really?' I was going to ask why, then something that flashed for a moment into his eyes, a secretive sort of joy, gave me the answer.

'You're going to have a –'

'Ssh! Don't tell anyone, but yes. Freddie says it's too soon to say anything. She doesn't want people to fuss.'

'I promise I shan't tell a soul. But how lovely!'

'Actually, of course I meant you to guess. I've been longing to tell someone for days.' Vere smiled. 'It makes it seem much more likely.'

'I know what you mean.'

'Can anyone play the piano?' called Georgia. 'If we roll up the rug the floor's perfect for dancing. Would you mind, Sir Oswald?'

Sir Oswald waved assent with the hand that was not caressing Cordelia's.

'I'll play, if you like.' Archie put down the cards and went over to the piano. He ran his hands up and down the keys experimentally and struck some chords. 'What shall it be?'

Georgia put some music in front of him. 'Something lively to start with. I'm feeling energetic.'

Archie obligingly began to play 'La Cucaracha'. Georgia wiggled her hips and clicked her fingers in front of Max, who stood watching her with an expression that seemed to me slightly derisive. Possibly this was wishful thinking. Cordelia got up at once, casually discarding Sir Oswald's hand, and began to jig about in time to the music. We watched them gyrating and jerking, hopping up and down and waving their arms.

'Does that dance have a name?' asked Vere. 'When I left England a decade ago everyone was making serious efforts to master the intricacies of the Twist. Now the object seems to be to look as though you're signalling a ship from a desert island, having been castaway with a dreadful bore for several years.'

'It's an age thing,' I said. 'That sort of dancing looks attractive and fun when a pretty young girl does it, but pathetic – almost ludicrous – when an older woman tries to do it.'

'Ow-how! You almost make me sorry for the ghastly woman.'

'Sorry,' I giggled. 'That *was* bitchy.'

Vere pointed to Max, who was now dancing with Georgia. 'Tell me, Miss Harriet Byng – as you're such a severe critic, you won't spare me, I know – does the older man look equally silly?'

'We-e-ll. Somehow not *so* bad.'

Max was weaving about rather gracefully, actually, with enough self-parody to stop him looking ridiculous. Emilio had joined the others on the improvised dance floor and was rolling his hips and wagging his head in front of Cordelia. He accidentally trod on Dirk's tail where it lay limp and unattended while its owner slept before the fire. Dirk woke and, taking exception to Emilio's attentions to Cordelia, whom he counted as one of his own, snapped at Emilio's ankle.

'Do you know,' said Mrs Mordaker to me, when the ankle had been examined and found free from so much as a tooth mark, 'I'm not at all sure that young man,' she cast her eyes in the direction of Emilio, who had resumed dancing, 'is quite all *there*. First of all he accused me of disturbing his sleep. I've no idea what he meant. And then he said something about – well, you know his accent's very odd – my *calves*. I thought he said that they were two pillars of pleasure.' We both looked down at her stout legs encased in gingery stockings. 'What *could* he have meant?'

'Harriet.' Jonno was upright now and plucking at my sleeve. 'What shay we cut the rug?' He swayed forward on his feet and had to be pulled upright by Vere.

'Harriet's going to dance with me.' Max had materialised unexpectedly beside us. Archie was playing something more euphonious now and crooning along to it in a pleasant baritone.

'Shod it! I arshed first.' Jonno was indignant. 'Anyway, washo fucking great about a poxy actor, I'd like to know, that all you gerlsh have got the hotsh frim?'

'Young man!' Mrs Mordaker reeled back, either from the brandy fumes or the swearing. 'If you don't moderate your language I shall complain to your father.'

'Oh, shut up, you silly old moo! You oughta be arreshted, that'sh what!' He waved a weaving finger under Mrs Mordaker's affronted eyes. 'Arreshted for making people feel shick whenever they shee your ugly old mush!'

'How dare you!' Mrs Mordaker strode away on her twin pillars of pleasure.

Jonno broke into mocking laughter that quickly became tears. 'I'm sho shad, Harriet. Sho fucking shad! *No* one lovesh me.'

Vere took Jonno's arm. 'You've had a skin-full, that's all. I'll take you up to your room and find you some aspirin.'

'You're a fucking good bloke,' Jonno sobbed into Vere's lapel. 'You're the only pershon here that givesh a tosh what happensh to me. Harriet only wantsh to fornitake – forni – cake with that fanshy nanshy actor –'

Vere led him firmly away.

Max took my hand. 'That boy's a pest. He ought to be sent away somewhere to be dried out.'

Rupert was standing in the doorway of the drawing room. I watched as his glance went very deliberately about the room, resting first on Archie, who was singing 'Smoke Gets in your Eyes'. On Cordelia and Emilio dancing together, cheek to cheek. On Sir Oswald, who was watching Cordelia, a fatuous smile on his lips. On Miss Tipple, head back, knees apart, sleeping in her chair. On Annabel, who was kneeling down, tying together the laces of Miss Tipple's black brogues. On Georgia, who was leaning against the piano, smoking a cigarette and staring angrily at me. Then his gaze fell on Max's hand holding mine, where it remained.

I took away my hand. 'I must do something about Emilio and Cordelia. He's going to set her alight in a minute, if he goes on rubbing her bottom like that. He can't realise she's only twelve.'

'Don't be a spoilsport.' I thought I detected impatience in Max's voice. 'You can see she's enjoying it.'

Whatever justification I might have found for interfering with my little sister's pleasure was made superfluous by the arrival of Maggie, white-faced. She grasped Rupert's sleeve.

'What's the matter?' Rupert put his arm around her broad shoulders. 'You're trembling. What is it?'

'I'm that put about, I don't know whether I'm coming or going.' Her voice broke. 'Oh dear, oh dear!'

Rupert pushed her into the nearest chair and bent over her. 'Now, Maggie. Hysterics won't help.'

Maggie looked up into his face, her eyes distraught, the corners of her mouth turned down like a child's. 'Old Gally's arm. It's *gone*!'

TWENTY-FIVE

The confusion that followed the discovery of the disappearance of Old Gally's arm meant that none of us was able to
get to bed before midnight. First Maggie had to be calmed.

'Get her a brandy, someone,' commanded Rupert, as she
was still clinging to his arm.

Max went over to the decanter. The rest of us turned our
eyes as though mesmerised to act in concert, to Old Gally's
chair. It looked its usual unattractive, inhospitable self.

'Do you mean that dirty old thing from the Long Gallery,
that's supposed to bring bad luck?' Georgia shivered. 'I think
I'll have a brandy too.' When Max put a glass into her hand
she pressed a naked shoulder against him. I would have put
her down as thoroughly hard-boiled but the knowledge that
the arm was missing seemed to have triggered a need for
masculine support. 'Silly of me, I know, but a girl feels
vulnerable when there are crazy people around. Who on
earth would have taken it?'

No one could, or would, answer this.

'I wish I knew what the fuss was about,' said Mrs Mordaker
in a forthright voice. 'Maggie, what *is* this nonsense? What's
missing and why has it upset you like this?'

Maggie made a gulping sound and shook her head, pressing her apron to her mouth. It was distressing to see her shaken from her usual calm competence. The growing tension drove Dirk to his loudest barks. Mrs Mordaker attempted to silence him with her patent method which, she had assured me several times, had never been known to fail. It consisted of hissing at maximum volume while touching his nose with an admonishing forefinger. I had tried it when alone in our bedroom with disastrous results. Dirk had been inflamed by the rain of saliva and the pressure of my finger to howl like a she-wolf separated from her young. Mrs Mordaker was equally unsuccessful on this occasion and we begged her to desist. She vented her temper on Maggie, saying she believed Maggie had overindulged in wine at dinner and her imagination had run riot in consequence.

'No, Rhoda, I never touched a drop and it weren't imagination. I do assure you of that.' Maggie spoke with certainty though she was still ashen-faced. 'I've had the key on my belt all day. Look.' She took hold of the chatelaine at her waist and sorted through the keys. 'Here it is, see? But, unless I've gone out of my wits – and I don't think I have – the padlock's been opened and the case is empty. And the Lord alone knows how. I'm ever so sorry to frighten you all but I dursn't say owt but the truth for fear that . . .' her voice trembled but she carried gamely on, 'harm may come to someone.'

'Maggie, be sensible' said Rupert. 'What possible harm could a bit of rusty old iron do? It's been locked up so long it couldn't even give you tetanus.'

'Oh, I beg you not to speak disrespectful of it!' cried Maggie. 'He's got ever such a nasty temper,' she added in a whisper.

Now I was sure that Maggie knew far more about the ghost of Galahad that she had been willing to admit.

'I agree with Maggie,' said Archie. 'Don't let's provoke it. Is there anything *particular* to fear?'

Maggie pressed her hands to her cheeks. 'It always turns up again. Always. It sort of hovers, though you can't see no one behind it. And it – points.'

There was something unpleasant in this idea.

'It's obviously a *very* badly brought up arm.' Archie sounded seriously rattled but one never knew whether he was teasing. 'Imagine if it were a codpiece. Now, that *would* be alarming.'

Mrs Mordaker frowned as she turned this idea over in her mind. I had an almost uncontrollable desire to giggle.

'The person it points to,' whispered Maggie, 'has terrible bad things happen to them. Divorce, disgrace, bankruptcy, illness – and then, in the end – worse.'

Everyone looked rather solemn. Everyone except Emilio, that is, who probably had not understood what Maggie was saying. He was trying to see down the neck of Cordelia's dress.

'Annabel, what do you know about this?' Rupert looked at her sternly. 'Have you been trying to frighten us?'

'I swear I haven't touched it!' Annabel appeared to be excited and alarmed. 'Hadn't we better go and look for it?'

'Do let's,' said Cordelia, not to be outdone in bravery.

'For heaven's sake,' cried Maggie, 'don't let the blessed lambs go off on their own with that – thing . . .' She faltered and looked up at Rupert with pleading eyes. 'Where's Freddie? And Jonno? Oh, if something should happen . . .' She had recourse to her apron once more.

'I'll go and look for them,' said Rupert. 'Not that I believe for one moment that there's any danger – just to reassure everyone that they're not going to be strangled in their beds.'

Maggie gave a gasp of dismay and Georgia shrieked. Even Mrs Mordaker put her hand nervously to her throat.

Rupert looked annoyed. 'There's nothing to scream about. I shall do a tour of the house and check on everyone not here and then there must be an end to this fuss.'

Maggie clutched at him. 'Whatever you do, don't go alone!'

Rupert looked down at her tired, frightened face and a softer note crept into his voice. 'All right, if it will reassure you. Who's coming with me?'

'I will,' said Max.

Archie said he feared it might bring on a laryngospasm if he was forced to leave the safety of the drawing room. Sir Oswald asserted with an air of gallantry that it was his duty to remain with those members of the fair sex who were most in need of his protection. His hand shook as he poured himself a generous measure of spirits. I did not blame him for this. No doubt he had heard tales of Old Gally's doings at his mother's knee. More reprehensibly Emilio claimed to have been crippled by Dirk. His big brown eyes with their strange canary-tinged whites were almost weeping with regret as he hobbled round in a circle to demonstrate.

Annabel and Cordelia begged to be allowed to join the search party but Rupert said they would be an appalling nuisance and forbade them to stir from the spot. Miss Tipple told anyone who would listen that the legend of Old Gally's arm was a paradigm of man's brutality, perfidy and stupidity.

'I entirely agree with you, Miss Tipple,' said Rupert. 'I'm absolutely certain that the theft of the arm is a joke – in questionable taste.'

'I'm coming with you,' I said.

'I think you ought to stay here,' said Max. 'Of course Rupert's right. It's a stupid prank. But you never know.'

'You're forgetting I'm the author of a celebrated weekly spine-chiller. What would my faithful readers think if it came to be known that the author of "Spook Hall" had skulked in the drawing room instead of risking life and sanity in pursuit of a vengeful limb?'

'Come on, then.' Rupert gave me a glance of approval.

'If Harriet's allowed to go I don't see why I shouldn't,' grumbled Cordelia.

'For one thing, I don't trust you not to have had a hand in this,' said Rupert sternly. 'It has all the hallmarks of the juvenile mind. For another, you're supposed to be convalescent. Come to think of it, it's after eleven and you ought to be in bed.'

Cordelia cast him a glance of pure despite but wisely said no more.

'Actually, neither Cordelia nor Annabel could have taken it,' I said as the three of us went into the hall. 'I passed it on my way downstairs from looking at Freddie's painting. The children were in the drawing room from the moment of my return until Maggie came in. So it couldn't possibly have been them.'

'What time was that?'

'About twenty minutes ago.'

'And you definitely saw the arm?'

'I didn't make a point of looking at it but I'd have noticed if it hadn't been there.'

'Damn!'

'Is that specially annoying?' asked Max.

'Don't you see? If it was one of the children who took it, it's just tomfoolery. If it was an adult the motivation becomes more complex. Let's have a look at the case.'

The lid was open and the coiled chain and open padlock lay beside it. The two-foot-long depression where the arm usually lay was a much darker red where the velvet had been protected from the light.

Rupert examined the padlock. 'No sign of it having been forced. No scratches round the lock. Someone had the key.'

'Anyone could have borrowed it,' said Max. 'Maggie presumably doesn't wear the keys in bed or in the bath. The most likely person is that ass Jonno. Typical adolescent attention-seeking.'

'He's my age,' I said, with dignity. 'Hardly adolescent.'

'Everyone knows that girls grow up faster than boys.' He ran his finger lightly down the hollow in the nape of my neck, which made me jump.

'Might we suspend the paddling of palms and pinching of fingers for the time being?' Rupert said coldly.

'*Othello*.' It was out before could stop myself. Being educated men, they both looked at me in pained surprise.

But Vere, whom we discovered unlacing a snoring Jonno's shoes in the latter's bedroom, ruled out the possibility that Jonno had taken it. He, Vere, had not noticed whether the arm had been in its case on the landing when he had passed it ten minutes ago. His attention had been fully engaged. Jonno's legs had refused to take him up the stairs and Vere had been obliged to give him a fireman's lift.

'He was asleep behind the sofa when I came downstairs,' I pointed out 'and didn't leave the drawing room until he went off with Vere. So it couldn't have been Jonno.'

Freddie was in her studio. She had been concentrating on Sir Oswald's chin and had heard nothing unusual. 'Actually you could have blown up the house and I wouldn't have noticed.' She put down her palette and began to wash the brushes. 'If not the children, then who? It would be funny if it weren't for Maggie being upset.'

'I know who it wasn't,' I counted on my fingers. 'Archie, Georgia, Emilio, Mrs Mordaker, and Miss Tipple were in the drawing room all the time. We can discount you and Vere, of course,' I added politely.

'There's Mrs Whale,' said Rupert.

'It couldn't possibly be her.'

'Why not?'

'She's much too devout. She'd never have the spirit. When Jonno swore the other day I saw her discreetly crossing herself. Honestly, she's practically a nun.'

'That only leaves Colonel Mordaker,' said Max. 'But he doesn't seem the kind of man to play a practical joke. I can't imagine him finding anything funny.'

'There's me, of course,' said Rupert. 'After the men left the dining room I went outside for a walk, alone. I've no alibi.'

'You're not taking this seriously,' I said accusingly.

'If you mean do I believe that the vindictive spirit of a long-dead Pye has returned to wreck the peace of his descendants, no, I most certainly do not. Someone very much alive has taken the arm, in order to put the fox among the hens and set up a cackling. It could have been me. I happened to know it wasn't but that's more than you do. Or your readers.'

'I'm supposed to be writing a ghost story, not detective fiction.'

'Suppose it was a stranger, someone from outside?' suggested Max. 'Are the doors kept bolted?'

'I went out through the front door,' said Rupert, 'and came in through one of the side doors. It was snowing just before I went out, which was helpful of it. If someone came in while I was in the garden there'll be footprints.'

We went down to see. As far as we could tell by the light of Rupert's torch and what gleams escaped the shutters, a single line of prints described one and a quarter circles round the house from the front door to the side door, just as Rupert had said.

'All right,' said Rupert. 'It's an inside job.'

'Must you talk like Fabian of the Yard?'

Rupert ignored me. 'Thanks to the snow we can also be certain that the arm is somewhere in the house.'

I was not particularly grateful for this information. Though

400

I was determined to maintain a spirit of sceptical inquiry I had to fight an inclination to spin round from time to time just to make sure there was nothing behind me.

In the kitchen Mrs Whale was standing at the sink, working her way through giant heaps of washing-up. Everything in the kitchen, including her face, was perspiring from contact with steam. When Rupert asked her if she knew anything about the missing arm her eyes registered alarm. She made the sign of the cross over her aproned chest with a hand encased in a soapy red rubber glove. 'Dark deeds can never be hid.' Her voice, usually low and flat, trembled with fervour. 'As the Good Book says, "Woe unto them that draw iniquity with cords of vanity, and sin as it were with a cart rope"!'

'Woe, indeed,' said Max pleasantly.

'I take it that means you can tell us nothing?' said Rupert.

Mrs Whale indicated the piles of plates and knives and forks already washed, dried and stacked on the table. 'Satan finds mischief for idle hands.' She turned her back to us and plunged a bundle of spoons into the foaming sink. I felt guilty, as I always did in her presence because my life was so much nicer than hers.

'You see, she couldn't have done it,' I said when we were in the hall. 'She's a paragon of godliness and moral rectitude.'

'The devil can cite Scripture for his purpose,' said Max. 'And that, you sinfully ignorant girl, is *The Merchant of Venice*. But it'll be a pleasure to take your education in hand. And other things besides.' He gave me a smile that, had I been less preoccupied, I would have found pretty devastating.

Rupert closed his eyes briefly. 'We'd better find Colonel Mordaker.'

'It's waste of time,' I said. 'The man hasn't an ounce of imagination. I *know* he didn't take it. I'm beginning to think I've got a scoop. For once, a manifestation of the supernatural that can't be explained by hot-water pipes or hysteria. Can't you sense something in the atmosphere? *I* can.' I was definitely beginning to see things out of the corner of my eye that vanished as soon as I looked directly at them. 'A paranormal force is at work here, some ancient mystery beyond our understanding. I've got a feeling that the doubting Thomases among us are in for something of a shock. Isn't it exciting?'

'Quite entrancing,' said Max.

'There's one born every minute,' said Rupert, not, I think, meaning the doubting Thomases.

The colonel was discovered in the library, asleep in an armchair. Several books lay open on the table beside him. As we looked at him his lower jaw dropped and he started to grunt like a pig scenting swill.

Rupert glanced at the pages of birds. 'He's been checking on Vere's blue-footed falcon,' he murmured.

The colonel stirred and smacked his lips together in his sleep. He said something indistinct that sounded like 'Attagirl, Lulu.'

'But for how long?' asked Max.

'Look at that.' Rupert pointed to an ashtray in which lay an inch of ash still attached to the stub of a cigar, now out. 'Cigars burn slowly when not drawn on. I'd say he's been asleep a good half-hour. And the fire's gone out too.' We looked at the fireplace where a few embers gleamed.

'Could he have been acting?' asked Max when we were back in the hall.

'I shouldn't have thought he had the brains to set it up,' said Rupert.

'Of course he doesn't,' I said. 'He's the dimmest man I've ever met. And, boy, that's saying something!'

Rupert laughed. 'Poor Harriet. If you want rattling chains, fingerprints on throats and flitting white shapes bent on fiend-ish retaliation, I'm afraid you'll just have to make it up.'

'What's worrying,' said Max 'is the malice behind it. The

theft of the arm was bound to upset Maggie. And it's enough to make some of the sillier women have nightmares.'

I was pleased by this indirect tribute. 'You don't mention the men who were thrown into a blue funk, I notice.'

'Is this the moment to wage a battle of the sexes?' Max smiled at me and I stared, fascinated, at the dent in the end of his nose. 'Besides, I concede. The men were a disgrace. You, Harriet, are an example to us all.'

Rupert made a sound like 'Tst', disdaining to take further notice of our trifling. 'I wish I knew how to convince Maggie, without evidence, that this is no more than a trick.'

'For some extraordinary reason she seems to set great store by your opinion.' This sounded ungenerous the moment I had said it. 'You can reassure her if anyone can.'

'The trouble is,' said Max, 'sooner or later it's going to turn up again, isn't it? I mean the point wasn't just to steal it, but to give someone a hell of a fright with a reprise of The Finger of Doom.'

As he said this I felt a definite shiver of apprehension.

'We'd better look for it in the morning,' said Rupert. 'We could search the bedrooms while everyone's at breakfast. Though in a house this size . . .' He shrugged and left the sentence unfinished.

I had already decided that I would make a thorough search of Cordelia and my room the minute I went upstairs, to ensure a decent night's sleep.

'Don't forget to look under the bed as well as in it,' said Max, who was obviously something of a thought-reader.

Those who had remained in the drawing room had, apart from Maggie, largely recovered their sang-froid. They had been distracted in our absence by having to search for Miss Tipple's shoes, unaccountably missing. Mrs Mordaker had accused Annabel of the theft and said such uncomplimentary things about spoiled, naughty children that Annabel had thrown a tantrum and flounced from the room. Eventually the shoes were discovered under a table in the jaws of Dirk, very much the worse for chewing. Mrs Mordaker said, several times, that dogs would be dogs, with which no one could possibly disagree. Regrettable though Dirk's behaviour was, it was useful in that it took people's minds off imminent death and disaster.

Rupert said that everyone was perfectly all right, just as he had expected, and there was nothing to worry about. If it would set Maggie's mind at rest, we could have an organised hunt for the arm in the morning. Meanwhile he was sure it was a childish jest, to be treated with the contempt it deserved.

'The dead are harmless.' Miss Tipple was scornful. 'It's men of flesh and blood one has to beware of. And I give due warning to whoever has been scratching at my door at dead of night that I intend to place a loaded service revolver – it belonged to my father and I always carry it with me – on my bedside table.' She glared at Colonel Mordaker, who joined us at that moment.

'Stuff and nonsense!' he roared when the disappearance of the arm was explained to him. 'If some ruddy perisher thinks he's going to get the better of H. R. G. Mordaker, MC, DSO, he's mistaken his man. Rhoda, where's m' duck gun?'

'In the car, Hereward, but is it wise –'

'Don't argue, woman! Now, listen to me, men.' I saw us bivouacking on a hillside somewhere near Anzio. 'I'm going to take the first shift, from twelve till two, positioning myself at the head of the stairs, and taking a recce every five minutes to check those rooms not on the main landing. Who'll do from two till four?'

'*Noth*ing would persuade me, Colonel dear,' said Archie into the silence that had fallen. 'My hands would tremble so much I'd never be able to pull the trigger. Besides, *think* of

Sir Oswald's plasterwork. It would be an act of *van*dalism to blast it full of holes.'

'Are there any *men* willing to share the watch with me or must I do it all myself?' The colonel's fierce little eyes fell on Max.

'I think the police might have something to say if we shot one of Sir Oswald's guests.' Max shrugged. 'Frankly I don't plan to spend the rest of my life in gaol because someone fancies a brandy and soda in the night.'

Then he looked at me and discreetly pressed his lips together to mime contrition. I grinned to show it was all right, though inevitably I had thought of my father and felt a stab of pain.

'No, no, no, no,' said Emilio as he caught the Colonel's eye. 'My leg ees *so* bad.' He took a step and staggered heavily. See, I am no useful. I regret but . . .' he spread his hands.

The colonel muttered something unflattering about dagoes that luckily Emilio had no chance of understanding. 'Well?' he demanded of Rupert. 'It's down to you, Wolvespurges. Or Gilderoy.'

Rupert smiled and shook his head. 'I'm an appallingly bad shot. And Vere, I happen to know, is a pacifist. It's against his principles to take up arms against his fellow man.'

'Damn it all, I'm not asking for crack marksmen. The gun's supposed to inspire respect, that's all.' When no one said anything, Colonel Mordaker said, 'Very well. I shall do the lot myself. A worse bunch of lily-livered weaklings I've never come across.'

'Oh, Hereward, I don't think it's a good idea,' protested his wife. 'Think of your heart. You'd better take a pill straightaway. You're looking flushed.'

The colonel bared his teeth at her and went out. We heard the front door slam moments later.

Maggie looked anxious. 'I must warn Janet to be careful when she takes up the morning tea.'

*   *   *

'You don't think it might really be Old Gally who's taken the arm?' asked Cordelia as we searched our bedroom later that night.

'Absolutely not,' I said with great firmness. I went to check in the closet, just in case. 'That's all hokum made up by someone to attract more visitors to the house.'

'But Annabel believes it.' Cordelia followed me in and together we sifted through piles of our clothes. 'She says Old Gally pointed his finger at her grandfather and he lost both legs in the war. He died a year later. And her great-great-grandfather was pointed at and *he* lost all his money and threw himself under a train. And one of her ancestors found the arm in his saddlebag. He was turned out of the house for drunkenness and debt and became a highwayman and was hung.'

'Hanged. But these things happen in every family. It has nothing to do with ghosts.'

'Annabel says there are lots more ghosts besides Old Gally. There's the Lady of the Moat. She lived here ages ago, and her husband threw her into the moat because she got smallpox and was hideously scarred and he didn't want to look at her any more.'

'How unkind and – wait a minute, there isn't a moat at Pye Place.'

'So there isn't. Perhaps it got filled in. Anyway, Annabel says she walks the house at dead of night, with her poor face hidden under a hat, leaving puddles of water everywhere.'

'You really mustn't believe everything –'

I was interrupted by a scream from Cordelia. 'I've found it! It's here! Under this blanket! Feel!'

Beneath several layers I felt something hard and knobbly, about two feet long with a bulge at one end. A moth fluttered up into my face and I screamed too.

'I don't want to die.' Cordelia spoke with conviction. 'I'm going to stand over here so that it can't point at me.' She moved to the doorway and stared with scared eyes. 'Unless it swivels round – ugh! Leave the horrible thing alone, Hat! I don't want it to point at you!'

'Nonsense!' Though my heart was turning backward flips I took a deep breath and threw back the blanket to expose Cordelia's Christmas stocking, which I had brought with me from London. I had hidden it there myself when I had unpacked and then forgotten all about it.

'Can I have it now? It's only fifteen minutes from being Christmas Day.'

'I'd completely forgotten that it's Christmas tomorrow.'

'*Can* I?'

'No. Get into bed.' I put the stocking back into the closet.

'How mean you are, and horribly bossy. Ophelia and Portia would have let me have it.'

'Possibly. But they aren't here.'

'I think being in love with Max has gone to your head. You may be in for a nasty surprise there.'

'In that case I'd better get some sleep to prepare myself.'

'It's awful having a big sister! Serves you right if it turns out he's in love with someone else.'

'Have you cleaned your teeth?'

'As it happens I have, though I don't see what business it is of yours.'

'Turn out the light, then.'

'You think he's been coming up here every day to look at *you*.'

'I think he's very kindly put himself out to entertain a bored and fractious child.'

'Child! We shall see.'

'Good night.'

'Huh!'

A few minutes later I heard the sound of a clock striking midnight. It seemed a pity to be quarrelling at such a moment. 'Happy Christmas, darling, anyway.' I murmured. 'Sweet dreams.'

Silence.

'Hat?'

'Mm?'

'Happy Christmas.'

'Mm. Thanks.'

'Hat?'

'What is it?'

'I think he *ought* to be in love with you but you know what men are.'

'Not really.'

'Oh dear. No one would think you were ten years older than me.'

Silence.

'Hat?'

'*What?*'

'It *was* kind of you to do me a stocking. I know Ophelia and Portia wouldn't have bothered. Sorry I was mean.'

'S'll right. Now go – to – sleep.'

Sound of a sob. 'I shall never – forgive myself – if he dumps you.'

'O-o-n urr-e.'

'What?'

'Go – sle-ep.'

'Promise you'll forgive me? I can't *bear* the thought of our being estranged for ever.'

I meant to reassure her that if ten thousand men cruelly scorned me for Cordelia I should remain a faithful and loving sister but sleep rolled over me and extinguished my powers of speech.

TWENTY-SIX

'Hat! Everything's lovely! The necklace is bliss! Oh, don't go back to sleep! I want you to see me wearing it!' I peeled open an eye and nodded approval. 'How can you possibly be tired? It's seven in the morning. Maggie's already been in and lit the fire. I've *never* opened my stocking so late. What do you think of the hat worn like this?' I got a vague impression of a white wool cap low over Cordelia's forehead.

'Terrific.'

'Or should it be further back?'

'Uh-hah.'

'I think I'll give Annabel my old navy one as a Christmas present. Poor kid, I bet she hasn't got a decent hat. Honestly, I'd rather go into dinner starkers than wear that awful green thing she had on last night. Do you think you might lend her something? Hat?'

'Mm?'

'Where did you get these lovely sparkly tights? They're in*cred*ibly sexy. Could we afford some for Annabel? Hat! Wake up!'

'Harrods, I think.'

I attempted to piece together fragments of recent memory.

409

My first coherent thought was relief that Cordelia, instead of despising her, had decided to take Annabel under her wing. I hoped she would not resent Cordelia's patronage. Then I remembered why I felt as though my eyelids had been steeped in starch.

Most unwillingly I had surfaced into consciousness some hours earlier just as the stable clock struck two. The ache from my shin suggested a kick from Cordelia as the instrument of my awakening. She turned her head, pressed her nose into my arm, and at once resumed the slow breathing of sleep. I had tucked the bedclothes around her shoulders and closed my eyes, hoping to fall back into oblivion.

The shutters had been left open and the moon was full. A beam like an interrogation tool bored through my clenched lids. Tiresomely my thoughts took shape and gathered pace. Would the charms of Fleur Kirkpatrick be sufficient consolation for my father, in prison on this day of all days when he was accustomed to rejoice in the bosom of his family? I thought of Maria-Alba, disturbed and frightened, warring with the nuns. I visualised poor darling Mark Antony pacing the empty house, wondering why he had been cruelly abandoned. Outside the wind tore at the trees as though trying to pluck them out of the ground. The imp of misery was making a feast of my stomach lining. How could I make sure Cordelia was happy, her first Christmas away from home? It does not matter how sternly you tell yourself that the crippling paranoia of the small hours of the night is due solely to body chemistry. You still feel absolutely miserable.

Then I remembered that Cordelia's stocking was still in the closet. Though she had not believed in Father Christmas for years, the ritual had to be observed. I tiptoed across the icy, boards, past Dirk, who lay bathed in moonlight by the long-dead fire, and opened the door. My own face with wildly disarranged hair made me start. The mirror, hanging at the back of the closet, always took me by surprise. I lugged the stocking over to the bed and laid it like a bolster down the centre. Shivering I got back into bed and tried to relax my mind and limbs and compose myself for sleep.

Half an hour later I was energetically reorganising my entire life, starting with a complete overhaul of face, figure and personality. It was a relief to allow my thoughts to wander into shameful reveries about Max, regardless of poor unhappy Caroline. I turned my pillow and pressed my cheek against its smooth coldness, telling myself that everything would look better in the morning. Just as my thoughts were beginning to blur I became aware of a need to go to the lavatory. I waited for ten minutes, hoping it would go away but of course it didn't.

Lights were burning dimly at intervals the length of the Long Gallery. I saw Colonel Mordaker sitting in a chair at the head of the stairs, with his back to me. I crept in the opposite direction towards the bathroom, wincing at every squeak of the boards, terrified of being blasted prematurely into the next world. In the bathroom I had a brief fantasy that my bottom had frozen to the seat and I would have to remain there until morning when an electric fire could be brought to thaw me out. But a minute later I was on my way back to bed.

I must have been about twenty feet from our bedroom door when I saw someone walking ahead of me. She was wearing a long robe and an old-fashioned headdress, a sort of a mob cap, pulled low over her brow. Something glistened on the floorboards in front of me. A wet footprint. I thought immediately of Annabel's story of the sadly disfigured Lady of the Moat.

I tiptoed behind her, conscious of an unreasonable dread of being discovered. Probably Mrs Mordaker, Maggie or perhaps Mrs Whale had woken up and fancied a bath. What though it was two o'clock in the morning? Having one bathroom between at least eight people meant there was always an undignified race to bag it. The day before, Mrs Mordaker had actually broken into a run, dressing-gown flapping, sponge bag swinging wildly on her arm, when she saw me approaching with the same object in view.

But I had just been in the bathroom and apart from me it had been empty. When the robed figure faltered and let out a small shriek, I very nearly followed suit. I hesitated, clinging to the darkness between the lights, telling myself not to be a coward. To very few people had such an opportunity been given. I owed it to science, to philosophy, to the *Brixton Mercury* to investigate further. But before I could muster my courage she had moved on, gliding swiftly and silently. When I came to the spot where she had paused I found a puddle of water.

The Lady of the Moat – I was almost convinced it was she – was speeding up as she approached the colonel. I dared not call out in case he was startled into emptying both barrels, with a complete disregard for plaster or flesh. Relief was quickly supplanted by fear as she passed the colonel's chair, almost brushing his arm, and disappeared down the stairs. He did not even turn his head.

I dashed into my bedroom, closed the door and with shaking fingers turned the key. I crept into bed with feet like fillets of frozen fish, angry with myself for being a deplorable coward. I had several times declared that I longed to see a ghost. Ah, but not in the middle of the night! A ghost in the bright light of day I was prepared for but darkness made everything frightful. The wind rose to a particularly loud hoo-hooing sound as it fought to bring down the chimneypots. I practised deep breathing and read myself a lecture.

Twenty minutes later, when my heartbeat and breathing

rates had slowed to normal, I was less certain than I had been that I had witnessed a visitation from the next world. But, whatever the facts, I could report what I had seen and make it gripping. With perhaps a few embellishments. I must turn this troublesome insomnia to my advantage and compose my masterpiece on the spot while the details were vividly before me. 'Her watery footprints gleamed silver beneath the moon like a snail's trail –' No, that sounded vaguely disgusting. 'The moon gleamed like a single eye on the silver river of prints –' No, a trickle was more like it. 'Her damp snails trailed . . .' I was asleep.

Breakfast had an air of gaiety about it. Along the table branches of larch were decorated with gilded cones, nut and orange pomanders, silver balls, dried pink roses and red lilies. In addition to the usual eggs, bacon, mushrooms and kedgeree, there were dishes of warm curd cakes, which melted in the mouth like snow. In honour of Christmas Day Sir Oswald came in to breakfast and was cordial with us all, particularly Cordelia. He cradled her hand between his fat paws and sniffed it like a police dog.

'It's my new Cherchez l'Homme soap,' explained Cordelia.

'*Il ne faut pas le chercher longtemps,*' he replied with a soulful look and a creaking of corsets.

After breakfast, to which everyone except Jonno and the colonel put in an appearance, groups were organised for church-going. Cordelia and Annabel disappeared immediately and I noticed that most of the men and Georgia had also slipped discreetly away.

'I so sad,' said Emilio, his eyes moist with sorrow. 'I am Catholeek. I cannot go to Eenglish service.'

'Oh, that's all right,' said Maggie with perfect innocence. 'Miss Tipple is also a Roman Catholic. You can take her in the Land Rover to the RC church in Bunton.'

Emilio's eyes dried immediately and became reproachful. Mrs Mordaker, Maggie and Freddie were to accompany Sir Oswald in the Rolls, which had been brought round to the front door by Dingle, who, on the few occasions Sir Oswald left Pye Place, acted as chauffeur. I assured Maggie with perfect truth that I was very happy to walk down with Mrs Whale and Dirk.

The morning was brilliant. The sun's rays shattered into spangles on the snow. The yew shapes, with their giant mushroom caps of snow, cast grotesque shadows on the glittering sea of white. Every leaf had its proportionate burden, every stalk its rim of crystals. The stone balls on the gate piers had shocks of white hair. Further down the lane long trickles of frozen water hung from the eaves of an old cart-shed. Our breaths streamed over our shoulders like smoke.

Mrs Whale walked beside me, gloved hands clasped across her stomach, the collar of her black coat turned up against the wind, which this morning was in a teasing mood, shooting cold draughts up our sleeves and skirts. Mrs Whale's complexion looked more faded than usual against the brightness of our surroundings. Deep lines were engraved between her brows and down her thin cheeks. The wind stood her shorn hair on end like a crest. Her eyes, which still had something lustrous and fine about them, were trained on the road. It was evident that the wintry scene had no power to engage her mind.

'We never have snow like this in London,' I said conversationally, when the crashing of the waterfall was sufficiently far behind us. I was keen to make headway with this woman who had so far resisted all my attempts to be friendly. 'Even in the park it quickly gets spoiled by footprints and turns to slush.'

'It's a nuisance when it gets trodden into the house.'

'I suppose so, but it's so pretty. And to have snow on Christmas Day! I shall always remember this.'

'The Lord made the earth beautiful to tempt us into misdoing, I often think.'

'Really? How could that be? Surely we ought to take pleasure in it.'

'Pleasure's a distraction from the duty we owe to Him.'

'But it's glorious to see such a wonderful sky going on and on for ever, so blue you could drown in it.' I drew in deep breaths of dazzling, freezing air. I wanted to skip or sing – to express my exultation. For once the imp of misery was ineffectual. I felt confident and optimistic. 'Look how perfect the snow is. It makes everything look so – well, it's a cliché I know – innocent.'

'You want to be careful, miss. Every year, just about, there's cases of snow blindness. Even local folk what ought to know better go missing in the hills 'cause they can't see nothing but white.'

My resolve to be kind and attentive to Mrs Whale weakened. But it must be difficult to be cheerful when you had to work hard all the time so that other people could be idle. 'Have you always lived in the High Peak?'

'I was born here, miss.'

'How lucky to have spent your childhood in such a beautiful, peaceful place.'

'I can't say as it felt all that lucky. I was brought up by my sister. She was a hard woman and rough-tongued. Our mother passed away with the cancer when I was four. She left six children. Snow meant the swedes were frozen in the ground and firewood was scarce. We went hungry to bed often enough. We slept head to toe, four in a bed, and that kept us from perishing with cold.' There was a subdued bitterness in Mrs Whale's voice that made me feel as though it were my fault. 'Our dad was a miner. He died of his lungs five years after our mother. I was in service from the age of fifteen till I married the head gardener at twenty.'

I felt the need of a little rhapsodising to lighten the gloom. 'I always think gardeners must be nice, contented people, tending the earth, making things grow – trees, lovely flowers.' I waved my hand in a vague, all-embracing way. 'Do you like gardening too?'

She lifted her eyes to engage them for the first time with mine. 'I hate it.'

'Oh.'

'It reminds me of him. He beat me. Sometimes I'd have to go to hospital. Then he tried to throttle me with twine. I've still got the scars.' She pulled down the neck of her black jersey and I saw a white line zigzagging across her throat.

'Oh, how terrible!' I had quite forgotten about the blueness of the sky and the innocence of the snow.

'I couldn't take it any more. I ran away. I found a room and a job in Sheffield.'

I was surprised that Mrs Whale, previously uncommunicative, seemed suddenly keen to tell me the story of her life. 'That must have been difficult with no one to help you.'

'I started in a factory, making clothes. I was good at sewing. But the factory went bust. So I went to work as wardrobe mistress in a theatre group.'

'Really? How interesting! My father's an actor. At least –' I stopped, wincing from the blow of remembering.

'I know about your father, miss. The name rang a bell with me at once when Lady Pye mentioned it and then I recognised you from your photograph in the papers. I'm sorry for it. Prison life is very hard. It can break your spirit.'

I was mildly surprised that someone so determined to shun the frivolous things of this world should have allowed herself to read the *Daily Banner*, which was what Colonel Mordaker would have called a 'scurrilous rag'. But perhaps it had come wrapped round pork chops or something.

'I liked it in Sheffield,' continued Mrs Whale, who seemed determined to unburden herself. 'I was happy for the first time. We toured the country and I saw a bit of life. I had a lover.'

'How very nice.'

'Yes, it was – very nice.' I did not think she intended irony. 'But my husband got to hear about it and came after me. There was a fight. I thought he was going to kill the only man I'd ever loved. So I took up my scissors and I stabbed him.'

I was shocked into speechlessness. Mrs Whale crunched through the snow beside me, head bowed, face impassive. 'Was he . . . ? Did he . . . ?' I asked when the silence became a burden.

'He died. I went to prison for ten years.' We trudged on a little way. The sun had gone behind a cloud and the snow no longer sparkled. 'It was what I deserved.'

'Any of us might have done the same to protect someone we loved. I think the sentence was rather harsh.'

'They'd only my word that was how it was. My lover went abroad and couldn't be got to testify. He'd been in trouble with the police before.'

'How mean!' I was disgusted.

Mrs Whale shrugged without lifting her eyes. 'Men are weak. It doesn't do to put your trust in them.'

'Surely they aren't all bad? You were unlucky.'

'I don't believe in luck, miss.'

'It sounds very sad,' I said inadequately. All my optimism had sunk beneath the weight of Mrs Whale's misfortunes. My feeble attempts to sympathise were obviously failing to cheer. I thought it might be a good idea to talk of pleasanter things. 'Look, a darling robin on a snowy branch just like a Christmas ca – Oh, Dirk! Did you have to bark at it?'

Dirk gave several more confirmatory barks. 'This must be the village. How pretty it looks from above, all those snowy rooftops clustered round the church.'

'Those years in prison broke my spirit,' continued Mrs Whale as though I had not spoken. 'Never alone, but always lonely, the cold in winter, the heat in summer, the dirt, nothing to look at that wasn't ugly as sin, nothing to hope for. But worse was feeling oneself a thing of contempt, as though one wasn't hardly human.' Her voice became a touch savage here and I felt alarmed.

'Don't let's talk about it if you'd rather not,' I ventured timidly. 'It must be painful.'

'It hurts all right. But that's my punishment. Only one person spoke a kind word to me in all those years and that was the prison chaplain. He said whatever I'd done I was still one of God's children.' Mrs Whale lifted her head to gaze heavenward and her voice trembled with feeling. 'He said, "Joy shall be in Heaven over one sinner that repenteth, more than over ninety and nine just persons, which need no repentance." It meant a lot to me, the idea that I belonged somewhere to someone. All the hate and hardness and despair fell away and I saw a shining light!'

I told myself it was shallow and unkind to feel embarrassed but I was. The nuns frowned on displays of excessive devotion. Expressions of religious fervour were considered to be 'putting oneself forward', than which there was no greater crime.

'Gosh!' I said.

'Yes. Gosh.' I might have suspected a little satire here had not Mrs Whale's expression been so absolutely solemn. 'I saw the chaplain every week after that and together we read the Bible and I learned about God's infinite mercy. When I came out of prison I wanted to join an Anglican order but Mother Superior wasn't sure of my vocation. She thought it might be wanting to hide myself away so's society wouldn't judge me. She said I had to spend a few years yet in the world, telling my story to anyone who'd hear it, in expiation of my great sin.'

'Well, I must say, that's pretty tough!' I was indignant. 'You'd already been miserable for ten years. I don't know why religious people have to be so jolly unforgiving.'

Mrs Whale smiled for the first time, a faint thinning of the lips. 'Strait is the gate and narrow is the way.'

Huh! I thought but did not say.

The Rolls was parked in front of the lichgate, forcing the rest of the congregation to squeeze past it in their best clothes, gathering snow from running boards and walls. There were mutterings and black looks.

I was ushered up a staircase and through a door into a private pew where those of the household who had been brought down by car were already assembled. Sir Oswald opened his eyes briefly to give me a smile of approval before closing them for the duration of the service. We could look through a screen down on to the congregation without being seen ourselves. We had cushions on our seats and our own small fireplace, filled with glowing coals. It seemed that as far as physical comfort went, things were strait and narrow only for *hoi polloi*.

The service was 'high' with plenty of incense and tinkling bells. Freddie and I sang with gusto but everyone else mumbled and groaned discreetly, ducking out of the top notes altogether. When the soloist began the anthem I looked through the screen to see Mrs Whale, mottled red and blue by sunbeams falling through stained glass, standing alone on the chancel steps, her cropped head thrown back and warbling like a thrush. During the sermon most of us followed Sir Oswald's example and closed our eyes. The vicar's theme of neighbourly love was well worn and had been proved to be unfeasible centuries ago. The vicar had a reedy voice that made Dirk bark until Mrs Mordaker hissed like a pit full of snakes and almost pushed his nose to the back of his head, which for once shut him up.

Afterwards Sir Oswald stood in the porch blocking the doorway, while he gave the vicar the benefit of his views on Uganda, the National Health Service, modern agriculture and the novels of Agatha Christie. I had never heard him so voluble. Behind him, in the shadow of his great bulk, the congregation grumbled to each other about turkeys and puddings being incinerated to blackened crisps while timers rang in unattended kitchens.

I was saved from more of Mrs Whale's oppressive conversation by Freddie's insistence that she preferred to walk back to the house. Mrs Whale was borne away in the Rolls with the others, looking anything but pleased by this addition to her comfort.

'Besides wanting your company, the smell of the cow byre coming from Dingle was so overpowering I thought I was going to be sick,' Freddie said as we strolled up through the village. 'Vere has gone to look for the falcons. We're leaving tomorrow morning, you know, so today's his last chance. The painting's virtually finished and I shall take it to the framer's next week.'

'I'm very sorry you're going. It's so lovely here, isn't it? I think house parties are an excellent thing. You can really get to know people.'

'I must admit I always rather dread them. The enforced intimacy day after day with people one mightn't like. I expect it's because I'm an only child. At parties I tend to get analytical, observing people rather than joining in. But naturally coming from a large family, you feel at home in a crowd.'

'Actually I often feel like an outsider myself. Sometimes even in my own family. They always seem somehow brighter, starrier, more – more visible than me. But it isn't that they stifle me. On the contrary, I wouldn't *be* me without them. That's what families do for you. They define you. The thought of being an only child is quite alarming. I shouldn't have the least idea who I was.'

'Well, friends define you as well. And husbands and lovers.'

I was silent for a moment, thinking. 'Of course I do have friends,' I said eventually, 'though I don't see them very often. And I did have a lover. But it's as though I've been half-turned away from everyone else, always looking back to my family. I think I've been too comfortable and contented to want to step outside the enchanted circle.' I was much struck by this idea. 'I didn't realise. This is the first time I've been away without them, the first time in my life I've spent time with people who didn't know that my father was a famous actor and I was the least remarkable member of his eccentric, glamorous family.' The idea gathered momentum. 'Or could it be that I've been too scared to be myself, by myself? Perhaps I've been like the froghoppers that live in the lavender bushes in our garden – a tiny grub happily munching at the leaf provided, protected from the elements by a ball of spit and thinking it's the universe.'

'You've got a job. There's self-definition through achievement. An attractive idea to the only child who shrinks from relying on other people.'

'I admit I do secretly feel extremely proud to have lasted several weeks at the *Mercury* in spite of ups and downs. I'm only an amateur writer, not a real journalist, but the fact that someone thinks I can do anything worth paying me for fills me with glee. The idea of being taken even a little bit seriously by other people is intoxicating.'

'The thing about a family, though,' Freddie slowed her pace

421

as the road became steeper, 'is that you can't have it on your own terms. I mean, you have to accommodate other people's follies and caprices. In a family you're thrown together with people you haven't chosen. And, whatever happens, you're bound to each other. Even if you row like blazes you're still brother and sister. There's a grounding reality about that I rather envy. And such useful early lessons in tolerance and love.'

'Didn't you love your parents?'

'I was nine when my mother died. I adored her. Fay appeared on the scene the day after the funeral. She resented having to look after me. My father took Fay's side. At least that's how I saw it then. I stopped even trying to love anybody for years.'

I put my arm through hers, moved by an inexpressible pity. 'You're making up for it now.'

'Yes.' Freddie's face had a rapt look, as though she still marvelled at her new found happiness. 'Vere said he'd told you about the baby.'

'I guessed, really. I hope you don't mind.'

'No, of course not. I don't mean to make a drama of it. It's just that I need time to get used to the idea myself.'

'I'm so pleased for you. I adore babies.'

'Do you know, I've never even held a baby.'

'There's nothing to it – looking after them, I mean. You just have to put yourself into their position. You have to look at everything as a baby might. Then you won't get at cross purposes.'

'That sounds to me like very useful advice. So,' Freddie said when we'd gone a little further in companionable silence, 'what actually do you write about in your newspaper?'

I outlined my brief as author of 'Spook Hall'.

Freddie seemed to find the idea amusing. 'I suppose it wasn't you who stole the arm just to have something to write about? No, of course not. You wouldn't want to frighten Maggie.'

'She looks awfully under the weather this morning. I think if I lived here all the year round, with the wind howling every second, my imagination would run away with me too. It's surpassingly beautiful. But it's not restful. There's something in the air that makes everything seem slightly distorted – perhaps intense is the word I'm looking for. Even my dreams are more vivid. And last night I really did believe I'd seen a ghost.' I told Freddie the story of the Lady of the Moat and described the woman I had seen. I tried to make it entertaining so Freddie wouldn't suppose I was completely unhinged and to my gratification she laughed until tears came into her eyes.

'Oh dear,' she said, at last, 'I do see how you thought – I'm so sorry to have frightened you. I'm afraid it was me.'

'What do you mean?'

'What a pity! I had no idea you were behind me.'

'You mean you were in the Long Gallery?'

'I couldn't sleep. So I decided to have another look at Sir Oswald's chin. I didn't mean to do any actual painting but I was suddenly inspired and the next thing, the stable clock was striking half-past one. I wasn't tired but I knew I ought to get some sleep. So I decided to have a quick bath to relax.'

'But I was in the bathroom.'

'Well, don't tell anyone but I've taken to bathing in the sink in the linen room. It fills up so much faster. And the linen room's so deliciously warm. Anyway, there's always someone else in the bathroom. I fetched my nightdress and towel but I forgot my slippers. So I had to walk back with bare feet. I ought to have dried them but I was in a hurry to get to bed. There's your Lady of the Moat.'

'But the mobcap!'

'I found an old rubber shower-cap on the back of the door so I borrowed it to save having to dry my hair.'

'The scream – the puddle of water!'

'I filled a hot-water bottle from the tap. But I hadn't pushed the cork in far enough. I was suddenly drenched in nearly boiling water.'

'But . . .' I was deeply disappointed to have my first super-natural experience exploded, 'how could you walk past the colonel without him seeing you? And why go downstairs?'

'I'd left my evening bag in the drawing-room. I'm fond of it and I didn't want D – any of the dogs to get hold of it. The colonel was sound asleep, his chin propped on the butt of his gun. Absolutely out for the count. When I came back upstairs he was lolling in his chair, with his head back, making a noise like water going down a plughole. Someone had tucked an eiderdown round him – Maggie, probably.'

'Well, damn! I really thought . . . Botheration! I'll have to cheat and pretend you haven't told me all that. In the interests of stimulating my readers' adrenalin flow and keeping my job, I'm becoming an out-and-out liar.'

'You'll be a journalist yet.'

Lunch – several raised veal and ham pies, a goose pâté, potato bread, a truckle of Lancashire cheese, fruitcake and a quince tart – was already on the table when we got in. Maggie explained that because of energetic nature of the afternoon's entertainment she had thought a light snack would be best. And there would be a large tea to accompany the opening of the presents under the tree afterwards. Apparently, down in the village by the mill the river had frozen to a depth that made it safe for skating. Cordelia's eyes were huge with excitement throughout lunch. She had fallen in love at an early age with Noel Streatfeild's novel *White Boots*. I could see she was planning to cut a dash before a marvelling world, as the beautiful, talented, tempestuous Lalla Moore.

The ice-bitten river was steel grey with a frothy surface of bubbles, twigs and leaves of various shades of brown, frozen into abstract compositions. The mill-pond had been very full before the freeze and made a perfect skating rink. The whole village had turned out to enjoy the fun. The few who possessed proper skates did figures of eight and spins in the middle where the ice was smoother. At the edge children made slides, towed one another along, pushed each other over and screamed with pleasure. The more daring launched themselves from the top of the hill on tin trays. Babies swaddled to the eyes were pulled up and down on homemade toboggans. Grandmothers and grandfathers sat on the wall that overlooked the mill-race, gossiping about the times when they had been young and foolhardy. It was exactly like those ice scenes that Dutch painters used to be so fond of.

Being strangers and also guests from the big house, our arrival caused something of a stir. I could see that we added fuel to the gossip. There were eight of us in the party. Archie had retired to his room, saying that he had a horror of his fingers being amputated by a passing blade. Mrs Mordaker volunteered to take Dirk for a walk. Vere and the colonel were both somewhere in the hills, stalking blue-footed falcons. Jonno had not come down from his room. Everyone else was too unfit, or in Maggie's case, too busy.

I put on the black skating boots I had chosen from the selection that had been brought into the hall at Pye Place. Annabel had her own pretty white ones and Cordelia and Georgia had argued about who should have the only other white pair but after an acrimonious session of trying-on, like the last act of Cinderella, they proved too small for Georgia.

Cordelia and I had spent many afternoons at the indoor rink on Queensway. We were able to go forward and backwards without falling over and revolve slowly on the spot but such things as toe-loops and axels were beyond our skills. Rupert and Max were competent skaters but Freddie, Georgia and Emilio were novices. I linked arms with Freddie and we skated slowly up and down until she began to get the hang of it.

'This is such fun,' she kept saying, even when a group of children banged into us and nearly knocked us down. 'I love doing physical things – perhaps because I so rarely do. I feel drunk with excitement.' After half an hour she bravely set out on her own. Her red hair flew out beneath her green woollen hat and on her generally pale cheeks were spots of colour. She circled round and round the pond, concentrating, in her own world.

Georgia clung to Max, squealing every time anyone went near them. She might have got on better if, instead of gazing into his eyes the whole time, she had watched her feet. Rupert tried to teach Emilio but as soon as the latter was hauled up he fell down again immediately, with cries of '*Madre de Dios!*' and 'Oop-la!'. He was good-natured and seemed not to mind the yells of laughter from the crowd that gathered to watch. 'We have not thees ice in Colombia,' he wheezed after the breath had been knocked out of him several times. When Emilio retired to sit on the bank, surrounded by a group of giggling girls, Rupert skated round fast on his own. Annabel, who watched him like a sheepdog alert for commands, followed, her thin legs flying out sideways in her effort to keep up with him. Cordelia soon gathered a group of adolescent boys who stumbled clumsily in her wake as though they were bear-cubs and she was smeared with honey.

I wanted to explore the river. Beyond the pond it ran between steep banks, from which drooped snow-burdened trees shedding flakes that drifted languidly in front of my face. It was delightful to be alone in this exquisite landscape. The Queensway rink had echoed with raucous music and shrieking voices. The silence of the countryside made this an incomparable experience.

The village was soon out of sight. Sudden prospects opened in the gaps between trees and rocks to reveal a sky slowly draining of blue. The horizon appeared as a smudged zigzag of ash and iron between the folds of the hills. Frozen reeds stood like glassy palisades. I imagined myself as an Anglo-Saxon or an Icenian skating down this river on slivers of bone, relishing this moment of freedom and solitude, snatched from a brief, barbarous, scavenging existence. Yet the poetry would perhaps be more thrilling because of that.

I heard the scrape of skates on ice behind me, like a knife being sharpened. An arm encircled my waist. I put my left hand in his. Together we skated faster, skimming over the ice, slicing through blue shadows, like birds piercing a cloud-patched sky. As in a dream, we swooped over the ground, the speed far surpassing the energy expended. Without effort we cut long curves in the ice, on, on, as though we were approaching some long-desired destination. I half-expected to rise above the ground, to fly, to cut the white bowl of the sky with giant arabesques. The boundless journey, the futility of thought, filled me with delight.

Now the banks became cliffs, the river more twisting, the landscape dramatic. A tree, snapped at its roots, lay in our path, its head buried in ice. We glided in a circle and stopped. Max put both arms round me. The whiteness of the light combined with the coldness of the wind made my eyes water and I closed them. Max rubbed away a tear with his finger. 'Darling. Darling Harriet.'

The sound of my name woke me from the dream. I was unable to forestall an abrupt and unwelcome return of self-consciousness. It shattered the idyll. I almost rebelled as I felt his lips touch mine but cowardice made me compliant. My, but he was a good kisser! And on skates too. The minute I thought this, I wanted to laugh. But at the same time the very idea of laughing when someone was trying to kiss me filled me with something like panic. Who could blame him for being angry? My family were right when they accused me of being too eager to please. I returned his kiss with passion to suppress the horrible laughter.

'God! You really are a siren.' Max held me tightly. 'Damn it, we're miles from anything like shelter. But I must have you, snow or not.' He pulled off his gloves, flung them down on the ice and began to unbutton my coat. This was tricky and we began to slide around. 'Stand still! Oh, Christ! This is bloody ridiculous.' Then he pushed me abruptly away and I had to twirl my arms to stop myself falling over.

'Hey!' I said, indignantly.

Then I saw Rupert skating towards us, hands behind his back, looking about him in a leisurely way.

'There you are,' he called. 'I thought I'd better come and warn you. There's a weir somewhere along this stretch. Apparently there have been several people drowned over the years.' He looked at me and I thought I saw amusement – or was it contempt? – in his eyes. 'They ought to put up a sign: "Deep Water". Or perhaps "Thin Ice".'

TWENTY-SEVEN

'There was a telephone call for you.' Maggie gave Max a piece of paper as we were blown in through the front door. 'She said it was urgent and you're to ring back today.'

I thought at once of Caroline. The telephone was in the inner hall where it was impossible to have a private conversation. I hurried to change my shoes but my fingers were numbed and slow. On my way to the drawing room I heard him say, 'Yes, of course, I see that, but it isn't exactly convenient . . . How long? . . . Well, I can't refuse, really, can I?' Then he laughed and said, 'That definitely sounds more like a threat than a promise.' I moved out of earshot.

I was disconcerted to find that as soon as Max's attention was turned elsewhere I longed for it to be given to me. But the minute it was, I became uneasy. On the walk back to the house Georgia had drawn his arm through hers and made him walk a little behind the rest of us. Oh, shameful vanity! I had felt certain he would have preferred to walk with me. All the time I was talking to Emilio – who seemed not to notice his fiancée's defection – I wondered what it would be like to make love with Max. Now, when he was talking to his wife, I felt the keen edge of jealousy.

I was careful not to look at him when he came into the drawing room.

'Hello, darling.' Freddie's face lit as Vere came in after him. 'We've had such a lovely time. Skating in a frozen landscape. It was incredibly beautiful.'

Vere kissed his wife and held her hand between both of his as he murmured in a low voice, 'Darling, should you have? You know you must be careful.'

She smiled. 'I'm tougher than you think.'

'All the same . . .' He left the rest unspoken.

'Did you have a good walk?'

'I found the remains of last year's nest.'

'Excellent.'

Freddie went away with his wet coat that he'd forgotten to take off. His eyes followed her to the door. It was a simple exchange, composed, tranquil, almost prosaic, yet the dullest student of human behaviour could not have failed to see how much love there was in it. I thought of the dynamic relationship my parents enjoyed and wondered if their flamboyant coquetry, played out before all the world, was a distracting cover to hide an emptiness within. The moment I thought this I felt as though I had carelessly injured something infinitely precious and the little beast residing in my digestive system gave me a particularly savage nip.

When the colonel returned a few minutes later, he was grim-faced and out of sorts. His hair clung damply to his reddened forehead and his hands were purple with cold. Ignoring his wife's words of greeting, he threw himself into a chair with a grunt of displeasure.

Archie was instantly alert. 'You're looking a little flushed, Colonel. I hope you haven't been overdoing it.'

Mrs Mordaker stood up. 'I'll just go and get your pills, Hereward. You'd better have a cup of tea straight away.'

430

'Don't fuss, woman.' The colonel's ungraciousness was remarkable but his wife seemed not to notice it.

'And did you see the blue-footed ones?' asked Archie, warming to his task of making the colonel lose his temper.

'No, I did not! If you ask me they don't exist!'

'Now, Colonel dear, there's no need to be cross.' Archie depressed his chin and looked reprovingly at him over his half-moon spectacles. 'It's unkind of you to give Vere the lie just because he's a more accomplished ornithologist.'

'Accomplished, my – Hrrr! I say there's no such thing! If there were I'd have seen 'em.' The rage in his voice woke Dirk, who began to howl.

'Didn't you just tell us,' Archie demanded of Vere, 'that you saw a flock of them this very afternoon?'

Vere raised his eyebrows and looked amused, which was probably more galling to the Colonel's pride than anything. I think he meant to be pacific, though.

'How *dare* you?' The colonel stood up suddenly and advanced a step towards Archie, fists clenched. 'I've had as much of you as I can stand. Men like you are an aberration. You ought to be locked up where your filthy practices can do no harm . . .' He paused to swat the air as he struggled for words.

'*My* filthy practices?' Archie did a wonderful imitation of bewilderment. 'What *do* you mean, dear boy?'

The colonel turned such a livid shade of mauve that I was really frightened he might have a heart attack.

'What's all the noise about?' asked Rupert, coming in then. 'Shut up, Dirk! Mordaker, have you taken leave of your senses? I can hear you shouting halfway up the stairs. You're frightening the children.'

I was certain that Annabel and Cordelia were enjoying the drama but the contempt in Rupert's voice was salutary. The colonel was the sort of man who divided people into those who were 'gentlemen' and those who were not, and he knew he was behaving badly. He stood clapping his hands feebly against his sides, looking a little ashamed. Awful though he was, I felt sorry for him.

'Here we are, dear.' Mrs Mordaker came in with the box of pills. 'Maggie's bringing the tea. Come and get warm.' The colonel seemed to deflate. Without protest he lowered himself stiffly on to the sofa, took the glass of water and swallowed the pill obediently. She gave his shoulder a little proprietorial pat. I saw then that she really did care about him. When she sat down beside him he gave her a grimace that might possibly have been an expression of gratitude, and made no demur when she tweaked his tie straight. A little later he allowed his hand to rest briefly on her knee. There are many kinds of love, I realised.

'Can we open our presents?' asked Cordelia when Maggie came in, bearing a loaded tray. 'You did say tea. We're simply dying to.'

'Speak for yourself,' said Annabel. 'I don't suppose I shall like mine anyway.'

Georgia, who had timed her arrival in the drawing room to coincide with Max's, whispered something to him about 'brats'.

'In my day children knew how to be grateful,' said Mrs Mordaker, unwisely.

'Gratitude isn't something you can *know*,' said Annabel instantly. 'You either feel it or you don't. I don't, particularly.'

'Please, Lady Pye,' Cordelia smiled winningly at Maggie. 'May we open them now?'

'Ravishing!' Sir Oswald opened his eyes and fixed them on Cordelia. She was looking particularly lovely in a dress of pumpkin-coloured silk made by my mother's dressmaker. 'Go on, my dear, and let's see what Father Christmas has been good enough to bring.'

Annabel ran into the hall and brought back an armful of parcels from beneath the tree, which she began to rip open. Cordelia brought in presents for the rest of us which she handed round with a pretty enthusiasm. I hoped she was unaware how effectively her own behaviour exposed Annabel's lack of decorum.

'A book!' Annabel threw it to one side. 'Boring! Books shouldn't be allowed at Christmas. A photograph frame! What am I supposed to do with that!'

Maggie looked defeated. I felt complete sympathy. Annabel needed a firm hand but Maggie's temperament was too compliant. And, naturally, she was reluctant to alienate her stepdaughter. Sir Oswald seemed quite uninterested in the child. I felt sorry for Annabel but there was a savagery about her moods that made me feel positively jaded.

'Annabel! Come outside.' Rupert, who had been sitting with a book open on his knee, hardly seeming to listen, got up suddenly.

'What? No! I'm opening my presents!'

'Now!' If Rupert had spoken to me in such a tone, jaded or not, I should have gone like a shot.

Annabel went slowly out.

'Oh, Lady Pye!' Cordelia, consummate actress that she was, looked at Maggie with shining eyes. 'A *Christmas Carol*! It's such a lovely story and now I've got my very own copy! I shall always treasure it!' She ran over to Maggie and kissed her cheek. 'It's so very kind of you.'

When I saw Maggie's kind face, bright with pleasure, I felt a tightness in my throat.

'An angel.' Sir Oswald's raddled cheeks flushed. He fidgeted about in his chair, crossing and uncrossing his legs.

After a few minutes Rupert returned, followed by Annabel. She seemed subdued. I watched her as she tore the paper from a small square parcel and saw a tear fall, which she brushed

433

away with the heel of her palm. She looked at the contents then got up and walked over to Maggie.

'Thank you,' She pecked her stepmother's cheek. 'It's a very nice sponge bag.' It was a pale copy of Cordelia but it was something.

'I hope it's what you like, dear,' Maggie said humbly.

It was a perfect example of people taking one at one's own estimate. Maggie thought nothing of herself and expected that others would discount her. So naturally they did.

I unwrapped a lovely calf-bound copy of Byron's poems.

'Dear, *dear* Maggie.' I kissed her heartily. 'You're so good to everyone. You should be canonised.'

'A charming thought – but you must be bones and worms first, I'm afraid,' said Archie, rather spoiling the compliment. 'It may be that a more immediate treat would be preferable.'

'I asked Rupert what you'd like.' Maggie looked pleased. 'It was his idea. I hadn't never heard of him.'

In the last days before leaving London, not knowing anything about my hostess, I had been much exercised about a suitable present. I had finally settled on an antique spectacle case, embroidered with flowers, hearts and doves. It was a little faded but extremely pretty. I saw Maggie pick it up more than once and stroke the flowers admiringly. I have always thought that there are few pleasures to equal that of giving, when you happen to have hit on the right thing.

Rupert's present to me was unconditionally the right thing. It was a Georgian inkstand. Two cut-glass inkwells with silver lids shaped like lions' heads fitted snugly next to a pen tray. The whole thing was mounted on silver lion's paws. Remembering that Rupert was apt to be annoyed when thanked effusively, I moderated my expressions of gratitude. But for many days afterwards, whenever I looked at it, I felt a sense of wonder that this lovely thing was actually mine. My present to him was meagre by comparison, a shagreen vesta case for keeping matches in, that I had found in an antique shop near the *Brixton Mercury*. Rupert thanked me and kissed me politely and briefly, much as one might kiss an ancient and slightly repulsive aunt.

For Archie I had found a wooden paperknife with a carved handle shaped like a dolphin. He gave me a beautifully illustrated copy of *Adam Bede*. 'I always give this novel to young women,' he explained. 'It's a very moral tale and shows what a bad end you'll come to if you allow gentlefolk have their wicked way with you.' He looked significantly at Max and then back at me. 'For your birthday, if things haven't improved, I shall give you a copy of *Tess of the D'Urbervilles*.'

Annabel looked sick with envy when Cordelia unwrapped the shoes Ma had given her. They were from Charles Jourdan, black suede with tiny heels. Cordelia put them on, pointed her toes and paraded about the room, to the evident delight of Sir Oswald, who seemed to be having trouble with the bottom buttons of his waistcoat. Annabel, her expression appalled, held up a grey dress with pink flowers embroidered on the collar and yoke. It was old-fashioned and childish.

'Isn't it right, dear?' Maggie peered through her spectacles at it. 'I got it at Tarrant's in Derby.'

'It's –' Annabel glanced at Rupert – 'OK.'

'It's very good quality wool,' said Maggie. 'I thought it would keep you warm next term when you're allowed to change out of school uniform.'

'I couldn't possibly wear it at school. The other girls would scream with laughter.'

Cordelia examined it critically. 'Do you know, Lady Pye, I think this *could* be a lovely dress. What it needs is a little of what Ma calls a *soupspoon d'élégance*. That's French for a hint of elegance,' she explained kindly. 'If you took off the collar and cut the neck down into a wide scoop, unpicked all the flowers, took out the gathers and made just a few wide pleats, with, um – let's see – perhaps a narrow scarlet sash over the hips, I think it would really be very smart.'

There was no doubt that Cordelia had inherited my mother's visual flair.

Annabel looked doubtfully at Maggie. 'Perhaps Mrs Whale could do it.'

'Bless you, my chick,' said Maggie holding out her hand for the dress. 'I don't like to put more on her, being as it's Christmas. But if it'll please you, I'll make the time myself. I see now what the young lady means. It *is* a bit old-fashioned. Those assistants in Tarrant's are that superior you dursn't go against them.' She took up the scissors from her work basket and began at once to unpick the flowers.

Freddie, who had only just returned to the drawing room, gave me a rectangle of white tissue paper. 'Oh!' I said. 'I haven't anything for you!'

'Of course you haven't,' she replied. 'You didn't know I was going to be here. This is an improvised present. The ink's hardly dry.'

I opened the parcel. It was a fine pen-and-ink drawing of a girl skating. Her long dark hair flew out behind her.

'How clever,' said Rupert bending over my shoulder to see. 'That's Harriet to a T.'

'Is it?' I studied the drawing, hoping to discover what *was* me, exactly. I caught Freddie's hand and pressed it. 'It's just marvellous! I simply love it!'

'There's one more present under the tree,' said Cordelia coming in with a small parcel in her hand. 'It wasn't there a minute ago. It's for you, Hat.'

I undid the white tissue paper, watched by the rest of the party who were suffering the anticlimax of having opened all their own presents. I lifted from the paper a gold necklace like a snake. Its body was made of finely wrought overlapping links that made it as thick as a man's finger, yet as flexible as a real snake. Its eyes were rubies.

'Crikey!' said Cordelia. 'Put it on! Or shall I?'

I felt self-conscious beneath the gaze of so many pairs of eyes. The necklace fastened at the front, the snake's jaws gripping its tail.

'It really is beautiful,' said Freddie. 'It must be terribly old.'

'Who gave it to you?' Cordelia shook out the wrapping. 'It doesn't say on the tag.'

Of course I knew who it was from and the knowledge sent my blood careering round my body until my face burned. Max was standing nearby, watching me. 'Thank you,' I said. 'It's much lovelier than I could possibly deserve.'

'It once belonged to a Mesopotamian princess,' he said. 'It's five thousand years old.'

Jonno, who had only just appeared, and who looked rather the worse for wear, rolled his bloodshot eyes. 'Is that a bribe or a reward, I'd like to know.'

'Think of the things that snake has seen,' said Freddie. 'Another world.'

I imagined the necklace around the throat of an proud, almond-eyed, raven-haired girl and her brown hand caressing it, thousands of years ago, as mine was now. Might there still be a few grains of sand from the shore of the Euphrates imprisoned between its links? I could not accept such a valuable thing. But I did not know how to refuse it in front of so many people.

Mrs Whale brought in champagne and everyone's mood grew gay. Even Annabel cheered up when she found Rupert had given her a wristwatch with the phases of the moon on the dial and a pale blue leather strap. She sat on her own in the far corner of the room, gloating over it. Archie played Victorian parlour songs on the piano and Jonno sang. He had a surprisingly beautiful voice, a refined tenor that was incongruous with the repulsive face furniture. Georgia told Max about her last holiday on St Lucia. Emilio flirted with Freddie and Vere talked *fortissimo* to Miss Tipple. Sir Oswald worked his way through my unoriginal, and perhaps unfortunate, present of a large box of chocolates while watching Cordelia, who was re-examining her loot. My hand went frequently to Max's necklace, which lay across my collarbones with a cold, insistent pressure.

Dinner was magnificent. Maggie and Mrs Whale must have slaved to produce *oeufs Richelieu* – soft poached eggs with truffles and prawns set in aspic – followed by sole on a bed of tomato mousse, and roast goose with soufflé potatoes and a sauce made from cherries. Sir Oswald's chin became very greasy and I saw him dab his brow with his napkin as he gobbled through large helpings of every course. Unfortunately those of us who had spent the afternoon skating or walking on the moor were exhausted by exercise and fresh air, and we had to struggle to maintain our part in the conversation. My eyes stung with tiredness and I noticed Freddie concealing huge yawns behind her hand. Cordelia and Annabel flopped over their plates and were silent.

While we ate our Christmas pudding Maggie's head, from more noble causes, drooped forward until her chin was on her chest and for ten minutes she slept. Georgia tried to set up a flirtation with Max but he was unresponsive. Only Archie, having spent all afternoon peacefully reading, was talkative and regaled us, Scheherazade-like, with an extensive repertoire of improbable stories. Our laughter woke Maggie and for a moment she looked around with bleary eyes and a startled expression at her guests seated round the candlelit table, as if she wondered what we were all doing there.

'This has been a wonderful Christmas,' said Max, the minute he saw his hostess was properly awake. 'You've been so kind and generous and I can't thank you enough. But, sadly, I must leave tomorrow. It was my agent on the telephone this afternoon. The Hubert Hat Company is taking *King Lear* on tour. It's all been put together at the last minute and they've had a struggle to replace absent members of the cast –' he looked apologetically at me – 'so I can't let them down. I've booked a taxi for the station in the morning, early. We're leaving for Australia tomorrow afternoon.'

'We could share your taxi,' said Mrs Mordaker, at once. 'It will save the man coming twice to the house. Besides it will be cheaper.'

'I'm afraid it will be too early for you. I'm leaving at six.'

'Hereward and I have always been early risers. I always say slug-a-beds miss the best part of the day.'

She gave Jonno, who was helping himself to another glass of wine, a disapproving look. He silently raised his middle finger in her direction, which luckily neither Maggie nor Sir Oswald saw. Mrs Mordaker's expression of outrage made Cordelia and Annabel explode with giggles throughout what remained of the feast, which was quite maddening for the rest of us.

I heard of Max's departure with mixed feelings. I was grieved that my father was to be left to drum his heels in prison while someone else took the stage as Gloucester. But I was glad it had not been Caroline on the telephone. I regretted that my flirtation with Max was being brought swiftly to an end but I was relieved that now I need not decide how it should be resolved.

'What a coincidence,' said Georgia to Max. 'I was planning to visit my sister in Melbourne in the New Year. You must let me have your address.' She shot me a triumphant look.

'I don't know how you've managed to meet so many people and do so many things,' I said to Archie as we dropped into chairs in the drawing room after dinner.

'You were all so *dull* I was obliged to entertain myself.

I merely recounted the plots of all the plays, novels and operas I could think of for a little mental exercise. Do you know, I shall miss the Mordakers. They are *so* amusing. *Don't* look now but Max and Georgia are having a row.' Archie looked slyly over my shoulder. 'He's said something unkind, I think . . . Yes, she's staring down at her glass, wondering whether to dash the contents into his face . . . She's thought better of it . . . She's trying tears. The *beast*! . . . He's laughing . . . She's slapped his face! No, Harriet! I for*bid* you to turn round. It would be indecent to crow over her humiliation.'

'I wouldn't dream of doing any such thing!'

'Nonsense. You're her rival and you've won. You mustn't pretend to be superhuman. Now Lancelot's looking at *you*. He wants you to approve his demonstration of fealty. He's making his way through the crowd to beg for your sleeve to wear in his helm . . . Don't look, here he comes . . . Ah, Max! Tell us about this Australian tour. Think of picturesque billabongs shaded by coolabah trees and *thronged* with muscular, perspiring sheep-farmers – you must be *so* excited.'

It appeared that Archie had appointed himself my moral guardian for he remained firmly at my side for the rest of the evening. The party broke up earlier than usual. I went upstairs with Cordelia, unable to make up my mind whether I was glad or sorry that there had been opportunity only for a decorous farewell kiss from Max in full view of the household. I was glad as we left the drawing room but sorry the minute Cordelia and I were tucked up with the lights out. When Max was out of my sight I could imagine myself as sexually liberated, with a devil-may-care attitude to adultery and fornication. Just.

I had been dreamlessly asleep for some time when something woke me. I resisted like mad but a faint, repeated noise dragged me towards consciousness. I lifted myself on one elbow and looked accusingly at Dirk. He slumbered innocently on, smacking his lips, and making pedalling motions with his paws. Beside me Cordelia lay without stirring. There it was again, a grating noise like fingernails being dragged slowly across wood. It came from the closet.

I thought of mice, deathwatch beetles, plumbing, even rats. I was not comforted. Then I thought of Old Gally's arm. This I had been trying, with everything in my power, to avoid doing. But with cruel insistence the horrid thing popped into my imagination. I pictured it sneaking round the closet door and cruising silently through the darkness over to the bed and slowly losing altitude to hover with its outstretched finger quivering just above my nose. That did it. I preferred to meet it on my own terms. I slipped out of bed, tiptoed to the closet door, stiffened my stomach muscles and pulled it open. A face that was not mine glared at me with crimson ferret eyes from the mirror at the back of the cupboard. I waited only long enough to see that it had a flowing wig beneath a feathered hat and a neck-ruff bedewed with glistening red. I slammed the door shut and flew out of the bedroom into the gallery.

Then, almost beside myself with indecision, I ran back in. I could not abandon my sister to Old Gally's murderous curses. But it was out of my power even to approach the closet. I did not scream or cry because I was too frightened. I had to find someone braver than me.

Rupert's room was next to mine. I opened his door a few inches, intending to creep in and rouse him gently. But there was no need. I heard muttered words, a groan or two, then Archie's voice saying, between moans, 'You brute – you *brute*! Hurt me – go on, *hurt* me!' I closed the door hastily.

I had come to rely on Rupert as a source of strength in times of need. He was so good at hiding his feelings that I had forgotten he must have needs of his own. I dithered, shivering with shock. I ran backwards and forwards a few paces in each direction, before deciding that, after Rupert, Freddie was the best person to help me. I sprinted down the landing. A gleam shone under the linen room door.

I burst in. 'Freddie! There's something horrible in my –' I stopped. Maggie lay with her head on the table before the sewing machine, her cheek resting on Annabel's dress, a pair of scissors in her relaxed grasp. She was so deeply asleep that I had to shake her quite roughly.

'Wha-ha? A-hoo? Oh, Harriet . . . I must have dropped off. What time is it? Is everything all right?'

She took off her spectacles. Her face was pale except for the red marks where they had gripped her nose. She rubbed her eyes and stared up at me, her expression apprehensive.

'Nothing's wrong,' I said after the briefest pause. 'But you ought to go to bed. It's after one, I think.'

She nodded. I kissed her good night and watched her stumble along the gallery, speechless with fatigue.

As soon as she was out of sight I knocked discreetly at the door I thought was Freddie's. I was rewarded eventually by a line of light appearing beneath it. I heard a key turn in the lock, then the door opened.

'Harriet!'

I was so confused and frightened that I did not immediately notice that Max was wearing only an eiderdown. We stared at each other for a moment or two. Then he grabbed my wrist and pulled me inside.

'I'm so sorry to wake you,' I said, almost weeping with fright. 'I thought this was Freddie's room. Only there's this man in my cupboard and I daren't go and see if he's still there but I can't leave Cordelia and I don't know what to do –'

'Shh!' He put his arms round me. 'Start again. Who's in your room? Not that donkey, Emilio?'

'No, Old Gally!'

442

'Old who?' Max put me at arm's length and examined my face.

'Old Gally. The Civil War one – the one whose arm it is – his ghost, I mean!'

Max began to laugh. 'Well, that's original, anyway.'

'Please come with me! I can't go on my own. It was so horrible. There was blood on his neck – oh, and his *eyes*!'

He looked at me doubtfully. 'You're shaking! You really are frightened.'

'Yes! Yes! Please come!'

'All right. You stay here. I'll go and see.' He pushed me down on to the edge of the bed and pulled a blanket round me. 'Just wait a minute. The cupboard in your room, did you say?'

I nodded, mute with fear and he went away, still wrapped in the eiderdown. I kept my eyes trained on the open door, expecting, any second, a hideous, headless corpse to come through it. In less than two minutes Max was back. He closed the door and locked it. I tried to read from the expression on his face what he had seen. He sat down beside me.

'No sign of the phantom rapist.' He spoke teasingly as though we had agreed it was a joke.

'Did you look –'

'I opened the cupboard door and I saw a mirror and myself reflected in it, rather the worse for too much champagne and not enough sleep.'

'Oh, I *am* sorry! But you must believe me! He was there. I *saw* him!'

'You had a bad dream, that's all. But I'm not complaining.'

'I was awake,' I said, perhaps a little sulkily.

'All right, I believe you.' It was perfectly obvious that he did not. 'OK, there's nothing to worry about. I looked everywhere, even under the bed. Cordelia's safe. Anyway she's got that hulking great dog in with her. Now, dear ...

lovely . . . Harriet.' He stroked my hair, then kissed me, first on the forehead and then on the lips. 'Let's forget all about him, shall we, and think about something more interesting?'

'Ah. Oh! But this isn't – You think I made it all up just to get into your room!' I struggled free and looked at him with reproachful eyes.

'Let's say it does look a little that way.' He pushed my head back gently so he could kiss my throat. 'But quite why you needed an excuse . . . I've been trying everything I know for days to get you in here. It needed only the lightest tap on my door.'

'Really, truthfully!' I clutched defensively at my nightdress, which he was unbuttoning. 'I did see him. I *did*!'

'All right, you saw him.' He pushed my hands away. 'Oh, what delicious little breasts you have. Exquisite. I hate making love to a Madonna.'

'I swear to you I thought this was Freddie's room.'

'Harriet. Enough.' He stopped suddenly and looked at me searchingly. 'You're not a virgin, are you?'

'Certainly not!' Then honesty compelled me to say, 'But I'm not very experienced. My first lover doesn't really count as the whole thing was a dreadful mistake and my second – ' I paused. Suddenly Dodge's enthusiastic puppy-like burrowings seemed friendly and safe.

'Only two! These days you probably qualify for the Sunday School Chastity Prize. That's perfect. We don't want to make a mess on someone else's sheets. You needn't worry about lack of technique. It's enough that you want me to make love to you.'

'But I wouldn't dream of trying to seduce you with a trick –'

'Why not? Anyway,' he let the eiderdown drop, 'you can see I'm willing.'

I could. He slid his hand through the opening in my

444

nightdress and started to caress my breasts and waist with deft fingers as though he were modelling the perfect woman out of clay. My body responded immediately. I felt my skin contract and grow hot, as the blood rushed faster through my veins. Adrenalin sent tremors of excitement through every organ, not least my heart, which beat as though trying to attract the attention of Rupert and Archie next door. Extraordinary sensations shot up and down my thighs. I was unable to resist when he laid me on the bed, for my muscles were quivering like those poor darling frogs' legs when the biology mistress passed a current through them in the lab at school.

'Oh, Harriet! Harriet, my darling!' he murmured into my ear as he lay beside me and pressed the length of his body against mine. 'Who will not change a raven for a dove?'

A piece of my mind – for, of course, though it felt entirely physical and involuntary, it was my mind that was largely responsible for these startling manifestations of passion – broke away from the rest and began an independent survey. Even while I ached to feel his body in mine, I was also thinking that this was not a good idea. His frequent use of my name was like the tugging of a thread that connected me to conscience and probity. Of course he did not know that quotations from Shakespeare were evocative of childhood and lisping innocence, of boiled eggs and soldiers, teddy bears and milky drinks, of young Harriet Byng in all her ambition, folly and ineptitude.

I struggled to resolve the dichotomy, to anaesthetise my mind was what my physical self stridently demanded, and it was cheered to the echo by the things he was doing with the tip of his tongue. One last fleeting thought hardened into an idea and hovered like a bird of prey above my scurrying emotions. If I, presumably, was the dove, who then was the raven? But now, as he brought matters to a head and I at once capitulated, it was too late to enquire.

TWENTY-EIGHT

Only the children and Rupert and Archie were in the dining room when I went down for breakfast.

Max had woken me at ten to six and we had said goodbye with kisses and hasty avowals of affection. He had been preoccupied with the business of chucking his things into a suitcase and I was entirely sympathetic as I have always hated packing. Cordelia was still asleep when I got back to my room. I waited until dawn before opening the closet door. I saw my own face, pale beneath hair tangled by lovemaking. Tentatively I put out my hand to touch the mirror. It was cold and solid.

Georgia entered the dining room as I was beginning my bacon and eggs. She looked very smart. Her head was wrapped in a turban of lime-green crêpe and she wore matching harem trousers. Her fingernails had been painted gold.

'Where's the kedgeree?' She looked accusingly round the table. When no one confessed to having it she took a spoonful of mushrooms and a slice of toast and ate them with an air of martyrdom.

'It's like the *Ten Little Niggers*, isn't it?' said Cordelia. 'People are disappearing fast. I don't care about the Mordakers but I wish Max hadn't gone.'

446

'Naturally we shall miss him,' said Archie, 'but those of us who have a tenuous relationship with sleep will find comfort in the cessation of traffic up and down the gallery all night long.'

The hypocrisy of it! I looked up, intending to brazen it out. But Archie was looking at Georgia. She lifted her eyebrows until they disappeared under the turban and smirked with an affectation of insouciance. An unpleasant idea lodged itself like a dart in my brain.

'What do you mean?' Annabel and Cordelia spoke in unison. I should have liked to know, myself.

'Three may keep a secret,' Archie leaned forward confidentially. The two girls looked excited. 'But only if *two* of them are dead.'

While the girls groaned I happened to catch Rupert's eye. He was looking at me over a copy of *The Economist* with that speculative gaze with which I was now familiar. Thankfully his sightline was interrupted by a dish of kedgeree carried by Mrs Whale.

'I'm sorry, madam,' she said when Georgia complained that it had come too late. 'Lady Pye's in bed and I've everything to do on my own. What with Sir Oswald's tray having to be punctual I couldn't get round to the kedgeree before.'

'Perhaps if you'd begun earlier –' began Georgia.

'What's the matter with Lady Pye?' asked Rupert.

'She's sick. I can't say what with. She won't have the doctor. I've Sir Oswald's tray to fetch, the drawing room to dust, the breakfast to wash up and the beds to make so I'll get on now, unless there's anything else you was wanting.'

'Has that wretched tin arm turned up yet?' Rupert changed the conversation abruptly.

'No, sir,' Mrs Whale looked immediately uneasy.

'Have you had a good look for it?'

'No. Begging your pardon, sir, but I dursen't.'

'You don't believe all that nonsense, surely?'

'No, sir. Only at night, when the wind's moaning and the house is creaking like a ship at sea . . .'

She left the sentence unfinished. It was obvious that she did believe it and I, for one, did not blame her.

'I think it might be a good idea to inform the police,' said Rupert surprisingly. 'Find me the number of the local station, would you, Mrs Whale?'

'Begging your pardon, sir, but Lady Pye won't like it. She'll think it's disrespectful to the – to Sir Oswald's ancestors. Come to that, Sir Oswald won't like it neither.'

'I'll take the responsibility.'

'Yes, sir.' She went away, her expression gloomy.

'Surely the police won't take it seriously?' I said.

'It falls into the same category as obscene telephone calls and poison-pen letters. An attempt to disturb the balance of someone's mind. I think they'll take it very seriously.'

'If she's ill Maggie won't be able to finish my dress before I have to go back to school.' Scowling, Annabel used the blade of her knife as a catapult to flip toast crusts on to the deck of the silver ship.

'Ow!' said Georgia as a piece of toast hit her face. 'Must you behave like a child of the gutter?'

'Must you be so ugly?' returned Annabel immediately.

'You foul little kid!' Georgia's aniseed-ball eyes narrowed with dislike. 'Someone ought to knock some decent manners into you!'

Rupert put down his cup and lowered his magazine. 'Annabel! Apologise. Now!'

'Shan't.' Annabel pushed out her lower lip and went very red. Slowly Rupert started to get up from his chair. 'All right! I'm sorry! So there!' she shouted. I wondered what she had imagined he was going to do. I had never been remotely tempted to discipline Cordelia with a display of

448

power, knowing she would instantly call my bluff. She was watching the interchange with keen interest.

Georgia threw down her napkin and stood up. Her cheek glistened with a smear of butter. 'You could be an exhibit in the Chamber of Horrors,' was her departing shot.

Rupert looked at Annabel. 'You're old enough to understand that you don't insult guests. Your behaviour to Georgia was gauche and unattractive. But worse is your grossly selfish attitude to Maggie. That really *is* ugly.' He returned to his reading.

Annabel gave a brave see-if-I-care smile and went on flicking toast, with greater accuracy. But after a while she began to sniff and a tear ran down her cheek. Poor little thing, I thought. She really does love him.

'*Il faut détourner la conversation,*' muttered Cordelia to me. It was what Ma always said when her guests became quarrelsome, as though they didn't all understand French perfectly well. I tried to think of something pacific to say.

'If you're going to sniff in that disgusting way,' said Rupert, without looking up, 'would you mind doing it elsewhere?'

Annabel burst into tears.

'I bet Max looks amazing in tights,' said Cordelia in her most grown-up voice.

'*I* prefer a little more beef and thewiness,' Archie responded in a tone of seriousness. 'The modern man is so girlishly skinny, as though at that moment prised from the rack. Also Max is just a little *too* clever. I like men to be blundering dolts as Nature intended. I speak romantically, of course. When it comes to conversation a sharp wit is agreeable.'

Annabel continued to weep, her head pressed into the circle of her arms. I felt sorry for her. She was still a child, with passionate feelings she could not control, and who lacked proper guidance. She had fastened her affections on a man who was indifferent to women – and certainly to little girls –

who was impatient, unsympathetic and emotionally inaccessible. Just as I was wondering how best to comfort her, Rupert closed *The Economist* with a sigh and said, 'Annabel, stop that hideous grizzling this instant before I lose my temper.'

I was shocked by such harshness. Had he quite forgotten what hell it is to be young? Annabel let out a low wail and then suppressed her weeping to hiccups.

'Good.' Rupert looked at her with cold detachment. 'If you want to stay with us in London you'll have to acquire a few civilised habits. I won't have scenes at breakfast. Nor at any other time, preferably. But first thing in the morning it's insupportable.'

'Will you really let me come?' Annabel lifted red eyes that were amazed.

'If you show me you can control yourself and not be a repulsive brat, you can spend the last night of the Easter holidays with us and I'll take you back to school myself the next day. But I shall want a good report from Maggie.'

Annabel's face was transformed from woe to delight. 'Could we go to the Motor Show?'

'Archie will take you. He likes cars. But only if you conduct yourself properly.'

'Oh, Rupert, I'll do anything you want. Anything!' She went to stand by his chair and put her small hand on his arm. 'Thank you for inviting me.'

'All right. We'll see.'

'What shall I do to start?'

'You must give Maggie all the help you can. And be polite and respectful to her.'

'I will, I promise! But can't I do something now to show you how good I can be?'

Rupert sighed again. 'I don't want a slave, just someone who's bearable to have around.' Annabel looked disappointed. 'Oh, all right. You can clean my car.'

Annabel shot off. Rupert tackled the buttery marks on his sleeve with his napkin.

'What diplomacy,' said Archie. 'I pray she doesn't get gravel in the sponge. But must we really have that little pest to stay? Annabel and the Motor Show! My God, I'd rather beat hemp.' Then he waggled his eyebrows at me apologetically as he remembered that my father was at this moment doing the twentieth-century equivalent.

'Not diplomacy,' said Rupert. 'Out-and-out bribery. I'm afraid we must. Now I'd better make some telephone calls.'

'He's going to regret taking that ghastly child on.' Archie helped himself to another cup of coffee. 'But lame ducks swim after Rupert as gulls follow the plough.' He smiled as though at a fond memory.

'I think the Byngs may well qualify as the most troublesome hangers-on,' I said. We were alone, Cordelia and Rupert having left the room. 'Archie, what did you mean about Max and noises in the gallery at night?'

Archie looked pained. 'My dear Harriet, if you want to persuade a man to give up a life of delicious self-indulgence, a bank balance in credit and his house just as he likes it to throw in his lot with you, you must learn not to take a chap up on casual remarks at breakfast.'

'You're prevaricating.'

'Yes, I am.'

'Please tell me.'

'On your own head be it. But no sudden yells or shrieks, please. My eardrums have been delicate from infancy.' I remained demurely composed. 'Well. Several times during the last few nights when a full bladder has required me to risk frostbite, I happened to run into Miss Bisset going *in*to or coming *out* of the bedroom of Max Frensham. In view of the risk he was running, I think the man is probably wildly oversexed, not to say satyric.'

'What's that?' I felt rather sick.

'Satyriasis, my innocent child, is a neurotic compulsion to have sexual intercourse as often as possible with as many women as possible. A masculine version of nymphomania and endemic among politicians. Fornicating with the Bisset was obviously inadvisable when a blindworm could have seen that Max's *chief* object was to spin his wheels with *you*. Of course, it's none of my business what you girls get up to but I hope he did not succeed.' Archie stretched the points of his waistcoat over his embonpoint and looked at me over his half-spectacles with a magisterial gaze.

'Certainly not!' I snapped, stifling a strong desire to cry.

'Oh dear! *Just* as I feared. Another notch on the Frensham bedpost. Harriet, do not attempt to follow your father on the stage. You'll never get further than Fifi, the French maid.'

'Are you sure it was Max's room you saw her coming out of? I mean,' I blushed, 'it would be easy to mistake one door for another.'

'A man of my years and experience makes it his business to know where guests at a house party are located,' said Archie solemnly.

I put my head in my hands.

'Oh now, *don't* take on, there's a good thing. The world won't end because Harriet Byng has been to bed with a bounder.'

I was confused by the sudden transposition of ideas. Max was not, after all, an ardent lover aspiring to possess my heart, but a common philanderer. Georgia was not a pathetic coquette. She had known precisely what she wanted and had got it. *I* was the dupe. How could I have been such a conceited, gullible idiot? When I put this question to Archie, I could not prevent a choke in the voice and a wateriness of the eye. He screwed up his face in dismay and came round the table to sit beside me.

'For one thing, Harriet, you're unassuming and that's very charming. You didn't think about protecting yourself. No doubt he *swore* eternal love. Surely your mother must have told you what fibbers men are? Are you in love with him? The truth now. Remember you have the acting ability of a jar of jam.'

I thought hard. 'No,' I said at last. 'I honestly think not. I found him very attractive but that was partly because I thought he was very attracted to me. I felt under some sort of obligation because he was so attentive. Crazy, I know.'

'If only boys were so sweetly grateful. But of course he *was* attracted to you. What red-blooded heterosexual man wouldn't be? I've no doubt he went to bed with Georgia because she was available. But anyone could see it was *you* who got his pistons pumping.'

I knew this was Archie being kind but none the less it did make me feel a little better.

'She's much more glamorous and fashionable than I am.'

'Pish! I admit she has a certain crude panache. As she's not actually good-looking, she has to knock our eyes out instead. Who'd notice a fat, plain man like me if I wore dull grey suits and behaved as other men?' Archie stroked the lapel of his red-and-black striped blazer with complacency. 'But *you*, Harriet, can afford to ignore the ploys of vulgar fashion. I don't want to turn your head.' I thought it was impossible that I should ever think well of myself again but as Archie was in full flow I did not interrupt him. 'No, your modesty is one of the many attractive things about you, and in this world of Bissets, unusual. But you also have the great gift of physical beauty. You must understand, now and for ever, that *style* is the aim in view and that fashion is the antithesis of style. Fashion is imitation. You must discover what is the *essence* of Harriet and cultivate it. Be yourself one hundred per cent. Dress as you think, as you feel, as you speak.' I sniffed noisily and tried to look as though I might possibly be the essential creature he described. Archie frowned. 'Until you know who you are, you'd better let *me* continue to have the dressing of you. I can assure you, at this moment you are the distillation of subtle elegance.'

'Thank you.' I mopped my eyes on my napkin. I had forgotten I was wearing mascara and was dismayed by the ugly black blotch on Maggie's starched linen.

'One wonders, though,' Archie smiled maliciously. 'Does Georgia know that you and she were turn and turn about? I'd have thought her as wily as a sack of foxes – up to every trick. But somehow I imagine even *she* has her pride and would revolt at the idea. The thing is he took you both in. He's an actor, after all. He wouldn't be much good at his job if he couldn't convince you that he was burning in hell for a glance from those beautiful dark eyes.' Archie tapped my cheek with his finger. 'Everyone makes mistakes in the bed department. When I think of some of the people I've woken up next to . . .' He shook his head until his cheeks quivered. 'No, I don't think I *will*, so soon after breakfast.'

This made me smile as it was intended to.

'That's a good girl. Uncle Archie says you're not to be a bore and *dwell* on it like a moon-sick maiden. I take it you weren't one?' I shook my head. 'Well, there's *that* to be thankful for.' He sighed. 'Do you know, I don't think I have the right temperament for an agony aunt. I'm too easily depressed by life's sordid cares. Which reminds me, you remembered, I'm sure, what you learned at school about the birds and the bees and the right and proper purpose of coition? And took care, accordingly?' I smiled weakly. 'Oh, *really*, Harriet! You're as helpless as a swaddled babe.' He resumed his former expression, as of a headmaster whose hopes in a promising pupil have been unexpectedly dashed.

'Actually I feel pretty sure it will be all right. I only had my per –'

'Stop there!' Archie held up his hand. 'Marjorie Proops is paid for it, after all.'

'I promise I won't pine. Not publicly anyway.'

'Excellent.' Archie patted my hand and beamed at me, his cheeks wrinkling up under the lenses of his spectacles. 'I shall hold you to that.'

'One thing, though, you won't tell Rupert, will you? I'm afraid he'd despise me dreadfully.' Archie's expression returned to its customary satirical sharpness. 'I mean, I don't think he'd understand how anyone could be such a fool.'

'I won't tell him if you don't want me to. But I wouldn't hold out much hope of putting one past him. He asked me only the other day why Frensham was laying suit to you.' I was much offended by this discounting of my power to charm but I concealed my indignation. 'He said he doubted whether Frensham was to be trusted. When I asked him why in that case he hadn't attempted to put you on your guard he said it was clear you were highly susceptible to Frensham's allurements. Any interference would probably only add to his appeal. Besides, he thought it might be a salutary experience and that you were *too* much inclined to live in a world of self-deception and make-believe.'

'He said that?' I stared at the bacon rinds amid the yellow blobs of egg on my plate while my bosom swelled with pain. 'I see.' Even then I recognised that there was some justice in what Rupert had said. But I was far from being prepared to admit it openly. Max had given my self-confidence a drubbing and Rupert's censure applied pressure to the bruise. 'Thank you, Archie, you've been more than kind. I'd better go and see how Maggie is.'

By unlucky chance, I met Rupert in the hall. I turned to the table to see if there was any post. Of course there wasn't because it was Boxing Day, but I had forgotten that.

'I'm going to London for a couple of days,' he said to my unresponsive back.

'Oh?' It came out like a snap.

'An emergency committee meeting of the board of the English Opera House. There's been a row. Hard words have been said and the two biggest cheeses have resigned. I'm supposed to draw out the thorns with a fomentation of shameless flattery and cajolery.'

'Oh.' His friendliness stung, now I knew what he thought of me. I turned, frowning. He looked at me quizzically, his eyes searching my face. 'I'm going by train,' he said, 'so that you and Archie can stay and help Maggie. She's not at all well.' I continued to look at him frostily. 'That's if you wouldn't mind.'

'I shall be delighted.'

The words came out like chips of ice. I thought I saw the suspicion of a smile hovering about his mouth. A faint scar showed on his upper lip. I remembered he had cut it years ago, when my father was teaching him to drive. Rupert had reversed at speed into a brick wall and gashed his face on the steering wheel. My father had banged his elbow. I must have been seven or eight at the time. I had gone with them in the taxi to the hospital, Pa groaning and weeping, Rupert white and silent with blood dripping from his chin. My father had entertained the staff of the casualty department with his entire vocabulary of pain and despair before being sent home with a sticking plaster. Rupert had borne six stitches without complaint. I had held his hand; then, when he asked me not to, his coat-tail. The memory might have softened my wrath, had he not assumed a comical expression of glowering resentment, imitating mine.

'What are you so huffy about? "Speak again, sweet Desdemona" –'

'Oh, shut up!'

TWENTY-NINE

Maggie's room was on the top floor. It was meanly proportioned with a view over the stable yard. The single iron bedstead and the chest of drawers and wardrobe made from varnished deal confirmed that this was a maid's room. The tiny grate was empty, the room was chilly and there was a smell of damp.

'Hello, my dear.' Maggie opened sad eyes in a face the colour of porridge. She had been lying flat on her back, but as I came in she tried to sit up. 'I'm ever so sorry to be laid up. I shall be better soon. Oh, lord!' She groped feebly for the bucket beside the bed and was sick on the eiderdown.

I held the bucket for her until she had finished vomiting. 'Lie down and don't worry. I'll find something to clean it up.'

In the corridor outside her room was a sink and next to it a cupboard containing brooms and dusters. I wiped the floor as well as I could. 'You must have some clean bedclothes. I know where. I won't be a minute.'

In Freddie's old studio I found an eiderdown and more blankets.

'You shouldn't have to do this,' murmured Maggie. 'I feel ever so ashamed.'

'Dear Maggie, it's a pleasure to look after you. Though I'm sorry you're ill, of course. But you ought to let Mrs Whale send for the doctor.'

'I don't want to be a trouble. I'll be better in a minute. Only when I lift my head the room does turn round so, I don't know which way up I am.' I noticed that Maggie's eyes were jerking the way people's eyes do when they look out of the window on trains. She groaned. 'How's Janet to see to everything? But I can't set foot to floor without falling over. I wonder if Sir Oswald's had his clothes put out for him? Could you ask Janet to do it, dear? I always lay out his tie and weskit first, then trousers and braces over them – carefully so's they don't crease – socks and shirt next and underpants and corset on top, so it's in order of putting on, see? Let me see, what's today? Tuesday, is it? Then it's his brown Tattersall check with the green and brown paisley tie.'

'I'll go and ask her.' I saw Maggie was shivering despite the extra bedclothes. 'And I'll bring you some tea.'

'I'm so sorry, pet, really I am.'

I met Freddie on the back stairs. She was carrying a tray of tea things and some buttered toast. 'Harriet, thank goodness!' she said when she saw me. 'Poor Maggie! But I've simply got to go. More snow's forecast and Vere's getting fidgety about his horses in case they aren't being properly taken care of. And we've left our darling old dog to be looked after by Vere's brother. He's a bit unreliable.'

I took the tray from her. 'Don't worry. I'll see to everything. You go.'

'Give Maggie my love. I've already thanked her and said goodbye but then I felt so unkind leaving her in that freezing room without even the comfort of a hot drink.'

'Goodbye, dear Freddie.' We kissed across the tray. 'I'm so glad we met properly at last.'

'Promise you'll come and stay this summer? I'm longing to

show you everything – our house and the valley and the river. There'll be haymaking and Vere's starting market gardening in the spring. I've so enjoyed our talks. I shall miss you.'

While Maggie drank her tea I looked out of the window and watched Freddie and Vere loading their luggage into a large black car that was parked in the yard. Though we had known each other only a few days I felt this friendship had the potential to develop and last. It's hard to say why with some people you could talk all day and all night, while with others it's a struggle to find enough to say during a single course at dinner.

With some people you can only have the sort of conversations that are exchanges of information – not just the death of your grandmother and the price of tomatoes but what conclusions you came to about Graeco-Roman architecture the last time you gave it any thought. Then they tell you what they think on the subject and you go on giving each other the benefit of your experience, which if you happen to be interested in the same things is a reasonable way of passing time. But with Freddie I seemed to have the best sort of conversations, where our talk became exploratory and would lead on to new ideas, like thinking aloud, and in the process of clarifying improvisatory theories I always made useful discoveries about what I thought and felt.

I watched them drive away with regret, wondering what it would be like to stay with Freddie and Vere in Dorset. I imagined myself as a Thomas Hardy heroine in a cotton sunbonnet and dimity dress, milking velvet-skinned cows in a flower-strewn meadow like Tess or, even better, as Grace Melbury strolling through the woods with the poetically rustic, noble-hearted Giles Winterbourne, his clothes sprinkled with pomace and apple-pips. My reverie was interrupted by Maggie being sick again, this time into the bucket.

'You poor thing! I'll get you some more tea. Do you think you could manage a bit of toast? It might help.'

'What's that, dear? I can't hear you. I seem to have gone deaf.'

I found Dr Parsons' number in the telephone book in the hall. He said he would come within the hour. When I went back upstairs, with some fire-lighters, matches, and a bucket of coal, Maggie seemed worse. She was delirious, falling into a doze, then waking with a start, muttering about potatoes and laundry and struggling to sit up. I lit the fire and drew the thin curtains to keep in the warmth when there should be any.

I was on my way downstairs again, trying to think of the best way to help Maggie, when I saw out of the corner of my eye that something in the Long Gallery was different. The glass case, home to Old Gally's arm, was once more bound by the chain and fastened with the padlock. I approached it with caution. The arm was back. It was rustier than ever and missing a finger. It had rather a pathetic appearance I decided, after the first recoil.

Mrs Whale was in the drawing room. She was kneeling before the grate with a shovel in her hand.

'Seems to me that chain and padlock's a waste of time,' she said, when I informed her that the arm had returned. 'There's forces that laugh at man's devices.'

'You mean the supernatural?'

'I mean,' she dropped her voice, 'the Devil.' She crossed herself twice.

'Mm, well, I expect so.' I had had many unsatisfactory conversations with Loveday about the existence, or not, of the Devil and I had no intention of beginning another. 'Maggie says would you mind putting out Sir Oswald's clothes?'

'Drat! I'd forgot them.' The ash from the fire rose in clouds.

She coughed and flapped her hand in front of her face. 'I've made the beds and swept the hall but I've the breakfast to wash up, the kitchen floor to scrub, the bathrooms to clean, the washing to put on and the water in the flower vases to change. That's before I scrub the vegetables for lunch. There's the table linen to see to and the silver to polish, what Lady Pye always does herself. besides the cooking. I'm not much of a hand at it and I've never pretended otherwise. I could do mince and potatoes. And rice pudding. But he'll not like it.'

'Couldn't the vases be left for one day?'

'Sir Oswald's most particular about the vases smelling fresh.' She lashed out with her duster at some floating particles of ash.

'Let me do some of the things. I could change the flower-water and scrub the vegetables.'

'Who's going to put out his clothes?'

'I don't think I could do that. I mean, I'd have to go into his room. And mess about with his underwear. It would be terribly embarrassing.'

Mrs Whale sat back on her heels and looked at me reprovingly. 'Lady Pye'll be vexed to death when she learns no one's done it.'

'Perhaps she won't find out.'

'She'll find out all right. The minute he's dressed he'll go and tell her, ill or not.'

I opened the door of Sir Oswald's room. The brilliant light from the snow-covered hills lay in broad bars across the floor. A bed at least fifteen feet tall was hung with crimson damask and handsome gilded tassels. White plumes sprouted from each corner of the gold-and-white canopy. A coat of arms was embroidered on the back panel, proud symbol of the sweltering mound completely covered by bedclothes that lay beneath it. Beside the bed was a breakfast tray on which were two disembowelled eggshells, toast crumbs and the remains of a pot of jam and a dish of cream. The mound moved rhythmically up and down and I heard a richly mucosal snore as I tiptoed over to the closet.

The shelves were filled with neatly folded garments, and a rack held coats and trousers. I found the items described by Maggie and gathered them in my arms to arrange them in order. I was just wondering whether men put socks on before or after their trousers when a voice said, 'Little girl, would you like a barley sugar?'

I spun round. Sir Oswald's reddened face was peeping from under the sheets, like a setting sun wreathed with cloud. He put out a plump hand and beckoned. 'I've a toffee if you'd rather.' I shook my head, put down the clothes and began to sidle over to the door. 'Just come and see the little doll I've got hidden here, in my bed.' The bedclothes rustled energetically. 'You can make it stand up all on its own if you're nice to it,' he called as I ran out and slammed the door behind me.

'Labyrinthitis,' said Dr Parsons as I escorted him downstairs. 'An inflammation of the inner ear. Lady Pye works too hard. She's run down. I've told her she should rest when she's ill and give her body a chance.'

'Is it serious?'

'Occasionally the deafness is permanent. But I've put her on a course of antibiotics, which ought to clear it up. She'll be unwell, with vertigo and nausea for several days. See she stays in bed and has nothing to worry her. I'll call again tomorrow.'

Keeping Maggie from worrying was beyond my power. There were eleven of us in the house after Rupert had been driven to the station by Archie. Luckily Georgia and Emilio were leaving at teatime. Out of the nine who would remain, three – Miss Tipple, Sir Oswald and Maggie – were entirely helpless. I decided to put the children to work.

'Oh, *why*? Why must we?' the girls whined in unison as I gave them dusters and the vacuum cleaner.

'Because it's the decent thing to do. Now stop grumbling. Anyone who does a good job can come with Archie and me to see *The Four Musketeers* at the cinema in Bunton tomorrow.' I hoped Archie would not object to this scheme. Not for the first time did I regret my inability to drive a car without hitting something.

Cordelia considered this. 'Can we have fish and chips afterwards?'

'Yes.'

'Popcorn during?'

'Yes.'

'Strawberry milkshakes?'

'If Bunton has such things.'

'The latest issue of *Metropolitan*? I saw it in the newsagent's at home. It's got an article in called "Sex without Guilt – The One-Night Stand", which looked interesting.'

'Well . . .' Too much information was generally better than too little. 'I suppose so.'

'A new jersey each?'

'Certainly not.'

'I just wanted to see how desperate you were.' Cordelia gave me a knowing look as she sauntered off, carrying the cleaning equipment. 'I'd say pretty.'

'Why should people feel guilty about sex?' I overheard Annabel asking Cordelia when I passed them ten minutes later, as they were polishing the banisters.

'Because beautiful people have so much and plain people not any,' replied Cordelia.

'What are one-night stands?'

'Goodness, don't you know anything? It's making love standing up. That way you don't get pregnant.'

This confirmed the advisability of more information.

I found Archie lying on the sofa in the library, reading a book and shedding tears. 'It's the life story of John Huss,' he explained, wiping his eyes. 'A protestant preacher in Germany in the fifteenth century. He was burned alive. As a toothless peasant hag, covered in warts and boils and reeking of urine, staggered forward beneath the weight of a huge faggot and threw it, cackling, into the flames, he cried out in his agony, "O holy simplicity." You have to admit it was forgiving in the circs. The man was a genuine saint.'

'Does it make it worse that she was ugly?'

'I think it gives it a little extra sanctity. And one would rather see someone good-looking, I suppose, in one's last few seconds. Actually I made up the boils and the urine. But still.'

'Anyway, I thought people being burned alive used to beg onlookers to stoke the fire to get it over with quickly.'

Archie snapped the book shut. 'If you're going to pour cold water on every little shred of romance in this sorry world, Harriet, I must beg you to leave me. I understand that the pain of betrayal may bring on a mood of cynicism –'

'Would you mind scouring the baths and basins?' I interrupted. 'Maggie says to pay particular attention to the plug chains. They have to be unhooked and soaked in a pan of disinfectant for an hour.' I held out a cloth and a bottle of Banoscum.

Archie looked at me in astonishment. 'Has misfortune in love turned your brain, my dear girl?' He gazed down at his immaculate Oxford bags and brown and white co-respondent shoes. 'I – to clean other people's tidemarks?' I explained what the doctor had said about Maggie not being allowed to fret. 'Of course I shall rally to the call. But not for anyone will I ruin my fingernails.' He swung his legs down from the sofa. 'I shall do the cooking.'

*   *   *

Lunch was half an hour late but when it came was unusual and excellent. Sir Oswald, who had been standing about with a glass of sherry complaining about the delay to anyone who would listen, ate greedily of the shallot and parsley soup and a most interesting pie made from chestnuts and a mystery ingredient. Archie explained that they were cardoons, which he had found in the kitchen garden, wrapped with thick brown paper to blanch them. He had cooked them, beneath a lid of delicious flaky pastry, with a bottle of pear wine he had discovered in the cellar.

Archie was modest when we praised him. 'Anyone can cook. It is merely a question of imagination and taking trouble. But I cannot cook meat. Veins, necks, tongues – these things are too much for my feelings.'

Maggie's mind was set sufficiently at ease by the discovery that Archie could cook to allow her to fall into a deep sleep all afternoon. I kept the fire well-stoked and the room became so warm that steam rose from the armchair as it dried out.

After I had helped Mrs Whale wash up the lunch things I took *The Small House at Allington* into the drawing room to read for half an hour before taking Dirk for his afternoon walk. I put a log on the fire and settled myself opposite Miss Tipple, who was dozing in her usual position with knees wide apart and the leg of one chewing-gum-pink bloomer, which had lost its elastic, trailing down her leg. Just as I was fancying myself as Lily Dale succumbing to the egregious charms of Adolphus Crosbie, Georgia came in.

'Have you seen Emilio?'

I closed my book politely, keeping a thumb in my place. 'Not since lunch.

'Oh.' She strolled towards the table, her long fur-trimmed coat trailing across the carpet, and looked in the cigarette box, which I had forgotten to fill. 'We're about to leave. I suppose he's saying goodbye to his latest conquest.' She laughed derisively. 'He thinks I don't know about his philandering. What's even more ridiculous, he thinks I'd mind.' I smiled to conceal my surprise, wondering who the object of Emilio's affections could be. There was no one remaining in the house who could possibly fit the bill. Miss Tipple was too old, beside being here in the room with us with us. Maggie was in bed. Surely not Mrs Whale? Then I thought of Cordelia. Luckily she and Annabel came in just then, before I had a chance to get angry and make an idiot of myself.

'We've finished mangling the washing. If we take Dirk out for you, will you promise we can go to the record shop before the flicks?'

I was so relieved to find she was not party to Emilio's leave-taking that I was willing to promise anything. The girls rushed off, exultant at this latest addition to the list of concessions.

'Sorry I haven't done anything to help,' said Georgia. 'Too busy packing.'

I had seen her lying on her bed, smoking and reading a magazine, as I had run past her room that morning bearing a pile of towels for the laundry room. I smiled politely for the second time and opened my book.

'I don't think I'll go to Australia.' Georgia found her cigarette case in her bag. As an afterthought she offered the case to me. I shook my head. She rummaged for her lighter. 'It's a mistake to run after men.'

'Probably.'

'They think they can treat you like shit.'

'Well, I imagine that has more to do with their attitude than one's own behaviour.'

'I see what you mean. Could be. Anyway, no hard feelings about Max?'

'None at all,' I said frigidly. 'Why should there be?'

'Oh, come off it! Your eyes were on stalks, like a love-sick snail, whenever he was around.'

'They were not!'

'Please yourself. I don't mind admitting I thought he was exceptionally luscious and extremely beddable.'

'Oh?' I was surprised that she should choose me of all people to confide in.

'Only, if I'm honest, when it came to it, he was something of a let-down.'

She blew out smoke and stuck out her chin, staring at me defiantly.

'Oh.' I said again. Against all odds I had clung to a ridiculous hope that Archie might have been wrong about Georgia and Max. This was now dashed and I was ashamed to feel a corresponding drop in spirits. 'I wouldn't know,' I lied without an ounce of shame. I saw Georgia was gratified by this information.

'Too bloody perfunctory by half. A girl wants a little attention, a little stroking and caressing, perhaps even a word or two of encouragement – not just to be climbed on and treated like a disposable semen receptacle.' This had not been my experience in bed with Max but I had no intention of saying so. 'You don't know it yet,' she continued when I remained silent, 'you're too young. But when you get to my age there are precious few decent men about. If they haven't already been scooped up they're mad or queer or have mothers with a capital M. I'm over forty, you know.'

'You don't look it.' Another lie.

'Any day now my jowls and boobs are going to droop and I'm going to develop a scrotum under each eye. I'm already having to dye my hair.' She patted her ash-blonde, stiffly-lacquered locks, which looked as though they had been chromium-plated.

'Really?'

'You get desperate.' I wondered again about Emilio. 'Invitations start dropping off. Suddenly there are long, lonely weekends when you're grateful to speak to the paper-boy. Emilio popped the question when he was trying to get me into bed. He didn't imagine in a million years I'd accept him. He lives with his aunt in a foul little hen-coop in Shepherd's Bush. Hasn't a penny. He's a gigolo with dwindling assets and built-in obsolescence. Not that I'm rich exactly but I've got a private income of a few thousand a year. I accepted him because I'm frightened of being an old maid.' She drew savagely on her cigarette and spat out the smoke. 'Bloody funny, isn't it? I expect you want to laugh.'

'No.' I didn't. It sounded painfully sad. 'But surely it's better to live alone than marry someone you're not in love with? Being an old maid is only an idea in people's minds. Can't you ignore what they think?'

'Can *you*?' Georgia lifted her pencilled brows and stared at me angrily. 'What are we anyway but what we seem to be to other people? If I'm in a room on my own I'm invisible. Nothing.' This was a new and interesting slant on the problem of identity.

'I think I'm more truly myself when I'm alone than at any other time. Then I'm not trying to impress or be liked.'

Georgia gave a sneering laugh. 'You think that because you're young and you've never been unhappy.'

I knew that this was absolutely not true, that since my father had been arrested I had been intimately acquainted with unhappiness. But I felt no inclination to confess this to Georgia, so either her misery was worse than mine or I wasn't the confiding type. 'As you say, there's a lot I don't know yet but one thing I've learned is that the best antidote to unhappiness is work.'

Georgia extinguished her cigarette in a pot of pale-pink hyacinths and threw the butt towards the hearth. 'Sitting in an office all day being ordered about by a common little man who has a business selling tin-tacks or motor axles!' She made a *moue* of distaste. 'Squabbling with a gaggle of suburban typists over whose turn it is to buy the biscuits. I'd rather marry Emilio.'

'Ah, but these days women don't have to do menial jobs. Why shouldn't *you* own the business selling tin-tacks? You could corner the market in tin-tacks – become the tin-tack queen. No one would think of you as an old maid then. And what a job does, above all, is stop you thinking about yourself all the time, which is a huge relief.'

Emilio came in then, which was a pity because I was just warming to my theme. I was surprised by how evangelical I felt about the value of work, having myself been gainfully employed for a period of not much more than a month.

'Aha, Señorita Harriet.' Emilio took my hand and covered it with noisy kisses from his fat purple lips, his brown eyes rolling about in his head like ball bearings in a bowl. He must have been at the brandy again for the whites were nearly gold. 'The sad time comes when I tear me away from you. I am pleasured to know you. A lovely mees, so pree-tty and swe-e-t –'

'Oh, for heaven's sake, Emilio.' Georgia snapped her bag shut and buttoned her coat. 'You could pour a tin of treacle over people – it would have the same effect. If you're coming back to London, let's go.'

'Oh, I come, Georgia. Do not fear, dear one, you have all my heart.'

'Yes.' Georgia looked at him as he minced across the room towards her. 'I believe I have, such a tiny thing as it is.' She cast a glance at me and shrugged. 'I'd better make the most of it. It's all I'm likely to have.'

'What you say?' Emilio asked politely, his head on one side like a parrot. 'I not unnerstand.'

She narrowed her eyes to peer at him more closely. 'You've got lipstick all over your neck.'

* * *

'Have they gone?' Jonno came into the drawing room just as I had imagined myself back on to Mrs Dale's croquet lawn at *The Small House at Allington*. 'Oogh! What a gruesome pair! They deserve each other.' Jonno looked pretty gruesome himself, haggard with red-rimmed eyes. He carried a plate of cold sausages and pickle, which he ate with his fingers, wiping them on his jeans when they got too greasy. It was an unattractive sight. 'Breakfast.' He offered me the plate. 'Want one?'

I shuddered. 'You know, you're going to kill yourself if you keep on drinking like that.'

'So? Who's going to care? Not me.'

'Self-pity's a great mistake. It kills off sympathy faster than anything.' Jonno scowled dreadfully but I pressed on, remembering Rupert's determination to domesticate Jonno. 'Your family would care. Maggie worries about you all the time. One of the reasons she's ill is because she puts everyone else's needs before her own.'

'Meaning I don't.'

'Not everything I say is solely about you.'

Jonno gave one of his speciality bitter laughs. 'I expect you're grumpy because Lover-Boy's buggered off. Well, if you're going to be poisonous, I'll bugger off too.' He turned to go, but when I made no effort to detain him he came back and sat down beside me, balancing the plate on his knee. 'Don't be nasty to me, Harriet. I feel so bloody miserable. And my head's beating like a tom-tom.'

'Why do you drink so much?'

'Why not?'

'Because it makes you ill and depressed. And a nuisance.'

'Am I really so hateful?' he said with a sigh that was almost a moan.

Part of me wanted to point out the absurdity of these histrionics but another part was touched by something genuinely

470

regretful in his voice. 'The sober you isn't hateful at all. I like what little I see of it. Everyone's boring when they're drunk.'

'Boring?'

'Dreadfully boring. A waste of time.'

I had intended to have an effect but I was appalled when he put his head in his hands and began to sniff. 'I wish – things were different,' he bleated. A tear fell through his fingers. I cannot see people crying without wanting to cry myself. My throat grew tight in sympathy. I stroked his ponytail. 'I *hate* myself for being so stupid and weak,' he went on in a voice that broke with emotion. 'I miss Kate so much. She was – the best thing – in my life.' He began to sob and I knew this was real, the pain of loneliness and desolation that alcohol could only temporarily deaden. 'Oh, oh!' he cried, 'I wish – I wish my mother hadn't died.'

Then he leaned his head against my chest and I cradled it in my arms, my own eyes pricking with tears. Dirk was roused from sleep by this unusual noise and padded over to see what was going on. He stared with puzzled eyes at Jonno and then, despite my frowns and silent mouthings, delicately extracted the last sausage from the plate and took it off to the hearth rug.

'Sorry,' Jonno said at last, pulling away to wipe his face on the sleeve of his shirt. He caught his nose chain on the button of his cuff and winced. 'You must think I'm unbelievably pathetic.'

'My father and brother often cry. We're a crying sort of family, generally. It's very good for you. You'll feel much better now.'

'Yes, I do, I think. Silly thing, though, to cry about something that happened so long ago.'

'Not silly at all. Tell me about your mother. If you'd like to.'

'I was twelve when she died. She was the most beautiful creature in the world. She was ill a lot and I think Dad made her unhappy too. But she said she felt quite safe with me to look after her. She called me her very perfect, gentle knight. It was from her favourite poem – I've forgotten what it was called. After she died I've never felt I was any good to anyone. Annabel had a nurse to look after her and in less than a year Dad married Maggie, who did everything for him – and everyone else. I was useless, pointless. As you say, a waste of time.'

'You know that's not what I meant.'

I tried to put some severity into my voice. I felt utterly sympathetic but I knew I should take advantage of a rare moment in which Jonno was neither drunk nor stoned. He was silent for a moment, thinking.

'Yes. I do know, really. I've got into the habit of playing dishonest games with myself, and other people. I wanted Kate to leave me so I could be miserable – have an excuse to be sorry for myself. I practically pushed her away. I knew I was hurting her but I couldn't stop.'

'I don't think you can afford to go on like that.'

'No.' He sat for a while thinking. Then he said, 'Promise you don't despise me for crying?'

'I like you better for it. Honestly.'

'How so?'

'Because you loved your mother so much. Now I know you really *do* care about other people.'

'I've tried not to. It always seems to end in pain.'

'That's not true. But even if it were, you can't protect yourself by becoming hard. That's cheating. Cheating yourself, I mean.'

'Harriet?'

'Yes?'

'Suddenly I feel I want to kiss you.'

472

I offered him my cheek.

'Actually I didn't mean in such a brotherly way. But I suppose you don't fancy me. I'm not as good-looking as Max Frensham.'

'You might be. It's hard to tell with so much camouflage. You could be rather handsome without that thing through your nose. And without the ponytail and that repulsive beard.'

Jonno looked offended. 'Some women go for the rebellious type.'

'I don't know about Manchester but in London Punk's already embarrassingly tired. Chains and safety-pins are about as excitingly sexy as zip-up slippers and knitted ties.' I remembered what Dodge had said. 'Punk's a corrupt nihilist movement without political meaning, motivated by an infantile need to shock.'

'That's the whole point – that it's pointless. There's no altruistic principle involved. It's intended to be deeply offensive to the Establishment, that's all.'

'Actually that nose-chain makes me think of our old district nurse. She looked after my mother when she was having Cordelia. Her name was Tabby and she was very tall and scrawny. I was fascinated by the veins in her legs that stood out like ropes when she'd been pedalling. Her bicycle chain was always coming off and we children had to put it back on for her. I suppose sausage fat's marginally more appetising than bike oil.'

Jonno laughed. 'OK. I was getting sick of it anyway. It catches on chairs and door-handles. Not only does it hurt but you look an arsehole. But what's wrong with the rest of me? Don't girls like virile, hairy men? Sort of caveman-cum-intellectual?'

'No doubt some do. I've a pathological hatred of beards. My father's an actor and he often grows one for a part.

He doesn't like false ones; he thinks glue's bad for his skin. As a child I dreaded being scratched when he kissed me. It's probably given me a Freudian aversion to them. And ponytails look wet to me. Sort of left-over sixties. I expect I'm in a minority, though.'

'Kate used to say she didn't like it either. But I felt I shouldn't give in.'

'Why not?'

'Because it would have seemed weak.'

'Frankly, I think having to be smashed out of your mind all the time is a darned sight weaker than doing something to please someone.'

'You really do know how to hit a fellow where it hurts.'

'Sorry.'

'No, you're right. That's why it hurts, of course.' He sniffed. 'Bloody hell! What's that burning smell?'

Until that moment we had been too busy talking to notice that wisps of smoke were rising from beneath Miss Tipple voluminous skirts.

'Georgia's cigarette end!' I looked helplessly about for something to smother the fire, not daring to use an antique needlepoint cushion or a silk Persian rug.

Jonno seized a vase of flowers, dropped to his knees and slooshed the contents over the floor beneath her chair.

'What? What?' Miss Tipple woke, seized her stick and cracked Jonno on the head with a force that was surprising in a very old lady. 'Get back, you sex-crazed beast! Help! Rape!'

THIRTY

Darling Maria-Alba,

This can only be a short letter because I'm so tired I can hardly hold the pen. I'm sitting up in bed writing this and Cordelia's asleep beside me. She's completely better and having a good time so don't worry about her. All the men admire her hugely and she and Annabel get on pretty well considering how different they are. Annabel is child of contradictions, something of a tomboy yet she hero-worships Rupert with an unshakeable passion. Cordelia says she found her crying fit to bust because Rupert had gone away without saying goodbye. Also she has a savage streak which I find rather disagreeable. Cordelia got very angry with her for trying to wring a chicken's neck. The poor bird was half-dead when Cordelia brought it into the kitchen but we put it in a box by the range and fed it porridge until it got better. Annabel said she had watched Dingle wringing their necks hundreds of times. I suppose this is the difference between a town childhood and a country one, and perhaps we should not have interfered. Anyway, Cordelia regularly patrols the hen-run now and counts them to make sure they are all there still. She and Dingle are sworn enemies.

The girls made up the quarrel eventually and this evening Cordelia lent Annabel some clothes and did her hair very prettily instead of the hideous plaits. She really will be a beauty when she learns to stand properly and to stop scowling. Her eyes are remarkable. Poor thing, she felt self-conscious when everyone commented on the improvement. She frowned and grimaced until Jonno said she looked a fright, then she ran off in a storm of tears. She is inclined to do this. Sir Oswald was moved to make Cordelia a graceful little speech of appreciation and said she was an angel of good influence. Sister Imelda would be thunderstruck. He can do that sort of thing rather well.

I debated whether to mention Sir Oswald's less attractive ways and thought better of it. Maria Alba always complained that the nuns were appallingly nosy and she was sure they went through her possessions when she was in the kitchen helping Sister Mary-Joseph. If they happened to read of Sir Oswald's paedophilia they would be dreadfully shocked.

Maggie is not at all well. She has an ear infection and can't get out of bed so we are doing the housework with the help of Mrs Whale. Imagine, all the ivory knife handles have to be rubbed with a cut lemon before being washed, to preserve them. And when I scorched a pillowcase Mrs Whale made a paste of something called Fuller's Earth with washing soda, vinegar and onions. The paste got the mark out brilliantly. Just as well, as I managed to scorch quite few. After tea – Archie made a superb chocolate and prune cake – I had to clean the skirting boards on the landing with a skewer wrapped in a cloth to get into the corners. This is done once a week regardless of it being the holidays. In the kitchen there is a huge old gas stove that makes our boiler seem space-age. Every Thursday the burners are taken off and boiled in soda water, then scrubbed and dried.

But if one discounts the time taken, it is quite satisfying doing things incredibly carefully and well. Everything is saved. Old bits of soap are stuffed into a tin that is attached by string to the kitchen tap. You swizzle it around in the washing-up water and hang up again afterwards. I was dying to ask Mrs Whale if money was very tight. After all, what could a bottle of Supersuds cost? But of course it isn't my business.

I must tell you something that happened that pleased me and then I'll get some sleep and prepare myself for another day of arduous housework. Also I have to begin my article for the next 'Spook Hall'.

I decided not to tell Maria Alba, who was extremely superstitious, that I had found the finger from Old Gally's arm in Maggie's handkerchief drawer. It had given me an unpleasant shock, like finding a scorpion in a shoe. Out of the case it did not look pathetic at all, but rather sinister. Also it left a nasty rust mark on one of the handkerchiefs, which had to be soaked off later in buttermilk. True to my mission as supernatural sleuth I screwed up my courage, picked it up without Maggie seeing, and put it in the pocket of my skirt. I needed to get hold of the key to put it back in its case but Maggie's chatelaine was nowhere to be seen.

I've told you about Jonno, the son, who drinks and is grubby and generally a bit of a pain. We had a serious talk this afternoon and I'm beginning to think there is something very likeable about him after all. When he isn't trying to be hard his eyes have a soft sweet expression. I think he's one of those men who's ashamed of being sensitive and so he covers it up with a brutish exterior. Well, anyway, I ticked him off about taking Maggie for granted and he took it without getting offended. He didn't drink at all at supper – lovage soup and seakale soufflé, followed by almond pudding – and afterwards he disappeared. I thought he must have gone to hit the bottle. But when I went up to say good night to Maggie, I found Jonno in her room, reading aloud a romantic novel called *Love is my Master*, all about a Victorian maid who falls in love with the boss of an iron foundry who's horribly scarred because he tried to save his brother who'd fallen into a vat of molten metal. But the fiancée of the dead brother is also in love with him and he feels guilty and – well, anyway, you get the gist. It was complete tosh but strangely enjoyable. I think Jonno enjoyed it too, though he'd never admit it. I could see Maggie was loving having him there. It's my first serious attempt at moral reform of anyone and I'm amazed to have been so effective!

Anyway, darling, your last letter sounded so cheerful I was really pleased. I'm so glad you've changed your mind about Mother Superior. I must say I've never thought her capable of drowning even a fly, let alone all the girl babies of Bushey Heath. Take great care of your dear, dear self and I'll write again very soon, Best love, Harriet.

I rose early the following morning to begin my list of tasks. Breakfast was late but no one listened to Sir Oswald's complaints so in the end he shut up and concentrated on getting down as many *oeufs frits à la Serbe*, as he could – which are fried eggs on a pilaff of rice with onion and raisins. It was unusual but agreeable. After I had scrubbed out the game larder with carbolic, which smelled terrible and seemed to get into my clothes and hair as well as my skin, I went upstairs to fetch Maggie's tray.

Mrs Whale was changing her bed and dusting her room. She straightened the pillows and tucked in her sheets so tightly that I wondered Maggie could breathe. Then she opened the window so wide that the fire smoked and all my efforts to warm the room were wasted.

'It'll get rid of the germs,' she said, beating the armchair cushions until the air was thick with motes before gliding to the door with her customary cloistral step without once glancing in my direction. I was sorry for this for I was keen to be friendly and show her that her confession had kindled sympathy, rather than censure, in my breast.

'Dear Janet,' said Maggie fondly, as soon as she had gone. 'I'm lucky to have someone so good to me.'

I closed the window and went to sit on Maggie's bed so I wouldn't have to shout as her deafness was, if anything, worse. 'Mrs Whale told me about what happened, about being in prison and everything. I feel very sorry for her. What can it be like to have done something so dreadful that one's life can never be the same again?'

Of course I was also thinking of my father. Everything always seemed to come back to him.

'She was ever such a pretty girl. Always chosen for the May Queen. The boys went for her in a big way. They never thought anything of me on account of I had glasses and my teeth stuck out. Janet always had the lead part in plays and she was captain of tennis and rounders. She was clever too, top of the class. She got a place at the grammar school but her mother couldn't afford the fares and the uniform so she went to the secondary modern with the rest of us. After she left school I didn't see her again for years until she sent me a letter, out of the blue, explaining she'd been in prison and why. She couldn't get a job because of it and her landlady had found out she'd been convicted of murder and told her to go. Such a sad letter, it made me cry to read it. I wrote back the same day and offered her a job and a home here with me. Funny, isn't it, the way some are unlucky? Her dad – father, I should say – died, while mine went on to make a fortune in carpets. Our dad couldn't go down the mine, see, on account of his chest was weak, so he went to work in a warehouse and he got on. He was always sharp and ready with an answer. He was a hard man but he meant to do right.' Maggie sighed. 'I were always that bit afraid of him. Mother worked here as cook before she married Dad. He hated her to talk of that after he made money. She was afraid of him too. That's how it most often is, I reckon.'

'My mother isn't the least afraid of my father. If anything it's the other way round.'

'You don't say?' Maggie's face looked especially defenceless without her spectacles. She smiled. 'I should like to see that. People's lives are so contrary, ain't they? Who'd have thought that I'd be living here in comfort, married to a gentleman and a baronet, while Janet's path's was such a stony one? But no life's without its thorns.' She stirred restlessly on her pillow. 'It was hard in the beginning being mistress of Pye Place. When Lady Pye died, the children's mother, that is – eh, but she was a sweet soul! – Dad knew how things were up at the big house. There weren't no money and everything was to be sold up. Sir Oswald had married for love the first time, see. She was the rector's daughter, respectable but poor. He always did like them tender and young.' She gave me a quick glance from her soft eyes. 'Well, that's the way men are. Dad said if Sir Oswald married me he'd give him three-quarters of the carpet fortune flat down on the day of the wedding.'

'Gosh! What did you think about that?'

'I begged Dad not to do it. I knew I wasn't good enough to fill the shoes of that lovely child. Ever so refined she was. I could have taken both her wrists in one of my great hands.' Maggie spread out her fingers, thickened by work and red against the whiteness of the sheet. 'But he never listened.'

'I honestly can't think of anyone I respect more than you,' I said. 'Please don't ever think you're not good enough for anybody.'

But Maggie seemed not to hear me. She had gone back into the past.

'Well, he took the money and he married me. I felt a right fool going up the aisle, all decked out in finery.' Maggie rolled her head to stare at the window as though the events of that day were pictured there. 'I was glad I couldn't see the faces of the people in church, on account of I wasn't wearing my glasses. They were gentry and what they must have thought of me, a common girl with a face like a plough horse crowned with orange-blossom, eh, I was scarlet as a turkey-cock with shame. I heard one or two tittering behind their hands but I couldn't blame them.'

'Oh, Maggie!' I was rendered practically speechless by the pathos of the scene.

'There was the wedding breakfast after, of course,' Maggie continued as though I had not spoken. 'That was worse in a way. But he tried. I'll give him that. He didn't go off with his smart friends. No, he stood by me and tried to make conversation but I was so awkward. I couldn't look at him for thinking what should come that night, when they'd all gone home. I'd never known a man, see, so it was doubly bad.' She turned her head on the pillow to look at me. 'I'm not upsetting you, talking about such things?'

I shook my head.

'Well, he stood his ground and no doubt he was thinking of it too, poor thing. Eh, what a contrast, that little lass and

481

me! He introduced me to all and sundry and they said how-do politely and flew away to talk to their own kind, like they were rooks and I were a scarecrow. All except Rupert. He brought me a dish of strawberries and took me out into the garden and we walked up and down together while he chatted of this and that and slowly, like, I started to feel easy with him. He asked me the names of flowers and I knew that. I've always had a soft spot for flowers. That gave me back a little bit of my own pride, see. He told me about himself, just as though we were friends, and what he'd seen and done in the world. Eh, I could have stayed out there with him all day and been happy.' Maggie's worn features were transformed by the recollection. 'Rupert was a young gentleman and handsome as a film star. He said he liked being out with me in the garden better than indoors talking to the fine folk. I didn't believe him but I loved him for it.'

'I can imagine.'

'There's some as think I'm a simpleton because I'm not educated but I can tell they look down on me for all it's Lady Pye this, Lady Pye that. I've learned not to let it hurt me. But Rupert's always been good to me. And what for? I asked meself time and time again.' Maggie turned to look at me again. 'I reckon it were sympathy. He saw how bad I felt and something in him came up to meet it.' She nodded her head. 'Yes, when all's said and done that's what saves mankind from being bad. 'Taint making paintings and bridges and books and that, though that's good in itself, but pride could do that. No, it's wanting to do something for someone cause you mind their hurt.'

I took Maggie's hand in mine. She gave it a little squeeze. 'Well, I thought of Rupert's kindness when it came to the night-time – to comfort me, like. I lay in bed with the lights out in a brand-new nightdress from Tarrant's – all slippery and cold, it was – and I was shivering, afraid of . . . Well, you know, dear. And worse, I was afeard he'd hate me for not being her, pretty and tiny with loving things to whisper. My head was going round and round, just like it is now. He came in and got into bed. Then I heard him weeping. "What's up?" I said. He said, "I can't do it. I'm so sorry." Then we lay side by side for the rest of the night, not speaking. I never slept a wink; nor, I don't think, did he. When it got light he started to snore and I got up and went down to make up the fires. That same day I moved my things up here, and here I've lain since.'

'Dear Maggie. I hope you haven't been too sad about – about not having –'

'Nay, lass. It was a relief, to say truth. I'm not that kind that men should love me. I've had my happiness looking after this dear house and him too. I love him, you know, oh yes, in my own way. I should hate for hurt to come to him. He's got old and fat and sad under my eyes and I'm ever so sorry, for he were a noble gentleman once. I remember well how he looked twenty sommat years ago, coming out of the church with that little girl, like a fairy, on his arm.' Maggie seemed to take pleasure in the memory. 'And now the carpet money's near run out, it's my duty to see he's looked after in the way he's used to. Yes, my life has its satisfactions, no doubt of that. It's those children as bother me. But last night, Jonno, you know what he said?' Maggie's eyes sparkled with sudden tears. 'He said, "Maggie," he said, "you've been a brick and I've been an idiot. I hope you'll forgive me." And I said,' Maggie's voice became fractured as she recalled the emotion of the moment, "Jonno," I said, "I hope you'll forgive *me* for standing in her place. I didn't want to do it but they was too much for me and I had to." He understood right enough what I meant though he didn't say nothing, just went red as though he were touched where it hurt. So he picked up my book and began reading the story, and it was like we'd taken a vow to do better between us.'

483

I stood up reluctantly, aware of a thousand jobs to do. 'Let's hope things will be better from now on. But it all depends on him not drinking.'

'I feel it will,' said Maggie. 'I don't know why but I feel certain of it.'

As it happened, what I attributed to optimism born of delirium turned out to be right. Jonno appeared in the hall just as I was on my way to polish the library floor. I looked at my watch. It was only ten o'clock. Furthermore, he looked clean, his ponytail and beard were combed and his nose was chainless. I knew from my dealings with Bron that one must never rush to praise or back-sliding will inevitably follow, so I gave him the mop and the jar of beeswax. He grumbled a little but I was firm. Then I detailed Cordelia and Annabel to dust the drawing room, brushing aside their protests in a brisk authoritative way.

Somehow, by default, the running of the household had fallen to me. Trifling though the latitude for exercising it might be, it was my first taste of anything like power. I found bossing other people about such a delightful novelty that I had to remind myself of Lord Acton's famous axiom about its tendency to corrupt. When Miss Tipple, forced to get out of her chair or be dusted by Cordelia, asked if there was anything she could do to help, I led her to the scullery and brought her knives, forks, spoons, salts and pepper-pots and silver wadding. She sat happily for hours, rubbing and rising. I overheard her singing 'Pale Hands I Love, Beside the Shalimar' in a wobbling soprano. It occurred to me that one of the worst things about being old must be the feeling of being no use to anyone.

I quickly discovered one of the major problems of captaincy: that one's crew members have widely dissimilar capabilities. Miss Tipple cleaned the silver beautifully and begged to be allowed to tackle the ship from the centre of the dining table, which she took apart and reassembled with the dedication of those Indian craftsmen who paint prayers on a grain of rice. But it was apparent that Jonno had never cleaned anything other than his own teeth before, and had no idea how to go about it. For one thing he began polishing the floor at the door instead of in the far corner of the room and then there was so much wax on the threshold that it almost sucked off one's shoes. I sent him to help Archie, who was getting temperamental about the lack of a sous chef, and finished the floor myself.

While I was disinfecting the telephone, I happened to see a note in Maggie's careful copperplate. Reasoning that it could not be private if left in so public a place, I read it. 'Porter and soup. Dinner, Thurs.' I remembered that porter was a vile drink which Mr Barrett had forced his invalid daughter, Elizabeth, to drink everyday before she wisely ran away to Italy and added Browning to her name.

'Ah,' said Maggie, when I took the cryptic note up to her for explanation, 'it was a lady that rang but I couldn't rightly hear what she was saying. It was a day or two ago and my ears were bad. I wrote it down and hoped the meaning would come to me. Most likely it was a shop about an order.'

I screwed up the note and forgot about it.

'If I have to clean one more blinking thing I'm going to run away.' Cordelia looked at me accusingly over lunch – a very good gratin of haricot beans with leek fritters. 'You ought to have a big drum so you can beat out the rhythm while we slave, like in the galley-ship in *Ben Hur* when Jack Hawkins orders Charlton Heston's leg to be unchained and saves him from being drowned. My favourite bit's when he finds out his mother and sister are lepers, and they have to live in this cave with some really grim people without noses and fingers . . .'

While Cordelia entertained her enthralled host and the rest

of the table, who were perhaps less enchanted, with a recital of the entire plot of what was an extremely long film, I began to compose my article for the *Brixton Mercury*. I could make much of the arm. But should I save up the Lady of the Moat for another time? And what about the face I thought I had seen in the closet mirror? As I remembered it I could not repress a shudder of revulsion, though I had several times given myself a stern talking-to about being a credulous ass. Then I remembered what had taken place afterwards. Anger with Max and with myself were about equal. No, I would not write about the events of that night until I could think about it calmly.

'I liked the bit where that man was chopped up by the chariot wheels best,' said Annabel. 'I'd like to race in the Circus Maximus. I'd easily win.'

'I suppose it would be hypocritical of me to urge you to be true to your sex and moderate your *blood*thirsty ways,' said Archie.

'She isn't so tough, really,' said Jonno, with typical brotherly unkindness. 'Don't you remember, Annabel, when I took you to the midsummer fair in Bunton last year and you insisted on going on the Dodgems on your own. Those boys from the comp jumped on your car and pulled your plaits and teased you until you cried. I had to rescue you and you blubbed like a baby just because they'd called you a posh bitch.'

Annabel flung down her knife and fork. 'I'm going to make you sorry you ever lived, Jonno Pye. I'm going to get Dad's gun.' She stormed out.

'What did I say?' Jonno looked amazed.

'Perhaps someone should go after her,' I said.

Because Cordelia was the youngest of a large family she was inured to teasing and always gave as good as she got. Poor Annabel was sensitive and did not know how to protect herself. She had no female role models except Maggie, whom she had been taught to despise. This, I suspected, explained her tearaway act. It was a desperate attempt to convince herself and others that she was as good as a boy.

'Don't look at me,' said Archie. 'If you had any idea how *drain*ing it is to be creative!'

Collectively we turned our eyes to Jonno.

'All right.' He stood up. 'I'll give her a pi-jaw and tell her not to be such a little silly. Luckily all the guns in this house are so rusty they wouldn't work even if there were any cartridges. But I'm such a black sheep myself, I'm not really in a position to preach.'

'Very true!' Miss Tipple lifted her chin from her plate to glower at him.

Sir Oswald, oblivious of what was going on around him, was massaging the pepper-pot vigorously and gazing at Cordelia as she continued to talk.

A new candidate for my column presented herself late that same night. In fact, if my stay at Pye Place did not make me master of my trade, there was no hope for me. Mrs Whale and I were making quick work of tidying the kitchen. Except for Maggie, Sir Oswald, Miss Tipple and Mrs Whale, the house party had enjoyed an outing to the Bunton Hippodrome, with fish and chips afterwards. Bouncer and Blitzen lay like pulsating balloons in their baskets with their night-time bones. Everyone else had gone to bed. I washed the drying-up cloths in detergent as instructed, rinsed them and put them in a laundry basket. The drying cupboard, at the foot of the back stairs, was reached by a stone corridor. Dirk ran ahead of me, then stopped abruptly a few yards from the kitchen and began to whine and sniff excitedly.

'Be quiet, Dirk,' I said as he started to bark. 'Must you be such a *noisy* dog –' I stopped because I smelled something so horrible that it made me gag: the awful stink of rotting meat.

I looked about for a dead rat or mouse. But the corridor was bare of decomposing flesh.

'Mrs Whale,' I called, 'do you mind coming here a minute?'

Her face wore its usual shut, suffering look but the moment she came within range of the smell, her expression changed to disgust.

'Oh, God!' she lifted her apron to cover her nose. 'It can't be!'

'What? What can't it be?'

'Oh – nothing. I don't know what I'm saying. I'm that tired.'

'What do you think it is?'

Mrs Whale shook her head and almost ran back to the kitchen. I heard feet padding down the stairs.

'Hello, Harriet. What are you up to?' It was Jonno. He had sat next to me in the cinema and held my hand through the second half of *The Four Musketeers*, which had distracted me from the film and provided a source of amusement for the girls.

'Can't you smell it?'

'What? Oh, Christ!' He had come within range of it. 'What the hell is that?'

'It's coming from this wall. But I can't see how. It looks solid to me.'

Jonno took a grimy handkerchief from his pocket and pressed it to his nose. 'Well, who'd have thought it?'

'Thought what?'

'You've obviously never heard of the ghost of Fanny Cost?'

'No! Who is she?'

'Let's go somewhere else. It's enough to make one shoot the cat.'

'I didn't know you had a – Oh, be sick, you mean. All right, tell me about her,' I insisted as we climbed the stairs. 'It would

488

be excellent if there was enough to make a separate article. So many ghosts are only good for a sentence or two – you know, the usual grey ladies and little black dogs and so on. They simple appear and disappear and it becomes boring.'

'How blasé commerce has made you,' complained Jonno. 'Have you forgotten the mysteries attendant on visitations from another world? Confirmation for a start that there's life beyond death and that we're under observation by vengeful spirits jamming up the ether? It gives a quite different slant to the question of good and evil if a hasty absolution isn't enough to guarantee safe conduct into eternity.'

'Oh yes, I know all *that* but I'm not paid to be philosophical. I've simply got to dish the supernatural dirt and make it snappy.'

'All right, hold the front page, here it is. Fanny Cost was a servant, sometime during Cromwell's rule. She had an illegitimate baby. Sir Oswald, the second baronet, and his wife were red-hot Puritans. Never off their knees. There are portraits of both of them in the gallery. Ghastly-looking couple like a pair of crows.'

'I thought the Pyes were royalists and catholics.'

'There were swingeing fines for being on the wrong side. Also you could have your head cut off. Anyway, poor Fanny's master and mistress were determined to make an example of the girl and her seducer. But before she could be made to tell who the father was, Fanny Cost disappeared, as did one of the grooms. Everyone concluded they'd run away together. But the other servants started to complain about a frightful stink and eventually they took down the walls in the servants' quarters and discovered her decomposing body with the dead infant in her arms. Sir Oswald was the local magistrate, conveniently. There was a trial, the missing groom was found guilty in his absence and placed under sentence of death should he return. But Old Gally's arm started wandering with awful regularity and it always pointed at the master of the house He fell ill and died soon after, confessing on his deathbed that he'd been the father of Fanny Cost's baby. He'd paid the groom to murder the girl and the baby, brick them up and make himself scarce afterwards. She's supposed to manifest herself by a smell of corruption. Of course it's a load of cobblers.' I thought Jonno looked uneasy.

'Of course it is. But don't tell Maggie.'

'You don't mean she believes in ghosts?'

'Yes. And it terrifies her.'

'All right.' He gave me an uncertain grin.

We had reached the head of the stairs. Our voices were thrown back in an echo that had lost all power to frighten me. I was practically convinced that the first time I had heard it, the voices had been those of Georgia and Max embarking on their flirtation and that's why they had not answered me. I felt angry all over again when I thought of it. Angry with myself, that is.

'What say we go to the drawing room for a snifter?' suggested Jonno.

'It nearly midnight. I'm going to bed. And so should you.' I took him by the arm and led him along the landing. 'What were you coming down for, anyway?'

'Oh, just a thimble of something to keep out the cold. I've been reading to Maggie about true love and its reverses, and that's thirsty work.'

'One thimble will become a jugful. You know that.'

'Bloody hell! You talk as if I was an alcoholic.'

'Aren't you?'

'No!' Then, less sharply, 'Am I?'

'If you can't manage without it, you are.'

We had reached the long gallery. 'I'll take my degenerate self off to bed then,' he said.

'Good night.'

I kept my face severe but then, because he looked so hangdog, I kissed his cheek in token of friendship. It was a mistake. Men aren't really very interested in friendship with women. Jonno put his arms round me and kissed me on the lips. All kinds of tenuous emotions and incoherent thoughts began to buzz in my brain, none of them anything to do with sexual gratification. I was afraid that outright rejection might set him back on the path to self-destruction. For some reason I felt a sense of responsibility, a strong desire to see him do better. Perhaps this was because he made me think of Bron, which prompted an affectionate, sisterly feeling. On the other hand it was impossible not to think of Max. After what I decided was a decent interval, neither rejecting nor encouraging, I drew back.

'Sorry. It's the beard.' This was partly true. It was horribly prickly, like pressing one's lips to a doormat.

'God, I hope you weren't imagining I was your father?' His voice was excited and he stroked my breast with a hand that shook. I was reminded that he was hardly more than a boy, actually a few months younger than me. Max had been so confident that I had felt like a timid teenager. With Jonno I felt like a sensible middle-aged woman with a subscription to the *Spectator* and a well-organised compost heap. 'No,' His voice took on its customary tone of self-loathing, 'I'm a fool. You were thinking of him, weren't you?'

'Who?' I asked to gain time.

'Don't be disingenuous.' He gripped my arm. 'Did you go to bed with him?'

'No.'

'Liar.'

'Look, Jonno, it really isn't any of your business whether I did or I didn't.' I decided to get angry.

'Isn't it? We'll see about that.' He gripped me harder. 'O-o-ow! What the hell is that? Something stabbed me.'

491

I felt in the pocket of my dress. 'Sorry. It's Old Gally's finger.' I held it out and we regarded it solemnly, unlovely object that it was. 'I found it this morning. I thought it was safer to keep it on me until I could decide what to do with it.' Also I had wanted to reassure myself that I was not afraid of it. I very nearly wasn't.

'You're chancing your luck, aren't you, carrying it around like a tube of fruit-gums? I hope getting pricked doesn't count as being pointed at. Suddenly I don't feel too good.'

'Really, Jonno! I'm surprised at you. Anyone can see it's just a bit of old tin incapable of doing anyone any harm –'

Just then the lights flickered and went out.

'All right, Harriet! Don't yell like that! It's only the generator. Mm! I must say it feels very nice to be clung to for a change instead of having to do all the clinging myself. Though that's a very odd scent you're wearing.'

Despite the beard I had clutched him instinctively and screamed with shock. 'Oh, Jonno! The finger! It's gone!'

'*No!* Oh, my *God*! Then it's all up with us! Prepare to meet thy doom! Oh, bother!'

The lights had come on again. I let go of Jonno, who was grinning. '*Now* who's a cowardy-custard,' he laughed. 'Not so sceptical now, are we?'

'I'm not too good in the dark. But what's happened to the finger?'

He dangled it in front of my nose. 'I consider it my manly duty to take charge of it from now on. You're only a sissy girl.'

'The beastly thing leaves rust marks on everything anyway.'

'As heir to the Pye fortune I really ought to find some way of getting rid of it. It might change my luck.'

'I think you've had very good luck,' I protested. 'You're strong and healthy with plenty of brains. Without the coconut matting, you'd be good-looking. You'll inherit a wonderful house in a beautiful part of England. What more could anyone want? As for happiness, you'll have to make it for yourself, like everyone else.'

'All right, Miss Pretty Perfect, get off that soap-box and let's be having some more of you.' He stopped and sniffed. 'There it is again. A phantom smell of – public lavatories.'

'It's carbolic. Look, Jonno, I'm so tired I can hardly think. I've got to go to bed.'

Hearing remonstrance in my voice, Dirk, who had been strolling about the gallery in a bored sort of way, sauntered over and began to growl.

'All right. One last kiss to show you aren't angry with me. Oh, bugger! Shut him up, Harriet! He'll wake the house.' Dirk had decided to draw our attention to the fact that he had become weary of this conversation. He threw back his massive head and let rip. His broad chest had acquired deep penetrating tones.

I hauled him away. 'Good night,' I called over my shoulder. 'See you on kitchen detail.'

'Good night, sweet Harriet.'

'Damn,' I said to myself as I lay in the darkness beside the sleeping Cordelia. 'Damn, damn, damn!'

THIRTY-ONE

'Hello? Hello? Would you speak up? The line's very bad.'

'Is that you, Harriet?' Rupert's voice on the telephone sounded impatient and preoccupied.

I expect mine sounded much the same. The morning had flown by, we were just about to have lunch and I had to choose between spending the afternoon dusting books in the library or writing my column, the sort of dilemma women have wrestled with for centuries. Also Cordelia had been nagging me for days to help her with her tapestry. Her ambitious attempt to render, in appliqué and satin stitch, her own sufferings as a bed-ridden invalid had resulted in something that looked like a screaming baby being roasted on a spit.

'Listen!' Rupert continued irritably, though I had not so much as breathed a word. 'I haven't time to explain. I've a meeting in three minutes. I'm coming back late tomorrow night. The train gets in to Bunton at eleven thirty. Meet it, will you?'

I was piqued by his peremptory tone. 'Actually, I've got an awful lot to do. I'll get Archie to collect you.'

'Don't argue. I particularly want you to come. Alone.'

'Flattering though that is,' my tone was sarcastic, 'I shall probably have my hands full. Not only washing up for a large number of people but my article to write. You seem to forget, I have a job.' I spoiled the loftiness of this by adding, 'Also, I can't drive.'

'What do you mean, you can't drive?'

'I haven't passed my test.'

'Oh, for heaven's sake! How old are you?'

'Twenty-two. I don't know what that's got to do with anything. You're thirty-two and you can't drive.'

'Of course I can.'

I was taken aback. 'Why don't you then?'

'Because Archie likes to. People are arriving. I must go. I'll take a taxi. But wait up for me, will you?'

'All right. But why me, particularly?'

There was a brief pause. 'I want to talk to you. How's Maggie?'

'Much better this morning.'

'Everything else all right? You sound harassed.'

'Everything's fine.'

'Good.' I could hear voices talking and laughing in the background. 'Don't forget.'

The receiver was put down. I might have enjoyed speculating about this enigmatic telephone call except that Cordelia was banging the gong and I had forgotten to put out ladles for the sauce boats.

Lunch was a very flaky leek and walnut strudel. It was impossible to talk and eat it, without blowing crumbs everywhere. Archie was increasingly inventive, partly because he was easily bored and partly because the Bunton shops were inadequately supplied with the kind of ingredients that appealed to his epicurean tastes.

'Do you know, it's only just occurred to me,' Jonno addressed me over the cheese and syrup pudding. A Jonno,

495

by the way, well-behaved and sober, who had done his best to be helpful that morning, turning fruit in the apple store, cleaning out the hen-house and bringing in logs. When not peevish with self-pity he was a good companion, amusing and jolly. I wished, though, he would not try to kiss me whenever we were alone. I had been embarrassed by Mrs Whale finding us in a clinch among the poor dangling corpses in the game larder. Also I felt anxious about whither this was tending. I was prepared to be kissed if that would encourage Jonno to believe that not all relationships were doomed to unhappiness but I drew the line at making love. 'If your brother's called Oberon,' said Jonno, 'and your sisters are Ophelia, Portia and Cordelia, why are you called Harriet? That's not a Shakespearean heroine.'

'It's my second name,' I said. 'Custard?'

'So what's your first name?'

'Come to think of it, why aren't you, as the eldest son, called Oswald or Galahad?'

Jonno made a face. 'John's *my* second name. I was ragged about the Galahad so I dropped it. OK, spill the beans.'

I told him what it was and he laughed until he was pink in the face. 'Ha, ha! Oh dear! Hee, hee! I can see why you abandoned it in favour of Harriet.'

'It *is* awful, isn't it?' said Cordelia with the conscious merit of one in possession of a decent name.

It is all very well for Shakespeare to say, 'What's in a name? that which we call a rose', et cetera. The answer is, quite a lot actually. William is a neutral, classless name. If Shakespeare had been obliged to go about introducing himself by a name that had people smirking and sniggering and had he been called Desperate Moaner by his classmates, he would have taken a very different attitude. When you think of someone, you create a sort of collage of the dominant characteristics of their face and figure, along with the background you most associate them with, and jumbled up in the picture is their name. In fact you can't think of them without it.

'My first name's Scarlett,' said Annabel.

'Really?' Cordelia was impressed. 'After Vivien Leigh in *Gone with the Wind*? I love that bit when Clark Gable picks her up and gallops off upstairs with her to – you know, violent her. Imagine if he'd tripped at the top!'

'She's fibbing again,' said Jonno. 'Come to think of it, if Annabel's first name really was Scarlett that would make her initials SAP. Rather suitable.'

Annabel brow blackened. She pushed back her chair and ran from the room.

'That gel has the manners of a Red Indian.' Miss Tipple was working her way enthusiastically through the pudding like a nesting vole, only occasionally coming up for air.

I wondered if Sir Oswald would be offended by this criticism of his daughter but he continued to look at Cordelia with a soppy smile on his face and to clasp his spoon convulsively.

'Your name must really be Archibald.' Cordelia addressed Archie. 'Luckily you aren't. Bald, I mean.'

'No,' said Archie in a superior way, drooping his silvered eyelids. 'Actually it's Archduke.'

'Within the case the thing lay with one metal finger outstretched like a finger-post to hell,' I wrote. 'A sickly phosphorescent light emanated from its rust and slime-clad shell, with an odour of corruption, like something that has been too long underwater. But worse was the reek of malevolence, detectable neither by the ocular nor the olfactory senses but by the impressibility of the mind. The propensity for wickedness, which is within all of us, leaped up like a flame in a draught in response to the evil that seethed within the loathed object. Even as I looked at it I felt my spirit grow meaner and falser and harder in sympathy.' Too much D. H. Lawrence? I wondered. Perhaps leaping flames sounded rather sexual. I crossed it out, chucked another log on the fire in the Little Parlour where I was working, and laboured on, while outside the wind groaned in sympathy with my efforts.

Two hours later I had completed another paragraph. My head was reeling with polysyllables and even my elbows were inky. But I was convinced that I had the bones of a really good spine-chilling article. Now that I had begun to describe the arm dragging itself inch by inch by its fingertips along the gallery I was starting at every movement of logs in the grate. Twice I had glanced rapidly over my shoulder, once to discover Dirk scratching his ear and the second time to see Mrs Whale standing in the doorway.

'Sorry to disturb you, miss.'

'It doesn't matter,' I lied.

'There's only two hours till dinner. I've the books to dust, the clocks to wind, and the sheets to iron. I'll not get the vegetables cleaned for Mr Archie unless I leave one of them jobs over. What'll it be?'

'Better leave the books.' I said absently, my mind still resonating with ghastly happenings.

'Sir Oswald is very particular about the books being speckless.'

'All right, don't iron the sheets. There's no one new coming to stay.'

'Lady Pye likes the beds ready and aired at all times, just in case.'

'Well, leave the clocks then.' I almost shouted, then remembered her sad life and managed not to.

'As you please. Only then some of them'll stop and being that old they don't always start up smooth. You have to take them slow through the quarter chimes –'

I threw down my pen. 'I'll dust the books.'

I was crossing the hall, composing a complicated sentence about the horror of being woken by the insistent tapping of a prosthetic forefinger on one's bedpost, when the doorbell clanged on its wire and made me skip with fright. I opened the front door a fraction and looked cautiously out into the freezing dark.

'Harriet! Darling!'

One of the two people who stood on the doorstep flung her arms round my neck. It was Portia.

'So you see, what with that beastly man threatening to press charges against Suke, it seemed best to avoid London for a bit and stop off here for a few days until tempers have cooled. I did ring a few days ago to ask if we could. I'm surprised Lady Pye didn't say anything. She sounded an absolute poppet. I hope you don't mind us muscling in on your scene?'

Portia and I were in my bedroom changing for dinner. Suke had declined to change, contending that the convention of putting on evening dress had been formulated with the sole purpose of exciting men to sexual congress later on and that therefore we should refuse to comply with it. I had pleaded rules of the house and received a scathing look. Portia and Suke had been wearing identical baggy boiler suits when they arrived, woven from something I think is called jute – anyway the colour of old sacks, no doubt from Suke's own loom. The excitement factor was certainly not evident. I was thankful that Portia had not followed Suke's lead and shaved off her hair. Suke's naked, veined head had a fierce, sculpted beauty like a statue of The Warrior in marble.

I remembered the note about porter and soup for Thursday dinner. 'Maggie hasn't been well. And no, of course I don't mind. I'm thrilled to see you. But what did Suke do exactly?'

'It was during the Authors' Convention in Edinburgh.

This man, a writer called Buck Blister, gave a talk about how all good thriller writers are men because female writers are incapable of understanding the amoral hero who only cares about winning the game. Women want to make him into a sort of Lassie, saving the weak and innocent and reforming everyone, with good finally triumphing. Whereas the proper hero mooches off alone at the end, even dirtier and more disorganised, having lost the woman he loved and quarrelled irreconcilably with his head of section, despising everyone except possibly Vladimir who he's just blasted to atoms.'

'Well, come to think of it, are there any good female thriller writers? I can think of masses of good detective writers like Dorothy L. Sayers and Margery Allingham and –'

Portia, who was brushing her hair, stopped to look at me in the mirror. 'For God's sake, don't let Suke hear you say that! When Buck got to the end of his talk she climbed on to the platform and hit him with the microphone until blood ran. He had to have stitches.'

'That was a bit rough wasn't it?'

'He asked for it.' Portia did not meet my eye. 'It was then I discovered that I'm not made for militancy. I actually felt sorry for him. Wasn't it wet of me?'

'Not at all! Any decent person would –' I hesitated – 'except Suke, of course, because she's so dedicated. But anyway if you don't like seeing people thrashed then that's how you feel and you shouldn't be ashamed of it.'

'Ah, but that's easier said than done, isn't it? Having the courage of your own convictions, I mean. You're usually the one bleating about that.' She smoothed down her dress – my dress actually. As Cordelia was already in my black, I had lent Portia my blue silk cloqué dress and my godmother's garnets. 'How do I look?'

'Terrific.' I did not exaggerate. Her lashes were the longest in the family and she had darkened them with mascara, which made her eyes look even bigger.

I put on a wool dress that was a becoming shade of blackcurrant. As Archie had chosen it I was confident that it suited me. Not that I minded about being outshone. I was entirely used to it. Actually I was proud of my sisters as we stood in the drawing room before dinner. It was just a pity the audience was so small. Only Miss Tipple and Annabel were there before us. I hoped Jonno was not in his room, getting drunk. When Sir Oswald came rolling in he was clearly much struck by Portia.

'So!' He nuzzled the back of her hand. 'Is there no end to this family of ravishing young creatures?'

'My sister Ophelia is generally considered to be the beauty,' said Portia, sounding rather Jane Austen-ish. 'It's so kind of you to have us at the last minute.'

Sir Oswald looked interested. 'Is Ophelia older or younger than you, my dear?' He pinched her bare arm in a friendly way, which made Portia jump.

'Older. My friend Suke's with me. Lady Pye said we might come. We really are grateful.'

'You need not thank me, my dear Miss Ping. The vitality of youth casts a vernal garland over these ancient walls –' His flowery prose suffered a check when Suke came in. 'Ah, here is your young friend.' His eyes ran over her gleaming cranium and the shapeless suit, and his face fell. 'Well, well.'

Despite the clothes and lack of hair, Suke had plenty of self-possession. She shook hands with Sir Oswald and thanked him for his hospitality in a manner that was not without charm. She had something of Joan of Arc about her, combined with the Boy David. She was tall and slender, her nose was sharp, her mouth firm, her chin decided. She stood with her feet apart and her hands clasped behind her back and her straight gaze told you there could be no compromise. I saw then what had made Portia fall in love with her. You knew at once that she would always tell you the truth, regardless of its palatability, or convenience to herself. She was strong in a way I deeply admired. I hovered nearby in case Sir Oswald should make a tactless remark and provoke Suke to hit him. I checked around for instruments to hand and while Suke was being introduced to Miss Tipple I hid the poker behind the sofa.

'Not Miss Ernestine Tipple!' cried Suke. 'The author of *The Fox and the Goose – an Analysis of Modern Marriage*?'

Miss Tipple bowed her head in acknowledgement.

'But that's extraordinary. It's practically been my bible. I've read everything you've ever written.'

Miss Tipple opened eyes colourless with age and fastened them hopefully on Suke's face. 'Even *The Speckled Band* – my work on venereal disease in women? For some reason that did not sell particularly well.'

'I found it very moving. A work of scholarship, I should say.'

'You appear to be a very intelligent young woman.' Miss Tipple uncurled until her spine was almost straight. 'I should like your opinion of my work in progress entitled *History of the Union of Female Franchise*. I have been many years already in its composition and I fear the end is not yet in sight. My eyes are troublesome and arthritis in my hand makes it difficult to hold a pen.'

'I should be honoured.' Suke stood with head flung back. I could not decide whether she most resembled Sir Lancelot or Robin Hood at that moment. She should have had a silver lance or a quiver of arrows.

'Marvellous, isn't she?' said Portia, to me in an undertone while Suke was offering her services as Miss Tipple's amanuensis.

'Marvellous. But I shouldn't like to get on her wrong side.'

'No.' Portia looked thoughtful. 'When she's disappointed in you that's almost worse than when she's angry. Like a bucket of freezing water. I'm afraid I haven't quite measured up.'

'Why not?'

'I'm much too frivolous. I can't be intense for more than two minutes together. And I don't really give a damn about things like being considered a sex object. Actually I quite like it. And I like men – though natch some are pigs. Also I do enjoy a good joke occasionally.'

I understood from this that Portia's *Schwarm* for Suke was largely over. I hoped there would not be trouble.

'Portia!' Archie, who had just that moment come in to the drawing room, embraced her warmly. '*Too* heavenly to see you. Harriet told me you were here. Luckily we're having *gannat de chou-fleur* which can be made to stretch. I need a drink.' He helped himself to champagne from the drinks tray nearby. 'I have wrestled with that beastly stove for two hours. Now I know how Hercules felt when he succeeded in slaying the Nemean Lion. Oo-hoo!' He executed a *grand battement* on seeing Suke. 'My dear,' he said in a whisper to me, 'I feel quite faint. I can see the blood vessels throbbing on her skull. Horrid, horrid, *horrid*! Please make sure we are at opposite ends of the table or I shan't be able to eat a *thing*!'

I was about to reassure him when Portia clutched my arm. 'Harriet! You mean thing, keeping him to yourself!'

She was staring in the direction of the door. There stood Phoebus Apollo, as though he had stepped through the frame of the portrait on the stairs, changed into black tie and come down to dinner. His ear-length wavy hair was the colour of butter and his clean-shaven, chiselled features would have driven Narcissus mad with envy.

'Greek god or what!' she breathed.

'Greek god,' I said. 'Definitely.'

Jonno, transformed almost out of recognition by the removal

of his beard and ponytail, glanced about the room. He saw me and grinned self-consciously.

'He's coming over.' Portia turned to face me. 'Please don't tell me he's queer. I couldn't bear it!'

'Ssh! He'll hear you. Not as far as I know. Hello, Jonno.' I signalled approval of his changed appearance with my eyes. 'Portia, this is Jonno Pye. Jonno, my sister Portia.'

Portia turned her head over her shoulder to look at him. It was a beguiling glance, demure beneath those fabulous eyelashes, like a shy woodland creature of leafy shadows and sparkling glades. Jonno sucked in his breath as though he had been winded.

'Hello.'

'Hello.'

They stared at each other. Jonno's cheeks, pale from the beard, gave a twitch or two as he clenched his jaw. His lips, beautifully moulded, parted with surprise as he gazed at Portia's lovely face.

'Portia's just come down from Scotland,' I said. 'From an authors' convention. With her friend Suke.'

'How – fascinating. Was it – snowing?'

'Snowing?'

'In Scotland.'

'Oh. No. Yes, I mean. Sleet. A blizzard actually.'

'How – wonderful.'

I left them still staring at each other with rapt expressions and went to rearrange the table plan. It seemed only kind to sit Portia and Jonno next to each other but, for different reasons, he, Portia, Sir Oswald and Archie all had to be as far from Suke as possible. After ten minutes of juggling place cards I was ready to blow my brains out.

I resigned myself to an evening of dullness. Suke and Miss Tipple, at my end of the table, spoke exclusively to each other about the great work. Annabel's only contribution to the conversation was to say several times that she had a great secret that would make us all sorry. She refused to be drawn further on this. Cordelia tossed me the occasional conversational crumb. I busied myself fetchign and carrying and composing sentences of my article. My consolation was that I need no longer hold myself responsible for Jonno's rehabilitation.

I was standing before the sink, rinsing a glass, when a hand reached over my shoulder and attempted to extract the mop from my fingers.

'I'll do that.'

I held on to it. 'It's very kind of you but I've got into the rhythm.' I smiled up at Suke but she gave me a look that seemed to assess and find me wanting.

'I like to do my equal share.' Her grip on the mop tightened so I let go rather than have an undignified contest.

'This is Mrs Whale,' I said as she came into the kitchen with the drying-up cloths. 'This is er . . . Miss . . .'

'My name's Suke.' She shook Mrs Whale's hand firmly. 'How do you do?'

Mrs Whale's eye ran over Suke's naked head and boiler suit. 'Very well, thank you, miss.'

'You mustn't call me that. I'm Suke to everyone. Social status has no place in sisterhood. I was indignant and ashamed that you served us at dinner, without sitting down to eat with us. Caste systems are symptomatic of a degenerate society.'

Mrs Whale looked as taken aback as I felt embarrassed. She picked up the glass Suke had put on the rack to dry, still dripping suds. 'Lady Pye likes her glasses rinsed in clean hot water, miss.'

'They're not Lady Pye's glasses. They belong to everyone. Property is theft.'

Mrs Whale drew her eyebrows together. 'I can assure you, miss, *these* glasses weren't stolen.'

'Oh, yes, they were. Stolen from the masses whose breath was choked out of them, grubbing up coal to keep the Lady Pyes of this world warm in their fine houses.' This had a familiar sound. Suke threw back her head and her pointed nose cleaved the air as she nodded to give her words emphasis. 'Stolen from those who laboured long hours in the field to put bread on her porcelain plate, from the women who got up in the freezing dawn to bring hot water and light the fires so that Lady Pye and her sort could lie in bed till noon –'

'But Lady Pye gets up to light the fires herself. At a quarter to six!'

'Well, in that case . . . good.' Suke was only momentarily deflected. 'But ask yourself, what has that obese creature gorging himself on brandy and chocolates in the drawing room – and lasciviously ogling an innocent, defenceless child into the bargain – ever done that we women should find ourselves drudging at his pleasure?' Suke seemed to have got Sir Oswald's measure straightaway. Perhaps not Cordelia's, though. Suke's voice had a penetrating quality that made my head ring. 'What has he done to benefit his fellow men? Answer me that!'

'If you don't mind, miss, I'll have that glass before it cools or it'll smear.'

I left them to it and joined the others in the drawing room. Archie laughed when I told him about the argument in the kitchen.

'The thing is, Suke's absolutely right,' I said. 'Every word she says is true and I respect her for speaking out when the rest of us pretend it isn't happening because it's easier that way. Suke made me feel ashamed. Why shouldn't Mrs Whale sit at the dining table with us?'

'She wouldn't be comfortable, for one thing.'

'But why not? Because of our horrible class system. Archie, it isn't right. Intelligent people do menial unrewarding jobs

506

in factories while the idiot sons of the rich spend their lives in pleasant places. It's so unfair!'

'I don't see why we shouldn't feel sorry for idiot sons as well.' He looked across the room to where Jonno and Portia sat together, talking in low tones as they had done throughout dinner, unable to drag their eyes from each other's face.

'I wouldn't call Jonno an idiot.'

'No, he isn't stupid, he just behaves stupidly. But *what* an improvement you've made! I hope you aren't sore at being cut out?'

'Not in the least. In fact it's a relief. And I find I can't begrudge Jonno his luck in being heir to this wonderful old house. It's different when you know someone and like them. But the flagrant immorality of the rich man in his castle and the poor man at his gate ought to be our first concern, shouldn't it? Of course *I've* never done anything to deserve having a family which values art and loves books.'

'I shall choose you an elegant hair shirt,' Archie said teasingly. 'Or better still, a sanbenito.'

'What's that?'

'A sort of yellow dressing gown with a red cross on the back, worn by penitents heretics during the Inquisition.'

I smiled in an absent kind of way because I was still contemplating with a jaundiced eye the swamping injustice of the world.

'You're depressed, Harriet. I wonder why.'

'What, me? No.'

'I'm a little depressed myself. I miss Rupert. Perhaps you do too.'

'Oh, Archie, I completely forgot! I'm so sorry. He rang this morning to say he'll be back late tomorrow night.'

A slow smile of satisfaction spread across Archie's face. He had remembered to renew his lipstick after eating, something I always forgot to do. It was an appealing shade of rich peony red. 'I hope not *too* late. I find anything after midnight really takes it out of me.'

'Actually, he asked me to wait up for him – alone.'

'Oh?' Was it my imagination or had Archie's face changed from cordial to hostile? His eyebrows sprang up towards his widow's peak. 'And why?

'He wants to talk to me. About Maggie, I think.'

Archie frowned, considering. 'Mm. That sounds dull. Not worth bags under the eyes. Very well.' He smiled at me, serene once more. 'Did he say how the meeting went?'

'He seemed to be in the middle of one. Is it important?'

'It could be. Very. Rupert's extremely ambitious. Yes, really,' he added, seeing my surprise. 'Not for money, of course. As you may know, his father left him enough capital to keep him in underpants, if not in yachts, until he dies. I think he'd be quite content with a lot less, materially, than he's already got. But he wants to *succeed*. He has things to prove to himself. Probably it has something to do with his childhood. He doesn't talk about it. But apart from your dear papa, it seems to have been singularly lacking in love.' I knew the passionate worship of a plain, fat toothless child was worth less than nothing in anyone's tally of love received, so I did not interrupt. 'Rupert *hates* to look driven and striving,' continued Archie. 'It's possible he may be ashamed of it. And, like everyone else, I suppose, he's afraid of failure, so he keeps his ambition under wraps. I love him for it. It's part of his complex nature.'

'It's never occurred to me that Rupert might have doubts and fears. Or even hopes. He seems so – confident. Invulnerable.'

'That's what he means people to think. He's the most secret, unfathomable, protected person I know. But that's not generally the sign of an invulnerable man. Rupert's as assailable as anyone, perhaps more than most, but he's adept at disguising his feelings.'

I tried to imagine Rupert as uncertain, even afraid. I had to give it up. For one thing, since my father's arrest I had come to depend on Rupert for my own sense of safety.

'I'm afraid I've come to rely on him rather a lot,' I confessed.

'Oh, *I* am as symbiotic algae on Rupert's coral reef. That's *my* weakness, if you like.'

'You know, I think something should be done about the drains.' Suke strode up to me and stood with her hands on her hips, a dark patch on the front of her trousers where water from the sink had splashed. 'There's a truly appalling stink in the corridor outside the kitchen.'

The next day was characterised chiefly by rows and dissension. Throughout lunch, Archie and Suke argued about what to cook for dinner. Suke approved the vegetarianism but she thought seakale *en robe de chambre* with *gugelhopf* – bread made with eggs and raisins – followed by a pudding of praline and cherries, an unnecessarily complicated bill of fare. She liked to show solidarity with the oppressed by dining simply. A cabbage stew or boiled potatoes and a lump of hard cheese was all that was necessary to sustain the body sufficiently to right wrongs. She was a girl of extraordinarily high principles. She was bossy – there was no other word for it – but it was very difficult, if not impossible, to refute her arguments.

'But it's so dull,' complained Archie to Suke's suggestion of steamed Brussels sprouts and a milk pudding. 'I am sensitive to being bored. It makes me ill.'

'Boredom is a symptom of profligacy.' Suke folded her arms across her chest and looked calmly at Archie. 'You wouldn't be bored if you were combing gutters for grains of rice for your starving children to eat.'

'If I couldn't feed them I shouldn't be so irresponsible as to have any children to starve,' retorted Archie. 'And can one comb gutters? You can comb fields and woods –'

Suke was not to be deflected. 'If sex was your only relief from grinding misery, I doubt if you'd show such marvellous self-control. Anyway, as a homosexual, you can afford to take this superior viewpoint because you run no risk of reproduction.'

Suke generally got away with laying down the law because most people, and this included me, were too intimidated by her plain-speaking to argue.

Archie, however, delighted in a call to arms. 'Though I cast my seed upon stony ground I claim an equal right to champion the downtrodden, the shiftless and the witless, if I choose. A head like a ripening pumpkin and the dress-sense of George Bernard Shaw does not give *you* the moral high ground.'

The argument continued in this vituperative vein. One could hardly blame the children for giggling irritatingly throughout the rest of lunch.

After washing up I lit the fire in the Little Parlour and settled myself to work. It was astonishing that the sentences I had liked best the day before now seemed dull and derivative. I began my article again, from the beginning, working all afternoon absorbed by the agonies and joys of creative effort, in the ratio, roughly, of five to one, stopping only to take Dirk for a walk.

During dinner, while we ate Suke's rissoles and boiled turnips, a brutal contrast to Archie's delectable first course of *oeufs Pascal*, Suke and Miss Tipple continued to discuss the *History of the Union of Female Franchise*. Suke proposed to write it herself, using Miss Tipple's material. I suspected that an uneasy debate was going on in Miss Tipple's mind. Her great labour – *HUFF* for short – had probably become, like poor Mr Casaubon's *Key to All Mythologies*, a troublesome, intractable burden. She was afraid she might not be able to bring it to a triumphant conclusion. But then, who was Ernestine Tipple, if no longer the author of a great work in progress? Just another feeble old woman waiting to die. A cipher, a recipient of charity and pity, perhaps even a downright nuisance. I wanted to urge Miss Tipple to battle on with *HUFF*, no matter what the final outcome, so she could face each day with a sense of purpose – until for her there were no more dawns. But I was much too frightened of Suke to contradict her.

I wondered where Suke got her self-assurance from and her enthusiasm for reform. A strict adherence to truth and principle was clearly no more effective a shield from the anguish of existence than my dissembling and equivocation. I had found her in tears in the kitchen before dinner and assumed she was crying about Portia.

'It *is* misery when things don't quite work out, isn't it?' I had said hesitatingly, not daring to be more explicit, certainly lacking the courage to put an arm round her. In my experience soft words, far from turning away wrath, frequently invite it.

She had pointed with her knife to a pan of onions stewing on the stove. 'They're a particularly vicious sort.' I was not convinced the onions were to blame. 'If you mean, am I wretched because Portia's gone off with Jonno,' Suke continued, 'I am not. Though I deplore her taste, she has every right to find her satisfactions where she likes. I don't believe in relationships held together by the glue of guilt and obligation. We're all free.' She blew her nose hard. 'Anyway, Portia basically likes men. I realise now she was just experimenting with me.'

I could not deny this. 'I know how much she respects you and values your good opinion.' Suke sniffed and attacked a heap of earth in which lurked the turnips. There was a stiff silence. 'I hope – I hope your feelings haven't been hurt?' I said, very stupidly.

She rounded on me with such savagery I knew they had been. 'Didn't I just say that I don't allow possessive feelings to corrupt my relationships with other people?'

'No. Right. Sorry. Shall I help you with those?' I indicated the turnips she was scalping. I hoped she was going to remove the tough skins and blackened, frosted places.

'Certainly not.' Suke hurled them in their blotched, filthy state into a pan of boiling water reducing it to a thick, bubbling scum like a sulphurous geyser. 'You've already done *more* than your fair share today. Sir Oswald, Jonno and Portia have not, as far as I know, done anything to help.'

This was certainly true. But I would always rather do things myself than have a row. Suke took me to task for this pusillanimity. She explained that this craven attitude reinforced bad habits, which ultimately were injurious for the people who had them. Suke was right, as always. She had worked out a rota for washing up and tonight it was Cordelia and Annabel's turn. I looked forward to seeing what would happen the following evening when it was the turn of Jonno and Sir Oswald. The coffee rota appointed Portia as chief percolator.

As supper had not appeared by eight o'clock and Miss Tipple and Sir Oswald were starting to get tetchy I again offered my services in the kitchen but Suke, pausing briefly in the process of giving something that resembled Dirk's Canomeat a punishing stirring, said they could manage. Archie gave me a meaningful glance behind her back and tapped his temple. Suke turned her head in time to see him do it. Her eyes became steely and her mouth a thin line. You would think that male and female homosexuals would be sympathetic to each other but it seemed not.

* * *

There was something to be said for Suke's system. It meant I could slip up to the Little Parlour straight after dinner and get on with my work. Gradually the party below dispersed. Miss Tipple went first, her elbow supported by Suke, who warned her about steps and uneven flooring in a nannyish, possessive voice. Portia and Jonno, yawning noisily with a pretence of lassitude that I am sure deceived no one, left the room immediately afterwards.

I had always envied Portia's ability to throw herself whole-heartedly into the business in hand. But I wondered if Portia's evident passion for Jonno was wise. I had watched them from my bedroom window that afternoon, capering hand-in-hand across the snowy fields like Zhivago and Lara celebrating the overthrow of the Bolsheviks. Jonno had been admirably restrained as far as drinking was concerned for the last forty-eight hours. Anyone could see he was, for the moment, drunk on love. But then everyone knows that wisdom has nothing to do with love.

What has it to do with, then? If not reason, is it purely a synergy of two sets of loins? I could answer that one. No. I had certainly desired Max. But even before I had found out about Georgia I had not begun to love him. I had to confess to myself that I had probably never actually been in love. I had been very fond of Dodge. I had admired his evangelical spirit and his ascetic way of life. He had seemed to me like a purifying fire in a world of hoggish dissipation. It had not occurred to me in those days to attribute his enthusiasm for political regeneration to a desire to lift himself from the dreariness of the workaday world.

Perhaps, I thought sadly, altruism was incompatible with the state of being human. It might not be possible to with-stand the cruel buffets of life without the soft garments of fantasy and self-deception. A footfall behind me made me spin round.

'I'll go to bed, now, miss, if there's nothing more.' Mrs Whale's habitual look of faded suffering had been replaced by one of lively annoyance. 'I've washed the dinner plates that the girls left greasy, glued the coffee cup back together, though I can't say if it'll be fit for use, unblocked the sink and cleared up the suds that was all over the kitchen floor. If you ask me, those Communists, or whatever Miss Suck calls herself, ought to learn to mind their own business.'

'Oh dear. I am sorry.'

'It's not *your* fault, miss.' I was pleased to detect a softening in her voice. Perhaps there was a chance we were on the way to becoming friends.

'I could have a word with Suke,' I suggested, without much conviction, 'explain to her that we've got into the habit of managing things a certain way.'

'You can try if you like but I doubt you'll do good. Once folks think they've got it in them to save the world it's my experience there's no doing anything with them. It's nothing more than conceit, if you ask me.' This summed up very neatly what my thoughts had been vaguely groping towards. 'But I'm talking out of turn. That's *my* pride speaking.' Mrs Whale lowered her eyes, as though suddenly recalling the blots on her own copybook. 'A haughty spirit goes before a fall, as the Bible says. It's my afternoon off, tomorrow, miss. I shall catch the one o'clock bus into Bunton.'

'Oh, good! I hope you'll have a lovely time. Are you going to see *The Four Musketeers*? It really was quite funny.'

'I'm going to see Father Terry at the deanery. He suffers badly from shingles, which makes him grumpy, and he can't seem to keep domestic help. I always boil his smalls for him on a Saturday.' Mrs Whale looked almost elated by this grim prospect. 'And he wants me to scrub the scullery and worm the cat.'

After she had gone I drew spider's legs round an ink stain

on my paper while I thought about her strange life – a lovely, intelligent woman reduced by cruel circumstances to a gruelling existence of spiritual struggle and self-repression. I drew an intricate web for the spider. It looked quite gothic so I added a pointed doorway with a skeleton arm waving from within. This reminded me that I was supposed to be working. I was not expecting Rupert for another hour and I must use the time profitably. 'A grey veil spun by long-dead spiders and thickened by the dust of ages draped the chained case like a pall . . .'

I was floating face down on a bed of snow. As I pushed my head into it I saw a whole world beneath, full of tiny people, getting on buses and hurrying into shops. It was not snow but cloud and I was the wind. I sucked in my cheeks and blew and the little people below me clutched at lamp-posts and ran after their hats. I felt guilty but it was fun. I blew harder and found that I could roar. Trees bent before the blast and chimneypots crashed from rooftops. A diminutive Dirk looked up at me, barking. I put down my giant hand from the sky and tapped him gently on the nose, hissing so sibilantly that people threw themselves flat on the ground with their hands over their ears. Dirk took hold of my finger between his teeth and pulled. I was falling from the clouds, faster and faster and the earth was spiralling up to meet me. I met it with a thwack on the side of my head and woke.

Something hard – the desk top on which my head had rested while I dozed – was hurting my jawbone, and my feet were numbed by cold. I sat up and looked at my watch. It was after twelve. I peered through the squint into the drawing room below. The electric lights had been turned off and a three-branched candlestick left burning on the table by Old Gally's chair. The fire had been recently tended and gave out a generous vermilion light. It stained the panelling with gold, put glints into the eyes of the faces in the portraits and lent warmth to the painted cheek. It required no effort to imagine the drawing room peopled by men in doublets and sugar-loaf hats, and women in embroidered coifs and farthingale skirts. Only a pile of paperbacks on the stool by Miss Tipple's chair spoiled the illusion that I had gone back three hundred years as I slept.

I thrust my head a little further out to check that someone had remembered to put the guard in front of the fire. Mingled with the odours of furniture polish, flowers and burning logs was the smell of tobacco. Had someone left a cigarette burning in an ashtray? I turned out the lamp on my desk. As my eyes adjusted to the change in the level of light, the features of the room below became more distinct. Old Gally's chair faced away from me towards the fire. From above its high back a long curl of smoke drifted upwards and feathered in the draught. I could just see the top of a head covered with very short white hair. I heard a creak as the occupant of the chair moved and a toe appeared as though the owner of the head had crossed one leg over the other.

An unexpected visitor had been left alone in the drawing room and had decided to pass the time with a cigarette, unaware that Old Gally's chair was off limits. This, I told myself, was the most likely answer. But the wind *would* howl like a demented soul suffering the torments of eternal damnation, making it impossible to believe in sensible, everyday solutions. Suppose . . . just suppose . . . I debated with myself. I could stay where I was until Rupert's return. Despite the cold, for the fire in the Little Parlour was out, this course of action, or non-action, recommended itself urgently. What I *ought* to do was to go calmly down and investigate. Was I a neck-or-nothing correspondent with a career to make or a contemptible coward?

I tiptoed down the staircase, wincing when my foot knocked against a riser. From the chair rose more spirals of smoke. I heard two prolonged sighs, the second of which was almost a groan. The lament of a troubled spirit, perhaps? I hesitated. The occupant of the chair began to hum, tunelessly at first, and then mournfully took up the words of a song.

'"The sigh of *mid*-night trains in emp-ty *sta*tions – silk *stock*ings thrown aside, dance in-vi-*ta*tions – oh, how the ghost – of – you *clings*, – these foolish *things* –" Harriet! Good God! Creeping up like that – nearly gave me a heart attack! Gently with the paternal neck – Now, now, my darling, there's no need to cry. Thank God, time and the hour, though they've taken their time about it, have finally run through the roughest – ahaa! hoo, hoo!' Whatever else my father might have been going to say was lost as he, too, succumbed to uncontrollable weeping.

THIRTY-TWO

The moment I woke I heard the changed note of the wind. It blew steadily but calmly, not rattling the windows but softly shaking the uppermost branches of the yews. My stomach felt light and empty. Then I remembered. Pa was free. Not only free but in this very house, in the Mordakers' old room. I turned on my side to tell Cordelia the marvellous news. Her cheeks were faintly pink, her eyelashes clinging together in sleep. It would be a pity to wake her. But I wanted to hear myself say it and then I could be certain it was true. I was tempted to run along the gallery, to open the door a crack and steal a look at him.

But last night, after the first electrifying moments of our reunion were over, it had become apparent how exhausted he was. Rupert had brought a decanter of brandy and a plate of cheese sandwiches into the drawing room just as Pa and I were struggling to pull ourselves together and behave like sensible people. We sat on the sofa, Pa's arm round my shoulder, my hand on his knee, and every minute or so he had pressed his handkerchief or his sleeve to his face. He had tried to be his old ebullient self but the act would not have deceived a baby.

'These sandwiches are terrible,' said Pa. 'I've just eaten a lump of butter the size of an egg. And the bread's as thick as a telephone directory. Rupert, my boy, you'll never make a cook.'

'I hope not.'

'I think they're delicious,' I said. My mouth was filled with food and my heart with gratitude because he had returned my father to me.

'You'll never make a liar,' said Rupert.

'We had a strange journey.' My father wiped his eyes again. 'There was a frightful woman sitting opposite us on the train with a parrot in a cage. It was completely fascinated by Rupert. It fixed him with its beady eye and lambasted him with impertinent comments. "Naughty boy. Bad boy. Give us a kiss then. Oh, you saucy thing!" People were staring, quite hypnotised. I think they were beginning to wonder if the parrot knew something the rest of us didn't.'

Rupert laughed. 'I must say, its attentions were so particular I started to feel quite uncomfortable.'

'It was the voice of conscience,' said Pa.

'I've always wanted a parrot.' I realised that my father was anxious to avoid anything like a serious discussion.

'Surely Dirk is enough for anyone,' said Rupert. 'Where is he, by the way? He made an awful racket when we arrived. The patent method still not mastered, evidently.'

'I was asleep. But I dreamed about him barking.'

'Sleep!' said my father. 'Now that's something I could do with. Any chance, Harriet, of a pillow on which to lay my head?'

I took him upstairs.

'Lovely. Marvellous old stuff, isn't it? Siberian temperature, though.' He prodded the mattress and yawned while I put a match to the kindling in the grate. 'I hope the Pyes won't be too put out to find an unexpected increase in the household.'

'Sir Oswald adores having people to stay. And Maggie's the kindest, gentlest person in the world. Besides, they'll be thrilled it's you.'

My father sighed. 'Will they? I wonder.' He took off his jacket. I opened his suitcase and laid his pyjamas on the bed with his dressing gown and slippers. 'Thanks, darling. No, I don't bother with a hairnet these days.' He rubbed his hand over his bristly white hair. 'Christ, I'm so bloody tired! I couldn't sleep at all last night, hoping – wondering if . . .' His eyes filled again.

I put my arms round him and kissed the top of his head, to hide my own tears. 'I'll get you some towels. Then I'll show you where the bathroom is.' When I returned he was lying on the bed, asleep. I wrapped the bedclothes around him, put a guard before the fire and turned out the light.

Downstairs I found Rupert pouring himself a second glass of brandy. 'I shouldn't be having this really. I'm shattered.' He stood before the fire, stretching his arms and back. 'It's been a long, long day.' He stirred Dirk's stomach with his foot. 'I found this hound from hell in the kitchen, polishing off the cheese which I'd forgotten to put away. He deserves to have nightmares.'

'Can you bear to tell me quickly what's been happening? I shall sleep so much better if I know . . . if I know . . . goodness, I'm sorry to be so wet. It's just that it's all been such a shock.'

He handed me his handkerchief. 'Don't apologise. And for heaven's sake, don't sniff!'

'Sorry. That's why you wanted me to wait up, wasn't it? So I could meet him without everyone else being there. It was so kind of you.'

'One hardly wants an audience for these things. I except Cordelia.'

I smiled. Selfishly I longed to pour out my gratitude and relief but I was certain he would dislike it.

'I couldn't say anything on the telephone,' he went on in matter-of-fact tones, unaware of my swelling heart. 'I didn't want to raise your hopes for nothing. It was touch and go whether he'd be let out today.' I dried my eyes and tried to be calm. Rupert rolled the brandy about on his tongue. 'I must say, Oswald knows a thing or two about cognac. Where were we? Ah, yes. Charles Foy was extremely helpful. If he hadn't spent half the day on the telephone, speeding things up, we wouldn't have made the train this evening. But you needn't worry. It's all over. It really is.' I bit my lip, unable to speak for fear of breaking down. Rupert glanced at my full eyes and then down at his glass. 'The press, naturally, are swarming. Foy set up a smokescreen so we could leave by a side door and be driven straight to the station. I'm afraid you're going to have to go through all that again.'

'It doesn't matter. We got used to it; we were quite friendly with some of them.' I thought I could even be pleased to see Stan now that Pa was free.

'It's lucky no one here has spotted you and tipped them off.'

'Mrs Whale did recognise me from my photograph in the newspapers. But she'd never do such a mean thing.'

'I hope you're right. As it happens, Waldo's gone from the top of the list of suspects to the very bottom. In fact, of the entire company your father is one of only four who *couldn't* have killed Basil.'

I begged him with my eyes to go on. Rupert put his hand into his inside breast pocket and took out a cigar. 'Mind if I smoke?' I shook my head. Rupert sat in Miss Tipple's chair and went through the process of lighting it. Then he prodded the fire into a volcano of sparks. I ate the last cheese sandwich, hoping it would have a calming effect. 'Foy's being

521

very secretive,' Rupert went on. 'It's important that no one says anything to the media.'

'Don't worry. I've learned my lesson.'

'He still doesn't know who murdered Basil,' Rupert went on, 'if it *was* murder. But he knows how Basil was killed. He gave me a hint and the rest is my own surmise. But it was clever!' He gave a short laugh. 'Very clever.'

'Might it have been an accident?'

'Foy's convinced it was deliberate But he's doubtful about being able to prove it. Forensic are working on it now. Of course, every judicial department was closed over Christmas, or Waldo would have been let out sooner.'

I was much too relieved that he was out now to nurse a grudge against the holiday-makers. Rupert blew a cloud and ran his hand over his forehead as though to smooth away the exhaustion of the day.

'You see,' he paused to savour the fumes from his glass, 'finding Waldo kneeling by the body, covered with blood, with a blood-spattered piece of metal in his hand was enough to blunt everyone's thinking processes. There was nothing else on the stage that could have been used to bludgeon Basil to death. The police not being theatre folk, an alternative weapon never occurred to them. But I must admit it I didn't think of it either, though knowing a little about the production, perhaps I should have.'

'The production?'

'The stage sets, particularly.' Rupert drew on the cigar until the tip glowed red. He put one arm behind his head, stretched out his long legs and stared reflectively at the ceiling. 'Lear is essentially a pagan play. The gods invoked are always generic and plural – Zeus, Apollo, Juno, Hecate and so on. Nature is presented as a wilful goddess, divinised by both Lear and Edmund at different stages in the play. The director of this production hit on the idea of doing a Lear in the Baroque style. A boldly unfashionable conception.'

I thought about this. I could not grasp the significance of what he had said.

'One of the remarkable things about this story,' Rupert went on, 'is that it was you who gave Foy the vital clue.'

'Me?'

'I must say I respect the man. Foy, I mean. Despite things looking so black for Waldo, Foy was prepared to back his hunch that he didn't do it, that he didn't have the right psychological profile for a murderer. When you told him about that séance, about Basil's spectral weather reporting, he didn't dismiss it out of hand as so much hysterical rubbish.' I crinkled cheeks that felt stiff with salt into a smile, to show I was not offended. 'He thought about it long and carefully. Despite being a policeman, Foy is a literary man. He got the feeling there might be something in the play itself that would give him the clue. So he went back to the theatre alone. He stood on the stage, on the spot where Basil was killed. He turned over in his mind all you'd told him. Like a bolt from the blue it came to him – the connection between the séance and the play. And then he looked up.'

'Yes?' I leaned forward, gripping the sofa arm. Several wild and half-formed possibilities filtered through my brain, none of them, as it turned out, anywhere near the truth.

'That's all he told me and I'm not going to say anything more. It's a triumph of inductive reasoning on Foy's part and I mustn't steal his thunder. I distinctly got the impression he wants to tell you himself.' Rupert twirled the cigar between his fingers, then looked briefly at me. Was there something speculative in that gaze?

'But what did you mean when you said that my father was one of the four people in the company who *couldn't* have done it? If I could only be sure that he was absolutely safe, I think I could bear to be left in suspense.'

'Remember the wardrobe mistress and the two understudies who were standing together behind the backcloth? The stage was invisible but they could see who went on and came off. They saw Waldo follow Basil. Those three can provide unshakeable alibis for each other and Waldo. Whoever killed Basil was *not* on the stage at the time.'

I breathed out slowly. 'Then it really is all right.' My brain was teeming with questions but I could see that Rupert was dog-tired.

'Let's go to bed,' I said. 'We can fill in the gaps in the morning.'

He threw his cigar into the fire. 'Filthy things. I don't know why I like them so much. I shall feel like hell tomorrow.'

'Rupert, I'm sorry I was cross before you went away.'

'Were you?' He looked surprised. 'Oh yes, you *were* grumpy and disagreeable, now I think of it. I assumed you were sulking because of Max Frensham's departure.'

'It wasn't that – at least, not in the way you think. I shouldn't have been angry with you. It was only hurt pride and I shan't be so silly again. It was ungrateful. I'm so conscious of how much I – we owe you, not just money but time and – and what a lot you've had to put up with –'

'That'll do.' Rupert turned away from me to rake out the embers with the poker. 'Grateful speeches may make *you* feel better – I'm sure I hope they do – but they're quite unnecessary. And rather tedious to have to listen to, frankly.'

'You really do know how to be abominably rude!'

'Uh-uh. Remember, you were never going to be angry with me again?'

I frowned but then spoiled it by laughing. 'All right. I won't be. But you oughtn't to be such a brute.'

'But it's so enjoyable.'

'Sadist!'

'You see. It *is* fun, isn't it?'

Breakfast was later than usual, to accommodate the weary travellers. When I came down Rupert was already in the dining room, firmly behind an open newspaper.

'Good morning,' I said brightly, longing to share my new-found happiness. 'Isn't it a lovely day?'

Rupert glanced towards the window. 'It's snowing.' He returned his eyes to the paper.

The main headline on the front page said 'Waldo Byng Innocent'. Beneath it was a photograph of Pa, taken several years ago when he was playing Shylock. In heavy makeup, wig and beard he looked sly and wicked, every inch a murderer. Unable to contain my curiosity I sat down next to Rupert, leaned low over the table and twisted my head at an angle so I could read the rest of the article. In smaller letters it said 'Triumph of Detective Work'. I felt a pleasurable pride in seeing Inspector Foy's brilliance trumpeted before the world. I rested my chin on the tablecloth so I could go on reading. 'London's theatre world has been in suspense since November when one of England's most famous actors, the Shakespearean tragedian, Sir Basil Wintergreen' – a fold in the page prevented me reading further. I prodded it gently with a finger.

Rupert lowered the paper. His expression was savage. '*Don't* do that!'

My father came in then, with Cordelia hanging on his arm. He looked pale and tired. He winked at me and laid a hand briefly on Rupert's shoulder. Rupert grunted in reply. Cordelia pulled out a chair for Pa, brushed away an invisible crumb and arranged a napkin over his knees. Then she ran to the sideboard to reel off the contents of the dishes in a loud voice as though announcing winners past the post. She made a terrible clatter with the lids, dropped a spoon, burned herself pouring coffee and complained loudly about the ensuing pain. I saw Rupert close his eyes and breathe deeply. Cordelia sat down beside Pa and, while he ate, sang 'See the conquering hero comes! Sound the trumpets, beat the drums!' to the tune of 'Hark! the herald-angels sing', tapping a teaspoon on a plate by way of accompaniment. Rupert threw down the newspaper and left the room.

I grabbed it. The article, despite running on to page two, was disappointingly vague when it came to facts, and the inspector's reported comments were cryptic, adding nothing to what Rupert had told me last night. But I was delighted by a fulsome description of my father's genius and by the paragraphs of tributes from his fellow actors that followed. They all insisted they had never for a moment believed him guilty and raved about his arrest and imprisonment being a disgraceful miscarriage of justice. You would have thought that instead of sending flowers and pretending urgent appointments elsewhere, they had been thronging his cell, bombarding newspapers with angry letters of protest and petitioning the Home Secretary to come to his senses.

'It's an odd photograph to have chosen. It isn't like you at all.' I held up the paper so he could see it. 'I mean, you're wearing a false nose.'

My father gave a bleat of a laugh, shaking his head when I asked if he wanted to read it. 'I don't think I'm quite ready yet for Waldo the Innocent. I've only just got used to being Waldo the Butcher.'

Cordelia refused to look at me. She was angry because I had denied her the chance to reprise the role of Roberta in *The Railway Children*, whose father had been wrongfully imprisoned. If I had been any sort of sister I would have arranged things so that she could have screamed '*Daddy*!

Oh, my *daddy*!' in front of the assembled household – into whose hearts the cry would have gone like a knife. Instead of which I had sent her in to see him alone before he came down, and a heaven-sent opportunity was for ever lost.

Portia had not been in her room, nor had her bed been slept in.

'Oh! Look!' My eye had fallen on a paragraph further down. 'How amazing! A picture of Rupert! Listen to this! "The English Opera House announced yesterday that Rupert Woovespurges –" they've spelled it wrong – "has been appointed its new artistic director. Wolvespugs, 32 –" golly, they've made even more of a mess of it – "is the youngest man to hold this prestigious title in this company's long and venerable history. Wolvyprigs's credentials are unusual in that he has never before held a permanent position but has several times been a guest director for highly acclaimed performances in London and New York. So far he has been unavailable for comment. He replaces Tristram Lobe, who resigned amid controversy recently and has been admitted to the Simmer Down Nursing Home in Sussex –" blah, blah, blah! *Well!* What a dark horse! Did you know, Pa?'

'He didn't say a word. I didn't even know it was a possibility! I've lost touch with things, rather.' He smiled. 'I'm extremely pleased for him. It's a great feather in his cap.'

I noticed, not for the first time, that Pa's smile was lop-sided now. It lifted only half his mouth while the other side remained turned down, as though he could not be wholeheartedly happy any more.

'Waldo!' Archie came in then, looking striking in an aubergine moleskin suit with black velvet lapels and cuffs. 'Rupert has told me the good news! I rejoice that you are no longer captive. And the *hair*!' He examined, from several angles, my father's head, which had a quarter-inch of growth like hoarfrost. Archie frowned so that his widow's peak was especially prominent, which gave him the appearance of a benevolent vampire. 'So chic! Fancy turning white overnight like Marie Antoinette! My dear, the ro*mance* of it!'

'You don't think it makes me look – old? I had thought of dyeing it.'

'Certainly not! It gives you a sort of *haute brutalité* – the women will adore it. As for the men –' Archie lifted his eyebrows and sucked in his cheeks.

My father shuddered. 'You'll forgive me, Archie, but at the moment I'm rather off men. Just in that way, you understand.'

'How *thought*less of me!' Archie smiled kindly. 'Of course, your poor nerves must be in *shreds*. All those violent, uncultured felons vying for your favours! Mm!' He fluttered his eyelashes. 'But we shall bring you round between us, never fear.'

Actually, I thought Rupert and Archie were probably the perfect couple to be with when one's tranquillity was overset. They were a wonderful blend of sly kindness hidden behind an unsentimental mocking toughness. I remembered with something almost like regret that this was our last day at Pye Place. Tomorrow we were returning to London, to resume our old lives. I asked myself why I did not feel positive joy at the prospect. Darling Pa would be once more at the centre of the family. That was such a marvellous transformation of events that I could not think of it without wanting to cry. Only – things could never be the same again. We must all have been changed irrevocably by the experience. For the first time I wondered why my father had not gone down to Cornwall to be with my mother. A small cloud drifted briefly over my happiness. Then it occurred to me that he had not been in a fit state to travel alone and I felt better.

'Look, Archie!' I held up the newspaper and tapped the photograph of Rupert. Archie took it and read. His normally sallow skin grew flushed. 'Callooh Callay!' he sang. 'And he didn't even mention it. The boy's a *genius*. I must find him at once.'

But Rupert came in just then with the post.

'*Ave, Caesar, te salutamus,*' said Archie, bowing low.

'Well done, Rupert.' My father dabbed his eyes with his napkin. 'I'm as proud of you as though you were my own son.'

'Does it mean you'll be able to boss everyone about?' asked Cordelia. 'Will they have to do whatever you say?'

Rupert smiled briefly. 'I expect they'll make it their life's work to thwart me on every possible occasion.'

'It's terrific news,' I said feebly, seeing that he was not particularly enjoying the praise.

Rupert put a letter on the table by my plate. 'Your post.'

'It's from Max.' Cordelia had forgotten she was not speaking to me. 'I recognise the writing. Can I read it?'

'Max? You don't mean Max Frensham?' My father looked his astonishment.

'Oh, you don't know, Pa,' said Cordelia. 'Max has been staying here and making passionate love to Harriet. This is probably a proposal of marriage. Shall I open it and see?'

'Don't be silly. It's nothing of the kind.' I knew I was blushing.

'Read it out then,' taunted Cordelia.

'Don't be a pest, darling.' My father tapped his youngest daughter on the head with the newspaper. 'You'll have lovers of your own before long. Then you'll know how it feels to be teased.'

'Oh, I've already had several.' Cordelia looked smug. 'In fact –' Whatever she was going to say, she evidently thought better of it.

'I think I'll go and stretch my legs.' My father got up. 'I fancy a walk.'

'Can I come?' asked Cordelia at once.

'Not, this time, darling.' He smiled at her. 'I need to be on my own for a bit.'

529

I had never, in twenty-two years, heard my father express a desire for his own company. Usually he complained that he was lonely if there were fewer than half a dozen people in the house. But, naturally, being mewed up day and night for weeks with unsympathetic strangers was bound to have affected him. I looked at him with eyes of love but he had turned away. He went into the hall.

'Pa! Oh, my darling, darling pa!' shrieked Portia's voice.

Cordelia threw me a look of hate.

I was putting knives and forks round the table for lunch, brooding over the last paragraph of my article and trying to think of another word for 'wraith', which was a favourite of mine and therefore a little overused, when a tap on my shoulder brought me abruptly out of my abstraction. Mrs Whale, wearing her black coat, a black headscarf, black gloves and an expression suitable for a funeral, had coasted silently up and was standing behind me.

'Excuse me, miss. I'm off to Bunton now. If it isn't taking a liberty, I thought your father might find this helpful. I know how hard it is.' She thrust a slim red book into my hand and was sliding away to the door before I could do more than call my thanks after her.

The volume was entitled *The Christian Way to Redemption. Prayers for the Sorely Afflicted.* It was well worn and some particular sentences were marked with a cross. I was deeply touched by this act of thoughtfulness from one whose reserves of strength were continually drained by her own spiritual struggles. I was confident that my father would know how to thank her for the book with melting charm. Also that he would not read a word of it. How hard it is to know our fellow men and women, I reflected. I was thoroughly ashamed of my former dislike of Mrs Whale.

THIRTY-THREE

'"I have be-dimmed the noontide sun,"' my father made a sweeping motion above his head with spread fingers, '"called forth the mutinous winds; And 'twixt the green sea and the azured vault Set roaring WAR. To the dread rattling THUNDER Have I given fire, and rifted Jove's stout oak With his own bolt."' He drove his hand swiftly downwards in imitation of lightning.

The applause, after he had finished Prospero's speech, was enthusiastic. Even Sir Oswald woke long enough to clap his pudgy hands together, making sounds like pistol-shots.

'That *was* lovely!' Maggie's eyes were glistening behind her spectacles. She had dressed and come down for lunch, protesting that she felt as right as rain. She was sitting in the comfortable chair by the drawing-room fire, Miss Tipple having graciously accorded precedence to the invalid. It was mid-afternoon and a light snowfall had kept us all indoors so my father had offered to entertain us. 'You make it come alive, Mr Byng. I could see the storm just as you said.'

'Waldo, please!' My father bowed gracefully.

'Wonderful!' Archie held his handkerchief to his eyes. 'Quite wonderful!'

'Bravo!' cried Miss Tipple, shaking her many chins with fervour.

Portia, Cordelia and I gave rousing cheers and Jonno whistled and stamped his feet.

My father acknowledged each of us in turn in a courtly fashion. Then his eye fell on Rupert. His expression grew doubtful. I did not recognise that look but it was consistent with his altered manner. Rupert handed his cup wordlessly to me. I got up to fill it. I would willingly have flown to China and picked the tea-leaves myself if only he would give a positive verdict.

Rupert nodded. 'Magnificent, Waldo!' My father continued to gaze at him anxiously. As Prospero he had been lordly, fiery, mischievous. Now his hands hung limply by his sides, the palms turned slightly out, which gave him an appearance of helplessness that cut me to the heart. Rupert nodded again. 'There is no actor alive who has your emotional range.'

'Encore!' called Jonno from the sofa where he had been entwined with Portia since lunch.

My father shook his head modestly and came to sit down next to me. I took his hand. It was cold and trembled slightly as I squeezed it. 'Cordelia!' he called gaily, in an attempt to recapture the Waldo of yore. 'Sing for Papa. One of Ariel's songs.'

Cordelia went to stand upon the hearth rug, her feet buried among the sleeping dogs and gave us 'Where the bee sucks' in a sweet soprano. Sir Oswald remained fully awake, staring at her, his eyes crossing and recrossing with desire.

'I haven't seen Annabel all afternoon,' I heard Maggie say to Rupert in an undertone. 'Not since she ran off in a pet.'

There had been several rows at lunch. Archie and Suke had quarrelled, yet again, about the morality of eating purely for pleasure. Archie maintained that a refined and inventive cuisine was the mark of a civilised nation.

'If there were enough food in the world for everyone then I might allow that. But,' Suke had turned in her chair to look at Sir Oswald, 'when half the world suffers from malnutrition, it ill becomes richer nations to fuss about soufflés and *court bouillons*. Gluttony is a moral crime.'

Sir Oswald, happily splashing through Archie's *crème de concombres*, felt all eyes upon him. He rubbed with his napkin at a spot of pale green that had fallen on to his paunch. 'A very good soup. Delicate flavour.' He smiled vaguely round the table. 'My congratulations to the cook.'

'But there are so many worse things than overeating,' I said, hoping to give the conversation a more general direction. 'I really think it's a venial sin. At least it doesn't hurt anyone else. Discounting the things that are actually against the law – well, there are awful cruelties like neglecting old people and letting them die of cold and loneliness, and making animals perform in circuses and –'

'Naturally those things are bad too.' Suke was relentless. 'But they don't cancel each other out. Besides, you're temporising again, Harriet. Trying to smooth things over. You'd do or say anything to avoid confrontation.' Yes, I jolly well would, I thought. 'I call that dishonest,' Suke continued with an earnest expression that I recognised was zeal for my good. 'Preferring to please people rather than tell the truth is a weakness. It will impede your spiritual and intellectual growth. Lies are fetters. Unless you're brave enough to make truth a priority you'll never be effective in fighting injustice.'

I caught Rupert's eye. It was amused. He raised a questioning eyebrow, waiting to hear my answer. I crumbled my roll while I tried to think of something to say in my own defence. It was most unfair. I had not on this occasion told a lie. But then I knew I would certainly have done so if it had suited me. Suke had unerringly put her finger on one of my chief defects, damn her.

'Harriet is deeply committed to social change.' My father's expression was solemn but I had seen mischief in his eyes. 'For two years now she has been a fully fledged anarchist.'

Everyone at the table had looked surprised, as well they might.

'If Harriet's an anarchist, I'm the Winter Queen of Bohemia,' said Archie.

Rupert continued to smile at intervals for the rest of lunch, as though recalling some private joke. Suke said nothing. But every time I glanced up her eyes were fixed on me with a look I can only describe as wondering.

After that the conversation had turned to Rupert's first venture as artistic director of the English Opera House, which was to be *Un Ballo in Maschera*. It seemed to have the most complicated plot, full of coincidences and mistaken identities. Rupert said it was far from his favourite Verdi opera but none the less it offered some interesting possibilities for interpretation. He and my father had an argument about whether jealousy was an indication of a deeply passionate temperament or of a cold, shallow one.

Everything had been going well until Suke told Annabel to think of starving children in India and finish her plateful of stewed chicken legs and beetroot, which was Suke's own contribution to the feast. Annabel had declared that it was disgusting – which indeed it was, containing not only grey pimply skin but also, on my plate anyway, a sad, scaly foot – and anyway she wasn't going to be bossed by a woman who looked like Telly Savalas. Rupert had been very sharp with her and Annabel had run from the room threatening to make us all sorry. We had heard the front door bang.

So when, after Cordelia's song, Maggie reminded us that Annabel had been missing for several hours, we began to feel worried. Cordelia went to look for her.

'That child is an infernal nuisance,' muttered Rupert when

she returned to say that Annabel was nowhere to be found. 'As for that stupid, meddlesome girl – by rights *she* should be sent out into the snow to look for her.'

I understood he meant Suke, who was in the library, working on *HUFF* with, I was prepared to bet, a delightful sense of being all square with the world. I looked about to see who might make up a search party. Jonno and Portia had disappeared, probably to bed. Sir Oswald and Miss Tipple were dozing by the fire. Pa had gone for a walk. Certainly Maggie should not be allowed to go out and I knew it was no good asking Archie. Cordelia, with her customary canniness, had melted away. Mrs Whale was busy with Father Terry's underpants in Bunton. That left Rupert and me.

He gave me a speaking glance before saying, 'I wonder if Annabel had any food on her.'

Dirk was sleeping before the fire, his muzzle quivering as he dreamed.

'It's worth a try. Let's find something of Annabel's to get him going.'

Dirk was reluctant to wake but ruthlessly we dragged him to the front door, thrust his nose into Annabel's riding boots and made noises of encouragement. I ought to have known. Just as I was fumbling with his lead, intending to clip it to his collar, Dirk went in half a second from a state of being hardly able to stiffen his legs to speedway racer.

'I'm awfully sorry,' I said as we watched him galloping down the drive.

We threw on coats and boots and went after him. Rupert refrained from comment on my stupidity but enlarged on Suke's until I began to fear for her safety, should we fail to find Annabel within the next hour. The falling snow inserted itself between our skins and our clothes with a fine disregard for our comfort. One of the standing giants shed its white mantle just as Rupert was passing, ennobling his shoulders with ermine.

From time to time I called Dirk's name and once he answered with a distant bark. We orientated ourselves by that bark and headed in the direction of two hills Rupert said were called The Cullions. The sky and snow-laden ground were indistinguishable, the horizon lost in shades of luminous grey from bone to lead. We walked briskly until I was glowing like the element of an electric fire. The snow melted on my heated forehead and ran into my eyes and my nose dribbled. Rupert walked a little ahead of me, muttering imprecations like an angry druid.

'Can I borrow your hanky?' I called in desperation, my gloves having reached saturation point.

Rupert stopped and gave it to me. While I blew and mopped he stamped his feet impatiently. 'This is a wild-goose chase. That bloody child is probably hiding somewhere, laughing her head off. Anyway, I don't know why I should feel obliged to take my hangover across inhospitable terrain in appalling weather to look for her, while her father and brother are snugly indoors, fornicating with your sisters.'

'You don't mean –' I began in alarm.

'No, not really.' Rupert looked exasperated. 'Do you honestly think I'd let that happen? Or, more to the point, that Cordelia would? Oswald's an idiot but he's a harmless one.'

'I hope so. But I do worry.' I told him what had happened in Sir Oswald's bedroom.

Rupert seemed to find it amusing. 'Even as a child you had an overdeveloped sense of danger. When Cordelia was a baby you were like a hen with one chick, following her about in case she stuck her finger in an electric socket or drank bleach. Clarissa wasn't the slightest bit interested in her until she grew some hair and could be shown off. A very pretty Italian au pair was supposed to look after her but she was in bed with Bron most of the time. Clarissa sacked her when she got pregnant.'

'Really? I never knew. Fancy you remembering that.'

'Bron came to me for help. He was very young. I didn't blame him. You used to carry Cordelia about everywhere, like Sindbad and the Old Man of the Sea. I don't suppose you've stopped worrying about her since.'

'Perhaps not.'

It was hardly a memory that flattered, but my vanity was gratified by Rupert remembering anything at all about me. I wondered how the problem with the au pair had been resolved and whether Bron had returned the money that must have been provided for its solution but before I could ask, Rupert said, 'It's stopped snowing.'

It had. The landscape, a moment ago a live, resisting, turbulent thing, was tranquil.

'Would you like it back?'

Rupert looked at the sodden handkerchief. 'Thank you, I prefer to drip. Call that blasted dog, would you?'

I wished, not for the first time, that we had found a name other than Dirk. He responded with several excited yips.

'He's found something,' I said with conviction. 'I recognise that note of self-congratulation.'

And indeed he had. As we climbed to the top of a bluff we found my father sitting on a rock, with Dirk prancing about him.

'Do take this animal away,' Pa said when we were near enough to speak. 'He has many square miles of emptiness to disport himself in. I can't see why he must do it exactly where I am. I've never liked dogs.'

He frowned at Dirk, who interpreted this as an instruction to bark in his ear.

'Sorry, Pa. He's thoroughly bad, I know. We're looking for Annabel. I don't suppose you've seen her? I could have sworn I heard a cry just then.'

'That was probably me. I was exulting in the silence and

communing with extravagant, tempestuous Nature when I felt a pang of hunger. Lunch being unsatisfactory I had provided myself with a small pabulum before setting out. I'd just put a chocolate biscuit to my lips when this great brute sprang out of nowhere and snatched it from my mouth. Naturally I yelled.'

'Listen! There it is again.'

Borne on the wind was a faint cry.

'I heard it that time.' Rupert set off towards it.

I clipped Dirk's lead to his collar and urged him to follow but he was reluctant to leave the contents of my father's pocket. In the end I persuaded Pa to part with a custard cream and by this means enticed Dirk onward. Several hundred yards ahead, in a deep gully, Annabel lay half-buried by snow. Rupert was leaning over her. I slithered down to join them. He had brushed away the snow, now a sinister pink in places, to expose the shining teeth of a mantrap that bit into the child's ankle and seemed to close through to the bone.

'The bastard who did this ought to be shot! All right, Annabel, keep still!' He stood up and pulled off his coat. 'Get this round her.'

I laid the coat over her. She seemed hardly aware of us and continued to scream at intervals. I wondered how long she had been lying there in agony, terrified that no one would find her. I held her head and murmured every consoling thing I could think of. Dirk lay down beside her and licked her face. Annabel turned towards him and put her hand on his great damp head.

Rupert was examining the trap. He was calm after the first outburst of anger. When he failed to get a purchase on the thing with his hands, he stood up and stamped hard with his heel. Annabel stopped screaming. She had fainted, but the trap was open.

'We need to stop the bleeding. Haven't you got a petticoat or something?'

Never having owned such a garment, I took off my skirt. Rupert bound Annabel's ankle and held the improvised bandage in place with my belt. Then he wrapped her in his coat and picked her up.

'You go ahead and telephone for an ambulance.'

I ran, stumbling over hidden rocks and twisting my ankles in holes. I saw the outline of my father still sitting alone on the top of his particular hill. I waved as I ran but he did not see me. Maggie came down to meet me as, barely able to speak, I came panting up the drive. I sat wheezing on a chair in the hall while she rang the hospital. Sir Oswald lumbered in and patted me kindly on the shoulder while I puffed out an explanation. He drew up another chair so he could sit beside me and hold my hand. I reminded myself that he was the father of the injured girl and allowed him to fondle my palm. I think he genuinely wanted to be comforting.

When Rupert arrived, he was in similar state of speechlessness. He was tall but not particularly muscular, and Annabel must have weighed five or six stones. He laid her on the extempore bed Maggie had made up on the floor and motioned to me to get off my chair so he could sit on it. He repulsed Sir Oswald's attempt to hold his hand, leaned his head back and took great gasping breaths.

'Maggie!' Annabel opened her eyes. 'I want Maggie.'

'I'm here.' Maggie was on her knees beside her in a trice. 'Eh, my duck, but you gave us a fright. If anything had happened –' she caught her breath. 'There now, my lamb, you'll be all right . . .'

'It hurts like stink,' Annabel wailed.

'You're a brave girl. I'm that proud of you.'

'It was me, Maggie,' said Annabel, between groans. 'I found the trap. In the stables. When I went to see if I'd caught anything I couldn't find it. It was covered with snow – and then I trod on it.'

'Whatever did you want to go and do that for?'

'I wanted to make you all scared.'

'You did that, right enough. I've been that worried. What was it you was going to ketch in the nasty thing?'

'I wanted something to put in the cupboard behind the Aga to make a horrible smell. I put in the meat I found in the paddock so everybody would think it was Fanny Cost's ghost.'

'Meat, dear? What meat's that?'

'It must be the chicken and cutlets I found in the fridge,' I said. 'And there was a rib of beef as well.'

Maggie looked at me, puzzled. 'You, dear?'

'You must have ordered it before you became ill. After Archie took over the cooking we didn't eat any meat. It was starting to smell so I chucked it into the field behind the stables for the foxes.'

'Eh, but, my lamb,' Maggie had turned back to Annabel, 'why did you want to scare us?'

'To show everyone, that's all. I was going to let you get really frightened and then I'd tell you it was me and laugh at the – the clots you'd made of yourselves. And I put the painting of Old Gally in the closet too.'

Maggie patted her tear-soaked cheek. 'I don't know what painting you mean, dear. No one's said anything about it to me. Perhaps you were dreaming.'

The little minx! I thought. Not only had she very nearly divorced me permanently from my wits but she had driven me panic-stricken and defenceless into the arms of – well, I could hardly blame Annabel for what had happened with Max. And, what was almost worse, it was another good story for 'Spook Hall' spoiled. Yet again, I should have to resort to imagination.

'I know what she means,' I said. 'But it isn't important. It was a jolly good joke, Annabel.' I smiled hypocritically, though, if it weren't for the wounded leg, I would willingly have put her over my knee and spanked her.

'But why did you do these nasty things, my precious?' asked Maggie. 'I can't understand why you wanted to frighten us.'

'You all think Cordelia's prettier and nicer than me.' Annabel let out a sob – whether of pain or jealousy I could not tell. 'But I'm cleverer than she is. Much!'

'My poppet, there's no gainsaying Cordelia's got very taking manners but no one thinks she's nicer nor prettier than you,' began Maggie.

'Daddy does!' cried Annabel. 'He loves her! And he doesn't care a bit about me.'

Sir Oswald drew in his breath and screwed up his eyes as though to reject the imputation. He stretched out a hand towards his daughter and patted the top of her head awkwardly. Annabel jerked her head away. The movement must have hurt her leg for she let out a shriek.

'Now, my dear,' Maggie stroked Annabel's forehead and brushed back wisps of wet hair. 'Be brave a bit longer. They're sending a helicopter special to take you to the hospital.'

Annabel let out another wail. 'And Rupert loves her too!'

'I – most – certainly – do – not!' These were the first words Rupert had spoken.

'Eh, of course he don't!' Maggie was firm, almost indignant. 'Not in the way you mean. I'm sure he's downright fond of both of you but Rupert's a sensible, grown man and he isn't going to be in love with any little girl, no matter how fetching her ways.' Maggie paused, perhaps reflecting that the same could not be said of Sir Oswald. 'You've let it all grow big in your mind and it just ain't true,' she went on. 'Now think what you'll be able to tell the girls at school about riding all the way to Sheffield in a helicopter.'

Annabel clutched Maggie's hand. 'Please – come to the hospital.'

'I'll come, don't you fret. Old Maggie won't leave you.' She bent to kiss the child's forehead. 'My pet, my pet.' I felt my chest tighten to hear the sound of love in Maggie's voice, at last allowed free rein.

Archie opened the drawing-room door, saw Annabel's leg trussed in my bloody skirt, shuddered and withdrew his head. Cordelia came running down the stairs.

'Crikey!' cried Cordelia. 'I've never seen so much blood before. Does it hurt like mad?' She bent over Annabel and examined her leg with morbid relish. 'I hope you get a doctor that looks like Dirk Bogarde in *Doctor in the House*. Only more experienced. It's all working out like in *The Railway Children*. They'll have to put your leg in plaster like the hound in the red jersey. Or,' her eyes grew bright with inspiration, 'have you seen *Reach for the Sky*? It's about Douglas Bader. He has a plane crash and they have to cut both his legs off.'

Annabel screamed long and loud, a sound that hurt my ears and made Sir Oswald sob. 'Maggie, don't let them cut my leg off! I won't go to hospital! I won't!' She screamed again with terror.

I shook my head at Cordelia and frowned.

'Annabel!' said Rupert. 'Stop that noise! I've examined your leg and I can assure you no one's going to amputate it. You'll be fine in a week or two. But if you scream *once* more I shall cut off your head myself.'

It was stern stuff but it worked. Annabel continued to whimper but she was calm.

'Listen, the helicopter's coming.' Maggie gently released the child's grip on her sleeve. 'I'd better get a bag packed.'

'Rupert!' Annabel twisted her head until she could see him. 'Hold my hand. Please.'

Rupert leaned forward and took her grubby fingers in his.

She pressed it against her cheek. It looked very large and dark against her white face with the stormy eyes softened by pain and love. Cordelia waggled her eyebrows and sent me conspiratorial looks.

'Maggie.' Sir Oswald spread his arms wide in a gesture of helplessness. 'What about me?'

'The child needs me, Oswald,' said Maggie. 'You must see that.'

'Don't worry, Lady Pye.' Suke had come into the hall from the library. 'You go with Annabel. I'll take care of everything while you're away. You needn't worry about a thing.'

'Bless you, lass!'

Sir Oswald's beaky upper lip trembled as he caught Suke's eye.

THIRTY-FOUR

As Maggie had gone to the hospital with Annabel, and Mrs Whale was still in Bunton pegging away at the jobs Father Terry was too spiritually exalted to do for himself, it fell to Suke and me to dismantle Annabel's recreation of the ghost of Fanny Cost. The old chimney flue that ran from the kitchen up to the dining room and presumably to several bedrooms above, must have been bricked up when the Aga was installed some years ago but a low door had been put in, probably to allow the flue to be swept.

We found a torch in one of the kitchen drawers, soaked handkerchiefs with disinfectant, held them to our noses, and crawled in. It was a strange otherworldly place of shadows and soot-laden cobwebs but you could stand upright and walk about in quite a large area. Patches of newer stonework and brick walls showed how the arrangement of rooms had been altered over the years.

'Look!' Suke shone the torch upwards and I saw pinpricks of light where the wall joined the ceiling. 'Airbricks. That's how the smell got into the corridor.' She swung the beam round. 'And here's the old fireplace still complete – ovens, grates, a spit and everything. They must have moved the entire kitchen some time this century.' She swung the light over our heads. 'Look at the maze of old flues leading off this one!'

Usually I am fascinated by lessons in social history but on this occasion the ghastly smell that was getting the better of the disinfectant made me less keen. It was easy to locate the shelf on which lay the rotting meat. The Aga on the other side of the wall kept it at a steady decomposing temperature. We had brought a bucket and a shovel with us and quickly we scooped up the putrefying flesh and poured water and disinfectant over the shelf.

'Well,' said Suke, as we walked through the freezing dusky air to the paddock to dispose of the bucket's contents, 'I bet that old bricked-up kitchen has seen a thing or two in its time. If only stones could speak.'

'Wouldn't it be marvellous to be able to go back in time for a few hours?' I was delighted that for once Suke and I were on the same wavelength. 'Think of all the conversations over cups of tea that have gone on round that wonderful old fireplace – confidences, jokes, quarrels, assignations, perhaps even lovers' vows exchanged.'

'There'd have been little time for all that while they were toiling every minute of the day to produce elaborate meals for their lords and masters. As for cups of tea – tea was hugely expensive and the mistress of the house kept it locked in a caddy for her own use. The servants would have drunk small beer.'

'Of course you're right. I wasn't thinking.'

'The work was hard and the hours were long.' Suke resumed her lecturing tone as we started to walk back to the house. 'Girls as young as twelve would stand in the freezing scullery, scouring pots with sand until their fingers were raw and they were weeping with tiredness. And boys the same age would be sent up the flues to clean them, scorching their hands and feet and scraping their elbows and knees until they bled. It was not unknown for children to get stuck in the chimneys and die.'

'Oh dear. How depressing. Thank goodness things are better now.'

'There's no room for complacency. There are sweatshops and carpet factories all over the world that use child labour. And child pornography and prostitution are commonplace. Everywhere the rich exploit the poor, the strong seize power to benefit themselves and the weak go to the wall.'

'Surely not in this country?'

The light from the back door, to which we had returned, gleamed on Suke's shaved head as she shook it sorrowfully. 'How little you know about how the other half live. Our inner cities are a disgrace – filthy slums crammed with illiterate paupers.'

'Well,' I resolutely put some cheerfulness into my voice, 'at least we don't use poor darling dogs and donkeys to turn spits any more.'

'Poor darling dogs and donkeys?' Suke looked at me with an expression of absolute contempt. 'Really, Harriet! I sometimes wonder if you are capable of seriousness.'

'What? But I *was* being . . .' I was talking to empty air as Suke had walked off.

Luckily Annabel's other amusing practical joke needed no deconstruction. The tremendous racket of the helicopter arriving to collect Annabel and Maggie had brought Jonno and Portia, a little tousled-looking, down from their bower of bliss. I had filled them in on the afternoon's events and later that evening the three of us went to see how Annabel had worked the trick of making Old Gally appear in the cupboard in my bedroom. In the room that had been the bishop's, next to mine, we discovered an identical cupboard backing on to ours.

'Ha!' Jonno lifted up a plain piece of wood that hung on the wall and turned it round. The other side was a mirror, our mirror. It had been covering a hole in the panelling. 'It's quite obvious how my bad little sister did it. This is a powder closet. In the days when people wore powder on their hair, they stuck their heads through this hole and their maids or valets dusted it – with a mixture of things like orris root and nutmeg – so it didn't get on their clothes. Peculiar idea, wasn't it? I suppose they wanted to keep the fleas at bay and conceal the stink of drains and BO.'

'Maggie must have put the mirror over the hole to save the bishop from the temptation of letting his eyes wander over your tender young limbs,' suggested Portia.

I could hardly believe I had been so easily taken in. 'So Annabel replaced the mirror with the portrait of Old Gally and then scratched at the panelling to draw Cordelia's attention to it. Pity she didn't know that Cordelia sleeps like the kraken. But there was blood glistening on the neck.'

When we examined the portrait in the long gallery with the aid of a torch we found flakes of red paint clinging to the canvas in the region of the ruff.

'You've got to hand it to Annabel,' said Portia, 'she's an ingenious child and a credit to the family.'

'It wouldn't be hard to be a credit to this family,' said Jonno. 'A worse set of wastrels and ne'er-do-wells you'd have to go a long way to find. We're in urgent need of reform.' His expression became soupy. 'Do you think, my darling Portia, you might find it in your heart to improve the stock a little?'

Finding myself suddenly surplus to requirement, I sidled off into my bedroom before they could discuss the subject further.

Despite Cordelia's persistent nagging I had refused to read

Max's letter until after she had gone to bed. When I was certain she was asleep I made myself comfortable in the chair by our bedroom fire and tore open the envelope. 'My darling Harriet,' it began.

Just writing your name excites me and brings back the exquisite pleasure of making love to you. God, I miss you more than I can describe. When I think of that soft place behind your ear, so pale with fine dark tendrils of hair, I feel weak. I can see your face very clearly, the big dark eyes, the lower lids curving up so sweetly at the outer corners, your long dark brows, that serious expression you have when watching other people as though you want to get to the heart of them. Your perfect slender nose above that full sexy upper lip. I want to run my hands again over your soft little breasts, to kiss your infinitely precious

I never discovered what else he was going to run his hands over and kiss because at that point I put the letter in the fire and watched the paper blacken and burn in seconds. Had he also written to Georgia, detailing her face and body and seducing her by post? I took the poker and prodded the flimsy ashes until they were atoms.

What added up to a few days of flirtation and an hour or so in bed was over. Max was my third lover in four years. But only with Dodge had there been anything that could be called a proper affair, a connection of minds as well as bodies. My mind slid away from thoughts of Hugo Dance. Apart from the fact that he had an unhappy wife, I knew nothing at all about Max. He had charmed me into acquiescence by flattery, both blatant and subtle, and such was my vanity that I had fallen for it. I did not seem very good at relationships with men. I wondered what was wrong with me.

The fire burned low and I came to no conclusion. I took up my sponge bag and towel. With any luck there would be no one in the bathroom. As I wandered the length of the Long Gallery, still cogitating on the mysteries of sexual attraction, I noticed almost subliminally that something was different. I turned back to look. On the chest lay the case, the chain curled beside it. Old Gally's arm had gone.

'Oh damn!' I said loudly, to reassure myself. 'Someone's playing stupid tricks again.'

I stared up and down the Gallery. The lights seemed to waver and dim. Probably the generator was struggling to digest a speck of dirt. It was unusually quiet. Even the wind was no more than a playful whisper and above it I could hear the sound of the waterfall. I set off purposefully for the bathroom. It seemed a long way. Something shimmered to my left. I turned my head quickly but it was only the Gorgon tapestry moving slightly in a draught. I smiled to myself. I had no intention of playing into the hands of some malicious practical joker. The bathroom door was clearly in view now. I quickened my step.

And then I saw it.

I had drawn the curtains in the large central bay myself, earlier in the evening, all fifteen feet of gold silk trimmed with tarnished silver *passementerie*. Now the curtains bulged out in the middle as though someone was standing behind them. And as I looked at them the silk began to billow and from the folds came the hand of Old Gally. Just before the lights failed altogether, a last beam glinted on its metal finger that pointed directly at my heart.

I didn't mean to scream but it was out before I knew it. By screaming I frightened myself even more. Abandoning calm good sense I broke into a run towards the bathroom with the sole idea of barricading myself in. But when I patted frantically all over the wall and the door and finally found the handle, the door was locked. I hammered on it, yelling with fear, and within a few seconds it opened, just as the lights came on again.

'How impatient you women are.' Rupert stood in the door-way in his dressing gown. 'In a house as poorly provided with bathrooms as this one, you must wait your turn.'

I grabbed his arm. 'He's there! Behind the curtains!'

'Who?'

'Old Gally!'

'Nonsense! Let go.' He shook off my hand. 'You're cutting off my blood supply.'

I relaxed my grip and contented myself with hanging on to his sleeve. When we reached the main bay I stood behind Rupert, hardly daring to look. The hand seemed to twitch as the curtains swayed. Slowly the finger swivelled towards us.

'Harriet, if you screech in my ear once more I shall lose my temper. It's been a long day, not helped by the ridiculous behaviour of several young women.'

Rupert went to the window and flung back the curtains. The arm remained suspended in mid-air but the body to which it belonged was invisible. I stuffed my hand into my mouth to stifle another scream.

'Just as I thought. Come and see.' Rupert took hold of the hand and pulled. 'Black cotton. Pinned to the curtain. Look here.'

Mystified, I stared at the safety pins attached to the lining. From them trailed long strands of thread. Another length was wound round the metal arm in several places, including the pointing middle digit. Rupert turned it over. It clanked with a dismal sound but all at once it had lost its power to frighten me.

He laughed. 'It's missing its index finger. Looks rather silly, doesn't it?'

I had to agree that it did. 'I found the finger in Maggie's

room. I hid it because I didn't want her to be scared. Jonno's got it now.'

'Here. You hold it while I close the window. There's a terrific draught. That's what made the curtains move.'

I examined the arm again, wondering how I could ever have been afraid of such a rusty, battered object. 'Who put it here, do you think?'

'It's pretty obvious, isn't it? Who's so jealous of Maggie that they'd want to frighten her? Who heard me suggest that we bring in the police and put the arm back in the case within the hour?'

I tried, and failed, to remember who had been in the dining room at breakfast on that particular morning at that particular time. 'How did they undo the padlock if the key was always on Maggie's belt?'

'Maggie catnaps constantly. Anyone could take it while she's dozing.' It was true. I remembered finding her in Freddie's studio, deeply asleep. 'Once the arm was back in its case I made Maggie give me the key. I took it with me to London. That's why the joker only had the finger to play with. I gave the key back to Maggie when I returned and it's on her chatelaine now. You left it in the hall.'

So I had. As Maggie was following the stretcher into the helicopter she had put the chatelaine with the keys into my hand, with instructions to give them to Janet. But Mrs Whale had not returned from Bunton by the time I went up to bed. I remembered noticing it on the hall table, still, when I went up to bed.

'But why go to all the trouble of setting this up? If you're right about Maggie being the one it was meant to frighten, everyone knows Maggie isn't here. Except, of course – Oh, but that's impossible!'

A faint creaking sound behind us made me spin round.

'You can come out now, Mrs Whale,' said Rupert without

raising his voice. There was a moment's silence. 'Either you come out of your own accord or I ring for the police.' Another pause. Then the door opposite the bay that had been Max's room opened and Janet Whale stepped into the gallery.

She looked shockingly different. She wore a gaudy scarf over a red dress, large gilt earrings and plenty of makeup. Her mouth was a scarlet line of scorn. 'Think you're clever, don't you! But Maggie'll never believe anything against me. She's known me all her life. We're old friends.' She put a weight of sarcasm on the last word.

'But why?' I was amazed. 'Why would you want to hurt Maggie – to frighten her? She's been so good to you!'

'You wait until you're in a position to have someone be good to you and see how you like it.' Mrs Whale was almost spitting with sudden temper. Her meekness had become flaring defiance. 'Why should *she* have all that money and a husband and this house and a respectable place in the world? *Lady* Pye.' She dropped a curtsy, her expression contemptuous. 'We used to laugh at her at school, she was so slow at lessons, and the boys used to call her Mag the Nag because of her ugly horse face. But the silly creature didn't mind. She was always soft and good-natured. Everyone took advantage of her. If her father hadn't made money with the carpets *she*'d have been the skivvy, while I – if I'd had better luck I might have stayed on at school, done my higher certificate. Perhaps even gone to university. I'd have seen the world and made a decent life for myself. Instead of which . . .' She sighed. 'Every day I wait on her at table. Every day I dust *her* things, I wash *her* crocks, I polish *her* floors. And *he*, why he's nothing but a bag of blubber. He don't even see me when I cross the room. I'm nothing to him. Though I'm cleverer than him by far, I have to wash the food off his clothes and carry in his breakfast while he snores in bed, and take the tray away again when he's guzzled it. And those children, they haven't respect for anyone. I've to live out my life in this place with the wind howling sometimes so's I can't hear myself think and be nothing to anyone.'

'But Maggie's so fond of you,' I said. 'And she works every bit as hard. It was such a cruel thing to do!'

Mrs Whale smiled. 'It did me good to see her worrying over it and turning it over in her mind. It made me laugh. Why shouldn't she know what it is to be unhappy? There was some justice in it, then.'

'Maggie's gone to the hospital with Annabel,' said Rupert. 'The child's had an accident. So this evening's little diversion was a waste of time. You can pack your belongings in the morning and leave first thing.'

'Why should I? Maggie'll never believe it was me. She's convinced Old Gally walks, the daft thing.' She grinned very unpleasantly. 'It isn't against the law to play a few tricks on a friend. I've done nothing wrong and you can't make me go.'

Rupert sighed. 'Maggie's told me your history. At least, she's told me the lie you concocted to win her sympathy. You didn't kill your ex-husband, did you? I had the police do a check on you. You went to prison all right but it was for murdering the old man you and your husband were supposed to be looking after. You wanted his money and you couldn't wait. Your husband's still serving his sentence.'

'I ought never to have married that fool. He never did anything right. I got twelve years for helping him. All I did was buy the weed-killer and wash up the cup afterwards. I wasn't even in the room when he gave it to the old skinflint.' Her expression was bitter. 'You don't know what prison's like. Scum of the earth, that's how they treat you. And that's how you feel. It's worse than death not to be free. I tried to hang myself but they cut me down. So I went religious and got parole. But there's no such thing as forgive and forget in *this* world.'

Rupert sighed. 'What do you think about going right away from here?'

'Where can I go? I've no references. If I do get a job, sooner or later people find out who I am. The newspapers see to that. They hound you until you've nowhere left to run. People are afraid I'm going to poison them. At least that's what they pretend. The truth is there's that amount of hate in folk they're glad to find someone they can hate and not feel guilty for it.' She laughed, a woeful sound. 'I'm a pariah.'

I felt some small return of sympathy. What must it be like to have put yourself, by some moment of weakness, of desperation, for ever beyond the pale?

'Maggie said you'd worked in the theatre,' said Rupert. 'Was that true?'

'Yes. I shouldn't ever have left it. Only *he* came whining round me and I was stupid enough to fall for him all over again.'

'A friend of mine's starting a new theatrical company, based in Birmingham,' said Rupert. 'They need a wardrobe mistress. He'll take you if I ask him. It'd be poorish pay at first but you could make something of it with hard work. Do you think you could make a fresh start?'

'You'd do that for me?'

'I'd do it for Maggie.'

She frowned. 'You wouldn't tell him about – about my past?'

'I'd have to. As you say, he'll find out sooner or later. But theatre people are more broad-minded than most. If you behave yourself, you'll get a second chance.'

She breathed in sharply and her eyes flashed. She must once have been a striking-looking woman. 'I'll do it. I'll be glad to get away from here and shake the dust of the mean, petty place off my shoes! I'll be glad not to have to run round after people that think they're better than me, though I can see what fools they are.'

'All right,' said Rupert. 'But the condition is that you leave tomorrow. You needn't say anything to anyone. I'll explain to the Pyes. You can go straight to Birmingham. I'll give you the address of some theatrical digs. And money to tide you over.'

'You won't want thanks as you aren't doing it for me.' Her passionate mouth stretched into a sneer. 'I wonder if you'd think so much of Maggie if she hadn't married Sir Oswald Pye of Pye Place. I don't think so, somehow.'

Rupert continued to gaze at her impassively and said not a word. So she lifted her chin and walked away, a splash of hard, bright colour against the faded beauty of her surroundings.

I felt angry but more than that, I felt sad. 'I'm amazed,' I said. 'I fell for her act completely. What made you suspect her?'

'A process of elimination, really. And she seemed a little too humble to be true. Truly pious people don't generally flaunt their humility. Call it intuition.'

'I thought women were supposed to be the intuitive ones.'

'You fell for it because you wanted to believe her. You're sympathetic by nature. I'm not.'

'Most people would have been much harder on her. Do you think she'll make a go of it?'

Rupert shrugged. 'No idea. Anyway, I'm not a policeman. It isn't my job to reward the good and punish the bad. I dislike examining the psyches of my fellow human beings. I've no desire to see into other people's minds and hearts.'

'Unless they're characters in an opera.' I was remembering the discussion at lunch. I thought I was beginning to understand Rupert. He tried to avoid intimacy with all but a few. It went against the grain with him to speak of his own feelings because he was afraid of weakening his defences. 'You prefer a world of make-believe, too.'

'What *are* you talking about?'

I smiled enigmatically and changed the subject. 'It was purest spite that made Mrs Whale torment poor Maggie. And after such kindness. But I feel sorry for her. Oh, look! Puddles of water! It couldn't be – the Lady of the Moat?'

'I was in the bath when you rattled the roof tiles with your screams,' said Rupert. 'I've been dripping gently ever since.'

'It's so disappointing. There's always the most prosaic explanation. Black cotton! It takes the excitement out of writing about it when I have to pretend. Thank goodness I finished my article about Old Gally's arm while I was still more than halfway to believing in it. But I shall have to invent mystery and terror when I write about Fanny Cost – and seeing Old Gally in the powder closet. You know, it never occurred to me that there might be two hoaxers.'

'Annabel's antics give a new meaning to the thoroughly tedious and typically pedagogic idea of burdening children with holiday projects. Surely you didn't really believe in either case that supernatural forces were responsible?'

'Well, it's extraordinary how different things seem when you're on your own in the dark.'

'Certainly, if you allow your imagination to run out of control.'

'Don't you ever get frightened?'

'It has been known. But not of ghosts. The living seem to me considerably more dangerous. So, are you pleased or sorry to have a rational explanation?'

'Mostly extremely sorry. I shall sleep better but, oh! what a let down! Imagine if we had conclusive proof that there *is* life after death!'

'Proof of the existence of ghosts wouldn't prove a continuation of consciousness. Spectral manifestations might be impressions left behind from past lives that we perceive intuitively – a sort of psychic dust. But even if one could prove that these emanations were genuine phantom angst – a guilty conscience or a cry for justice – a confirmation of life after death would mean the end of other kinds of philosophical possibilities. *Not* knowing, we have freedom to believe what we will. That seems preferable to me. I'm going to bed. If you feel another scream coming on perhaps you'll be considerate enough to stifle it till morning. Good night.'

Watching him walk away, I could not help contrasting his behaviour with Max's.

THIRTY-FIVE

'I wish we didn't have to go.'

Cordelia probably spoke for all of us as we drove down the winding hill towards the village. I had turned back for a last glimpse of the house and the waterfall to see a forlorn Sir Oswald waving his handkerchief on the doorstep. The minute Archie put in the clutch Portia and Jonno had rushed indoors. They were catching the train to Manchester that evening. She had embraced us all and sworn she would telephone but I knew her thoughts had flown ahead to life with Jonno.

Much of the sorrow in Cordelia's voice was attributable to the knowledge that, immediately following our return home, things would be said and done about schools. But also, like the rest of us, she had been happy at Pye Place. An atmosphere of unreality had prevailed that had served to stimulate the imagination and relax one's usual constraints. For a time we had been out of the ordinary world, transposed to somewhere savagely beautiful, where it seemed quite natural for behaviour to run to extremes. It was the first time I had spent any time with a family other than my own and it had shown me that context was of crucial importance to one's idea of oneself.

We had slowed to a crawl, waiting for a herd of cows to discover that there was no way to go but forward.

'Archie?'

'Harriet.'

'What was your childhood like?'

'I was an only child. I lived with my mother and her sister in a small house in Chelsea. At least Mother called it Chelsea. Others might have thought it was Fulham. I was spoiled and petted by all the women who came to drink tea and discuss the neutering of stray cats and the homing of kittens. Mother was de*vot*ed to felines but suspicious of men and thought my father had let her down badly by allowing himself to be killed in the war. How I came to be born at all is a mystery. When she spoke of my father – which was infrequently – she evoked a terrifying being of sordid and shameful habits. He had been a doctor, specialising in diseases of the bladder. Perhaps it was that she objected to. She *dread*ed the medical profession, and urologists in particular, and made me wear ladies' lock-knit drawers to keep my urinary tract warm.'

'You're making this up!'

'It's true. She hated boys' rough games and paid extra for me to learn music and needlework with the girls. I had a beautiful treble voice and once sang "O for the Wings of a Dove" at a concert, wearing a white nightdress of my aunt's and accompanying myself on the harp. The audience passed handkerchiefs up and down the rows. I went meekly along with my mother's commands and proscriptions – an innocent, curly-haired, harp-playing, slightly *sweaty* boy – because of the woollen underwear, you understand – until one day I met an artist who wanted to paint me in the *nude*.'

'Which one of you was nude?' put in Cordelia.

'Quite quickly we both were. Ah! At last that lummox of a boy has had the sense to drive those silly cows into a gateway.' He wound down the window. 'Young man,' he addressed the astonished drover, 'I intend to report you for appearing in public in a costume liable to incite lewd behaviour.'

The cowherd looked down at his khaki jersey, mud-splashed dungarees and gumboots in bewilderment as we accelerated away so fast that the entire herd turned tail and ran back up the lane.

Had Archie made up all that stuff about his childhood? I wondered. It would appear to be a pattern upbringing for a gay, exhibitionist hypochondriac. But when you knew Archie, those characteristics were almost the least important things about him. What had engendered his wisdom, wit and kindness? His moods, his sensitivities, his predilections? I wondered if families might be less important, when it came to the shaping of personality, than I had previously thought.

'What did Sir Oswald give you?' Cordelia interrupted my speculations. 'I saw him tuck something into your glove on the doorstep when you kissed him goodbye.'

'I haven't looked.' I turned over the little green box in my hand.

'Well, go on.' She gave me an impatient nudge with her elbow, which hurt as she was practically sitting on my knee. Rupert, because of his length of leg, was once more in the front passenger seat. Pa, Cordelia, Dirk and I were squeezed into the back. Dirk seemed to have doubled in size in ten days. His head hung over Rupert's shoulder and from time to time he gave his ear an exploratory lick.

Our discomfort was greatly added to by being miserably cold. Pa said he was sorry but he had developed raging claustrophobia during his spell of imprisonment and being cooped up in a car with four people and an enormous dog would, he feared, bring on a panic attack unless we had all the windows open. Rupert and Archie were wonderfully good about this. I saw Rupert several times hitch his scarf closer round his ears – or it may have been a defence against Dirk's tongue – but he had said not a word of protest. Archie had taken from his luggage a splendid old-fashioned motoring cap with ear-flaps, which he had fastened beneath his chin. Leaning forward, clutching the wheel and baring his teeth, he looked more than ever like Mr Toad.

'Well?' said Cordelia. 'What is it?'

I opened the box. It was a charming little brooch, a silver acorn cup set against an oak leaf. The acorn was a pearl. 'It really *is* beautiful. How good of him.' I was delighted and moved. And sorry that I had sometimes entertained unkind thoughts about this most generous of hosts. 'I must write and thank him as soon as we get home.'

'Huh! That's nothing,' said Cordelia. 'Wait till you see what he gave me.' Cordelia fished about in her coat pocket, banging me in the eye and causing Dirk to thrust his claws into my leg. 'Get a load of this!'

She held up a two-strand necklace of the most beautiful, lustrous pearls. A clasp of emeralds and diamonds winked as they blew about in the blast of freezing air.

'Cordelia! Oh, my heaven! It must be worth thousands. Archie, stop the car! We must turn round and go back. We can't possibly accept such a valuable thing!'

'We?' Cordelia was indignant. 'He gave it to *me*! And I'm going to keep it. Actually I don't like it much but I'm certainly not giving it back.'

'Make her see that she must, Pa,' I said urgently. 'It's probably an heirloom. It ought to go to Annabel. It would be very wrong to keep it.'

'Annabel's got masses of stuff to inherit.' Cordelia spoke before Pa could answer. 'I saw what was in the box when Sir Oswald got it out. Piles of things. Besides, he won't want it back. It was the price of my silence.'

'Cordelia! What do you mean?'

'I bloody well earned it.' Cordelia put her nose in the air

and glanced sideways at me, enjoying my consternation. I caught Rupert's eye in the rear-view mirror. His expression was unreadable.

'What did he make you do?' I demanded.

'Oh, not what you're thinking.' Cordelia stuck out her tongue. 'So there, Miss Fussy-Knickers. And we all know who got into yours.'

'Cordelia! Tell me at once! Or Pa will make you.'

My father looked at me inquiringly.

'All right,' she said. 'Don't get so uptight. It was yesterday while you and Rupert were out searching for Annabel. Sir Oswald asked me to come upstairs to his bedroom.'

'Cordelia, you must *never* go into a bedroom alone with a man again. Promise me you won't!'

'Don't be silly. My husband's going to be pretty annoyed on my wedding night if I say I can't go into a bedroom alone with him because I promised my sister. Or perhaps you'd like to come in with us to make sure I'm all right?' Cordelia could be maddeningly sarcastic when she wished. I wanted to shake her.

'She's got a point there.' I could see my father was trying not to laugh.

I gave him a furious look. 'This is serious. What did he make you do?'

'Nothing much. He made me lie on his bed. He stroked my hand and looked soppy and grinny. You know how men do when they fancy you.'

I heard something like a snort from the front of the car, which I ignored.

'Go on,' I said.

'He went on about me being an angel and said he wanted to show me how to fly with him up to heaven. I thought, if you think I'm going along with that you've got another think coming. It was incredibly boring, so after a bit I started to get up. Then he unzipped his trousers and got his thing out.'

I groaned and put my head in my hands. 'Why didn't you tell me? I feel so responsible.'

'That's bilge! I suppose you didn't tell Sir Oswald to fall desperately in love with me? *Some* people always want to make themselves out to be important even when they had nothing to do with it. Anyway, I said, "Put it away. It's horrible. I don't want to see it. If you don't I shall scream for help and you'll be arrested because I'm underage and it's called peedo – something." Sir Oswald started to cry and said he was very sorry and he knew he shouldn't have but he was so much in love with me that he couldn't help himself. So I said, "Stop crying, it's all right and I won't tell anyone if you never, ever do it again, not just to me but to any girl because no one likes looking at such a revolting thing." He promised he wouldn't. So you see,' she smirked at me triumphantly, 'I've probably saved some poor girl less intelligent than me a very nasty shock.'

'I must say Cordelia, you seem to have handled the situation with remarkable aplomb,' said my father. 'Though,' he assumed a look of mock-severity, 'you have already broken your word about not telling.'

I gave him a burning glance of reproach. 'But suppose he hadn't co-operated? Another man might well have tried to – force himself on her.'

'I'd have kicked him where it hurts,' said Cordelia promptly. 'I know it's absolute agony if you do that. And they can never have sex ever again. They're importunate for the rest of their lives.'

This was too much for Rupert and Archie. They almost yelled with laughter. I did not know what to say. If such a thing had happened to me at the age of twelve, I would have been horribly frightened, agonisingly embarrassed and probably put off sex for good. Cordelia had evidently been none of these things. Perhaps some innate wisdom had told her that Sir Oswald was a feeble, unhappy man – harmless, as Rupert had said. Perhaps she was, as she so often claimed, more able to deal with life than I, more perceptive of human strengths and weaknesses. Was I making too much of it? No harm had been done. But it could so easily have been disastrous. But then, one could say this of nearly every situation in life. I was baffled.

'That necklace must go back,' I said.

As we left the High Peak behind and the roads became straighter Archie drove faster. He kept his hand more or less continuously on the horn through towns. When we overtook a bus on the brow of a hill my father was moved to protest that as his hair could not turn any whiter, presumably its next reaction to severe shock would be to fall out altogether. And he feared the love of his life might revolt against a man with a pate as bald as a baby's. I felt a trickle of pain when he said that. He had been very busy on the telephone before we left. His voice had been charged with enthusiasm and he had laughed a lot in a bright, eager way, which made me certain he was not talking to Ma. I closed my eyes in order not to see lorries with huge radiators and sixteen enormous wheels coming straight towards us and tried not to think about the future.

We stopped for lunch at the same hotel. As we entered the dining room, a stunned silence was swiftly followed by an excited hum of talk. I overheard snatches of conversation as we were shown to our table.

'It *is* him. I'm sure of it. You remember. Waldo Byng – oh, yes, he murdered that actor – now what was his name? No, he didn't, you silly, at least he got away with it. Extraordinary people he's with – that man with the cloak – isn't it called an Inverness cape? – but, my dear, purple eye shadow! Do look

564

at that child – perfectly angelic – I wonder who that tall, distinguished-looking man is? – vaguely familiar – didn't I see him in the newspaper the other day?'

My father, aware that many eyes were upon him, straightened up and put on his Henry V face – all keen, boyish charm. 'Waiter!' he called. 'Dom Pérignon, *prestissimo, per favore*. The '68 will do. And bring the menu at once.' He rubbed his hands. 'Give us great meals of beef and iron and steel. We will eat like *wolves* and fight like *devils*!'

The waiter looked alarmed. I hoped Rupert was not expected to pay for this performance with a hefty bill.

'That's Shakespeare,' a superior-looking woman informed the rest of her table. 'One of the history plays.' Throughout lunch they sat with their heads inclined towards us, like seedlings growing towards the light, hoping for more snippets of culture.

'Harriet, you cannot possibly have tomato juice and a plain omelette.' My father's voice must have been audible in the kitchen. 'Never let it be said that a child of mine was a killjoy. You'll offend the cook.' He called the waiter back. 'Madam will have the *fritto misto*, followed by the *tournedos Rossini*, rare, with *pommes noisette* and a green salad. There!' He beamed across the table at me. 'That will put colour in your cheeks. You're looking quite pinched.'

I expect I was. My blood was gelid due to the interior temperature of the car. I glanced apologetically at Rupert, but he was frowning over the wine list.

We reached London by the late afternoon. The champagne and the enormous quantity of food we had eaten meant that we all, except Archie luckily, slept for the remainder of the journey. I woke suddenly to see that we were bowling down The Avenue only yards from our house. I experienced the customary rush of pleasure on seeing it. As Archie gave the brake a violent jab with his foot, the squeal of tyres and the restraining clutch of seat belts woke the others. Mark Antony, about whom I had had many anxious thoughts during the last ten days, was on the doorstep flanked by a couple of photographers, who were leaning against the columns of the porch, reading newspapers. The faces of the latter were transfigured by joy as they came galloping down the path.

'Is my hair sticking up?' My father tried to see himself in the rear-view mirror.

'There isn't enough of it to stick up, Pa,' said Cordelia with the grumpiness of the just-woken. 'Hat, open the door and let Dirk out. He's crumpled my skirt and dribbled all over it.'

My father smoothed a licked finger over his eyebrows and took several measured breaths. 'Mi, mi, mi, mi!' he sang before stepping out of the car. 'Good evening, gentlemen.'

'Sir! Mr Byng, sir! Look this way!' Cameras flashed. 'Great! Lovely! How are you, sir? How does it feel to be a free man again? Crikey, is that a dog or a horse? Let's have one of you with the girls. Happy family reunited. That's right – closer – smile, young ladies. That's great! Thanks, and another. Who are these two? Give us a photo, gents.' Archie posed in his motoring cap and cape. Rupert pushed past the photographers and walked up to the front door. I followed him, fumbling in my bag for the door key.

'They'll be ages.' I said. 'We might as well go in and get some fires going. Darling Mark Antony, I've missed you so much.' I picked him up and kissed him between his ears. He struggled in my arms and, the minute I put him down, stalked round to the back of the house. I knew it would be at least twenty-four hours before he would forgive our desertion and consent to be properly friendly again.

I could hear the telephone ringing as I turned the key in the lock. I kicked my way through a heap of letters on the doormat and went to answer it. It was Dilys Drelincourt, my father's agent. She sounded excited. It took a degree of persistence on my part to get Pa away from the cameras.

'Hello, Dil darling, how are you ... I'm fine ... Yes, tremendous form ... What? ... Wait a minute, say that again ... No! you're kidding ... Really? ... Oh, my God, but that's marvellous! Abso-ruddy-lutely marvellous!' Pa smacked his forehead with his hand and began to pace the floor to the length of the telephone wire, his eyes bright with excitement. I waited in the hall with him, longing to hear whatever this good news was and knowing he would want someone to tell immediately. 'OK, OK ... yes, right ... Ring them at once and say yes ... Good girl, Dil! We'll show them! Ha! Ha!'

At last he put the telephone down, threw his arms round me and danced me up and down the hall. 'Harriet! Darling girl! They're putting on a new production of *Othello* at the Kemble. A superb cast. Roderick Ripple's to play Iago, Lynda Layover's Desdemona. And,' his mouth trembled and his eyes filled with tears, 'guess who's going to be Othello?'

'Oh, Pa, Pa! My clever brilliant Pa!' I kissed him again and again. 'I'm so proud of you!'

My father wept a little. 'I thought no one would want me – I expected to eat the bitter bread of banishment – but Dilys says audiences will be sympathetic, she thinks it'll be an added draw. She's already had offers of other parts. They're clamouring for me.' He wiped his eyes and looked solemn. 'Sweet are the uses of adversity, which like the toad, ugly and venomous, wears yet a precious jewel in his head.' Then he snatched up the telephone. 'I must ring Fleur at once and tell her.'

'But what about Ma? Aren't you going to tell her first?'

My father paused in the middle of dialling. He looked at me and something like guilt crept into his expression. 'Of course. Now, let me see, where's the number?'

I pointed to it on the pad. My father made comic faces at

me while he listened to the telephone ringing miles away in Cornwall.

'Hello? Can I speak to Mrs Byng? . . . Waldo Byng . . . Yes, it is, actually . . . Thank you, thank you . . . Yes, it certainly is . . . You're very kind . . . Thank you . . . Oh, I see . . . No, that's all right. I'll try again later. Just tell her when she comes in that I rang will you? Thanks. Goodbye.'

He put down the telephone. 'She and Ronnie have gone for a walk.' He sighed, his hand still on the receiver. Then he looked down at the table. 'Harriet, I can't think of a gentle way to say this, but you'll have to know some time. I'm so sorry, darling. I know of all of you it's going to hurt you the most. In fact I don't expect the others will mind too much. I hope not, anyway.' He winced and continued to stare at the pad on which the Cornish number was written. 'You see, what happened – my going to prison, I mean – well, it sort of pointed the way. It wasn't that that did it. We've been drifting apart for a long time, years really, but we were both too lazy, and perhaps too comfortable, to do anything about it. But while I was in prison I had a chance to think about things. And your mother did too. She's a marvellous woman – God, there's no one lovelier and more accomplished than Clarissa. I've been a lucky man, a very lucky man, to be married to her all these years. We'll always be the best of friends. But you see,' he gave a laugh that sounded rather sad, 'for a long time your mother hasn't wanted sex. She says she's bored with the whole thing. She can't be bothered with the mess and she doesn't like her hair getting tangled. Naturally I respect that – but, well, I'm a man. There's life in the old dog yet –' he laughed again – 'and Fleur and I, well, not to put too fine a point on it, we're in love. You'll love her too, I'm sure, when you get to know her. She's so fine and intelligent and beautiful.' At that moment he looked up and saw my face. 'Well, naturally, you may not feel – just at first . . .' He closed his eyes for a second and swallowed. 'Harriet, my darling, your mother has agreed to a divorce.'

I knew I ought to say something but I had no idea what. My face, in fact my whole body, had become absolutely rigid and all the time my muscles were pulling tighter and tighter like ropes round a windlass until I thought they might be going to snap. My limbs began to tremble with the tension. My mind said, this isn't true. It's all right – nothing's going to happen. This is nothing but a dream. You've always been so frightened of this and now you're dreaming about it. But it isn't true.

'I've got the fire going.' Rupert came into the hall from the drawing room. 'I think Archie and I'll push off now. I've got some calls to make and we're having dinner with some of the EOH committee. What's the matter?' When neither of us said anything, Rupert said impatiently, 'Harriet, you're absolutely white. What's the matter with you?'

I moved my hand experimentally. It jerked unnaturally as though operated by strings.

'Guess what, Rupe!' My father's voice was ringing with good cheer. 'I've been asked to play Othello at the Kemble!'

'Waldo! A coup indeed!' Rupert shook my father's hand and then they embraced. 'That'll be something to look forward to! I'm absolutely delighted.'

'You'll review it kindly, I hope.'

'I rather think my reviewing days are over.'

The front door opened to admit Archie and Cordelia. My father gave them the good news about *Othello* and there was further congratulation. Then Cordelia saw Mark Antony on the stairs and ran up in pursuit.

'We'll give you a hand with your cases.' Rupert's voice reverberated oddly in my ears. He seemed to be standing very far off.

'Bye, Harriet, dear girl.' Archie kissed my cheek. 'My, what glacial flesh! Be circumspect and mean with your favours until

569

we meet again. Remember that the primrose way leads to the everlasting bonfire.'

I smiled – it felt like a gape, a rictus.

The front door closed behind the three of them. I heard Cordelia upstairs, opening bedroom doors, calling Mark Antony. I walked stiffly into the drawing room as though on stilts. The firelight gave a pleasing glow but could do nothing for my frozen body. I went to the window and looked into the street.

My father was talking to Rupert and Archie. The street lamp was on now and their faces were cast into high relief. Pa ran his hand over his white bristly head then spread his arms wide and shrugged. He was telling them that he and my mother were going to divorce, that never again would we live together in this house as one large happy family. That was over; it was already something to be remembered only with pain. What had been most precious to me, what had kept me safe, what had been utterly to be relied upon, my prop and stay, my happiness, had been destroyed. My parents no longer loved each other. It was over.

A spasm of something like terror made my knees shake. I dropped on to the window seat and lowered my head until my forehead was pressed against the cool silk of the cushion. It was real. The thing I had feared all my life was going to happen. My parents were going to divorce.

Something swelled in my throat. It was a sob. Once I let it out more followed, like toads dropping from the mouth of the bad princess. I longed for tears but there was only a dry painful wrenching. I heard Pa walk into the room. I knew it was selfish of me to let him see how much I minded but I could not help myself. The dreadful sounds, sounds of weakness and misery, burst out of me. A hand rested for a moment on my head.

A voice – not my father's – said, 'Poor Harry.'

Then the footsteps went away.

THIRTY-SIX

'Sorry I'm late,' I panted as I dashed up the aisle of the Phoebus Theatre auditorium. 'Traffic jam. The bus was hours getting here.'

Inspector Foy was standing on the stage. Its darkness was pierced by a single beam of light that made a small bright circle, roughly in the centre. 'It doesn't matter a bit.' He bent and stretched out his hand to hoist me up. 'It's always a pleasure for a theatre buff to have a chance to wander about the place. I wonder sometimes if I shouldn't have followed my first inclination to be an actor. There's too much reality in a policeman's life.'

I had forgotten how his ears turned over at the top, rather sweetly, like a breaking wave. I discovered I was extremely pleased to see the inspector again. His presence had the old calming affect.

'It's good to see you, Harriet.' He smiled and looked as though he meant it. 'I was never so delighted in my life as when I signed those papers of release.'

'It's wonderful to have Pa home. Though we don't see much of him. The telephone never stops ringing with people swearing eternal friendship, wanting him to star in their plays, be godfather to their children or go on yachts with them.'

Actually, since we had come home two days ago, my father had been out nearly all the time. He looked so guilty when he came back that I was careful to conceal any appearance of curiosity. I assumed he had been with Fleur. We were treating each other with polite circumspection, not talking more than was necessary, avoiding eye contact.

'It's surprisingly tiring.' I smiled.

I had lain awake the last two nights while adrenalin coursed through my body and made my heart pound until I felt ill. Towards dawn I had slept uneasily, dreaming of people and places of indefinable menace. Ma had rung the day before. Neither of us mentioned the divorce by name. She had talked of the house she had persuaded Ronnie to buy with his savings, which had turned out to be surprisingly substantial. The savings, that is. 'Such a darling house, Harriet, like a large cottage orné – eighteenth-century Gothick with ogee windows, painted palest pink – its own little cove, sandy beach, cliffs, woods – you never saw such a delicious place. We're going to let rooms to our friends for enormous sums. Such fun – imagine the parties. You must come down and see it soon, darling.'

'I'd love to, when I next get some holiday.'

'Ronnie'll be thrilled to see you. Between you and me, I think Bron and the others frighten him a bit. But I can tell he's got a soft spot for you. I could be jealous – except he's such a silly old thing.' She laughed complacently and I realised she sounded happier than she had done for ages. 'He's so loyal, you know. Of course he doesn't have your father's magnetism – who does? – but it's rather nice being the only pebble on the beach for a change. Relaxing. The only thing we quarrel about is Ronnie's appalling stinginess. The other morning I turned out his pockets and found the salt and pepper pots from our table in the hotel dining room. He said we might need such things if we're going to run a rest home for out-of-work actors. I said undoubtedly we would but he'd better think again if he imagined I was going to have EPNS rubbish on my tables. I made him put them back at lunchtime.'

My mother chattered in this vein for some time and finally rang off, promising to call again soon. I was glad she was happy, I told myself fiercely. But how could she endure the prospect of leaving for ever the dear old house in which she had brought us up? All those glorious occasions when she had created such a vibrant and original atmosphere, when she and Pa had blown kisses to each other down the length of the table, when they had laughed themselves into a state of helplessness at a favourite joke. Those rapturous moments of reconciliation after one of them had wandered, when they had seemed to fall back in love with renewed fervour. Had it meant so little, after all?

The inspector was saying something about being glad that things had worked out as they had. I made myself concentrate. 'I particularly wanted to show you how it was done,' he said. 'We needn't expect anyone else, I take it?'

'Pa's seeing his agent,' I explained. 'Besides, he doesn't like talking about anything to do with the recent past. Bron and Ophelia are still away. She's coming home tomorrow. And Portia's in Manchester. Cordelia's at home, making herself a pair of pedal pushers – it's a kind of trouser.'

As Pa no longer needed it to brighten the walls of his cell, the tapestry had been abandoned. This was a relief as it had taxed my paltry needlework skills to the limit. I had tried to persuade Cordelia that trousers were tricky and it would be much easier to make a skirt but she had been adamant that she could do it. I had to admire her self-confidence. She had cut up an old seersucker tablecloth striped in lurid shades of pink. Unfortunately the pedal pushers had given trouble from the start and Cordelia had been looking rather black by the time I set out.

'Oh well.' Inspector Foy resigned himself gracefully to an audience of one. 'You'll be able to explain to the others. Now,' he shot his cuffs and made conjuring motions with his hands, 'allow me unfold the mystery. This is more or less as the stage was when it happened.'

There were a few books and some tins of paint in one corner and a Thermos flask and what looked like an old coat in the other. A newspaper had separated into crumpled sheets towards the backcloth, which was nothing more than a sketched outline of trees and bushes. A theatre that is dark – that is, without a production running – is a melancholy place. It is cold and echoing, with the characteristic smell of glue and paint and dust that had been in my nostrils from babyhood.

'The body of Sir Basil was discovered here.' He pointed to the centre of the stage where so many famous actors had taken their final bow. The beam of light picked up a dark stain that was both sad and horrible. Basil's bow had been more final than is generally the case. I had never liked him, but one cannot help having tender feelings for anyone meeting a violent end. 'You know what a *deus ex machina* is?'

'Literally, the god out of the machine. A sort of artificial device to resolve a play.'

'That's right. Zeus or the personification of an abstract idea, Peace or Justice, something like that, is lowered on to the stage – in a throne or a chariot or a sunburst – to reward the good characters, punish the bad and deliver a judgement. The Greeks and Romans were very keen on it and it had another burst of popularity in the seventeenth century.' I nodded dutifully. 'You remember in King Lear there's a violent storm at the end of Act Two and for a lot of Act Three?'

'It's always my favourite bit. I can't stand the gouging scene. Nor Cordelia being hanged.'

'This was to be a Baroque production. The director decided to represent the storm by dropping a canvas of thunderclouds amid the appropriate flashes of lightning and cracks of thunder. Seated among the clouds was to be a personification of Nature wearing widow's weeds and holding an amphora of dry ice. Nature in mourning because of the forces of evil and destruction released by Lear's misguided actions at the beginning of the play. You get the picture?'

'I remember Pa telling us something about it. He thought it was very effective.'

'Just stand there a minute and whatever you do *don't* move from that spot. Keep well away from the centre of the stage. Promise?'

I promised. The inspector disappeared into the wings. A delay was followed by a discreet whirring, then my eye was drawn by something moving high up above my head. Slowly it descended. As soon as it hit the beam of light I saw that attached to the base of a boldly painted canvas of black, purple and grey swirling clouds was a prong of metal. It was bent into a zigzag with a dangerously sharp tip. Abruptly the canvas gathered speed and dropped the last ten feet with a mighty thwack. It stopped some three feet above the stage, quivering with the violence of its descent. The lightning shaft pointed like an accusing finger at the circle of light.

The inspector reappeared, an expression of modest triumph on his face. 'Simple, wasn't it? The thing is controlled by ropes and counterweights. According to your father, in rehearsal a few days before Sir Basil's death, it came down too fast because one of the stagehands had mistakenly removed a weight from the counterbalance. Fortunately no one was standing beneath it then. That's how the murderer got the idea, of course. The shock of Sir Basil's death drove what had been a minor incident out of everyone's heads. It was clever in its absolute simplicity. But none of us thought of it. The moment the blow had been dealt, almost splitting Sir Basil's skull in two, the murderer simply hoisted the canvas back into the flies. Then your father came in, stumbled over the body, and you know the rest.

'Our chaps did a fingertip search of the stage, the wings, the green room, the dressing rooms, the traps, every inch of the place. But not being theatre people it didn't occur to them to look up. It didn't occur to me either until I came back here on my own about three weeks ago. You'd told me about the séance. I was inclined to disregard it but we had so little to go on. So I turned it about in my mind. I made the connection with the storm and that's when I looked up and saw it. After that, everything was clear. Forensic found dried blood of Sir Basil's type all over the shaft.' The inspector detached it from the canvas. 'Exhibit A, if we ever get to a trial. I brought it over just to show you.'

'The cunning of it!' I was admiring. 'And how clever of you to guess!'

'I realised, when your father told us about the single spotlight, it was probably a marker. That helped to persuade me that he hadn't done it. He would hardly have brought it to our attention, if so. But that seemed to suggest pot-shots from the back of the theatre. It didn't seem to fit with a hand-to-hand encounter.'

'I see. Whoever did it must have been in the fly tower at the crucial moment. Then they probably rushed on stage with the others when my father started shouting. So it could be anyone in the company – apart from Pa and the three women. But Rupert said it might have been an accident.'

The inspector looked rueful. 'Well, yes. I don't believe it was for a moment but it's going to be very difficult to prove it was murder unless, of course, I can get a confession. There is just a possibility it fell accidentally on Sir Basil. And that someone innocently hauled it back up without realising what damage it had done. But the spotlight, which unfortunately only your father remembers, seems to me an important piece of evidence.'

'Wouldn't the murderer have come back and cleaned the bolt of lightning?'

'I expect he'd have liked to. But I put a man on to watch the place. The caretaker who let you in is PC Willett.'

'I thought he seemed a bit brisk and efficient. Theatre staff are generally garrulous characters. It's a lonely job so they make you stop and chat so they can tell you what they think about everything. You know, like taxi-drivers.'

Inspector Foy sighed. 'Probably our murderer thought the same. That was a bad mistake on my part.'

'Are you going to interview everyone again?'

'I shall try. But half the suspects are scattered all over the world by now. I can't say I'm at all pleased with the way things have turned out.'

'Do you mean you won't be able to catch the murderer?'

'It looks rather unlikely. We'll go on trying, of course. We'll go back over all the old ground and try to establish a motive. But you see the difficulty. Your usual murder is something done in the heat of the moment: husband whacks wife in a temper; jealous boyfriend stabs unfaithful lover. What we call a "domestic". Then there are gangland killings, usually involving drugs. Sometimes there are contract killings. Occasionally there's a madman on the loose – a psychopath who strikes at random. Paedophiles, rapists, sexual perverts – their victims have simply been in the wrong place at the wrong time. But the calculated murder of one individual by another is comparatively rare. In those cases the motive is usually money. Less frequently love or jealousy.'

'Who profits by Sir Basil's death?'

'His Jack Russell terriers and Battersea Dogs' Home. I think we can safely rule them out. There were a few small bequests to friends but nothing worth killing him for.'

I thought of Sir Basil's flabby cheeks, his angular body, his large bald forehead. 'I can't imagine anyone being jealous of his love.'

The inspector shook his head. 'According to his house-keeper, when not at the theatre, Sir Basil spent most of his time quietly at home with his dogs. He almost never entertained callers of either sex. I admit it's a puzzler. Unless . . .'

I waited for him to go on. 'What?'

'Unless we admit the possibility that Sir Basil was not the intended victim. That X was waiting for someone *else* to come on to the stage and stand on that spot. X had to keep out of sight of the wardrobe mistress and the understudies so he might not have had a clear view of things. The lighting, as we see it now – as it was on that morning – is sharply chiaroscuro. He saw a man on the marker and assumed it was *his* man. He let the canvas fall, bang! Only to find Sir Basil lying dead with a smashed skull and no chance of a replay.'

I thought about it. I felt suddenly sick. 'You mean . . . you mean . . . Pa?' I almost whispered it.

'Your father was in the habit of running through scenes on his own while waiting for rehearsals to start. He told us so himself. Probably everyone in the theatre knew that.'

'But who would want to kill Pa?'

'Ah! Now you're asking. I hoped you might be able to tell me.'

'Pa hasn't any money. He's always spent whatever he's had. Our house is mortgaged. Our only car is Bron's and he hasn't finished paying for it yet. My mother's jewellery is paste.' The inspector did not look surprised. It occurred to me that he must have acquainted himself with our financial standing weeks ago. 'So –' I was reluctant to say it – 'if it was anything, it was – probably – love.'

I stared at the inspector's shoes. They were black, highly polished, the laces tied into neat double knots. The list of my father's amours was lengthy. Doubtless there were as many again that I had known nothing about.

'I'm not asking you to betray him.' Inspector Foy's voice was patient. 'I've already asked him if he could think of anyone who might be nursing jealousy or thoughts of revenge. He was very co-operative. Laudably frank, in fact.' I bet he was, I thought. There were few things my father enjoyed more than reminiscing about his former conquests.

'I understand that you might not wish – perhaps it's unfair of me to ask you – it's just that sometimes men aren't very good at seeing what's under their noses when it comes to other people's feelings. I've always found women much more acute. I only ask if you're aware of anyone who might hate your father enough to kill him.'

'I don't think there was anything between him and Marina Marlow. She only wanted the publicity.'

'So he said.'

'There was Patsy Pouncebox last year. But she went to New Zealand.'

'She could have come back.'

'But she wasn't the type to kill anyone – if there is a type. She was neurotic but kind-hearted. Always crying, poor thing. You couldn't help liking her, really.'

'Husband?'

'No. That was the trouble, I think. She hoped that Pa –' I stopped. I had been going to say that she had hoped my father would leave my mother, which was ridiculous, when I remembered with a pinch of agony in my stomach that that was exactly what he was going to do. I was back in the cycle of forgetting, remembering, and then trying to come to terms with the facts.

'Before Patsy it was someone called Fenella Fanshaw.'

'Your father didn't mention her. Is that significant, I wonder?'

'I shouldn't think so. I expect he's just forgotten. She married soon after it broke up. There's Fleur Kirkpatrick.'

'As far as I know they met after your father was arrested.'

'Of course.' How stupid of me to forget. Misery filled me and I felt very, very tired.

'He's told me they intend to marry.' How kind his voice was! 'That must be difficult for you.'

My face had become stiff. I grimaced, trying to stretch the muscles. 'I'd better go. There's only me to cook supper. And I need hours to do it, in case I have to throw everything away and start again.'

He looked disappointed. 'It was good of you to let me show off my powers of detection. I'm sorry to have kept you so long.'

'Why don't you come and have supper with us tomorrow?' I was surprised the moment I issued the invitation and even more surprised when he said, 'Thanks. I'd like that.' I hadn't made it sound very enticing, after all.

'Seven thirty, then.' I smiled and turned away to avoid seeing the sympathy in his eyes, which made me want to burst into tears.

THIRTY-SEVEN

It was during this period of my life that the blessedness of having a job to do was brought fully home to me. Muriel and Eileen had obviously read their newspapers over the Christmas holiday for when I arrived at the office they almost curtsied. Mr Podmore, sitting behind his desk, grunted when he saw me, snorted disgustingly into his handkerchief and held out an impatient hand for my 'copy'. I saw he had added something extra greasy, perhaps goose fat or brandy butter, to his waistcoat. His pencil ran through my beautiful sentences and arrows turned my article on its head. After he had, as far as I could see, rewritten the entire piece, he fixed his little blue lenses momentarily on my face.

'Odd. Deb Attracts Spectral Phenomena. You don't seem the psychic type.'

'Well, of course, in the end they weren't spectral at all only I thought it would be a pity to spoil it –'

'Not at all bad, Hilary. Keep it up. Not so many adjectives.'

'Harriet,' I said to his back, for already he had turned to a pile of papers behind him and was riffling through them. 'And I've never been a debutante.'

He did not seem to hear me.

'Like a nice Chocolate Oliver, dear?' asked Muriel when I returned to the office. 'My niece gave them to me for Christmas. They're ever so luxurious.'

I took one. I have always thought it undignified to bear grudges. Besides, they are my favourite biscuits. Mr Podmore came in while we were munching.

'You.' He looked at Muriel. 'Break-in in Baker's Row. Pensioner in Shock. Burglar Exposes Himself. Possible tie-in with Jack the Zipper.'

'Oh, that old chestnut,' muttered Muriel. 'Jack the Zipper must be a hundred and forty by now. *If* he ever existed.'

But Mr Podmore had already slammed the door of his sanctum. A few wisps of smoke drifted out and Eileen coughed delicately into her cupped hand. Usually Muriel would have sent me on such a pedestrian story but this time she put on her coat, fastened her headscarf under her chin and went, grumbling fearfully, to Baker's Row.

Mr Podmore appointed me to do research for a series of articles he was writing, about the breakdown of community spirit. This week it was the Nuisance of Noisy Neighbours. Luckily, as it was a cold wet afternoon, I could do most of it by telephone. I got the street directory and started ringing people up.

It was extraordinary how willing people were to fill me in on the intimate doings of their neighbours. Nobody had a good word to say for anybody else. It turned out that most of these upright citizens were living next door to men who regularly put their wives into hospital with multiple fractures, received pantechnicons of stolen goods and were frequently seen digging six-by-two-by-six-shaped holes in their back gardens at dead of night. As for next-doors' wives, it seemed they only stopped battering their children and entertaining tradesmen in scarlet underwear – the wives not the tradesmen – in order to nip down to the off-licence to lug back crates of gin.

Certainly these people led colourful lives. Drugged practically senseless, they thieved, fornicated and held orgies throughout the livelong day. At night they did the same but with devil-worship thrown in. Travelling home that evening on the bus through these same dull grey streets I looked in vain for even one lighted window where the inhabitants were not sitting immobile in front of their televisions with trays of chips on their knees. But until the bus drew up at the bottom of our road I had not thought once about the divorce and had been free all day of nagging unhappiness. Cordelia met me on the doorstep.

'You're late. That sewing machine is the most stupid thing ever invented. You've got to help me.'

'All right. But you've got to help me, then. Inspector Foy's coming to supper.'

Cordelia brightened. 'Oh good. He's rather yummy, I think. And not queer.' She looked thoughtful. 'It's a pity my trousers won't be finished. But there's always your black.'

I unpacked the food I had bought on my way home. Cordelia helped herself to one of the grapes I had intended to go with the cheese. To my dismay, she shuddered and spat it out. 'Sour as pickled onions.'

'Oh, blast! Really?' I started to feel harassed. We put the grapes on the windowsill for the birds. A blackbird flew down at once, gave them a peck and flapped off in disgust. While Cordelia peeled potatoes I struggled with the sewing machine, which had made an annoying tangle on the underside of the seersucker. I had to admit defeat but Cordelia had been put into a good mood by the imminent arrival of the inspector. When he came she met him on the doorstep and led him at once into the drawing room where she gave him a drink and entertained him with grown-up conversation. I heard snatches of it as I rushed up the basement stairs flinging off my apron as I went.

'So sorry,' I panted. 'You know what cooking's like – so much last-minute stuff.' Actually I had been chasing Mark Antony through the maze as he made off with the salmon from which I had carelessly averted my eyes for a moment. It was looking a little the worse for wear, not only minus its head but its gleaming silver sides marred by teethmark and by the battering it had received against the yews. I had given it a good wash before putting it into the fish kettle, making a mental note to come down in three minutes to turn the gas down in order to achieve a gentle simmer.

'I was telling Charles about our delightful stay with Sir Oswald and Lady Pye.' Cordelia looked at me critically. 'You've got fish scales on your cheek.'

'Char . . . ? Oh, yes.' I had forgotten that this was the inspector's name.

'I'd like it if you'd call me Charles, too.' He got out his pipe, waved it at me for permission to smoke and on receipt of my nod began to pack the bowl with tobacco. He was looking remarkably different in a black blazer, blue shirt and jeans. Despite the pipe he looked younger and more – less like an uncle, certainly.

'Cordelia's been telling me about the glittering social scene in Derbyshire.' Despite the perfect solemnity of his delivery I could tell that the inspector – that Charles – was amused. But he was much too kind a man to wound Cordelia's feelings by not appearing to take her seriously. 'Lords, bishops and baronets. Film stars and foreign princes. Dancing every night. It sounds very glamorous.'

Cordelia looked quickly at me and blushed a little.

'My goodness, yes,' I said. 'It was. And Cordelia's hand was sought for every dance.'

'Harriet looked very nice too.' Cordelia paid off her debt.

'And Portia, once she got rid of the cement-coloured Babygro.'

'Well,' said Charles, 'Derbyshire must have been knocked sideways by so much beauty.'

I left them talking while I went to answer the telephone.

'Sorry I haven't rung before.' Portia's voice sounded excited and happy. 'We've been busy looking for somewhere to live. We've found a tiny cottage just outside Manchester. It's got a stream beside it and it's incredibly primitive but cheap. Next to a field full of divine cream-coloured cows. It's called Nightingale Cottage. Isn't that romantic? Two rooms downstairs and one upstairs, right in the roof. Jonno can't stand up straight in the bedroom because of the slope.' She giggled. 'He says he intends to be lying down in it most of the time, anyway. You have to wash in the kitchen sink. The lav's outside but it flushes, thank God. Honestly it really is rather a love's-young-dream, roses-round-the-door sort of place. Damp as hell but there's a huge fireplace, bigger than the kitchen actually. How are you?'

'Fine.'

'Good. You've no idea how much fun we've been having. Jonno's got to see his tutor tomorrow and start doing some work but while he's in the library I'm going to be helping the farmer·who owns our cottage, milking the cows and things. Only it seems it's done by machine these days, which is a disappointment. I rather fancied myself as Tess of the D'Urbervilles.' It was good to know we still shared fantasies, at least. 'Still,' Portia continued, 'a pound an hour isn't bad. Jonno has an allowance from his father so we won't starve. And the farmer's going to teach me how to shear a sheep. Imagine me, a farmhand! Isn't it priceless, when I can hardly tell a hen from a goose? There are ducks on the stream and I want to train them to come up to the door. You're not saying much.'

'I'm listening to you. How's Jonno?'

'I'm crazy about him. This is it, Hat. This is love. But it isn't what I'd thought it would be. We spend most of the time we aren't in bed laughing hysterically. He's my friend as well as my lover. The very best friend I've ever had. He says he feels the same. He hasn't been drunk once. He says he doesn't want to drink when he's with me. It wouldn't matter if the rest of the world flew off to another planet. We don't need anyone else.'

There was much more in this vein. As I listened I was hoping that nothing would happen to destroy the dream. Portia had been *aux anges* before and it had not lasted. She and Jonno were alike in being reckless and impulsive. I did not know if this was a good or a bad thing.

'Yes, I really do like him. Very much,' I said in answer to her question, 'but Portia, listen a moment. There's something I ought to tell you. Brace yourself, darling. It'll be a bit of a shock. But don't worry, I'm sure it'll all be fine. We've just got to get used to the idea. Ma and Pa – they've decided that they can't make each other happy in the old way and they think perhaps it might be a good idea to live apart for a bit.'

'You mean they're going to split? Get a divorce?'

'Yes. I'm so sorry to have to tell you, darling, but I didn't want you to read it in the papers. The journalists keep asking me if the rumours are true and –'

'Has Pa got somebody new?'

'Yes. A lawyer called Fleur. He says it's serious.'

'And Ma'll stay with Ronnie?'

'They seem to be rather happy. They're going to buy a small hotel in Cornwall.'

Portia was silent for a moment. Then she said, 'It isn't a total surprise, is it? I mean, they haven't been together really for ages. In body but not in soul. The heat went out of the thing years ago. I tell you one thing, Hat, I'm not going to mess about – with other men, I mean – and I'm not going to

586

let Jonno do it with girls, either. It just hurts too much and you can't go on really loving someone when they hurt you. You have to bank down the fires or you're too vulnerable. I want something much better than that.'

I was impressed by Portia's solemn tone. 'I hope you make it work. I'm sure you're right. But you're so young to forswear all others. It won't be easy.'

'No. But I've always got our parents as a shining example of how *not* to do it. Does Cordelia know? About the divorce, I mean.'

'None of the others do. Bron and Ophelia are still away. Pa asked me if I'd tell them when the moment seemed right. It hasn't so far with Cordelia.'

Portia's voice became sharper. 'Why are *you* supposed to do our parents' dirty work?'

'Pa says he can't face it. He's not in very good shape, you know. He gets very agitated about things. Yesterday Cordelia slammed a door and Pa had to go and stand in the garden for half an hour. When he's here we have to have all the doors open all the time.'

'Mm. I hope this Fleur creature is long-suffering.'

'I haven't met her.'

'Well, it's a mess. I'm glad I'm out of it.' There was a silence. 'Sorry, that was rather selfish of me. Of course you're right in it. Don't get gloomy.'

'I'll try not to. I'm going to throw myself into my work. And there's a lot to see to here. I'll be fine.'

'We're not on the telephone at the cottage, natch, but I'll let you have the farm number when I know it, so you can always get a message through if it's vital.'

'Thanks. I'd better go now. Charles Foy's here for supper.'

'Who? Oh, an inspector calls. That's good. I've sometimes thought he's taken a shine to you. You'd better look out. Or not as the case may be. He's quite a duck. Though really your fond little heart's already given away, isn't it?'

'What do you mean?'

'If you don't want to tell me, I'll keep quiet and pretend not to know anything about it.'

'I really don't know what you're talking about.'

Afterwards, when we'd said goodbye, I realised that I had forgotten to tell her how the murder had been done. If it was murder. Portia had promised to telephone at least once a week. I found myself wishing she was not so far away. The sound of a key in the lock of the front door broke into my thoughts.

'Hello, Harriet. Give me a hand with my cases, would you? The taxi-driver's being bloody. I shan't give him a tip.'

Ophelia put down her bag and took off her coat. She looked sleek and elegant. She offered her cheek for me to kiss.

'How was Sussex?'

Ophelia rolled her eyes. 'One useful thing's come out of it. Apart from my fee, that is. I'm prepared to look a lot more kindly on home and all its squalid little ways. My dear, they were so pure and good. A strange religious sect, a cross between the Mormons and the Plymouth Brethren. And yet they've got pots of money! It's extraordinary.'

'I don't know why rich people shouldn't be religious.'

'I've always thought religion was a consolation for being plain and poor. It seems I was wrong. The Drosselmeyers have mink-lined and gold-plated everything but they don't drink, they eat only boiled chicken and fish and they go to bed at nine o'clock. The only thing they *do* do is screw like mad. He has three wives and twenty children. Horrible little things. The boys wear miniature suits like their father's and the girls wear strange missionary caps. They all have an intimate knowledge of the Old Testament and a distressing habit of quoting it on every possible occasion.'

'Poor Ophelia. No champagne after all. We must have some this evening to make up. Charles Foy's here.'

'Ah. The great detective. When Pa rang me he seemed to think we ought to get up a subscription for a statue in the park.' She shrugged. 'Naturally I'm glad Pa's out of that ghastly hole but I'm so bad at being grateful. And he – Foy, I mean – disapproves of me so much I can't resist behaving badly just to tease.'

'Can I help you with your luggage, Miss Byng?'

The inspector – Charles – came into the hall. He must have heard what she said but he smiled very charmingly.

'Oh, thanks.' She was off-hand. 'There are two more cases in the cab. If you wouldn't mind.'

She turned her back on him haughtily but as she passed me on her way to the stairs she winked. Poor Charles struggled in a few minutes later with her baggage. I only found out much later that he had to pay the cab fare as well.

'I ought to investigate these cases.' He put them down and flexed his arms. 'There must be at least one dead body in each.'

'Better have another drink. Oh my God – the salmon!'

I had been so distracted by Portia's telephone call and Ophelia's return that I had quite forgotten about turning down the gas. The fish kettle had boiled dry and the underside of the salmon was stuck to its base.

'Can I help?' Charles had come down into the kitchen. 'I don't need to be treated with ceremony, you know.' He peered into the kettle. 'Mm. Here, let me.' Masterfully he took over and got the fish onto a plate and the kettle cooling in the sink. 'I think you can scrape off that burned bit and the rest will be perfect.'

'It doesn't look quite as I'd hoped.'

'Smother it with slices of cucumber. It'll be fine. The taste's the thing. Now, give me a job.'

'Why've I been left all on my own in the drawing room?' complained Cordelia, coming down to find Charles putting the finishing touches to the *risi e bisi* which we were having for a first course while I struggled with the hollandaise sauce. 'I've eaten all the peanuts and now I feel sick. I shan't be able to eat any supper.'

'Just as well.' I looked sadly at the sauce. 'This beastly stuff's gone greasy and lumpy suddenly.'

Charles peered into the pan. 'I think it's curdled. Sorry I can't help you. I'm only a coarse cook. That's too advanced for me'

'Damn! That was the doorbell. Pa must've forgotten his key. Cordelia, could you go?'

'I'm feeling much too sick. I finished the bread sticks and the olives as well.'

She did look rather green. I ran up and flung open the front door. Rupert and Archie stood on the doorstep.

'Oh, how lovely!' Actually I wanted to kiss them both passionately, having missed them a surprising amount although it had only been a few days. But, mindful of their possible distaste for the female embrace, I offered a chaste peck. 'What a marvellous surprise! I'm thrilled to see you!'

'I hope not as surprising as all *that*.' Archie was looking particularly fine in a claret-coloured velvet frock-coat. 'Waldo rang yesterday and asked us to come to supper.' He sniffed. 'An interesting smell. Fish. With a *hint* of scorch.'

'How bad of him not to tell me!' I was distraught. 'Come in. It's salmon. Only I forgot to turn the gas down. Will you help yourselves to drinks while I have another go at the sauce?'

'A speech calculated to make a guest's spirits droop.' Archie strode towards the stairs. 'You'd better let *me* see it.'

In the kitchen Charles was disentangling the sewing machine. I introduced him to Archie.

'Good evening.' Archie bowed. 'I have heard your praises

sung.' He stood with his hands on his hips examining Charles, who remained calm. 'Hm. A real detective. I call that in*tense*ly stimulating. If not inflammatory. However, you'll forgive me if for the moment I concentrate on Harriet's sauce?' He beckoned to me to come closer. 'You've let it overheat. You must begin again over hot water with a fresh yolk. Apron!'

'There was too much tension in the upper thread,' explained Charles to Cordelia. He showed her how to adjust it, then did some experimental runs on a spare piece of fabric. 'It should be all right now.'

'You aren't gay, are you?' I heard Cordelia ask him, sternly.

'Not in the least. I have a manly way with machinery, rather than a flair for dressmaking.'

Archie raised his eyebrows and gave me a discreet thumbs down.

'I mean, I really love queers but obviously they're no good as husbands.'

Charles retained his sang-froid despite the heady atmosphere of latent seduction. 'If you'll take my advice you won't think of marrying a policeman. Very unsociable hours. And our conversation isn't up to much.'

When things was more or less under control I sent everyone upstairs to join Rupert in the drawing room with fresh supplies of wine and peanuts so we could have another shot at elegance. Pa had not come home yet so I decided to wait another five minutes. Before leaving for work I had laid the table in the dining room and arranged some hellebores from the garden with sprigs of mistletoe, now out of season and therefore cheap on Brixton market. I put out two more sets of knives and forks and lit the candles. Really, it did look rather pretty.

We began dinner without Pa. Conversation sparkled. I

591

began to feel that intoxication which overcomes a hostess when she sees her party is a success. Ophelia, looking breathtakingly lovely, drank a great deal of champagne and was very entertaining at the expense of the Drosselmeyers. Then Charles told the tale of the bolt of lightning and those who had not previously heard it were electrified. Sorry about the pun. I could see Cordelia was making up her mind to disregard his advice as to the unsuitability of policemen as husbands. She propped her chin on her hand and ate him with her eyes, quite forgetting her *risi e bisi*, which, incidentally, was not at all bad.

'So what are the chances of catching the murderer?' asked Rupert as I sent Cordelia down to bring up the salmon, not quite a *pièce de résistance* but the cucumber slices had worked wonders.

'Slim, I must admit.' Charles got up to help me stack the dirty plates on the dumb waiter as though he had known us for years. He really was an exemplary man. 'If you look at murder from the murderer's point of view, obviously the main problem is getting rid of the body. One is rather conspicuous shoehorning a corpse into the boot of one's car. And it's a lot of work digging what has to be a large, deep hole in the garden. Corruption makes hiding it in cupboards or under floorboards impractical unless you live the life of a hermit. Hence acid baths, joints in deepfreezes and so on. But if the body is found at the scene of the crime and nothing particularly points to you – if you've time to wash off blood and hair, dispose of the weapon and bloodstained clothing then, if the truth be told, you're in a position to sit tight and laugh at the police. In this case the weapon was effectively hidden for a sufficient period of time and the murder was done at such a distance that X had nothing to hide. Our only chance is to find the motive, bring in X and extract a confession. But these days we're not allowed to torture suspects. The nastiest thing we can do is give them a plastic mug of canteen coffee with a grubby spoon. If they're cool customers with a good solicitor they can, literally, get away with murder.'

The salmon beneath its thatch of cucumber slices was an odd shape, even odder than I remembered it, but it tasted all right. Also there seemed to be less of it but as Cordelia refused to have any it went round easily. The primrose-coloured sauce was unctuous and the vegetables were unexceptionable. I relaxed.

'The table looks lovely, Hat,' said Ophelia. 'The mistletoe is quite original.'

Ophelia's encomiums were greatly valued by me as they were so rare. Sussex seemed to have had a mellowing effect.

'Every Christmas a bunch is hung over my door at the police station, creating much merriment and innuendo,' said Charles. 'I always try to skip past it pretty quickly. There are some frighteningly big girls in uniform these days.'

'Traditionally it's supposed to be unlucky to put mistletoe on the table,' said Rupert. 'According to Norse legend, the berries are the tears of Freya, the goddess of love. When she wept for her lover – whose name I've forgotten – her tears turned into pearls. She suspended them between heaven and earth with a warning to mortals that if they would guard themselves from the torments of love, they must hang it out of reach.'

'So, Harriet, you have set us all at grave risk from the barbs and pestilences of passion.' Archie looked portentous. 'For myself I cannot be *too* grateful. Life without love is a cup of cold tea. Give me a rummer of the stuff that scorches and sets one's veins on fire. Hello, what's this?' He held up something on the prongs of his fork, then leaned over and put it on my plate. It was a small triangle of seersucker.

'I can't imagine how it got there.' I was mortified.

'I know,' Cordelia whispered in my ear as we loaded up the

dumb waiter again. 'When I went down I found the salmon under the table among all the bits of stuff. Dirk was licking it. I put it back on the plate with some more cucumber to hide the bits he'd eaten. Supposing someone's actually swallowed some of it – the fabric, I mean?'

'What's all this whispering?' called Archie. 'You know I can't bear to be left out.'

I was horrified to see on the edge of Rupert's plate one of Dirk's little bone-shaped biscuits. It was good of him not to have said anything.

'Cheese, everyone,' I cried distractedly. I heard the front door open. 'Cordelia, run down and see if there's any *risi e bisi* left for Pa. And check that Dirk hasn't got into the larder with the *Budino Diplomatico*,' I added in a lower tone. This was an Italian trifle, very easy, which I had learned to make at Maria-Alba's knee. I was confident it would make up for the salmon.

'Hello, everyone,' said Pa's voice. 'Sorry we're late.'

I extracted my head from the interior of the dumb waiter. Preceding my father into the dining room was a woman with dark hair winged with streaks of silver and held in place by two small black patent bows. She wore a smart red suit and very high heels. After the men had got up with a scraping of chairs, a hush fell on the dining room.

'Fleur, this is Harriet, my second daughter.' Pa began with me because I was nearest. He looked nervous.

'It's so lovely for me to meet Waldo's girls at last.' Fleur's voice was incisive, not loud but penetrating, with a strong transatlantic accent. 'You must be the journalist.'

'Of a kind.' I gave her a wide smile, hoping to get it into my eyes.

'What kind is that?'

'The incompetent kind.'

Fleur smiled back, showing quite a bit of gum. Her eyes

were pale blue and catlike. 'I'm sure you're a very good little writer.'

'And this is Ophelia.'

'Hi, Ophelia!' Fleur clacked across the room in a cloud of scent to shake her hand. 'I'm charmed to meet you. Waldo's told me so much about you all. Now let me see, you're the one who does clever things with cushions and toast-racks. Though why you sweet young things want jobs, I don't know. It's plain old girls like me who have to sharpen their brains and make a career for themselves.'

'How do you do?' Ophelia seemed to be examining the wall directly behind Fleur's badger-striped head.

'Nonsense, darling.' My father took Fleur's hand and kissed it. 'You know quite well how beautiful you are, besides being the most brilliant woman in London.'

Fleur put her head on one side and grinned until her eyes were slits. 'You're so sweet to me, Waldo,' she cooed. 'I'm just the luckiest woman in the world.'

While further introductions were made I struggled with the ropes of the dumb waiter. This gave me time to compose my feelings. I must give Fleur a chance. For Pa's sake I must try to like her. The *Budino Diplomatico* came up with a note. 'HAD AN ACCIDENT WITH THE PUD. SORRY.' It seemed to have acquired many more cherries and pieces of angelica since I had last seen it.

'*No*, thank you,' I overheard Fleur say, when Ophelia offered her the remains of the first two courses. 'Waldo and I had an *enorm*ous lunch and we have to watch our figures.'

This made me think of Wallis Simpson who, if report is true, weighed herself three times a day. Fleur had the same band-box appearance and professional charm behind which, one knew in one's bones, was a cold and calculating mind. Fleur was much prettier than Mrs Simpson, I forced myself to admit. But she had turned my father into someone as pea-brained as poor old Edward VIII. He was almost drooling over her arm, snuffing up her heavy scent as though he were a pig seeking truffles. I reminded myself that I was supposed to be giving Fleur a chance.

I decided to serve the *Budino* from the sideboard, just in case. I sliced into it with a spoon. It should have been elegant layers of brandied sultanas, jam and *crema bavarese* – brown, pink and yellow stripes. Instead it was a swirl of sludge colours. Cordelia mimed heartfelt apology when she came up from the kitchen.

'How do you do?' she said politely to Fleur. 'I am Cordelia, Waldo and Clarissa's youngest daughter.'

'Oh, my! What a pretty child, Waldo.' She ran her eyes over Cordelia's dress – my black. 'And *so* glamorous.' Fleur's laugh was deep and not unattractive except perhaps in being a little too self-assured. She gave my father's cheek a playful tweak. 'Honey, you ought to have told me this was to be a grand party. I feel quite cast in the shade by your gorgeous girls.' My father made mewing noises of protest and appreciation while Fleur turned back to Cordelia. 'So you're the baby of the family. But I can see you're very grown up, dear. How old are you?'

'Fourteen,' replied Cordelia without a moment's hesitation.

'And is it usual in England for fourteen-year-old girls to wear Givenchy? In the States kids of fourteen are in jeans and sneakers mostly.'

'It isn't everyone who can carry it off.' I could tell Cordelia was beginning to resent such concentration on her age.

'I should think not. Your poor Pappy's gonna have to work *aw*fully hard to keep you in *haute couture*.'

Cordelia considered Fleur gravely in silence. Then she said, 'How *brave* of you to wear scarlet.'

I saw Fleur's smile shrivel for a moment before it became broader than before. 'Waldo, will you change places with me, honey? I'm just a little in the draught from these marvellous old windows.' Her gaze roamed round the room and rested for a moment on the half of a gondola from *The Merchant of Venice* that served as a sideboard. 'My, what a quaint house this is. I just adore you English eccentrics.' She shivered. 'But isn't it a mite expensive to heat?'

I happened to look at Rupert. He caught my eye and smiled, his dark eyes sharp with amusement. I felt suddenly better.

I gave Fleur some pudding. She took a mouthful and put down her spoon. 'So nice. But perhaps a little rich. Have you some fruit?'

'I'll get you some grapes.' Cordelia was out of her chair and running down the stairs before I could stop her.

'I don't know when I've eaten a more delicious pudding,' said Charles. He looked at me as I raced about with plates and raised his glass. 'In fact this was a dinner fit for a prince. I can't remember when I've enjoyed myself so much.'

'O*ho*!' said Archie in an undertone to Ophelia. 'I hear the laughter of the goddess.'

THIRTY-EIGHT

It was not to be expected that we would welcome Fleur with
open arms, but as the weeks passed we came to accept her
after a fashion. To be fair, few women newly engaged would
be positively pleased about the prior existence of five children.
I don't believe she meant to be actually unpleasant but she
wanted to show us that my father belonged to her. That they
were besotted with each other was apparent to all the world.
Pa was much more confident when she was with him. This
ought to have pleased me, I know.

Fleur constantly petted him, stroking his cheek, smoothing
his hair and straightening his collar, which had the effect of
making the rest of us feel excluded. Of course, I was sensitive
to the least fault. Her continual carping about how hard he
was having to work to support us all grated, considering we
were doing our best to alleviate the situation by our own
efforts. She had a special voice for talking to Pa, a husky
croon, like Billie Holiday with a sore throat. She assumed a
habit that we all loathed, of calling him 'Sweetness'.

She and Ophelia went several rounds in the struggle for
supremacy and Ophelia won by dint of outright rudeness.
Fleur grew afraid of her and kept out of her way as much as

possible. She quickly gave up attempts to patronise Cordelia and instead, seeing that Pa was devoted to his youngest child, thought it expedient to win her over with flattery. Cordelia called her Pussyfoot behind her back because of her crude blandishments but was reasonably polite to her face. By contrast I felt Fleur's manner to me tended towards the dismissive but I probably asked for it. I was so anxious to conceal my real feelings that I was always conciliatory in her presence and she took this for weakness. As it probably was.

Fortunately, Fleur and Pa were working so hard in their respective spheres (he began rehearsals two weeks after our return) that they preferred to spend what few hours were left, alone together at her flat. After a week or two of token nights at home, he gave up all together the pretence of living with us and returned only to fetch clothes and books. Fleur always came with him. On the grounds that her stomach was 'faddy' she avoided having dinner with us but sometimes they had a drink and an attempt was made by all of us, except Ophelia, to pretend that these were relaxed and friendly get-togethers. Sometimes Rupert and Archie were there, which helped enormously. And Charles Foy came almost as often.

It was on one of these occasions, some time in late March, when Pa, Fleur, Charles and I were making conversation in the drawing room, while Ophelia and Cordelia lurked upstairs until Pussyfoot should have gone, when we heard a dramatic *vroom, vroom* from the road. My spirits lifted, thinking it was Rupert and Archie, but when I went to the window I saw an unfamiliar red sports car parked outside.

A pair of legs the thickness of cocktail sticks swung out of the passenger seat followed by a body clad in a coat of black and yellow fur, striped like a bumblebee. Above this was a bob of scarlet hair. I could not see her face because of a gigantic pair of dark glasses. My attention was distracted by the emergence of the driver on the other side.

'Bron!' I cried. 'Oh, Pa, it's Bron!'

We had had one telephone call from him since Christmas, in which he said he was fine and wasn't coming back to England for a bit and he'd read about Pa being let out of prison in the Italian papers so that was fine, and he hoped we girls were fine too. I had told him about the divorce and he had said, 'Fine, fine,' as though we were discussing the weather. It was altogether an unsatisfactory conversation.

I ran to the front door.

'Don't crush the suit, there's a good girl.' Bron returned my kiss and straightened imaginary creases from his immaculate coat. 'You're looking terrific, Hat. What a transformation!'

I had forgotten that the last time he had seen me I was wearing my anarchist uniform.

'Rupert bought me these things. Wasn't it kind?

'What some men will do in order to get their oats! Now me – I like it the other way round. This is Letizia.'

He put out his hand to embrace the tiny waist of the woman who had scampered up the steps like a daddy-longlegs fluttering to the light. I remembered that Letizia was a divinity of the fashion world and Bron's employer. Close to I could see that her face – what was visible round the enormous specs – was a cracked riverbed of wrinkles.

'*Ciao, cara.*' Letizia smacked the air with lips like a rouged rubber band. She spotted the Anubis hat stand. 'This we must have. For the fashion shoot.' She pushed past me into the house. 'Yes, *perfetto* for the beach collection. Pay anything they want.'

Bron took a wallet from his pocket. 'What do you say, Hat? Five hundred?' He held out a fistful of notes.

'What? For the hat stand? But, Bron, it isn't mine to sell. Besides, I'm very fond of it.'

Bron took out more notes and slapped them down on the table. 'A cool thousand. What Letizia wants Letizia gets,

600

sweetie. Luckily she wants yours truly.' He gave me a fiendish grin and followed her into the drawing room.

'And this is Papa. *Ciao*.' Letizia embraced my father. 'Now I see where my darling boy gets his good looks.' She gripped Pa's cheek between thumb and forefinger and waggled it. He looked bemused. 'The famous actor, ah yes, I remember now. The man that was assassinated. In Italy we understand these things but the English – pooh! – they make such a fuss!'

'Actually, I didn't –' Pa began but Letizia had gone on to Fleur. 'And this is Mama.' She kissed Fleur enthusiastically. 'I have to thank you for bringing in the world the beautiful Bron who has made me *so* happy. I owe you a great – word, *caro*?' She snapped her fingers at Bron.

'Um, debt?' supplied Bron, getting out the wallet again.

'*Sì, sì*. But I did not mean – *va bene*,' she shrugged. 'What matter?'

Bron slapped down another pile of notes.

'I am not this man's mother,' began Fleur, pardonably annoyed as she was thirty-five, less than ten years older than Bron. 'In fact I never saw him before in my life.'

'Ah, you are American,' said Letizia, who had been doing a quick circuit of the drawing room. 'That answers it.' She gestured with a hand like a collection of leafless twigs towards Fleur's very smart tailored dress. 'You Americans have no history, poor things. You have to try too hard. The hair is not bad. But not the little black bows. Too much. And you,' she darted towards me, 'this is much better. You have the style.' She veered away on her tiny insect legs. 'That sofa – *perfetto* with the fur collection. In fact I make you an offer.' She turned back to Fleur. 'Fifteen thousand for the whole furniture of the house. You have a taste with the decoration. What you say?'

Fleur looked at Pa. 'Sweetness –' she began in a dangerous voice.

601

'Now, my dear Miss Letizia,' began my father obediently, 'delighted though we are to see you, I'm afraid we have no intention of selling our furniture to a complete stranger.'

'But, *tesoro mio*, I am not a stranger. No. I am your – word, *caro*,' she snapped her fingers at Bron.

'Daughter-in-law,' supplied Bron. 'We were married in Rome last week.'

'But, Bron,' I said, later as we stood in the kitchen while Letizia had a bath to wash away the rigours of air travel, for they had come straight from the airport to see us. 'Isn't she just the tiniest bit – old?'

'She's fifty-eight. I found her passport the other day. But I'm not supposed to know.'

'Thirty-two years!'

'So what? She's as energetic in bed as a sixteen-year-old. She likes to dominate. I don't have to do a thing, except roll over occasionally. It's exactly what I like.'

This I could imagine. 'But there's more to marriage than sex.'

'She's got loads of dosh: And a genius for making more. And she likes nothing better than to spend it on little old me.'

'But what about all the other things that are important in marriage?'

Bron looked puzzled. 'Like what?'

'Well, companionship, shared tastes, um, principles.' It was difficult to think of things under Bron's insouciant gaze. 'Children. You won't be able to have any.'

'Thank God, no. What would I want them for?'

I had to admit I could not see Bron as a father. 'What about when she's old and you're still a comparatively young man? Supposing her health breaks down?'

'I shall get in a very young, very pretty nurse.'

I gave up. Perhaps this was, after all, the best thing for Bron.

He certainly looked happy. And when Letizia came down to the kitchen after her bath, I saw quite quickly that they were, in an odd way, well suited.

'Dear ones, what are you making?' she fluttered over the pans. 'Pasta? Good, I make it for you. You, Bron, sit there so I can see your beautiful face. And, Harriet,' she turned me round, unfastened my apron, put it on herself, and gave me a little push, 'you sit next to your brother and enjoy him while he is here. Tomorrow we go to Paris so it is sad for you. Bron has said to me how you love him. I have a big family and I see them not enough. Now where is the storeroom? *Eccola!*' She bolted into the larder and came out with several packets. 'I love to cook but I do not have the time. Excellent *pasta asciutta*. And *ceci*, *peperoncini* and *polenta*. You have an Italian cook?'

I explained about Maria-Alba.

'The poor thing! *Va bene*, this is life.' Letizia looked sympathetic for one and a half seconds before launching herself on the ingredients. She chopped, fried, stirred, blanched, steamed and whipped at breakneck speed while I watched in amazement and Bron got quietly sozzled. From time to time she bent to kiss him as she whirled past and he exerted himself so far as to pucker his lips.

In less time than it would have taken me to make a straightforward *spaghetti con pomodori* Letizia had prepared five courses, beginning with an *insalata di fagioli e tonno* and ending with *zabaglione*. All the time she kept up a friendly discourse on next season's fashions, the difficulty of finding good cutters, her Italian childhood, journalism, the film industry, world politics and space travel. Between pronouncements she twirled Bron's hair into a spike, chucked him under the chin and tweaked his ear until he protested that she would make it red. For some reason when Letizia did these things I did not feel in the least excluded.

603

'Careful, old girl,' he said after a particularly vigorous caress. 'You'll get polenta on my nice new tie. You know, that apron is rather sexy? Now I understand why men fantasise about girls dressed up as parlour-maids. Pour me another, will you?' Carelessly he held out his glass though the bottle was nearer to him than her.

'He is so utterly bad, *vero*?' Letizia giggled and stopped her whisking to fill his glass. 'He is the first man I meet who has no conscience, *assolutamente*. I like that. I see clearly what he thinks. If he looks at another woman I stop his money and this he knows and he likes money more than sex, just a little bit, so we understand each the other.'

As Rupert was responsible for bringing Letizia and Bron together I had telephoned to ask him and Archie to join us for dinner. I was laying the dining table for ten people – Pa having persuaded Fleur that their presence was required at this feast of celebration – when I heard Charles and Ophelia quarrelling in the hall.

'I don't care! I'm going out. I can't stand another minute of that frightful Pussyfoot. She positively mauls Pa as though he's a gazelle and she's going to tear him into bits for her cubs.'

'I know it's difficult but it's as hard for the others, especially Harriet. She needs your support.'

'She can come to the cinema with me, if she wants.'

'She won't do that because she feels guilty about your father and everyone disliking Fleur.'

'She hates her, herself.'

'That makes her feel worse.'

Ophelia's voice became jeering. 'If Harriet wants to be elected to the communion of saints, that's her lookout. Anyway, what business is it of yours? I wonder if your motives are quite so pure as you like to make out.'

Charles was furious now. 'You really are intolerably

selfish . . .' They moved away just then into the drawing room so I missed the rest.

Rupert and Archie arrived a minute later and I offered them my usual restrained greeting. Not so Letizia, who hurled herself on them both.

'*Ruperto*, how wonderful to see you.' She kissed him fervently. 'And, Archie, *tesoro mio*, how beautiful is the outfit. *Molto originale*. Particularly the pink coat, like the English hunting costume.'

'I felicitate you, Letizia.' Rupert gave her a charming bunch of roses and hyacinths. 'I hope you'll both be very happy. Congratulations, Bron.'

'Bron, my darling boy, I tell you something.' Letizia linked her arm through Rupert's. 'I have been in love with *Ruperto* for years but he won't – word, *caro*?' She snapped her fingers at Bron.

'Fuck you?' he suggested.

Letizia screamed with laughter. 'Oh, he is so bad, the angel! No, no, it is something like play the games. Rupert likes to be the boss too well. I expect he is right. We should not go well together for long. But I love him.' She stroked Rupert's sleeve. He made no response but looked down at her, with an enigmatic smile. 'I tell you a warning, *caro*, if ever I leave you it will be for this man.'

'Okey-doke,' said Bron with almost offensive good humour.

'To be blunt, Letizia,' Rupert removed her arm from his and gave it to Bron, 'fond of you though I am, and much though I appreciate your many talents, I couldn't stand the noise on a permanent basis.'

This made Letizia hold her sides with laughter. I found myself liking her more and more. Ophelia did stay to dinner after all, though she sulked through the first course. The champagne Rupert had brought thawed her sufficiently to make her laugh at one of Archie's stories and by the time we

605

waved Bron and Letizia off, just before midnight, she seemed to have forgotten her grievance and said goodbye to Charles with perfect politeness.

Things went on much the same for another month. I worked hard and sometimes earned a word or two of praise from Mr Podmore. Ophelia got a commission to decorate a house in Mayfair for a rich banker and this put her in a very good mood. She became friendlier, and sometimes even asked me how I was getting on at work. On one occasion, when she found me sitting alone in the dining room writing to Maria-Alba, she patted the top of my head and asked me to send her love to the poor mad old thing. Once I came across Ophelia in the kitchen singing 'Oh What a Beautiful Morning' at the top of her voice, which seemed remarkably out of character. She was making toast, which was the nearest she ever got to cooking. I asked her what she was so happy about.

'I haven't any idea. Perhaps it's spring, perhaps it's having money I've earned myself.'

'It *is* a good feeling, isn't it? What a lot those previous generations of women missed. I know now that even if I became supremely rich – unlikely, I know – I'd always want to go on working. It's being deeply engaged with something. And it gives such a savour to everything that *isn't* work.'

'To think I used to believe that the only possibility for happiness was a rich husband.' Ophelia took a bite of toast but continued to talk, spraying crumbs. 'Not that I wouldn't still like that but I can see now it isn't the be-all and end-all.' I looked at Ophelia in astonishment, hardly able to believe what I was hearing. From the time she had been old enough to understand the concept of husbands Ophelia had set her heart on marrying a rich one. 'I don't want to be bought,' she continued. 'I want to be more important than a car or a house or a set of golf clubs. I've proved to myself I'm not just

606

a beautiful face and a good body. Now someone's got to have much more than bags of tin. He's got to be my equal. Crispin and the others were so hopelessly wet I could walk all over them. Perhaps I won't even bother to marry. I could take over Fay's business. She's getting on a bit, losing her touch. The other day she suggested pine when a client moaned about the cost of walnut. *Pine*!' Ophelia spoke the word with absolute disgust as though Fay had suggested painted cardboard. She looked at her watch. 'I must run. My little banker wants me to choose him some flower vases. My influence is such he daren't buy so much as a potato peeler without consulting me.' She let herself out of the house a few minutes later, humming 'Hooray for Love'.

I found a school that would take Cordelia in September. I worried about her missing two entire terms but it seemed there was nothing to be done. I arranged for her to take Italian lessons at the local polytechnic. Because of Maria-Alba she already had a smattering of the language. Otherwise Cordelia spent most of her time in the greenhouse with Loveday or making patchwork curtains for her room, the pedal pushers having been abandoned at last as a hideous fashion fit only for sad old women.

Portia rang occasionally. She was enraptured by her new life and she and Jonno were thinking of getting married. Foolishly I begged her to wait a little longer and she got cross, so after that I just listened and sympathised. Ma also rang infrequently. She and Ronnie were in a frenzy of decorating. Four of my family had flown the nest and they all appeared to be exquisitely happy as a result. The house seemed very empty without them. I gave up dusting their bedrooms.

'You seem a little melancholy,' said Charles one evening as we sat alone in the garden.

It must have been about the beginning of May. I happened to be wearing a very pretty dress of dark lavender linen acquired on a recent shopping trip with Archie. I had no idea how much had been spent that day because Archie said he could not bear sordid discussions on what ought to be an occasion of delicious enjoyment but I was certain that my indebtedness had risen by a terrifying amount. My clothes were both a joy to me and a reproach.

Rupert and Archie were in Italy, fitting in a last holiday before the rehearsals of *Un Ballo in Maschera* began in earnest. Archie said it was to recover from having Annabel to stay. She had apparently behaved reasonably well but the Motor Show had taken its toll on Archie.

According to Annabel, things were going tolerably well at Pye Place. Suke and Miss Tipple were still there. When Suke wasn't writing the *History of the Union of Female Franchise* she was helping Maggie. Suke had tried and failed to make Sir Oswald do his share of the housework but she had taken a firm stand on the question of his diet. Sir Oswald had kicked up terribly about being served watery stew accompanied by lectures on the Third World. He had lost his temper and finally asked Suke to leave his house but Suke had been unmoved. Presumably innate chivalry made it impossible for Sir Oswald to summon the police to hurl her into the street. He had been forced to submit.

A ray of light had been the parties of deprived inner-city children that Suke had organised to spend weekends at Pye Place, to give them a wholesome taste of the countryside. According to Annabel, Sir Oswald had been surprisingly responsive to the idea and had condescended to show them his domain personally, the girls anyway. Suke had great plans to charge foreigners exorbitant sums to stay at the house and dine with the baronet. She had sent for her loom and was turning the stables into a craft centre. All this Archie had elicited by cross-questioning, while he and Annabel queued for an hour for a chickenburger at the Motor Show which had looked and tasted, he said, like a bread-crumbed beer mat.

Rupert had had a great deal to bear from Annabel's head mistress. As ill luck would have it, she had been looking out of the window just as Annabel was driven up to the school's front door by a darkly handsome man in an expensive-looking car. To the head mistress's absolute disgust she had seen the child fling her arms round Rupert's neck and kiss him passionately on the lips. Rupert had been summoned to her study where she had subjected him to an impertinent inquisition, convinced he was Humbert Humbert to Annabel's Lolita. Only Rupert's sternest manner and iciest satire had prevented her from sending for the police.

We had not seen Pa for nearly a week.

Anyway, when Charles asked me if I was feeling melancholic, we were lounging in deck chairs on the remaining small square of grass not yet incorporated into the maze, drinking prosecco. I ate olives while Charles smoked his pipe. The evening sun gilded a few powder-puff clouds and threw the yew hedges into sharp relief. The clash of Loveday's shears made a sort of syncopated background music to our conversation. Now and then a spume of chopped leaves would spurt up from the bushes as Loveday shook them vigorously. We were alone, Ophelia not having returned from the banker's house in Mayfair. Cordelia was machining squares together at the kitchen table.

'Not really,' I said. 'I was just thinking – there's a thrush that comes every year and sings on the tree outside my room. He hasn't come so far. I hope nothing's happened to him.'

'Oh dear. Poor Harriet.' Charles sounded sympathetic. 'Another defection.'

My pride was piqued by this harping on my lack of *joie de*

vivre. It was time I stopped wearing my heart on my sleeve. 'How are you getting on with interviewing suspects? Any motives yet?'

'No, nothing really to work on. I'm thinking of flying out to South Africa, but as we don't know for certain even that it *was* murder, it's hard to justify the expense. Most of the Hubert Hat Company's there now with *King Lear*. Did you know?'

I did as it happened. Only that morning I had had a letter postmarked Johannesburg and addressed to me in Max's elegant writing. I had put it unread into the boiler, as I had done with his other letters. He was persistent, I had to admit. I was no longer angry with him – well, not much anyway – but I could not forgive myself for playing so completely into his hands. I still blushed to remember that night of passion. Passion on my part, anyway. He had probably been rather bored.

'But, Harriet, there's something I've been wanting to talk to you about.' I brought my attention back to what Charles was saying. He knocked out the dottle from his pipe and buried it in the earth with a convenient twig. 'I've been putting it off in rather a cowardly way.'

I looked at him, surprised. His voice had acquired a new timbre with that last sentence. Hesitant. Almost troubled. He abandoned his excavating and threw away the twig. Then he pom-pommed up and down the scale a few times as was his habit when he needed time to think exactly what he wished to say. Charles was always so confident, so self-possessed, that I had come to consider him as a sort of bulwark – there to protect the public from themselves and me from anything like uncertainty. I felt a clutch of fear. 'What is it? It's nothing to do with Pa?'

'No, no. It's nothing to do with the case. Your father's absolutely safe, I promise you. Believe me, you can put all

610

that right behind you.' In his eagerness to reassure me he had put his hand on mine. It felt warm and agreeable. I let it stay there. 'It's something quite different. I – I – oh, damn it, it's not easy to say. You're a bright girl. It must have occurred to you that my frequent visits here aren't solely in pursuance of my duty as a member of the Metropolitan Police?'

'I supposed we were friends.'

'Well, yes. Of course we are. And I value that dearly. This house has become something of a second home. Whenever I walk in through the front door, no matter how bloody the day, my spirits lift. I'm deeply fond of it and everyone in it. I'm even fond of Dirk.'

Dirk, lying at my feet, stirred at the mention of his name.

'I don't know why you say "even". I think he's adorable.'

'All right. Especially Dirk. But there are degrees of liking and loving. And I find myself, bewilderingly, at the extreme of love.'

My heart beat rather fast at this. My instinct was to stop him saying anything more. I did not like to think of him as someone in the grip of emotion, a rudderless barque.

'I've tried to fight it.' Charles had removed his hand and was staring down at his glass, at the bubbles that rose to pop on the greenish-gold surface of the wine. 'I've told myself I could never be successful; that there are too many differences. I'm thirty-nine – too old for hopeless passions.' He made a derisive sound. 'But the age gap isn't the worst of it, I know. I'm married to my job – how could I expect any woman to put up with the long hours, the unglamorous slog, the unpleasantness of the worst aspects of human nature in which I'm deep-dyed? And yet,' he went on before I could say anything, 'recently I've thought – I've hoped – God, I must be crazy. Is this what insanity feels like? Harriet,' he turned to look at me, 'I'm sorry. This isn't how I meant to say it. I'm very conscious that you'll feel I'm trying to shatter the fragile peace

611

you've constructed for your family. I can guess how much you were hurt when your father was put in prison. And now he's trying to recover his self-confidence by throwing himself into a love affair, which must be a terrible blow to you. But, selfishly, I feel I've got to speak about my own feelings. I'm like a man possessed. Half the time at work my concentration goes and I wonder whether . . . Do you think –'

'This looks very cosy. Am I *de trop*?' Ophelia, whose approach had been muffled by the grass, threw herself down in a third deck chair without waiting for an answer. 'My God, I'm shattered. I must have a drink.'

I got up quickly. 'I'll get you one. No, honestly,' as Charles began to get up, 'I want to do something about supper anyway. You sit and talk to Ophelia. It's only bacon and pea risotto but do stay, if you'd like to.'

'On condition you let me help you.'

'All right.'

I took Ophelia a glass and gave Charles another chilled bottle of prosecco and the corkscrew and went upstairs to my room to change into jeans and a jersey as the evening was beginning to cool. The minute I shut my bedroom door I put my head in my hands and groaned aloud. I was seized by paralysing conflict. What was I to do? What was I to say? Who could have imagined such a thing? Oh God, what an intolerable mess feelings make of our lives! If we were only creatures of reason and intellect, what a delightful episode we might fashion of our brief period of existence. As it was, oh horror! I took myself to task. Was I guilty of having given him the wrong signals? I had really believed we were good friends. Perhaps that was an impossibility between heterosexual men and women. I had thought I could be as unguarded with Charles as I was with Rupert and Archie. I must be dangerously naïve.

'Hat?' Cordelia turned the handle of my door and, finding it locked, rattled it hard. 'That beastly, bloody sewing machine's gone into loops again. It's the complete end and I hate it! Do come and help me.'

'All right. Just a minute. Go and chop a couple of onions, will you?'

I heard Cordelia go grumbling away. I must think, decide what was the best thing to do. Of one thing I was sure: though I was enormously fond of Charles, I was not in love with him. I had no uncles, both my parents being only children, but if I had, Charles would definitely have been my favourite. Oh, what was I thinking about – uncles? This was ridiculous. I must be calm and behave like a sensible person. I must temper the blow but leave him in no doubt that I might possibly change my mind. I groaned again, almost screamed as I imagined his face as I told him the dreadful truth. No, I absolutely could not go through with it. I would have to do whatever he wanted. I liked him so much, what would it matter? People went to bed with people they weren't in love with all the time. I might even learn to love him. 'Harriet,' I said aloud, 'you're a complete idiot!'

'Who are you talking to?' Cordelia was rattling the door again. 'I can't find the onions. You've *got* to help me or I'm going to have to join Maria-Alba and the nuns.'

I unlocked the door. 'You can come in. I'm just getting changed.'

'You're looking quite red in the face. What's the matter?'

'Nothing.' I disappeared for a moment inside my jersey. 'How are the curtains? Did you find something else to cut up for squares?'

'Well, as she obviously isn't coming back I cut up Portia's green dress, you know the velvet one.'

I pulled on my jeans. 'Was that wise? I seem to remember it was one of her favourites.'

613

'I shall make the rest of it into a cloak for parties. With a Russian hood, perhaps.'

I had to admire Cordelia's unwavering confidence. We went downstairs together. I managed to put right the sewing machine without calling on Charles's manly expertise. Through the window I saw the top of his head above the deck chair, the occasional puff of smoke from the pipe and his gesturing hand as he talked to Ophelia. I hoped they were not quarrelling. My ideas were still rioting as I chopped onions and bacon and grated parmesan. Thank goodness, he had forgotten his promise to help.

Making a risotto is a calming exercise. A simple, undemanding process of adding ladlefuls of stock and stirring. Cordelia whirred away on the machine, talking all the time but I hardly heard a word she said. I was rehearsing something kind but firm to say, something affectionate and pride-saving. We were not talking about a proposal of marriage, after all. No doubt men had sexual advances turned down all the time. By thirty-nine they must be used to it. I had made far too much of the whole thing. But he had talked of love . . . Oh, Harriet, for heaven's sake, get a grip!

After half an hour of rambling thus, the risotto was ready. I loaded the dumb waiter and went upstairs to the dining room. I dressed the salad, put wine and water on the table and called Cordelia. I opened the dining-room window, which looked out over the back garden to call the others. I very nearly fell out in surprise at what I saw. Charles and Ophelia were no longer in their deck chairs. They were standing in the heart of the maze. And they were kissing.

There was nothing avuncular about that kiss. It was as passionate as anything I had ever seen, either on the screen or in real life. They paused briefly and Ophelia pressed her face against Charles's chest. Then they began all over again.

'I'm going to take that bloody machine round to Oxfam

first thing in the morning,' said Cordelia, coming into the dining room.

'Quick!' I said, beckoning her over. 'Take a look at this!'

'If it's that thrush you're always on about I'm not specially interested – Blimey!' Cordelia clutched my arm. 'Golly, no wonder she's been so cheerful lately. She's had a pash on him the whole time. That's why she was always so jolly rude to him, I suppose.'

Yet again Cordelia's sagacity amazed me.

'I had no idea. I've been so stupid.' I started to laugh. The sensation of relief was marvellous.

'Look, they're getting awfully excited,' Cordelia leaned further out. 'I expect they think no one can see them. I wonder if they're actually going to make love? I'd better make myself watch. It'll be useful experience.'

'Supper, you two!' I shouted.

Charles lifted his head and they looked up, startled.

'Oh God! I might have known,' I heard Ophelia say. 'There's no privacy in this wretched family.'

Charles waved. He looked thoroughly pleased with himself. I waved back.

Supper was a strange affair. Charles and Ophelia were obviously present only in body while their minds were floating in some empyrean that we lesser mortals could not reach. Whenever they looked at each other a round tale of love was told and Cordelia and I were obliged to talk almost exclusively to ourselves. Whenever I thought of the fool I had so nearly made of myself I had to bite my lip to stop myself laughing aloud. I was deeply touched that Charles had considered my feelings enough to feel some compunction about putting his love for Ophelia to the test.

'No one's listening to me,' complained Cordelia at last. 'I don't see the point of pretending we didn't see you two kissing. Are you going to get married?'

Ophelia sat silent, hanging her head. I was astonished to see my proud sister brought to such a state by love.

'I hope so.' Charles looked at Ophelia, his face bright with desire. 'I do hope so. But perhaps not immediately.'

'The quicker the better, as far as I'm concerned,' said Cordelia. 'Have you got any younger female relations who might want to be bridesmaids?'

'Um, yes, two nieces.'

'What do they look like?'

'Let me think – ginger hair and braces on their teeth.'

Cordelia smiled. 'Poor things.'

The minute we finished coffee, Charles stood up and said, 'That's was excellent, Harriet. Thank you. If you'll forgive me, I've some urgent business to attend to.'

He held out his hand to Ophelia in a masterful way and she rose, blushing – something I never remembered her doing before – and allowed herself to be led off. We heard the front door shut and Charles's car accelerate away.

'Phew!' said Cordelia. 'I couldn't have stood the strain much longer.'

I stopped dusting Ophelia's bedroom.

'You know, the change that's come over that girl is incredible,' said my father several days later, about Ophelia. 'She's even more beautiful but she's almost submissive. I'm not sure I approve.'

We were gathered in the drawing room for one of our uneasy cocktail hours which Pa evidently felt obliged to keep up, in order to do his duty by Cordelia and me. Ophelia and Charles had been on a flying visit to collect some clothes. She had kissed all of us goodbye, even Fleur. She had actually hugged me and asked me to come and have supper at Charles's flat the following week.

'It's happiness,' I said. 'I think it's marvellous.'

'But why him?' said Fleur. 'He's OK-looking, quite a peach – but a policeman!'

'He's a chief inspector, not a bobby on a bicycle,' I said, perhaps a little too fierily. 'He's very, very clever and well educated and thoroughly decent –'

'Well, well, I'm sure we're all delighted,' Pa said pacifically.

Ophelia had talked to me about Charles on her last visit. 'He's the only man I've ever met who didn't believe I was a cold-hearted bitch,' she said. 'And so I've practically stopped being one. It's extraordinary how we all feel compelled to live up to other people's idea of us. Charles was so tough with me, I couldn't help falling in love with him. Though I fought against it like mad. But he was stronger. I'd almost given up hope of finding a man who was determined enough. He says he fell in love with me the minute he saw me but that was only my face. Then he started to enjoy the tussles. Now,' she blushed again, 'he says he loves the challenge of knowing that I'll be hateful if he drops his guard for a moment. He says I frighten him more than the most hardened criminals he has to deal with.'

'But would you? Be hateful, I mean.'

'Actually, no, probably not.' Ophelia giggled, also a first. 'I'm absolutely crazy about him. But I'm not going to let on.'

I thought she was letting on probably more than she imagined.

'We're a bit worried, though, about you and Cordelia all alone here,' Ophelia went on. 'Are you really all right?'

'Completely all right. It's quite cosy actually, with just the two of us. Cordelia goes every day to the language lab. Her Italian sounds pretty good to me. And I'm making progress

617

with the job. Mr Podmore said he thought I might have the makings of a journalist.'

What he had actually said was, 'Deb Shows Promise.' High praise indeed.

'Oh, that's all right then. I know what a home girl you are – how much this house means to you.' She had looked about. 'Come to think of it, it looks a lot better than I've ever seen it.'

'I learned how to do housework in Derbyshire.'

'Really?' She made a face. 'What a strange holiday it must've been.'

'Fleur and I have been talking,' Pa smoothed down his hair, still white but longer now and rather distinguished, 'and it seems to us – of course we're very willing to hear what you have to say – but we think it's pretty silly, just you two girls in a great big house like this.' He examined his hands, always one of his good points. 'It seems to be fulfilling the function of a rather expensive wardrobe for the rest of us. The estate agent – just a preliminary talk, of course – says we could sell the leasehold for quite a large sum. It would be useful at the moment. Fleur and I have seen a house we like in Hampstead. It's lovely but not cheap. And I shall have to settle some money on Clarissa.'

He looked at me hopefully. I tried not to appear utterly miserable.

'What about us?' Cordelia put down her knitting – her latest creative project, the curtains having lost the lustre of novelty – and turned first to me, then to Pa. 'Where will we live?'

'Well. That's up to you, naturally.' Pa beamed uneasily. 'You might like to come to Hampstead with us. It's a pretty house and there are two spare bedrooms.'

Cordelia looked doubtingly at Fleur.

'That would be so nice,' said Fleur. 'Such a treat for us.

618

But, Sweetness, have you forgotten that Harriet's job is in Brixton? And Cordelia's new school is in Fulham, isn't it? We can't expect the girls to wear themselves out with so much travelling. Besides there's only a small yard. They'd have to find new homes for the cat and dog.'

'I'll go down and get another bottle,' I said.

I ran down to the kitchen. Mark Antony was dozing on the kitchen table in a ray of sunlight. The familiar pockmarks in the red Formica top that made the table so difficult to clean properly suddenly seemed inexpressibly dear to me. Next to him was the butter, which had a smooth, sculpted shape with distinct tongue marks.

'You bad boy!' I kissed his head and fondled his ears. 'You shan't be given away!' Mark Antony shook his head and got down. He hated being disturbed when he was sleeping. I found the corkscrew and struggled for a while with a cork that had broken in half. When I finally got it out I was crying tears of frustration. I dried my eyes on the drying-up cloth and left streaks of mascara. 'Bugger, bugger, bugger!' I said just as the doorbell rang. Then next moment I heard Archie's voice raised in protest at being jumped on by Dirk. I took up two more glasses.

'Harriet, my dear girl!' Archie was so brown that the whites of his eyes gleamed like lamps in the darkness of the hall. 'You're looking gorgeous! Give Uncle Archie a buss just here.' He pointed to a tawny cheek.

'You look gorgeous yourself.' I obliged with the kiss. 'Absolutely the colour of the dining table.'

'It took a *great* deal of work. I had to turn myself every few minutes to avoid burning. Exhausting. But it was worth it.' He admired himself in the mirror. 'Do you like my Nehru coat?' He stroked the sleeve of his embroidered jacket. 'I'm thinking of a turban. With a large jewel right *here*.' He indicated the place on his brow with a mahogany forefinger.

'Like that toad of adversity Pa's always quoting,' suggested Cordelia, who had let them in.

'Hm, not *quite*.'

'Hello, Rupert,' I said. 'How was Italy?' He was only lightly tanned but he looked very relaxed in an open-necked blue shirt.

'Good.' He examined my face. 'What's the matter?'

'Rupert *nev*er stopped working.' Archie saved me the trouble of answering. 'He sat in the shade surrounded by scores and manuscripts. The youthful talent of Tuscany paraded before him in various states of undress but he never looked up. There was one poor girl who tried *every*thing to get him to notice her. She asked him to rub suntan oil on her back. Rupert summoned one of the waiters to do it. She did cartwheels round the pool. He put his hat over his face and went to sleep. Finally she contrived to drop her towel and stand *butt*ock-naked before him. He trained his field glasses on a circling buzzard for the next ten minutes.' Archie laughed. 'Oh, it was *cruel*!'

'It was a bloody nuisance,' said Rupert.

'Pa and Fleur are here.'

I led the way into the drawing room. My father seemed delighted, almost relieved, to see them.

'What's *this*?' Archie picked up Cordelia's knitting, a fast-growing garment in red and white.

'It's for Ophelia's baby.'

'Ophelia's going to have a *baby*?'

Astonishment registered on both their faces. I explained about the latest development in the Byng family's love life. Rupert and Archie took some convincing that I was serious. 'They're still in the first throes of passion,' I said. 'Cordelia's just perfecting her skills. There's no question of babies yet.'

'There jolly soon will be,' said Cordelia darkly. 'They absolutely radiate sex.'

Archie was examining the piece of knitting. 'But it's got *four* legs!'

Cordelia giggled. 'Two of those are arms, silly.'

'If you ask *me*, something's gone wrong with the pattern.'

After polite enquiries had been made about health and holidays, Pa said, 'Now you'll have something sensible to contribute to the discussion, Rupert. I've just been talking to Harriet about selling the leasehold of this house.'

'Ah,' said Rupert noncommittally.

My father set forth his reasoning. 'So you see, it makes sense really, doesn't it, if we can find somewhere for Harriet and Cordelia to live? They might live with Ophelia and Foy, I suppose?'

'Not on your life,' said Cordelia at once. 'It'd be like being in one of those films by Tendency Williams about the Deep South. People sweating a lot and having conversations you can't understand.'

'Or they could have a little flat and be independent.'

'That's a great idea,' said Fleur. 'Or a couple of rooms in a boarding house, maybe?'

Cordelia set her jaw and stabbed with a needle at a ball of red wool.

'I think,' said Rupert, 'they had better come and live with us.'

THIRTY-NINE

Rupert was accommodating beyond the call of duty about Dirk and Mark Antony, only insisting that they must be kept out of his work-room or fur would fly – theirs, with them in it. He drew the line at taking in Loveday. He said one look at the labour necessary to keep the maze in trim would convince the new tenants of Claremont Lodge that they must keep Loveday on. Besides, he would pine if separated from his masterwork.

I broke the news of our departure to Loveday as gently as I could. He stopped clipping long enough to wipe away a green goatee of clippings and said, 'I knew that. I cast the runes afore Yuletide. The serpent's got its tail in its mouth and we've come full circle.'

'We'll be so sorry to say goodbye to you, Loveday.'

'I dare say ye will. An artist dusna come mickle cheap. The worth of a thing is best known by the want o' it.' He snipped at a fragment of yew near my nose. By this I understood that he felt we were the losers, which was just as it should be. My father gave him a generous cheque, which Loveday accepted with condescension and so we parted.

It was not possible to get through the packing-up without

the shedding of many tears but I was conscious of disloyalty to the dear old house when I could not altogether suppress a pleasurable anticipation at the idea of living with Rupert and Archie. My mother said she was too busy decorating the cottage orné to come up to town and that she was indifferent to the fate of the old furniture. So Pa accepted Letizia's offer to buy the contents. This made moving much easier, but as I closed the door for the last time on the Anubis hat stand I did feel pretty bleak. But a toot from the car accompanied by a howl from Dirk made it impossible to indulge melancholy thoughts, and in no time we were scorching down The Avenue for the last time, on our way to a new life.

I had not been to 10 Horn-on-the-Green, Richmond, which was Rupert's house, since the night of the party, six months before, when I had gone to beg for his assistance to repair the shattered Byng fortunes. I was able to appreciate its superior beauty now the house was empty of people. Situated in the middle of a row of terraced early Georgian houses and faced by an almost identical terrace on the other side of the canal, it was the only one that was double-fronted. They were all built of pinky-red bricks and the windows and doors were painted uniformly dove grey, which was tranquil and elegant. The canal was a glassy olive-coloured seam between green velvet banks and two rows of trees that were now frosted with delicate white blossom. Archie explained that the residents of the street had formed a preservation society to maintain its fidelity to the Age of Elegance. Nowadays a single red begonia in a window box was enough to bring down upon the transgressor the full weight of the Society's opprobrium.

Cars were allowed only in the mews behind so we carried our suitcases through the garden, an intricate parterre of box hedges and rills, punctuated by urns on pedestals. Dirk bounded over the borders, planted all in white and blue, and put to flight a flock of doves that had been sauntering around a trellis arbour.

Rupert was admirably restrained, merely saying, 'I expect they'll get used to one another.'

Inside the house we released Mark Antony from his basket. He prowled about, keeping low to the ground with his ears flattened, examining every inch of every room. For two days he was ruffled and upset, and kept up an unpleasant yowling as a protest at being kept indoors. After that we could stand it no longer and let him out through the front door. He strolled to the edge of the canal to look into the murky waters. His brass-coloured eyes lit with a rabid gleam on seeing the tiny brown fish that swam backwards and forwards. He crouched, front paw extended. From that moment on he was a stickleback junkie, rarely leaving his post except to feed and relieve himself.

When Ophelia paid her first visit to Horn-on-the-Green, I took her upstairs to see my bedroom and she was perfectly silent for several minutes in homage to its style. The wallpaper was Chinese, hand-painted with birds and butterflies. The bed was a half-tester hung with ice-blue taffeta and all the furniture was satinwood.

'Happy, Hat?'

It was the first time she had asked me such an intimate question. 'Yes.'

'What about Ma and Pa?'

'They both seem ecstatic.'

'I meant, how do *you* feel about the divorce?'

'Oh. Well. The good thing is that it no longer terrifies me. I thought it might destroy me and I find it hasn't. I can go on working, looking after Cordelia, even forgetting about it for quite long periods. No one could live with Rupert and Archie and not find a great deal to be happy about. They're both expert practitioners of the art of enjoying themselves.

I've discovered it's a skill and I intend to master it. I find I'm still me, and that whatever me is, there's enough of it to sustain independent existence. That's given me confidence. But, if I'm truthful, I'll never be able to think of the divorce without sorrow. It's changed the way I think about my childhood. I know it's irrational but it's as though a dark veil has been thrown over my memories of that time. I can still recall it and I know it was lovely but always now I see it with the end, like an angel of death, hovering in view. The death of the child in me, I suppose. Stupid, I know.'

'You always were a hopeless romantic. I don't believe for a moment that child's gone. You look older but you're a kid, really. Wait until you meet someone you can make your own life with. You won't need to cling to the past then. You can grow up.' I was too grateful that Ophelia had bothered to consider my life at all to resent the unflattering imputations. Perhaps she was right. 'Where's Cordelia?'

'Rehearsals for the school play.'

At breakfast the day after we moved in, Rupert had announced that he had arranged for Cordelia to attend the local comprehensive.

'I refuse to go,' said Cordelia at once.

'Then you will go and live with Waldo and Fleur.'

'I'd rather cut my throat.'

'You'll find a suitable implement in the kitchen. But don't make a mess.'

'You . . . you . . .' I saw she did not quite dare to call him names, 'mean thing!' she concluded feebly.

Rupert looked up from his paper. 'If you want to live here with us you'll go to school. You're quite free to choose to live with your father or your mother or either of your sisters, if they'll have you. And there's Bron, of course.'

Cordelia left the table and marched upstairs to her room, banging the dining-room door.

'I'm awfully sorry –' I began.

Rupert looked up briefly. 'Let's not make a drama of it.' He returned his eyes to the paper.

That evening Cordelia tried a different tactic. She waited until Rupert had washed and changed and poured himself a drink. We were sitting in the drawing room, looking out at the garden through the French windows. A pair of goldfinches sipped from the edge of the fountain. The setting sun shone on the surface of the water, transforming it into a shining gold disk.

'It's very kind of you to worry about my education, Rupert,' said Cordelia.

Rupert smiled, caressing the stem of his glass with long fingers. 'I don't know that I'd call it kind. Practical, rather. You'll be at a disadvantage next September, if you miss two-thirds of the year, that's all.'

'I'm sure you're right, though I could do some reading at home and the girls'll probably be pretty dim. Actually, I met Drusilla Papworth the other day – she was in my class at St Frideswide's – and she told me that our old headmistress, the one Harriet got stroppy with, has left. So I could probably go back there.'

'Sister Imelda?' I was astonished. It was impossible to imagine the place without her.

'Drusilla said she had a nervous breakdown soon after I got expelled.'

'I don't suppose the two things were connected,' said Rupert.

But I was not so sure. I remembered with a painful sense of guilt my cruel taunt about her relationship with Sister Justinia.

'St Frideswide's is too far away.' Rupert picked up a

book as though to end the conversation. 'Anyway, it's all fixed.'

'But I'd rather not go to a state school.'

'Why not?'

'Well, I never have. None of us have.'

'It'll be good for you to have to fit in.'

'How unfair! Harriet's never had to fit in.' Cordelia was indignant.

'Then she's missed out on a valuable experience. What makes you different from other children that you have to have special treatment?'

'I bet you've never been to a state school!'

'No. And it took me a long time to realise that public school had made me arrogant. These distortions of reality are a disadvantage.'

'I wouldn't call Harriet arrogant.'

'No. Harriet has an in-built corrective to assumptions of superiority. She has an innate respect for truth.' I was delighted by this unexpected praise. 'And,' Rupert continued, 'a lack of self-conceit that amounts to what psychiatrists call an inferiority complex.'

This was not so good.

'Well, I don't know why I should have to make up for *you* being arrogant,' said Cordelia resentfully. '*I'm* not conceited.'

Rupert smiled enigmatically. 'I appreciate the effort you're making to be reasonable, Cordelia, but I assure you nothing will make me change my mind. If you want to live here with us you'll start at the Arthur Brocklebuck Comprehensive tomorrow morning.'

'Tomorrow!' Cordelia began to cry. 'Oh no! Please, Rupert, no! I couldn't bear it. Let me have a week or two to get used to the idea. It's too cruel!' She clasped her hands together and dropped on her knees before him, huge tears rolling down her cheeks. 'I've got to get used to being the product of a broken home,' she wailed. 'I'll do anything to please you. I'll bring you tea in bed and embroider you a pair of slippers. I'll do all the washing-up. I'll scrub the bath. I'll even wash your socks –'

'Now look, Cordelia.' Rupert spoke firmly 'These touching offers of self-sacrifice are unnecessary. I'm not a despotic paterfamilias who has to be propitiated. Besides, we have an excellent daily help and she'd be very annoyed to be interfered with. All I ask is that you stop play-acting. Save it for the stage. There's nothing wrong with feeling things strongly but don't pretend what you don't feel.'

Cordelia stopped crying. She got to her feet and stood, head erect, mouth quivering, a picture of wounded innocence. 'One day, Rupert Wolvespurges, you'll be very, very sorry you've been so beastly to me. You're the most acrominious man I've ever met!'

Rupert was merciful enough to wait until she was upstairs, out of earshot, before giving way to laughter.

The next morning Cordelia, mute with resentment, walked with me to the unprepossessing brick-and-glass edifice that was the Arthur Brocklebuck Comprehensive. We had been asked to come early, before school began, so she could be given books and a desk and a tour of the school. The empty building smelled of linoleum and lavatory cleaner. Miss Savage, the deputy headmistress, was hirsute, with big hips. She looked tired and bad-tempered. I was dismissed peremptorily, as though I was a particularly badly behaved and time-wasting pupil. Cordelia had looked at me with eyes that spoke of perfidy. But when, filled with trepidation, I went to meet her at the end of the first day I had been astonished to see her walking down the road towards me swinging her satchel, a skip in her step and a smile on her lips.

'How was it?'

'Interesting.'

'Nice girls?'

'All right, I suppose.'

She seemed hardly to be listening. I tried again.

'How were the teachers?'

'The usual pathetic collection. Sad, really. The drama teacher is all right.'

'Oh good. You'll like the chance to do some acting.'

'Mm.'

This did not seem enough to account for the gleam of satisfaction in her eye, not unlike that in Mark Antony's after a particularly enjoyable day of stickleback surveillance. 'Did you have someone to talk to during break?'

'Oh, yes. When I could get a word in edgeways. They were so keen to tell me about themselves. Those that weren't silently worshipping.'

'Worshipping? You mean they've found out about Pa?'

Cordelia looked disdainful. 'Certainly not. You know I never name-drop.' I knew no such thing. 'It was me they were worshipping. Jason said I was the most luscious bird he'd ever seen.'

Foolishly, it had not occurred to me that there would be boys. Ma having favoured a convent education on the grounds that Roman Catholicism had a certain artistic caché, we had no experience of co-educational schools. 'Ah. Is Jason in your class?'

Cordelia looked at me with pitying patience. 'You don't think I want to go out with twelve-year-olds, you idiot? Jason's the head boy.'

'You mean he's eighteen?'

'Actually, I didn't ask to see his passport,' Cordelia drawled sarcastically. 'But he shaves and his voice has broken.'

I decided friendly curiosity was the best approach. 'Is he good-looking?'

'Not bad. But not a patch on Zak.' She closed her eyes and drew a deep breath. 'He's Captain of Games and all the girls are in love with him. He's taking me to the cinema on Saturday.'

'What are we going to do?' I asked Rupert that evening after answering the telephone to four eager adolescent male voices, asking to speak to Cordelia.

We were sitting in the arbour, drinking Chablis and eating delicious walnut sablés, made by Archie. The sunshine was warm. The doves were cooing round our feet, hoping for crumbs. Dirk lifted his lip when they came too near but forbore to chase them, he and I having had strong words on the subject.

'Do? I suppose I had better have another line put in.'

'I mean about all these boys running after Cordelia.'

'There's nothing to be done about that. It's been going on for several hundred thousand years apparently.'

'But she's only twelve!'

'It'll be invaluable experience. You can't teach people things by shutting them up. Make sure she knows about pregnancy and diseases. You can tell her about the inexorable drive of testosterone in the young male, and the difference between lust and love.'

Archie sighed. 'I wish someone would teach *me* what the difference is. If it's possible for a twelve-year-old to know, I must really be lacking in discernment. I keep thinking I've got the hang of it but time and again I'm proved wrong.'

I looked sternly at my sablé, embarrassed. It seemed then that Rupert and Archie had an 'open' relationship. Of course I knew that, by repute anyway, male homosexuals were promiscuous. But I could not imagine Rupert enjoying a brief, bawdy fling. Or perhaps I did not want to. Naturally it was not to be supposed that either of them sought sexual satisfaction in public lavatories. Perhaps they met handsome young men at parties and brought them back to Horn-on-the-Green. There had certainly been nothing like that since Cordelia and I had been living there but it had only been two days. Perhaps our presence was a tiresome impediment to their usual manner of conducting themselves.

I stole a glance at Rupert. He was looking at me through half-closed lids. He smiled and I had an uncomfortable idea that he had guessed what I was thinking. I felt myself flush to the roots of my hair.

'That's the telephone again,' I said on hearing it ring. 'I'll go. I expect it'll be for Cordelia.' I was glad of the excuse to take my hot face indoors.

'Hello?' I said.

'Who's that?' It was a female voice. Sharp, almost accusing.

'Harriet.'

'Harriet who?'

'Harriet Byng.'

There was a brief pause. 'I want to speak to Rupert.'

'I'll get him. Who's calling?'

'Leah. If that's any of your business.'

I put the receiver on the little fruitwood writing desk that Archie said was called a *bonheur du jour* and went out into the garden. 'It's Leah.'

Rupert groaned. 'You didn't say I was here?'

'I implied it.'

'Well, say I've gone out, will you?'

I went back to the telephone. 'He's gone out, I'm afraid.'

'I don't believe you. I'm coming round.'

I heard the click of the receiver.

'She didn't believe me. She's coming round,' I repeated dutifully, on going back into the garden.

Rupert swore under his breath. 'I refuse, I absolutely refuse to have a scene. I've had an exhausting day. The lead French horn was drunk again and we had to find a replacement. Amelia, the heroine, has hardly stopped crying since she discovered last week that her lover – the baritone singing Renato – has been sleeping with the entire chorus. She's been eating so much in compensation that Wardrobe have had to let out her costume to the last thread. Riccardo fell downstairs yesterday and now he limps and has a black eye. He's supposed to be the tragic hero. He looks ridiculous.'

'Oh dear, and you've had so much trouble over Cordelia's school,' I said, feeling thoroughly guilty.

'Don't you start,' said Rupert, very unfairly. He looked his most saturnine.

'We can refuse to let her in,' suggested Archie. 'There's a gloomy-looking youth mooching about the canal, probably one of Cordelia's *aficionados*. They can mooch together.'

I wondered who Leah could be and what was the urgent business that demanded she present herself, uninvited, at Rupert's door. Rupert picked up a book of Rochester's poems and read them with a frowning face while finishing the Chablis.

When Cordelia came out to say that someone was knocking the front door down and should she answer it, Rupert said grumpily, 'Let her in. We'll get it over with.' He looked at us with raised eyebrows. 'If you wouldn't mind taking yourselves off for a minute, I think I'll be able to get rid of her more easily if she has no chance to sit down.'

He put his glass on the table and went to stand by the fountain, arms folded, expression inimical. Archie and I almost stuck in the doorway as we rushed to remove ourselves from the scene, but not before I caught a glimpse of a tall girl with a haughty face and long blonde hair striding through the hall.

'Who is she?' I asked the minute Archie and I were alone down in the kitchen.

632

'Leah Wyldbore-Pater. The most *terr*ifying woman. Sculpts. *Scalps* more accurately. A praying mantis.'

'You don't like her very much?'

'I *told* Rupert to have nothing to do with her. Better mate with Lilith, I said, than Miss Wyldbore-Pater. But who ever listens to good advice?'

'You mean Rupert had an affair with her?'

'In*cred*ible, isn't it? You'd think he'd know better. *I* could see she was trouble from the moment she came up to us at a party and pretended she'd met Rupert before. But then, to be fair, lust did not cloud my judgement. I must admit to making some bad mistakes myself when swept along by the current of desire.'

It was incredible. But not for the reason Archie thought. There were bisexuals in the theatre as elsewhere, but to me they were an unknown quantity. As I thought of it, Rupert, or rather my idea of him, seemed to shimmer and shift, and the end result was something much more threatening. And potentially hurtful. There had been a bitter-sweet poignancy in thinking of him as a man ever beyond reach. Now, in theory, anyway, he wasn't, and the abrupt realisation of various possibilities plunged me into a state of painful suspense and at the same time depressed me unutterably.

'Oh, yes,' I said, eventually, aware that Archie was standing with potato-peeler poised, looking at me. 'Of course. I made a fool of myself over Max. I expect everyone does it.'

'Mm.' Archie continued to look at me. 'I can see it has shocked you to discover that Rupert is like any other man – impulsive and liable to blunder in the bedroom department. You have probably confused a *horr*or of melodramatics with a lack of carnal desire. Rupert has spent most of his life with theatre people, who indulge every emotional caprice, each tug on the heartstrings until they have wrung from it every *nu*ance of sensibility. Not being a performer himself he finds it wearing. He makes an exception in *my* case because he knows I don't expect a full-bore response to my dramatics. Also I cook and drive and organise the day-to-day running of his life, which he doesn't want to have to do for himself. Also,' Archie tried to look modest, 'I think I *may* say with truth that he is fond of me.'

'I'm sure of that,' I said warmly.

A sudden shout – of fright or was it anger? – came from outside. Archie shot me an excited glance.

'A little hot in here, don't you think?'

He sashayed to the window and opened it. In a second I had joined him and we were both listening for all we were worth. The kitchen was in the basement and the window was screened by a box hedge on the other side of the area. We could hear every word without being seen.

'. . . *dare* treat me like this!'

'Like what?' Rupert managed to sound both bored and annoyed.

'You think you can pick me up and drop me like a soiled glove!'

'I seem to remember you picked *me* up.'

'You *pig*! I didn't exactly have to drag you to bed, did I?'

'I agree I came willingly.'

'You were like a dog after a rabbit! You took what you wanted and then left without a backward glance.'

'It lasted several weekends, didn't it? I wasn't aware I had signed up for anything more.'

'You're like all men. Only interested in one thing – a fuck and then it's goodbye.'

'If you wanted something else you should have told me at the beginning.'

'And I suppose you'd have promised love and then dropped me the minute you'd got what you wanted.' Leah sounded livid.

'If you'd told me you wanted love, then I hope I'd have declined the rest, tempting though the offer undoubtedly was. I can't swear to altruism but I think a sense of self-preservation would have made me draw back.'

'So you think I'm good enough to screw but not to love!' Leah was shouting now.

I imagined the members of the Horn-on-the-Green Preservation Society sitting in their several gardens, clucking with disapproval at this breach of the peace.

'No doubt my views are entirely unrepresentative,' said Rupert with deceptive mildness.

A sound like a smack rang out.

'If you hit me again I shall hit you – hard.' I could tell he was really angry now.

'Oh, Rupert, I'm sorry.' Leah was suddenly tearful. 'If you only understood how much it hurts. I'm in love with you. Please. Take pity on me.' Then in a lower tone, throbbing with emotion, 'Kiss me.'

Archie and I exchanged glances.

'If I believed that you really meant that,' said Rupert in a softer tone, 'I should be desperately sorry to have made you unhappy.' Archie and I clutched each other and held our breaths. 'Luckily I don't. Love isn't something that springs up over a few weekends. We hardly know each other.'

'Oh, how cruel you are!' She was sobbing. 'You're breaking my heart! I'm busting up inside. My life isn't worth living. What did I ever do to make it impossible for you to love me?'

'Well,' Rupert spoke with deadly effect, 'I think moral blackmail is pretty unappealing. And I dislike clichés, both in speech and behaviour.'

'You absolute *bas*tard! I must have been crazy to think I was in love with you. Goodbye, Rupert Wolvespurges, and I hope you rot in hell!'

The sound of footsteps running through the house was followed by a slamming of the front door that made the house shake.

'Bravo!' shouted Archie.

Rupert's face appeared over the box hedge. I saw a pink mark on his cheek. 'How dishonourable of you both to listen to what was a painful and private exchange. Harriet, I had thought better of you.'

'Sorry. But you were very good. Though – poor girl – I feel awfully sorry for her.'

'Don't be.' He patted his face gently. 'She nearly broke my jaw. I wonder where she learned to hit like that.'

'I think it's incredibly sexy,' breathed Archie. 'I'm racked with jealousy.'

After that things bowled along smoothly for a while. Rupert said several times that he repented having another telephone line connected for both rang with tiresome consistency and we got into the habit of unplugging them after eight o'clock to be able to enjoy the evening in peace. Cordelia finished the red-and-white garment and began to knit a rainbow-striped cot blanket. After the first few rows it started to develop a strange trapezoid shape. Archie said we had better waste no time looking for a lozenge-shaped cot to match it. Luckily Cordelia's tranquillity was undisturbed by Archie's teasing. In fact she seemed to take it as a tribute.

She and Rupert, however, had another falling-out. To my surprise, when Zak presented himself at the house with the intention of escorting Cordelia to the cinema, Rupert asked him to come into his work-room. Archie and I tried to listen at the door but they made them to fit in the eighteenth century and we heard only a low rumble.

'I merely asked him if he knew how old Cordelia was,' said Rupert when we questioned him later. 'Apparently Cordelia told him she was sixteen. She explained her presence in the lower second form by claiming to have spent several years in a Swiss sanatorium with TB, which had put her behind with her school-work. I suggested to Zak that a romantic encounter with a twelve-year-old might be detrimental to his public image and reminded him that the law took a dim view of sex with children. He seemed anxious to leave after that.'

The scene that followed when Cordelia came downstairs dressed to slay, only to find her *cavaliere servente* gone, was bloody but brief. It is difficult to continue to shriek at someone who waits politely for you to finish, then goes back to reading his book without comment.

The following day, when Cordelia was pale and exhausted from alternately sulking and sobbing, Rupert had a talk with her. From what she told me afterwards, I was much impressed by his ingenuity. Apparently he had told her that love affairs rushed into without forethought and with persons lacking experience and finesse would destroy the exquisite bloom of romance for ever. There were subtleties and refinements that one needed maturity to master and it would be a pity for a great beauty to throw herself away on the first grubby schoolboy who offered himself. It would not make inspiring reading in later biographies. It was a good thing Cordelia had not heard the exchange between Rupert and Leah or she might have been less inclined to take his word for it.

Anyway, the end result was that Zak circulated Cordelia's real age among his contemporaries and the bigger boys stopped calling. Cordelia had no intention of squandering her loveliness on fourth-formers, now she had set herself to learn the arts of coquetry. Archie gave her a book about geishas, which absorbed her for several weeks. As she was to be Viola in the school production of *Twelfth Night*, she had enough for the moment to occupy her thoughts.

We all worked hard at our various callings and when we

came home, inspiration spent, energies depleted, Archie had wine cooling in the fridge and delicious things cooking on the stove. Because Rupert was in a crucial period of rehearsal we entertained no one but Pa and Pussyfoot occasionally and, more often, Ophelia and Charles. Rupert said he felt like a voyeur whenever they came to dinner. It was obvious that they had got out of a rank, enseamèd bed to come to Horn-on-the-Green and that the moment they left us, they dashed back into it.

It was, looking back, a time of real happiness spoiled only by occasional reverses, such as when Mr Podmore opened his office door long enough to shout, 'Deb Dismissed for Overwriting,' before slamming it so hard that our eardrums practically bled. I quite believed my career was over and started to pack up the tools of my trade – a Biro, two pencils and an India-rubber – which I could hardly see through a blur of tears. Muriel told me to take no notice. He had at one time or another sacked everyone on the staff but nothing ever came of it. Anyway, the union would have something to say if it did. Eileen made us all a cup of tea and opened a new packet of caramel wafers, which we worked our way through as a cosy threesome with a sense of solidarity that was actually rather enjoyable. An hour later Mr Podmore sent me out to report on the Brixton Rodent Show as though nothing had happened.

The letters from Max came less frequently now. The last one was postmarked Rio de Janeiro. I threw it away unopened.

Maria-Alba continued to write, more and more sensibly. At last she wrote to say that she had decided to become a noviciate, having been promised sole reign in the convent kitchens, Sister Mary-Joseph's arthritis having become troublesome. My first reaction was dismay. Initially I thought my uneasiness was for Maria-Alba's sake but, when I had a chance to think about it, I realised my distress was entirely selfish. After all, if there were enough faith to sustain it, life in a closed order must be a haven for sufferers of severe agoraphobia. The family she loved was scattered, her home disbanded. I quickly came to see that it was the best possible solution.

In her letter Maria-Alba said she had made her peace with God since he had been kind enough to put her in charge of an enormous kitchen. Her only regret, she was kind enough to say, was parting from our family and me in particular. She would be allowed a few visitors to say goodbye. Would I come?

Of course I did go, the next week. The convent was a grim Victorian building but in the courtyard, surrounding the life-size statue of the Virgin in painted azure robes, were glowing orange nasturtiums and scarlet zinnias. It was cheerful and reassuring, just the sort of thing Maria-Alba liked. The nuns greeted me like an old friend, their smiling faces unlined by doubt or sorrow. I was shown into the visitors' room. Maria-Alba, from now on to be known as Sister Veronica John, was waiting on the other side of a grille. The bars reminded me, most unpleasantly, of visiting my father in prison.

We wept on seeing each other. Maria-Alba had loved me unconditionally all my life and I owed her more than I could possibly tell. But she assured me she was happy. She looked beautiful in the plain grey habit. She had stopped taking sedatives and anti-depressants and her skin had lost its yellowness. It was odd but delightful to see her cheeks faintly flushed with pink. She already knew all the family news from my letters, and in this context our worldly concerns seemed irrelevant. On every wall were images of the crucifixion and pictures of the Christ and the Virgin. It was natural that we should talk about God and the eternal verities and things that really mattered. I came away feeling that though Maria-Alba and I would never see each other again, we thoroughly loved and understood each other and that this union of hearts and minds was as much as anyone could possibly ask.

I cried all the way home on the bus, not from sadness but because I was deeply moved. Also another part of my childhood was gone for ever. Fortunately I was able to creep into the house and remove all sign of tears by supper-time so as not to annoy Rupert.

FORTY

It was the opening night of *Othello*. I felt sick all day with sympathetic butterflies. My father suffered agonies from stage fright on first nights. Before the first performance of every play he would announce at breakfast that someone must ring the understudy as he, Pa, was incapable of putting even a toe on the stage that evening. He was not an actor, he was a talentless sham, whom the audience would boo and the critics rip to shreds. He would dry, he would faint, he would freeze with a *petit mal*. Pa had never been epileptic but one of his many phobias was that he was about to become one. He could not eat, could barely sip a glass of water. As a child I used to stand outside the bathroom door weeping tears of fellow-feeling while he retched fruitlessly into the lavatory.

Years ago, when he was due to go on as Romeo, he had suddenly decided that he was too old for the part – he was thirty-five then but actually could pass for twenty in makeup – and that the critics were certain to ridicule his interpretation. He had locked himself in my bedroom and threatened to throw himself out of the window. The fire brigade had come round with a canvas sheet in which to catch him and Loveday had become violent with one of them for trampling on his yew

641

cuttings. After a couple of hours of coaxing and threatening, my mother had hit on the clever scheme of getting Bron to puff cigarette smoke under the bedroom door while shouting that the house was on fire. My father, who also had a phobia about being burned alive, came out at once and was bodily carried downstairs by the firemen.

On every first night our long-suffering GP was summoned to prescribe beta-blockers and my father would deliberate for hours about whether to take them. He always ended by flushing them down the lav rather than risk taking the edge off his performance. By the time the director shoved him on stage we were all nearly demented with the strain.

Pa had not yet recovered from his prison horrors. He could not use lifts, or even trains in case they went into tunnels. Being in small rooms with lots of people made him panicky. He could not lock the lavatory door or even close it. He had perfected whistling the triumphal march from *Aida* as a warning that he was enthroned.

Would Pussyfoot manage to calm him, I wondered. Should I go round to her flat and offer assistance? Selfishly I shrank from the idea. I had been there only once and had not enjoyed it. From the moment the door opened to envelope me in fumes of Nuages, which was the scent Pussyfoot wore in bucketfuls, I had felt profoundly depressed and had to stick a stupid grin on my face all the time so they wouldn't see how I hated it. It was partly because in this domestic setting they seemed very much a couple. Also Pussyfoot was very house-proud. She asked me to take off my shoes in the hall, though I noticed she and Pa were wearing theirs and that his were not particularly clean. One is somehow at a disadvantage being the only one in stockinged feet. Also before I sat down she whisked away the silk cushion from my chair and threw it on an unoccupied sofa, as though my clothes were dirty or I might be sick on it. She put a coaster under my glass in case

642

I marked the table and moved a sort of air-freshener thing in a plastic cone right next to me.

Pa never noticed these things, of course. He was too busy pretending they were delighted to see me. I honestly think she was hardly aware of doing them herself. Her subconscious was protesting against the invasion of the enemy. While Pa and I talked, Pussyfoot had looked at her fingernails, hummed, stared out of the window and started every time either of us spoke to her as though her thoughts were miles away. Then she began to yawn until her eyes ran. I made an excuse and left.

No, I would not go to Pussyfoot's flat. Luckily I had to go to work anyway so I was able to survive until five o'clock with an assumption of composure though I had a stomachache on and off all day. When I pushed open the door of 10 Horn-on-the-Green, my nostrils were greeted by a mixture of a sharp cologne and the familiar scent of Cabochard.

'Here she is!' Ronnie got up from his chair and came to greet me with open arms. A sprucer Ronnie whose elegant clothes displayed a trimmer paunch. 'How are you, my dear? You're looking quite marvellous! Isn't she, Clarissa?'

'She certainly is.' Ma ran her eyes over me from crown to toe before offering me her cheek. 'My word, darling, what an improvement! Turn round so I can see you.'

I pirouetted, enjoying the unaccustomed warmth of maternal approval. 'How lovely to see you both! What a wonderful surprise!'

'Darling, old habits die hard. I couldn't let Waldo have a first night without being there to support him. I had a dreadful nightmare last night that he'd dried, and this morning Ronnie said, "If it worries you so much let's go up to town and cheer the old boy on." Wasn't that sweet of him?'

'Very.' I looked affectionately at Ronnie, who beamed at these words of praise. Probably they were in short supply. I felt like hugging them both for coming but I knew that Ma wearied quite quickly of demonstrations of affection.

'So,' my mother continued, 'I telephoned Rupert to see if he could get us tickets and he asked us to come and stay here. I must say it's pretty stylish.' She looked about her with an appreciative eye, admiring the pale-green painted panelling, the rose-coloured sofas, the group portrait by Zoffany above the chimneypiece, the collection of Chelsea botanical plates in the alcoves on either side. 'Of course, queers have no one to spend their money on but themselves. They can be deliciously selfish.'

'Actually Rupert's already spent a fortune on us,' I said. 'He's been incredibly *un*selfish, paying our bills while Pa was – away and giving me these lovely clothes and having Cordelia and me living here. And there was her school uniform – the blazer was twenty pounds and goodness knows what it added up to with a new hockey stick and a tennis racquet. And four hundred pairs of navy knickers.'

'It was only a casual remark, darling.' My mother raised her eyebrows. 'No need to get het up. I'm sure he's been perfectly angelic. I can assure you that I'm very ready to overlook any disagreements we may have had in the past –'

'Hello, Clarissa. Hello, Ronnie.' Rupert had come in through the French windows. I wondered if he had overheard. 'Sorry I'm later than I meant to be. The meeting went on longer than I expected.' He shook Ronnie's hand and looked uncertainly at my mother. She rose and placed an affectionate hand on his shoulder while kissing both cheeks.

'So divine of you to have us at short notice, Rupert. Archie's made us feel utterly at home. I'm completely in love with this house. You're a very clever boy.' She gave him the benefit of her most seductive smile and the moment his back was turned gave me a conspiratorial wink.

Cordelia arrived home a few minutes after Rupert and was

thrilled to see Ma and Ronnie. Archie brought in champagne and *diablotins*, which are tiny puffs of pastry filled with whatever you like – in this case, a mixture of Roquefort, shredded mushrooms and courgettes. At six o'clock we went to change and at seven we were driven to the Kemble Theatre where we were to meet Ophelia and Charles in the bar. An admiring throng gathered round Ma and Ronnie in the foyer.

'Do look!' I overheard someone say. 'It's that actor Ronald Whatshisname who was Bonnie Prince Charlie. My mother's been in love with him for years.'

'Ooh, yes,' said another, 'And isn't that Vanessa Redgrave on his arm?'

Upstairs the crowd parted respectfully to let Ma and Ronnie through, affording us a glimpse of a familiar rear view seated on a stool at the bar.

'Bron! Oh, my darling boy!' Ma ran in slow motion towards him, her beautiful dress floating out behind her like an advertisement for chocolate. The other theatregoers were all eyes and all ears. 'I've missed you so much, my angel.' They kissed each other with consummate grace. 'And you never telephone! You've no idea what a mother's feelings are! Where are you staying? Is Letizia with you? Oh, my sweetest boy, it's such heaven to see you!'

'Hello, Ma. You're looking top-hole. Letizia sends her love but she's got a show on and couldn't spare the time. I told her I *had* to be here for the old man's first night so she agreed to let me off the leash just for this evening. I'm flying back tonight. But why don't you and Ronnie come and stay as soon as the show's over? Say next week? We're renting a palazzo near Rome for few months.'

'What bliss, darling! We'd love to. If you're sure I wouldn't cramp Letizia's style? It isn't every young bride who wants her mother-in-law to stay just when she's getting to grips with housekeeping.'

It occurred to me then that there was quite a lot about Letizia that Bron hadn't told Ma.

'Oh, Letizia doesn't worry about that kind of thing. The villa's well-staffed, including two cooks, so we'll be fairly comfortable, I should think.'

'I must say that's a very tempting invitation,' said Ronnie, looking eager. 'Speaking for myself I could do with a break from decorating –'

'Stop grumbling, Ronnie,' cut in Ma. 'Of course we shall come. It's so wonderful to see you, sweetest boy! Shall we have a chance to talk afterwards? What time is your flight?'

'Oh, any time I like. Letizia has her own ducky little jet. It's waiting for me at Heathrow.'

There was more in this vein. By the time Ophelia and Charles arrived, everyone standing near us had given up any pretence of talking to each other. They were gripped by the impromptu entertainment provided by my family.

The first bell rang and at once, with a spurt of terror, I was brought back to the present. We went to our seats in the front half of the stalls. My knees were weak and ached with fright for my darling father, who I knew would be shivering in the wings. Just as the lights were going down and a hush was falling over the auditorium, there was a disturbance behind as some latecomers scrambled along the row. I recognised one of the voices muttering, 'Excuse me . . . Sorry . . . Thanks . . .' I turned round and saw Portia and Jonno.

The curtain went up and we were engulfed by that familiar rush of cold air from the stage, which always wrought my nerves to their highest pitch. I had forgotten how long the first scene of *Othello* is – or so it seemed to me now – in which Iago declares his hatred for his master and plots his downfall. Cordèlia who, she said, could take Shakespeare or leave him – preferably the latter – made so much noise tearing out a page of her programme and pleating it into a fan, that the woman in front turned round and glared. For the rest of Scene One Cordelia dropped little bits of torn-up paper into the folds of the woman's shawl collar. In the end I had to take the programme away from her. I sensed that the audience was restless. Everyone had come to see the man whose wrongful imprisonment had made him the focus of intense interest and public sympathy. At last the flats did a cunning little twist about and the backdrop lifted to indicate a new location for Scene Two. Now was the moment for Othello's first entrance.

The audience leaned forward in their seats. The spotlights dimmed. Servants ran on to the stage bearing torches and then Pa strode forth from the wings, magnificent in crimson and silver. A collective murmur of 'Aah' broke out spontaneously and a current of excitement shot through the theatre.

''Tis better as it is.' Pa's voice boomed out . . . 'Let him do his spite.'

As the play unfolded I could hardly believe this man was my own dear father. Not only because he was as dark and glistening as a Sachertorte, but because he was the embodiment of martial swagger and barely restrained violence. In real life Pa was a man whose pain threshold was zero. He had to be completely anaesthetised before the dentist was allowed even to look into his mouth. When Ma had babies he had to be exiled from the house until it was over, lest he should hear anything like a moan and be precipitated into full-blown madness.

But as Othello he bore himself like a man who would knock you down if he disliked the colour of your hat. And then repent of it afterwards. A man of supercharged energy whose instincts were to react first and think second. A bear of a man, fiery of temper, always running to extremes. A man more at home in a sea-battle than in the bedroom with a beautiful young wife. He could command legions of

647

rough men but he was a child when it came to understanding women.

And yet how tender he was with Desdemona. When he took her in his arms to say, 'I cannot speak enough of this content: it stops me here', and put his hand on his heart, he was humble, tamed, his voice tremulous, at the point of tears. His inability to articulate the strength of his love for her was touchingly at odds with the fluent tales of his adventures at sea, his descriptions of 'hairbreadth scapes i' th' imminent deadly breach'. Like Desdemona, the audience listened with a greedy ear.

Othello is often played as a man of neurotic insecurity, distrustful and uneasy in a white man's world. Pa showed us why Desdemona loved him. He charmed us like birds to his hand and won our allegiance so that as we watched him degenerate by degrees from ecstatic lover to afflicted wretch and then to monster and murderer, we could not withhold our pity. We saw how his reason was destroyed by the conflict between love and jealousy. When he smothered his innocent wife, his suffering was unbearable to behold. His remorse was so frightful, his suicide so tragic and calamitous yet so inescapable that tears poured down my cheeks. Othello and Pa had merged in my mind as victims and outcasts. Great unhappiness cannot all be wept away at once.

As the curtain closed on the three corpses you could have heard a fly buzz. Then a trickle of applause began that rapidly became a roar. The curtain was slower than usual to reveal the cast. The audience grew clamorous. When it parted all the actors were on stage except for Pa. Ophelia and I looked at each other in alarm. What could have happened to him? He explained afterwards that when he had thrown himself on the body of Desdemona to die in her arms he had cut his head on the bedpost and there had been a panic backstage to find a sticking plaster. The delay served him well. The audience had worked itself into a frenzy of impatience and when at last he appeared it started to bellow. Everyone from stalls to amphitheatre leaped up to give him a standing ovation, stamping, throwing flowers, whistling and shouting their appreciation.

This went on unabated for what seemed like ages while Pa stood uncharacteristically still, not bowing or kissing his fingers to them as he usually did but looking around at the excited smiling faces as though dazed. Then he held up his hands for silence and slowly the noise died.

'Dear friends,' began Pa. 'I am emboldened by your generosity to delay you for a few moments.'

'Hear, hear!' Another burst of applause.

Pa smiled and waited for them to be silent. 'It will not be news to many of you, perhaps, that until recently I was detained at Her Majesty's pleasure in the insalubrious building known as Winton Shrubs.' There was a jocularity in this that made the audience titter uncertainly. A few clapped and then broke off, abashed. 'More than enough has been recorded in the press about my own tribulations and it is not of them I wish to speak. You can guess that I found myself in unfamiliar company. Men who, if report were true, had done terrible things. Murderers, violators and thieves. Initially I shrank from them in horror. But when you are locked up together, twenty-three hours a day, in a room the size of a cupboard you cannot help falling into conversation. And what I heard made for pretty uncomfortable listening, I can tell you. We think we can imagine what it must be like to be born poor and unfortunate – deprived of those things that everyone in this theatre takes for granted. But what these men had to tell defied imagination. I had not guessed the half of it. When they spoke of their experiences in childhood and early youth, my blood ran like fire, then ice. Life is a merciless bully for children born into circumstances of grinding poverty, to unhappy families broken apart by crime, drugs, alcohol. It brutalises the affections, cramps the intellect, destroys aspiration. It grinds Beauty and Truth under its heel.' Pa paused for a moment, visibly moved. 'These men talked tough, but who were they kidding? They weren't even any good at being *bad*. Until you spend time in prison you can have no idea of the sort of living death it is. The claustrophobia, the boredom, the ugliness, the dirtiness, the inhumanity. Ladies and gentlemen, these men were on the whole bad but they were not wholly bad. Are some babies born cruel, avaricious, evil? I don't believe it for a moment! Misfortune makes men bad and prison makes them worse.'

He paused and coughed, wiping his eyes on the sleeve of his sumptuous black and gold tunic. Several people around us were sniffing. I found I was biting my handkerchief until my jaw ached.

'So what happens when the sentence is served and the gate swings wide? Many prisoners have lost touch with family and friends. They go out into a world which is at best indifferent to their fate. A lonely bedsitter, the old familiar poverty, ugliness, meanness of spirit. Beauty and Truth have made themselves scarce yet again. And to compound the misery, they are marked for ever as the dregs, the scum, the detritus of society. The only people who do not heartily distrust and despise them are other ex-prisoners. Is it any wonder that the majority reoffend and find themselves in the grim cycle of crime and punishment? Ah yes, you would say. But it's their own fault. And of course it *is*. But where would any of us be, without good luck behind us? A kind parent, an inspired teacher, an agile mind, good looks, some power to attract, enough money for the simple pleasures of life, to escape the squalor of base existence. Speaking for myself I believe I could have been the lowest villain imaginable if I had undergone the misery and degradation of those men.' Pa's voice broke here and he began to weep openly. There was a general rustling as people groped for handkerchiefs. 'So, with these thoughts in mind, I hope you will not object when I tell you that the entire cast and theatre management have most generously agreed that all receipts from tonight's performance are to be donated to the Waldo Byng Ex-Prisoners' Centre.'

There was a moment's silence and then a great cheer went up with more whistles and stamping, and such was the collective enthusiasm for the cause I was prepared to bet that for a brief while there was not a man or woman in the auditorium who would have objected to find an ex-con waiting for them at home, sipping their whisky and wearing their own fireside slippers.

'Magnificent, Waldo! Annihilating! I was scorched to my very bones!' Ma swept into his dressing room and everyone in it apart from Pa crowded back against the walls. I had noticed before that my mother always took up a surprising amount of space for one so slender and lissome. Pa and Ma embraced each other fervently as though they were lovers from rival families who had been kept apart by vindictive relations. But I knew it meant little. The old French saying, *Toujours il y a l'un qui donne la baisée et l'autre qui tend la joue*, is probably true. In my parents' case they both offered the cheek and it was this need to be the object of whatever adoration was going, that made them fundamentally incompatible.

After an effusion of compliments they embraced for the last time and Ma made a graceful exit. The two commissionaires who had been appointed to stand guard at the door of Pa's dressing room and keep out undesirables, temporarily lost control and a heaving, babbling throng pressed forward. Poor Pussyfoot was shoved into a corner and almost forced to sit in Pa's wash-basin. Her face had been glazed in a mirthless grin as she watched my mother's performance. I felt quite sorry

651

for her. I was standing just inside the doorway, having been recognised and approved by one of the doorkeepers. I took a step in Pa's direction and felt my progress impeded by a clutch on the back of my dress. I turned to see, above the epaulettes of the bouncers, the top half of a face I recognised. It was Caroline Frensham. She had squeezed her arm between their uniformed chests and was hanging on to my beautiful gooseberry-green silk taffeta with a determined hand.

'Harriet! I've got to talk to you!'

I had read somewhere that in New Zealand there are 'strong-eye dogs', trained to control sheep by staring fixedly at them. Caroline's eyes were small but fierce. Obediently, like a lamb to the slaughter, I turned and pushed my way under the locked arms of the guardians of Pa's sanctum. I had been haunted by Max's wife to such an extent that, on finding myself actually in her presence, I did consider making an undignified dash for it. But such was the crowd in the corridor, flight was impossible. Also Caroline's face was miserable. I thought she looked ill. I had behaved very badly. It was time to atone.

Together we elbowed through the mob until we reached a place of relative calm. I started to say, 'Caroline, you must believe how sorry I am. It was a dreadful mistake –'

But she wasn't listening. 'Harriet! I'm desperate! Just desperate.' She clutched at a button on the coat that lay over my arm, as though I might fly from her. But this I now had no intention of doing, provided she did not become violent. 'I've got to see him! I can't go on like this!' She started to cry.

'But – truthfully – I don't know where he is. Well, somewhere in South America, I think,' honesty compelled me to admit, 'but really I've had no contact –'

'What? Oh, you mean Max. He's in Brazil. But I'm not talking about *him*. It's Waldo. I've just *got* to see him! Oh, hell, Harriet, you're a big girl now. He and your mother have

652

an understanding – I'm sure you know all about it.' It was more of a statement than a question. I half nodded, half shook my head but she carried on talking at speed anyway, almost gabbling. I assumed she was still taking pills. 'OK, so Waldo and I have been having an affair. I know he feels bad about wrecking my marriage, but I've made up my mind to divorce Max, whatever. He's never been faithful – he even slept with my bridesmaid the night before our wedding – he's incapable of passing up a chance of a fuck. All he ever wanted from me was my money. When I fell in love with Waldo I realised what a fool I'd been, putting up with that *bas*tard all these years. Waldo's everything I've always wanted in a man – tender, sincere, unselfish. You know, he's returned every present I've ever given him? He's so high-minded. I just worship the ground he walks on.'

In her urgency Caroline increased her grip on my button and it came off. It was carved jet and I knew I'd never be able to match it but it would have seemed heartless to appear concerned.

'Harriet!' Caroline's red-rimmed eyes were boring into mine. 'You've got to help me! I've done everything Waldo asked. While he was in prison I stayed with my sister in New Zealand so the papers wouldn't write him up as an adulterer and prejudice his case. But now he's free what harm can it do? When I call him he always says to wait a while longer till the fuss has died down.'

I remembered Pa complaining, while he was in prison, of a tiresomely persistent girlfriend who showered him with unwanted presents. If only he had told me then that it was Caroline Frensham.

'It's been damn near six months! I'm so lonesome without him!' More tears fell and she rubbed her nose with the back of her hand, turning it into a scarlet blob. 'But when I rang his apartment yesterday, a woman answered. She told me there was no point in calling any more. She said Waldo wasn't interested in me.' Caroline laughed, a desperate sound. 'Well, I knew better than *that*. I just got on a plane and came straight over. I mean, who *was* that woman? Not Clarissa, that's for sure! Sounded like a Yank to me. Those guys on the door wouldn't let me backstage before the performance. And now they want to stop me even speaking to him. I'm going crazy!'

I thought she did look mad. Her eyes were staring and there was a fleck of foam at the corner of her mouth. I noticed that her coat was fastened on the wrong buttons, her hair looked limp and greasy and her hands were shaking. I wondered what I ought to do. I could tell her point-blank about Pussyfoot. Supposing she went off and killed herself? Max might have been telling me the truth about her suicidal impulses. I could not take the risk.

'Why don't you go home, Caroline? I *promise* I'll get him to telephone you. You must be very tired if you've just got off the plane. Wouldn't it be better to get a little sleep before you see him? You really don't look well.'

'Oh. Yeah.' She looked down at herself in a bewildered sort of way and I felt a brute, stringing her along just like Pa. 'Yeah, I'm bushed. Guess I look pretty rough, eh? Perhaps I'll go back home and lie down a bit.' She put up her hand to her hair. 'And I'll get my hair fixed. I want him to see me look my best. That's a good idea, Harriet. You're a peach!'

Oh no, I said to myself silently. I'm a selfish coward. 'I expect he's got your number?'

'Yeah. Tell him to call me first thing tomorrow.'

Now that I had suggested she might be tired she seemed hardly able to keep on her feet. She was swaying and her lids were drooping. Gently I uncurled her unresisting fingers and extracted my button. 'Can you get a taxi all right?'

'I've got a car and a driver waiting. I'll be OK. Thanks, Harriet. You're a pal.'

I watched her staggering along the corridor, with feelings of sorrow and dread on her behalf. I would speak to my father at once and make him see that he must, as gently and kindly as possible, tell her that the affair was all over. But when I fought through the crowd and at last got near enough to press my lips to his sooty cheek, Pa gripped my arm. 'Harriet, thank God! Get them out of here, will you?' Sweat was making rivulets through his makeup and his eyes were terror-stricken. 'I think I'm going mad!' he whimpered. 'I want to go home!'

Bron, who was standing nearby, overheard. 'Don't blame you. It's a deplorable crush. Somebody's trodden on my new crocodile shoes. It'll be a miracle if they haven't ruined them.'

Living with Letizia seemed to have made a new man of Bron. While I was trying to think how to dispel the fawning crowd without hurting anyone's feelings, my brother, with uncharacteristic purpose, extinguished his cigarette in his neighbour's glass of champagne and clapped his hands.

'All right, everyone. Din-dins is on me at Crillons. *Presto pronto.* Last one there's a sissy!'

FORTY-ONE

The reviews of *Othello* were uniformly ecstatic. Pa's performance was 'profound', 'elegiac', 'intense' and 'percipient'. He had given 'a transcendent interpretation of good and evil rarely seen on the English stage'. He was 'magnetic and puissant'. He had 'redefined Shakespeare's dramatic purposes for a whole generation.' He was even 'the greatest Shakespearean actor of the twentieth century'. He was inundated with offers of parts. There were rumours of a knighthood in the next honours list.

Suddenly my father could do no wrong. Newspapers reported his separation from my mother with unusual discretion and pleased Ma by mentioning that she had been 'an unforgettable Rosalind' and publishing a photograph of her that was at least ten years old. She and Ronnie had hurried back to Cornwall the day after the first night to oversee the plasterers. Portia and Jonno returned to their cottage, which currently had an infestation of squirrels and flooded after every rainstorm, but they swore that having ducks swimming round the kitchen table was indescribably romantic. Bron had overdone the Moët et Chandon at Crillons and had been carried off by two charming Italians and flown back to Milan.

Ophelia and Charles resumed their satisfactory careers and sizzling love-life. Cordelia went back to school and had her own first night before the end of term, when she took the house by storm as Viola in *Twelfth Night*. I was so proud of her. Watching the skill with which she beguiled the audience into believing her to be by turns an enigmatic boy-servant and a girl on the verge of womanhood, I was inclined to believe in Cordelia's prophesy that she had a brilliant future before her. Even Rupert was moved to comment, saying that she had the rare power to absorb the eye. Naturally Cordelia was thrilled by her own success. Every member of my family seemed deliriously happy.

Except me.

During former turbulent times I had often thought that if my parents and siblings were happy I should have nothing more to wish for. But of course I was much more selfish than that. I was not so miserable that I drenched my pillow with tears at night and dreaded to face each day. No one living with Rupert and Archie in that charming house, with every sense deliciously catered for, could have been anything other than entertained and gratified, superficially at least. No, the cause of my gnawing unhappiness lay deep, and every time I started to examine it I was so appalled by what I discovered that I gave it up at once. But one thing bothered me so repeatedly and insistently that I decided to do something about it.

The nearer we got to the first night of *Un Ballo in Maschera* the more distracted Rupert became. Sometimes we had to repeat things two or three times before he heard them. He wandered about, muttering to himself and almost gave up eating and sleeping. He looked pale and large-eyed, and after one particularly long telephone call from a member of stage management he shut himself into his work-room for several hours and not even Archie could get a monosyllable from him.

'It's because he's so buttoned-up,' complained Archie as we sat by ourselves in the arbour. Cordelia was in the kitchen, making herself a kimono. 'If *only* he'd throw a tantrum he'd release some nervous tension. Or take some woman to bed.'

'That might create more problems,' I said. 'Remember Leah.'

'Certainly. And Celia, Beatrice and Pascale. *Not* to mention Anna, Esther and Hildebrand.'

'You just did.'

'What?'

'Mention them. Anyway, who are they?'

'The most recent of Rupert's women.'

I was aware of a sick feeling. It is not pleasant to have one's gods dethroned. I knew Rupert sometimes drank too much, that he was bad-tempered in the mornings, that he could be hard and unsympathetic, and yet . . . I pulled myself together. If he chose to behave like a sottish Lothario that was entirely his business. It was nothing to me.

'Hildebrand. What an awful name.'

'It's Teutonic for war sword. He met her when she was a Valkyrie in a production he reviewed at Bayreuth so it's quite apt. Thick blonde hair and a chest that required specially forged outsize armour.'

I suspected Archie of teasing but anyway it seemed more dignified to be indifferent. 'I'm delighted Rupert has so many women he can call on for consolation.'

Archie paused in the act of pouring himself another glass of wine. '*Oho!*'

'Oho what?' I said, perhaps snappishly.

'Oh – nothing.' Archie's eyes wandered to the mossy statue of a woman, who stood ankle-deep in some pretty dark purple flowers with a scent of plums, at the end of an avenue of pleached hornbeams. 'That's Clytie,' he said. 'She was a sea-nymph in love with Helios, the sun-god. He deserted her for another woman. So she went into a huff. According to Ovid, she lay naked on the ground for nine nights and days, quenching her thirst only with her own tears. Then her limbs took root in the soil, a mortal pallor spread over her and her body became a colourless stalk. Her head turned *bright* violet. Now, though she's fastened to the ground she turns her face always in the direction of the sun, which she never ceases to worship. That flower you see there is the heliotrope, named after her. A sweet tale but a reminder that we must be careful where we lay our loves for clumsy feet to trample on.'

I waited for him to tell me what had brought this story to mind but he changed the subject. 'We must be *very* careful not to make demands on Rupert until the first night is over. You might have a word with Cordelia to that effect.'

This chimed in so neatly with what had been depressing my spirits that I went indoors almost at once and began to write the article I had been brooding over for the last week. It was a review of Pa's *Othello*. I wrote the first draft straight off with hardly a pause. Because I was discussing abstractions – love, honour, courage, jealousy, and so on – I found the words came more easily than when I was trying to describe supernatural happenings and make them live in the reader's mind. When I read the piece through, it seemed not entirely hopeless. I polished it carefully over the next couple of evenings, typed it out during one lunch hour and that evening posted copies of it, along with my 'Spook Hall' articles, to the three provincial newspapers I had heard of.

The truth was, the burden of indebtedness had become too much to bear. Though I gave Rupert my mite – three-quarters of my earnings at the *Brixton Mercury*. – I knew it was a fraction of what Cordelia, Dirk, Mark Antony and I must be costing him. My clothes alone came to a terrifying total. I tried to be economical but money had never been something I had much idea of. When Archie found me standing at the kitchen sink trying to stuff a tin with soap, as Maggie did at Pye Place, using scraps of Camay I had saved from the loos at work, he had been indignant.

'In Dante's *Inferno* there's a special place in the fourth circle of Purgatory reserved for skinflints. They're forced to roll weights up and down a hill in company with the profligate, each group hurling insults at each other as they pass. You will *not* like it.'

'I know, but I'm so conscious of how much Rupert spends on us. I feel horribly guilty.'

'Ah. So *that's* why you've been nibbling cheese rinds, eating apple cores and refusing second helpings. At first I feared your peculiar behaviour might be because you were *enceinte* with a tiny Frensham.'

'Thank God, no! That's one thing to be grateful for.'

Archie looked at me consideringly. 'Why the tone of despondency? I should have thought there were plenty of things in your young life to make you *skip* for joy. Anyway, if you want to save money I suggest you discourage Dirk from chewing. He's just destroyed my chamois moccasins embroidered by a now-extinct Indian tribe, of which I was extremely fond.'

'Oh, no! Has he? He's such a bad dog. I'm dreadfully sorry. Is there any chance I could get them repaired for you?'

'Not the slightest. They're in at least twenty pieces, not counting the morsels in Dirk's stomach.'

'Oh, dear. And yesterday he ate the belt of Rupert's mac. He didn't say anything when I apologised but I could see he was very annoyed when Dirk threw up the buckle on the Savonnerie rug. I still haven't got the stain out.' I paused, my fingers a sticky mess of slivers of soap that refused to adhere. 'Rupert's the sort of person everybody runs to for help. I don't know why they do. I can't work it out because it's not as though he's exactly friendly – unless he's in the mood. And

660

he's got such a strong sense of duty that he always does help. When he was a boy we were always interrupting him and asking him to do things, though I could see sometimes that he wanted to be alone. But he invariably did them. None of my family has any sense of duty, so I was always very aware of that. Now I feel as though I'm taking advantage of him.'

'You mustn't be earnest, Harriet. You'll get *terr*ible frown-lines and look a hundred and forty when you're only twenty-three,' was all Archie would say.

The provincial newspapers were maddeningly slow to respond but eventually after nearly three weeks had gone by I received a letter from the *Manchester Sentinel* inviting me for an interview. I took a day off work and caught the train to Manchester without telling anyone where I was going. I was very nervous but the three people I spoke to at the *Sentinel* were genial and extremely keen to talk about Pa. It was immediately obvious that being the daughter of the most popular actor in England was my best card and I played it for all I was worth. After another week of waiting, I got a letter appointing me assistant deputy arts sub-editor at a salary that was double what I was earning at the *Mercury*. I was enormously pleased. Well, pretty pleased, anyway. Any cowardly reluctance I might have felt about leaving London and beginning a new life I did my best to suppress the minute it threatened to surface.

Besides, I would not be alone. I intended to take Cordelia with me. It was hard on her having to change schools again just when she had settled at the Arthur Brocklebuck Comp but I thought this would be better than living with Pussyfoot, who very definitely did not want her, or with Ophelia, who might not make a very good job of pretending she did. Pussyfoot complained constantly about the expense of doing up the new house in Hampstead in an attempt to forestall demands from us children but I was prepared to do battle on Cordelia's behalf. Pa must make her an allowance until her education was finished.

Of course, I would not ask for anything for myself. I would be twenty-three in September and should have been earning my living years ago. Now I could not understand how I had existed for so long in a fantasy world without purpose or responsibility. With my new salary I could probably afford to rent a double room, not too distant from the premises of the *Sentinel*. With care I could make my beautiful clothes last several years. In time, if I worked hard, we might progress to a small flat. To one so thoroughly spoilt as I had been, there was something melancholy in this prospect but it was a challenge and I knew I enjoyed working. Also we would be near Portia and Jonno. Naturally they would be very much bound up in each other but we could meet often. Occasionally, anyway. And I would know she was not far away, which would make the whole thing seem much less lonely. And Dirk and Mark Antony would make the most dreary lodgings seem like home.

Cordelia, when I told her the plan, took a less sanguine view. 'Manchester! You must be barmy! We're doing *North and South* at school. It's all smoky and Mrs Hale dies of lung cancer and there are strikes and everything's covered with soot! I'm not going!'

But when I discussed the alternatives she was equally firm. 'I won't go and live with Ophelia and Charles. I'd be left out all the time. Beside Charles's flat's only got one bedroom. Where would I sleep? I'd hear them having sex, night and day. I'd be as mad as the Lady of Shallots in a week.'

When I suggested Pa and Pussyfoot in Hampstead Cordelia became scathing. 'It'd take about a week of Pussyfoot grumbling about me wearing out the chairs and breathing up her oxygen before I chucked myself under a train like Anna What'shername and if you remember how much you cried when Greta Garbo did it; think how much worse it'll be when it's your own sister, much younger and even more beautiful.'

'Very well, then Manchester it must be.'

'But why can't we stay here?'

This was Archie's question when I told him of the projected move while we were in the kitchen, making supper.

'Because I can't go on being a parasite. I must learn to be independent. You and Rupert have been so good to have us. But you must be allowed to have your house to yourselves again.'

'Right.' Archie carefully unmoulded a tomato and anchovy mousse. It looked very pretty on its bed of orange and chicory. I felt disappointed that he had not attempted to argue me out of my decision to leave, though I had spent the day marshalling reasons why I must. '*There*! I think a little cold soup to begin, perhaps pea and lettuce, and I've made *pêches au Château-Lafite* for pudding.'

'That sounds wonderful.'

'It *does*, doesn't it?' Archie smiled with satisfaction.

'I shall miss your marvellous suppers. And all the fun we've had. And you.' I was close to tears.

Archie frowned, his widow's peak prominent above his white face. 'What are you talking about? Oh that. Rupert'll deal with that little flight of insanity. Only you mustn't push him too far, remember. He's under great pressure. On the other hand perhaps it'll do him good to think about something else.'

'No, but I mean it. I really must go –'

'Ssh!' Archie held up a hand with silvered nails and a ring of yellow sapphires. 'I *must* concentrate on the soup. Unless you've anything sensible to say?'

I went upstairs to change. When Rupert came home he was mute with exhaustion. We had supper in the garden and the warmth of the evening, the scent of the flowers and the sweetness of the birdsong seemed to revive him. Colour returned to his face and he began to talk about the production. They had had their first fully staged, fully costumed rehearsal that afternoon when it was discovered that the woman playing Ulrica, the fortune-teller, was too fat to get through the door of her fortune-telling hut. Ulrica had wept tears of humiliation and locked herself in her dressing room. Rupert had had to plead with her through the door to return to the rehearsal. Finally she had allowed him to come in and then thrown off her dressing gown to convince Rupert that she was not in the least fat but merely big-boned.

'Good heavens, the woman was a sea of billowing flesh! Whole tribes of cannibals could have dined off her for weeks!' Rupert shuddered. 'It's a sight I can't get out of my mind. But I persuaded her that the set designer had made a mistake in the measurements of the hut door. In our absence the carpenter had managed to pare away an inch or two from the lintels and Ulrica was just able to force her way in.'

'Supposing she has a fish-and-chip supper just before the performance,' I said. 'It's going to be rather embarrassing if she gets stuck. Can't she have her crystal ball in a shady grotto instead?'

'Unfortunately, the hut's an essential part of the plot. Amelia, the soprano, is also enormous and it was touch and go whether *she* could get inside to have her future foretold. To my great relief she did but then, unfortunately, with both of them inside, the door couldn't be opened wide enough to let either of them out. The rehearsal had to be stopped again while the door was taken off its hinges. By this time the rest of the cast was scarcely able to stand up for giggling, let alone sing. The whole ridiculous episode wasted nearly an hour and both Amelia and Ulrica were moody as hell afterwards. We're going to have a curtain over the door instead.'

'It's hardly high art, is it?' said Archie.

'No, but it's just what putting on an opera entails. The art bit – the singing and playing – you don't have really to worry about. The singers take their careers very seriously and spend far more time nurturing and training their voices than one could reasonably ask. They know their stuff. You can hold forth as much as you like about motivation and message but hardly any of them can act anyway. And the orchestra is so competent that mostly the musicians play with the same degree of emotional intensity as if they were turning out the garden shed. Sometimes the conductor can make them catch fire, sometimes something magical happens which sets it all alight, but you have to leave that to chance. The best you can do in try to build a seamless performance which looks good and makes sense.'

Rupert, I was certain, was deliberately understating his own importance. He had worked so hard on this production that he had scarcely been aware of anything else. Nations might have gone to war, thrones might have toppled and the entire population of England have been converted to Confucianism without him knowing. But tonight he seemed happy and expansive. He leaned back in his chair, breathing in the dropping honey from the jasmine that covered the arbour, a glass of Château-Lafite in one hand, a cigar in the other, content with the world.

'I've got a new job,' I said, feeling that this was as good a time as any to get his attention. 'As assistant deputy arts sub-editor on the *Manchester Sentinel*. Starting next month.'

Rupert turned his gaze slowly to my face and looked at me as though I had announced that I intended to earn my bread playing a comb and paper in Oxford Street. '*What* are you talking about?'

'My new job. In Manchester. The salary's pretty good. I shall be able to afford a room and food, and I hope Pa will make Cordelia an allowance. It's a pity she's got to change schools again but she seems quite good at making friends. I'm going to try and get a ground-floor room so that Mark Antony can go in and out by himself. Dirk'll be the biggest problem but if the room isn't too far away I can come back every lunchtime to walk him –'

'Have you had too much sun, Harriet?' It was a pity the good humour had been so swiftly banished. Rupert was looking very cold now, almost angry. 'You seem to be babbling. Perhaps you ought to lie down.'

'I'm perfectly all right. You've both been angelically good about having us to stay but of course things can't go on like this for ever. We've loved being here. How ever much I tried I could never tell you how grateful we are –'

'Please . . .' Rupert closed his eyes and put up his hand as though he were shutting me out. 'You know I hate that kind of thing. I'm tired and I'm incapable of thinking about anything much. Whatever's brought on this maudlin fit, just skip it, would you mind? I don't want you to be grateful. Even less do I want you to tell me about it.' He put down his glass and put his head in his hands. 'Can't you be reasonable and just get quietly on with your life, at least for the time being until this production's over?'

'I'm being perfectly reasonable!' I felt myself growing hot. 'This needn't disturb you at all. Cordelia and I can just slip away and you probably won't even notice we've gone. I should think you'll be delighted not to have Dirk chewing everything and Mark Antony digging holes in the garden. To say nothing of the telephone ringing and the sewing machine going at all hours of the day.'

For a moment Rupert sat silent, smoking his cigar and frowning at a bee that was buzzing about a dish of peach stones. He looked so far away that I wondered if he had stopped listening.

'Do you really think,' he said at last, in tones of wounding contempt, 'that you're going to be able to find a landlady who'll tolerate an enormous dog and a large cat on the premises? Really, Harriet, I wonder sometimes if you're fit to be allowed out on your own.'

'I hadn't thought of that.' My spirits, already sinking, were further dashed. 'But some people are mad about St Bernards. They'll probably like him better than us. Anyway, that just shows what a lot I've got to learn about being independent and looking after myself. You're always saying I don't live in the real world. I shall put aside a certain amount to pay back everything I owe you. It'll take rather a long time, I'm afraid, but –'

'I don't want to hear any more about it!' Rupert stood up suddenly and threw his cigar into a rose bush. He turned on me a face that was transfigured by what looked like fury, almost hatred. 'Go, if you want! Go to hell, if you like – the sooner, the better – but leave me in peace!' He marched into the house.

Archie went to retrieve the cigar butt. 'We don't want Dirk to eat it. He'll only be sick again.' I could feel that he was looking at me. My face was burning. 'That didn't go too well, did it?'

I gave a shaky laugh. 'Not very.'

'Don't take it to heart, my girl. He's not sleeping very well and he has to deal with everyone else's nerves at work and bind their psychic wounds. As soon as this thing comes off, he'll be himself again and then he'll be sorry he lost his temper.'

'I'm the one that's sorry. Sorry that I upset him. Sorry that we've been such a nuisance – all along really, ever since I came to your party when Pa was arrested. Poor Rupert's been badgered mercilessly by the entire family, but most of all by me. Of course I understand what he's feeling. He's afraid the opera might not be a success.' I managed some sort of smile though my heart was sore. 'I want to help him, not make things worse.'

'It's only two and a half weeks until the first night. You'll see, if the notices aren't too bad, he'll be back to normal in no time. And I've had an in*spired* notion! We'll have a party afterwards to celebrate. That'll put him right. A sort of catharsis. Drinking, dancing and fornication.'

It had always seemed to me that Archie enjoyed parties more than Rupert did but I bowed to his superior knowledge. 'What sort of party?'

'A drum! A rout! Let me see. Stop that, you *brute*!' Archie threw a peach stone at Mark Antony, who was starting to dig a hole among the regal lilies. 'The performance will end at about half-past ten. They'll need a few minutes to get their breaths back. Transport will have to be organised. *Char-à-bancs*, I suppose. They'll get here about half-past eleven. *Per*fect! They'll be drunk already on excitement. We shall dance until dawn!'

'Won't they all be too tired to perform the next day?'

'An opera house isn't like a theatre, with the same play on every night throughout the run. They mix up two or three operas and often ballet as well. There won't be another performance of *Un Ballo in Maschera* for at least a week. It's the *ideal* moment for a ball.'

'A ball!'

'It's the obvious thing. And it'll save changing.' Archie sighed with satisfaction and chucked another stone at Mark Antony, who was beginning on the Japanese anemones. 'We shall give a masked ball!'

668

FORTY-TWO

During the watches of the night, I wondered if Rupert was awake too, and if occasionally his mind ceased to wrestle with the problems of the production and perhaps turned to thoughts of me. I told myself that this was most unlikely, and anyway, it was a deplorable kind of egotism on my part to want it. But when I went down for breakfast there was a note, with my name on it, propped against my cup. Archie, in a magnificent red silk dressing gown embroidered with fans, was frying eggs. There was no sign of Rupert.

Archie gave me a plate. 'You look as though an inebriate husband has blacked both your eyes. Pillow uncooperative?'

'Like a hot iron,' I admitted, unfolding the note.

'Forgive the tantrum. Too much to drink combined badly with a trying day. Of course you must go and if I can help, please ask. Congratulations on the new job. R.'

'A pipe of peace, I take it?' Archie peeled a pear with finesse.

'Yes.' I folded the piece of paper and put it in my pocket. 'He's very kind.'

'M-hm.'

'He says congratulations on the job.'

'Uh-huh.'

'He's sorry he was cross.'

'Good.'

'He says of course I must go. So that's all right,' I smiled as brightly as I could manage. Which perhaps was not very. Archie put down the pearl-handled knife, folded his hands and looked at me over the top of his half-moon spectacles. 'Archie . . .' I hesitated.

'Harriet.'

'Don't you mind about Rupert sleeping with girls? I mean, don't you feel even the tiniest bit worried that one day he may actually like one of them enough to . . .' I paused.

'You mean, Rupert might want to make little Wolvespurgeses with some fresh-faced, flaxen-haired Brünnhilde? Of course that's always been a possibility. But it's just as likely that I may want to set up an antiques shop in the Cotswolds with Siegfried. We have to take that as it comes. Rupert and I aren't lovers. As far as I know, he's never had sexual congress with a man. Naturally people assume that two men living together are buggers but the truth is that it suits us both to let the world think that. It appeals to Rupert's sense of humour and, more importantly, it gives him protective colouring. Women are fascinated by him – I suppose it's his reserve they find challenging. He likes taking them to bed but he doesn't want emotional ties. Living with me he has all the pleasures of domesticity and companionship without the histrionic episodes and sentimental assurances that women require. In my case it makes me look much sexier if I can hint of a handsome younger man as a conquest.'

I digested this. Rupert and Archie were not lovers. Rupert wasn't gay at all. I did not know whether joy or despair was uppermost in my mind. Perhaps an uncomfortable mixture of equal amounts of each. Then I remembered something.

'But just a minute. At Pye Place I opened the door of

Rupert's room and overheard what sounded like – things said that strongly suggested that you and he . . .' I felt my face grow hot. 'I mean, you were making love. I heard you.'

'Ha, Ha! I see!' Archie laughed until his mascara ran. 'The fact is, Rupert and I changed rooms. Mine was shockingly draughty. My throat is susceptible to inflammation, you know. Rupert is not sensitive to such things. You must have heard me dallying with the gallant Emilio – not a catch I'm especially proud of but he had a certain Hispanic lustre that was appealing. And he was *willing*. I haven't shocked you, have I?'

'Not at all.' I gave further thought to this new interpretation of events. Archie and Emilio. I ought to have guessed. Poor Georgia. I felt so sorry for her that I completely forgave her for sleeping with Max. Of course I knew the whole thing was Max's fault anyway and not hers, but one is only human. 'Archie . . .'

'Harriet.'

'You're rather hard on women, aren't you? Histrionic episodes and sentimental reassurances – we don't *all* want to live in a ferment of false emotions.'

'I'm only explaining how Rupert thinks. I *like* the company of women. For me life would be hideously dull without melodrama and theatricality. But I'm rarely serious. And then only when I'm coming down with a cold. Rupert's *mad*ly intense. Poor boy, he can't help it. He's *terr*ified of being overwhelmed by love.'

'I can understand that.' I put my head in my heads. 'It *is* frightening to feel that all your happiness is bound up in another person. That without them you don't – you don't particularly want to live.'

'Oh, Harriet! *Harr*iet! My poor child, you *have* got it bad!'

There was a sympathetic silence while I got control of my

face. Then I lifted my head and smiled bravely. 'I feel such a fool,' I said. 'I don't know how I've let myself get into this ridiculous situation.'

'I don't suppose this is all about *Max*, is it?'

I shook my head.

'I thought not. Will you let Uncle Archie give you a bit of advice?'

I nodded.

'There's a tide in the affairs of men which taken at the flood, leads on to fortune. Now don't say *Othello*, because it's *Julius Caesar*,' he added quickly. 'Shakespeare understood that the art of living consists in playing your cards right. Bugger beauty and truth. Remember, he goes on to say, if you omit to catch that tide, all the voyage of your life will be bound in shallows and in miseries. Doesn't sound too good, does it? In other words, you've got to get the timing right. It's clever of you to be going away. *That*'ll do it, if anything will.'

'It isn't cleverness. Just that I hate to be a burden. And I don't think I could bear it if I had to stand and watch some girl – even if I knew it wasn't going to lead to anything permanent – well, you know . . .'

'My dear, don't *speak* to me of jealousy. Horrid, horrid, *horr*id!' Archie made a face of abhorrence. 'Now listen. Be as blithe as you know how. Don't be seen to mope. Let him brood on your bold new independence. Pretend you're stalking a very rare, shy camelopard. You *must*n't startle him. Men are frightfully stupid creatures in these matters. Sometimes I'm tempted to lose all patience. Ideas trickle into their minds like silt drifting to the bottom of a pond. Finally you get something you can call mud. Bide – your – time!'

'You're the kindest, dearest man, Archie. Would you mind if I kissed you?'

'I should be absolutely de*light*ed. Provided you keep it dry and don't knock me off my chair.'

That afternoon Archie rushed round to the printers with the invitations he had designed – a black card with information about the party written in silver – and, while Archie addressed envelopes, Cordelia and I spent all evening cutting the cards into mask shapes. We could do several at once so this wasn't as labour-intensive as it sounds. But we rebelled against cutting in eyeholes, which was much too difficult, and compromised by sticking two eye-shaped lozenges of glitter on each card, instead, which was fun to do and looked very effective. Rupert, when told of the proposed celebration, confined his comments to suggesting we get in chairs with solid seats and strong legs. The fortuneteller's hut had had to be completely remade in the shape of an Eskimo tupik to accommodate the lead tenor.

The discovery that Rupert was neither homosexual nor emotionally committed to Archie really changed nothing. I felt even more of a nuisance. Sometimes when I answered the telephone a woman's voice would ask for Rupert. I always said he was out, as I had been told to do. The voice would become suspicious, even tetchy. One girl asked outright what I was doing there.

When a Leah lookalike – Rupert's taste seemed to be for tall blondes – escaped Archie's vigilance and sneaked into the house behind Cordelia, she was clearly annoyed to find me in residence. She cross-questioned me in a manner bordering on the accusatory about my relationship with Rupert, and chain-smoked without bothering to extinguish the last cigarette properly so the atmosphere in the drawing room was like a Highland black house by the time he came home. When he saw her, he said, 'Oh. Virginia. I wasn't expecting you,' in a voice that lacked even the faintest suggestion of pleasure and flapped his hand about in front of his face. I went to help Archie in the kitchen. Ten minutes later Virginia left the house.

'All right, you disgraceful pair.' Rupert called down to where Archie and I had been jostling for position out of sight round the bend in the stairs. 'I know you were listening. Well, what's the verdict? Did that go better?'

'Certainly it was effective as a temporary measure,' said Archie. 'I wonder if she'll continue to believe that your doctor has prescribed absolute rest to avert a nervous crisis, when she receives an invitation in tomorrow morning's post with your name on it, requesting her to jitterbug till dawn in less than two weeks' time?'

Rupert groaned. 'Why on earth did you ask her?'

'I remember you were quite keen on her at one time. And I thought we could do with a few more girls with waists.'

'At least she didn't break your jaw,' I said comfortingly.

Archie invited everyone who lived in the street to the ball, thereby ensuring the co-operation of the Horn-on-the-Green Preservation Society, of which he was, anyway, chairman. He planned to have a fifteen-foot wide, sprung dance floor on the grass the full length of the canal and a marquee for food and drink on the common at the end of the cul-de-sac. That way there would be plenty of room for everyone to dance and drink and eat without disturbing the decorum of number 10. This would be used for sitting out only. Where the fornication – declared by Archie to be a key component of the evening's fun – was to take place, I could not imagine. I decided to lock the door of my bedroom just in case.

Archie worked tirelessly to ensure the success of the celebration. The music was the most taxing element to get right. Minuets, pavans and galliards would be in keeping with the period but no one would know the steps. Disco dancing would be contrary to the spirit of the occasion. Country dancing would be fun but perhaps too energetic for the stouter guests. In the end Archie decided on a thirties swing band to get the thing off to a lively start, giving way to a more sultry jazz band just before dawn, when we would unmask. Fortunately he had an extensive network of contacts. He knew just the girl to do the food, was on familiar terms with a most obliging wine merchant, and had met the very person to put up a marquee. As we had so little time it was as well that one afternoon on the telephone settled every major requirement. Then we came to what we all agreed was the most important item on the list – what we were going to wear.

'I fancy something in black leather, very tight,' said Cordelia, whose ideas were rapidly changing under the influence of the Arthur Brocklebuck Comp.

'You must wear white.' Archie spoke decidedly. 'It may remind some of the worst roués of your virginal condition. We want it to stay that way if at all possible.'

'I'm not at all sure that it will be a suitable –' I broke off and clapped my hands over my ears as Cordelia began to scream.

'– and if you *don't* let me come I shall go to bed with one of the boys at school and get pregnant immediately,' I heard when I unblocked my ears. 'Or perhaps it'd better be the art master. He's crazy about me and at least he could afford a pram. I hope they won't send him to prison for underage sex. It wouldn't be a very good start for the poor baby, would it? I shall tell it as soon as it's old enough to understand about its wicked Aunt Harriet who was so mean she wouldn't let me –'

'Oh, all right!' I gave in with ill grace. 'But you mustn't drink anything – nothing alcoholic, I mean – and you must be in bed by twelve.'

'All right,' Cordelia said with great sweetness. 'Anything you say, dear sister.'

I was not fooled for a moment by this. I made a mental resolve that I would not let her out of my sight. This would curtail my own enjoyment but the idea of struggling in a bedsitter in Manchester with Cordelia, Dirk, Mark Antony *and* a tiny baby was not appealing.

'Something Empire for Cordelia,' mused Archie. 'High-waisted diaphanous muslin with tiny puffed sleeves and a low neck. Not *too* low,' he added, catching my eye. 'A green sash, a sprinkling of flowers and a silver mask sewn with crystal beads. No jewellery. We want to suggest something vernal, *burg*eoning. Flora and the country green. Botticelli's *Primavera*.'

Cordelia's eyes grew dreamy. 'I like the sound of that.'

'And for Harriet it *must* be gold brocade. A young Elizabeth, not knowing from day to day whether she is to be queen of all England or have her head cut off. One of those tight bodices with a pointed waist and scalloped tabs, a low square neck, tight winged sleeves and a wheel farthingale skirt. A gold mask – everything gold except the lining of the skirt, which will be crimson. A flash of dark red as you dance suggesting the hidden *fires* within. Your hair dressed simply, gathered at the crown and then falling down your back.'

'That sounds glorious,' I breathed, much taken with the idea. 'But where can we find such beautiful dresses?'

'Mrs Wapshott will make them. She is an elderly widow who lives round the corner and once worked for Balmain. There is nothing that woman cannot do. She has already begun my own costume.'

Archie refused to be drawn on what he was intending to wear. Instead he went shopping on our behalf for fabrics, lace and ribbons, and Mrs Wapshott was set to work. Fitting sessions began a few days later. Mrs Wapshott, a bent, bony old lady with hair dyed startlingly black, spent most of the time on her knees and never spoke because her mouth was always full of pins. She studied the detailed drawings Archie had made, draped our bodies with cloth and then attacked it in a frenzy, her scissors snapping like the beak of a large bird. We might have been tailors' dummies for all the attention she gave us. I cannot remember that she ever looked me in the eye. I am certain she did not know my name.

The construction of the wheel farthingale was a challenge she enjoyed. She confessed to Archie that never in her long life as a seamstress had she been asked to make such a thing. A whalebone hoop like a wheel – my waist being the hub – was suspended by cotton straps, like spokes. The whole structure was covered by a long skirt of gold brocade, the flat top of which was surmounted by a ruff-like frill. It was like wearing a small table but it did miraculous things for my posture. Our dresses, when they were finished, surpassed our imaginings and were a great joy during a time of trial.

Rupert had been right when he said that landladies would be reluctant to give shelter to Dirk and Mark Antony. I answered every advertisement in the 'To Rent' section of the *Manchester Sentinel*. From their aggrieved tones before they slammed down the telephone you would have thought I was asking them to harbour plague rats complete with fleas. I took another day off work and tramped the streets of Manchester. At last I found a house in quite the wrong area, miles from the *Sentinel*, which stank of cats the minute the landlady opened the door. She looked so like a witch I was afraid to go in. Her hair was long and grey and her nose curved down nearly to her chin. She was toothless and cackled. But she had three cats and three dogs of her own and was amenable to one more of each. The room was, frankly, horrible. It smelled of mould as well as of urine, it was dark, badly furnished, and looked out on an area filled with overflowing dustbins. In the train back to London I tried to think of ways to make it look more attractive. It must do as a temporary home until we could find something better.

When I told Mr Podmore that I was handing in my notice with effect from the first of September I was astonished by his reaction. He put down his pencil, took off his blue spectacles and leaned back in his chair with his hands clasped behind his head.

'All right. How much?'

'How much what?'

His small, toffee-coloured eyes were cynical. 'Let's not play games. How much do you want?'

'Do you mean money?'

'I certainly don't mean sexual titillation.'

I began to think that Mr Podmore was one of the most unpleasant men of my acquaintance. 'I don't want money, thanks. At least not more than I'm getting. I've got a job with the *Manchester Sentinel*.'

'Have you, indeed? Deb Shuns Social Whirl for Smoke Stacks. So what have they offered you?'

I did not think this was any of his business but I told him anyway, hoping to rise in his estimation.

'I'll double that.'

I stared at him, unable to believe I was hearing properly.

'Well?' He cleaned out an ear with the point of his pencil. 'What do you say?' Then, when I still said nothing, he added, 'I'll move Tremblebath in with the old dragons and you can have his office. And an expense account of . . . um, twenty pounds a month. Now I can't say fairer than that, can I?'

'You mean . . . you really want me to stay?'

'It looks like it, doesn't it?'

'But why?'

'All right, Hilary. You want me to spell it out. You're a tougher cookie than I took you for.'

'Harriet. I've no idea what you're talking about.'

Mr Podmore waved his hand at a pile of papers on his desk. 'Readers' letters. All about "Spook Hall". Wanting to know the whereabouts of the house with the dummy arm, the exact consequences of the pointing finger, the name of Sir Galahad's favourite hunter, the bust measurement of the Lady of the Moat. What sort of pinny the serving girl was wearing when she was bricked up. Every psychical research society in the country seems to have read your stuff and they all want information. Apparently every maiden aunt with nerves and every schoolboy with a ghoulish imagination finds it impossible to get through the weekend without his or her copy of the *Brixton Mercury*. The circulation's gone up by several thousand in the last few weeks. Don't tell me this is news to you because I shan't believe you.'

In the bus, on the way home, I was unable to keep an imbecilic grin off my face. Partly because I kept seeing Mr Podmore's incredulous expression when he realised that nothing he could offer would persuade me to stay but mostly because I was cock-a-hoop at my own success. Of course I knew that it would have required little in the way of sensation to bump up the circulation of the *Brixton Mercury*, which was essentially a dull record of small-time news, gossip and events within a depressed locality, hardly more interesting than a parish magazine. If there was any credit going it was due to Mr Podmore for having the idea of 'Spook Hall' in the first place. And it had been a lucky fluke to find myself spending a holiday at Pye Place, where there was standing room only for the restless dead.

Still, I was inclined to congratulate myself on having at least made a sustained effort. I had learned the valuable lesson that sitting down and doing the thing, however ill-conceived and badly executed, is half the battle. Now I had to learn how to write. Already my first attempts seemed laughably bad, though I did not yet know how to make them better. Rupert often said, probably as a hint to me, that to write well it is essential to read well.

I was disturbed in the mental composition of a programme of intensive study by a tap on my shoulder.

'Harriet Byng? It is you. I thought so.'

I turned to see a woman with short grey hair, pale, unfriendly eyes, an aquiline nose and a mouth compressed into a thin disapproving line. It was a very familiar face, yet I could not put a name to it.

'Hello!' I smiled, trying to look pleased, hoping to be enlightened.

'I wasn't sure at first. You've changed your way of dressing. And you've got more poise.' When I continued to stare, she said, 'It's Sister Imelda.'

I gulped and almost swallowed my tongue in fright. It was no good reminding myself that I had left school years ago and was beyond her jurisdiction. Her cold gaze seemed to accuse me of irresponsibility, insubordination and cheating on my bus fare. Then I remembered our last conversation. She had made unkind remarks about my family and I had returned the unkindness with a cruel taunt about her relationship with Sister Justinia. I was tempted to jump up and hurl myself from the moving bus.

We stared at each other for a while without speaking. Without a wimple she looked naked, almost indecent. I felt ill at ease to see her neck and ears plainly on view. On Sister Imelda the pale blue scarf knotted round the neck of her neat grey blouse seemed as licentious as a peekaboo bra.

'Perhaps you didn't know I'd left the order?'

'Cordelia did say something . . .' my voice tailed away.

'I've been ill. But I'm all right now.'

'Oh. Dear.' I must try and pull myself together. 'Sister Imelda, I'm afraid when we last spoke I said some unfor-givable things –'

'No. That's why I wanted to speak to you. You see, it was you that began it all. Giving up my vocation, I mean. I thought of writing, but then I heard you'd moved away. I read about your father, of course, in the newspapers. I'm glad he didn't do it. It was difficult for you – and – perhaps I might have been more sympathetic.'

'Please don't worry!' I was eager to make things easy for her. I was sorry to see her somehow diminished, humble, without identity. It was too confusing. I preferred to think of her as a caricature of authority, someone remote, faintly ridiculous and forever beyond intimacy. 'I *am* sorry to have hurt you –'

'No,' she said again. 'I was angry – very angry. You were insolent. And cruel.' For a moment the steel returned to her eyes. 'But you were quite right. People *were* talking. For a while I tried to deny it, asking God to give me strength to confront my adversaries and confound them.'

'Really, I was only trying to defend myself. I just said the first thing that came into my head. It wasn't worth being upset about –'

'Ah, but though you spoke in ignorance – and, shall we say, malice – you happened to be speaking the truth. I did love Sister Justinia, with a love that ran counter to my love of God.'

'Surely God doesn't mind –'

'You don't know what you're talking about, Harriet.' Sister Imelda spoke with her old acerbity. 'I loved Sister Justinia as a woman, not as a sister in Christ. I still do. And I'm very glad to say that she loves me.' A smile broke across Sister Imelda's face. I was startled by the change. Her eyes were soft, her face flooded with colour, she looked blissfully happy. 'We've got a nice little flat just down the road from here. I have a job as head of a department teaching adult literacy. Sister Justinia – it's Alice, now – is working for a children's charity. We're very contented.'

'I'm so pleased.'

Sister Imelda – no doubt she had another name now but I was destined never to know it – stood up.

'This is my stop. Goodbye, Harriet. I'm glad we had a chance to talk. I don't suppose we'll meet again. I hope you'll keep a watch on that temper. It may not always be a force for good.'

I watched her bustling along the pavement, her thin legs striding briskly beneath her sensible pleated skirt, scarf flapping. The relief of not having her on my conscience was tremendous. But the metamorphosis of my old, much-feared enemy was too much to take in at once. I tried to imagine the two ex-nuns sitting in comfortable chairs each side of a cosy fire, talking, sharing a joke, perhaps watching a gardening programme on television. Eating oatmealed herrings or pickled beetroot or perhaps a casserole. Making cocoa, going to bed . . . the vision faded here. God had lost the exclusive services of Sister Imelda and Sister Justinia but had gained those of Maria-Alba. I hoped that, like me, he would think things had worked out rather well. For at least half an hour I forgot the dingy, malodorous room in Manchester that awaited us, and the imminent parting from nearly everything that was infinitely dear to me, and felt almost cheerful.

The preparations for the ball were a welcome distraction from present uneasiness over future privations. Visiting the dressmaker, grooming the garden to perfection, and debating with Archie and Cordelia whether to have fireworks, acrobats, lute-players, harpists or performing pigs, left little time during the day to brood.

It was my idea to have a fortune-teller. I found the telephone number of Madame Xanthe – palmist, astrologer, crystal gazer, tarot reader and dowser – in the small ads of the *Brixton Mercury*. As the cosmos was an open book to Madame Xanthe, it was perhaps surprising that she lived modestly at 27B Nipper Lane, Kensal Green. But I reminded myself that some people very properly despise the material things of this world. Archie hired a small tent for her, then had a crisis of confidence and exchanged it for a larger one.

The great day dawned. We had worried continuously about the weather but the sky was blue and cloudless, the sun hot. We suppressed our excitement at breakfast for Rupert's sake. He was silent and looked terribly strained. He tried to behave normally, putting up his usual newspaper barrier against conversation but I noticed he did not once turn the page.

Finally he threw down the paper. 'There is nothing more to be done,' he announced to no one in particular. 'Everything has been thought of, every last detail rehearsed. It's in the lap of the gods now. I've told the cast to spend the day resting and forbidden them to even think about the performance tonight, and I shall take a leaf from my own book.'

'Good,' said Archie. 'You can help us with the lights and the flowers. *What* am I saying? You can't arrange a bunch of buttercups. But you could at least carry buckets of water that'll be too heavy for the girls.'

But Rupert had already wandered off to his work-room and when I looked in, an hour later, he was busy tinkering with the models of the sets and making sketches. He stared at me with unseeing eyes when I asked him if he wanted lunch and said, 'Perfectly, thanks. But I'd better leave a quarter of an hour earlier so I can have a word with the chorus.'

The plan was for Archie to drive Cordelia and me to the theatre. The second the curtain came down on the last act we would rush back to Richmond to oversee the final preparations and change into our costumes. Rupert, having taken a taxi to the theatre earlier, would return on the coach with the cast and musicians. He had claimed his privilege as host not to dress up.

'Like Max de Winter,' Cordelia had said. 'But you aren't so grumpy. Not all the time, anyway. If I'd been that girl, the one he marries after Rebecca – Joan Fontaine, I mean – I'd have chucked everything with an R on it on to the bonfire. And I'd have told Mrs Danvers to stop mooning about in the west wing and bloody well get on with the housework.'

The marquee and the dance floor arrived in the morning, blocking the mews with lorries, but as the other residents were anticipating an evening of rare excitement they accepted the inconvenience cheerfully. Cordelia and I carried buckets of flowers about to Archie's dictation.

'We want to suggest Arcady – pagan pastoral, with an underlying sophistication,' he said. 'Luckily I have generous friends with country gardens. Shop flowers are so *trite*. You girls can divide the alchemilla, catmint and cotton lavender more or less evenly between the vases. Leave the roses to me. Remember, simple yet sumptuous.'

Simple it may have been but he got very snappy with us for not arranging our flowers with sufficient artistry.

'No, no, *no*! Not stiff, not symmetrical. It should be graceful, natural! As though you've picked a handful at random and just *hurled* them into a vase.'

'That's exactly what we *have* done,' protested Cordelia.

There was much *sotto voce* grumbling and tense badinage before Archie pronounced himself satisfied. The marquee, pretty striped in white and green looked like a bosky bower from *A Midsummer Night's Dream* when he had finished, and the scent from the pale pink and dark red roses was intoxicating. Bees and butterflies abandoned ragwort and nettles on the common and zoomed about inside the tent, delighted to find an unexpected epicurean feast. By the time the glasses and silver wine coolers had been set out on damask cloths, and gilt chairs and small tables arranged for those whose costumes or physiques might prevent them from picnicking on the banks of the canal, we were intoxicated by our own cleverness.

The orchestra was warming up as we entered our box in the Grand Tier. In the car I had forgotten about our wonderful party and thought only of Rupert and the agonies of creation with which I was, in a small way, familiar. Pa and Pussyfoot were conspicuous in the stalls, surrounded by worshippers. In the balcony I spotted Ophelia and Charles. They were talking intently to each other. Rupert's chair between Cordelia and me remained empty.

'Of course he's not going to miss it,' said Archie, but I thought he looked anxious.

'I hope he hasn't fainted in the lavs,' said Cordelia.

This had once happened to Pa when playing Petruchio in *The Taming of the Shrew*. The start of the performance had been delayed by nearly an hour while they searched for him and the scene shifters had threatened to strike because of union rules about overtime. The cast had collectively gone to pieces and the audience had to be bribed to wait with the promise of half-price tickets. But in the end Pa had been discovered, revived and thrust on stage, and the play had been, ultimately, a triumph.

Just as the lights were going down Rupert entered the box.

The first notes of the overture made my scalp prickle. It was my first experience of real, live opera. Until now Shakespeare had taken up all my theatre-going energies. When the curtain went up I was thrilled by the vastness of the stage and the spectacular scenery. The subordination of the acting to the music made it an entirely new experience. The extraordinary beauty of the singing demanded, from the beginning, complete emotional engagement. Rupert had been critical of the opera as being weak of plot and not the best of Verdi's music, but I was entranced.

As the story of conspiracy, assassination and forbidden love unfolded, I lost the thread several times but I abandoned myself to the sheer loveliness of the sight and sound of it. The scene on the quay when Riccardo, surrounded by fishermen, sings his beautiful aria was staged with consummate skill, all flickering firelight, moonlight and starlight. The forest scenes were enchanting with spreading trees, sunlit glades and a real donkey, and no one got stuck in the fortuneteller's hut.

Rupert spent the interval backstage so we had no chance to ask him how he thought it was going. At the end of last act when the betrayed lovers sing their final duet, they seemed to me to speak of the grief of all lovers, everywhere, who must part. I stole a glance at Rupert. He was leaning on the edge of the box with his chin in his hand, his expression dreaming, his eyes very bright.

FORTY-THREE

'May I have the pleasure of this dance, Harriet?' A man in a dark green tail coat, ivory knee-breeches and a black mask, bowed and offered me his arm. 'You're looking perfectly stunning.'

'Hello, Charles. You're the spit of Beau Brummell. But how did you know it was me?'

'It's my job to deduce these things. An ink-stain on the middle forefinger of the right hand, a slight fraying of the cuff, a crumb of marzipan – no, truthfully, I asked Rupert which was you. How did you know it was *me*?'

'I've always admired the way the tips of your ears turn over.'

'Really? I wondered if Ophelia's noticed. You look like a Spanish infanta in that dress. And that necklace is really something.'

Archie had insisted I wear the snake torque that had been Max's Christmas present. Despite my protests that I intended to send it anonymously to Caroline Frensham, since I was certain that she had unwittingly paid for it, Archie had stood firm. He offered to put it in the post for me the very next day if that would appease my conscience but I must, must,

687

must wear it one last time to perfect the creation that was his brain-child. I had given in rather than quarrel just as the Polite World was gathering at our door. It felt cold and heavy against my throat.

'It's five thousand years old and was probably stolen from the tomb of a Mesopotamian princess. I only hope it hasn't got a curse on it. Ophelia looks very lovely.'

'Oh, yes.' Charles turned his head to seek her out in the crowd. 'But she even looks marvellous with her head in a towel and wearing my old jersey, up a ladder with a paint-brush.'

I was quite unable to imagine Ophelia in such a situation. 'Aren't the lights pretty?'

Paper lanterns concealed light bulbs. In the ultramarine glow that passes for night in London they looked like floating pink and green moons among the branches of the trees that lined the canal.

'Very. I hear you're going away. Rupert told me. He said you'd got a new job. Congratulations.'

'Thanks.'

'You don't sound very happy.'

'Oh, I am. Blissfully. But I shall miss London and – everyone.'

'We'll miss you too. But you'll come back for our wedding?'

'Oh, Charles, I'm so pleased about it! When's it going to be?'

'November. It's usually a quiet time for crime. Villains like to draw breath before the Christmas rush.' Charles gave my waist a brotherly squeeze. 'God, Harriet! I'm the luckiest man alive!'

'Well, yes, I think you probably are. But she's very lucky too.'

We did a twirl or two before Charles said, 'I'm having such

a glorious time I nearly forgot what I wanted to tell you. Yesterday a colleague of mine arrested Madame Eusapia and her assistant, Miss Judd. I happened to see the report.'

'No! Why?'

'Several people put in a complaint about them. So a plainclothes police officer went to one of their séances. He caught Miss Judd crawling round the room, head to toe in black except for gloves impregnated with luminous paint. The overhead light had a loudspeaker hidden in it and there was a tape recorder screwed to the underside of the table. Yards of butter muslin were stuffed down the front of Madame Eusapia's dress and the canary's cage was full of whistles, bells and fake cobwebs.'

'Oh, damn! How disappointing! What a workaday world this truly is. If only there weren't a rational explanation for everything! A part of me really did think she might be genuine.'

'The performance was hopelessly corny, apparently. These old girls never try anything original.'

'But, just a minute, that doesn't explain everything, does it? OK, I accept she knew who I was. Either Mr Podmore told her or she recognised the name. We were in the newspapers every day just about then. She mugged up the Shakespeare and put it on tape, perhaps took snippets from Sir Basil's own recordings. I think the moustached man was in on it too, because he and Sir Basil – Madame Eusapia, I mean – had a sort of conversation, obviously planned. I suppose she thought I'd have contacts with the press and people with money and could get her publicity. But that doesn't explain how she knew that Sir Basil was killed by the bolt of lightning.'

'That's exactly what's been puzzling me.'

'So what have you decided?'

'I think it *must* be co-incidence. She picked the storm bits because they were highly dramatic. They just happened to be spot on. Extraordinary co-incidences *do* happen. Or . . .'

We stared at each other. The effect of the mask was to make Charles's eyes glitter in a most effective way. 'Or . . . ?' I repeated.

'Or she really does have second sight but resorts to tricks to boost the takings.'

'I'd love to think so. I really would!'

'Don't breathe a word to anyone but so would I. I sometimes get very tired of facts.'

'What an excellent brother-in-law you'll make.'

'O rose of May! Dear maid, kind sister.' He laughed. 'For some reason Ophelia attributes all Shakespearean quotations to *Hamlet*, and for once she'd be right. What are you smiling about?'

'Oh, nothing.'

'Hello, daughter dear. Luckily I recognised you before I made a pass. You're looking quite bewitching.'

'Hello, Pa. Not nearly so magnificent as you.' The handful of press gathered round the gated entrance to the street had got busy with their cameras when Pa arrived in medieval battledress. 'But isn't it rather uncomfortable?'

'I wore this armour for Henry V at Agincourt. I hoped I'd have an opportunity to put it on again. I particularly like the crowned helm. And the visor makes a perfect mask. It's made of aluminium so it's very light.'

'P – Fleur's dress is charming.'

'Do tell her so, will you? She's so sensitive. She thinks you don't like her. I tell her it's nonsense. But she's naturally modest. I must say I find that very attractive. And yet she's so bright she makes all other women seem like fools.'

There was much in this to annoy but fortunately my beautiful gold kid, silk-lined loo mask concealed my expression. I

690

kept my lips in a curve. 'I'll make a point of telling her. Have you seen Cordelia? She was here just a moment ago.'

'Isn't that her with the man in the elephant's head? What a lovely child she is! In fact all my children are raving beauties. I used to think you were the ugly duckling but you've turned out a fully fledged swan after all.'

I turned to see Cordelia slipping away into the relative darkness of the common.

'I'd better go and check on Cordelia.'

'Don't fuss, darling. What can possibly happen to her?'

'I just want her first experience of love to be wonderful and memorable, with someone she adores, not an ugly, mechanical fumble. Besides, she's much too young.'

'Of course. She's a child!'

'She's twelve, extremely precocious in some ways and immensely attractive to men.'

'Well, in that case you'd better run. I can see what looks like a trunk waving near that little group of trees.'

I came panting into the copse to find a perfectly strange couple groaning with desire while struggling to undo the plackets, ribbons, whale-boned corsets and hidden zips of each other's costumes. There was no sign of Cordelia or the elephant. I hurried back to the canal, where the banks were swarming with guests. Being surrounded by masked faces is fun but also disconcerting. Even on the edge of being alarming. Eyes seen through mask-holes are expressionless but, if you allow your imagination free rein, they can seem mocking and hostile. Fortunately everyone's mouths were talking and laughing and the music was gay. But a few bars of those horror film clichés – an out-of-key fairground tune or a whispered nursery rhyme – would have changed the atmosphere from jolly to jolly sinister in a moment.

Archie had instructed the carpenter to make a narrow bridge, its makeshift rails hung with twinkling lights and entwined with greenery, so that our guests could cross the canal. I was halfway over when I met a man in a scarlet soutane and cardinal's broad-brimmed hat, elaborately tasselled. We drew in our stomachs and essayed to pass.

'One moment, *mam'zelle*,' said a marked French accent. 'My crucifix is attached to ze *coiffure*.' The bridge sagged a little under our combined weight. 'I zink we must go on land to undo ourselves. We do not want to upset.' Once on the bank it took a while to separate us. 'A thousand pardons, I do not want to pull ze hair. *Voilà!* It is done. Will you give me ze absolution for such a clumsy zing and dance wiz me?'

He wore a scarlet full mask, which I believe is called a vizard. It was stern, with narrow eyes and a turned-down, censorious mouth but his voice was friendly and agreeably flirtatious.

'I'd love to but first I must find my little sister. I saw her a short while ago with an elephant.'

'*Mais oui*, it is there.' The cardinal pointed to a group on the opposite bank. To my relief I saw Cordelia and the elephant among them, talking to Rupert. 'You wish to return across?'

'Oh, no. I just wanted to make sure – Never mind.' The band was playing 'Beyond the Blue Horizon'. I had already drunk two glasses of champagne and suddenly I caught the general mood of frivolity and frolic. 'Let's dance.'

It was heavenly to be sweeping across the floor under the stars. The air was balmy and smelled of earth and leaves and scent and the excited buzz of happy voices lifted my spirits. The cardinal danced well and the weight of my skirts gave an additional languorous pleasure to the sensation of swinging and circling.

'You dance *divinement*,' he said. 'Is it permitted to know ze name of ze beautiful stranger?'

'Excuse me,' said a familiar voice. 'My turn, if you don't

mind.' The elephant thrust his trunk between us and, ignoring the cardinal's protests, took me in his arms and waltzed me away. 'Hello, Harriet. Aren't you surprised to see me?'

'Jonno!'

'The same.'

'Oh, how lovely! Where's Portia? I thought you had to stay up for the Long Vac.' Jonno had failed his second-year exams, the appeal of being in bed with Portia having triumphed over writing essays in a dim, dusty library. He was to be allowed to stay on, on condition he worked during the summer holidays.

'So I do, but the invitation was so tempting we decided to dash down for tonight. We rushed round to the fancy dress shop just before it shut. Portia's over there.' He pointed to a slender marmalade cat, standing with her tail over her arm, talking to Pa. 'I'm afraid our costumes rather let the side down but we're having such a good time, who cares! It's a brilliant party.'

'It's all Archie's doing. Cordelia and I only did as we were told. It *is* lovely, isn't it? I shall be so sad . . . You know we're coming up to Manchester?'

'I'm really pleased. You're my second favourite woman. In fact, you look so inviting, if I wasn't wearing a rubber trunk I'd be dangerously tempted to give you an incestuous kiss. But you've made a bad mistake about choosing a place to rent. It's a very rough area, not suitable at all.'

I explained the peculiar constraints that had led me to select the vilest part of Manchester to live in.

'Still, you'd better think again, you know.' He waved his trunk at me. 'I've only just got the hang of this. I might try sucking up water and blowing it out when I'm sufficiently drunk. Trouble is, it isn't at all easy to drink the ordinary way. It may take me some time.'

'Darling Hat!' The ginger cat flung her arms round me. It

693

was odd being kissed by a plastic mask with whiskers like the bristles on a yard broom. Her suit was made of orange-and-black striped fur that had seen better days. 'Such bliss! I feel drunk already. Let's all go and have our fortunes told.'

'You girls go ahead,' said Jonno. He lifted a glass and held up his trunk. 'I've some catching up to do.'

Inside the fortune-teller's tent it was dark except for a glowing crystal ball round which fluttered a cloud of frustrated moths. The overpowering smell of incense and patchouli made me cough.

'Come in, young lady.' Madame Xanthe was tiny, her chin reaching only a few inches above the table-top. She wore a shiny satin robe. Round her neck was a fox-skin, its tail between its jaws, a modern version of my necklace. Its boot-button eyes stared at me angrily. 'Sit down, dear.'

Madame Xanthe peered at me with little wrinkled eyes that blinked upwards like a tortoise's. The beads in her head-dress sparkled as she bent forward to examine the crystal ball. She passed her hands over it several times

'Ooh, this is a turn-up for the books! Well I *never*! You're a very unusual young lady!' I felt rather flattered. 'You've got the gift. Tell me now, dear, have you had any strange experiences? Anything paranormal, I mean?'

'Well, yes and no. It's hard to be sure. I mean, a lot of things that happen in life are rather strange –'

'Yes, you've had many trials and tribulations, I can see.' Madame Xanthe was clearly not interested in philosophising chitchat. 'A lot of heartache. He that was all in all to you has abandoned you. And there will be no return. That avenue is closed to you for ever.' She glanced up at me. 'Can you think who that man might be, dear?'

I shook my head.

'That's surprising. It's here very definite. An older man.

Perhaps a relation.' I smiled politely. 'But you're a lucky girl! I can see here very plain you're about to get your heart's desire. A tall, dark, handsome man's going to sweep you off your feet.'

'Really?' Though I knew it was all nonsense, my heart did speed up a bit.

'Oh yes. He's very passionate and he worships you.' This seemed highly unlikely. She pointed to the shining globe. 'There he is! Oh, he's very clever and successful. You're going to live together very happily until a ripe old age and have two children. A boy and a girl.' She frowned and stared. 'And a pig.'

'I'm going to have a pig?' I was startled.

'No, dear,' said Madame Xanthe a little impatiently. 'I see a large animal – perhaps it's a donkey – or a large dog.'

'I do have a St Bernard.'

'There you are then.'

'Is that all you can see?'

'That's all, dear.' She examined the globe again. 'Good health, just the usual minor ailments. You want to be careful driving a car. You aren't very good at it. You're going to have a nice house in the country and Mr X, your hubby's, going to grow potatoes. Or is it dahlias?'

'But what will *I* be doing?'

'I can't see that, dear. You're busy with the children.'

'I'm not going to be a writer, then?'

'I can't tell. The picture's gone, I'm afraid. And it wasn't very clear.'

I waited outside the tent while Portia's fortune was told. Might I really have psychic powers? I could not imagine myself living with a man who grew prize dahlias. But Madame Xanthe *had* seen Dirk in the crystal ball. I was mildly depressed that she had not also seen me sitting in an office

695

with 'EDITOR' written on the door. But what of the passionate, worshipping man who was to sweep me off my feet?

Portia came out of the tent.

'Well? What did she say?' I asked with some eagerness.

'The usual nonsense. Something about being abandoned by an older man, who'd once been everything to me. I can't think who that could be. Unless it was Pa. She said I'd been through many trials and tribulations. Well, that's true of everyone. And that I was going to be seduced by a tall dark handsome stranger. I hope not. Jonno'll be furious. What did she say to you?'

'Exactly the same.' I was conscious of disappointment. 'Where's Cordelia?'

'She *was* dancing with the executioner. Look, isn't that her going into the marquee?'

Inside the marquee we saw Archie, surrounded by an admiring crowd. He beckoned to us.

'Come, Harriet, and let these good people feast their eyes on you. And who is the pussy with mange?

'Hello, Archie. It's Portia. It's all I could find to wear at the last minute. I prefer to think of myself as a cat with a past. You look amazing.'

Archie made a minute adjustment to the folds of his enormously wide culottes of silver brocade trimmed with gold ribbons at the waist and knee. 'I had Mrs Wapshott copy a painting of Louis XIV. My *fav*ourite king. He never did things by halves. They're called petticoat breeches. Practically drag, dear girl, but the royal connection makes it respectable.' Above them he wore a coat and waistcoat of the same brocade with gold lace and gold buttons. A hat trimmed with huge feathers was perched on his white full-bottomed wig, which sparkled with diamonds. A single ruby-red glass tear, the only point of colour, clung to his silver mask. He dazzled and glittered and shimmered, and you could hardly look at him without blinking.

Archie waved a jewelled hand. 'It's so romantic not knowing who anyone is. One's imagination garbs them with fabulous beauty, excoriating wit and acute sensibility. I dread my appointment with reality in the morning.' He murmured in my ear, '*Un succès fou*, I think we can safely say.'

'The food looks so gorgeous, it really a pity to eat it.' Portia pointed a paw at the buffet table, laden with succulent dishes. Candlelight touched the ice sculptures with flashes of gold. There was a giant water lily, a Chinese pagoda and a dragon with a long tail. We had got them cheap because the young Finnish artist who had executed these marvels had succumbed to Archie's charms. I had seen them earlier together on the dance floor, snaking hips in unison.

'Do you know, I feel quite twenty again,' Archie gave a sigh of pleasure. 'Pinkki – that's my new friend from Lapland – is the most ravishing boy. He must be the tall, dark, handsome stranger authorised by Madame Xanthe to sweep me off my feet. She was spot on, too, about the older man. Though it was so long ago, I shall never forget those thrilling sessions in the map cupboard with the geography master.'

I examined the crowd. 'I can't see Cordelia.'

'What a worrier you are, Harriet.' Archie tapped my cheek. 'I saw her only a minute ago slipping into the fortune-teller's tent with that quaintly lubricious cardinal. I hardly think he'll try to seduce her in the presence of the sibyl from Kensal Green. You need food to subdue that cankerworm within.'

He was right. I was fussing unnecessarily. I must recover my party spirit. I drank another glass of champagne rather fast and took a plate of tiny purple artichokes. I was about to help myself from a tureen of hollandaise when a tiny hand shot out and gripped the ladle. Madame Xanthe's other hand had a firm grasp on a plate almost as big as herself, piled high with food. I put down the artichokes and dashed off to her tent. I pulled open the flap, hardly knowing what I expected to find. Cordelia and the cardinal were sitting either side of the table, playing an energetic game of snap with tarot cards.

'Ah, ze big sister come to make certain you are OK.' The cardinal spread his hands wide, his expression sour, his voice gay. '*Voilà*! Nozing in my sleeve, no tricks. Mam'zelle is safe.'

'I nearly wasn't,' said Cordelia. 'That bloke in the executioner's costume was trying to get his hand down my front. Snap!' Triumphantly she laid The Hanged Man on top of the pile.

'I see this happening and I menace him wiz his own axe.'

The cardinal and Cordelia seemed to find this very amusing.

'I'm sorry to break up the game but it's nearly one o'clock and you promised you'd be in bed an hour ago.'

'Oh, please, Harriet! I'm having such fun.'

The cardinal waved a finger at Cordelia. 'I give you a penance. You have one dance wiz me and then you go to bed. What do you say, Mam'zelle Harriet? I swear to take care of *la petite fille*.'

'It's very kind of you. Well, all right.'

The party was afloat on excitement and champagne. I saw Pa and Pussyfoot dancing together, her arms clasped tightly about his armoured neck. Portia and Jonno revolved rapidly across the floor, his trunk flying out, her tail fastened round his waist. Ophelia and Charles moved very slowly amid the whirling revellers, gazing intently into each other's eyes. Rupert, the only animate, human face in the crowd, ambled languidly about in the arms of a tall blonde girl whose *décolletage* revealed much bosom.

I experienced again that sense of the grotesque, as though the merriment was the obverse of something ominous. The fixed expressions of exaggerated mirth or pain were sinister, like puppet figures of the Grand Guignol. I felt a sensation of something almost like fear. The necklace seemed to tighten round my throat. There was a shout of laughter as the executioner, obviously drunk, fell over and rolled down the bank into the canal. He emerged, smiling good-humouredly despite the weeds hanging from his ears and took off his mask. It was Hugo Dance.

I looked about anxiously. There was no sign of Cordelia. I pushed my way through the crowd towards the front door of number 10. Inside, the house was silent. It seemed deserted but, unusually, the door of Rupert's work-room was open. I went in. The room was dark but enough light came through the window from the gas flares to pick up the red of the cardinal's soutane, which lay crumpled on a chair by the window, his hat thrown carelessly on top. Propped against a cushion the mask stared up at me, its saturnine expression mocking.

The treacherous bastard! How could I have been so stupid as to trust him? I practically snorted with rage as I imagined my sister in the arms of her bogus protector. Then I heard the door close softly behind me and the key grate in the lock. I turned quickly. Though the light was dim, the man who had been standing behind the door, waiting for me, had so often been the object of my covert scrutiny that I recognised him at once, just from the shape of his head and the shadows of his face.

'Max!'

FORTY-FOUR

'Hello, Harriet.'

'What are *you* doing here? I thought you were in South America!'

'There are such things as aeroplanes.'

'Cordelia –'

'Brushing her teeth, I expect. You needn't have worried. Little girls don't tempt me in the least.'

I continued to stare at him, bewildered. 'But why are you here?'

'Quite a few people in the Hubert Hat company had invitations. It sounded a good party. I decided to gate-crash. I wish you'd take off that mask. I want to see you properly.'

I had forgotten what a beautiful voice Max had. It was persuasive. I undid the strings obediently.

'That's better,' he said. 'Come here.'

He walked over to the window. I followed him but positioned myself so that Rupert's desk was between us. He smiled.

'All right. So you're feeling unfriendly. Tell me, why didn't you answer my letters? I rather thought when we said goodbye at Pye Place that your feelings towards me were – affectionate.'

'They were.' Slowly I was gathering my wits. 'But then I didn't know about Georgia.'

'Georgia?'

'You were good enough to divide your favours between us, I believe.'

'Ah.' Max frowned and stared down at a pot of pencils, pens and brushes. Now my eyes had adjusted to the light I could see what a beautiful colour his hair was, like beech leaves in winter. 'Supposing I tell you it isn't true.'

'I shan't believe you.'

'You'd condemn a man without hearing the evidence?'

'I don't want to know any more about it.'

'Who's been blackening my character?'

'Archie told me.'

Max laughed. 'So you'd believe that ridiculous oversexed hermaphrodite rather than me. Malicious gossip is meat and drink to men like that.'

'Archie happens to be one of my very best friends. And I do believe him. Also Georgia herself admitted it.'

'Did she?' Max stopped smiling. 'All right, Harriet. I don't want to lie to you. It's true I bedded Georgia. Don't go!' I had turned away, suddenly angry with myself for even listening, but Max leaned forward and grabbed my arm. 'Just a minute. Let me talk to you. Please. I've been wretched, wondering why you didn't write. I've flown thousands of miles just to see you. Can't you give me a chance to explain?'

I had forgotten how fine-drawn his face was, with large eyes that seemed to burn with a sort of saintly asceticism. And there was that fascinating dent at the end of his long, elegant nose.

'Let go of me. I must stop Dirk barking.'

I had shut Dirk in the kitchen with a dish of bones before the party began. Now, having detected my presence in the house, he was emitting screeches like chalk on a blackboard.

'In a minute. I understand why you're angry. It was incredibly stupid of me to sleep with Georgia. Particularly as I didn't specially want to.' He shrugged. 'I don't enjoy hurting people's feelings, even when they're as manipulative as Georgia. It's hard for a man to say no when a girl throws herself at him. And men, after all, are conditioned by society to treat all attractive woman as potential sexual partners. Most women want to be admired and flirted with. If we only wanted to discuss poetry and the devolution of Wales you'd all be pretty annoyed. We're damned if we do and damned if we don't. It seemed easier to go to bed with her than keep fighting her off. But that last night, when she came to my room, I told her it was no go. Though I'd given up the idea of making further progress with you at Pye Place, I knew you were important to me. Very important. I resigned myself to a night of frustration. Then you appeared so unexpectedly and –' he smiled, 'I got my reward.'

He stroked my arm and then moved his hand down to take mine. I remembered how he had comforted me when I was unhappy about Pa. How kind he had been to Cordelia. I knew his explanation was reasonable and I believed it.

'Be fair, Harriet. I bet you can't think of a single man you know who'd have behaved differently.'

I admitted – strictly to myself – that I couldn't. Bron would not have hesitated to take advantage of sex freely offered with no strings attached. I guessed that Pa also would have availed himself of a quick tumble without a second thought. I wondered about Rupert. He certainly seemed to prefer relationships with women that were brief, casual and impersonal. It was an undeniable fact that few men would have refused such an invitation. Looked at from Max's point of view I could see my anger was hardly justified.

But suppose – just suppose for one moment – that appalling fantasy, that freak of fancy which had taken shape a few weeks ago and lingered disquietingly in my thoughts ever since, were true? I could forgive Max for sleeping with Georgia. If that were all, we might have been friends, though I had no desire to get into bed with him again. But that other crazy idea, which now sprang into the forefront of my mind – I almost shuddered to find myself alone with him. It couldn't be true! It must be the result of an overactive imagination and too much third-rate journalism. Rupert had said I lived in a world of make-believe and he was right. Now Max was in the room with me, so plausible, so charming, his smile – his voice – so winning, I doubted my own reason.

Max came round to my side of the desk. 'Can't you understand that I'm a man like any other, weak, faulty, vain, if you like, but a man who's very much in love with you?' He put up his hand to stroke my cheek, then ran it down to caress my throat. 'Darling, I've missed you terribly. When I saw that necklace I did allow myself to hope that you still cared for me just a little. Let me prove to you that I can be as faithful as any woman could possibly desire – to the point of satiety.' His lips brushed my forehead. 'Damn this dress. It's like trying to embrace someone who's wearing a chest of drawers.'

He pulled me closer, forcing the hoop of my skirt to stick up behind like a preposterous bustle. In other circumstances the situation would have been absurd enough to make me laugh but I was not in the mood to find anything funny.

'I'd have to be mad to even think of anyone else,' he murmured. 'I'm wild about you. Don't you realise how happy we could be if you could only put that stupid business with Georgia out of your mind?'

'Perhaps,' I said, pushing him far enough away so that I could see the expression in his eyes. 'But the trouble is I don't think I could ever quite put out of my mind the possibility that besides being good-looking, charming and obviously a very talented actor, you're also –' I took a deep breath – 'very likely a murderer.'

Max stopped stroking, murmuring, even breathing. If I had doubted before, those few seconds of stillness turned my suspicion into certainty. I saw in his eyes a look that was unmistakably fear.

'Is that a joke?' He laughed and regained his composure instantly. 'Sweet girl, you'll never be dull.'

He tried to kiss me but I twisted my face away.

'I'm not joking. It *was* you, wasn't it, who shone the spotlight on the stage to mark the spot where someone had to stand to be killed by the lightning bolt? You were at the rehearsal when it came down by accident and that gave you the idea of the perfect murder. You took the weights off the counter-balance so it would come crashing down and kill poor old Basil. But of course it wasn't Basil you wanted to kill. Caroline was in love with my father. She wanted to divorce you and marry him. You didn't give a damn about Caroline – but you wanted to be able to go on spending her money – all that stuff you told me about liking to be ordinary and wearing scruffy clothes and living simply was a lie, like everything else.'

'What a provocative creature you are!' Max took my face between his hands. 'A little crazy but that's exciting.'

'I'm right, aren't I? And what's really ironic – what would make it funny if so many people hadn't been so hurt by it – is that Pa had no intention of marrying Caroline. He didn't even like her very much. But he was too cowardly to tell her. He's going to marry P – Fleur Kirkpatrick. So it was all for nothing – all the trouble you went to, pretending to be interested in me – and I was stupid enough to think you really liked me.'

'You're raving, my darling. You've had too much to drink and you don't know what you're saying. My poor girl, you

704

badly need someone to take care of you. I'm going to start by making love to you. I've been wanting to do that again for a very long time.'

I struggled to free myself but he held me firmly. He tried to kiss me but I turned my face away. I remembered what Portia had once told me about kneeing men in the groin but this was impossible with the hoop and several metres of embroidered brocade and petticoat between us. Max put both hands around my neck. The torque cut into my throat as his grip tightened. I could not breathe. I felt a tremendous pressure in my ears and the music and Dirk's barking grew faint. I tried to pull his hair with one hand while hitting him with the other but I was weak from lack of oxygen. His tongue was in my mouth and I was suffocating, unable to scream. The room began to swim. What a fool I've been, I thought as everything went dark, I'm too young to die and there's so much I don't know – and who's going to look after Cordelia – and Dirk and Mark Ant – suddenly Max let me go. I heard a crash as of furniture breaking, followed by the smashing of china.

I took a gulp of air. It took me a little while to focus my eyes. Max was lying full length on the floor, surrounded by pieces of Sèvres and the legs of a Sheraton table. I held my throat in one hand and my head, which was throbbing, in the other.

'You were only just – in time,' I meant to say but it came out as an unintelligible croak.

'A fine example to set your little sister,' said Rupert. 'A-how!' He was nursing his right hand in his armpit. 'I've never hit anyone before. I certainly shan't do it again. It's bloody agony.' He groaned and sucked his knuckles. 'Next time you decided to entertain a lover alone in a locked room, make sure you want to go through with it. It was lucky I had a spare key.'

'I didn't – know it was Max – I wanted to see that Cordelia–' was what I intended to say but my larynx was on fire.

'Did he hurt you?'

'He was trying to – kill me,' I squawked.

'Speak up. I can't understand you.' Rupert's voice was level but there was a hint of impatience in it. I could only whimper, inarticulately. He frowned. 'You're really upset, aren't you?'

He put his arms round me. I pressed my head against his chest and would have sobbed if I had had breath enough. Rupert held me stiffly, in a manner to discourage hysterics. 'Come on, Harriet. You're quite safe. He's hardly going to rape you while I'm here. Anyway, I seem to have knocked him out cold.'

'Not – rape!' I gasped.

'You mean you wanted him to? God! I shall never understand women.'

'Has anyone seen Pinkki?' Archie stood in the doorway. 'I told him to wait for me in the garden but – *Oho*! So you've *finally* got round to it. Well, thank goodness for that. It's been a long time brewing but – What's Frensham doing here? I didn't send him an invitation.' Archie went to stand over Max. 'He's not *dead*, is he?'

Rupert pushed me to one side and crouched over Max's motionless body. 'He'd better not be! Get some water from somewhere. I'll loosen his collar.'

The idea that because of me Rupert might have to spend the rest of his life in a tiny cell in Winton Shrubs spurred me to action. I picked up a vase of sweet peas and dashed the water – and the flowers – on to Max's white, unconscious face. It seemed to have no effect so I hurled after it the remains of a pot of tea – cold, fortunately – and the contents of the inkwell.

'That'll do. You're making a horrible mess. He's coming to.'

'What the – Oh, Christ! Harriet . . . Fuck! I think my jaw's broken.' Max lay with his eyes open, looking up at us, his hand clasping his chin. 'What happened?'

'I hit you,' said Rupert. 'I mistook passion for resistance. I'm sorry. Can you open and close your mouth?'

Max did so, wincing. 'It's OK, I think. What's this?' He picked a flower from his shirt-front and looked at it, puzzled. 'I'm soaking wet. Jesus! I'm covered with blood!'

'It's red ink. Harriet got carried away.' Rupert was looking amused now. 'Fortunately, her aim isn't too good.'

Max was a shocking sight. Not only was his hair dripping and his chest sprinkled with flowers and tea-leaves but one side of his face was stained bright red. Rupert helped him up. Max got out his handkerchief to mop his face. He caught sight of himself in the mirror above the fireplace and groaned.

'I suppose the ink was permanent?'

I examined the bottle. 'I'm afraid so.'

Max looked at Rupert and then at me. I guessed he was wondering what I had told him.

'Harriet – Look, I got carried away.' Max gave a mirthless laugh. 'You shouldn't lead people on, you know. You don't know what power a beautiful woman has over a man. I'm sorry.'

I said nothing. My mind was jumping from one idea to another and I was unable to make sense of anything.

Max grinned at Rupert in a man-to-man way. 'I can see I've made an awful mess of things. Let me speak to Harriet alone, will you? One doesn't want an audience if one's going to crawl.'

Rupert looked at me. I shook my head. 'Don't mind me.' Rupert folded his arms and leaned against the desk.

'I shan't breathe a *word*,' said Archie. 'At least only to a few discreet friends.'

Max bit his lip. 'Come outside with me, Harriet, will you?

You'll have hundreds of chaperones. If I get another rush of blood to the head you can push me into the canal.'

'Go away.' I had recovered my voice sufficiently to speak distinctly. 'I hope I never see you again.'

Max took a step towards me but I moved closer to Rupert and took hold of the fingers that stuck out from under his folded arms. They closed reassuringly on mine.

'So that's it.' Max gave a ghastly smile. 'I ought to have known.' He managed another attempt at a laugh. For once his acting was not up to much. 'You've been consoling yourself in my absence with home comforts. I suppose the director of a world-famous opera house is more of a prize than a humble actor. But I'd be careful if I were you. He's not the marrying kind.'

Rupert pinched my fingers hard which I took as a warning to say nothing.

Archie held open the door. 'Time to go home, Max dear. I should get a pack of frozen peas on that jaw. You're beginning to look like Desperate Dan.'

Max paused on the threshold. He looked white and sick, and despite everything I almost felt sorry for him. 'Good luck, Harriet. You're going to need it.'

The front door slammed moments later.

'I don't know why people can't shut doors quietly,' said Rupert. 'It's very bad for the locks.'

'That was Max, wasn't it?' Cordelia came running in. 'He might have waited. Can I go after him?'

'He's got a plane to catch,' said Rupert. 'Besides you're undressed.'

Cordelia was wearing pyjamas.

'So are lots of the guests,' she argued. 'There's a trouserless man in the garden, trying to make love to the statue.'

'That's my Pinkki.' Archie rushed out.

I came to my senses. 'Darling, go straight to bed. And don't look out of any more windows. Rupert, do you think you might say something to Archie? Suggest they go indoors?'

'Thanks, but I've performed my quota of chivalrous actions for this evening. My hand is throbbing like hell. Go and draw the curtains if you think it matters – No, wait! I want to talk to you. Good night, Cordelia,' he added pointedly, seeing she was disposed to linger. 'Now,' he said as soon as we were alone, 'what was that business with Max about? When I came in it looked as though you were reluctant to be ravished. Did I misread the signs?'

'No. But it was worse than that.'

When I told Rupert I thought Max had been trying to strangle me, he laughed so much that tears came into his eyes. He had to sit on the desk to steady himself.

'You're drunk.' I said, annoyed that he seemed to find my nearly being throttled so entertaining.

'I believe I am. I don't think it would occur to me to knock anyone out cold if I were sober. Or even to imagine that I could. Put it down to relief that the first night's over. And it's a beautiful night. And – put it down to anything you like. Now what were you saying?'

'Max tried to kill me. At least I think he did.'

Rupert assumed a more or less straight face when he saw my expression of pique. 'Don't be silly, Harriet. People don't go around strangling girls because they refuse to go to bed with them. And certainly not in the middle of parties when they're likely to be interrupted at any moment.'

'We were locked in.' I pointed out. 'Come to think of it, why did *you* come in?'

'I wanted a cigar. Also to make a few notes. I realised suddenly what had been bothering me about the lighting in the last act.'

Evidently the proximity of the large-breasted girl he had been dancing with had not been wholly distracting.

'Well, it was lucky for me you did. Everyone thinks Max is in Rio de Janeiro. He could have pushed my body behind the desk, put on his costume, locked the door behind him and left the party with no one any the wiser. My corpse might not have been discovered until morning. By which time he'd be on a plane back to South America. There'd be nothing to connect him with the murder. No motive. He could easily have got away with it.'

'You've become obsessed with the *modus operandi* of homicide. You'd better put it to good use in your journalism. Why on earth would Max want to murder you? I mean, I've a quick temper myself but you haven't yet driven me to strangle you.'

'I wish you'd be serious. It was because I accused him of trying to murder my father.' I explained my theory. 'It came to me in a flash as soon as I met Caroline Frensham and she told me she was madly in love with Pa. Charles is always talking about motive. Don't you see? Max couldn't bear to lose all that money. That's why he was so keen to take up with me. I couldn't understand it, then. He was always saying how much he worshipped Pa. He hoped I'd tell him what the police were doing, which naturally I did because then he had a cast-iron alibi. But he was a liar from beginning to end. Of course I can't prove it. But do you think we ought to tell Charles and stop Max getting on the plane?'

Rupert took a hole-puncher from his pen tray and began idly to make holes round the edge of a piece of paper. Small white circles fluttered down and mingled with the water and ink on the carpet. 'No,' he said at last. 'For one thing, as you say, there's not a particle of proof.'

'But when I said it he sort of froze and I looked right into his eyes and I knew, I absolutely *knew* I was right.'

'Intuition doesn't count as evidence. And if it did, what would another court case do to Waldo? He'd be the key witness, being both the intended victim and Caroline's lover.

710

He's only just getting right again. There'd be questions, cross-examinations, police stations, lawyers . . . I don't think he could take it.'

'I hadn't thought of that. You're right. He can't look at a budgerigar in a cage or a goldfish in a bowl without bursting into tears. But supposing Max is insane? He might try to kill someone else.'

'About one in ten murders are solved. *Ow*!' Rupert put down the hole-puncher, having drawn blood from his thumb. 'That's leaving corpses at the bottom of the Thames or set in concrete under motorways that no one knows anything about, out of the equation. The world is teeming with killers on the loose. And we don't know that Max *is* one. He might be completely innocent. Anyway,' he added seeing that I was about to protest, 'I don't see myself as a Fury, avenging wrongdoing and bringing the perpetrators to justice. I can live with the doubt if you can. I realise you're more emotionally involved than I am.'

'Only because he tried to kill Pa. I don't give a damn about Max.'

'Don't you? I thought you did. In fact you gave a very good impression of being pretty infatuated.'

'I never was! I admit I was attracted to him – because I thought he liked *me*.'

'And of course he did, you owl. Why come back otherwise? It would have been much safer to stay in Rio. He came because of you.'

'But he tried to *kill* me. I *think*, anyway.'

Already the idea seemed ridiculous. I could tell Rupert thought I was being hysterical.

'Men do sometimes kill the thing they love. As a fan of *Othello* you ought to know that.'

I tugged ineffectually at the necklace, 'I wish you'd undo this beastly thing.'

Rupert switched on the desk lamp. 'It's an ingenious mechanism. But what a weight! No wonder you thought . . .' Rupert stopped speaking as he examined my neck. He touched my throat lightly. 'Sorry. Did that hurt?' he asked unnecessarily as I squealed. 'There's some very bad bruising starting to come up.'

He continued to peer at my throat, frowning. I loved the way his eyebrows lay like straight black brushstrokes along his brow bone. I had a mad impulse to stroke them, which I naturally resisted.

'My God! I thought you were exaggerating. But this looks like – Supposing I hadn't come in! You might have been – Harriet!' He folded his arms again and looked at me severely. 'You took a terrible risk coming in here with him. What if I hadn't decided to have a cigar? Supposing I hadn't had a spare key? If you thought he was dangerous, it was foolhardy, to say the least.'

'Of course I didn't *mean* to be locked in with him. I had no idea the cardinal was Max. I was checking on Cordelia.'

'Don't go to Manchester.' Rupert looked serious. His chin was already dotted with five o'clock shadow, only, of course, it was half-past one in the morning. I could have kissed every one of those darling burgeoning bristles. 'I agree with Max about one thing. You don't realise how powerfully men are attracted to you.' He sighed. 'Your unwillingness to believe in your own beauty makes you vulnerable to the worst sort. Look, if it's money that's bothering you, you can get a better job in London and make a bigger contribution to expenses. Though, God knows, it isn't important.' When I said nothing but went on looking at his chin with an expression I hoped was not actually hungry, he said, 'Is there something else that makes you feel you must go away? Something other than pride?'

Pride! What was he talking about? I wanted to put my

arms around his infuriatingly wonderful neck and never let go. I had as much pride as Dirk on seeing a bone. I hoped I wasn't dribbling.

'What is it then?' he persisted, poor dumb creature that he was. 'I know you and Archie are fond of each other. And Cordelia's settled down now. Is it me?' He must have taken my continued silence for assent. 'We've always been friends, haven't we? Even when we were children. Do you remember, you used to come to me if you grazed your knee and I used to pretend I was going to cut it off?'

Of course I remembered. Every single memory of Rupert was inscribed in scarlet capitals in the register of my childhood.

'I used to draw a dotted line on your leg and get out my penknife and you'd always stop crying and start laughing. You were such a bright little thing. I was fond of all the Byng children in limited doses, but I always liked you best. You were the plain one but you had more brains and feeling than all the others put together. Now you're the beauty of the family.'

'Don't tease me. I know I'm not.'

Rupert sighed. 'What will it take to convince you? Some people may prefer the conventional good looks of Clarissa and the other girls, but for me, and I suspect many others, you have an altogether superior fascination.' I debated this, wonderingly. No doubt he was being kind. 'Look,' he continued, 'I know I'm impatient and grumpy in the morning. And I'm sarcastic and – well, some women have accused me of being heartless. You of all people might understand why I hate scenes. Can't you overlook my deficiencies?'

I could have, oh, how easily I could have, if only – What deficiencies? I couldn't think of one. To my horror I felt my eyes fill with tears of hopeless love. I stared hard at a spot of blood on his dress shirt which must have come from his thumb.

713

'What have I done to drive you away?' I could have stamped on his stupid, uncomprehending foot. 'I don't want to make you unhappy. Far from it. I actually like having you here. In fact, since you told me you were going I've had to face up to – well,' he laughed, 'I do believe I'm about to make a scene myself. Actually for quite a while I've been aware . . . I've wanted to – tell you . . .' He looked almost stern, suddenly. 'I'm very bad at talking about these things. I suppose that's why I love the theatre. I can indulge my emotions without self-betrayal. Anyway,' he took a cigar from the box on his desk, rolled it between his fingers, stared at it as though surprised to find it in his hand and put it back, 'until now, I haven't exactly been tested. I've wanted to make love to some women because they were beautiful and I've wanted to talk to others because they were agreeable, intelligent people. I'd given up hope of finding someone in whom those qualities were united. But love isn't like that, is it? It isn't a question of totting up desirable attributes. If anyone asked me what it is about you – well, I suppose I'd have to say – leaving looks aside – you're unselfish, you're tender-hearted to a fault, you make me laugh, and by nature you're transparently truthful.'

I could hardly believe my ears. A foolish hope drew its first lungful of breath and fluttered into life. I resolved never *ever* to tell another lie.

'But these things on their own could never be enough. Perhaps one loves someone because their presence colours the world and makes it beautiful. Beauty and truth,' he mused. 'Keats was right. They *are* indivisible. Someone, I think it was de la Bruyère, said that love always begins with love. The warmest friendship cannot change even to the coldest love. Do you think that's true?'

I shook my head. Anyway, as far as I was concerned it was quite irrelevant. I had nursed my secret and incurable passion

714

for Rupert since I was old enough to whistle through the gap where my front teeth ought to have been.

'I hope not,' continued Rupert, 'because – do look at me. Fond though I am of the top of your head I'd like to see your face.' He put his hand under my chin. I shut my eyes too late. A treacherous tear dropped down my cheek.

'What's the matter? Did I hurt your neck?'

The man I loved was an idiot.

I took courage and opened my eyes. We stared at each other. Heavens! Such is the power of love that I thought lightning flashed between us, burning his image on my gaze, my mind, my soul.

'Harry!' His arms were round me, holding me close. 'Darling!'

Seconds later there was a terrific crash of thunder. It was a summer storm. Outside the merrymakers screamed and the rain began to patter against the window.

The door opened. 'Let's go in here,' said Archie's voice. I turned to look. Behind him were the slightly squinting eyes of an otherwise flaxen-haired Norse god. 'O*ho*! Our arrival is infelicitous. Come, Pinkki, we'll try upstairs. *Do* get on with it, you two,' he threw over his shoulder. 'At this rate you'll both be crooked and blind before you can consummate.'

Rupert laughed and tightened his hold on me.

'I can't sleep in a thunderstorm.' Cordelia came in, carrying Mark Antony. 'Can I sit up and – Blimey! Rupert! Why've you got your arms round Hat? You were going to snog! You aren't stuck on each other? Oh, no!' She groaned. 'I don't think I can stand it. It's going to be like Ophelia and Charles again. Soppy grins and heavy breathing and nobody able to think about anything but sex.'

'In my case that will certainly be true.' Rupert let me go. He took Cordelia firmly by the shoulder and walked her to the door. 'Now, my dear Cordelia, I want you to go downstairs and calm the dog. Then you can start making plans for redecorating your bedroom. You were talking, the other day, about something you'd admired in a friend's house.'

'You mean Tracy Betts's that's like a Spanish hathy – hathy whatever-it's-called – bumpy walls like porridge hung with guitars and castanets and a wishing well that's really a pop-up bar?'

'Not the bar.'

'Well, but the red and black curtains in sort of tiers like a flamenco dancer's dress?'

'Fine.'

'Golly! You really *have* got it bad.'

'I have. Now be a good girl and push off.'

Cordelia went, her eyes ablaze with creativity.

'Now.' Rupert surveyed me with amusement. 'It's a very fetching frock but it presents something of a problem. But if the Elizabethans managed it, so can I.'

Again I heard the key turn in the lock but this time I did not object to being taken prisoner. In fact, I had every intention of serving a life-sentence.